IEE TELECOMMUNICATIONS SERIES 44

Series Editors: Professor C. J. Hughes
Professor J. D. Parsons
Professor G. White

DIGITAL SIGNAL FILTERING, ANALYSIS AND RESTORATION

Other volumes in this series:

DIGITAL SIGNAL FILTERING, ANALYSIS AND RESTORATION

Jiří Jan

Translated from the Czech original
Číslicová filtrace, analýza a restaurace signálů
(Vutium Press, Technical University of Brno)

The Institution of Electrical Engineers

This edition published by: The Institution of Electrical Engineers, London, United Kingdom

Číslicová filtrace, analýza a restaurace signálů
originally published in Czech by Vutium Press
(Technical University of Brno), 1997

The Institution of Electrical Engineers,
Michael Faraday House,
Six Hills Way, Stevenage,
Herts. SG1 2AY, United Kingdom

British Library Cataloguing in Publication Data

A CIP catalogue record for this book
is available from the British Library

ISBN 0 85296 760 8

Printed in England by TJ International Ltd., Padstow, Cornwall

Contents

Introduction

Signal processing is an important and fast developing area with applications in very different regions of human activity – from traditional communications and multimedia technology through measurement evaluation and system identification in mechanical, civil, electrical or chemical engineering, in physical as well as human sciences, in medicine and biomedical applications, ecological and economic analyses and futurology. The traditional concept of signals as continuous functions of time (so-called analogue signals) has gradually widened to include signals formed by discrete series and even multidimensional discrete signals. These discrete signals may, although not necessarily, originate from continuous-time (or continuous-space) signals by means of sampling. As proven in signal theory, the original continuous signal can be perfectly recovered from samples under certain conditions, and therefore the information value of the discrete form is equivalent to that of the continuous function. It follows that all the results achievable by classical continuous-time methods can in principle also be obtained by discrete processing. However, discrete methods offer much more: complex and demanding methods can be realised that would be unreliable or even not actually feasible in the continuous version (e.g. adaptive and learning methods); signals, the continuous versions of which do not exist (e.g. sequences of economic data), can be effectively processed and analysed. Also, if the discrete values are expressed as numbers, the signal processing system can cooperate directly with digital information systems which provide time-unlimited mass memory in data archives. These features have led to the gradual replacement of analogue signal processing methods by discrete techniques in many application areas, and also to the spreading of modern signal processing methods into nontraditional fields. However, this does not mean that classical methods are going to disappear completely, only that their application will gradually focus on areas where discrete methods cannot compete for principal reasons: signals at the interface with the real, predominantly 'analogue', world, i.e. mostly weak signals before digitisation, power-output analogue signals after digital to analogue conversion and also very high-frequency signals of hundreds of MHz and above.

Although the title of this book implies a bias towards digital representation of the discrete data, much of the knowledge presented can also be applied more generally to discrete signals with analogue representation of samples, for example to charge-coupled technology. This is supported by the fact that we are not going to analyse in detail the problems arising due to finite precision number presentation, as the practical meaning of rounding-error analysis is markedly decreasing owing to the availability of ever more sophisticated technical means such as modern signal processors using high-precision number representation.

The purpose of this book is to give a continuous explanation of the basic theory of digital signal processing and analysis, focusing primarily on one-dimensional signals to enable the reader to gain a good comprehension of individual terms and concepts. The author has based the book conception on his personal confidence that understanding theoretically formulated concepts in the field is the base of any solid application, and that an awareness of the application possibilities of specialised methods as well as the design or selection of proper approaches is substantially facilitated by knowledge of the basic concepts. This opinion is supported by the fact that specific application information usually has only a rather short-lived validity and is better available from journals and conference proceedings. The content of the book and depth of the individual chapters is determined mainly by this approach, but also by an attempt to embrace all fundamental concepts forming the generally applicable core of the field, not just the areas historically considered to be basic, i.e. classical digital filtering and discrete transforms. Our starting position is that, today, a basic knowledge of the principles of the digital processing and analysis of signals (or data sequences) belongs to the essential outfit of every engineer or scientist and, consequently, it is appropriate to treat the material in a more general way. Application notes advise, although only on a general level, on the usefulness of individual methods not only in the field of classical communications but also in measuring and instrument technology, in technical cybernetics for system identification and digital control and in computer science for the analysis of mass data or processing of multidimensional signals, such as in multimedia applications.

In order to be reasonably self contained, the book presents, in its first four chapters, an overview of the fundamental theory of discrete systems, processes and signals. The reader is only expected to be familiar with mathematics to the level of introductory university courses in engineering (science or economics); useful but not necessary will be a knowledge of the elements of signal theory. The extensive Chapter 5 is then devoted to an explanation of the principles of classical digital filtering including the basic realisation structures and design methods, and Chapter 6 presents averaging methods to improve the signal-to-noise ratio of repetitive signals. Digital compared to analogue representation allows effective processing of complex signals; the principles of the corresponding methods are described in Chapter 7. The following two chapters, 8 and 9, are devoted to fundamental approaches to signal analysis – correlation and spectral analyses and the possibilities for their use in different areas. Chapters 10 and 11 describe methods for estimating an unknown signal on the basis of its version distorted, for example owing to transfer through a distorting and noisy channel, or as provided by similarly imperfect measurement. Estimates based on *a priori* knowledge of signal statistics (Wiener filtering) as well as methods based on signal-generation models (Kalman filtering) and adaptive methods, which gather the information on signal properties during processing, are discussed. A note on the principles of signal data compression appears at the end of Chapter 10. A separate chapter, Chapter 12, is devoted to a brief introduction to nonlinear processing, in particular to homomorphic filtering and its application. Taking into account their increasing practical meaning, basic neuronal networks as signal processors and analysers are treated in Chapter 13. Chapter 14 generalises the previous concepts to the multidimensional case, that is to basics of digital two-dimensional image processing.

Presentation of the information tries to emulate the purpose of the book, and therefore a deeply rigorous mathematical treatment – definition, lemma, proof – is not given, but rather a continuous explanation considered more acceptable for a nonmathematical reader. In spite of this less formal approach, it is hoped that there are no logical discontinuities or unclear concepts. This should prevent any obscurities that, as experience (as well as some published papers) shows, often remain in seemingly trivial facts or principles. All the presented results have been derived although often the proof is hidden in an informal explanation; if some generally known initial relationship and rules are presented without proof, this is usually explicitly said. It is a consequence of deriving all the results, including those that are repeatedly cited in the literature, that, in some places, the explanation deviates from the traditional interpretations or conclusions which have appeared to the author as being imprecise or misleading. The aim is that the reader should be familiar with the terms and concepts described – not only believe the conclusions but be able to derive them himself, although by informal reasoning. He should also be able to interpret the results 'physically'. Let us say here that in several places we shall refer to the physical meaning of the conclusions; this notion is used rather arbitrarily. The purpose of such interpretations is to show what the mathematical formula means in relation to the signal, its frequency or information content etc., not to relate the signal values to a specific physical quantity.

An understanding of the material presented in this book will be substantially eased by practical experience, to which the figures presenting the results of computer simulations should contribute. Unfortunately, examples that could be solved by the reader with only a pen and paper have to be too simplified to be realistic and are of only scholastic character; valuable experience can be gained by solving concrete tasks *via* simulation programs on a computer. There are numerous signal-processing programs available, some in educational or simplified free versions, using a user-friendly block-diagram interface which enables easy and comprehensible task formulation. It is strongly recommended that the reader devote attention to such practical verification of the studied theory.

With respect to the character of this book, only literature used as immediate sources or recommended for further study is cited, which is therefore not usually in the form of original papers.

The notation and terminology are a compromise between the practices of the different fields included in the book. This leads to notation varying somewhat between individual chapters or to some symbols having different meanings in different parts of the book. It is hoped that the relevant explanations or definitions prevent any confusions or conflicts.

The author would like to express his sincere thanks to all who contributed to its present shape. The primary thanks belong to both reviewers, Dr-Ing Robert Vich, D-Sc (Czech Academy of Sciences, Prague, Czech Republic) and Prof. Dr-Ing Dušan Levický (Technical University, Košice, Slovakia), who contributed to enriching the text and to the correction of some misprints. Without the patient support of my family, especially during the times when the word-processor used presented some of its less agreeable attributes, the book would not have been finished.

The author sincerely hopes that, in spite of possible (and unfortunately probable) oversights, the reader will find the material interesting and the study of it therefore intellectually rewarding. Should the basic knowledge gained become a key to solving practical application problems, or the starting point for studying more advanced methods, the mission of the book will have been fulfilled.

Brno (CZ), 1997

A comment for the English edition: This new edition appears owing to the joint effort of two publishing houses: the IEE publishing department in Stevenage and VUTIUM, the publisher of the Technical University of Brno. It is my opportunity here to express sincere thanks to both institutions for all the effort which they have devoted to issuing this book. Besides correcting some misprints and omissions and reformulating some explanations, some topics have been added to the previous edition: sections on the cosine transform, on the principles of wavelet transforms and on the Karhunen–Loeve transform. Also, a note on signal and image-data compression has been appended to the chapter on signal restoration.

Brno (CZ), 2000

Chapter 1

Properties of discrete and digital methods of signal processing

1.1 Basic concepts

Let us start by introducing some basic terms and concepts that will be used repeatedly in this book. Nevertheless, the following descriptions are not precise definitions in the mathematical sense but rather mutual demarcations of terms, their relationships and areas of use.

The *continuous signal* is a piecewise continuous function $f(x)$ of a continuous variable x that mainly has the physical meaning of time but can also be a space distance or other physical quantity. The physical quantity expressed by the signal values (e.g. electrical voltage) has for the most part no significance in our discussions. Note: often such signals are called continuous-time signals but obviously this is less general, although perhaps more precise in the particular sense of common signals.

The *discrete signal* is an ordered sequence of values $f_i = f(i)$ which is a function of the integer-valued variable index, i. From a theoretical point of view, the origin of the sequence is irrelevant; most frequently it is a series of some measurement values.

A note on *sampling*: quite often, the discrete signal describes values of a function $f(t)$ which is continuously (perhaps piecewise continuously) variable in time measured (sampled) in time instants, $t_i, i = 0, 1, \cdots, n, \cdots$. The sampling is mostly regular, i.e. periodic with the sampling period T so that $f_n = f(t_n) = f(nT)$. In this case, we are considering sampling rate or *sampling frequency*, f_s or f_v, and the corresponding angular sampling frequency $\omega_s, \omega_v = 2\pi f_v$. It is often useful to relate the actual frequency of signal components to the sampling frequency; the corresponding dimensionless ratio valued in the range $\langle 0, 2\pi \rangle$ is then called the *normalised frequency*.

The *digital signal* is a discrete signal, the values of which are expressed by numbers which belong to a finite number set (e.g. the set of integer numbers $-32\,767, \cdots, +32\,767$ when using sixteen-bit representation). Its is important to stress that the discrete character of not only time (or other independent variables) but also of signal values is a substantial property of digital signals which, in some situations, influences the results of processing to a significant extent.

A note on *sample precision*: it is obvious that, in general, the digital signal can only express samples of a continuous signal approximately; the differences between the precise values and the closest values expressible by the numbers from the given set form a sequence called *quantisation noise*. Currently, owing to the development of digital technology, it is usually possible to use a number representation of such precision that the quantisation noise is negligible in the given application; we will not therefore deal with problems concerning quantisation noise in greater detail. The sample values of a discrete signal can also be expressed in ways other than by numbers, for example by the height or width of electric-voltage impulses or by the magnitude of electrical charge. In this case, the set of signal values is continuous (if we neglect the quantum character of electricity), but the precision of samples is limited by other phenomena (such as thermal noise) and, with the current level of technology, it is usually lower than that of digital representation.

Continuous processing of (time-dependent) signals consists in their transfer through physical systems which work continuously in time and have defined one or several inputs and outputs of continuous (so-called analogue) signals. Such *continuous-time systems* are characterised mathematically by differential equations, the analysis of which provides information on the input–output behaviour of the systems that is interesting from the point of view of signal processing (e.g. impulse or frequency responses). An example of such a system is an RLC serial circuit with an input which is the voltage of the complete serial combination and outputs which are the current in the circuit and the voltage on the capacitance. An example of such a time-independent continuous (two-dimensional) system is an optical Fourier transformer.

Discrete signal processing can be characterised by recalculation of the input sequence of values into the output sequence. Systems realising such computations are denoted as discrete systems; they are mathematically described by difference equations the analysis of which leads to information on systems properties with respect to signal processing. The calculation mentioned can be performed either in an analogue way (for example in switched-capacitor circuits), or digitally by means of a computer running suitable programs.

If an analogue signal, $x(t)$, should be processed by a discrete system in order to obtain the output signal, $y(t)$, again in the analogue form, the first element in the processing chain is a *sampler* which provides samples x_n of the input in the given time instants t_n; the samples then form the input sequence for the discrete system. Based on the output discrete sequence $y(n)$ provided by the discrete system, the continuous function $y(t)$ must be reconstructed by means of the *reconstruction interpolator* (see Figure 1.1 in which the discrete system is within the dotted frame). As already stated, the discrete system can be (and commonly is) realised digitally, as in Figure 1.1; should it accept samples of the analogue input signal and provide an analogue output, the core computing

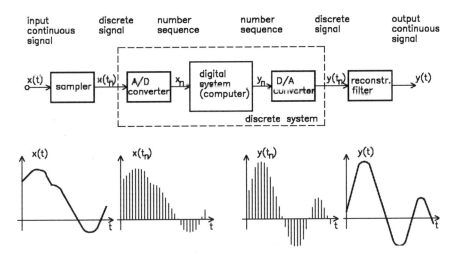

Figure 1.1 Chain of digital processing of an analogue signal

device must be preceded by an analogue-to-digital converter and followed by a digital-to-analogue converter.

The digital system itself is a computer which, as far as time-sequence processing is required, must work in real time, i.e. it must be powerful enough to complete the algorithm needed for calculation of an output sample in the time between two samples. The calculation can be performed by a general-purpose computer controlled by a suitable programme, or by utilising specialised computing structures (e.g. signal processors or matrix computers) optimised for the types of operations prevailing in signal processing.

1.2 Areas of application and stages of signal processing

Digital signal processing is very widely used in today's technology, and even the enumeration of more important areas goes beyond the extent of this introductory and rather theoretical book. Individual concrete applications can be found in many publications, particularly in journals. It seems more useful to characterise the individual stages of signal processing and discuss some typical application areas:

1 *Processing* (in a narrower sense, sometimes described as preprocessing) is characterised by both input and output data being signals. The purpose of processing is to provide a signal that is in a sense better or more appropriate than the input signal. In many applications, the result of this stage is the desired final product and no follow-up stages apply. It is probably the richest and most structured application group. Typical tasks are:

- separation of a useful component out of a mixture of signals (typically referred to as frequency filtering in communications);
- synthesis of combined signals (modulation, mixing, frequency-division or time-division multiplexing in communications, synthesis of speech signal etc.);
- elimination or suppression of noise (in all types of measurement, technical diagnostics, radio engineering, audio and video, medical signals and images);
- correction of signal deterioration (correction of nonlinearities in sensors, deconvolution – compensation of distortion by linear systems, demultiplication etc. in measurements, signal communication, in diagnostics of technological and biomedical systems etc.).

A particular type of processing is *signal restoration*, which aims towards reconstruction of an original signal based on its distorted and noisy replica; predominantly *a priori* information is used on the character and parameters of the distortion and noise involved. The methods applied for this purpose are, in principle, the same as those for other processing applications; the difference is in the formalised design of the parameters of the processing methods (e.g. of frequency responses of the used filters) exploiting the results of a preliminary identification of the kind and degree of the distortion.

2 *Analysis* often serves as the preparation for restoration or classification of a signal, or also for identification of the properties of its source or the environment (system) through which the signal was transferred and thus influenced. The input of analysis is the analysed signal and the output is a description of it in the form of a set of suitable parameters. The following tasks are typical:
- frequency or time–frequency analysis (as applied for identification in automatic control, speech recognition, adaptive correction in audio-technology, biomedical diagnostics or analysis in economics and management);
- signal decomposition into independent or only weekly mutually-dependent components with the aim of data reduction, i.e. for the subsequent economical transfer or archiving of signals (with applications in telecommunications, multimedia computer applications, hospital and other databanks, audio and video technology);
- correlation and autocorrelation analysis (applied, for example, for system identification in technical and biomedical fields, detection of weak telecommunication signals in noise, radar technology and biomedical engineering, analysis of economic relations);
- spectral analysis as a part of the preparation for signal restoration;
- so-called amplitude-interval description (detection and determining of occurrence time of prominent waves, their amplitudes, mutual time relations etc., e.g. analysis of ECG and EEG signals in medicine).

3 *Recognition and classification* determines to which one of a set of classes, admissible to a particular problem, the signal belongs. The input of this stage is the description of the signal obtained usually in the second stage; the output is the label of the class to which the signal has been found to belong. This problem usually involves steps which can be characterised as intelligent decision making and, if it is done automatically, it belongs rather to the field of artificial intelligence. Often, trained neural networks are used here which can, in a sense, also be considered to be signal processors. As the area of automatic recognition and classification is beyond the scope of this book, we will not deal with signal classification in any detail. Let us only present some typical examples:
   • recognition of phonemes and words, or even the speaker, based on time–frequency description of the speech signal;
   • discrimination of physiological forms of ECG signal from the pathological forms, eventually with a suggestion of diagnosis, according to amplitude–time description;
   • nondestructive diagnostics of mechanical systems, such as vehicles, on the basis of spectral or time–frequency analysis of acoustic signals generated by running the system;
   • discrimination of a radar response from the noise background, a moving target from a stable background, an allied target from the enemy one;
   • identification and localisation of defects on a communication line on the basis of correlation analysis;
   • scene recognition based on segmentation and geometrical analysis of a two-dimensional image signal;
   • fingerprint or face recognition based on preliminary feature analysis.

The described sequence of processing stages is naturally rather simplified and many approaches incorporate features of two or even all three stages without it being possible to separate them clearly.

1.3 Classification of discrete methods of signal processing

It is useful, initially, to introduce ways of classifying the described methods according to different aspects, although more precise definitions of some groups or classes will only follow from later chapters. We will also state to what extent the individual classes of methods are the subject of this book. Discrete signal processing methods can be classified according to many different features, namely:

1 **Linearity:**
   • *linear* methods for which the *principle of superposition* applies:

$$G\left(\sum_i a_i s_i(nT)\right) = \sum_i a_i G(s_i(nT)),$$

where G is an operator realised by the processing system and $\{s_i(nT)\}$ is a finite set of signals multiplied by corresponding scalar constants, a_i.

Linear systems can be modelled and analysed mathematically relatively easily, and routine approaches have been worked out for their design and analysis. They are commonly available, and therefore the majority of commonly-used technical systems are treated as linear; also, this book deals mainly with linear methods. Examples: linear filtering, linear discrete unitary transforms including the discrete Fourier transform (DFT), averaging;

- *nonlinear* methods are such methods and systems that do not conform to the superposition theorem. With respect to this negative demarcation, they cannot be mathematically characterised in a unified way nor is a unified analysis available. Only certain classes of nonlinear methods have so far been developed into practically useful forms; the use of nonlinear methods is therefore less frequent. One of the well established classes is homomorphic systems which are characterised by having separated all the nonlinearities into input and output blocks while the core of the system remains linear. Examples: function converters, including correctors of sensor nonlinearities, some modulators, demultiplicative filters etc.

2 **Inertiality:**
   - *memoryless systems* which utilise only instantaneous input values for calculation of the output, the examples being function converters, nonlinearity correctors; an example is a multiplier;
   - *systems with memory* which contain delay elements, i.e. memory registers in digital systems, are subdivided into:
     - *nonrecursive systems* which use only input values in the output calculations (including delayed ones); they are systems without feedback, for instance most finite impulse response (FIR) filters, see Section 5.2;
     - *recursive systems* which calculate the output with the use of both the input and delayed output values; therefore they are systems with feedbacks, i.e. infinite impulse response (IIR) filters, see Section 5.3.

3 **Dimensionality:**
   - *one-dimensional methods and systems* working with signals dependent on one independent variable only, in most cases on time;
   - *multidimensional systems* operating on signals which depend on two or more variables, e.g. the image data of a static image represents a two-dimensional signal dependent on two space variables. Working with

multidimensional signals is practically feasible (apart from very special cases such as optical processors) only in digital systems.

4 **Variability of the operator in time:**
- *time-invariant systems,* the parameters of which are constant in time; most common methods are of this type;
- *time-variant systems*, the parameters or even algorithms of which vary in time, e.g. in adaptive filters.

5 **Type of realisation:**
- *digital methods/systems* in which the samples of signals are usually represented by binary coded numbers, and the computation is realised by a digital processor;
- *discrete analogue systems* with sample representation by analogue quantities (e.g. by electric charges in the switched capacitor circuits); the calculation, naturally discrete in time, is then realised by analogue means (usually by cumulating products with constant parameters).

1.4 Advantages and disadvantages of discrete and digital signal processing

Discrete and digital processing methods have both advantages and disadvantages when compared with historically older analogue (that is continuous-time) methods.

The limitations of discrete and digital methods are:

1 A principal limitation of all discrete methods is the *limited frequency range* of processed signals which (except for rather special cases of narrowband undersampled signal processing) must not exceed the Nyquist limit. With *uniform sampling* the only form of sampling covered in this book, the upper frequency limit of the processed signal is equal to one half of the sampling frequency. Technically feasible sampling frequencies have been growing enormously owing to hardware development, so that currently (2000) they can achieve a range of several hundreds of MHz in high-end digital applications. With the exception of the frequency region of radio frequencies of decimetre and shorter waves, digital methods can therefore be applied in all signal-processing applications, at least in principle.

2 Should an analogue signal be processed, the *analogue-to-digital and digital-to-analogue converters* must be included in the processing chain at the input and output, respectively. If it is not clear that the input signal is band limited, so that the sampling theorem is fulfilled with respect to the chosen sampling frequency, then the analogue lowpass *antialiasing filter* must precede the A/D converter. In addition, an *analogue amplifier* may be needed before

digitisation in the case of weak signals which cannot be D/A converted precisely enough. At the output, an *interpolator* (reconstruction filter) may be needed to provide a continuous signal based on samples. These devices make the process more complicated in comparison with straightforward analogue processing. On the other hand, owing to the development of very large-scale integration (VLSI) technology, the converters and other circuitry are available with sufficient precision and speed in the form of clearly defined and user friendly chips, suitable for most applications. The necessity of inclusion of the antialiasing filter is often prevented today by choosing a sufficiently high sampling frequency at D/A conversion followed by digital lowpass filtering and *decimation* (leaving only every kth sample) of the discrete signal.

3 Until the 1980s, the main obstacle to the general use of digital methods was the high price of the equipment. Owing to the development of VLSI technology, this obstacle is gradually disappearing, and today, there are many applications using digital processing not only for its better technical properties but also for economic reasons. The original narrow field of only demanding scientific and military applications and investment units has gradually widened so that now it includes a substantial part of multimedia applications. In this way, digital processing penetrates into consumer electronics (e.g. compact-disc technology, DAT, DVD, digital video, digital broadcasting) and personal computer technology (graphics and sound cards, analogue interfaces and digitisers, scanners etc.), with mass production reducing the price still further.

However, discrete and digital methods have some substantial advantages:

1 Flexibility of processing given by the fact that the characteristics of a discrete system are determined only by algorithms and numerical parameters, which can both be easily changed. A change, for example, of frequency response can be made by changing constants in the system's memory or even by merely changing the sampling frequency. The discrete-system function is determined by its inner programme so that arbitrary changes of behaviour and consequently of system characteristics can be achieved by changing the algorithm as, for example, is the case with complicated types of adaptive filtering.

2 *Stability of properties in time,* particularly in the case of digital processing, is also given by the fact that system properties are determined only by programmes and parameters saved in memory which cannot spontaneously change. Therefore, when the system is in working condition, its characteristics cannot change without intervention into the system information. There is no ageing or wear, so that any adjustment, tuning and balancing, needed in most analogue systems is unnecessary; the maintenance is limited

to diagnosing the mere functionality. Digital processing is therefore perfectly reproducible.

3 *Time-unlimited memory* of digital systems provides an easy way of processing very slow signals. This can be seen, for instance, in the control of extensive production units where time constants can be from seconds up to weeks, or even in the processing of historical, economic or astronomical data sampled over years. And digital elements are far more reliable for long time periods and are incomparably easier to construct than cumbersome analogue memory elements acting as energy stores (e.g. inductances and capacitances).

4 Digital systems, as a matter of general principal, do not suffer from the problems connected with mutual influencing of co-operating blocks which complicate the design of analogue systems. One-way digital connections, being simply data communications, exclude any mutual influence of the function of connected digital blocks unless gross design errors (overload, extremely bad impedance matching) are involved.

5 Possibility of reliable realisation of complicated processing methods that are difficult to realise or are practically infeasible in an analogue version (for instance, advanced adaptive processing, higher methods of analysis in real time, multidimensional processing etc.).

6 Compatibility with information systems enabled by a similar type of data processing and the possibility of using compatible data representations are important features used by integrating signal and measurement data processing into automatic control and management systems, such as in automatic production, air traffic control, in hospital information systems for intensive care monitoring and computer-assisted diagnostics etc.

7 Possibility of multiplex operation: the digital processors with a higher computing capacity than necessary for a given signal-processing task can be used in time sharing for more tasks without introducing any interference among the individual tasks. (For example, one signal processor can realise the complete filter bank, or even different processing phases such as the filtering of a signal, its frequency analysis and real-time classification).

Current use of digital signal-processing methods and the positive trend of application quantity and complexity give testimony to the claim that their advantages already outweigh the drawbacks in many practically important fields.

Chapter 2
Discrete signals and systems

2.1 Sampling and reconstruction of signals

Let us repeat that we understand *a continuous, one-dimensional signal* to be a piecewise continuous real or complex function of one continuous real variable, t. Usually the dimensionality will not be emphasised as, with the exception of Chapter 14, we will deal exclusively with one-dimensional signals. Note that the number of independent variables is not, in principle, limited; we can have two, three or multidimensional signals. Signals that are continuous (according to our definition) are also called analogue signals as they can be represented by time courses of physical ('analogue') variables (t then specifically means time).

The independent variables usually have a physical meaning of time and therefore such signals are sometimes called *continuous-time signals*. The name can be restrictive as, in a more general sense, the variable can also, for example, have the meaning of a space variable, however, it also includes functions which are not piecewise continuous. In the interests of simplicity, we will limit ourselves to piecewise continuous signals and to some important signals which, although not piecewise continuous, will be interpreted as limit cases of piecewise continuous signals.

Sampling serves to express the continuous signal $f(t)$ by its discrete samples $f_n = f(t_n)$ for specified values t_n of the independent variable t. Usually, the samples are equidistant so that $t_n = nT$, where T is a suitable real constant denoted as the *sampling period* so that

$$f_n = f(nT).$$

It will be shown that the discrete representation formed by the theoretically infinite sequence $\{f_n\}$ can carry, under certain circumstances, the complete information on the continuous signal. The assumptions enabling the exact reconstruction of the continuous signal from its samples will also be determined.

A comment on the *Dirac distribution*: a very useful signal in theoretical considerations is the Dirac distribution $\delta(t)$ (sometimes also called the analogue *unit impulse*):

$$\delta(t) \to \infty \text{ when } t = 0, \quad \delta(t) = 0 \text{ when } t \neq 0, \quad \text{while } \int_{-\infty}^{\infty} \delta(t)\, dt = 1.$$

Although this is obviously a continuous-variable signal, it is not continuous in our defined sense. It can, nevertheless, be interpreted as the limit case of a continuous signal $d(t)$ for $h \to \infty$:

$$d(t) = h \text{ for } t \in \left\langle 0, \frac{1}{h} \right\rangle, \quad d(t) = 0 \text{ for } t \notin \left\langle 0, \frac{1}{h} \right\rangle$$

(which obviously fulfils the requirement of unit integral weight). The interpretation of the Dirac impulse as the limit case of the function enables us to interpret it as a *quasicontinuous signal* and therefore to treat it exactly in further relations, for example to calculate its Fourier transform which is not defined in the usual sense, also by means of a limit.

The properties of Dirac distribution are as follows:
1 Shift of the impulse: $\delta(x - \xi)$ is nonzero just for $x = \xi$, where ξ is an arbitrary real number.
2 Sifting property: $\int_{-\infty}^{\infty} f(t)\delta(t - \tau)\, dt = f(\tau)$.
3 The spectrum (in the sense of the integral Fourier transform) is, as follows from the sifting property,

$$\Lambda(\omega) = \int_{-\infty}^{\infty} \delta(t - \tau)e^{-j\omega t}\, dt = e^{-j\omega\tau},$$

especially when $\xi = 0$, we have $\Lambda(\omega) = 1$.
4 Energy of the impulse: $E_\delta = \int_{-\infty}^{\infty} \delta^2(t)\, dt = \lim_{h \to \infty} h^2.1/h = \lim_{h \to \infty} h = \infty$.

It is worth noting that the Dirac impulse can depend on a variable representing any physical quantity, namely on frequency.

Using the Dirac distribution, the ideally sampled signal can be expressed as a quasicontinuous signal. Let us introduce the *sampling signal*

$$v(t) = \sum_{i=-\infty}^{\infty} \delta(t - iT) \tag{2.1}$$

with sampling period T and therefore *circular sampling frequency* $\omega_v = 2\pi/T$ (Figure 2.1). Then, the sampled signal can be expressed as a product of the continuous (analogue) signal and the sampling signal

$$f_v(t) = f(t).v(t) = \sum_{i=-\infty}^{\infty} f(iT)\delta(t - iT). \tag{2.2}$$

All the information on the signal samples is obviously contained in this signal, and in this sense it is equivalent to the *discrete signal* $\{f_n\} = \{f(nT)\}$. On the other hand, it is a quasicontinuous signal – dependent on continuous time –

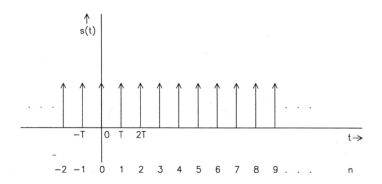

Figure 2.1 Sampling signal

which can be interpreted as a limit case of the height modulated impulse signal with a constant impulse width, which in the limit approaches zero, the weights of impulses remaining unchanged. Figure 2.2 should be interpreted in this sense; the arrows indicate that the values of the impulses approach infinity and the arrow heights represent the weights of the individual impulses which are equal to values of the discrete sample values.

The *sampled signal spectrum* (i.e. continuous (integral) Fourier transform $\mathbb{F}(.)$) will be expressed in terms of the original analogue signal spectrum. We shall utilise the elements of continuous signal theory, namely the *convolution theorem*

$$F_v(\omega) = \mathbb{F}\{f(t).v(t)\} = \frac{1}{2\pi} F(\omega)^* V(\omega) = \frac{1}{2\pi} \int_{-\infty}^{\infty} F(\omega - u) V(u)\, du, \qquad (2.3)$$

where $F(\omega)$ and $V(\omega)$ are *spectra* (*integral Fourier transforms*) of the continuous signal and sampling signal, respectively; for example for the original signal we have

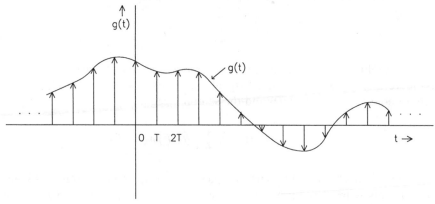

Figure 2.2 Sampled signal

$$F(\omega) = \mathbb{F}\{f(t)\} = \int_{-\infty}^{\infty} f(t)e^{-j\omega t}\, dt. \tag{2.4}$$

The spectrum $V(\omega)$ cannot be determined directly from the definition expression of the Fourier transform because $v(t)$ is not an absolutely integrable function. Therefore, we shall proceed by the method used in signal theory to determine the integral spectrum of periodic functions. Let us first state that the sampling function $v(t)$ is periodic (with period T) originating from regular repetition of the unit impulse. It can therefore be expressed by a Fourier series

$$v(t) = \sum_{k=-\infty}^{\infty} c_k\, e^{jk\frac{2\pi}{T}t} = \sum_{k=-\infty}^{\infty} c_k\, e^{jk\omega_v t}$$

where

$$c_k = \frac{1}{T}\Lambda\left(k\frac{2\pi}{T}\right) = \frac{1}{T} \tag{2.5}$$

according to the theorem of the relationship between the Fourier-series coefficients and the spectral density of the original (nonrepeated) signal

$$\mathbb{F}\left\{\sum_k c_k\, e^{jk\omega_v t}\right\} = 2\pi \sum_k c_k \delta(\omega - k\omega_v),$$

(which can easily be proved by the inverse transform utilising the sifting property of the impulse), so that

$$V(\omega) = \mathbb{F}\{v(t)\} = \mathbb{F}\left\{\sum_k \frac{1}{T} e^{jk\omega_v t}\right\} = \frac{2\pi}{T} \sum_{k=-\infty}^{\infty} \delta(\omega - k\omega_v). \tag{2.6}$$

The spectrum of the sampling signal is thus formed by an infinite sequence of real impulses of weight $2\pi/T$ (Figure 2.3).

Substituting (2.6) into eqn (2.3) we obtain, after interchanging the operations of integration and summation,

$$F_v(\omega) = \frac{1}{T}\int_{-\infty}^{\infty} F(\omega - u)\sum_k \delta(i - k\omega_v)\, du = \frac{1}{T}\sum_k \int_{-\infty}^{\infty} F(\omega - u)\delta(u - k\omega_v)\, du$$

and, utilising the sifting property,

$$F_v(\omega) = \frac{1}{T}\sum_{k=-\infty}^{\infty} F(\omega - k\omega_v). \tag{2.7}$$

An important result has been obtained: the spectrum of an ideally and regularly sampled signal is formed by the sum of the infinite number of the original spectrum (Figure 2.5) replicas which are mutually shifted by integer multiples of

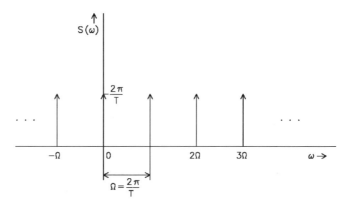

Figure 2.3 Spectrum of sampling signal

the sampling frequency (Figure 2.5, 2.6). In order to prevent any loss of information, every replica must carry the complete information on the original signal, and this is obviously only possible if no overlap of the spectra and consequently no distortion of the partial spectra takes place. Hence, the following conditions for reconstruction of a continuous signal from its samples must be fulfilled:

- the analogue signal must have a limited spectrum, i.e. it must be a band-limited signal with maximum frequency ω_{max},

$$F(\omega) = 0 \text{ outside of the interval } \langle -\omega_{max}, \omega_{max} \rangle, \tag{2.8}$$

- the sampling frequency must fulfil the following condition (*sampling theorem*):

$$\omega_v > 2\omega_{max}. \tag{2.9}$$

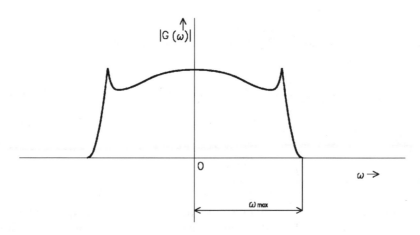

Figure 2.4 Example of spectrum of a bandlimited continuous signal

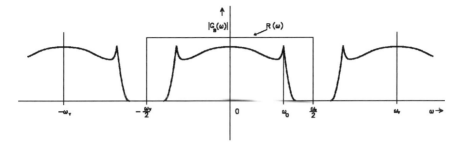

Figure 2.5 Spectrum of sampled signal when the sampling theorem holds

The first condition depends on the character of the processed signal. If the signal originates in a physical system as one of its physical variables (e.g. electrical voltage), or if it has been transferred *via* such a system, it may always be expected that the high-frequency components are, starting from a certain frequency limit, sufficiently small to consider the condition to be fulfilled with acceptable precision. If such a situation cannot be assumed, or the signal, although band limited, has such a high ω_{max} that the available technical means do not allow the fulfilment of the second condition, then the signal spectrum has to be limited artificially by means of a lowpass (antialiasing) filter before sampling. A similar situation occurs when a relatively low sampling frequency is chosen because the higher frequency components of the signal are irrelevant with respect to the purpose of the processing.

The *sampling theorem* stated in the second condition (also referred to as Nyquist, Kotelnikoff or Shannon's theorem) determines the lowest sampling frequency to be used. Nevertheless, it is usually necessary in practice to fulfil the condition of eqn (2.8) with considerable reserve in order to take into account the imperfect possibilities of signal reconstruction.

It should be emphasised that all these considerations do not apply directly to the discrete signal $\{f_n\}$, which cannot be transformed by the integral Fourier

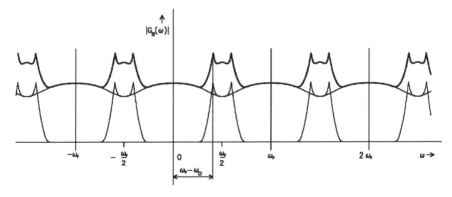

Figure 2.6 Spectrum of an undersampled signal

transform, but rather to the quasicontinuous signal $f_v(t)$. Both these signals carry the same information and are consequently mutually convertible, needing the same sampling rate. (On the subject of identical information content, we have assumed that the discrete sequence is supplemented by information on the value of the sampling frequency, as this is not a part of the digital sequence itself.)

The spectrum given by eqn (2.7) can, taking into account the linearity of the Fourier transform, be expressed also as a sum of spectra of individual shifted and weighted Dirac impulses,

$$F_v(\omega) = \sum_{n=-\infty}^{\infty} h_n\, e^{-j\omega T}. \tag{2.10}$$

Reconstruction is the inverse of the sampling process, hence it provides the continuous signal $f(t)$ on the basis of its sampled version $f_v(t)$. It can obviously be visualised in the original domain as interpolation among the sample values, but it can also be formulated precisely in the frequency domain: if we can change the spectrum of the sampled signal $F_v(\omega)$ into the spectrum of the original signal $F(\omega)$, it will naturally correspond to a perfect reconstruction of the desired signal. It is therefore required that

$$F_r(\omega) = R(\omega)\frac{1}{T}\sum_{k=-\omega}^{\omega} F(\omega - k\omega_v) = F(\omega),$$

where $R(\omega)$ is the frequency response of the reconstruction filter.

It is obvious that it suffices to suppress completely all the replicas of the spectrum except the basic one in the frequency range $\langle -\omega_v/2, \omega_v/2 \rangle$. This can be done (if the sampling theorem has been fulfilled so that no aliasing appears) simply by transferring the signal *via* a lowpass filter with the limit frequency $\omega_v/2$. The frequency response of such a filter should be ideally $R(\omega) = T$ for $|\omega| \leq \omega_v/2$, and equal to zero outside of this band. As such an ideal reconstruction filter cannot be precisely realised (as will be seen in the next paragraph), certain safeguard bands must be provided encompassing the transient areas of the filter's frequency response between the pass and stop bands (Figure 2.7). This again calls for fulfilling the sampling theorem with a sufficient reserve.

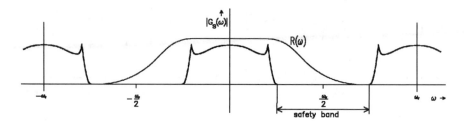

Figure 2.7 *Reconstruction as interpreted in the frequency domain*

In the original (usually time) domain, the reconstruction process, correspond-ing to the mentioned multiplication in the frequency domain, means the convolution

$$f_r(t) = f_v(t)^*r(t) = \int_{-\infty}^{\infty} f_v(\tau)r(t - \tau)\, d\tau$$

$$= \int_{-\infty}^{\infty} \left(\sum_{i=-\infty}^{\infty} f(iT)\delta(\tau - iT) \right) r(t - \tau)\, d\tau$$

$$= \sum_{i=-\infty}^{\infty} f(iT)r(t - iT), \tag{2.11}$$

where $r(t)$ is the impulse response of the ideal reconstruction filter,

$$r(t) = f^{-1}\{R(\omega)\} = \frac{1}{2\pi} \int_{-\infty}^{\infty} R(\omega)e^{j\omega t}\, d\omega = \frac{T}{2\pi} \int_{-\omega_v/2}^{\omega_v/2} e^{j\omega t}\, d\omega$$

$$= \frac{T}{2\pi} \frac{1}{jt} (e^{j(\omega_v/2)t} - e^{-j(\omega_v/2)t}) = \frac{\sin\left(\frac{\omega_v}{2}t\right)}{\frac{\omega_v}{2}t}. \tag{2.12}$$

This impulse response is obviously a suitable interpolation function as it has zeros at all sampling points except for the origin of the time axis. The result (eqn 2.11) expresses this interpolation (Figure 2.8). However, the function $r(t)$ is not exactly realisable by a real filter, as it is noncausal. Therefore, the realisation requires a causal approximation consisting in principle in intro-ducing some delay, thus shifting the response to the right, followed by cutting

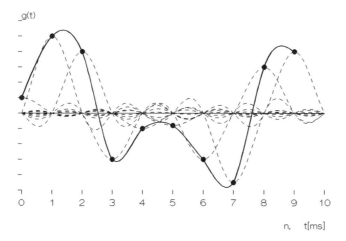

Figure 2.8 Ideal signal reconstruction from samples as interpolation in the original domain

off the part remaining to the left of the time origin. This or a similar approximation causes the previously mentioned frequency-response distortion of any realisable reconstruction filter.

2.2 A note on the Z-transform

The Z-transform is an important means of analysing discrete systems (e.g. systems with discrete time). It can be characterised, from an application point of view, as the counterpart of the Laplace transform which finds its use in the analysis of continuously working systems. We shall state here only the most important properties of the Z-transform, which will be used in the following explanation of discrete system theory.

Definition: The Z-transform of a sequence $\{x_n\}$ of numbers $x_0, x_1, \cdots, x_n, \cdots$ is the complex function

$$\mathbb{Z}\{x_n\} = X(z) = \sum_{n=0}^{\infty} x_n z^{-n}, \tag{2.13}$$

where z is a complex variable. (This is the so-called one-sided Z-transform; other alternatives will not be used in this book.) Sometimes, $X(z)$ is called the image and the sequence $\{x_n\}$ is then called the original.

Domain of definition: If the substitution $u = 1/z$ is introduced, $X(z)$ is obviously a power series in u. The radius of convergence of this series is $R = 1/l$, where $l = \lim_{n \to \infty} \sqrt[n]{|x_n|}$ or, equivalently, $l = \lim_{n \to \infty} (|x_{n+1}|/|x_n|)$). The series converges, therefore, for $|u| < R$, that is for $|z| > 1/R = l$. The functions $X(z)$ are holomorphic and can be analytically extended across the whole z plane.

Z-transforms (images) of some elementary sequences are as follows:

- the discrete unit impulse $\{u_n\} = 1, 0, 0, \cdots$ has the transform

$$U(z) = 1.z^0 = 1,$$

- the discrete unit step $\{s_n\} = 1, 1, 1, \cdots$ is transformed into

$$S(z) = \sum_{n=0}^{\infty} 1.z^{-n} = \frac{1}{1 - z^{-1}},$$

- the discrete causal complex harmonic function $\{x_n\} = e^{jn\omega T}$ for $n \geq 0$ is transformed into

$$X(z) = \sum_{n=0}^{\infty} e^{jn\omega T} z^{-n} = \frac{1}{1 - e^{j\omega T} z^{-1}}.$$

Inverse Z-transform: should $X(z) = \mathbb{Z}\{x_n\}$, the inverse Z-transform is the operator providing $\{x_n\} = \mathbb{Z}^{-1}\{X(z)\}$. The expression for calculation of a general term of the original sequence from the corresponding transform is, without proof,

$$x_k = \frac{1}{2\pi j} \oint_c X(z)z^{k-1}\, dz, \qquad (2.14)$$

where the integration path c must lie within the region of convergence of the series $\sum_{n=0}^{\infty} x_n z^{k-n-1}$ (without utilising the possibility of analytic extension) and must surround the point $z = 0$. The integral can usually be calculated simply by means of residual theorem. (We will not use other methods of the inverse transform.)

Basic properties of the Z-transform (providing existence of the individual transforms) are:

- the Z-transform is a linear operator; for any complex numbers c_i it is valid:

$$\mathbb{Z}\left\{\sum_{i=1}^{K} c_i{}^i x_n\right\} = \sum_{i=1}^{K} x_i\, \mathbb{Z}\{{}^i x_n\}. \qquad (2.15)$$

- transform of a shifted sequence: for any integer n and k, $n \geq k$ (for delayed sequence), this is valid:

$$\mathbb{Z}\{x_{n-k}\} = z^{-k}\left(\mathbb{Z}\{x_n\} + \sum_{m=-k}^{-1} x_m z^{-m}\right), \qquad (2.16)$$

where the sum on the right-hand side is zero when the original input sequence is causal and therefore has nonzero elements only for nonnegative indices.
   Indeed:

$$\mathbb{Z}\{x_{n-k}\} = \sum_{n=0}^{\infty} x_{n-k} z^{-n} = z^{-k}\left(\sum_{n=k}^{\infty} x_{n-k} z^{-n+k} + \sum_{n=0}^{k-1} x_{n-k} z^{-n+k}\right),$$

which gives the expected result after the substitution $m = n - k$. The sum on the right-hand side expresses the influence of the eventual nonzero terms of the signal $\{x_n\}$ before the time origin, which of course do not enter the Z-transform of the shifted sequence.
   The other alternative is the transform of a sequence shifted to the left (i.e. anticipated),

$$\mathbb{Z}\{x_{n+k}\} = z^{k} \cdot \left(\mathbb{Z}\{x_n\} - \sum_{n=0}^{k-1} x_n z^{-n}\right);$$

here, on the contrary, the influence of the terms that are before the time origin must be subtracted.

• convolution theorem: the sequence

$$\{y_n\}: y_n = \sum_{m=0}^{n} x_m h_{n-m} = \sum_{m=0}^{n} x_{m-n} h_m$$

is referred to as the plain or linear *discrete convolution* and denoted symbolically $\{x_n\} * \{h_n\} = \{x_n * h_n\}$. The following important relation called the *convolution theorem* is valid,

$$\mathbb{Z}\{x_n * h_n\} = \mathbb{Z}\{x_n\} . \mathbb{Z}\{h_n\}. \tag{2.17}$$

Indeed, the product of the transforms $X(z) = \mathbb{Z}\{x_n\}$ and $H(z) = \mathbb{Z}\{h_n\}$ is

$$X(z)H(z) = [x_0 + x_1 z^{-1} + x_2 z^{-2} + \cdots] . [h_0 + h_1 z^{-1} + h_2 z^{-2} + \cdots]$$

$$= x_0 . h_0 + (x_1 h_0 + x_0 h_1)z^{-1} + (x_0 h_2 + x_1 h_1 + x_2 h_0)z^{-2} + \cdots$$

$$= \sum_{n=0}^{\infty} \left(\sum_{m=0}^{n} x_m h_{n-m} \right) z^{-n} = \mathbb{Z}\{x_n * h_n\}.$$

This theorem has a fundamental importance; it is often used in linear system and signal analysis.

2.3 Discrete linear systems – models and characteristics

2.3.1 Input–output models and basic characteristics

A discrete linear time-invariant (LTI) system (also referred to as a convolutional system) is generally described by a difference equation of mth order

$$y_n = \sum_{i=0}^{r} L_i x_{n-i} - \sum_{i=1}^{m} K_i y_{n-i}, \tag{2.18}$$

to which the structure (signal flow diagram) depicted in Figure 2.9 corresponds. This general structure contains feedback and, if at least one of the coefficients K_i is nonzero, the system is called *recursive*. When all the coefficients $K_i = 0$, $i = 1, 2, \cdots, m$, the second term falls out and the simplified system, the structure of which does not contain feedback (Figure 2.11), is then described as being *nonrecursive*.

When eqn (2.18) is Z-transformed term by term, utilising the theorem (2.16), on the transforming of shifted sequences, we obtain

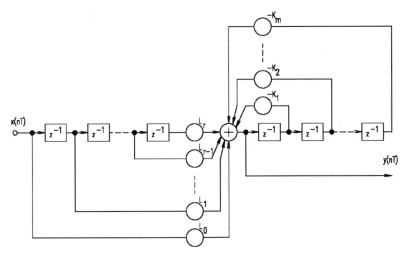

Figure 2.9 Direct realisation of a general recursive system

$$Y(z) = \sum_{i=0}^{r} L_i X(z) z^{-i} - \sum_{i=0}^{m} K_i Y(z) z^{-i} + \sum_{i=0}^{r} L_i \left(\sum_{k=-i}^{-1} x_k z^{-k-i} \right)$$

$$- \sum_{i=1}^{m} K_i \left(\sum_{k=-i}^{-1} y_k z^{-k-i} \right),$$

where the last two terms on the right-hand side express the influence of initial conditions given by the state of the delay elements before the start of work of the system (i.e. before the time origin). From this algebraic equation, the image $Y(z)$ of the output sequence can be expressed as

$$Y(z) = \frac{\sum_{i=0}^{r} L_i z^{-i}}{1 + \sum_{i=1}^{m} K_i z^{-i}} X(z) + \frac{\sum_{i=0}^{r} L_i \left(\sum_{k=-i}^{-1} x_k z^{-k-i} \right) - \sum_{i=1}^{m} K_i \left(\sum_{k=-i}^{-1} y_k z^{-k-i} \right)}{1 + \sum_{i=1}^{m} K_i z^{-i}}.$$

$$(2.19)$$

The first term of eqn (2.19) expresses the component of the complete response which is evoked by the samples of the input signal starting from the beginning of the system's work, and the second term is the component caused by nonzero initial conditions. The sequence corresponding to the second term is a transient as far as the system is stable, that is it becomes negligibly small after sufficient time has elapsed since the start of work. Considering this fact and, also, the fact that the selection of the time origin is arbitrary, it is often not necessary to analyse this component. We shall therefore limit ourselves to the analysis of the system response, and its properties, under zero initial conditions, as described by the first term only. Notice that the image response to the initial conditions is obviously given by the same coefficients as the response to the input signal from which the important system characteristics will be derived, namely the impulse and frequency responses. Therefore, these characteristics are closely connected with the character of the response to the initial conditions.

Under zero initial conditions, eqn (2.19) reduces to

$$Y(z) = H(z)X(z), \tag{2.20}$$

where $H(z)$ is the *transfer function* of the system, sometimes called the image transfer, or transfer in z,

$$H(z) = \frac{\displaystyle\sum_{i=0}^{r} L_i z^{m-i}}{\displaystyle\sum_{i=0}^{m} K_i z^{m-i}}, \quad (K_0 = 1). \tag{2.21}$$

Recursive systems usually have $m \geq r$; then the polynomial in the denominator has all powers of z and low-power terms are missing in the numerator polynomial. Both polynomials can be factored into products of root factors (when multiplicative constants are factored out and their ratio denoted A), as

$$H(z) = A \frac{z^{m-r} \displaystyle\prod_{i=1}^{r} (z - n_i)}{\displaystyle\prod_{j=1}^{m} (z = p_j)}, \tag{2.22}$$

where n_i, p_j are the roots of the polynomials in the numerator and denominator, respectively. The transfer function is therefore a fractional rational function (a proper one if $m > r$) of the continuous complex variable z; the *zero points* and *poles* of the function are n_i, p_i, respectively. The multiplicative factor A is the so-called *gain factor* (more precisely, *amplification*) of the system. It is therefore possible to characterise a discrete linear time-invariant system either by the system constants L_i, K_i or alternatively also by the pole–zero configuration in the z-plane together with the gain factor. It is obvious that a recursive system has the number of poles, as well as of zeros, equal to the order of the system m; if $m \geq r$ then the transfer function has a multiple zero of the multiplicity $(m - r)$ in the origin of the z-plane. As for all polynomials with real coefficients, the roots are either real or complex numbers, in the latter case in complex conjugate pairs; this therefore also applies to zeros and poles of a system with real system constants.

The relation of eqn (2.20) enables us to find the image response to any input signal for which its Z-transform exists (which are, among others, all finite sequences). Let us determine the response of the system to the discrete unit impulse $\{x_n\} = 1, 0, 0, \cdots$, the image of which is obviously $X(z) = 1$. Then, $Y(z) = H(z).1$ so that the output sequence is $\{y_n\} = Z^{-1}\{H(z)\}$. Hence, the system response to the unit impulse is given by the transfer function in a unique way. As the correspondence is inversible, the system is also fully defined – as far as the input–output description is concerned – by this response which is called the *impulse response* (or *impulse characteristic*) and is usually denoted by $\{h_n\}$. The impulse response and the transfer function of a system form a Z-transform pair,

$$\{h_n\} = Z^{-1}\{H(z)\} \quad \text{or} \quad H(z) = Z\{h_n\}. \tag{2.23}$$

The impulse response of recursive systems is usually infinite in time owing to the effect of feedback, although usually the amplitudes of the samples are essentially decreasing with time; such systems are called systems with infinite impulse response (*IIR systems*). As we shall see later, the impulse response of all non-recursive and of some rather special recursive systems terminates completely after a precisely defined time; then they are systems with finite impulse response (*FIR systems*).

It follows from the convolution theorem and eqn (2.20) that the output sequence of a discrete linear system under zero initial conditions is given by the convolution of the input signal and the system's impulse response,

$$\{y_n\} = Z^{-1}\{H(z)X(z)\} = \{h_n * x_n\}, \quad \text{i.e.} \quad y_n = \sum_{m=0}^{n} h_m x_{n-m} \tag{2.24}$$

as far as the system is time invariant, that is its impulse response sequence $\{h_n\}$ doesn't change in time. This result can be interpreted in a very comprehensible way by using the principle of superposition: let us decompose the input signal $\{x_n\}$ into its individual terms x_i. Each term, appropriately positioned on the time axis, will be considered as an independent input signal $\{{}^i x_n\} = [0, \cdots, 0, x_i, 0, \cdots]$, which is in fact a unit impulse weighted by the constant x_i and delayed by i sampling periods. Every such impulse produces, at the system output, its own properly weighted and shifted impulse response; the responses to all the partial signals sum together. The convolution generally has a number of terms equal to the order n of the calculated output sample so that the length of the sum grows without limit. Therefore, the convolution expression (2.24) is not a suitable formula for practical computations (except for FIR systems).

Let us analyse further the response of the system to the harmonic signal

$$\{x_n\} = \{\cos \omega n T\} = \left\{ \frac{1}{2}(e^{j\omega n T} + e^{-j\omega n T}) \right\},$$

which can be considered as a sampled version of the continuous signal $\cos \omega t$, $t > 0$. The expansion into two complex components according to Euler's equality enables us to simplify the mathematical notation by analysing the response to each component separately and consequently to sum the partial responses weighted by 1/2. For the first component $\{^1x_n\} = \{e^{j\omega nT}\}$ is then (by using the Z-transform definition and calculating the sum of the infinite geometrical series)

$$X_1(z) = \mathbb{Z}\{e^{j\omega nT}\} = \frac{z}{z - e^{j\omega T}},$$

so that, with zero initial conditions, the partial image response is

$$Y_1(z) = H(z)\frac{z}{z - e^{j\omega T}}.$$

The elements of the corresponding time sequence can be obtained by the inverse Z-transform (using the unit circle as the closed integration path which, as we shall see later, encircles all the poles of every stable system)

$$
\begin{aligned}
{}^1y_n &= \frac{1}{2\pi j} \oint_c H(z)\frac{z^n}{z - e^{j\omega T}}\, dz \\
&= \sum_i res\left[H(z)\frac{z^n}{z - e^{j\omega T}}\right]_{p_i} + res\left[H(z)\frac{z^n}{z - e^{j\omega T}}\right]_{e^{j\omega T}} \\
&= \sum_i \lim_{z \to p_i}(z - p_i)H(z)\frac{z^n}{z - e^{j\omega T}} + \lim_{z \to e^{j\omega T}}(z - e^{j\omega T})H(z)\frac{z^n}{z - e^{j\omega T}} \\
&= \sum_i \frac{\prod\limits_{j=1}^{r}(p_i - n_j)p_i^{m-r}}{\prod\limits_{j=1}^{i-1}(p_i - p_j)\prod\limits_{j=i+1}^{m}(p_i - p_j)}\frac{p_i^n}{p_i - e^{j\omega T}} + H(e^{j\omega T})e^{j\omega nT}.
\end{aligned}
\tag{2.25}
$$

We have supposed, for the sake of simplicity, only simple poles. An eventual occurrence of multiple poles in $H(z)$ would lead to only a slightly more complex derivation with a qualitatively similar result.

The interpretation of the result is interesting. The first term is a sum of signal components which all decrease exponentially with time providing that $|p_i| < 1$, $\forall i$ which, as we shall see later, is a necessary (and sufficient) condition of the system stability. (Notice that only the numerator of the second fraction is dependent on n, i.e. on time, and the remaining parts of every component are complex constants dependent only on pole and zero positions and on the signal frequency.) The first term becomes, therefore, negligible after a certain time from the start of system operation and thus it can be said that it is a transient response to suddenly connecting the signal to the input. The second term is obviously given by the product of the nth element of the input signal $\{^1x_n\}$ with the complex quantity $H(e^{j\omega T})$ which is independent of n and therefore also of time. This quantity which is dependent on signal frequency will be called the *frequency response* of the system at frequency ω and will usually be denoted $G(\omega)$.

The physical meaning of the frequency response will be apparent when we have finished the derivation of the system response to a real harmonic signal by adding the response to the other input signal component $\{^2x_n\} = e^{-j\omega nT}$. The calculation of the response to this input is quite analogous to that for the first component and after neglecting the transient part we obtain

$$^2y_n \cong H(e^{-j\omega T})e^{-j\omega nT} = H^*(e^{j\omega T})e^{-j\omega nT},$$

where the transition from the first to the second expression follows from the assumption that $\{h_n\}$ is a real sequence. If the frequency response is expressed as

$$G(\omega) = H(e^{j\omega T}) = |H(e^{j\omega T})|e^{j\varphi(\omega)},$$

where $\varphi(\omega) = \text{Arg}(H(e^{j\omega T}))$ is the phase and $|G(\omega)| = |H(e^{j\omega T})|$ the modulus of the frequency response, we obtain the elements of the resulting output signal as

$$y_n = \frac{1}{2}(^1y_n +{}^2y_n) = |G(\omega)|\left(\frac{e^{j(\omega nT + \varphi(\omega))} + e^{-j(\omega nT - [-\varphi(\omega)])}}{2}\right)$$

$$= |G(\omega)|\cos(\omega nT + \varphi(\omega)) \tag{2.25a}$$

It can therefore be seen that the *dynamically stable* (nondecaying) component of the response of a discrete linear time-invariant system to a real harmonic signal of a certain frequency ω is again a harmonic signal of the same frequency. The output is nevertheless time shifted with respect to the input, which is expressed by the phase shift $\varphi(\omega)$, and its amplitude is $|G(\omega)|$ times greater. This is why the module of the frequency response is sometimes referred to as amplification at the particular frequency (naturally, it can also be $|G(\omega)| < 1$). Notice that in the case of the harmonic signal unlimited in time, that is when it has started in time $-\infty$, the transient is not present at all and the output is precisely given at any time instant only by the dynamically-stable component. This is, for example, also the case for the harmonic signal components determined by spectral analysis, as we shall see later.

It is evident that the values of the frequency response are given by the transfer function values on the unit circle at the points $z = e^{j\omega T}$, the position vector of which contains the angle ωT with positive direction of the real axis. As the frequency can be chosen arbitrarily, it is possible to determine the frequency response for all the frequencies $\omega \in \langle 0, \omega_v/2\rangle$ admissible for the input harmonic signal according to the sampling theorem, that is to ascertain the values of the transfer on the whole half circle for $\omega T \in \langle 0, \pi\rangle$. The transfer is obviously dependent on the angle and therefore, with a fixed sampling period, T, on the frequency ω; the function $G(\omega)$ formulated in this way may be called the *frequency characteristic* (or response) of the system.

Of course, it can be expressed as

$$G(\omega) = H(z)|_{z=e^{j\omega T}} = \mathbb{Z}\{h_n\}|_{z=e^{j\omega T}} = \sum_{k=0}^{\infty} h_k e^{-j\omega Tk}, \tag{2.26}$$

where we can recognise the last sum as a Fourier series, the coefficients of which are given by the values of the impulse response. It follows that the frequency response of a linear discrete system is a periodic function with a period length equal to $2\pi/T$, that is the sampling frequency ω_v. As the complex conjugate terms (for $k < 0$) are missing, the values of the series, i.e. of the frequency response, are complex with the interpretation of the modulus and phase as explained in the previous paragraph. Notice that $G(\omega)$ is a continuous-frequency function, as the signal frequency may be arbitrary.

Substituting expression (2.22) into eqn (2.26), we obtain

$$G(\omega) = \frac{e^{j\omega(m-r)T}\prod\limits_{i=1}^{r}(e^{j\omega T} - n_i)}{\prod\limits_{i=1}^{m}(e^{j\omega T} - p_i)}, \tag{2.27}$$

where the individual factors in the products are complex numbers which can be represented in the z-plane by vectors between pole or zero position and the point $e^{j\omega T}$ on the unit circle representing the frequency axis in that plane. If the lengths of such vectors, or angles included between them and the real axis, are denoted, respectively

$$|e^{j\omega T} - n_i| = d_i, \ |e^{j\omega T} - p_i| = l_i,$$

or

$$\arg(e^{j\omega T} - n_i) = \varphi_i, \ \arg(e^{j\omega T} - p_i) = \psi_i,$$

then the modulus and argument of the frequency response can be expressed as

$$|G(\omega)| = \frac{\prod\limits_{i=1}^{r} d_i}{\prod\limits_{i=1}^{m} l_i} \quad \text{and} \quad \arg(G(\omega)) = (m-r)\omega T + \sum\limits_{i=1}^{r}\varphi_i - \sum\limits_{i=1}^{m}\psi_i. \tag{2.28}$$

Hence, it is also possible to determine the modulus and phase frequency characteristics on the basis of the geometric configuration of poles and zeros of the system. This approach is useful for simple estimates of the frequency response of a system, based on the knowledge of its pole–zero configuration (Figure 2.10). On the other hand, use of eqn (2.28) enables distribution of the poles and zeros intuitively, with respect to the required properties of the resulting frequency response, when starting to design a system (see Section 5.3.2.1).

A very important property of discrete systems is *stability*, which can be understood as the tendency of a system to react adequately during a lasting stimulus and to return to its initial state after the extinction of that stimulus. In input–output analysis of systems, which we most commonly apply, stability is more

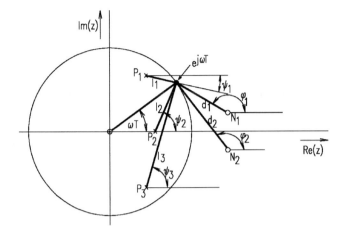

Figure 2.10 Estimate of frequency response based on pole–zero configuration

formally defined as follows (bounded input–bounded output – **BIBO** definition): the system is stable if it responds to any bounded input sequence $\{x_n\}$
(i.e. limited as far as sample values are concerned) by a bounded output
sequence $\{y_n\}$.

It is obvious that, according to this definition, only instability can be directly
confirmed. To this end, it is sufficient to find a single value-limited input
sequence to which the system responds with a sequence containing at least
one element with unlimited magnitude. Testing of systems by some selected
test signals (e.g. by the unit impulse or unit step) can only verify, for a finite
time interval, that the response is limited for these special signals, which is
only a necessary but not a sufficient condition of stability.

A number of necessary and sufficient criteria of stability have been found
theoretically, and can be used in practice; we shall present the two which are
most frequently applied.

1 *Stability criterion in the original domain* (Hurewitz): a linear discrete time-
   invariant system is stable if and only if its impulse response fulfils

$$\sum_{n=0}^{\infty} |h_n| = V < \infty, \tag{2.29}$$

i.e. if the series derived from the impulse response is absolutely convergent.
To prove the criterion, we shall first derive its sufficiency. Let us have a
bounded signal $\{x_n\}$, which fulfils $|x_n| < L < \infty$; for generality, let us say
that it can have nonzero values even to the left of the time origin, $x_n \neq 0$
for $n < 0$. The output is given by the convolution $y_n = \sum_{k=0}^{\infty} h_k x_{n-k}$ (the

infinite upper limit comes from the possibility of the signal starting any time before the time origin) and consequently

$$|y_n| \le \sum_{k=0}^{\infty} |h_k||x_{n-k}| < L \sum_{k=0}^{\infty} |h_k| = LV,$$

so that the output is definitely bounded.

The condition is also necessary as shown by the following argument: suppose that the criterion is violated, i.e. $\sum_{k=0}^{\infty} |h_k| = \infty$. Consider the output value y_n if the input signal consists of the sequence of values

$$x_k = \text{sign}(h_{n-k}), \quad \text{i.e. } x_{n-k} = \text{sign}(h_k).$$

Then

$$y_n = \sum_{k=0}^{\infty} h_k x_{n-k} = \sum_{k=0}^{\infty} h_k \,\text{sign}(h_k) = \sum_{k=0}^{\infty} |h_k| = \infty$$

and the system is unstable in the sense of the BIBO definition.

2 *Stability criterion in the image domain (pole configuration criterion)*: a linear discrete system, the transfer function of which is a fractional rational function, is stable if and only if all poles p_i of its transfer function are situated inside the unit circle,

$$|p_i| < 1, \;\forall i.$$

The proof will again be divided into verifying of necessity and sufficiency.

Sufficiency: if $H(z) = P(z)/Q(z)$, where $P(z)$ and $Q(z)$ are polynomials, then $H(z)$ has no other singularities than the poles $p_1, p_2, \cdots, p_m$ which are the roots of $Q(z)$. Therefore, $H(z)$ is holomorphic outside of the region encompassing the poles, i.e. for $|z| > r$, $r < 1$. As $H(z) = \sum_{k=0}^{\infty} h_k z^{-k}$, this series is convergent in the mentioned region and because it is a polynomial (in $1/z$), even absolutely convergent, i.e. $\sum_{k=0}^{\infty} |h_k z^{-k}| < \infty$. The point $z = 1$ belongs to the region of convergence and thus the series $\sum_{k=0}^{\infty} |h_k|$ is also convergent, so that the system is stable according to the previous Hurewitz criterion.

Necessity: let the Hurewitz criterion be fulfilled, $\sum_{k=0}^{\infty} |h_k| = V < \infty$. Let us admit that the system image transfer $H(z)$ has a pole on, or outside of, the unit circle. The previous sum can be rewritten as $\sum_{k=0}^{\infty} |h_k z^{-k}||_{z=1}$; it follows from its convergence that this polynomial in $1/z$ must converge for all $|1/z| < 1$, i.e. for all $|z| \ge 1$. As this is in conflict with the supposition on the pole position, the requirement of poles being inside the unit circle is necessary.

Stability is a crucial requirement of proper functioning of discrete systems in most applications so that the analysis or ensuring of validity of any of the mutually equivalent stability criteria is a necessary step in every design.

Up to this point the considerations in this chapter have referred to generic systems modelled by eqn (2.18), that is both recursive and nonrecursive. We will now deal specifically with nonrecursive systems which are a special case, and are simpler in having all the feedback coefficients equal to zero. Consequently, their specific properties have certain advantages, and they also simplify the considerations concerning their design and use. The direct realisation corresponding to the difference equation

$$y_n = \sum_{i=0}^{r} L_i x_{n-i}, \tag{2.30}$$

which is a simplification of eqn (2.18), is depicted in Figure 2.11. Equation (2.30) obviously represents the directly calculated convolution with a finite number of summed terms.

The transfer function (2.21) or (2.22) simplifies to

$$H(z) = \frac{1}{z^r} \sum_{i=0}^{r} L_i z^{r-i} = \frac{A}{z^r} \prod_{i=1}^{r} (z - n_i), \tag{2.31}$$

so that, disregarding the r-multiple pole at the origin of the z-plane, the transfer function is only defined by the configuration of r zero points. Because, on the other hand, $H(z) = Z\{h_n\}$, we find that

$$H(z) = \sum_{i=0}^{\infty} h_i z^{-i} = \sum_{i=0}^{r} L_i z^{-i}, \tag{2.32}$$

and, by comparison of coefficients of both polynomials, we find that $L_i = h_i$ for $i \in \langle 0, r \rangle$ and $h_i = 0$ for $i > r$. Hence, the system constants of a nonrecursive system are equal to the values of the corresponding impulse response, which is finite and of the length $r + 1$. Further, from eqn (2.31) it follows that the frequency characteristic of a nonrecursive system is given by a finite Fourier series

$$G(\omega) = H(e^{j\omega T}) = \sum_{k=0}^{r} h_k e^{-jk\omega T}. \tag{2.33}$$

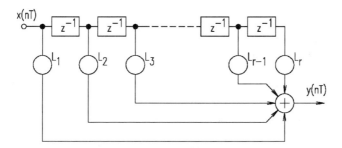

Figure 2.11 Direct realisation of a general nonrecursive system

Finally, it is an important property of nonrecursive systems that they are *absolutely stable*. Indeed, the Hurewitz criterion of (2.29) is always fulfilled because the impulse response is finite; similarly, the image-domain criterion cannot be violated, as all the poles are concentrated in the origin.

Let us conclude this section by noting that, as we have shown, all the non-recursive systems have finite impulse responses, i.e. they are of FIR type. Nevertheless, the inverse statement doesn't generally apply: as we shall see later, recursive systems exist which have finite impulse response, because of mutual compensation of poles and zeros. It follows that the classification of the systems into FIR and IIR classes does not generally agree with the division into non-recursive and recursive systems.

2.3.2 State models

So far, we have described discrete linear systems by means of an input–output model eqn (2.18). There exists another type of model that is in some instances more generic – the *state model*. It enables us to work with vector (parallel) inputs and outputs and describes even the values (so-called *state variables*) in selected inner points of the system structure. In addition, it enables the basic realisation structure of eqn (2.18) to be transformed into other structures which are equivalent in terms of input–output correspondence and may be advantageous in implementation. The usual form of the state model is

$$\mathbf{q}_{n+1}, = \mathbf{A}\mathbf{q}_n + \mathbf{B}\mathbf{x}_n$$

$$\mathbf{y}_n = \mathbf{C}\mathbf{q}_n + \mathbf{D}\mathbf{x}_n \qquad (2.34)$$

where $\mathbf{q}_n = [^1q_n, {}^2q_n, \cdots, {}^kq_n]^T$ is the column vector of state variables (the symbol T denotes transposition), $\mathbf{x}_n = [^1x_n, {}^2x_n, \cdots, {}^px_n]^T$ is the vector of input values and $\mathbf{y}_n = [^1y_n, {}^2y_n, \cdots, {}^ly_n]^T$ is the output vector. The symbols $\mathbf{A}, \mathbf{B}, \mathbf{C}, \mathbf{D}$ denote matrices of corresponding dimensions defining a concrete system. It can be seen that the state model counts with systems which can have more than one (scalar) input and/or output. The model given by eqn (2.34) is obviously a vector difference equation of the first order.

The name of the model is derived from the concept of state variables which are saved in the system memory (as far as digital systems are concerned). The vector $\mathbf{q}_n$ of values of all the state variables determines the so-called *state of the system* in the nth sampling period. The present state determines, together with the incoming input signals $\mathbf{x}_n$, according to eqn (2.34), the state $\mathbf{q}_{n+1}$ in the next period and the present output $\mathbf{y}_n$ (see Figure 2.12). The reader who is familiar with the basic theory of finite automata will certainly notice the similarity with the generic functional scheme of a finite automaton. He will realise that a discrete system is a special case of such an automaton, the input, output and state alphabets of which are formed by sets of values of the signals $\mathbf{x}, \mathbf{y}, \mathbf{q}$ (sets of admissible numeric vectors in digital systems) and with transient

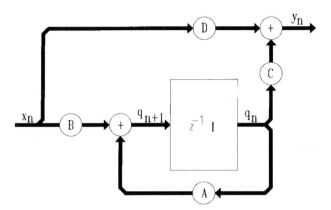

Figure 2.12 Discrete system in state representation

and output functions which are formed by the matrix relations of the state model.

We shall show that there exists a state model equivalent to our previously used (less generic) model (2.18), which is a scalar difference equation of mth order. Let us define the state variables as states of all $m + r$ memory elements, i.e. the delayed values of signals $\{x_n\}$ and $\{y_n\}$:

$$^i q_n = y_{n-i}, \quad i \in \langle 1, m \rangle$$

and

$$^i q_n = x_{n-(i-m)}, \quad i \in \langle m+1, m+r \rangle.$$

The (scalar) output signal is obviously $\mathbf{y}_n = [y_n] =^1 q_{n+1}$; the input signal also has only one scalar component $\mathbf{x}_n = [x_n]$. The state model matrices of the system described by eqns (2.34) are then

$$
\mathbf{A} = \begin{bmatrix}
-K_1 & -K_2 & \cdots & -K_m & L_1 & L_2 & \cdots & L_r \\
1 & 0 & \cdots & 0 & 0 & 0 & \cdots & 0 \\
0 & 1 & \cdots & 0 & 0 & 0 & \cdots & 0 \\
\vdots & \vdots & \ddots & \vdots & \vdots & \vdots & \ddots & \vdots \\
0 & 0 & \cdots & 1 & 0 & 0 & \cdots & 0 \\
0 & 0 & 0 & 0 & 0 & 0 & 0 & 0 \\
0 & 0 & \cdots & 0 & 1 & 0 & \cdots & 0 \\
0 & 0 & \cdots & 0 & 0 & 1 & \cdots & 0 \\
\vdots & \vdots & \ddots & \vdots & \vdots & \vdots & \ddots & \vdots \\
0 & 0 & \cdots & 0 & 0 & 0 & \cdots & 1
\end{bmatrix}, \quad
\mathbf{B} = \begin{bmatrix}
L_0 \\
0 \\
0 \\
\vdots \\
0 \\
1 \\
0 \\
0 \\
\vdots \\
0
\end{bmatrix},
$$

$$\mathbf{C} = \begin{bmatrix} -K_1 & -K_2 & \cdots & -K_m & L_1 & L_2 & \cdots & L_r \end{bmatrix}, \quad \mathbf{D} = \begin{bmatrix} L_0 \end{bmatrix}.$$

This model describes the same structure of function blocks as does the original scalar equation, and obviously they are therefore mutually equivalent.

It is not so far clear from the discussion whether or not there is always a possibility of an inverse transform, that is a transform from a state model into an equivalent scalar model. We will show in the Section 5.3.3 for a system of state equations that, by solving it *via* the Z-transform, we obtain the transfer function $H(z)$ in the usual form of a fractional rational function with the polynomials of corresponding order. Thus, it will be seen that the system of m interconnected and simultaneously working subsystems of the first order is equivalent to a simple recursive system of the mth order. It can be proved generally that an equivalent input–output model (2.18) can be found for any state model (in the sense that their input–output behaviour is identical), as the model corresponds to the mutual equivalence between a simultaneous system of first-order equations and a single difference equation of a higher order. The state model thus does not generalise the class of signal-processing systems from the point of view of their external behaviour and therefore we will not discuss them in greater detail (apart from the mentioned exception).

2.3.3 Connection of systems

The final part of this chapter will be devoted to the interconnecting of systems in order to build hierarchically more complex systems, the characteristics of which can be determined on the basis of the knowledge of characteristics of subsystems.

Cascade (serial) connection means that N subsystems with the individual transfer functions $H_1(z), H_2(z), \cdots, H_N(z)$ are interconnected in a chain so that ${}^i x_n = {}^{i-1} y_n$, $i \in \langle 2, N \rangle$ where ${}^i x$ and ${}^i y$ are input and output signals of the ith subsystem. The input of the first subsystem is considered to be the input x of the complete system, and similarly the output of the Nth subsystem means the external output y (Figure 2.13 where the last index should be N). In the Z-transform domain, the external output can be expressed as

$$Y(z) = Y_N(z) = H_N(z)Y_{N-1}(z) = H_N(z)H_{N-1}(z)Y_{N-2}(z)$$

$$= \cdots = \left(\prod_{i=1}^{N} H_i(z) \right) X_1(z)$$

$$= H(z)X(z).$$

The resulting transfer function of the serial system is therefore given by the product

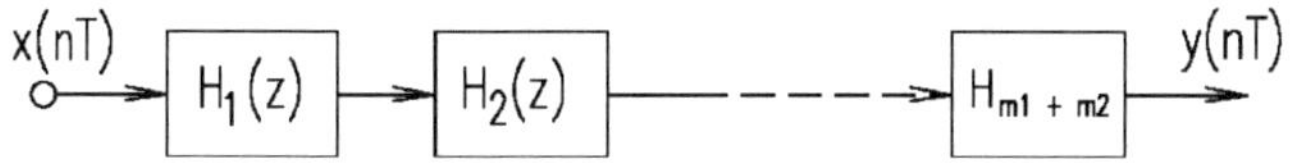

Figure 2.13 Cascade connection of subsystems

$$H(z) = \prod_{i=1}^{N} H_i(z).\tag{2.35}$$

It follows that the frequency responses are multiplied in the same way,

$$G(\omega) = \prod_{i=1}^{N} G_i(\omega).\tag{2.36}$$

It can also be seen that the set of poles and zeros of the complete system is formed by the union of the corresponding sets of the partial systems (it is said that each of the subsystems 'covers' some desirable resulting poles and zeros). A possible exception is the case when the positions of a pole and a zero coincide so that they cancel each other out and thus disappear from the resulting set. As there are no resulting poles other than those that were already in the partial subsystems, the resulting system is stable if all partial systems have been stable. From eqn (2.35) it follows, based on the convolution theorem, that the resulting impulse response of the cascade is given by the convolution of partial impulse responses,

$$\{h_n\} = \{^1h_n * {}^2h_n * \cdots * {}^N h_n\}.\tag{2.37}$$

Parallel connection of N partial systems is defined as an interconnection (Figure 2.14, again $m1 + m2 = N$) where the inputs of all subsystems are connected together and form the external input, $^ix_n = x_n, \forall i$, with the external output given by the sum of the output of the partial systems, $y_n = \sum_{n=1}^{N} {}^iy_n$. (Notice that digital outputs cannot be directly interconnected.)

In the Z-transform domain, we have for the transformed output (with zero initial conditions)

$$G(\omega) = \sum_{i=1}^{N} G_i(\omega) Y(z) = \sum_{i=1}^{N} Y_i(z) = \sum_{i=1}^{N} (H_i(z)X(z)) = \left(\sum_{i=1}^{N} H_i(z)\right) X(z).$$

The transfer function of a parallel system is therefore given by the sum of the partial transfers,

$$H(z) = \sum_{i=1}^{N} H_i(z),\tag{2.38}$$

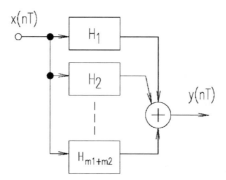

Figure 2.14 Parallel connection of subsystems

and, consequently, the frequency characteristics are also summed,

$$G(\omega) = \sum_{i=1}^{N} G_i(\omega). \tag{2.39}$$

As far as the resulting pole and zero configuration is concerned, it is obvious that the resulting set of poles is the union of sets of poles of the subsystems (apart from the unlikely case of a pole being cancelled by a zero generated by the connection). The parallel system is therefore also stable if all the subsystems are individually stable. Concerning the zeros, a rule similar to that for the poles does not apply because a zero of the complete system can be generated only in places where there is a zero sum of all partial transfer functions. The set of zeros therefore contains the intersection (usually empty) of zero sets of subsystems, in union with new zeros generated by the cooperation of all the subsystems; these are placed at positions in the z-plane that need not correspond to any of the original zero points.

The impulse response of a parallel system is, owing to the linearity of the Z-transform and according to eqn (2.38), given by the sum of partial impulse responses,

$$\{h_n\} = \sum_{i=1}^{N} \{^i h_n\}. \tag{2.40}$$

The *feedback connection* of two systems (Figure 2.15) is defined by the following relations:

$$y_n = {}^1 y_n, \quad {}^2 x_n = {}^1 y_n, \quad {}^1 x_n = {}^2 y_n + x_n,$$

where y_n, x_n are the values of external output and input, respectively, and indexed values belong to individual subsystems. In the Z-transform domain, we have, then, under zero initial conditions

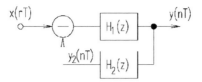

Figure 2.15 Feedback connection of subsystems

$$Y(z) = H_1(z)[H_2(z)Y(z) + X(z)],$$

so that the resulting transfer function is

$$H(z) = \frac{Y(z)}{X(z)} = \frac{H_1(z)}{1 - H_1(z)H_2(z)}. \tag{2.41}$$

It can be seen that the resulting feedback system can be unstable even if both partial systems are stable, because new poles can be generated by the interconnection.

Chapter 3
Discrete linear transforms

3.1 A note on the Fourier transform of discrete signals

The spectrum as defined by the integral Fourier transform for continuous signals does not exist for discrete signals. However, in Section 2.1 we introduced the notion of quasicontinuous signals which enable us to generalise the definition of the transform even to the discrete signals interpreted as limit cases of certain continuous signals. The relation (2.7) then gives the sampled-signal spectrum as an infinite sum of mutually shifted replicas of the original continuous signal spectrum.

The spectrum of the same signal can, with respect to the linearity of the Fourier transform, also be expressed as the sum of spectra of shifted and weighted Dirac impulses representing the individual samples,

$$F_v(\omega) = \mathbb{F}\{f_v(t)\}$$

$$= \mathbb{F}\{\cdots + f_{-1}\delta(t+T) + f_0\delta(t) + f_1\delta(t-T) + f_2\delta(t-2T) + \cdots\}$$

$$= \cdots + f_{-1}e^{j\omega T} + f_0 \cdot 1 + f_1 e^{-j\omega T} + f_2 e^{-j\omega 2T} + \cdots$$

$$= \sum_{n=-\infty}^{\infty} f_n e^{-j\omega nT}. \tag{3.1}$$

It is obvious that this expression is only based on the sample values and can therefore be calculated for a discrete signal in the form of a number series. The spectrum determined in this way could therefore be interpreted in the above-mentioned sense as the spectrum of the quasicontinuous signal. Based on these considerations is the following definition.

The Fourier transform of a discrete signal $\{f_n\}$ (or DTFT, *discrete-time Fourier transform*) is given by the expression

$$\mathbb{DTFT}\{f_n\} = F(\omega) = \sum_{n=-\infty}^{\infty} f_n e^{-j\omega nT}. \tag{3.2}$$

The transform is defined in the usual sense if the infinite sum converges for all real values ω, for which $\sum_{n=-\infty}^{\infty} |f_n| < \infty$ is sufficient. As every signal of a finite length (with a finite number of samples) fulfils this requirement, the transform is defined for all finite signals (among others).

Let us notice first that, as (3.2) is a Fourier series in the exponential form, this transform is a continuous and periodic function of the frequency ω with the period $2\pi/T$. The spectrum values are complex, because generally $f_n \neq f_{-n}$. If the signal is *causal* (i.e. limited from the left, $f_n = 0$ for $n < 0$), it is

$$F(\omega) = \sum_{n=0}^{\infty} f_n e^{-j\omega nT}, \tag{3.3}$$

which is obviously $\mathbb{Z}\{f_n\}|_{z=e^{j\omega T}}$. The spectrum of a discrete signal, which is zero for negative indices, is therefore given by the values of its Z-transform on the unit circle; a point on the circle determined by the position vector with the angle ωT corresponds to the frequency ω. If $F(z)$ is a fractional rational function and all its poles lie inside the unit circle, the finite sum exists everywhere on the unit circle, hence also the transform (3.3).

The corresponding inverse transform, IDTFT, is given by the expression for the Fourier series coefficients,

$$f_n = \frac{1}{2\pi} \int_{-\pi/T}^{\pi/T} F(\omega) e^{j\omega Tn} \, d\omega, \tag{3.4}$$

with the integral taken over one period $\langle -\omega_v/2, \omega_v/2 \rangle$ of the spectrum.

Some useful signals do not have the DTFT in the usual sense (for instance, the unit step obviously doesn't fulfil the finite-sum requirement). In such cases, it is necessary to generalise the definition. The DTFT spectrum (in a wider sense) could then be defined as a function, of which the inverse DTFT transform (3.4) gives the original signal sequence, providing that such a function exists. Alternatively, the signal to be transformed might be formulated as the limit case of a series of signal sequences such that each has its DTFT in the usual sense. The transform is then defined as the limit of the corresponding series of spectra (if such a limit exists).

Note that the values of the DTFT can be numerically determined only at a finite number of discrete points in the frame of one period of the spectrum. Should we decide to use the equidistant division of the frequency axis, that is to divide the interval $\langle -\omega_v/2, \omega_v/2 \rangle$ into N equal parts of width $\Omega = 2\pi/NT$, eqn (3.3) modifies to

$$F(k\Omega) = \sum_{n=0}^{\infty} f_n e^{-k\Omega nT}, \tag{3.5}$$

which is the discrete version of the DTFT. Specifically, if we use exactly N signal samples for the calculation, which is equivalent to the case when the signal is zero for all $n \geq N$, we obtain the *discrete Fourier transform* (DFT),

$$\mathbb{DFT}\{f_n\} = F_k = \sum_{n=0}^{N-1} f_n e^{-jk\Omega nT}. \tag{3.6}$$

This transform provides, in a mutually unique way, a correspondence between the sequence of N signal samples in the original domain and the sequence of frequency-domain (spectral) coefficients of the same length. The properties and calculation of the DFT, in the context of its practical use, will be considered in Sections 3.3.3 and 3.3.4.

3.2 General unitary transforms

The discrete linear transform is a mapping $\{x_n\} \to \{X_k\}$, from the original domain (generally, a vector space $\mathbf{C}^{N_1}$ but usually $\mathbf{R}^{N_1}$) to the transform domain (a vector space $\mathbf{C}^{N_2}$ or $\mathbf{R}^{N_2}$) according to the relation

$$X_k = \sum_{n=0}^{N_1-1} a_{k,n} x_n, \quad k \in \langle 0, N_2 - 1 \rangle, \tag{3.7}$$

or, in vector form,

$$\mathbf{X} = \mathbf{Ax}, \tag{3.8}$$

where the matrix $\mathbf{A}$ of the dimension $N_2 \times N_1$,

$$\mathbf{A} = \begin{bmatrix} a_{0,0} & a_{0,1} & \cdots & a_{0,N_1-1} \\ a_{1,0} & a_{1,1} & \cdots & a_{1,N_1-1} \\ \vdots & \vdots & \ddots & \vdots \\ a_{N_2-1,0} & a_{N_2-1,1} & & a_{N_2-1,N_1-1} \end{bmatrix}, \tag{3.9}$$

is the core of the transform, the elements of which can be real or complex numbers.

Usually, $N_1 = N_2$; the matrix $\mathbf{A}$ is then a square matrix and if it is non-singular, i.e. $|\mathbf{A}| \neq 0$, the transform is *reversible*, meaning a mutually unique correspondence between the original and transformed number sequences. The output sequence $\mathbf{X}$ of the transformation is called the *discrete spectrum*. The inverse transform is obviously given by the equation

$$\mathbf{x} = \mathbf{A}^{-1}\mathbf{X}. \tag{3.10}$$

A linear discrete transform is *unitary* if its core fulfils the relation

$$\mathbf{A}^{-1} = m\mathbf{A}^{*T}, \tag{3.11}$$

where m is a real number and the symbols $*$, T denote complex conjugate and transposed matrices, respectively. Should $\mathbf{A}$ also be Hermitian, $\mathbf{A}^{*T} = \mathbf{A}$, then the inverse transform becomes identical to the forward transform (disregarding, perhaps, eventual multiplication by a constant). *Orthogonal transforms*, which are a special case of the unitary transforms, are characterised by core matrices with only real elements, so that $\mathbf{A}^{-1} = m\mathbf{A}^T$. If the matrix $\mathbf{A}$ is symmetrical with respect to the main diagonal, the inverse transform is again (disregarding multiplication by a constant) identical to the forward transform.

Several examples of commonly used transforms follow:

1　*Hadamard transform* is characterised by having all core elements real numbers, $a_{k,n} = \pm 1$, so that the result of the transform is a real sequence. The transform is very fast, as the calculations do not contain multiplication. The core of the transform is given recursively:

$$\mathbf{H}_2 = \begin{bmatrix} 1 & 1 \\ 1 & -1 \end{bmatrix}, \quad \mathbf{H}_{2N} = \begin{bmatrix} \mathbf{H}_N & \mathbf{H}_N \\ \mathbf{H}_N & -\mathbf{H}_N \end{bmatrix}. \tag{3.12}$$

Thus, for example for $N = 8$, it is

$$\mathbf{H}_8 = \begin{bmatrix} 1 & 1 & 1 & 1 & 1 & 1 & 1 & 1 \\ 1 & -1 & 1 & -1 & 1 & -1 & 1 & -1 \\ 1 & 1 & -1 & -1 & 1 & 1 & -1 & -1 \\ 1 & -1 & -1 & 1 & 1 & -1 & -1 & 1 \\ 1 & 1 & 1 & 1 & -1 & -1 & -1 & -1 \\ 1 & -1 & 1 & -1 & -1 & 1 & -1 & 1 \\ 1 & 1 & -1 & -1 & -1 & -1 & 1 & 1 \\ 1 & -1 & -1 & 1 & -1 & 1 & 1 & -1 \end{bmatrix} \begin{matrix} 0 \\ 7 \\ 3 \\ 4 \\ 1 \\ 6 \\ 2 \\ 5 \end{matrix}.$$

The individual rows of the matrix represent the so-called basis functions to which the transformed signal is being decomposed. On the other side, these functions are linearly combined in a weighted sum during the inverse transform to reconstruct the original signal. The numbers to the right of the matrix mean the number of sign changes in a row. It can be proven that every integer in the range $\langle 0, N-1 \rangle$ will appear just once. Further, it can be shown that the Hadamard transform is (in a wider sense) orthogonal and hence, as its core is a symmetrical matrix, it represents a case of identical algorithms of forward and inverse transforms $(\mathbf{H}^{-1} = (1/N)\mathbf{H})$.

2　*Walsh transform* can be derived from the Hadamard transform by only interchanging rows in its core so that the number of sign changes increases monotonically with the row index. The purpose of this modification is to achieve a rough similarity with the discrete Fourier transform, where frequency, and consequently the number of basis-function sign changes, also increases monotonically. It should be said that attempts to use the Walsh transform as an easily calculated replacement of the DFT (or of power spectrum) in spectral analysis of signals have generally been unsuccessful in trials as the approximation is quite rough.

3   *Discrete Fourier transform* is defined by the core

$$
\mathbf{A} = [W^{kn}] =
\begin{bmatrix}
W^0 & W^0 & \cdots & W^0 \\
W^0 & W^1 & \cdots & W^{N-1} \\
\vdots & \vdots & \ddots & \vdots \\
W^0 & W^{N-1} & \cdots & W^{(N-1)^2}
\end{bmatrix}, W = e^{-j\frac{2\pi}{N}}. \tag{3.13}
$$

The basis functions are sampled complex exponential functions which, when combined in a similar way to that used when deriving eqn (2.25a), can be used for the synthesis of real discrete harmonic functions. The corresponding discrete spectrum is generally a complex sequence. We will deal with this transform in detail in Section 3.3.

4   *Haar transform* is similar to the Hadamard transform in having piecewise constant (rectangular) basis functions, but its character is different, as can be seen from the example of core matrices for $N = 4$ and $N = 8$:

$$
\mathbf{H}_4 =
\begin{bmatrix}
1 & 1 & 1 & 1 \\
1 & 1 & -1 & -1 \\
\sqrt{2} & -\sqrt{2} & 0 & 0 \\
0 & 0 & \sqrt{2} & -\sqrt{2}
\end{bmatrix},
$$

$$
\mathbf{H}_8 =
\begin{bmatrix}
1 & 1 & 1 & 1 & 1 & 1 & 1 & 1 \\
1 & 1 & 1 & 1 & -1 & -1 & -1 & -1 \\
\sqrt{2} & \sqrt{2} & -\sqrt{2} & -\sqrt{2} & 0 & 0 & 0 & 0 \\
0 & 0 & 0 & 0 & \sqrt{2} & \sqrt{2} & -\sqrt{2} & -\sqrt{2} \\
2 & -2 & 0 & 0 & 0 & 0 & 0 & 0 \\
0 & 0 & 2 & -2 & 0 & 0 & 0 & 0 \\
0 & 0 & 0 & 0 & 2 & -2 & 0 & 0 \\
0 & 0 & 0 & 0 & 0 & 0 & 2 & -2
\end{bmatrix}. \tag{3.13a}
$$

Except for the first row which defines the mean signal value, basis functions can be characterised as providing weighted and scaled differences of sample averages. These are differences between the left and right half of the signal (second row), between the first and second quarter (third row) and the third and fourth quarter (fourth row) etc. The last $N/2$ rows provide differences of the neighbouring samples in all possible $N/2$ shifted positions. The transform coefficients can thus be interpreted as describing scaled differences. Notice that not only a different scale in time is used, corresponding roughly to the notion of 'speed of changes' in time or 'frequency', but signal changes are also localised in time by being primarily detected by the closest basis function. In this way the obtained spectrum not only provides information about the 'frequencies' in the signal course, but also information on the location of signal changes (edges, one-shot waves) on the time axis. From this point of view, the Haar transform is historically the first transform to enable directly a rough time–frequency analysis. We shall return to it later in Section 3.5 on wavelet transforms, as Haar basis functions can also be interpreted as an orthonormal scalable wavelet set.

Generally it can be said that, as far as discrete transforms are reversible, there is no loss of information during the transformation in either direction. Therefore, only the use to which the results are put determines whether it is more advantageous to use the original sequence or its spectrum. The choice of transform type also depends on the particular problem; the applications of the transforms are versatile:

- spectral analysis, which serves to determine the magnitudes and time relations of elementary components (corresponding to the chosen basis functions) of the analysed signal; decomposition into harmonic components is usually understood by spectral analysis, i.e. the DFT is then applied;
- realisation of some mathematical operations more easily in the frequency domain; for instance, so-called fast convolution *via* the frequency domain needed in e.g. signal filtering, or correlation as used in signal analysis can effectively be done by means of the DFT;
- signal data compression aiming to reduce redundancy, which is, for many practically important types of signal (e.g. image and audio data), more effectively realisable in the frequency domain. The basis for this is that the transformed data items are generally less mutually correlated than in the original data and, consequently, can be coded more effectively. Moreover, the energy of the signal, usually uniformly distributed among original-space samples, becomes concentrated in only a small part of the corresponding spectral coefficients, so that some of them may be neglected or only roughly represented. The compression of signal and namely image data is the main application field for cosine transforms, and, lately, also for wavelet transforms;
- signal transfer/communication *via* a noisy channel which may be more robust with respect to interference if the discrete spectrum is transferred instead of the original sample sequence. Naturally, it is followed by the corresponding inverse transform at the receiving end. Here any transforms, including the simplest ones, find a use.

When the application requires both the forward and inverse transforms, it is particularly advantageous if the algorithms of the transform are basically identical in both directions.

We may conclude this brief overview with the statement that most of modern signal processing is based to some extent on the use of unitary transforms. It was, in fact, the advent of fast transforming algorithms which started the huge development in digital signal processing. The most frequently used transform is undoubtedly the DFT, followed nowadays by the cosine transform

(CT) which is extensively used in signal data compression. Time–frequency analysis includes the application of different types of wavelet transform which are also used in modern data-compression methods. The following sections are devoted to a description of the basic properties of some of the most important transforms; the final part of the chapter concerns the theoretically interesting although computationally inefficient Karhunen–Loeve (eigenvector) transform which provides a golden standard in decorrelating data sequences.

3.3 Discrete Fourier transform

3.3.1 Definition and properties of the DFT

The *discrete Fourier transform* (DFT) is defined by eqn (3.6), the genesis of which is explained in the Section 3.1.3, or by the equivalent expression (3.8) with the core matrix given by eqn (3.13). The definition relations are therefore

$$\mathrm{DFT}\{f_n\} = \left\{ F_k = \sum_{n=0}^{N-1} f_n W^{kn} \right\}, \quad W = e^{-j\frac{2\pi}{N}},$$

$$\mathrm{DFT}^{-1}\{F_k\} = \left\{ f_n = \frac{1}{N} \sum_{n=0}^{N-1} F_k W^{-nk} \right\}. \tag{3.14}$$

It can be seen that the transform is a defined algorithm operating above certain number vectors, the physical meaning of which is entirely irrelevant. However, we primarily work with signals regularly sampled in time, with the sampling period T. Then it is both possible and useful to interpret the transform in a way similar to the concept of the spectrum of continuous-time signals, that is as a function of frequency (discrete, as explained). In this case, it is advantageous to write the definition relations in the following equivalent form,

$$F(k\Omega) = \sum_{n=0}^{N-1} f(nT)e^{-jk\Omega nT},$$

$$f(nT) = \frac{1}{N} \sum_{k=0}^{N-1} F(k\Omega)e^{jnTk\Omega}, \tag{3.15}$$

because it is clear here that the spectral coefficients belong to certain frequencies, $k\Omega$, and the signal samples to certain time instants, nT. In addition, the meaning of the basis functions is more obvious: the product of frequency $k\Omega$ and time nT, similarly as in the continuous-time case, gives the argument of each complex exponential function.

To begin with, we shall prove that the DFT is reversible, i.e. that $\mathbb{DFT}^{-1}\{\mathbb{DFT}\{\mathbf{f}\}\} = \mathbf{f}$ and that the second of the relations in eqns (3.14) and (3.15) is really the inverse transform. Actually, we obtain by substitution

$$f_l = \frac{1}{N}\sum_{k=0}^{N-1} F_k e^{jlk\frac{2\pi}{N}} = \frac{1}{N}\sum_{k=0}^{N-1}\left(\sum_{n=0}^{N-1} f_n e^{-jkn\frac{2\pi}{N}}\right) e^{jlk\frac{2\pi}{N}}.$$

Interchanging the order of summations then gives

$$f_l = \frac{1}{N}\sum_{n=0}^{N-1} f_n \left(\sum_{k=0}^{N-1} e^{j(l-n)k\frac{2\pi}{N}}\right) = \frac{1}{N}\sum_{n=0}^{N-1} f_n \frac{1-e^{j\frac{2\pi}{N}(l-n)N}}{1-e^{j\frac{2\pi}{N}(l-n)}} = \frac{1}{N} f_l N.$$

Here, we first use the fact that the inner sum for k adds together N terms of a geometric series (with the first term equal to 1 and the quotient $e^{j\frac{2\pi}{N}(l-n)}$). Then we notice that the value of the resulting fraction becomes N if $n = l$, and zero for all other terms of the sum.

Let us now derive the main properties of the discrete Fourier transform:

1   The DFT is *linear*, as follows from the definition relation.

2   The DFT is a *unitary* transform (in the wider sense) as, with $\mathbf{A} = [W^{nk}]$, the core of the inverse transform is

$$\mathbf{A}^{-1} = \frac{1}{N}[W^{-nk}] = \frac{1}{N}\mathbf{A}^* = \frac{1}{N}\mathbf{A}^{*\mathrm{T}},$$

with respect to the symmetry of $\mathbf{A}$. Hence, it is possible to use almost the same algorithm for both the forward and inverse transforms, the only difference being the opposite sign of the imaginary parts of all the core elements, and the multiplicative constant.

3   The transform relations in both directions are obviously represented by a Fourier series and they therefore yield *periodic sequences*. The signal sequence in the time domain has the period NT, which is the length of the processed signal (nothing is known about the real signal-sample values outside the interval $n \in \langle 0, N-1\rangle$), and the period in the frequency domain is $N\Omega = \omega_v$ as it corresponds to the periodicity of the sampled-signal spectrum. The valid extent of variables in both domains is therefore satisfactory with respect to their physical interpretation; a smaller extent would lead to a loss of information and a greater extent would result in redundancy.

4   *The relation to Z-transform*: The DFT of a signal means the sample values of the Z-transform of this signal, equally spaced on the unit circle in the z-plane (Figure 3.1):

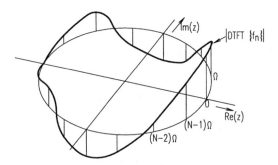

Figure 3.1 Values of the DFT in the z-plane (example)

$$\mathbb{DFT}\{f_n\} = \left\{ F_k = \sum_{n=0}^{N-1} f_n e^{-jkn\frac{2\pi}{N}} \right\} = \mathbb{Z}\{f_n\}\Big|_{z=e^{jk\frac{2\pi}{N}}}.$$

5   *The spectrum of a discrete harmonic signal* $f(nT) = e^{j\omega nT}$ *of an arbitrary real frequency* $\omega = q\Omega$ *is given by*

$$F(k\Omega) = \sum_{n=0}^{N-1} e^{jq\Omega nT} e^{-j\Omega Tnk} = \sum_{n=0}^{N-1} e^{j\Omega T(q-k)n}.$$

There are two seemingly distinct cases of such a signal representation in the DFT. For any integer q (i.e. when ω is one of the frequencies $k\Omega$), the sum is equal to N for $k = q$ and zero for all other k. Thus, there will be only one nonzero spectral line at the proper frequency $k\Omega$ in the spectrum (Figure 3.2a). When q is noninteger, i.e. when ω is not the frequency sampling point,

$$F(k\Omega) = \frac{1 - e^{j\frac{2\pi}{N}(q-k)N}}{1 - e^{j\frac{2\pi}{N}(q-k)}},$$

which is a function similar to the function $\sin(x)/x$. All the spectral coefficients $F(\Omega)$ will be nonzero in this case. Nevertheless, the coefficients closest to ω on the frequency axis will acquire the maximal two values, so that it is still possible to determine the frequencies of signal components with a precision corresponding to the value of N used (Figure 3.2b), unless the frequencies of the components are too close to each other.

6   *Circular (periodic) convolution as represented in DFT (circular-convolution theorem)*: let $\mathbf{x}$, $\mathbf{y}$ be two original sequences of the same length N, the DFT spectra of which are $\mathbf{X}$, $\mathbf{Y}$. Let us formulate a new spectrum, $\mathbf{V}$, as the vector of products $V_k = X_k Y_k$ and find the corresponding original sequence $\mathbf{v} = \mathbb{DFT}^{-1}\{V_k\}$:

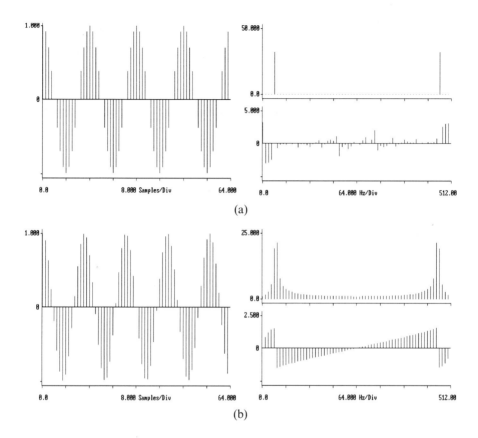

Figure 3.2 Discrete real harmonic signal and its DFT spectrum in the range $\omega \in \langle 0, \omega_v \rangle$
    a   Integer q
    b   Noninteger q
    (Upper part of spectra – magnitude, lower part – phase)

$$v_l = \frac{1}{N} \sum_{k=0}^{N-1} (X_k Y_k) e^{jlk\frac{2\pi}{N}}$$

$$= \frac{1}{N} \sum_{k=0}^{N-1} \left(\sum_{n=0}^{N-1} x_n e^{-jnk\frac{2\pi}{N}} \right) \left(\sum_{m=0}^{N-1} y_m e^{-jmk\frac{2\pi}{N}} \right) e^{jlk\frac{2\pi}{N}}.$$

By rearranging the terms we obtain

$$v_l = \frac{1}{N} \sum_{m=0}^{N-1} \sum_{n=0}^{N-1} x_n y_m \left(\sum_{k=0}^{N-1} e^{j(l-m-n)k\frac{2\pi}{N}} \right) = \sum_{m=0}^{N-1} x_{[l-m]} y_m. \qquad (3.16a)$$

Here we have used the fact that the sum for k is equal to N, if $(l - m - n) = pN$ (integer p); else it is zero. Hence, $n = (l - m) + pN$, where p can be chosen so that $n = [l - m] = (l - m) \bmod N$ and consequently $[l = m] \in \langle 0, N - 1 \rangle$, which is the so-called principal index value. Should m be calculated instead of n, an equivalent expression is obtained,

$$v_l = \sum_{n=0}^{N-1} x_n y_{[l-n]}. \tag{3.16b}$$

This expression is the *circular or periodic convolution* $x \circledast y$. The convolution property of the DFT is very useful in practice and used extensively in many applications. We shall discuss (in Section 5.2.3.2) the methods enabling us to utilise circular convolution for calculations of elements of the finite linear convolution; i.e. to prevent the distortion caused by the periodicity inherent in the DFT.

7   Important relations between originals and transforms apply in special cases:

original	spectrum
real	complex: real part even, imaginary part odd
real even	real even
real odd	imaginary odd
complex: real part even, imaginary part odd	real
complex, real part odd, imaginary part even	purely imaginary

Here, a discrete function is considered odd (or even), with respect to the periodicity, when it fulfils, respectively,

$$y_n = -y_{[-n]} \quad \text{or} \quad y_n = y_{[-n]}.$$

8   *The relation between DFT and harmonic analysis*: Harmonic analysis expresses a periodic and piecewise continuous function $f(t)$ by its Fourier series

$$f(t) = \sum_{k=-\infty}^{\infty} c_k e^{jk\Omega t}, \tag{3.17}$$

where $\Omega = 2\pi/\tau$, τ is the function period; the generally complex coefficients are given by

$$c_k = \frac{1}{\tau} \int_0^\tau f(t) e^{-jk\Omega t} \, dt. \tag{3.18}$$

Supposing that the frequency content of the function is limited from above by ω_m, let us sample one period of the function by exactly N samples, i.e. with the sampling period $T = \tau/N$. The number of samples N has to be chosen such that the sampling theorem is fulfilled, i.e. $\omega_m < \pi/T = N\Omega/2$. It will be proven in Section 9.1.1 that, under the above mentioned assumptions,

$$c_k = \frac{1}{N} F_k. \tag{3.19}$$

The DFT therefore provides exact values of Fourier coefficients under these conditions. (At first sight, it is surprising that the values of the integral (3.18) are given by finite sums; it can be shown that this is a consequence of the special type of integrated functions.)

9   The relationship between the DFT and the integral Fourier transform will be analysed in detail in Section 9.1.2.

3.3.2 Methods of fast DFT calculation

Values of the DFT can, of course, be calculated according to the definition expression

$$F_k = \sum_{n=0}^{N-1} f_n W^{nk}, \quad W = e^{-j\frac{2\pi}{N}}, \tag{3.20}$$

where the coefficient values W^{nk} can be retrieved from a table of sine values for a quarter of a period. Apart from the sine table, the algorithm requests N memory registers for the input sequence (if it is real, as is usual, but $2N$ for a complex sequence) and $2N$ registers for the complex output sequence. For evaluation of the computational demands, the set P of one complex multiplication and one complex addition will be used as a unit. Expressed in this way, the workload for calculating one spectral coefficient according to eqn (3.20) is NP, hence the work to calculate the complete transform (N values of the spectrum) is N^2P. This quadratic computational complexity is unpleasant as it causes high requirements when performing transforms for practical values of N of the order of 10^2–10^5.

With respect to the practical importance of the DFT, more effective algorithms have been developed in the course of time; of them, Goertzel's algorithm based on linear filter theory deserves a note here. This algorithm consists in principle of a bank of bandpass filters; each of the filters is designed so that it provides one spectral coefficient F_k after accepting N samples, i.e. the complete signal sequence. Obviously, N such filters working in parallel are needed to provide the complete transform at any one time. It can be shown that this

algorithm may save up to 75 per cent of the load in comparison with the definition expression, but unfortunately the quadratic dependence on N remains. The
algorithm is nevertheless advantageous for two reasons: its effectiveness in cases
where only a few spectral coefficients are needed, and its ability to calculate the
transform in real time, namely, when a series of spectra in time development are
needed.

The fundamental step which drastically decreased the computational requirements of the DFT was the invention of a fast algorithm for DFT computation in
1965 (Cooley and Tukey). This discovery contributed substantially to the
expansion of DFT applications as well as to the development of digital signal
processing in general. It is interesting that similar algorithms had been
published earlier, several times since 1903, but they didn't find any interest.
A broad family of modifications to this algorithm is known today, all of which
are brought together under the name of the *fast Fourier transform* (FFT). All
these modifications only provide effective computation of the same DFT as
defined above.

Fast algorithms for DFT computation can be interpreted in terms of the
factorisation of the core matrix into a product of sparse matrices, which
excludes most unnecessary operations. In the following sections, the basic
approaches will be simply explained in an alternative way to show the principles
of workload reduction as well as the basic algorithmic details. Two basic types
of fast algorithms will be presented: decimation in time, and decimation in
frequency domain.

3.3.2.1 Decimation in the original domain

The original sequence $\{f_n\}$ of the length N (N even), the DFT of which is given
by eqn (3.20), is divided into two sequences, $g_l = f_{2l}$ (i.e. even terms of the
original sequence) and $h_l = f_{2l+1}$ (odd terms). Each of these sequences has, of
course, its own DFT:

$$G_k = \sum_{l=0}^{\frac{N}{2}-1} g_l(W^2)^{lk}, \quad Hk = \sum_{l=0}^{\frac{N}{2}-1} h_l(W^2)^{lk}, \quad W^2 = e^{-j\frac{2\pi}{N/2}}, \quad k \in \left\langle 0, \frac{N}{2} - 1 \right\rangle. \quad (3.21)$$

The complete transform can be expressed in terms of these two partial
transforms:

$$F_k = \sum_{n=0}^{N-1} f_n W^{nk} = \sum_{l=0}^{\frac{N}{2}-1} (g_l W^{2lk} + h_l W^{(2l+1)k})$$

$$= \sum_{l=0}^{\frac{N}{2}-1} g_l(W^2)^{lk} + W^k \sum_{l=0}^{\frac{N}{2}-1} h_l(W^2)^{lk},$$

where summing in pairs has been used when passing from the first to the second expression. Therefore

$$F_k = G_{k'} + W^k H_{k'}. \tag{3.22}$$

The index extent of F_k runs until N, while the indices for G_k and H_k have only a range up to $N/2$. To provide the necessary values, the periodicity of the latter indices is utilised: the indices $k' = k \bmod (N/2)$ will be used.

Should the partial transforms have been already calculated according to the definition expression, the resulting workload is given by the sum of the workloads for both partial transforms plus the overhead needed to combine them according to eqn (3.22),

$$2 \times \left(\frac{N}{2}\right)^2 \times P + NP.$$

It can easily be seen that the reduction in comparison with the original workload $N^2 P$ is almost 50 per cent. But if $N/2$ is again even, each of the partial transforms can be subdivided in the same way, which again approximately halves the effort etc. It is therefore advantageous to select $N = 2^m$, m integer; it is possible then to carry out the decimation completely until the last stage, when transforms of length 2 are calculated. In such a case, there will obviously be m levels of decimation. Figure 3.3 presents the signal flow diagrams resulting from such a gradual decimation for $N = 8$. The blocks symbolise the DFTs which are not yet decimated; the nodes of the graphs represent the sums of their inputs and the coefficients at the edges denote multiplications by constants (for typographical reasons, W^i is written as wi). By inspecting the last, completely expanded, graph, the resulting workload can be determined exactly: in each of the three layers there are N nodes, of which each, together with a coefficient, represents the unit work P. The conclusion can easily be generalised; the total workload is clearly

$$P \times N \times m = P \times N \log_2 N. \tag{3.23}$$

This expression grows, for large N, almost linearly with the number of samples and hence its value is markedly less than that for the original quadratic expression. Evaluation shows that, while for $N = 8$ the total reduction is about 60 per cent, for $N = 1024$ it is already 99 per cent and for $N = 131\,072$ as much as 99.99 per cent. The computational acceleration is therefore quite high for practical values of N, by several decimal orders.

Let us also notice some details of the algorithm that can be seen on the graph. Although the output sequence is ordered naturally, the inputs are in so-called bit-reversal order. (The order of the inputs is given by their original indices when expressed in direct binary code and read with inverse weight of individual bits – the most significant bit as the least significant one etc.) This phenomenon requires presorting of inputs before calculation.

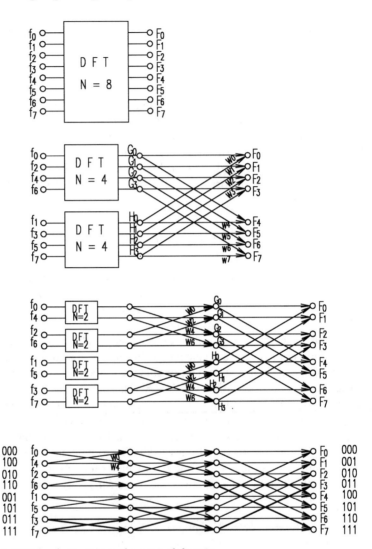

Figure 3.3 FFT by decimation in the original domain

Another interesting feature of the algorithm is the existence of repeating 'butterflies' – structures of four nodes and four edges (some are accented by thick lines). It is clear that only the values of a butterfly's input nodes are needed for the calculation of its two outputs. Hence, only two registers are needed for the realisation of a butterfly; they can be shared by both the input and output so that, apart from two buffers for temporary results, only *N* main memory registers are needed. This feature is called *computation in place*.

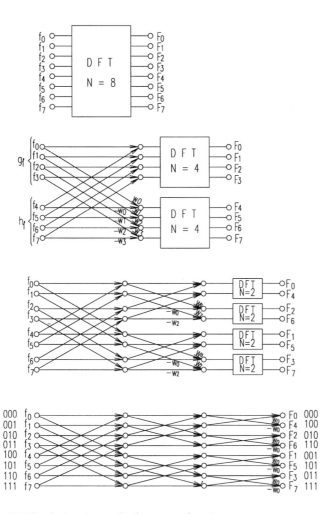

Figure 3.4 FFT by decimation in the frequency domain

3.3.2.2 Decimation in the frequency domain

The sequence $\{f_n\}$ is divided into two partial sequences following one after the other, $g_l = f_l$ and $h_l = f_l + N/2$, $l \in \langle 0, N/2 - 1 \rangle$. Summing again in pairs, the complete DFT can obviously be expressed as follows,

$$F_k = \sum_{n=0}^{N-1} f_n W^{nk} = \sum_{l=0}^{\frac{N}{2}-1} \left(g_l W^{lk} + h_l W^{(l+\frac{N}{2})k} \right) = \sum_{l=0}^{\frac{N}{2}-1} (g_l + e^{-j\pi k} h_l) W^{lk}.$$

Taking into account that the exponential factor is either 1 or -1 for k even or odd, respectively, we obtain for the even spectral coefficients

$$\left\{ F_{2k} = \sum_{l=0}^{\frac{N}{2}-1} (g_l + h_l)(W^2)^{lk} \right\} = \mathbb{DFT}\{g_l + h_l\},$$

and for odd spectral coefficients,

$$\left\{ F_{2k+1} = \sum_{l=0}^{\frac{N}{2}-1} (g_l - h_l) W^l (W^2)^{lk} \right\} = \mathbb{DFT}\{(g_l - h_l) W^l\}.$$

The complete transform is again divided into two partial transforms of halved length, but this time the overhead calculations must be performed on the input side. Figure 3.4 presents such a decimation in the frequency domain, again for $N = 8$. It can be seen that the resulting workload is basically the same as that for the previous method but there is a difference in the ordering of the sequences: now, the input sequence is ordered naturally while the output sequence has bit-reversal order. Computation in place is again possible, the butterfly as the building block of the algorithm being preserved.

Many modifications of these algorithms have been published in the literature, providing some advantages at a price of other less favourable features. For instance, modifications are available with the natural order on the opposite side than that which corresponds to the explained way of decimation (e.g. Figure 3.5), with a natural arrangement of both input and output (thereby losing the calculation-in-place feature, Figure 3.6), algorithms for cases when N is not an integer power of 2 but can be factored into prime numbers (Figures 3.7 and 3.8) etc. Algorithms of a completely different conception, based on the results of number theory, also exist, but this rather specialised area is beyond the scope of this book.

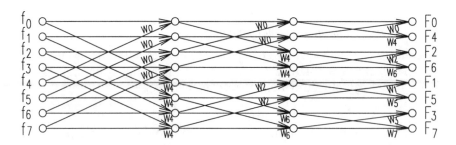

Figure 3.5 Modified FFT by decimation in the original domain with naturally ordered inputs

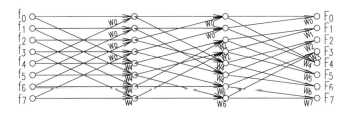

Figure 3.6 Modified FFT by decimation in the original domain with both input and output naturally ordered

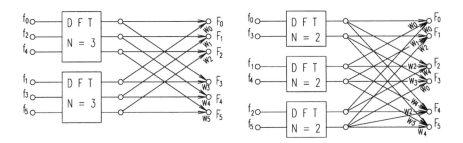

Figure 3.7 FFT for N = 6 by decimation in the oridinal domain, two transforms with N = 3 or three transforms with N = 2

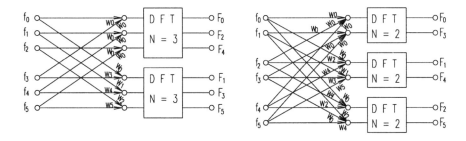

Figure 3.8 Two alternatives of FFT for N = 6 by decimation in the frequency domain

3.4 Cosine and sine transforms

The *discrete cosine transform* (DCT) originated, and can most easily be understood, on the basis of the discrete Fourier transform. One of the drawbacks of
the DFT is that the spectral coefficients are complex and, therefore, most algorithms are forced to make all the computations in complex representation, even
in the common case of real signal samples. Thus, the primary motivation for the
DCT was to develop a transform providing real spectra. We will now show that
this is easily possible based on DFT properties.

As we have seen, the DFT spectrum is real if the signal is symmetrical with
respect to the time origin; the input signal must be an even function. In this
case, the spectrum also becomes symmetrical. Obviously, any finite signal can
be extended to become symmetrical (without any loss or gain in information
content) by simply complementing the original sequence by a time-inverted
sequence, appended left of the original. The symmetry may be either even
(the originally first sample is doubled) or odd (the first sample of the original
remains single and forms the centre of symmetry). We will use only the first version; for an original signal of N samples, $\{f_n\}$, $n \in \langle 0, N-1 \rangle$ the symmetrical
sequence thus will be $\{_{sym}f_n\}$, $n \in \langle -N, N-1 \rangle$. Notice that the centre of symmetry, considered to be the origin of the time axis, is now the point
$n = -1/2$. According to definition (3.14), the discrete Fourier transform of
this sequence is

$$\mathbb{DFT}\{_{sym}f_n\} = \left\{ F_k = \sum_{n=-N}^{N-1} f_n W^{k(n+\frac{1}{2})} \right\}, \qquad W = e^{-j\frac{2\pi}{2N}}. \qquad (3.24)$$

We may observe immediately that, in comparison with the DFT of the original
sequence, the number of spectral coefficients has been doubled (but it can be
shown that the frequency resolution remains the same because the new coefficients are only interpolated). Using the signal symmetry and the complex-
conjugate symmetry of the transform-core factors, we may calculate the sum
in pairs, obtaining

$$F_k = a_k \sum_{n=0}^{N-1} f_n \cos\left(\frac{\pi}{N} k\left(n+\frac{1}{2}\right)\right), \qquad a_0 = 1, a_k = \sqrt{2}, k \neq 0. \qquad (3.25)$$

This formula, operating only on the original sequence, obviously provides real
transform values and it may therefore be considered to be the definition expression of the discrete cosine transform.[1] Obviously, the DCT core matrix of size
$N \times N$ is given by

---

[1] Often a normalised version of (3.25) is applied, which is divided by $\sqrt{N}$, as well as the inverse transform expression; to maintain consistency with the previous DFT definition, we include the resulting
factor $1/N$ only for the inverse transform.

$$\mathbf{C} = [c_{k,n}] = a_k f_n \cos\left(\frac{\pi}{N}k\left(n + \frac{1}{2}\right)\right). \qquad (3.26)$$

The matrix is nonsingular and unitary. The inverse transform can similarly be derived as

$$f_n = \sum_{k=0}^{N-1} a_k F_k \cos\left(\frac{\pi}{N}k\left(n + \frac{1}{2}\right)\right), \quad a_0 = \frac{1}{N}, a_k = \frac{\sqrt{2}}{N}, \; k \neq 0.$$

Again, obviously, the inverse DCT is almost identical with the forward DCT, which simplifies the implementation. Fast algorithms exist for the DCT and IDCT based on the same principle as for the DFT, i.e. with the computational complexity of the order $N \log_2 N$.

The discrete cosine transform is real, $\mathbf{C} = \mathbf{C}^*$, as required and orthogonal, so that $\mathbf{C}^{-1} = (1/N)\mathbf{C}^T = (1/N)\mathbf{C}$. The transform provides very compact spectral representation, i.e. the signal energy is compressed almost completely to only a few spectral coefficients, especially when applied to signals with highly correlated samples. In this case, it is a very good approximation of the decorrelating Karhunen-Loeve transform (Section 3.6).

The DCT finds its most important use in the field of signal (and image) data compression owing to its excellent energy-compaction and decorrelation properties.

In a similar way, the *discrete sine transform* (DST) can be derived, the core matrix of which is

$$\mathbf{S} = [s_{k,n}] = \sqrt{2} \sin\left(\frac{\pi(k+1)(n+1)}{N+1}\right). \qquad (3.27)$$

The properties of the DST are similar to those of DCT, including the compaction and decorrelation abilities. The sine transform is a very good approximation of the Karhunen–Loeve transform for sequences with lower inner correlations.

Still another real transform, in a way similar to the DFT, is the *Hartley transform*, the core matrix of which is defined as

$$\mathbf{H} = [h_{k,n}] = \sin\left(\frac{2\pi nk}{N}\right) + \cos\left(\frac{2\pi nk}{N}\right). \qquad (3.28)$$

It can be proved that the basis functions given by eqn (3.28) are orthogonal; in fact they are again real harmonic functions but phase shifted by $-\pi/4$ with respect to the cosine basis. In this sense, the Hartley transform is a compromise between the sine and cosine transforms. Its advantage in comparison with the DFT is that the transform values are real; the complexity of computation is similar.

3.5 Wavelet transforms

Wavelet transforms (WT) have emerged recently as an alternative to classical transforms. Although the principle of expanding the given signal into a linear combination of basis functions which form an orthogonal-function family remains unchanged, the basis is being chosen such that it would enable time location of events even in the obtained spectrum. Wavelet transforms thus enable, to a certain extent, what is commonly called *time–frequency analysis* (see also Section 9.2.3).

What distinguishes the wavelet basis from all the previously mentioned transform bases is that every basis function – *wavelet* – is supported on only a finite time interval (or it is negligible outside of such an interval). Thus, only the properties of the corresponding section of the analysed signal influence any concrete spectral value based on such a wavelet. Conversely, the properties described by a particular value of the spectrum can be attributed to that particular time interval, which is naturally impossible with classical transforms. This is the main difference to, for example, the Fourier transform with its harmonic basis functions that are nonzero on the whole time axis so that every spectral value is influenced by the complete signal of theoretically unlimited time extent. The wavelet-transform basis functions cover by parts the whole time extent of the analysed signal so that complete information is preserved. (In respect of enabling time location of spectral events, WTs are similar to short-time (windowed) Gabor–Fourier transforms, in digital form arranged into so-called spectrograms – see Section 9.2.3.).

To describe the main properties of the wavelet transform briefly it is perhaps best to start from the notion of the *continuous wavelet transform* (CWT)

$$S_{CWT}(a, \tau) = \int_{-\infty}^{\infty} s(t) \frac{1}{\sqrt{a}} \psi\left(\frac{t}{a} - \tau\right) dt, \quad a > 0, \ \tau \in R. \quad (3.29)$$

Obviously, the two-dimensional transform value $S_{CWT}(a, \tau)$ is given by the correlation integral between the analysed signal $s(t)$ and the basis function $(1/\sqrt{a})\psi(.)$, which is a concrete wavelet. It is a characteristic of all wavelet transforms that the basic functional prescription (mother wavelet) $\psi(.)$ is fixed for all vectors (a, τ); the real shape of a concrete wavelet on the time axis nevertheless depends on both parameters. It can easily be seen that the parameter a called *scale* controls dilatation of the function (for $a > 1$, the wavelet is stretched a times); dividing by $\sqrt{a}$ provides for preserving the wavelet energy. On the other side, the parameter τ causes a time shift of the function along the time axis by the amount τ. Changing this parameter thus enables the complete time range of the signal to be covered gradually, although the wavelet has a finite duration. Time identification of the spectral values is naturally possible with a precision corresponding to the length of the concrete wavelet version. An example of a mother wavelet $\psi(1, 0)$ and the modified versions $\psi(2, 2)/\sqrt{2}$ and $\psi(4, 5)/2$ are depicted in Figure 3.9.

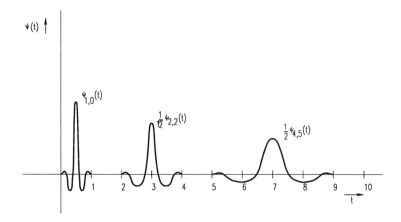

Figure 3.9 A mother wavelet and its modified versions

According to Fourier transform properties,

$$\mathbb{F}\left\{\psi\left(\frac{t}{a}\right)\right\} = a\Psi\{a\omega\}, \quad \text{where} \quad \Psi(\omega) = \mathbb{F}\{\psi(t)\},$$

i.e. the Fourier spectrum of the wavelet shrinks by the scale factor a when the wavelet is dilated by a. Providing that the wavelet is chosen so that its spectrum also has important values only at a finite interval of ω, the border frequency(-ies) will be shifted correspondingly. In this way, the frequency range covered by a particular wavelet, is determined by the scale parameter a. Therefore, the spectrum in the space (a, τ) actually describes both the frequency and temporal properties of the signal concurrently. Obviously, there is a limit on available resolution in both coordinates, linked to the Heisenberg uncertainty principle: the more compact the wavelet description in one domain, the more dilated it is in the other, as can be seen from the above equation.

Common wavelets are designed as fast oscillating functions of short duration, thus enabling the detection of local details on the signal course or, in other words, mediating response to only high-frequency components of the signal. (What the high frequency means depends, of course, on the chosen scale a.) It turns out that for many types of practical signal, a wavelet-type description is more suitable than a classical description, as it provides a good signal approximation with only a low number of terms. The reason is that the signals often contain sharp edges, impulses or discontinuities which need very many Fourier (or other classical) spectral components to be expressed, but only a few wavelet components are needed for the same purpose. The result is good energy compaction properties in spectral representation which are needed for signal data compression, and this is the field in which the different WTs now find important applications.

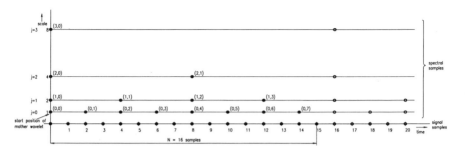

Figure 3.10 Dyadic sampling in the scale–time space

Although they can be chosen with a high degree of freedom, wavelets forming the transform basis have to fulfil certain rather strict requirements. Should the transform be invertible, they have to be mutually orthogonal and zero mean. In order to fulfil the requirements of time–frequency analysis, both the time domain as well as spectral representations of the wavelets should be compact (although only one of them may theoretically have finite support). The theory of wavelet design is based on a rather intricate mathematical background which goes beyond the scope of this book, but established wavelet families (Haar, Daubechies, biorthogonal, coiflets, symlets etc.) are defined and available. We shall, as with the previously discussed transforms, limit ourselves to describing a generic discrete version of the transform and the basic properties of WTs, thus presenting the wavelet-transform concept. Details and application comments can be found in specialised literature, e.g. Reference [33].

The two-dimensional continuous transform $S_{CWT}(a, \tau)$ must somehow be sampled in order to provide a discrete spectral representation. It has been found that, from several aspects, a suitable sampling method is the dyadic sample choice,

$$a = 2^j, \quad \tau = k2^j = ka \quad \text{for} \quad j, k \text{ integer}, \ j \geq 1. \tag{3.30}$$

This means that the scale is sampled in a dyadic (octave) sequence and the time axis is divided linearly. If the mother wavelet $\psi(1, 0)$ is supported on $t \in \langle 0, 1 \rangle$, the shifting step in time is equal to the length of the wavelet in any scale. It can be shown that, under very general conditions, the set of discrete spectral values in the sample points (Figure 3.10) carries the complete information on the original signal, which can therefore be reconstructed from the coefficients $S_{CWT}(2^j, k2^j)$.

The sample density in time (and thus time resolution) of discrete spectral values decreases with increasing scale a; this is obviously physically necessary as the longer wavelets need a correspondingly longer time period to establish the resemblance index $S_{CWT}(a, \tau)$ by correlation. An example (family of the first 15 Haar wavelets for analysing a finite signal section) can be derived as the continuous version of basis functions corresponding to the Haar transform

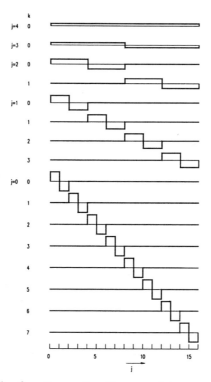

Figure 3.11 Family of continuous-time Haar wavelets

mentioned in Section 3.2 (Figure 3.11). Notice that here, the last eight lines represent wavelets for $a = 1$, with τ increasing in steps of 1 from 0 to 7, the next four lines above are wavelets for $a = 2$ and $\tau = 0, 2, 4, 6$, etc. The first line, providing the mean value of the signal as the first spectral coefficient, is in a sense a counterpart to the maximally dilated wavelet with $a = 8$, $\tau = 0$ on the second line.

The next step in developing the dyadic *discrete wavelet transform* (DWT) is sampling the analysed finite-length signal with a sampling period T, using discrete wavelets, and consequently replacing the definition integral by a sum. It is common to then work with variable indices j, k belonging to the dyadic scheme instead of the corresponding variable values a, τ:

$$S_{DWT}(j, k) = \sum_{n=0}^{N-1} s_{n} \cdot {}_{j,k}w_{n}, \quad a = 2^{j}, \ \tau = k2^{j}, \tag{3.31}$$

where $s_{n} = s(nT)$ are signal samples, ${}_{j,k}w_{n}$ is the nth sample of the kth shifted version of a 2^{j} scaled discrete wavelet, N is the number of signal samples. The last spectral coefficient formally denoted $S_{DWT}(\log_{2} N, 0)$ reflects only the signal mean, thus the relevant sequence ${}_{\log_{2} N+1,0}w_{n}$ is to be defined as all 1s. As there are then obviously $\log_{2} N + 1$ different scales, i.e. $j = 0, 1, \ldots, \log_{2} N$

and the number of spectral values on a particular scale level is $N/2^{j+1}$, the discrete spectrum will have N values (including the signal mean). This is, of course, much more efficient than calculating and saving N^2 values on a rectangular grid, and still preserves the complete information as the values of the dyadic choice have been shown to be sufficient for reconstruction of the original signal sequence $\{s_n\}$. When defined in this way, a (complete) wavelet transform is a unitary transform and can therefore be expressed by the generic vector formula (3.7) with the core matrix (3.9) given by samples of dilated and shifted wavelets. An example of such a DWT is the already mentioned discrete Haar transform (surprisingly quite practical and widely used nowadays as a WT, although known since 1906); rows one to seven of the matrix (3.13a) obviously contain sample sequences of the discrete scaled and shifted wavelets.

The *inverse discrete wavelet transform* (IDWT) can be expressed as a linear combination of the wavelets used

$$ s_n = \frac{1}{N} \sum_{j=0}^{\log_2 N} \sum_{k=0}^{\text{int}(N/2^{j+1})} S_{j,k}\,_{j,k}w_n. \tag{3.32} $$

Equivalently, realising that the $_{j,k}w_n$ are just elements of the core matrix (indices j, k determining the row index and n the column index), the IDWT can be expressed, as any inverse unitary transform, by eqn (3.10). Therefore, we see that discrete wavelet transforms are a class of unitary transforms as defined in Section 3.2. Notice that we have again left the normalising factor fully in the inverse transform in order to maintain consistency with previous sections.

Having clearly defined the family of wavelet transforms consistently in the frame of unitary transforms, we could stop here, as this knowledge should suffice for well understood, straightforward applications. Nevertheless, the dyadic DWT and IDWT are more often expressed as fast algorithms in terms of a certain type of filter bank. We shall briefly explain this concept because it enables another practically useful interpretation of the transformed values as a hierarchical decomposition and also allows partial (incomplete) transforms. As this explanation, although avoiding any details, is based on elements of discrete FIR filtering, the reader who is unfamiliar with this matter is advised to study first Sections 5.1 and 5.2 of this book before continuing here.

The correlation expression (3.31) can be equivalently substituted by a discrete convolution

$$ S_{DWT}(j, k) = \sum_{n=0}^{N-1} s_n\,_j h_{k-n}, \tag{3.33} $$

where the sequence $\{_j h_n\}$ for a constant j is the impulse response of an FIR filter. The length of the filter M_j is equal to the length of the nonzero part of the corresponding wavelet; the impulse response is the time-inverted sequence of the wavelet, $_j h_n = {}_{j,0}w_{M_j-1-n}$.

Thus, on the initial (0th) level, we can calculate the coefficients $S_{DWT}(0, k)$ by simple filtering of the signal by convolution with ${}_0h_n$ and taking every second sample of the filter output ${}_0y_n$, as $S_{DWT}(0, k) = y_{M_0 + 2k}$, considering the delay by M_0 periods introduced by the filter. Notice that, obviously, there will be $N + M - 1$ samples in $\{{}_0y_n\}$; this signal sequence will be denoted as *details* on the level $j = 0$. By subtracting the details from the (adequately delayed and decimated) signal s_n, we could obtain a coarser signal description, which may be described as the zero-level *approximation*.

In this way, we have provided the first $N/2$ of all spectral (DWT) coefficients. Similarly, we could provide the rest for other values of j, by filtering the signal s_n also with all 2^j times longer impulse responses, and taking then adequately every 2^{j+1}th output sample. We would altogether need $\log_2 N$ different filters with increasing lengths (plus an averager to calculate the mean). However, a better alternative is offered by utilising the results of the theory of quadrature-mirror filters [25], the basic idea of which can be explained as follows. The signal approximation can be derived as a lowpass filtered part of the signal, and the details as a highpass filtered part. Although the filtering cannot be perfect in separating completely the high-frequency from the low-frequency components, we will explain the principle of the algorithm as if it were so. When the wavelets are properly designed (this can be taken for granted), the consequences of the frequency-response overlap will cancel out in the course of processing.

Let us take a couple of filters as on the upper part of Figure 3.12, the frequency responses of which are schematically depicted below and together just cover the useful range of frequencies $\langle 0, \omega_s/2 \rangle$. The response $H(\omega)$ represents

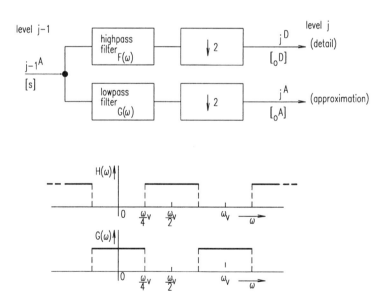

Figure 3.12 Decomposition by a couple of quadrature-mirror filters

a highpass filter corresponding to convolution with $_0 h_n$; $G(\omega)$ is a complementary lowpass response. It can be shown that the impulse response of the lowpass filter may be derived as $_0 g_n = (-1)^n {_0 h_{M_0 - 1 - n}}$; the filter couple is then called a *quadrature-mirror filter*. Obviously, the output signals of the filters describe details and approximations of the signal at the level 0, as above. As the frequency bandwidth of each of the subsignals is only $\omega_s/4$, both signals may be resampled with the half sampling rate, i.e. we can preserve only even samples while discarding the odd, exactly as already mentioned. This operation is indicated by downsampling blocks '$\downarrow 2$'. In this way, we obtain the DWT coefficients $S_{DWT}(0, k)$ in the highpass channel, and these we shall call *detail coefficients* $_0 D_k$; the even samples in the lowpass channel output may be called *approximation coefficients* $_0 A_k$. If we ignore the small influence of the (short) length of the filters, the number of coefficients after the filtering stage is (almost) equal to the original number of signal samples, N.

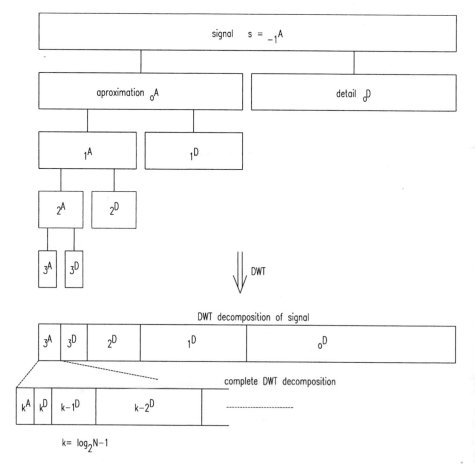

Figure 3.13 Dyadic DWT decomposition of a signal

The same procedure can be applied recursively to levels $j = 1, 2, \cdots$, as schematically depicted in Figure 3.13. On every next level, the number of processed samples is halved in comparison with the previous one. This is not only advantageous from the computational point of view, as unnecessary samples are not calculated, but it also enables the same filters $_0h_n$, $_0g_n$ to be used on all subsequent levels. The dilation of the filters is provided for by successively decreasing the sampling rate thus increasing the effective real-time length of the filters automatically as required; also, amplitude normalisation is arranged automatically. Thus the impulse responses h_n, g_n need not be indexed by j and they describe the chosen type of DWT completely.

We see that the signal can be decomposed into a sequence of complementary couples of subsignals $_jD_k, {}_jA_k, j = 0, 1, \cdots, N - 1$. As no information is lost in any filtering stage, it is possible to stop the decomposition process at any suitable level, say J. The signal is then described by its approximation vector $_J\mathbf{A} = \lfloor _JA_k \rfloor$ and all its detail vectors $_j\mathbf{D} = [_jD_k], j = 0, 1, \cdots, J$; this is *hierarchical wavelet decomposition* of the signal. In many applications the approximation at a certain level does not need to be further analysed, or it is just what is needed as a suitable signal description. Then a further advantage of the filterbank realisation of a DWT is that it enables such an *incomplete transform*. Obviously, if $J = N - 1$, we arrive at the *complete* unitary DWT transform as defined above; the approximation $_{N-1}A$ is then a scalar and equal to the signal mean.

The above procedure provides the signal description in the time–frequency domain which may itself be the final goal, for example in analysing the signal properties or as a feature set for a following recognition phase. Nevertheless, there are many instances, when, usually after some modification of the DWT spectrum, the signal must be reconstructed, for example in noise-suppression or data-compression applications. We shall show how this can be done, again by use of a suitable filter bank. It can be proved that, on any level, the higher-level approximation can be obtained from the relevant approximation and detail subsignals by means of the procedure schematically depicted in Figure 3.14. Both subsignals are here upsampled, i.e. zeros are inserted as the odd-indexed elements of the new twice-as-long sequences. These are then filtered again by members of a couple of quadrature mirror filters, the impulse responses of which h'_n, g'_n are simply time-reversed versions of the responses of

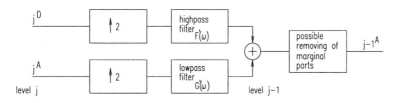

Figure 3.14 A reconstruction stage

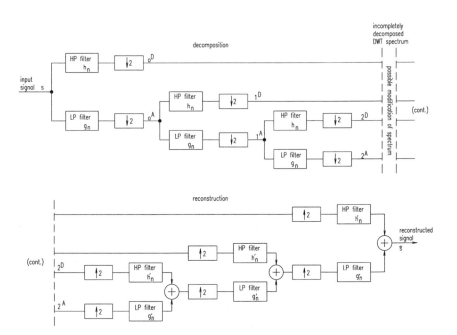

Figure 3.15 A multirate system: incomplete decomposition of signals until level 2 and corresponding reconstruction after a possible modification of spectrum

filters in the corresponding decomposition stage, $h'_n = h_{M-1-n}, g'_n = g_{M-1-n}$. The outputs are summed yielding the higher-level approximation (after removing marginal parts afflicted by border distortion). When applied recursively, this procedure can consecutively recover the approximations $_{J-1}A, _{J-2}A, \cdots, _{-1}A = s$; obviously, the last 'approximation' recovered from $_0A$ and $_0D$ is the original signal s. The system of decomposing and reconstructing structures as in Figure 3.15 is an example of a *multirate system* where different sampling rates are used concurrently. It is a fundamental result of the theory of multirate processing that a perfect reconstruction is possible in spite of the aliasing, which will inevitably appear owing to frequency-response overlap of the filters.

3.6 Karhunen–Loeve transform

The Karhunen–Loeve transform (KLT), in its discrete version, also known as the Hotelling transform, is a unitary transform which, in contrast to all previously discussed transforms, is case dependent. More precisely, its core matrix must be derived based on the statistical properties of the class of signals to be processed. The transform is designed based on the requirement that it will produce decorrelated signal components, that is it will reduce the autocorrelation matrix of the signal-generating process into a diagonal correlation matrix of the corresponding spectral coefficients.

Let a discrete, random finite-length signal be represented by a column vector **u** of N elements, the autocorrelation matrix of which is the ensemble mean $\mathbf{R}_{uu} = \mathbb{E}\{\mathbf{u}.\mathbf{u}^T\}$. We are looking for such a unitary transform matrix Φ that would produce the discrete spectrum $\mathbf{v} = \Phi\mathbf{u}$, the elements of which are mutually uncorrelated spectral coefficients v_k. The autocorrelation matrix of the spectrum is then obviously

$$\mathbf{R}_{vv} = \mathbb{E}\{\mathbf{v}.\mathbf{v}^{*T}\} = \mathbb{E}\{\Phi.\mathbf{u}.\mathbf{u}^{*T}\Phi^{*T}\} = \Phi\mathbb{E}\{\mathbf{u}.\mathbf{u}^{*T}\}\Phi^{*T} = \Phi\mathbf{R}_{uu}\Phi^{*T} = \Lambda, \quad (3.34)$$

where Λ denotes a diagonal matrix. As the transform is to be unitary, $\Phi^{-1} = \Phi^{*T}$, the equality of the last two forms can be rewritten as

$$\mathbf{R}_{uu}\Phi^{*T} = \Phi^{*T}\Lambda. \quad (3.35)$$

As known from matrix theory, this equation will be satisfied when the matrix Φ^{*T} is formed of columns φ_k that are eigenvectors of the matrix $\mathbf{R}_{uu}$ (notice that this is not the only possible choice).

These are obtained as follows: the *eigenvalues* $\lambda_k, k = 0, 1, \cdots, N-1$ of the autocorrelation matrix that are roots of the characteristic polynomial equation $\det(\mathbf{R} - \lambda\mathbf{I}) = 0$ are to be calculated first and sorted according to their values in descending order, $\lambda_k > \lambda_{k+1}$. Then the set of corresponding vector equations, i.e. linear equation systems

$$\mathbf{R}_k = \lambda_k\varphi_k, \text{ or equivalently } (\mathbf{R} - \lambda_k\mathbf{I})\varphi_k = \mathbf{0} \quad (3.36)$$

is to be solved successively for all λ_k, yielding the eigenvectors $\varphi_k, k = 0, 1, \cdots, N-1$. The matrix Φ^{*T} may then be formed from the columns φ_k as

$$\Phi^{*T} = [\varphi_0, \varphi_1, \cdots \varphi_{N-1}]. \quad (3.37)$$

A matrix constructed in this way is called the eigenmatrix of $\mathbf{R}_{uu}$. (Recall that the eigenmatrix is not the only matrix fulfilling eqn (3.35), i.e. other totally decorrelating transforms exist.) The sought transform, the discrete Karhunen–Loeve (or Hotelling) transform, is therefore given by

$$\mathbf{v} = \mathbb{DKLT}\{\mathbf{u}\} = \Phi\mathbf{u}, \quad \mathbf{u} = \mathbb{DKLT}^{-1}\{\mathbf{v}\} = \Phi^{*T}\mathbf{v}. \quad (3.38)$$

The discrete Karhunen–Loeve transform has several interesting properties:

1   The elements of the transformed vector – DKLT spectrum – all have zero mean and are mutually uncorrelated,

$$E\{v_k\} = 0, \forall k \quad \text{and} \quad \mathbb{E}\{v_k v_l\} = \lambda_k\delta(k-l), \forall k, l$$

A proof is unnecessary, as this property was required when deriving the transform matrix. This is a very important property, enabling the optimization of signal data compression, adaptation algorithms etc.

2   The error caused by shortening the spectrum (setting higher-indexed spectral coefficients to zero), the so-called basis restriction error, is minimal among all $N \times N$ transforms. More precisely, consider a sequence of three operations, a forward transform, a nonlinear operation of omitting higher spectral coefficients and an inverse transform,

$$\mathbf{v} = \mathbf{Au}, \quad \mathbf{w} = [w_k]: w_k = \begin{cases} v_k, \, k \in \langle 0, m-1 \rangle \\ 0, \, k \geq m \end{cases} \quad \text{and } \mathbf{z} = \mathbf{Bw}.$$

The error caused by such shortening of the spectrum can be evaluated by the mean-square value of the error vector $\mathbf{u} - \mathbf{z}$,

$$\varepsilon^2 = \frac{1}{N} \mathbb{E} \left\{ \sum_{n=0}^{N-1} |u_n - z_n|^2 \right\} = \text{Trace}(\mathbb{E}\{(u - z)(u - z)^{*T}\}). \tag{3.39}$$

It can be proved that the error achieves its minimum value when the Karhunen–Loeve transform is used, i.e. when

$$\mathbf{A} = \Phi, \quad \mathbf{B} = \Phi^{*T} \quad \text{so that } \mathbf{AB} = \mathbf{I}.$$

We shall skip the rather intricate proof which can be found e.g. in Reference [10].

3   The DKLT has an excellent compaction property: among all the unitary transforms described by matrices $\mathbf{A}$, it packs the maximum average power into any chosen subset of first spectral coefficients $v_k, k = 0, 1, \cdots,$ $m \leq N - 1$. When defining the average power of a single spectral coefficient and the total power of the limited spectrum, respectively,

$$\sigma_k^2 = \mathbb{E}\{|v_k|^2\} \quad \text{and} \quad P_m(\mathbf{A}) = \sum_{k=0}^{m} \sigma_k^2, \tag{3.40}$$

it can be proved that, for any m, the power packed into the first m samples is maximum for the DKL transform,

$$P_m(\Phi) \geq P_m(\mathbf{A}).$$

Again, the proof, dependent on the previous derivation, will be skipped.

The discrete Karhunen–Loeve transform (3.38) thus provides a golden standard in several respects, including some not mentioned here. Unfortunately, in its exact form it is difficult to apply in practice. Primarily, it is a case-dependent transform, the core matrix of which must be derived individually for every class of signal based on the autocorrelation matrix of the background stochastic process. It is often not easy or even not feasible to identify the signal properties that deeply. In addition, an exact fast algorithm for the DKLT does not exist.

The exact Karhunen–Loeve transform therefore remains more a valuable theoretical tool and a standard against which other methods, using less effective transforms, may be compared. On the other hand, it has been found that the DKLT can be closely approximated by transforms based on harmonic functions, namely by the cosine transform (DCT) and sine transform (DST). For signals that can be modelled by Markov sequences of bounded values, which is the case, for example, for many types of image, these transforms represent an excellent approximation of the DKLT: particularly the DCT in cases of background Markov sequences with highly correlated neighbouring elements and the DST in cases of more loosely correlated elements.

Chapter 4
Stochastic processes and their characteristics

4.1 Stochastic signals and processes

So far we have worked with the notion of *deterministic signals* characterised by certain known functions of an independent variable, usually of time; hence, in the discrete version, $f_m = f(t)$, $t \in \{t_m = mT, m \text{ integer}\}$. Nevertheless, in technical practice it is usually only meaningful to analyse signals, the values of which are not known ahead of time, as is obviously the case with received telecommunication signals, with sequences of measured data etc. It is useful to consider such signals as being *stochastic*, that is to take every processed signal as a concrete realisation of a stochastic process.

Let us go through the concept and properties of a *stochastic process*, which is the cornerstone of the theory of the analysis and restoration of signals, in slightly greater detail in order to understand the concepts in this particular area.

To this aim, we shall introduce the notion of a *family of functions* $f_w(t)$, that is a set $\{f_{w_k}(t)\}$ of functions mutually distinguished by the parameter $w_k \in W$, where W is a countable set (therefore possibly even an infinite one). This family – *the basis of the stochastic process* – contains all the possible shapes of signal which can be expected in a given application. Which of the functions becomes the actual received or measured signal – the *realisation of the stochastic process* – depends on the result, w_k, of the associated random experiment.

An elementary example of such a function family is an indexed set of K plots of functions which serves as a source base of a stochastic process (see Figure 4.1, where the discrete functions are represented by their envelopes for the sake of clarity). The kth function, which will become the actual realisation, is selected from the set according to the result, w_k, of an associated random experiment, for example, as a number k tossed as one of the lots indexed $1 \ldots K$. Usually, the random experiment is hidden in the mechanism of generating the signal, which can be of a rather complex physical background. As a typical example, the thermal noise voltage on a resistor in a certain time interval is such a stochastic signal. A concrete random constellation of instant positions and movements of elementary particles, the behaviour of which is itself controlled

result of
associated
experiment   realisation of stochastic process

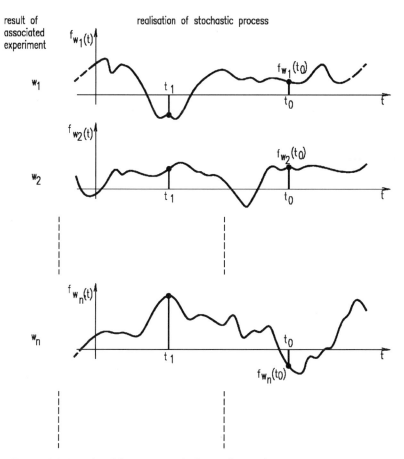

Figure 4.1 Family of functions as the base of a stochastic process

by quantum rules and therefore is stochastic in time, selects it from a practically infinite set of possible noise realisations.

When selecting a particular time instant, t_m, the corresponding function value $f_w(t_m)$, which may be briefly denoted $f_w(m)$ or even f_m, is obviously a random variable dependent on the result, w, of the associated experiment. Every such random variable can be described by the standard probabilistic character-istics, usually called *local* or *instant characteristics* as they refer to a concrete independent-variable localisation, e.g. a time instant, t_m. The most common characteristics are the distribution function, the probability distribution and its moments.

The *distribution function* $P_f(z, m)$ describes the probability $\mathbb{P}$ of the individual realisation sample f_m becoming at maximum the value of the real parameter z,

$$P_f(z, m) = \mathbb{P}\{f_m \leq z\}. \qquad (4.1)$$

Note that either the real value f_m can be from a continuous interval, or it may become one of the discrete values $f_m \in \{z_j, j \in J \text{ integer}\}$, as can be the case resulting from digitising quantisation. In the first case, it is referred to as a continuous stochastic variable, and in the latter a discrete variable. From now on, we shall only deal with *fully discrete processes* where both the set of time instants and the function values are discrete. Then, both sets are usually finite for practical reasons: only finite sets of samples (finite signal sections) can be practically processed. Also, the value extent clearly must be finite and the sample values have to be expressed by finite codes, enabling only a limited number of quantisation levels. It also follows that the number of fully discrete process realisations is finite under the given limitations, although it is usually very high from a practical point of view.

The probabilities of individual discrete function values z_j,

$$P_f(z_j, m) = \mathbb{P}\{f_m = z_j\}, \tag{4.2}$$

can be described by a finite table for every m. Obviously it is

$$P_f(z, m) = \sum_j p_f(z_j, m), \quad j \in \{j : z_j \le z\}. \tag{4.3}$$

The most commonly used moments of the distribution are the *local (instant) mean*

$$\mu_f(m) = \mathbb{E}_w\{f_m\} = \sum_{j \in J} z_j p_f(z_j, m) \approx \frac{1}{M} \sum_{w=w_1}^{w_M} f_w(m), \tag{4.4}$$

where $\mathbb{E}_w\{.\}$ is the operator of (ensemble) mean that can be approximated by the corresponding ensemble average for a great M as presented in the last part of the equation, and the *local (instant) variance*

$$\sigma_f^2(m) = \mathbb{E}\{|f_m - \mu_f(m)|^2\} = \sum_{j \in J} (z_j - \mu_f(m))^2 p_f(z_j, m),$$

$$\sigma_f^2(m) \approx \frac{1}{M} \sum_w |f_w(m) - \mu_f(m)|^2. \tag{4.5}$$

The local (instant) characteristics naturally do not express the relationships between the different time instants of a stochastic process. To describe such relationships, the *joint probabilities* of signal values, becoming certain given levels in two (or even more) different instants of one realisation of the process, must be taken into account. In the simplest case, this leads to the two-dimensional probability distribution

$$p_f(z_j, z_k, m, n) = \mathbb{P}\{f_{w_l}(m) = z_j, f_{w_l}(n) = z_k\}, \tag{4.6}$$

which describes the probability of the event that the signal will have, in a concrete realisation w_l, the value z_j at the instant t_m and the value z_k at the instant t_n.

These probabilities are described by a two-dimensional table of the variables z_j and z_k. If the random variables f_m and f_n are independent, then of course

$$p_f(z_j, z_k, m, n) = p_f(z_j, m) \, p_f(z_k, n).$$

Should they be dependent, as is the more general case, according to Bayes theorem conditional probabilities are involved:

$$p_f(z_j, z_k, m, n) = p_f(z_j, m) \, p_f(z_k | z_j, n)$$
$$= p_f(z_j | z_k, m) \, p_f(z_k, n).$$

By generalisation, we arrive at the r-dimensional probability distribution

$$p_f(z_{j_1}, z_{j_2}, \ldots, z_{j_r}, m_1, m_2, \ldots, m_r)$$
$$= \mathbb{P}\{f_{w_i}(m_1) - z_{j_1}, f_{w_i}(m_2) = z_{j_2}, \ldots, f_{w_i}(m_r) = z_{j_r}\}. \tag{4.7}$$

Notice that, while the two-dimensional characteristics describe relatively simple and rather generic properties of the stochastic process, increasing r leads to an increase in the complexity and information content of the characteristics. On the other hand, the significance of a single characteristic for the characterisation of the process rather decreases with r, as is clearly shown by the extreme case $r = N$. Then, the probabilities of occurrence of concrete sequences of N sample values are sought, i.e. the probabilities of individual complete realisations – possible signals.

An analogous approach can also be applied to the analysis of mutual relationships between two different processes $f_w(t)$ and $g_w(t)$ that are controlled by the same associated random experiment with the general result w. For brevity, such processes will sometimes be called *concurrent processes*. The joint probability of a pair of values – one being from the process $f_w(t)$, the other from the process $g_w(t)$, both from realisations belonging to the same result, w_i, of the associated experiment – is given in analogy to eqn (4.6) as

$$P_{fg}(z_j, z_k, m, n) = \mathbb{P}\{f_{w_i}(m) = z_j, g_{w_i}(n) = z_k\}. \tag{4.8}$$

By further generalisation we would arrive at multidimensional probabilities of occurrence of more selected values in chosen time instants in the two corresponding realisations; nevertheless, such characteristics are rather infrequently used owing to their rather high complexity.

4.2 Correlation and covariance functions

Although multidimensional probability distributions provide the most complete description of stochastic processes, experimental determination of them by means of ensemble averages presents a challenging task from a practical point of view; usually, it is so cumbersome that it is not feasible. Even estimates of local probability distributions tend to be very demanding in the general case (namely with nonstationary processes – see later). Thus we usually have to be content with estimates of low-order moments of the distributions – local means and local variances according to the last expressions in eqns (4.4) and (4.5). When analysing the mutual relations of signal values among different time instants, we usually have to limit ourselves to the case of only two different instants. Even then, the complete distribution is normally not provided but, instead, only the mixed moments are analysed. As these are of extraordinary importance in contemporary signal theory, we will discuss them in more detail. They are the correlation and covariance of a couple of values, or correlation function and covariance function in the case of analysing sets of such couples.

Correlation of a couple of two random variables f_m, f_n is the (ensemble) mean value of their products (i.e. over all possible realisations), which can be estimated approximately on the basis of the corresponding ensemble average,

$$R_{ff}(m, n) = \mathbb{E}\{f_w(m)f_w(n)\} \approx \frac{1}{M} \sum_{w=w_1}^{w_M} f_{w_i}(m)f_{w_i}(n). \qquad (4.9)$$

Covariance, in the same situation, is the mean of products of the corresponding centred variables, i.e. the variables after subtraction of the local means. It can be estimated similarly,

$$C_{ff}(m, n) = \mathbb{E}\{(f_w(m) - \mu_f(m))(f_w(n) - \mu_f(n))\}$$

$$\approx \frac{1}{M} \sum_{w=w_1}^{w_M} (f_{w_i}(m) - \mu_f(m))(f_{w_i}(n) - \mu_f(n)). \qquad (4.10)$$

Rewriting the second expression, taking into account the linearity of the mean operator, we obtain the relation between correlation and covariance,

$$C_{ff}(m, n) = \mathbb{E}\{f_w(m)f_w(n)\} - \mu_f(m)\mathbb{E}\{f_w(n)\} - \mu_f(n)\mathbb{E}\{f_w(m)\} + \mu_f(m)\mu_f(n)$$

$$= R_{ff}(m, n) - \mu_f(m)\mu_f(n), \qquad (4.11)$$

so that when knowing both local means, the two quantities provide the same information. For autocovariance, it can be vividly seen what kind of information is conveyed. Let us call such variables positively related, the differences of which from respective mean values will probably – in most cases – be of the same sign. Should both variables be closely related and the relation be positive, then obviously most of the products in the mean or average in eqn (4.10) will be positive, so that the estimate of the covariance will also be positive. On the contrary, if the relation is basically inverse (or negative, the signs of differences will be mostly different), this will be made obvious by the negative covariance. It can be proven that the covariance is always zero if the random variables are independent, as both polarities of the products are then equally probable; the opposite is not necessarily true. Nevertheless, if the estimated covariance is about zero, it can be expected that the relation is probably weak or does not exist at all. The variables, the covariance of which is zero, are called uncorrelated; among them, independent variables are a special case.

The absolute value of covariance does not quantify the degree of the relation; more quantitatively it can be characterised by the *correlation coefficient*

$$\rho_{ff}(m, n) = \frac{C_{ff}(m, n)}{\sqrt{\sigma_f^2(m)\sigma_f^2(n)}}, \tag{4.12}$$

which assumes values between ± 1, the extremes corresponding to the linear (positive or negative) mutual dependence of the two concerned variables.

As the independent variables i.e. time instants t_m, t_n may be chosen arbitrarily in the frame of the analysed process section of N samples, the expressions (4.9) and (4.10) can be regarded as functions of the two discrete variables (or of the corresponding integer indices m, n). Then, these expressions define the *correlation function* or *covariance function*, respectively. With respect to the discrete character of both variables, the definition region of the functions is given by the Cartesian product of the sets of both indices. The function values can therefore be arranged into the *correlation –* or *covariance – matrix* of size $N \times N$. The matrices are obviously symmetric with respect to the main diagonal as the operation of multiplication in the definitions of functions is commutative.

Functions defined in this way are important characteristics of a stochastic process; often they are denoted as *autocorrelation-* or *autocovariance functions* in order to emphasise that internal relations of a process f are analysed. We shall discuss the properties and use of these functions in more detail in Chapter 8 on correlation analysis of signals. Let us only state here intuitively that the distribution of function values indicates the distribution of mutual relations among the random quantities constituting the process elements. In particular, the extent of such relations (in terms of number of samples, meaning e.g. time differences) or whether there are any long-distance relations such as a consequence of periodicities can be estimated.

When analysing mutual relations of two processes $f_w(t)$ and $g_w(t)$ associated with the same random experiment, w, we can define the *crosscorrelation function* in an appropriately modified way in parallel to the definition of the auto-correlation function (4.9) as

$$R_{fg}(m, n) = \mathbb{E}\{f_w(m)g_w(n)\} \approx \frac{1}{M} \sum_{w=w_1}^{w_M} f_{w_i}(m)g_{w_i}(n). \tag{4.13}$$

Similarly, the *crosscovariance function* is defined as a modification of (4.10),

$$C_{fg}(m, n) = \mathbb{E}\{(f_w(m) - \mu_f(m))(g_w(n) - \mu_g(n))\}$$

$$\approx \frac{1}{M} \sum_{w=w_1}^{w_M} (f_{w_i}(m) - \mu_f(m))(g_{w_i}(n) - \mu_g(n)). \tag{4.14}$$

Crossfunctions are used in a similar way to the autocorrelation and auto-covariance functions, with the difference of describing *mutual* relations or influences between two concurrent processes. It should be emphasised that the order of correlated processes is important ($R_{fg} \neq R_{gf}$) and, consequently, the *cross-correlation* and *crosscovariance matrices* are not symmetrical with respect to the main diagonal. The elements of these matrices can be estimated on the basis of ensemble averages as presented on the right-hand sides of eqns (4.10), (4.11) or (4.13), (4.14). The estimation procedure is usually very demanding, as it needs to measure a high number M of realisations of the analysed process for the autofunctions or couples of realisations for the mutual (cross-)functions.

Notice that the correlation and covariance functions are deterministic functions as follows from the definition expressions and from the nonrandomness of the (theoretical) mean value. Nevertheless, the estimates of the function values based on ensemble averages are always erratic to a smaller or greater extent because the approximation of a mean by the corresponding average suffers from a random error; consequently, the estimates are also random functions. As we shall see later, this property is usually taken into account as a source of possible imperfections which can be analysed in detail utilising the information on the processes and estimation procedures used. The estimated functions themselves are commonly used rather as deterministic functions in the sense of signal theory.

4.3 Stationary and ergodic processes

So far we have spoken about generic, generally nonstationary, stochastic processes that are characterised by having the local probabilistic characteristics different for different time instants (or more generally, for different values of the independent variable). The correlation function is also of local character as its values correspond to concrete couples of time instants. On the most generic level, the property of nonstationarity is expressed by the multidimensional probability distributions (4.7) depending on concrete time instants. It is nevertheless intuitively felt that this concept is often too generic and that the local characteristics of many stochastic processes are invariable in time or that they are changing slowly in comparison with the signal development. This observation has led to the formulation of the notion of stationary stochastic processes.

A *stationary stochastic process* (in the strict sense) is defined by having all its multidimensional probability distributions of any order invariant with respect to time shift. This means that the distributions will not change if all the analysed time instants are shifted by the same interval,

$$p_f(z_{j_1}, z_{j_2}, \ldots, z_{j_r}, m_1, m_2, \ldots, m_r)$$
$$= p_f(z_{j_1}, z_{j_2}, \ldots, z_{j_r}, m_1 + d, m_2 + d, \ldots, m_r + d), \qquad (4.15)$$

for any integer d. It follows from this requirement that all the characteristics of stationary processes are independent of the selection of the time origin.

Verification of the property (4.15) for concrete processes is unfortunately very difficult if not impossible in practice. That is why a weaker definition of *wide-sense stationary processes* (sometimes called 'weakly stationary') is widely accepted. This only requires that the local mean and the autocorrelation function are time-shift invariant in the above mentioned sense, i.e.

$$\mu_f(m) = \mu_f(m + d) = \mu_f$$

and

$$R_{ff}(m, n) = R_{ff}(m + d, n + d) = R_{ff}(m - n), \qquad (4.16)$$

which can be verified much more easily. As is obvious, the autocorrelation function then becomes a function of only a single variable – the time difference between the analysed instants (or the difference of the corresponding indices). This is a very welcome simplification useful both for identification of the function as well as for its interpretation because it is now described by a vector of $2N - 1$ values instead of by a matrix of N^2 elements. Should $m = n + \tau$, then

$$R_{ff}(\tau) = R_{ff}(m - n) = \mathbb{E}\{f_\omega(n + \tau)f_\omega(n)\} = \mathbb{E}\{f_\omega(n)f_\omega(n + \tau)\}$$
$$= R_{ff}(n - m) = R_{ff}(-\tau), \qquad (4.17)$$

which shows that the autocorrelation function is even; only N values are therefore sufficient to describe it.

In some applications, it may be useful to enhance the weak definition by imposing additional requirements: e.g. that the variance or even the complete local (one-dimensional) probability distribution also be time-shift invariant. On the other hand, on other occasions only one-dimensionality of the autocorrelation function is required without the requirement of time-shift invariance of the local mean. Such modified definitions are only rarely used.

When investigating the relationship between two concurrent processes it is of course also useful if the crosscorrelation function is dependent on only a single variable – the time shift (more generally, on the difference of the independent variables). This is possible if the function is invariant in the above-mentioned sense,

$$R_{fg}(m, n) = R_{fg}(m + d, n + d) = R_{fg}(m - n). \qquad (4.18)$$

Two such stochastic processes f, g fulfilling this condition are called *mutually stationary* (or cross-stationary) *processes*. As the interchange of factors in the product (possible in eqn (4.17)) is not possible in crosscorrelation functions, the order of variables is important and consequently $R_{fg}(\tau) \neq R_{gf}(\tau)$. The crosscorrelation function is thus not even and its complete description vector has $2N - 1$ components.

Imposition of the stationarity requirement has not removed the necessity to base the identification of properties of stochastic processes, described by estimates of their probabilistic characteristics, on the *ensemble averages*. It is nevertheless often difficult or even infeasible in practice to provide a greater number of realisations of a process or pairs of realisations in the case of two related processes. Then we need to determine the process properties as precisely as possible on the basis of a single available realisation, which causes the difficult problem of finding a substitute for unavailable ensemble averages. *Time averages* are the only alternative in such a case. It is primarily obvious that stationarity is a necessary condition for such an approach, because any time-dependent parameters cannot be identified by time averages. It is, however, not a sufficient condition, as the following elementary example shows. If the mean is estimated as the time average of N values of one realisation w_i, i.e. $\hat{\mu}_f \approx (1/N) \sum_{m=1}^{N} f_{w_i}(m)$, instead of the ensemble average $\mu_f(m) \approx (1/M) \sum_{w=w_1}^{w_M} f_w(m)$, the result may be false. This is because stationarity does not exclude the case when the mean values in the individual realisations differ, perhaps to a great extent. Nevertheless, in such cases the ensemble average still provides an approximately correct value (for large M) because it is possible to accumulate the information from many realisations. It is clear that the use of time averages will yield reasonable results only for a subclass of stationary processes which have some special properties. This subclass comprises processes that will be called ergodic.

We shall arrive at a definition of *ergodic processes* in the following way: let us define the time average for every realisation w_i as

$$E_{w_i} = \lim_{N \to \infty} \frac{1}{N} \sum_{n=1}^{N} f_{w_i}(n). \tag{4.19}$$

It is obviously generally a random variable dependent on the realisation, that is on the result of the associated random experiment. If it is valid that

$$E_{w_i} = E_{w_j} = \mu_f, \quad \forall i, j, \tag{4.20}$$

i.e. all the limit time averages of individual realisations are mutually equal and, at the same time, they are equal to the mean of the stationary process according to eqn (4.4), then the process is called ergodic with respect to the mean.

Similarly, the process, ergodic with respect to the autocorrelation function, is characterised as follows: all the time-based estimates of the function as determined from individual realisations,

$$R_{w_i}(\tau) = \lim_{N \to \infty} \frac{1}{N - \tau} \sum_{n=1}^{N-\tau} f_{w_i}(n) f_{w_i}(n + \tau), \tag{4.21}$$

are identical and equal to the autocorrelation function of the process defined by eqn (4.13), i.e.

$$R_{w_i}(\tau) = R_{w_j}(\tau) = R_{ff}(\tau), \quad \forall i, j, \tau. \tag{4.22}$$

Mutually ergodic processes are defined in an analogous way, but with respect to the crosscorrelation functions as determined from couples of realisations. The same approach can also be applied to other probabilistic characteristics of a process, but the ergodicity with respect only to the mean value and correlation function is usually sufficient for practical problems.

Ergodic processes are therefore stationary processes, the probabilistic parameters of which, estimated by means of time averages, are approaching the theoretical (ensemble-mean based) values for sufficiently long processed sections of the individual realisations. The probability of any chosen nonzero difference between the parameter estimated on the basis of time average and its theoretical value approaches zero as the processed signal length increases towards infinity, if the signal-generating process is ergodic. We say that the time averages converge to the proper values with respect to probability.

The above discussion explains the substance of the notion of ergodicity. Nevertheless, it does not instruct the user on how to decide whether a concrete analysed process is ergodic, if only a single realisation (or perhaps a small number of them) is available, which is exactly the case when the concept is needed. In some practical cases, the stationarity and ergodicity of a process follow from its physical principle. If this is not the case, then the only option is to accept a heuristic hypothesis that the analysed process is ergodic. The parameters, estimated as time averages (sometimes called *empirical parameters*), should then be tested by practical utilisation. Should the results be consistent with other results of the experiments or with theoretically-derived values, then the hypotheses may be considered proven at least in the frame of our knowledge. Otherwise, the hypothesis must be rejected and the analysis improved by, for example, providing better or more measurement data.

4.4 Spectra of stochastic processes

4.4.1 Power spectrum of a stochastic process

Deterministic discrete signals can be described in two equivalent ways: either in the original (mostly time) domain by sequences of sample values, or in the frequency domain by their Fourier spectra, usually in the sense of the DTFT spectrum (eqn 3.2) or its discrete version – DFT according to eqn (3.6). When working with stochastic signals, the spectrum $F_{w_i}(\omega)$ or $F_{w_i}(k\Omega)$, $k = 0, 1, 2, \cdots, N - 1$ can be calculated for every individual realisation $f_{w_i}(n)$, $n = 0, 1, \cdots, N - 1$, which is a deterministic signal selected out of the set of possible realisations by the result, w_i, of the associated random experiment. The spectra of different realisations are, of course, mutually different, $F_{w_i}(\omega) \neq F_{w_j}(\omega)$ when $i \neq j$. In spite of this, we can often discover, when providing a sufficiently high number of realisations of a particular process, some features common to all the individual spectra calculated from the realisations.

These similarities are expressed as enhancements or suppressions of certain frequency regions, visible on the amplitude spectra even when the variance of spectral values among individual realisations is high. Corresponding similarities are usually not evident in the original domain.

It is a tempting idea to find a characteristic spectrum of a process by averaging the spectra $F_{w_i}(\omega)$ for different w_i. Unfortunately, this is useless, as the averages of complex numbers with random phases converge to zero and the individual phase spectra expressing the relative time shift of the frequency components have, as a rule, purely random character. On the other hand, it is possible to average the absolute values, i.e. the amplitude spectra, or squared amplitudes $|F_{w_i}(\omega)|^2$; these frequency-domain functions can be denoted as *power spectra of individual realisations* (after multiplication by $1/N$). The connection with the notion of power follows from the idea that the signal values can be represented by a physical quantity (e.g. electrical voltage), the square of which is proportional to its instant power; therefore, the squared amplitudes of harmonic components also correspond to their power. The individual power spectra of two realisations of the stochastic process, generated as random white noise shaped by being passed through a certain bandpass filter, are depicted in Figure 4.2 (in the frequency range $\omega \in \langle 0, \omega_v/2 \rangle$).

The *power spectrum of a stochastic process* is defined as a function given by the ensemble mean

$$S_{ff}(\omega) = \mathbb{E}\left\{\frac{1}{N}F_w(\omega)F_w^*(\omega)\right\} = \mathbb{E}\left\{\frac{1}{N}|F_w(\omega)|^2\right\} \approx \frac{1}{M}\sum_{w-w_1}^{w_M}\frac{1}{N}|F_{w_i}(\omega)|^2; \quad (4.23)$$

here, the right-hand side expresses the estimate of the function by an average of a finite number of realisations. Such a concrete estimate, based on 100 realisations of the process which generated the spectra of Figure 4.2, is on the right of Figure 4.3. We can see that such an averaged estimate is markedly closer to the theoretical function shown on the left-hand side than the individual spectra. It should be said, nevertheless, that even such an estimated averaged spectrum could still be rather erroneous owing to the variance of averages for an acceptable value of M.

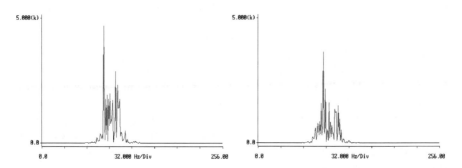

Figure 4.2 Individual power spectra of two realisations of a process

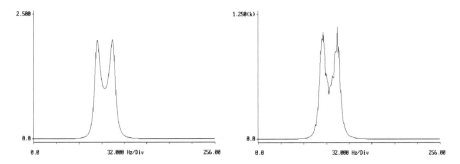

Figure 4.3 Theoretical power spectrum of a process and its average-based estimate

As the Fourier transform removes the dependence on time, it is sensible to characterise only those processes in the frequency domain, that have probabilistic characteristics which do not vary in time, i.e. stationary processes. In this way, the individual spectra describe the properties of the complete realisations (principally not limited in time) in the frequency domain and, consequently, the complete process is described by the resulting mean power spectrum.

There is an important relationship between the power spectrum of a stationary stochastic process and its autocorrelation function, called the *Wiener–Kchintchin theorem*. Its version for discrete processes of a finite length N is as follows,

$$S_{ff}(\omega) = \mathrm{DTFT}\{w(\tau)R_{ff}(\tau)\}, \quad \text{or} \quad S_{ff}(k\Omega) = \mathrm{DFT}\{w(\tau)R_{ff}(\tau)\}, \quad \tau \text{ integer}, \quad (4.24)$$

where $w(\tau)$ is a weighting function – a triangular window of the width $2N - 1$ with the central weight equal to 1. The *weighted* autocorrelation function and the power spectrum thus form a transform pair in the discrete Fourier transform.[1] Indeed, for an arbitrary process of a finite length N,

$$S_{ff}(\omega) = \mathbb{E}\left\{\frac{1}{N} F_w(\omega) F_w^*(\omega)\right\}$$

$$= \frac{1}{N} \mathbb{E}\left\{\left(\sum_{n=0}^{N-1} f_w(n) e^{-j\omega nT}\right)\left(\sum_{m=0}^{N-1} f_w(m) e^{j\omega mT}\right)\right\}$$

$$= \frac{1}{N} \sum_{n=0}^{N-1} \sum_{m=0}^{N-1} \mathbb{E}\{f_w(n) f_w(m)\} e^{-j\omega(n-m)T}$$

$$= \frac{1}{N} \sum_{n=0}^{N-1} \sum_{m=0}^{N-1} R_{ff}(n, m) e^{-j\omega(n-m)T}.$$

---

[1] Many authors define the power spectrum by an expression similar to eqn (4.24), and the relation (4.23) is then interpreted as a property which is a consequence of the Wiener–Kchintchin theorem.

If the process is stationary, the relation $R_{ff}(m, n) = R_{ff}(m - n)$ applies. Further, by introducing the substitution $m - n = \tau$, we obtain (taking into account that there are n^2 terms in the double sum of which, for a certain τ, $N - |\tau|$ terms contain $R_{ff}(\tau)$)

$$\sum_{\tau=-N-1}^{N-1} w(\tau)R_{ff}(\tau)e^{-j\omega\tau T} = \mathbb{DTFT}\{w(\tau)R_{ff}(\tau)\}, \qquad (4.24a)$$

where $w(\tau) = (N - |\tau|)/N$. Note that the discrete version of the Wiener–Kchintchin theorem is usually cited in the literature without the explicit weighting function, which is confusing if no explanation is given. We shall return to the practical consequences of explicitly mentioning the window in Section 8.2.

Notice that, as a consequence of the even symmetry of the weighted autocorrelation function, the power spectrum as its Fourier transform is real (zero phase) which is in accordance with the definition (4.23). Also note that, for ergodic processes, the limit values of a correlation function as calculated by means of ensemble averages and time averages are identical, so that the previous derivation includes validity of eqn (4.24) even for autocorrelation functions defined by time-course mean values.

The Wiener–Kchintchin theorem is one of the fundamental pieces of knowledge of signal theory and leads to further important theoretical considerations. Among others it enables, in principle, estimation of the power spectra of stationary and namely ergodic stochastic processes *via* their autocorrelation functions. We shall deal with the questions of random-signal spectral analysis utilising both aforementioned classical approaches as well as by means of other methods in detail in Section 9.2.

4.4.2 Cross-spectrum of a pair of processes

In a similar way as we introduced the power spectrum in the previous section, we shall present the notion of *cross-spectrum*. It characterises, in the frequency domain, the relationship of two concurrent stochastic processes, $f_w(n)$, $g_w(n)$, controlled by the same associated random experiment w, and is defined as

$$S_{fg}(\omega) = \mathbb{E}\left\{\frac{1}{N} F_w^*(\omega)G_w(\omega)\right\} \approx \frac{1}{M}\sum_{w=w_1}^{w_M}\frac{1}{N}F_{w_i}^*(\omega)G_{w_i}(\omega). \qquad (4.25)$$

Here, $F_{w_i}(\omega)$ and $G_{w_i}(\omega)$ are the spectra of realisations that correspond to the same result, w_i, of the associated experiment. The spectra $F_w(\omega)$ and $G_w(\omega)$ are therefore random functions of frequency and it can be observed that eqn (4.25) provides the value of their correlation also as a function of frequency.

The interpretation of this function deserves a level of attention which is usually not devoted to it in the literature. The correlation $S_{fg}(\omega_j)$ for a concrete frequency ω_j is, as seen, the mean value (or average, in an estimate) of products of complex numbers so that it is a complex quantity. Let us investigate when this quantity will assume extreme values.

It would be zero or near to zero primarily when most of the contributions to the average are zero. It appears if, for different w_i, at least one of the factors $F_{w_i}(\omega_j)$, $G_{w_i}(\omega_j)$ is almost always zero, which means that the component of a particular frequency ω_j is mostly missing in one of the spectra under comparison. In such a case, any important mutual relationship at this frequency obviously does not exist. However, the frequency correlation can also be zero when the given frequency components are present distinctly almost always in both signals but the phases of the products entering the sum are so different that their contributions mutually cancel. The phase value of a particular product is given – one of the factors being complex conjugate – by the difference of the corresponding phase-spectra values of both realisations. The zero average at a frequency then means that there is no important (prevailing) phase relationship at that particular frequency between the components under discussion. In this case, it is also appropriate to say that there does not exist any relationship between the analysed processes at this particular frequency.[2]

On the other hand, the correlation reaches its maximum (at a frequency) if there is a fixed phase relation of the components at the particular frequency – the difference of values $\arg\{F_{w_i}(\omega_j)\}$, $\arg\{G_{w_i}(\omega_j)\}$ in the couples of the phase spectra (at the given frequency ω_j) will be a constant in all realisations. The mean (or average) result will in this case be a complex number with a phase equal to the mentioned difference and with the module given by the mean (or average) of products of amplitude spectra values $|F_{w_i}(\omega_j)|$, $|G_{w_i}(\omega_j)|$.

The cross-spectrum enables only relative comparison of the relationships of the two processes on different frequencies. To assess the degree of the phase relationship quantitatively and absolutely, the normalised quantity – *coherence spectrum* – is used,

$$\kappa_{fg}(\omega) = \frac{|S_{fg}(\omega)|^2}{S_f(\omega) . S_g(\omega)}. \qquad (4.26)$$

The coherence spectrum, independent of the magnitudes of the power spectra $S_f(\omega)$, $S_g(\omega)$, obviously takes on the extreme value 1 at frequencies at which the corresponding components in both analysed processes have a fixed phase relationship, the so-called coherent components. The value of the coherence spectrum decreases with an increase of variance in the phase difference; in the extreme case of equal probability of all phase differences, it becomes zero.

---

[2] It can be argued that the mere existence of a frequency component in most of the concurrent realisations may still indicate a certain type of a relationship even when no fixed or prevailing phase relationship between the components is present. Should such relationships be investigated, it would be possible by introducing the frequency-dependent correlation of amplitude spectra:

$$\mathbb{E}\{|F_w(\omega)||G_w(\omega)|\} \neq |S_{fg}(\omega)|.$$

In analogy to what we have derived for the power spectrum, for the cross-spectrum we can write

$$S_{fg}(\omega) = \mathbb{E}\left\{\frac{1}{N}F_w^*(\omega)G_w(\omega)\right\} = \frac{1}{N}\mathbb{E}\left\{\left(\sum_{n=0}^{N-1}f_w(n)e^{j\omega nT}\right)\left(\sum_{m=0}^{N-1}g_w(m)e^{-j\omega mT}\right)\right\}$$

$$= \frac{1}{N}\sum_{n=0}^{N-1}\sum_{m=0}^{N-1}\mathbb{E}\{f_w(n)g_w(m)\}e^{-j\omega(n-m)T}$$

$$= \frac{1}{N}\sum_{n=0}^{N-1}\sum_{m=0}^{N-1}R_{fg}(n,m)e^{-j\omega(n-m)T}.$$

If both processes are mutually stationary with respect to correlation, again, after introducing the substitution $n - m = \tau$, we obtain

$$\sum_{\tau=-N-1}^{N-1}w(\tau)R_{fg}(\tau)e^{-j\omega\tau T} = \mathrm{DTFT}\{w(\tau)R_{fg}(\tau)\}.$$

Therefore, an analogue of the Wiener–Kchintchin theorem applies to the relationship of the cross-spectrum and the crosscorrelation function,

$$S_{fg}(\omega) = \mathrm{DTFT}\{w(\tau)R_{fg}(\tau)\}, \quad \text{or} \quad S_{fg}(k\Omega) = \mathrm{DFT}\{w(\tau)R_{fg}(\tau)\}, \quad \tau \text{ integer}. \quad (4.27)$$

The substantial difference from eqn (4.24) is in the asymmetry of the crosscorrelation function with respect to the time-origin in the general case. Therefore, its spectrum – i.e. the cross-spectrum of the two concerned processes – is generally complex, as also follows from the previous discussion. As the crosscorrelation function is always real, the spectrum is symmetrical in the sense $S_{fg}(-\omega) = S_{fg}^*(\omega)$ and, moreover, as can easily be verified, $S_{gf}(\omega) = S_{fg}^*(\omega)$.

4.5 Transfer of stochastic signals via linear systems

As shown in Section 2.3, a linear discrete time-invariant system is characterised, as far as its input–output behaviour is concerned, by the impulse response $h_n = h(n)$ or alternatively by the Z-transform of it – the transfer function $H(z)$ or also by the frequency response $G(\omega) = H(e^{j\omega T})$. When discussing the transfer of a random signal through such a system, we consider the following.

The system's input is fed by a realisation $f_{w_i}(n)$ of the process $f_w(n)$. The realisation, arbitrarily chosen out of the possible realisations of the process by the associated random experiment, is obviously an ordinary deterministic signal from the point of view of the system. The system responds at its output by the output sequence according to the convolution expression (2.24),

$$y_{w_i}(n) = f_{w_i}(n) * h(n). \quad (4.28)$$

(We suppose for simplicity that a sufficiently long time has elapsed since the beginning of the system's operation so that the responses to the initial conditions as well as to the start of the signal are already negligible.) This relation is naturally valid for any concrete realisation so that it can be considered as a family of equations

$$y_w(n) = f_w(n) * h(n), \tag{4.29}$$

describing the behaviour of the system with respect to the whole stochastic process. It should be emphasised that the system can only deal with the individual realisations of the process. The output process $y_w(n)$, the base of which is constituted from the responses to all admissible realisations of the input process $f_w(n)$, is evidently controlled by the same associated random experiment as the input process, and therefore the processes are concurrent. We are now interested in determining the probabilistic characteristics of the process $y_w(n)$ when knowing the corresponding characteristics of the process $f_w(n)$. Regarding the genesis of the output process the output process can be interpreted as having been derived by the linear system from the input process; in this sense, we may speak about the change of (auto)parameters of a process when 'transferring' it through the system. It will also be interesting to find the mutual (cross)-characteristics of the input and output processes.

The (ensemble) mean value of the generally nonstationary output process is

$$\mathbb{E}\{y_w(n)\} = \mathbb{E}\{f_w(n) * h(n)\} = \mathbb{E}\left\{ \sum_{l=0}^{\infty} f_w(n-l)h(l) \right\}$$

$$= \sum_{l=0}^{\infty} \mathbb{E}\{f_w(n-l)\}h(l) = \mathbb{E}\{f_w(n)\} * h(n). \tag{4.30}$$

This sequence of local mean values at the output is therefore produced by the convolution of the input mean-value sequence with the system's impulse response, i.e. by the same convolution that produces every individual output realisation. Similarly, we obtain for the output autocorrelation function (in the general case of nonstationary processes)

$$R_{yy}(m, n) = \mathbb{E}\{y_w(m)y_w(n)\}$$

$$= \mathbb{E}\left\{ \left(\sum_{l=0}^{\infty} f_w(m-l)h(l) \right) \left(\sum_{k=0}^{\infty} f_w(n-k)h(k) \right) \right\}. \tag{4.31}$$

If the input process is (weakly) stationary, it follows from the previous equations that the output process is also stationary as, according to eqn (4.30), the output mean will be constant and, with respect to eqn (4.31), the output autocorrelation function will depend on only a single variable $m - n$. In this case, the power spectra for the input process as well as for the output process according to eqn (4.24) exist. The Fourier (complex) spectrum of an individual input realisation is modified in agreement with eqn (2.20), i.e. $Y_{w_i}(\omega) = G(\omega)F_{w_i}(\omega)$, therefore also $Y^*_{w_i}(\omega) = G^*(\omega)F^*_{w_i}(\omega)$. The power spectrum of an individual realisation at the output of the system can thus be written

$$\frac{1}{N}|Y_{w_i}(\omega)|^2 = \frac{1}{N}Y_{w_i}(\omega)Y^*_{w_i}(\omega) = \frac{1}{N}G(\omega)G^*(\omega)F_{w_i}(\omega)F^*_{w_i}(\omega)$$

$$= |G(\omega)|^2\frac{1}{N}|F_{w_i}(\omega)|^2.$$

Applying the operator of the mean value to both sides of the equation yields

$$S_{yy}(\omega) = \mathbb{E}\left\{\frac{1}{N}Y_w(\omega)Y^*_w(\omega)\right\}$$

$$= |G(\omega)|^2\mathbb{E}\left\{\frac{1}{N}F_w(\omega)F^*_w(\omega)\right\} = |G(\omega)|^2 S_{ff}(\omega). \qquad (4.32)$$

Hence, the power spectrum is modified so that it is multiplied by the squared-amplitude frequency response of the system. The autocorrelation function is modified correspondingly,

$$w(\tau)R_{yy}(\tau) = \mathrm{DTFT}^{-1}\{S_{yy}(\omega)\} = \mathrm{DTFT}^{-1}\{|G(\omega)|^2 S_{ff}(\omega)\}$$

$$= \mathrm{DTFT}^{-1}\{|G(\omega)|^2\mathrm{DTFT}(w(\tau)R_{ff}(\tau))\} \qquad (4.33)$$

therefore

$$w(\tau)R_{yy}(\tau) = \hbar(\tau) * (w(\tau)R_{ff}(\tau)), \quad \hbar(\tau) = \mathrm{DTFT}^{-1}\{|G(\omega)|^2\}. \qquad (4.34)$$

Naturally, the sampled version of DTFT, i.e. the discrete Fourier transform (DFT) will be used in practice to analyse the sampled finite signal sections.

The cross-spectrum describing the relationship between the input and output processes in the frequency domain is

$$S_{fy}(\omega) = \mathbb{E}\left\{\frac{1}{N}F^*_w(\omega)Y_w(\omega)\right\}$$

$$= \mathbb{E}\left\{\frac{1}{N}F^*_w(\omega)G(\omega)F_w(\omega)\right\} = G(\omega)\mathbb{E}\left\{\frac{1}{N}|F_w(\omega)|^2\right\} = G(\omega)S_{ff}(\omega).$$

When expressing the spectra using the Wiener–Khintchin theorem, we see that this relationship enables us to identify the frequency response of a linear system by means of correlation analysis,

$$G(\omega) = \frac{\mathrm{DTFT}\{w(\tau)R_{fy}(\omega)\}}{\mathrm{DTFT}\{w(\tau)R_{ff}(\omega)\}}. \qquad (4.36)$$

It should again be emphasised that the results of this calculation, as well as those of other identification procedures based on statistical methods, are always distorted by an error caused by using only imprecise estimates instead of theoretical correlation functions. Notice that although eqn (4.36) provides the complete information on the frequency response, including the phase characteristic, the ratio of power spectra (4.32) can only yield the amplitude frequency response.

4.6 A note on the principle of orthogonality

Estimation of random values of stochastic processes, based on some other values of the same process or of other related processes, is frequently used in different methods of stochastic signal processing and analysis. The task can always be reduced to the isolated problem of estimating a single random quantity, u, on the basis of values of other N random variables forming a vector $\mathbf{x} = [x_1, x_2, \cdots, x_N]^T$ (the symbol ^{T} denotes a transposition). Only the linear estimate is, as a rule, mathematically tractable,

$$\hat{u} = \sum_{i=1}^{N} a_i x_i = \mathbf{a}^T \mathbf{x}, \tag{4.37}$$

where the vector of weights $\mathbf{a} = [a_1, a_2, \cdots, a_N]^T$ is to be found such that a suitable error criterion is met. It turns out that, considering different views and needs, the mean quadratic error

$$\varepsilon = \mathbb{E}\left\{\left(u - \sum_{i=1}^{N} a_i x_i\right)^2\right\} \tag{4.38}$$

is found to be a suitable criterion to be minimised. Its zero gradient, as a function of the weight vector,

$$\nabla \varepsilon(\mathbf{a}) = 0,$$

is a necessary condition for the minimum. Expressing it in components gives

$$\frac{\partial \varepsilon}{\partial a_i} = \mathbb{E}\left\{\frac{\partial}{\partial a_i}\left(u - \sum_{i=1}^{N} a_i x_i\right)^2\right\}$$

$$= \mathbb{E}\left\{2\left(u - \sum_{i=1}^{N} a_i x_i\right)(-x_i)\right\} = -\mathbb{E}\{(u - \hat{u})x_i\} = 0. \tag{4.39}$$

Thus, we obtain a system of N equations

$$\mathbb{E}\{(u - \hat{u})x_i\} = 0, \quad \text{for} \quad i = 1, 2, \cdots, N, \tag{4.40}$$

which is called the *principle of orthogonality*. It can be interpreted as follows: should the estimate be optimal in the above sense, the error $u - \hat{u}$ of the estimate must be uncorrelated with (i.e. statistically orthogonal to) each of the random variables x_i on which the estimate was based. This important theorem will be utilised repeatedly in subsequent chapters.

The system of linear equations formulated by the principle of orthogonality,

$$\mathbb{E}\{(u - \hat{u}(\mathbf{a}))\mathbf{x}\} = 0, \tag{4.41}$$

can, in principle, be directly solved with respect to the components of the vector **a**, i.e. the weights of the optimum estimate according to eqn (4.37) can be found, providing the problem enables us to determine the estimates of the mean values appearing in the equations. This would occur when the values of all variables x_i and the corresponding values of u can be repeatedly measured for many realisations; then the aim is to determine the weights for a future estimate when u may not be observable. Nevertheless, more commonly, the weights, or the values resulting from them, are determined either analytically using the principle implicitly or by iteration, e.g. by minimisation of the gradient by the steepest-descent method.

Chapter 5
Linear filtering of signals and principles of filter design

5.1 General note on linear filtering

Filtering is usually formulated as a type of process that selects certain components out of a mixture of signals and suppresses other components. More generally, filtering can be understood as a means of changing the properties of individual components, e.g. their relative magnitudes and the mutual time or phase relations in the resulting signal.

The components of the processed signals are commonly understood or formulated in the frequency domain – they are then harmonic components the amplitudes and initial phases of which are modified by the filtering. The effect of a filter is thus expressed by two frequency characteristics: amplitude frequency response, and phase frequency response. As the filters under discussion are discrete, their characteristics are periodic and it is sufficient to define them only in the frequency range $\langle 0, \omega_s/2 \rangle$ where ω_s is the angular sampling frequency.

A special type of filters are the *band filters* which ideally have unit amplitude transfer in frequency passbands and zero transfer in stopbands; the transitions between both types of band should ideally be of zero width. Ideal characteristics of basic kinds of band filters are depicted in Figure 5.1 (the missing type – bandstop – would be the reverse of a bandpass filter). The responses of realisable filters only approximately approach the ideal responses. The flatness of the characteristics inside the bands and the steepness of the continuous transitions between the stop and passbands serve as quality criteria of the filter. Apart from the design method, they can be influenced primarily by the degree of complexity of the filter.

Linear phase response is usually desirable for band filters and many others. This requirement follows from the need to preserve mutual time relations among signal components of different frequencies, i.e. to introduce the same delay (which is necessarily nonzero owing to physical reasons) to all the signal components. The phase response is naturally more or less unimportant in stopbands. Deviations from the linear phase function are acceptable in some applications, such as the filtering of acoustic signals, but are critically disturbing in

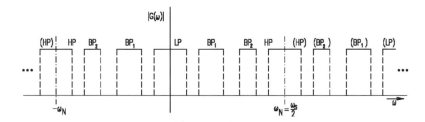

Figure 5.1   Amplitude frequency responses of basic discrete band filters (LP – low pass, HP – high pass, BP – band pass)

the processing of other signals, e.g. composite video. On the other hand, there are some applications where the phase response is designed to be nonlinear on purpose, e.g. in phase equalisers.

   Linear time-invariant filters are the main application field for discrete linear systems. By definition, they realise the discrete linear convolution of their impulse responses with the input signals. The systems can be equivalently characterised by any of their characteristics in the time, frequency or Z-domain. Practical tasks are usually, but not necessarily, expressed as requirements in the frequency domain; less frequently, the needs may also be expressed either in the time domain or in the Z-plane. In this Chapter, we shall show the fundamental properties of linear filters of both types – FIR and IIR. We shall also introduce the basic design methods, leading to the determination of the filter-realisation structure and its parameters on the basis of prescribed properties of filter characteristics.

5.2 Finite impulse response (FIR) filters

5.2.1 Basic properties of FIR filters

A finite impulse response (FIR) filter is fully defined by N values of its impulse response which, at the same time, form the vector of the system constants $\mathbf{h} = [h_n]$, $n \in \langle 0, N-1 \rangle$. The difference equation of an FIR filter expresses the finite discrete convolution

$$y_n = \sum_{k=0}^{N-1} x_{n-k} h_k, \qquad (5.1)$$

which also describes the algorithm of the so-called direct realisation method of the filter. Therefore, the values of the filter-realisation constants are equal to the sample values of its finite impulse response. The transfer function of the filter is obviously

$$H(z) = \sum_{n=0}^{N-1} h_n z^{-n}. \tag{5.2}$$

The pole–zero configuration in the z-plane is then described by positions of zeros only and the sole (multiple) pole at the origin of the coordinates only expresses the time delay or, equivalently, the corresponding phase shift. Consequently, FIR filters are *absolutely stable*. The frequency response

$$G(\omega) = H(e^{j\omega T}) = \sum_{n=0}^{N-1} h_n e^{-j\omega n T} \tag{5.3}$$

is clearly a periodic function with the period $2\pi/T$ expressed by a Fourier series with coefficients h_n. This direct relationship between the frequency response and the system constants enables a well understandable and relatively simple design of filters of this type. As the number of terms in the Fourier series is finite, the frequency response is a continuous function with accordingly limited possibilities of forming sharp edges at the boundaries of frequency bands.

FIR filters can be designed in such a way that their phase response is *exactly linear*. To have this property, it is sufficient to ensure that the impulse response fulfils one of the conditions

$$h_n = h_{(N-1-n)} \quad \text{or} \quad h_n = -h_{(N-1-n)},$$

which are the so-called *symmetrical response* (Figure 5.2a) or *antisymmetrical response* (Figure 5.2b), respectively.

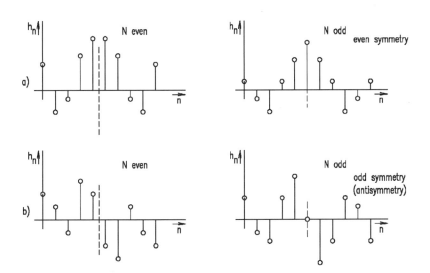

Figure 5.2 *Examples of impulse responses of linear-phase FIR filters*

Indeed, for N even, summing in the expression (5.2) by pairs for indices n and $N - 1 - n$, we obtain

$$H(z) = \sum_{n=0}^{N/2-1} h_n(z^{-n} \pm z^{-(N-1-n)})$$

$$= z^{-\frac{N-1}{2}} \sum_n h_n\left(z^{-(n-\frac{N-1}{2})} \pm z^{(n-\frac{N-1}{2})}\right), \tag{5.4}$$

where the subtraction applies to the case of the antisymmetrical impulse response. Use of Euler's equality leads to the expression for frequency response

$$G(\omega) = H(e^{j\omega T}) = e^{-j\omega\frac{N-1}{2}T} \sum_{n=0}^{N/2-1} 2h_n \cos\left(\omega T\left(n - \frac{N-1}{2}\right)\right) \tag{5.5}$$

in the case of the symmetrical impulse response, and

$$G(\omega) = je^{-j\omega\frac{N-1}{2}T} \sum_{n=0}^{N/2-1} 2h_n \sin\left(\omega T\left(n - \frac{N-1}{2}\right)\right) \tag{5.6}$$

for an antisymmetrical response. As the sum contains only real terms, the factor in front of the sum expresses completely the filter's phase response, which is obviously a linear function of frequency. The corresponding constant time delay is one half of the length of the impulse response (that – in the case of N even – means a noninteger number of sampling periods). Note that the phase will differ further by π in frequency bands where the sum is negative (usually in stopbands). Similarly, for an impulse response with an odd number of coefficients,

$$H(z) = \sum_{n=0}^{\frac{N-1}{2}-1} h_n(z^{-n} \pm z^{-(N-1-n)}) + h_{\frac{N-1}{2}} z^{-\frac{N-1}{2}}$$

$$= z^{-\frac{N-1}{2}} \left(h_{\frac{N-1}{2}} + \sum_{n=0}^{\frac{N-3}{2}} h_n\left(z^{-(n-\frac{N-1}{2})} \pm z^{(n-\frac{N-1}{2})}\right) \right), \tag{5.7}$$

so that the frequency response in the case of the symmetrical impulse response is

$$G(\omega) = e^{-j\omega\frac{N-1}{2}T} \left(h_{\frac{N-1}{2}} + \sum_{n=0}^{\frac{N-3}{2}} 2h_n \cos\left(\omega T\left(n - \frac{N-1}{2}\right)\right) \right). \tag{5.8}$$

For a system with an antisymmetrical response of odd length we obtain

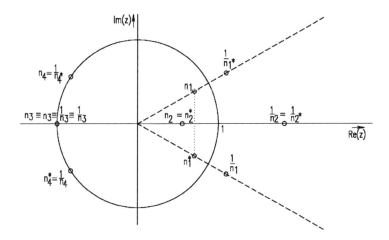

Figure 5.3 Quadruplets of zeros for a linear-phase, real coefficients filter

$$G(\omega) = je^{-j\omega\frac{N-1}{2}}T\left(\sum_{n=0}^{\frac{N-3}{2}} 2h_n \sin\left(\omega T\left(n - \frac{N-1}{2}\right)\right)\right), \tag{5.9}$$

taking into account the fact that the antisymmetry implies $h_{(N-1)/2} = 0$. Obviously, the time delay determining the slope of the frequency phase response is, for systems with N odd, equal to an integer multiple of T.

It can be shown that the symmetry conditions mentioned above are not only sufficient but also necessary, that is every *linear-phase filter* has to have either a symmetrical or an antisymmetrical impulse response. Obviously, this condition can be precisely fulfilled only for finite impulse response filters.

All linear-phase filters have a special configuration of zeros n_i of their transfer functions: if $H(n_i) = 0$, then $H(1/n_i) = 0$ and, for systems with real coefficients, $H(n_i^*) = H(n_i) = H(1/n_i^*)$; therefore the zeros are grouped generally into quadruplets (Figure 5.3). Indeed, let's disregard the exponential factors on the right-hand sides of eqns (5.4) and (5.7), which express only the time delays corresponding to the multiple poles at the origin of the z-plane. Then the remaining expression, say $H_2(z)$, representing the zeros of the transfer function, has the form of a linear operator

$$H_2(z) = L(z^{-\alpha} \pm z^{+\alpha}) = \pm L((z^{-1})^{-\alpha} \pm (z^{-1})^{+\alpha}),$$

and, consequently:

$$H_2(z)|_{z=n_i} = H_2(z^{-1})|_{z=n_i} = 0.$$

5.2.2 *Basic methods of FIR filter design*

5.2.2.1 *Frequency-sampling method*

Starting from the characterisation of an FIR filter by the vector **h** of its N impulse-response coefficients, we can describe it, owing to the reversibility of DFT, uniquely also by N values F_k of the discrete Fourier transform of the sequence $\{h_n\}$,

$$F_k = \sum_{n=0}^{N-1} h_n e^{-jk\Omega nT}, \quad \Omega = \frac{2\pi}{NT} = \frac{\omega_s}{N}. \tag{5.10}$$

Comparing this expression with (5.3) we see that $F_k = G(k\Omega)$, $k = 0, .. N-1$, are equidistant samples of the filter's frequency response in the interval $\langle 0, \omega_s - \Omega \rangle$.

Thus, if the desired frequency response in the basic range of frequency $\langle 0, \omega_s \rangle$ is given (e.g. as a plot against continuous frequency), a corresponding FIR filter can be designed by using the following steps:

1   The frequency interval is divided into N subintervals and the desired (generally complex) values F_k of the frequency response at the appropriate sample frequencies are read.
2   The inverse discrete Fourier transform of the sequence $\{F_k\}$ provides the sequence $\{h_n\}$ giving the (generally complex) values of the filter coefficients, e.g. the components of the vector **h**.

Obviously, filter coefficients obtained in this way give a warranty that the frequency-response curve will go exactly through the desired points at the frequencies $k\Omega$; nevertheless, nothing has been said so far about the form of the curve between the samples for other frequencies ω. Preliminarily, we can estimate that the approximation of the desired response will be better the smoother the desired curve is with respect to the density of sampling; increasing N leads therefore to an improvement in the approximation.

Let us derive more precisely the way in which the curve is interpolated between the samples. In order to do this, we determine first the transfer function of the designed filter in terms of the given samples of the frequency response:

$$H(z) = \sum_{n=0}^{N-1} h_n z^{-n} = \sum_{n=0}^{N-1} \mathrm{DFT}^{-1}\{F_k\} z^{-n}$$

$$= \sum_{n=0}^{N-1} \left(\frac{1}{N} \sum_{k=0}^{N-1} F_k W_N^{-nk} \right) z^{-n}, \quad W = e^{-j\frac{2\pi}{N}}. \tag{5.11}$$

Interchanging the order of summations gives

$$H(z) = \frac{1}{N} \sum_{k=0}^{N-1} F_k \left(\sum_{n=0}^{N-1} (W^{-k}z^{-1})^n \right) = \frac{1}{N} \sum_{k=0}^{N-1} F_k \frac{1 - z^{-N}W^{-kN}}{1 - W^{-k}z^{-1}}$$

$$= \frac{1 - z^{-N}}{N} \sum_{k=0}^{N-1} \frac{F_k}{1 - W^{-k}z^{-1}}, \tag{5.12}$$

where we determined the inner sum as the total of a finite geometric series and utilised the equality $W^{-kN} = 1$. Note that the last form of eqn (5.12) provides a clue to an interesting recursive realisation structure for FIR filters (see Section 5.2.3). Substituting $z = e^{j\omega T}$ we obtain, after certain simplification,

$$G(\omega) = \sum_{k=0}^{N-1} F_k \Phi \left(\omega T - k \frac{2\pi}{N} \right), \tag{5.13}$$

where the interpolation function,

$$\Phi(\omega T) = \frac{1}{N} \frac{\sin \left(\omega T \frac{N}{2} \right)}{\sin \left(\frac{\omega T}{2} \right)} e^{-j\omega T \frac{N-1}{2}} e^{j\pi k(1 - 1/N)}, \tag{5.14}$$

ensures that the resulting frequency response has the desired values at the sample frequencies. Inside the subintervals, the response is interpolated in a similar way to the continuous signal, when interpolated ideally from samples (the fraction has – owing to an N-times faster changing argument in the numerator than in the denominator – a similar, although periodic, character to the function $\sin(x)/x$. This justifies the intuitive assumption that the density of sampling in the frequency domain must correspond to the required steepness of change in the frequency response. This statement could be formulated more precisely in the form of the modified sampling theorem for the frequency domain.

Usually, filters with real coefficients are required. To achieve this, even symmetry for the amplitude frequency response (or for the real part of the response in the Cartesian representation) must be ensured as well as odd symmetry for the phase response (or for the imaginary part). This means that samples F_k are only needed for $k = 0, 1, \cdots, \text{int}(N/2)$ and the remaining values of the range $\langle 0, \omega_s \rangle$ can be computed according to the relation $F_{N-k} = F_k^*$.

Should we further wish to obtain, as is most commonly the case, a causal linear-phase filter, the desired phase would have to fulfil, according to eqns (5.5) to (5.9), the requirements for the desired type of filter, i.e.

$$\arg(F_k) = -k\pi(N-1) + a \frac{\pi}{2}, \tag{5.15}$$

where $a = 0$ or $a = 1$ for filters with the desired symmetrical or antisymmetrical impulse response, respectively. An equivalent but simpler approach is to require

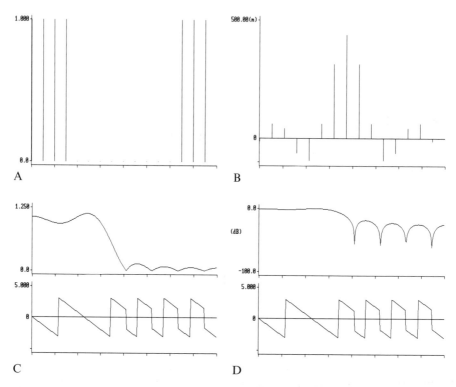

Figure 5.4a An example of a lowpass filter design based on the frequency sampling method
(N = 16)
A – Samples of frequency response in the frequency range ⟨0, ω_s⟩
B – Calculated impulse response
C, D – Resulting amplitude and phase frequency responses of the filter in the
range ⟨0, ω_s/2⟩ (amplitudes in linear and logarithmic scale, respectively)

preliminarily zero-phase response, which leads to a noncausal (zero-delay) filter. Delaying the resulting impulse response by the time interval of $0.5T(N-1)$ may be used afterwards to convert the response into a causal response. Note that when using common-type DFT and DFT^{-1} algorithms, we should remember that these count on causal vectors in the time domain. The impulse response symmetrical around the time origin can then be obtained utilising the periodicity of the resulting time-domain sequence.

An example of a lowpass filter design using the frequency-sampling method for two values of N can be found in Figure 5.4a, b. It can be clearly seen that increasing N together with including half-value samples at the edges of the frequency bands (respecting the gentle transient between pass and stopbands) leads to a considerable improvement of the filter properties.

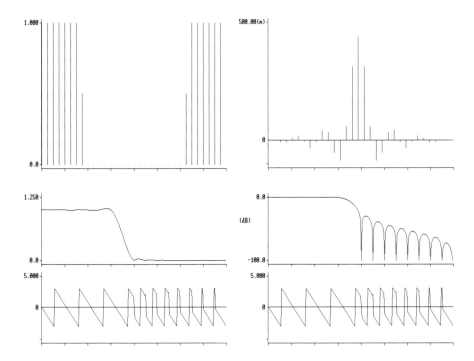

Figure 5.4b The same example as in Figure 5.4a but for N = 32

5.2.2.2 Windowing method

The method of FIR filter design by windowing the impulse response presupposes knowledge of the unlimited impulse response $\mathbf{h}_d$ exactly respecting the desired (naturally periodical, otherwise arbitrary) frequency response of the filter. As the requirements for the filter are usually specified in the frequency domain, the first step of the method is then the calculation of the precise values of the infinite impulse response on the basis of the given frequency response. If $\mathbf{h}_d$ is known, such as in the case of transforming an IIR filter into an FIR filter, the first step does not take place.

First step: the desired frequency response $G_d(\omega) = H_d(e^{j\omega T})$ is a periodic function of frequency (with the period $2\pi/T$) and therefore can be expressed by a generally infinite Fourier series

$$G_d(\omega) = H_d(e^{j\omega T}) = \sum_{n=-\infty}^{\infty} h_d(n)e^{-j\omega nT}, \qquad (5.16)$$

the coefficients $h_d(n)$ of which are clearly the values of the ideal impulse response $\mathbf{h}_d$ which, as seen, may be generally noncausal and infinite. These values can be exactly determined according to the relation for the calculation of Fourier series coefficients,

$$h_d(n) = \frac{T}{2\pi} \int_{-\pi/T}^{\pi/T} G_d(\omega) e^{j\omega nT} \, d\omega, \tag{5.17}$$

if an analytical formula is available for H_d, as is the case for bandpass and band-stop filters. Of course, only a finite number N of coefficients, which are really needed in the second step, will be calculated. In the case where only discrete samples of the frequency response can be provided in place of the formula, the integral computation (5.17) can be substituted by an approximate calculation using the DFT of vectors of length M, $M \gg N$. The order M of the transform has to be chosen such that the coefficients $h_d(n)$ for $n > M - 1$, which will not be calculated, would be negligibly small and consequently the calculated coefficients would differ from the exact values of (5.17) by only negligible errors.

Second step: in the second step, the impulse response sequence $\mathbf{h}_d$ is weighted by a time window in order to limit its length to the selected range of N components. The shortening of the sequence leads to the consequences which will follow from the next considerations.

The frequency response (5.16) is also the spectrum of the infinite quasi-continuous signal

$$h_d(t) = \ldots + h_{-2}\delta(t + 2T) + h_{-1}\delta(t + T) + h_0\delta(t)$$
$$+ h_1\delta(t - T) + h_2\delta(t - 2T) + \ldots \tag{5.18}$$

the length of which will be limited by multiplying it with a finite-window signal $w(t)$ of the length of N samples,

$$w(t) = \sum_{n=n_0}^{n_0+N-1} w_n\delta(t - nT), \tag{5.19}$$

where n_0 in the case of a real frequency response must obviously be $-N/2 + 1$. The spectrum of the product $h(t) = h_d(t)w(t)$ of the two signals is of course the convolution of their individual spectra,

$$G(\omega) = \frac{1}{2\pi} \int_{-\infty}^{\infty} G_d(\omega_0) W(\omega - \omega_0) \, d\omega_0. \tag{5.20}$$

This formula describes the resulting frequency response of the designed system, the impulse response of which is

$$\{h_n\} = \{h(n)\} = \{h_d(n)w(n)\}. \tag{5.21}$$

The purpose of the design is that the differences between $G(\omega)$ and $G_d(\omega)$ would be acceptable. With a chosen length of the window, N, the result can be influenced substantially by the window shape, i.e. by the weighting coefficient sequence $\{w_n\}$. The standard, frequently-used windows are depicted, together with their spectra, in Figure 5.5. We can see that the simple rectangular

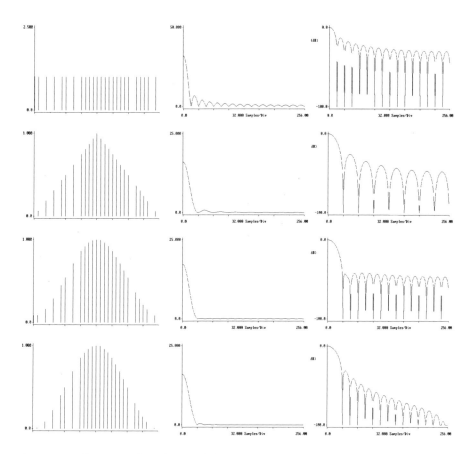

Figure 5.5 The standard windows and their spectra
Rectangular window
Bartlett window
Hamming window
Hann window

window, corresponding to a mere shortening of the sequence $\mathbf{h}_d$, may lead to a considerable deterioration of the resulting frequency response. This is due to its spectrum, which is of the shape of $\sin(x)/x$ and accordingly has large sidelobes, causing 'leakage' of every value of $G_d(\omega)$ into even distant regions of ω. The selection of the window is thus an important decision. When the vector $\mathbf{h} = [h_n]$ is determined according to eqn (5.21), the design is finished.

An example of the design of a bandstop filter by the mentioned method is shown in Figure 5.6. As can be seen, application of the Hamming window instead of the rectangular window substantially reduces the ripple of the amplitude response in both the pass and stopbands. This is achieved at the cost of certain deterioration of the transient steepness at the boundaries between both regions.

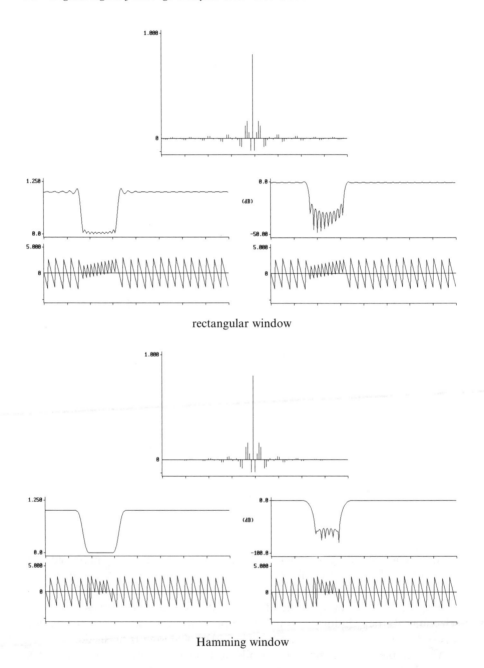

rectangular window

Hamming window

Figure 5.6 Example of a bandstop filter design by the windowing method. Upper part: rectangular window applied; lower part: Hamming window applied. Depicted: resulting impulse response and frequency response (amplitude curves in linear and logarithmic scales)

5.2.3 Realisation of FIR filters

5.2.3.1 Realisation in the original domain

The basic structure of an FIR filter is a direct realisation derived from difference eqn (5.1), which is the nonrecursive part of a generic realisation of discrete systems (Figure 2.11); sometimes it is called a *discrete convolutor* or, according to the structure, a tapped delay-line filter, or also a *transverse filter*. The system coefficients of this structure are given directly by the components of the vector **h**.

The structure can be further simplified in the case of linear-phase filters utilising the symmetry or antisymmetry of their impulse responses, as shown in Figure 5.7, where the additions (differences) correspond to filters with a symmetric (antisymmetric) impulse response, respectively. The latter filters with N

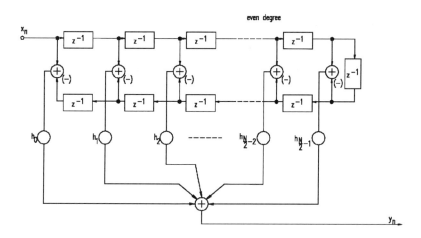

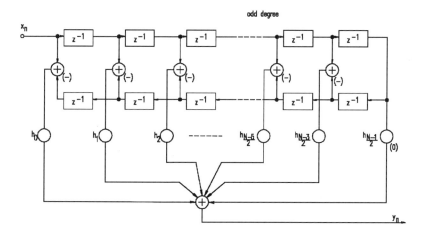

Figure 5.7 Direct realisation structures of FIR linear-phase filters

odd also have the middle coefficient always equal to zero, as shown in the brackets. The derivation of these structures is straightforward and evident. Their advantage is in halving the number of multiplications, which is particularly advantageous with common hardware where a multiplication is a long operation (i.e. in most systems except for dedicated signal processors).

An alternative structure is the cascade connection with a nonrecursive and a recursive part as shown in Figure 5.10, which is derived from the transfer function as expressed by eqn (5.12). The fraction preceding the sum represents a nonrecursive structure of a so-called *comb filter* which is depicted in Figure 5.8. As can easily be shown, it has equally spaced zeros on the unit circle with the first zero at $z = 1$ ($\omega = 0$). Owing to symmetry, the frequency response of the comb filter consists of a set of N repeated equally high lobes. The following sum represents a parallel connection of N digital resonators of the first order, each having a single pole at W^k (thus, the resonators would have complex coefficients). The poles are situated in the same positions as are the zeros of the comb filter and consequently they are cancelled out. The resulting all-zero configuration is thus generated by parallel cooperation of the resonators. The resulting filter is therefore of the FIR type, although the structure is recursive. It is evident that the system realisation constants are given directly by the sample values F_k of the desired frequency response. The synthesis of the impulse response **h** is thus not needed; obviously, the system has the impulse response **h**, which we would obtain by the process described in Section 5.2.2.1.

The described structure is quite generic and can realise a filter corresponding to any set of frequency samples, even from asymmetric frequency responses. Should we limit ourselves to filters with real elements of **h**, the system coefficients must fulfil the requirement $F_k = F^*_{N-k}$. The resonators with complex poles can then be combined by couples into resonators of second order with real coefficients, having a pair of complex conjugate poles (see Figure 5.9 for symmetrical **h**, when $F_k = F_{N-k}$). In this way, the system is simplified both as far as hardware is concerned and also from an operational point of view: only one half of the frequency samples has to be assigned to the system. Notice that the frequency response of this type of filter can be very easily

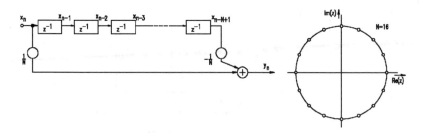

Figure 5.8 Structure of a nonrecursive comb filter and its zero configuration for $N = 16$

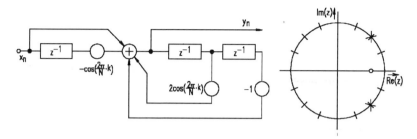

Figure 5.9 Structure of a digital resonator and its configuration of poles and zeros

adjusted in this flexible way, without any design procedure transforming the frequency-domain requirements into system constants. The resulting frequency response is naturally interpolated among the given frequency-domain samples according to eqn (5.13) by the functions defined by (5.14) for $k = 0, 1, \cdots,$ int$(N/2)$.

A comment on the stability of the system: it is perhaps surprising that the system, containing resonators at the limit of stability, the impulse response of which is not only infinite but even undamped, has, as a whole, a finite impulse response. The explanation is in the combination of the resonators with the comb filter, the impulse response of which, $\mathbf{h}_1$, is formed by two nonzero impulses of the same amplitude but opposite sign, $h_1(0) = 1$ and $h_1(N-1) = -1$. After

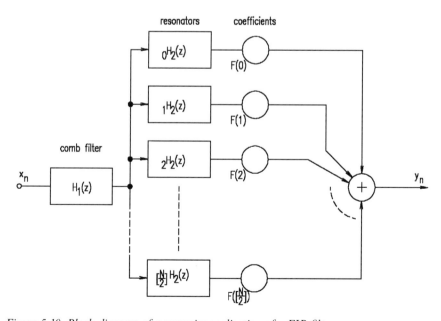

Figure 5.10 Block diagram of a recursive realisation of a FIR filter

excitation of the system by a unit impulse, the first output of the comb filter, $h_1(0)$, initiates oscillations in all the resonators, and the other impulse $h_1(N-1)$ stops them after exactly an odd number of half periods by super-imposing oscillations of the same amplitude but opposite phase. It is evident that the exact FIR function will only be achieved when the poles exactly coincide with the zeros, for which exact values of the internal system coefficients in the resonators are needed. If the coefficients are not absolutely precise, the system will behave more or less differently.

5.2.3.2 *Realisation* via *the frequency domain (fast convolution)*

Realisation of an FIR system *via* the frequency domain utilises the similarity of nonperiodic (linear) convolution (5.1) as realised by FIR dynamic systems, $y_n = \sum_{p=0}^{N-1} x_{n-p} h_p$, and that of the circular convolution

$$y_n = \sum_{p=0}^{M-1} x_{[n-p]} h_p, \tag{5.22}$$

which can be obtained as the original sequence corresponding to the spectrum consisting of the term-by-term product of spectra of both operands (Figure 5.11),

$$\{y_n\} = \mathbb{DFT}^{-1}\{X_k H_k\}, \quad \{X_k\} = \mathbb{DFT}\{x_n\}, \quad \{H_k\} = \mathbb{DFT}\{h_n\}. \tag{5.23}$$

The length of the sequences to be transformed is denoted M and the symbol $[l]$ means $(l \bmod M)$. If a fast algorithm (FFT) is used for the calculation of the DFT, the overall calculation load is, for longer sequences, substantially lower than when using the direct formula (5.1); therefore, this method is sometimes called the *fast convolution*. Obviously, only sequences of identical length M can be processed according to (5.23), so that we need to lengthen both the finite signal and the impulse response to a common length by padding them with zeros. (It will be shown in the next paragraph that it is necessary to have $M > N$.)

Let us compare the processing of a finite signal section of K samples by a filter with the response $\{h_p\}, p = 0, 1, \cdots, N-1$, which realises the linear convolution formula, with the processing by the circular convolution. They differ in the number of summed terms and in the indexing of the signal. Nevertheless, the number of nonzero terms in both sums, determined by the length of the impulse response N, is obviously the same. Thus, if we can achieve $x_{[n-p]} = x_{(n-p)}$ for all used indices, the values of y_n provided by eqn (5.22) would be identical to those calculated according to the nonperiodic convolution (5.1).

The sequence $\{x_k\}$ as used in eqn (5.23) is, owing to the indicated indexing, obviously a periodic version of the original sequence $\{x_k\}, k = 0, 1, \cdots, M-1$. When trying to find a condition for the identity of the results, the problem reduces to finding such a minimum period M which still prevents the

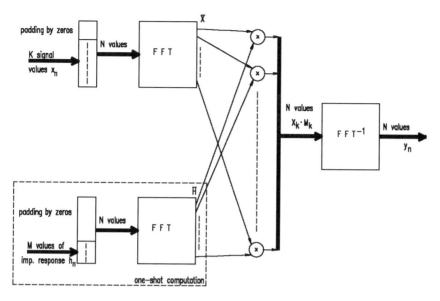

Figure 5.11 Calculation of convolution via *frequency domain*

interperiodic interference. For nonnegative values of the index $n - p$, the equality $[n - p] = n - p$ is always valid in the possible range of indices, so that these terms cannot cause any difference. For negative values $[n - p] = (n - p) + M$, which means that, instead of *a priori* zero values of x_k for $k < 0$, the values from the end of the period enter the calculation. It is therefore necessary to ensure that the concerned values are zero. The worst case appears for $n = 0$ when there is only one nonzero term in the sum, so that $(N - 1)$ zero values of x_k for $k = M - 1, M - 2, \cdots, M - N + 1$ are needed. It follows that the required length of the period, i.e. of the transformed sequences, is

$$M \geq K + N - 1, \tag{5.24}$$

which in the boundary case means exactly the length of the response of an FIR filter to the finite signal.

Obviously, it is only possible to process the input signal in a batch mode – a vector of K samples at a time, rather then processing every sample individually. This implies that it is always necessary to wait until the complete section of K signal samples arrives, which requires a buffer memory at the input and inserts a delay of KT at minimum. Should the result be presented at the output again as a time sequence, there would also have to be a buffer memory at the output. The output samples must be then retrieved and sent away at the pace of the sampling frequency (Figure 5.12).

When the signal is long or time unlimited, it can only be processed by parts with length K which is to be chosen as a compromise between as large as

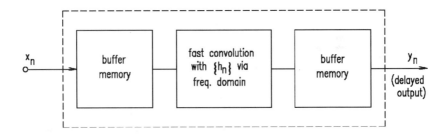

Figure 5.12 Fast convolution of long time-sequences

possible a segment length (positively influencing the relative effectiveness of the fast convolution) on one side and yet an acceptable delay on the other. Nevertheless, we must take into account the fact that the results of a particular segment are related to both neighbouring segments. The last $N-1$ samples of the previous segment influence the initial part of the selected segment and, similarly, the fading of the response to this-segment-input still influences the next $N-1$ initial output samples of the next segment (Figure 5.13). As the input signal has, thus, the length $K+N-1$, the period (transform length) $M \geq K+2N-2$ should be selected in the sense of the previous discussion, which would lead to an increase in computational complexity. We shall now describe two methods of preventing this by preserving the period length only according to eqn (5.24).

Overlap save method
As illustrated in Figure 5.14, we need just K output samples of the chosen segment so that the previous as well as following samples are useless. It is then possible to admit interference among the initial and ending $N-1$ samples

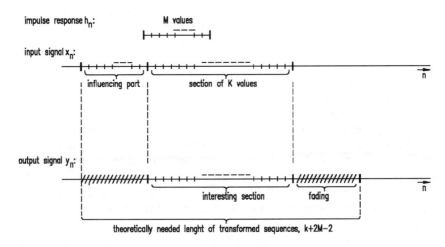

Figure 5.13 The relationship between segments in segmented fast convolution

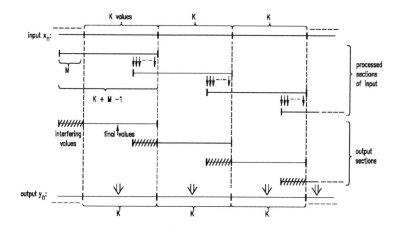

Figure 5.14 Segmented fast convolution by overlap save method

of each period (hatched parts of the output in Figure 5.13). The period may thus be limited to $M \geq K + N - 1$ even if the input signal segments have the same length – the input segments are extended by $N - 1$ previous samples and therefore no further padding by zeros is needed. The useless (and erroneous) initial parts of the output segments, i.e. $\{y_n\}$, $n = 0, 1, \ldots, N - 1$, will be discarded. It is clear that, for the calculation in each segment, $N - 1$ previous input values must be known (the so-called overlap) which must be saved from the previous segment; this has given the method its name.

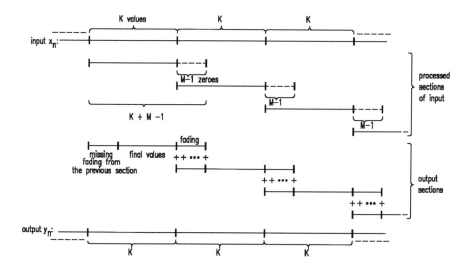

Figure 5.15 Segmented fast convolution by overlap add method

Overlap add method

Depicted in Figure 5.15, the overlap add method uses only the input values belonging to the selected segment. These are padded by zeros from the right so that the length of the period is naturally only $M = K + N - 1$. The result therefore only gives a response to the input belonging to the given frame; the response also includes the fading already belonging to the next frame. Thus, the output overlap from the previous segment (fading) must always be added to the initial part of the fast-convolution output of every segment.

Both these methods are equivalent as concerns the resulting values and the computational complexity.

5.3 Infinite impulse response (IIR) filters

5.3.1 Basic properties of IIR filters

Infinite impulse response filters are always recursive as only systems with feedback can generate an infinitely long response to a finite stimulus. Their possibilities are generally richer that those of FIR filters owing to the fact that the transfer function has not only zeros but also poles which can be positioned in the z-plane. Although the poles always have to be situated inside the unit circle with respect to the requirement of stability, the zero points can be both inside and outside. The shift of a zero from a position n_i into the position $1/n_i$ does not cause any change in the amplitude frequency response but influences the phase response. This leads to the possibility of designing variations of filters which all have the same amplitude response but different phase responses. The extreme cases are *minimum-phase* filters which have all the zeros inside or on the unit circle and *maximum-phase* filters with all zeros outside (or on) the unit circle. Other filters which have some zeros inside the unit circle and others on or outside of it are called *mixed-phase* filters. Couples of a pole situated at, say, p_j and a zero placed then at $1/p_j$ are characterised by compensation of the pole effect on the amplitude response by the effect of the zero; such a pair does not influence the amplitude response at all and it can therefore only be used to correct the phase response. Filters comprising only such pairs have a constant amplitude response and their phase characteristic can approximate the design requirements when placing the couples properly. Such filters are called *phase correctors*.

In comparison with filters of FIR type providing a comparable quality of signal processing and design flexibility, we find that IIR filters, apart from having the mentioned advantages, are by one to two orders of magnitude less demanding in terms of computational complexity. This enables us to realise them on less powerful hardware. Conversely, the positive properties are balanced, to a certain extent, by the more complicated relationship between the desired frequency response and the realisation (system) parameters which leads to less straightforward design procedures. IIR filters may also suffer in principle from instability when the design is improper and by a higher sensitivity to errors owing to the digital principal of realisation (cumulating of rounding and quantisation errors). Therefore, it is necessary to attest the stability and precision in every concrete realisation. A fundamental disadvantage of IIR filters is that they always have, as a principle, only a nonlinear phase response, although a reasonable quasilinearity can be achieved by a suitable design in the appropriate frequency bands.

   IIR filters as time-invariant discrete linear systems are described by generic recursive equations of the form (see Section 2.3.1)

$$y_n = \sum_{i=0}^{r} L_i x_{n-i} - \sum_{i=1}^{m} K_i y_{n-i}, \tag{5.25}$$

where L_i and K_i are the system parameters in feedforward and feedback connections, r and m are the numbers of delays in the nonrecursive and recursive parts of the system, respectively, m also giving the order of the system (usually, but not necessarily, $r \leq m$). The transfer function

$$H(z) = \frac{\sum_{i=0}^{r} L_i z^{m-i}}{\sum_{i=0}^{m} K_i z^{m-i}} = A \frac{\prod_{i=1}^{r}(z - n_i)}{\prod_{i=1}^{m}(z - p_i)} \tag{5.26}$$

is given by the ratio of polynomials in z, which are defined by the system constants L_i and K_i ($K_0 = 1$); the expansion of polynomials into products of root factors enables the filter to be characterised by its configuration of poles p_i and zeros n_i complemented by the amplification (gain) factor A. The frequency response is mediated by the values of $H(z)$ on the unit circle,

$$G(\omega) = H(e^{j\omega T}), \tag{5.27}$$

therefore, it is also given by the same system constants; however, the relationship is complicated. It is easier to investigate the relationship between the frequency response and the configuration of poles and zeros on the basis of the expressions for the amplitude and phase responses,

$$|H(e^{j\omega T})| = A \frac{\prod_{i=1}^{r} d_i}{\prod_{i=1}^{m} l_i} \quad \text{and} \quad \text{Arg}(H(e^{j\omega T})) = \sum_{i=1}^{r} \psi_i - \sum_{i=1}^{m} \varphi_i. \tag{5.28}$$

Here, d_i and l_i are the distances (in the z-plane) between the point $e^{j\omega T}$ on the unit circle representing the frequency axis, and zeros and poles, respectively. The quantities φ_i and ψ_i are the angles of the corresponding difference vectors with respect to the real axis. This approach will be used for the design by interactive placement of poles and zeros.

5.3.2 Basic design methods for IIR filters

5.3.2.1 Optimisation approaches

5.3.2.1.1 Interactive design, based on pole–zero configuration

A straightforward IIR filter design by interactively positioning the poles and zeros of the transfer function in the z-plane leads, by iterative approximations, to the desired amplitude frequency response with acceptable tolerances. Nevertheless, the design procedure is rather heavy going and the result definitely will not be optimal, as far as the complexity of the filter for the given requirements is concerned. The approach is based on the relationship between the geometric distribution of roots of transfer-function polynomials and the frequency response according to eqn (5.28). The simple concept and transparency of the method make it a suitable didactic introduction to more sophisticated automated optimisation methods. The design consists in the following steps:

1   Intuitive initial layout of couples of complex conjugate poles and zeros in the z-plane according to the desired amplitude response.
2   Calculation of polynomial coefficients (i.e. the system parameters) based on root values, corresponding to poles and zeros, followed by the computation of $|G(\omega)| = |H(e^{j\omega T})|$ according to eqns (5.26) and (5.27), or (5.28).
3   Comparison of the achieved amplitude response with the desired response:
    - if the requirements are not met with an acceptable precision, intuitive corrections of the pole–zero layout and even addition of further couples of poles or zeros or deletion of them; back to step 2;
    - when the result is satisfactory, continue.
4   Calculation of the phase response arg $(H(e^{j\omega T}))$ according to eqns (5.27) or (5.28) and its evaluation:
    - should the phase characteristic be unsatisfactory, try to change the positions of some zeros to inverse ones and go back to step 2; if no further changes of this kind are possible, either accept it 'as is' or try a new layout going back to step 2;
    - when the phase response is acceptable (or unimportant), continue.
5   End of design. The last achieved system constants are valid and can be used for realisation. If need be, the gain of the system can be adjusted by suitable scaling of the coefficients.

Comments:
- The method is suitable only for simple problems, namely for the design of band filters. In such a case it is recommended to place initially a zero on the unit circle in the centre of every stopband and similarly to place a pole at a radius 0.6–0.96 from the origin of the coordinates at the frequency angle corresponding to the centre of every passband.
- The mentioned range of radii of pole positions is also suitable for the singularities added in step 3. The minimum of the range is given by the

requirement that the pole would have an appreciable influence on the shape of the response, the maximum by the requirement of stability even when the realisation precision is low. (At the same time, the mentioned maximum ensures that the impulse response of the designed filter will not have important samples for pro $n > 128$, and it can therefore easily be visualised.) Placing of a pole on a radius vector of the angle ωT causes an increase of the magnitude transfer at, and in the neighbourhood of, the respective frequency; the gain and the influenced frequency band are about inversely proportional.

- The zero points always cause an increase in attenuation (i.e. decrease of transfer) in a band surrounding the frequency of their position. As the pole-position limitations concerning the stability do not apply to zeros, they are usually best positioned directly on the unit circle to achieve maximum attenuation. If a zero is placed directly on the unit circle it provides, according to eqn (5.28), zero transfer and a phase jump by π on the respective frequency. When modifying the amplitude and especially phase characteristics, a reasonable range of zero radii is about 0.5–2.0.

- Interesting results can be achieved by pole–zero couples where both elements are placed on the same radius vector. If the pair is close, its influence is negligible at greater frequency distances, but in the close vicinity of the respective frequency, the influence of the element, which is closer to the unit circle, dominates. Thus, it is possible to form narrow amplification or rejection bands or to make local corrections of the characteristics. Another interesting case is the previously mentioned zero–pole couple in which the positions are in inverse relation; these are only used for local correction of the phase response.

- Needless to say, if as a rule, the designed system should have only real coefficients, the poles and zeros must always be added in complex conjugate pairs unless they are positioned on the real axis.

- The number of complex conjugate pairs of zero points or poles in practical cases usually does not exceed about 20 in order to maintain manageability of the manual design.

- It is useful to use different scales for evaluation of the amplitude-response ripple in the passbands (fractions or units of dB) and in the stopbands (tens to hundreds of dB). The logarithmic scale is advantageous in both cases.

5.3.2.1.2 *Optimisation design according to frequency-response specification*

At present, when sophisticated optimisation methods and algorithms are available, the conceptually simplest and most transparent method of IIR filter design is the optimisation approach which can take into account all the required aspects. We will present here, as an introduction, a simple method of minimising the differences between the desired amplitude frequency response and the one really obtained by the design of a system of a chosen order.

The desired amplitude frequency response is given by a set of desired values $|G_d(\omega_i)| = |H_d(e^{j\omega_i T})|$ for generally nonequidistant frequencies $\omega_i \in \langle 0, \pi/T \rangle$, $i = 1, \ldots, M$, perhaps complemented by the admissible tolerances. The error criterion to be minimised is the expression

$$E = \sum_{i=1}^{M} w_i(|H(e^{j\omega_i T})| - |H_d(e^{j\omega_i T})|)^p \to \min, \qquad (5.29)$$

in which the weights w_i enable us to take into account the importance of ith value precision (higher weights given to frequency samples of high importance will force the optimisation to increase the precision here at the cost of other frequency samples). The even exponent p enables us to influence the uniformity of errors – the higher p the more equally the errors will be distributed among the frequency-response samples; usually, we are satisfied with the quadratic criterion, $p = 2$.

Let us suppose that the transfer function of the system under design is in the form of a product of second-order terms (we shall see later that this corresponds to the so-called cascade realisation),

$$H(z) = A \prod_{k=1}^{K} \frac{1 + a_k z^{-1} + b_k z^{-2}}{1 + c_k z^{-1} + d_k z^{-2}}, \qquad (5.30)$$

specified by the vector $\mathbf{F} = [A, a_1, b_1, c_1, d_1, \cdots, a_K, b_K, c_K, d_K]$ of $4K + 1$ parameters F_j that have to be determined by the design. The frequency response of the system is, of course

$$H(e^{j\omega T}) = A \prod_{k=1}^{K} \frac{1 + a_k(e^{j\omega T})^{-1} + b_k(e^{j\omega T})^{-2}}{1 + c_k(e^{j\omega T})^{-1} + d_k(e^{j\omega T})^{-2}}. \qquad (5.31)$$

Substituting it into eqn (5.29), we have $E = E(\mathbf{F})$; this scalar function of the parameter vector is to be minimised.

The minimisation can be formulated as the solution of a system of nonlinear equations: the necessary condition for the minimum to be at $\mathbf{F}_{opt}$ is the zero-valued gradient $\nabla E(\mathbf{F}_{opt})$, i.e.

$$\frac{\partial E(\mathbf{F})}{\partial F_j} = 0, \quad j = 1, 2, \ldots, 4K + 1. \qquad (5.32)$$

This is a system of the required number of nonlinear equations, by solution of which we can obtain in principal the parameters of the designed filter in a closed form. It is necessary to take into account the possibility that some of the system poles may appear outside of the unit circle as the stability aspect is not included in the formulation. In such a case, it is possible to stabilise the system by moving the pole to the inverse position, which would not change the amplitude response.

Solving such systems of nonlinear equations is not a simple problem, however. This is why iterative optimisation procedures are often preferred, such as the method of steepest descent, where the minimum is approached by a sequence of small steps against the local gradient. Unfortunately, being trapped in a local minimum is then not excluded, so that the solution fulfilling eqn (5.32) will be only locally and not globally optimal. On the other hand, if the initial estimate of parameters will characterise a stable system, every successive approximation including the final one will be stable: the criterion E grows over every limit when a pole approaches the unit circle, which thus forms an impassable barrier when the steps are sufficiently small.

The connection between this method and the previous intuitive approach is obvious: in both cases, an initial estimate must be provided which is subsequently improved by partial steps. While the intuitive approach relied on theoretical knowledge and experience, and the expected result was a not-fully-optimised system of any reasonable order, the optimising algorithm aims at every step towards the fastest local improvement, and globally to the optimum for a chosen system order. However, the global optimum cannot be guaranteed.

The described method disregards any requests for the phase response. It is nevertheless possible to include a quantity reflecting the phase requirements, e.g. group delay (derivative of phase), to the criterion, with the requirement to be as constant as possible in the passbands, and to improve the solution in this respect.

5.3.2.1.3 *Optimisation design according to impulse response specification*

The following method does not suffer from the complications connected with solving a system of nonlinear equations. Nevertheless, it is limited to the design of purely recursive filters and needs the less common specification in the time domain so that the frequency-domain requirements must first be transformed.

The specification is formed by the first L samples of the desired impulse response, $h_d(n)$, $n = 0, 1, \cdots, L - 1$. The next samples remain undefined and it is only supposed, on the basis of the stability property of the filter, that their values are small and generally decreasing with n.

The criterion, to be optimised, is derived as follows. Let us imagine that the filter of the desired transfer function $H_d(z) = \mathbb{Z}\{h_d(n)\}$ is connected as the first block in a cascade with the following filter the transfer of which is the inverse of the designed filter, i.e. $(H(z))^{-1}$ (Figure 5.16). If the unit impulse $\{u_n\}$ is

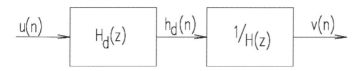

Figure 5.16 Conceptual cascade connection serving to derive the method

brought to the input of such a cascade, it will respond with an output sequence $\{v_n\}$, which approximates the unit impulse with increasing accuracy the better $H(z)$ approximates $H_d(z)$. In an ideal case, $v_0 = 1$ and $v_n = 0$ for all $n > 0$. The error criterion can therefore be formulated as follows:

$$E = \sum_{n=1}^{\infty} (v_n)^2 \rightarrow \min, \quad \text{or rather} \quad E_L = \sum_{n=1}^{L-1} (v_n)^2 \rightarrow \min, \tag{5.33}$$

with respect to the limited length of the specified part of the impulse response.

The transfer function of the designed filter is supposed to be in purely recursive form

$$H(z) = \frac{b_0}{1 - \sum_{r=1}^{m} a_k z^{-r}}, \tag{5.34}$$

so that the z-domain image of the output signal as a response to the unit impulse is

$$V(z) = H_d(z) \frac{1}{H(z)} U(z) = H_d(z) \frac{1 - \sum_{r=1}^{m} a_r z^{-r}}{b_0} .1,$$

and, after the inverse Z-transform,

$$b_0 v(n) = h_d(n) - \sum_{r=1}^{m} a_r h_d(n - r).$$

A natural demand is that the $\{h_d\}$ be causal and that $v(0) = 1$, so that $b_0 = h_d(0)$. The vector $\mathbf{a}$ of coefficients a_r of the designed filter can be provided by solving the system of equations obtained by substituting into the error criterion,

$$b_0^2 E = \sum_{n=1}^{L} \left(h_d(n) - \sum_{r=1}^{m} a_r h_d(n - r) \right)^2$$

$$= \sum_{n=1}^{L} h_d^2(n) - 2 \sum_{n=1}^{L} \left(h_d(n) \sum_{r=1}^{m} a_r h_d(n - r) \right) + \sum_{n=1}^{L} \left(\sum_{r=1}^{m} a_r h_d(n - r) \right)^2.$$

The first term is independent of $\mathbf{a}$ and may thus be omitted; let us denote the remaining expression E'. The necessary condition for the minimum is again $\partial E'/\partial a_i = 0$ for $i = 1, 2, \ldots, m$. By differentiating, we obtain after simplification

$$\sum_{r=1}^{m} a_r \Phi(i, r) = \Phi(i, 0), \quad i = 1, 2, \ldots, m, \tag{5.35}$$

which is the required system of linear equations. Its coefficient values,

$$\Phi(i, r) = \sum_{n=1}^{L} h_d(n - r)h_d(n - i),$$

are given entirely by the specified values of the desired impulse response. It is obvious that compiling the equations is easy, as is solving such a standard equation system.

5.3.2.2 Approaches based on similarities with analogue systems

5.3.2.2.1 On similarity and analogue filters

The theory of analogue filter design is extensively elaborated in the literature, especially regarding band filters, and it is therefore useful to use these results – namely, the well tried approximation formulae – even for digital filter design. Particularly in the early days of digital filtering, these method were the only available ones which led to quality results. The importance of them is, nowadays, decreasing with the development of modern, sophisticated optimisation methods; however, they still form a practically important and routinely used way, offered by most automated systems, for the design of digital filters. The principles should therefore be well understood.

The importance of this approach is, however, primarily in bringing forward the possibility of finding variously defined analogies between the functioning of continuous-time systems and of discretely working systems, especially digital systems. Particularly when using systems involving both continuously and discretely working parts, it is important to grasp the relationship of (and differences between) both types of systems. This is, for example, common in automatic control and robotics, where the controlled processes and actuators are often working continuously in time and the analysis and control are typically realised digitally in contemporary installations. The oversimplified view that the digital system with 'sufficiently dense' sampling behaves almost as a continuously working system is often fundamentally misleading, as will be shown in the next section, and can even lead to functionless designs. But even in more successful cases, this idea often leads to ineffective designs working with excessively large amounts of data and requesting unnecessarily high computing power for a given application.

It should be declared at the beginning of the discussion that *no equivalence* exists between continuously and discretely working systems, simply because the principles of their operation are different. On the other hand, it is possible to find many analogies which allow us to state that digital systems can usually successfully simulate, in a sense and under some limiting assumptions, the behaviour or properties of continuous-time systems. In the opposite direction, the simulation would be much more difficult, because of the complexity of today's digital systems. In particular, as far as signal processing is concerned, we will be interested either in similarities in the frequency domain (frequency responses or the pole–zero configurations which determine them) or in the time domain, namely in the similarity of impulse responses and consequently of complete time behaviour. For nonlinear systems, the similarity of the character of nonlinearities may also be interesting etc.

Comment (on basic types of analogue filters): every analogue filter, as a linear time-invariant continuous-time system, is characterised by its impulse response $h_a(t)$, that is its response to the Dirac unit impulse $\delta(t)$. Alternatively, it can be described by a rational fractional function called the image transfer function (in Laplace transform)

$$H_a(s) = \mathscr{L}\{h_a(t)\} = K \frac{\prod\limits_{i=1}^{r} (s - n_i)}{\prod\limits_{i=1}^{m} (s - p_i)},$$

where n_i, p_i are zero points and poles of the transfer, respectively, K is the amplification (gain) and m is the order of the filter, $m > r$. The frequency response of the filter is given by

$$G_a(\omega) = H_a(j\omega) = K \frac{\prod\limits_{i=1}^{r} |j\omega - n_i|}{\prod\limits_{i=1}^{m} |j\omega - p_i|} e^{j\left(\sum_{i=1}^{r} \varphi_i - \sum_{i=1}^{m} \psi_i\right)},$$

where φ_i and ψ_i are angles of radius vectors of zero points and poles starting at the point $j\omega$. This formula enables us to estimate the frequency response on the basis of the zero–pole configuration in the s-plane. It can be shown that stable filters have all their poles in the left half plane, $\mathrm{Re}(p_i) < 0$, $i = 1, 2, \ldots, m$.

Common filter types are extensively described in the literature by design formulae and tables. These enable us to determine a suitable type of filter, its order and system coefficient values, given the boundaries of the frequency bands, the steepness of the transition from stop to passbands and the acceptable gain ripple inside the bands. The fundamental types of filter are Butterworth, Chebyshev and elliptic filters; it is sufficient to mention only the lowpass modifications of these types, on the basis of which it is possible to design digital lowpass filters. Should we need another band-type filter (highpass, bandpass or bandstop), this can be obtained from a lowpass model by means of frequency transforms (Section 5.3.2.3).

The magnitude of the frequency response of the *Butterworth lowpass filter* of mth order is given by the expression

$$|G_a(\omega)|^2 = \frac{1}{1 + \left(\dfrac{\omega}{\omega_0}\right)^{2m}},$$

where ω_0 is the boundary (cut-off) frequency defined by a 3 dB decline of the maximum gain at zero frequency. The amplitude frequency response is maximally flat (monotonous function with zero derivatives at zero frequency until mth order). It can be shown that poles of such a filter are in the left half of the s-plane, on a semicircle centred around the origin of coordinates and with a radius of ω_0.

The *Chebyshev lowpass filter* of the order m has the characteristic

$$|G_a(\omega)|^2 = \frac{1}{1 + \varepsilon^2 C_m^2\left(\dfrac{\omega}{\omega_p}\right)},$$

where the parameter ε indicates the response ripple in the passband, in which the amplitude transfer varies between the maximum of 1 and the minimum value $1/\sqrt{1 + \varepsilon^2}$, ω_p is the cut-off frequency at which the response leaves this tolerance field and C_m is the Chebyshev polynomial of the mth order. The amplitude response of the Chebyshev filter is rippled in the passband and decreases monotonically in the stopband; a modification exists with both properties interchanged. The main advantage of this filter type is the higher slope of the transition from pass to stopband. The poles of its transfer function are situated on a half ellipse in the left half plane of s; the greater half axis is vertical and equal to the radius of the circle of the corresponding Butterworth filter; the pole positions are horizontal projections of the Butterworth's poles to the ellipse. The eccentricity of the ellipse increases with ε, as well as, consequently, the slope of the transition, which is positive, while the subsequent increase in passband ripple is a negative phenomenon.

An *elliptic filter* of lowpass type has the amplitude characteristic

$$|G_a(\omega)|^2 = \frac{1}{1 + \varepsilon^2 E_m^2\left(\dfrac{\omega}{\omega_p}\right)},$$

where E_m is the Jacobi elliptical function of the order m. Owing to the properties of this function, the transfer of the elliptical filter is, in contrast to the previous two types, a fractional rational function so that the frequency response is given by both poles and zeros. The zeros are situated on the frequency axis $j\omega$ in the stopband so that they increase the slope of the transition as well as the suppression at certain frequencies in the stopband, at a price of causing a ripple there. As the analytical design of the elliptical filter is complicated, sometimes an approximation is used instead, derived from Chebyshev filters with a corresponding configuration of poles complemented by adding zeros, suitably placed in the stopband on the frequency axis. Naturally, even the response in the passband may be notably influenced by this modification. It is therefore necessary to verify the resulting response and, if need be, to revise the zero positions, and perhaps even the pole placement.

5.3.2.2.2 *Impulse invariance*

Impulse invariance is, intuitively, the most acceptable definition of similarity among analogue and discrete systems in the time domain. It requires that the impulse response $\{h_n\}$ of the discrete system be formed by regularly spaced samples of the impulse response $h_a(t)$ of the corresponding analogue system,

$$h_n = h_a(t)|_{t=nT}. \tag{5.36}$$

Let us investigate the properties of discrete systems designed in this way in comparison with those of analogue models.

Let us state first that the image transfer function of such a discrete system is

$$H(z) = \mathbb{Z}\{h_n\} = \sum_{n=0}^{\infty} h_n z^{-n}, \tag{5.37}$$

and its frequency response is therefore

$$G(\omega) = H(z)|_{z=e^{j\omega T}} = \sum_{n=0}^{\infty} h_n e^{-j\omega nT}. \tag{5.38}$$

Further, we shall express this frequency characteristic in terms of the analogue system characteristics. We will use the knowledge of sampling theory; the sampling will be expressed by multiplication of the continuous impulse response, $h_a(t)$, which is a continuous signal, by the sampling sequence of Dirac impulses, $v(t) = \sum_{n=-\omega}^{\infty} \delta(t - nT)$. The procedure yields a quasicontinuous signal

$$h_v(t) = h_a(t) \cdot v(t) = \sum_{n=0}^{\infty} h_a(nT)\delta(t - nT), \tag{5.39}$$

where the lower limit of the sum is given by the supposed causality of $h_a(t)$. The spectrum of this signal can be expressed in two alternative ways: either by exploiting the linearity of the Fourier transform, as the sum of spectra of individual terms of the sum (5.39),

$$G_v(\omega) = h_0 \cdot 1 + h_1 e^{-j\omega T} + h_2 e^{-j\omega 2T} + \ldots = \sum_{n=0}^{\infty} h_n e^{-j\omega nT}. \tag{5.40}$$

Alternatively, it can be expressed as a convolution of the spectra $G_a(\omega)$ and $V(\omega)$ of both factors in the first representation in eqn (5.39), as was derived when analysing the process of sampling in Section 2.1,

$$G_v(\omega) = \mathbb{F}\{h_a(t) \cdot v(t)\} = \frac{1}{2\pi} G_a(\omega) * V(\omega) = \frac{1}{T} \sum_{k=-\infty}^{\infty} G_a(\omega - k\omega_v), \tag{5.41}$$

where $\omega_v = 2\pi/T$.[1]

---

[1] In order to prevent confusion with the symbol of the variable s, we denote the sampling frequency by ω_v, following the convention of Section 2.1.

From comparison of the right-hand sides of eqns (5.38) and (5.40) it follows that the frequency response of the discrete system is identical to the spectrum of the sampled impulse response of the analogue system, thus also to the expression (5.41). It follows, then, that the frequency response of the discrete filter, designed by means of impulse invariance, is given by infinitely many replicas of the frequency response $G_a(\omega)$ of the analogue system, mutually shifted by integer multiples of the sampling frequency ω_v.

Interpretation of this important result is as follows: considering the close similarity of behaviour of both types of systems in the time domain according to eqn (5.36), it could have been expected that their behaviour in the frequency domain would also be accordingly similar. However, we find that this is generally not true. The basic difference of the frequency response $G(\omega)$ of a discrete system is in its periodicity. Nevertheless, even in the limited basic (working) range of frequencies $\langle -\omega_v/2, \omega_v/2 \rangle$, the response of the discrete system generally differs from that of the analogue system in the corresponding frequency range, which is surprising at first sight. The reason is that the values in the basic range as valid for the analogue system, $G_a(\omega)/T$, may be substantially modified in case of the discrete system due to adding further (shifted) replicas of the infinitely extended characteristic $G_a(\omega)/T$. The exact identity will only be achieved when

$$G_a(\omega) = 0 \quad \text{for} \quad |\omega| \geq \omega_v/2, \tag{5.42}$$

in which case the contribution of the shifted versions into the basic range is zero; this is never exactly valid for any analogue system. An acceptable similarity can be reached if $G_a(\omega)$ is negligible for high frequencies (and if the sampling frequency is properly chosen); it is nevertheless only possible for filters with a limited frequency band, such as for sufficiently good lowpass or bandpass filters. It is therefore not possible to design a digital highpass, bandstop or allpass filter using the method of impulse invariance.

Furthermore, by generalising the previous discussion, we shall analyse the relationship between the transfer functions of both types of systems. Notice that the frequency response $G_v(\omega)$ of the 'sampled' continuous-time system is also determined by the transfer function $H_v(s)$, specifically by its values on the imaginary axis,

$$G_v(\omega) = H_v(j\omega). \tag{5.43}$$

So far we have derived the validity of eqn (5.41) only for $s = j\omega$, i.e. on the imaginary axis in the s-plane, but it is easy to show that the relationship can be generalised to the whole s-plane, i.e. that it is valid:

$$H_v(s) = \frac{1}{T} \sum_{k=-\infty}^{\infty} H_a(s - jk\omega_v). \tag{5.44}$$

Indeed, the function $H_v(j\omega)$ is a rational fractional function of $j\omega$, the form of which is unique. Thus, $H_v(s)$ must have the same form (in the variable s) in order to ensure that $H_v(j\omega) = H_v(s)|_{s=j\omega}$, and even the equivalent expression for the same function, i.e. $\sum_{k=-\infty}^{\infty} H_a(s - jk\omega_v)/T$, must express the same values on not only the imaginary axis but everywhere on the s-plane.

We have arrived at the conclusion that the transfer function of the original continuous-time system was modified by sampling in such a way that the new transfer $H_v(s)$ is given by the sum of an infinite number of replicas of the original transfer $H_a(s)$ mutually shifted by an integer number of $j\omega_v$. This means that every original singularity will appear in the resulting function infinitely many times with the mentioned shifts. *Vice versa*, singularities that were outside the so-called *basic stripe* of s: $\text{Im}(s) \in \langle -j\omega_v/2, j\omega_v/2 \rangle$ in $H_a(s)$, will also be projected into it. This indicates, too, that the frequency response in the working range of frequencies may be substantially modified by the sampling.

In order to quantify the relationship between both transfer functions, we shall show that the discrete system has all the mentioned properties, if for its transfer $H(z)$ is

$$H(z)|_{z=e^{sT}} = \frac{1}{T} H_a(s), \tag{5.45}$$

which represents a mapping of the s-plane onto the z-plane according to the transform relation

$$z = e^{sT}, \tag{5.46}$$

(complemented by multiplication of transformed values by $1/T$).

Actually, providing validity of eqn (5.42), the equality of frequency responses in the working frequency range really applies: substituting $s = j\omega$ into eqn (5.45), we obtain

$$H(e^{j\omega T}) = \frac{1}{T} H_a(j\omega). \tag{5.47}$$

Furthermore, rewriting $s = \sigma + j\omega$, i.e. $e^{sT} = e^{\sigma T} e^{j\omega T}$, we find the following properties of the mapping (Figure 5.17):

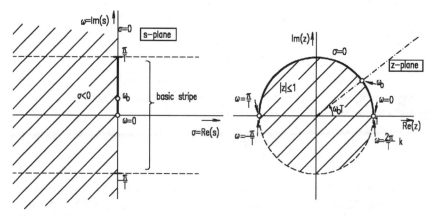

Figure 5.17 Mapping $z = \exp(sT)$

1   Frequency axis: imaginary axis of the *s*-plane, $\sigma = 0$, is mapped onto the unit circle of the *z*-plane, $z = e^{j\omega T}$. The range $\langle 0, j\omega_v/2 \rangle$ is transformed onto the complete upper half circle starting from point 1, and the range $\langle 0, -j\omega_v/2 \rangle$ is similarly mapped onto the lower half circle. This corresponds to a linear (uniform) frequency transform with the ratio of frequencies in both systems equal to 1, and enables the equality of the frequency responses according to eqn (5.47) as far as eqn (5.42) is fulfilled. The remaining parts of the imaginary axis of the *s*-plane are mapped periodically onto the unit circle of the *z*-plane, as corresponds to the expression (5.41).

2   Area of poles in the case of stable systems: the left half plane of *s*, i.e. $\sigma < 0$, obviously maps onto the inside of the unit circle $|z| = |e^{\sigma T}| < 1$. Therefore, as far as the analogue system was stable, even the derived discrete system is stable.

3   Mapping of poles: a pole in the position $p_s = \sigma_p + j\omega_p$ is transformed into a pole $p_z = e^{\sigma_p T} e^{j\omega_p T}$ which lies in the *z*-plane at a radius vector corresponding to the frequency ω_p of the pole position in the *s*-plane; the closer to the unit circle the nearer the original pole was to the imaginary axis in the *s*-plane. The poles are therefore mapped by the transform eqn (5.46) with the only unlikely exception that there would be an opposite pole of the same order mapped onto the same position, owing to the infinite sum of eqn (5.44). A complex conjugate pair of poles obviously preserves this property even after the transform.

4   Transformation of zeros: zeros are generally not transformed onto the positions corresponding to eqn (5.46), as they are overlaid by nonzero values from nonbasic stripes of the *s*-plane, which are mapped onto the same areas of the *z*-plane. On the other hand, there may (and usually do) appear new zero points owing to mutual compensation of the complex contributions according to eqn (5.44). These appear in positions on the *z*-plane to which basic-stripe nonzero values of the *s*-plane correspond.

5   The transform relation (5.46) is unambiguous in the direction $s \rightarrow z$ but not in the opposite direction, which means that there exist in principle more than one analogue system fulfilling the impulse invariance requirement with respect to a given discrete system. This is quite natural, because the continuous impulse responses can interpolate variously among the discrete samples.

It is evident that $H(z)$ derived from $H_a(s)$ complies with all the requirements following from the impulse invariance design according to eqn (5.36). Thus, the mapping (5.46) is the sought transform between both complex planes which describes this discrete-system design method based on an analogue model. It can be proved that it is a unique transform so that the requirement of eqn (5.36) is also fulfilled only when the transform (5.46) applies. The transform relationship, sometimes called the *direct transform*, explains in a clear way the relationship between the *s* and *z*-planes when there is a uniform (1:1) linear correspondence between frequencies in both corresponding systems that are related also by the impulse invariance condition. On the other hand, the transform cannot be directly utilised to derive $H(z)$ based on $H_a(s)$ because the periodicity of the former means that there is an infinite number of contributions to each point of the z-plane according to the transform relation (5.46).

A practical approach to the design of a discrete system by means of the impulse invariance method is based on the following reasoning.

As known from continuous-time system theory, the impulse response of an analogue system can always be expressed as a finite sum of complex exponential functions:

$$h_a(t) = \sum_{k=1}^{m} A_k e^{p_k t} \quad \text{for} \quad t \geq 0, \tag{5.48}$$

where p_k are generally complex parameters and m is the order of the system. It follows from the requirement of impulse invariance that

$$h_n = h_a(nT) = \sum_{k=1}^{m} A_k e^{p_k nT}. \tag{5.49}$$

Term-by-term Laplace transform of the expression (5.48) yields

$$H_a(s) = \sum_{k=1}^{m} A_k \frac{1}{s - p_k}, \tag{5.50}$$

and from the Z-transform of eqn (5.49), also term by term, follows

$$H(z) = \sum_{k=1}^{m} A_k \frac{1}{1 - e^{p_k T} z^{-1}} = \sum_{k=1}^{m} A_k \frac{z}{z - e^{p_k T}}. \tag{5.51}$$

By comparing $H_a(s)$ and $H(z)$ we find that the poles are transformed according to eqn (5.46), as we expected, while the zeros generally are not. The design procedure is as follows:

1   The given image transfer function $H_a(s)$ (rational fractional function) will be expanded into partial fractions in the form of (5.50).
2   Mechanically rewriting the previous result according to the above deduction, i.e. only substituting the coefficients A_k from eqn (5.50) into eqn (5.51), provides $H(z)$.
3   This expression for $H(z)$ will be converted into a suitable form with respect to the intended type of realisation. In this step, the pairs of complex conjugate system coefficients can usually be merged so that real coefficients are provided.

5.3.2.2.3 *Direct transformation of zero points and poles*

The method of direct transformation of poles and zeros of an analogue model onto the z-plane is conceptually very simple. It is partially similar to the previous method of impulse invariance in that it also provides linear uniform frequency correspondence. The method also takes for granted the fact that all the important poles and zeros of the analogue system, influencing the frequency response, lie in the basic stripe of the *s*-plane. These significant points are transformed to the *z*-plane according to the relation (5.46) and the transfer function $H(z)$ is then calculated from their positions (except for a multiplication constant, which has to be determined based on the required gain of the filter). It is obvious that the poles are transformed in the same way as by the previous method; but, in contrast, zero points are also mapped according to the same relation. The basic idea of the method is as follows: it can be expected that the frequency response of the digital system in the working range of frequencies will be basically similar to that of the analogue model when the poles and zeros are distributed around the frequency axes in the *z* and *s*-planes analogously. On the other hand, the impulse invariance will not be preserved.

5.3.2.2.4 *Bilinear transform*

The method of the bilinear transform is motivated by a desire to formulate the transfer function of the discrete system directly by means of a simple transform of the analogue-model transfer function. Such a mapping from the *s*-plane onto the *z*-plane, $z = g(s)$, should fulfil the following requirements:

- the entire *s*-plane must be mapped onto the entire *z*-plane and the mapping must be reversible, i.e. must be unique in both directions;
- the imaginary axis of the *s*-plane must be mapped uniquely and monotonously onto the unit circle of the *z*-plane and *vice versa*;
- the left half of the *s*-plane must be mapped onto the inside of the unit circle in the *z*-plane;
- the transformation used must transform a rational fractional function $H_a(s)$ reversibly into a rational fractional function $H(z)$.

The meaning of the first requirement is obvious. The second condition means that every value of the frequency response of the analogue system becomes just one value of the frequency response of the designed discrete system. As the 'analogue' frequency axis is infinite while the 'discrete' axis is limited, a distortion will appear in the sense that the mentioned identical values will generally correspond to different frequencies on each of the axes. This phenomenon is called *frequency-axis distortion*. Fulfilling the third requirement ensures preserving the stability: if the analogue model is stable, even the resulting discrete system will be stable. The fourth requirement follows from the fact that the transfer functions of both the analogue and discrete systems are exclusively of the rational fractional type.

Should we find a transform function of the required properties, the transfer functions will obviously fulfil the equation

$$H(z) = H_a(s)|_{s=g^{-1}(z)} = H_a(g^{-1}(z)). \tag{5.52}$$

Thus, by mere substitution of the argument of the analogue-model transfer function by the inverse-transform formula, we obtain the discrete-system transfer function in the variable z. A suitable algebraic manipulation will then provide the form of the transfer function describing the desired type of realisation.

One such transform function fulfilling these requirements is the so-called *bilinear transform*

$$z = g(s) = \frac{1+s}{1-s}, \quad \text{or inversely,} \quad s = g^{-1}(z) = \frac{z-1}{z+1}, \tag{5.53}$$

which, as a rational fractional function, obviously fulfils the first and the last of the conditions (Figure 5.18).

We shall first investigate the frequency-axes transform; a notation will be introduced denoting the frequency in the analogue system by ω_a, and the frequency in the discrete system by ω_d. As $s = j\omega_a$, the following obviously applies,

$$z = \frac{1+j\omega_a}{1-j\omega_a} = 1.e^{j2\alpha} \tag{5.54}$$

where $\alpha = \arg(1+j\omega_a) = \arctan(\omega_a/1)$. Based on this, we can first state that the imaginary axis of the s-plane is transformed onto the unit circle in the z-plane. As the frequency ω_d is determined by the radius vector of a point on the unit circle, with respect to eqn (5.54)

$$\omega_d T - 2\alpha = 2\arctan(\omega_a). \tag{5.55}$$

Therefore, $\omega_a = 0$ corresponds to $\omega_d = 0$, and for $\omega_a = \pm\infty$, $\omega_d = \pm\omega_v/2$ (i.e. $z = -1$). The infinite analogue-system frequency axis has thus been transformed into the finite discrete-system axis formed by the unit circle on which the positive

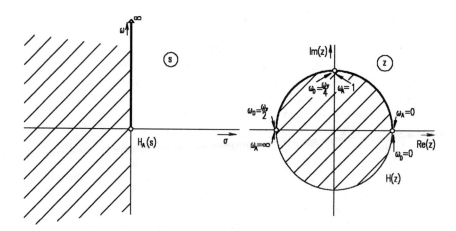

Figure 5.18 Properties of the bilinear transform

frequencies are represented by the upper and the negative ones by the lower half circle. Then, $\omega_a = \pm 1$ corresponds to $\omega_d = \omega_v/4$ (i.e. $z = \pm j$). A considerable distortion of the frequency axis can be observed which is given by the tangent function: the representation of identically-broad 'analogue' frequency bands will be gradually more and more compressed with the increasing frequency on the 'discrete' frequency axis. As far as band filters are to be designed, this is of no harm, as the widening or narrowing of the pass and stopbands can be compensated for in advance by prescaling the frequencies of the band boundaries. For a discrete filter to have a desired boundary frequency ω_{dm} (e.g. cut-off frequency), the analogue model has to have the corresponding boundary frequency

$$\omega_{am} = \tan\left(\frac{\omega_{dm}T}{2}\right). \tag{5.56}$$

The procedure of recalculating the 'analogue' boundary frequencies according to eqn (5.56) is called *prewarping*. This complication is the price of gaining reversibility of the frequency-response mapping.

The condition of stability preserving is also fulfilled by the bilinear transform: if $s = \sigma + j\omega$ is coming from the left (or right) half plane, i.e. $\sigma < 0$ (or $\sigma > 0$), then $|z| < 1$ (or $|z| > 1$), respectively; this can easily be shown when we rewrite the transform formula as $z = (1 + \sigma + j\omega)/(1 - \sigma - j\omega)$ and calculate the absolute values of both numerator and denominator in each of the two cases. The left (right) half of the s-plane is therefore transformed into the inside (outside) of the unit circle in the z-plane, respectively.

The design procedure for a discrete filter by means of the bilinear transform is as follows:

- the requirements are expressed by the desired prominent frequencies of the resulting digital filter (e.g. the band-boundary frequencies of band filters);
- prewarping: calculation of the corresponding frequencies of the analogue model according to eqn (5.56);
- the analogue filter is designed with the desired (prewarped) properties, i.e. the model transfer function $H_a(s)$ is determined (commonly by means of a routine procedure using formulae and tables taken from a catalogue of filters);
- the resulting transfer function $H(z)$ of the discrete filter is found by substituting $(z - 1)/(z + 1) \to s$ into $H_a(s)$;
- the resulting transfer function formula is converted into a form corresponding to the intended realisation structure.

Examples of bandstop filter design by the bilinear transform method based on Butterworth and Chebyshev filters can be seen in Figure 5.19*a*, *b*. The characteristic features of both types of filter influence the resulting properties of the designs: the smoothness of the Butterworth amplitude response in contrast to

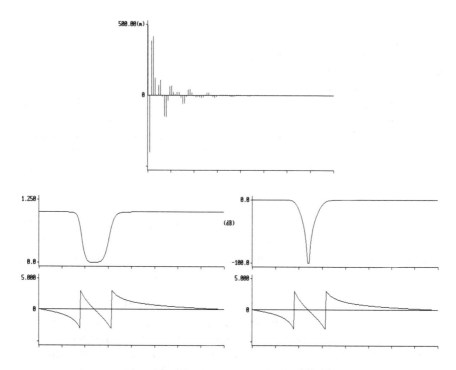

*Figure 5.19a Example of a bandstop filter design by bilinear transform, analogue model:
Butterworth filter; depicted: resulting impulse response (initial 512 samples),
amplitude and phase frequency response in the range ⟨0, ωᵥ/2⟩, with its
module in linear and logarithmic (dB) scale*

the visible ripple of the Chebyshev response, which, on the other hand, has
steeper and narrower transient regions between pass and stopbands.

5.3.2.3 Frequency-response transformations of discrete systems

The idea of mapping the transfer function, that has been used for the digital
filter design based on analogue models, can be used more generally, including
to formulate a new transfer function $H'(z')$ a discrete filter on the basis of
another discrete filter (model) with the image transfer $H(z)$. The practical meaning of such transforms is found in the possibility of deriving many different
types of filter from a certain model type. Such *frequency transforms* are currently
used namely to design band filters. Based on the image transfer of a standard
lowpass filter with a normalised cut-off frequency, it is easily possible to
derive transfer functions of lowpass filters with another cut-off frequency or
highpass, bandpass and bandstop filters with any desired boundary frequencies.

The requirements for mapping $z' = g(z)$ from the z-plane into the z'-plane are,
for the mentioned purpose, as follows:

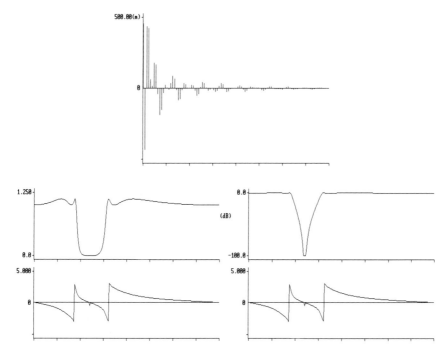

Figure 5.19b Example of similar design as in Figure 5.19a; analogue model: Chebyshev filter

- the entire z-plane must be mapped onto the entire z'-plane;
- the entire unit circle of the z-plane must be uniquely mapped onto the entire unit circle in the z'-plane (the inverse mapping need not be unique);
- the inside of the unit circle must be transformed onto the inside of the unit circle in order for stability to be preserved;
- the mapping used must transform the rational fractional function $H(z)$ into another rational fractional function $H'(z')$ in order that it could be realisable by a linear time-invariant filter.

Should such a function be available, the new transfer function is determined as

$$H'(z') = H(z)|_{z=g^{-1}(z')} = H(g^{-1}(z')). \qquad (5.57)$$

Let us state without proof that the above requirements are fulfilled by the family of rational transformations

$$z = g^{-1}(z') = \pm \prod_{i=1}^{k} \frac{1 - \alpha_i z'}{z' - \alpha_i}, \qquad k = 1, 2$$

where α_i are suitable constants. The requirements are even fulfilled by some simpler mappings, such as $z = -z'$ or $z = z'^2$ which are limit cases of the generic ones.

Table 5.1 Frequency transforms to transform a lowpass filter to other type filters

Target	Mapping formula	Auxiliary quantities
lowpass filter	$(z^{-1} - \alpha)/(1 - \alpha z^{-1})$	$\alpha = \sin((\beta - \gamma)/2)/\sin((\beta + \gamma)/2)$
highpass filter	$-(z^{-1} + \alpha)/(1 + \alpha z^{-1})$	$\alpha = \cos((\beta + \gamma)/2)/\cos((\beta - \gamma)/2)$
bandpass filter	$-\dfrac{z^{-2} - 2k\alpha z^{-1}/(k+1) + (k-1)/(k+1)}{z^{-2}(k-1)/(k+1) - 2k\alpha z^{-1}/(k+1) + 1}$	$\alpha = \cos((\gamma_u + \gamma_l)/2)/\cos((\gamma_u - \gamma_l)/2)$ $k = \tan((\gamma_u - \gamma_l)/2)\tan(\beta/2)$
band reject filter	$-\dfrac{z^{-2} - 2k\alpha z^{-1}/(k+1) + (1-k)/(1+k)}{z^{-2}(1-k)/(k+1) - 2\alpha z^{-1}/(1+k) + 1}$	$\alpha = \cos((\gamma_u + \gamma_l)/2)/\cos((\gamma_u - \gamma_l)/2)$ $k = \tan((\gamma_u - \gamma_l)/2)\tan(\beta/2)$

β is the characteristic (cut-off) frequency of the lowpass model filter
γ is the desired characteristic frequency of the filter to be designed
γ_u, γ_l are the desired upper and lower characteristic frequencies of the new filter

We will not deal in greater depth with the theory of these transforms, which provides the detailed formulae for the types of transform given in Table 5.1; more details are e.g. in Reference [16]. Rather, to clarify the principle of this approach, we will present three elementary examples:

1   The simple substitution $z \to -z'$ provides a highpass filter based on a lowpass model, or *vice versa*. This substitution moves all the zeros and poles into positions that are centrally symmetrical with respect to the original locations. For systems with real coefficients that have all the poles and zeros in complex conjugate couples, it means reversing the configuration of poles and zeros with respect to the imaginary axis. Consequently, the new frequency response is the mirror image of the original response, with the symmetry axis at the frequency $\omega_v/4$ (Figure 5.20).

2   Changing one characteristic frequency of the frequency response from ω_0 into ω_1 (e.g. the cut-off frequency of a low or highpass filter without changing the filter character) can be obtained by the substitution (see the first line of Table 5.1)

$$z \to \frac{1 - \alpha z'}{z' - \alpha}, \quad \alpha = \frac{\sin\left(\dfrac{\omega_0 T - \omega_1 T}{2}\right)}{\sin\left(\dfrac{\omega_0 T + \omega_1 T}{2}\right)}.$$

This mapping results in a nonlinear conversion of the frequency axis at which its ends ($\omega = 0$ and $\omega = \omega_v/2$) are fixed. An example of shifting a point of zero transfer of a simple lowpass filter from the frequency

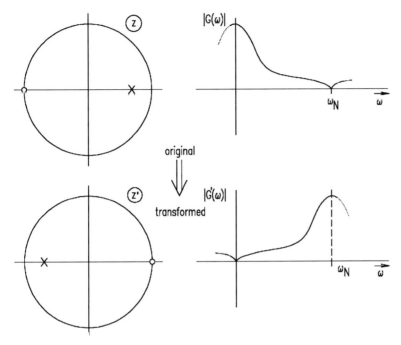

Figure 5.20 Example of converting the frequency response by the substitution $z \rightarrow -z'$

$\omega_0 = \pi/2T$ into $\omega_1 = \pi/4T$ ($\alpha \cong 0.4142$), which leads to narrowing of the passband, is shown in Figure 5.21.

3 Conversion of filter character by the transform $z \rightarrow \pm z'^2$ is documented in Figure 5.22. Here, the lowpass model filter has been converted into a bandpass or bandstop filter. The conversion can easily be explained: the mapping is characterised by the frequency in the z'-plane being one half of the frequency in the z'-plane, so that every value from the unit circle in the z-plane appears twice on the unit circle in z'-plane. The simple starting lowpass filter (*a*) is transformed, depending on the sign of the transform expression, either into a bandstop filter (*b*) when arg(z) varies in the range $0 \ldots 2\pi$ while arg(z') in the range $0 \ldots \pi$, or into a bandpass filter (*c*) when arg(z) varies in the range $-\pi \ldots \pi$ for the same extent of arg(z').

5.3.3 Realisation of IIR filters

5.3.3.1 Direct realisations

The structures of direct realisations are derived in a straightforward way from difference equation (5.25), the coefficients of which, K_i and L_i, are also the

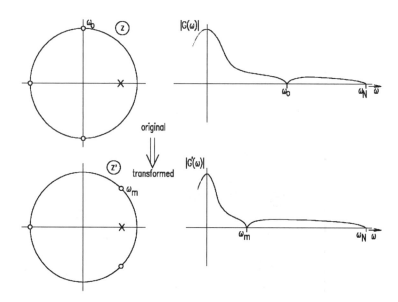

Figure 5.21 Example of nonlinear conversion of the frequency axis

realisation constants of the system. The so-called *direct form I* (Figure 5.23) corresponds directly to the form of the equation. It is obvious that this type of realisation requests $r + m$ delay elements (e.g. memory registers).

The *canonical realisation* (direct form II) utilises the fact that the sequence of involved cascaded blocks is irrelevant (if rounding errors can be neglected). Both parts of the system can therefore be interchanged so that the recursive part is the first in the chain, followed by the nonrecursive part. If we say

$$H_1(z) = \frac{1}{\displaystyle\sum_{i=0}^{m} K_i z^{-i}} \quad \text{and} \quad H_2(z) = \sum_{i=0}^{r} L_i z^{-i},$$

then, according to eqn (5.26), $H(z) = H_1(z)H_2(z)$. Let us further denote

$$W(z) = H_1(z)X(z) \qquad (5.58)$$

then, obviously

$$Y(z) = H_2(z)W(z). \qquad (5.59)$$

If the last two expressions are converted by means of the inverse Z-transform into the time domain, we obtain

$$w_n = x_n - \sum_{i=1}^{m} K_i w_{n-i} \quad \text{and} \quad y_n = \sum_{i=0}^{r} L_i w_{n-i},$$

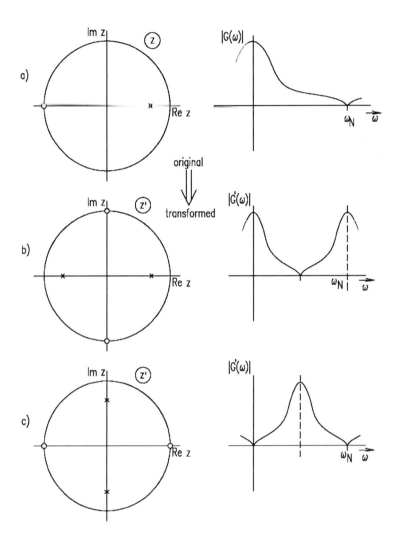

Figure 5.22 Example of conversion of the filter character
   a Model lowpass filter
   b Derived bandstop filter
   c Derived bandpass filter

respectively. Each of these partial equations is directly realisable and by noting that the same delayed signal values are used in both realisations, we can use the same delaying chain for both parts of the system (Figure 5.24). It can be seen that the canonical realisation is more economical as it needs only $\max(m, r)$ memory registers and, at the same time, the number of operations per sample is the same as for direct realisation I.

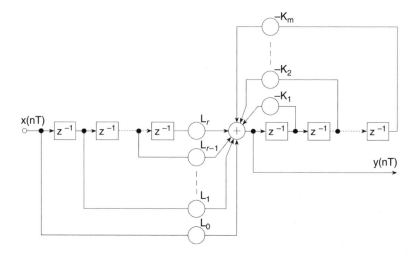

Figure 5.23 Direct realisation (1) of an IIR filter

The direct realisations are vivid in concept but they have a drawback in their considerable sensitivity to rounding errors owing to complicated feedbacks. Due to these, the errors circulate in the system, they may accumulate and, consequently, when the computational precision is insufficient, cause undesirable effects (e.g. so-called deadbands, limit cycles or even instability). Nevertheless, owing to the high precision of number representation in contemporary systems, the influence of these nonlinear phenomena is already rather limited in practice.

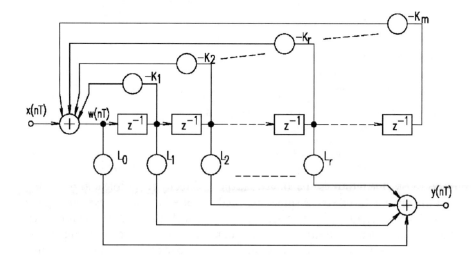

Figure 5.24 Canonical realisation of an IIR filter

Figure 5.25 Cascade realisation of an IIR filter

Note: several other canonical forms exist that are equivalent in terms of transfer function. All need the same minimum number of delay elements; we will not deal with them in this book.

5.3.3.2 Combinations of second-order systems

Another approach to the realisation of recursive systems is decomposition into the simplest possible subsystems by interconnection of which the requested transfer function is obtained. Such an arrangement helps to provide good insight into a system which has explicitly only second-order feedbacks and is therefore less sensitive to rounding errors.

The *cascade (serial) realisation* (Figure 5.25) comes out of the transfer function (5.26). When the polynomials are not factored thoroughly into root factors, as on the right-hand side of this expression, but rather into real root factors and nonfactorable second-order polynomials, we obtain

$$H(z) = \frac{P(z)}{Q(z)} = A \frac{\prod\limits_{i=1}^{r_1} (z^2 + a_i z + b_i) \prod\limits_{i=1}^{r_2} (z - e_i)}{\prod\limits_{i=1}^{m_1} (z^2 + c_i z + d_i) \prod\limits_{i=1}^{m_2} (z - f_i)} z^{m-r}. \qquad (5.60)$$

Here, A is the gain factor, $2m_1 + m_2 = m$ is the order of the system, $m \geq r$. The system is built as a serial connection of subsystems the transfer functions of each of which,

$$H_k(z) = \frac{1 + a_k z^{-1} + b_k z^{-2}}{1 + c_k z^{-1} + d_k z^{-2}},$$

are formed by second-order polynomials (nonfactorable quadratic trinomials or products of root-factor couples). The number of such sections, the system constants of which are given by the coefficients of the partial polynomials, is of course $\operatorname{int}((m+1)/2)$. Each of the sections generates, or 'covers', generally two poles and two zeros of the complete transfer (often complex conjugate pairs of such points). The structure of all such sections of a system is usually identical, and commonly canonical, with respect to its economy. The identity of all the sections eases the realisation both in the form of integrated circuits

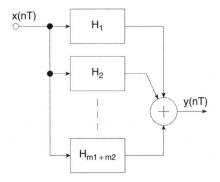

Figure 5.26 Parallel realisation of an IIR filter

or as software. Hardware realisation of identical sections can be formed by repeated structures on a chip. Alternatively, should the circuitry be powerful enough with respect to a particular signal, the same processor can be used in time sharing to emulate all the sections with different system constants being repeatedly retrieved from memory.

Parallel realisation (Figure 5.26) uses decomposition of the transfer function into the sum of partial fractions. Providing the numerator polynomial of the transfer has a zero at the origin of its coordinates, the ratio of polynomials can be rewritten into a true rational fractional function,

$$H(z) = \frac{P(z)}{Q(z)} = z\frac{P_1(z)}{Q(z)} = \sum_{i=1}^{m_1} \frac{z(A_i z + B_i)}{z^2 + c_i z + d_i} + \sum_{i=1}^{m_2} \frac{zF_i}{z - f_i}. \tag{5.61}$$

Here, again, $2m_1 + m_2 = m$ is the order of the system. The individual sections, the number of which is $\mathrm{int}((m + 1)/2)$, have their partial transfer functions in the form

$$H_k(z) = \frac{A_k + B_k z^{-1}}{1 + c_i z^{-1} + d_k z^{-2}};$$

the subsystems of the first order corresponding to the terms in the last sum of eqn (5.61) are again merged in pairs. It can be seen that each section generates two poles of the original complete transfer, while the zeros of it are produced by the parallel interaction of all the sections. The individual sections are somewhat simpler to those in the cascade realisation – there is only a first-order polynomial in the numerator. However, this is balanced by the sum operation at the output and by the necessity to weight the individual section outputs by the coefficients A_k, B_k. The advantage of parallel realisation is the possibility for all the sections to work in parallel when realised in a suitable hardware.

5.3.3.3 Realisations based on state description

As has been shown in the overview of the theoretical background (Section 2.3), linear discrete systems can be described by a more general mathematical model than the input–output model (5.25), i.e. by a so-called *state(-variable) model*

$$\mathbf{q}_{k+1} = \mathbf{A}\mathbf{q}_k + \mathbf{B}\mathbf{x}_k, \quad \mathbf{y}_k = \mathbf{C}\mathbf{q}_k + \mathbf{D}\mathbf{x}_k. \tag{5.62}$$

Here, $\mathbf{A}, \mathbf{B}, \mathbf{C}, \mathbf{D}$ are matrices of coefficients of the state-formulated system, $\mathbf{q}_k$ is the vector of state variables (i.e. the outputs of the memory registers) in the kth sampling period, $\mathbf{x}_k$ and $\mathbf{y}_k$ are vectors of components of the input and output signal, respectively. As can be seen, both external signals are generally of a multicomponent type. If the input and output signals are both scalar, it can be shown that every system realised according to eqn (5.62) with any matrices of coefficients can be transformed into a functionally equivalent system according to eqn (5.25). This is thus a special case and leads to a simpler realisation. It is obvious that the more general structure, according to the state equation, will have a generally great number of coefficients (i.e. also operations of multiplication and addition per sample). On the other hand, even the possibility of selecting different combinations of zero and nonzero coefficients leads to enormous flexibility for designing different structures which are functionally equivalent or properly approximate the requested function. The selection of a suitable structure, optimal for a required task under given technical conditions, available processing blocks, precision of computation and coefficients etc., is of course not a simple task. Some classes of such realisation structures (e.g. wave filters, ladder structures etc.) have been widely studied and the respective design procedures are well prepared for users.

We will not deal with these special realisation forms of discrete linear time-invariant systems in this book, because they do not contribute any new options for the single-signal processing methods concerned. Specialised publications are devoted to the design and analysis of their properties, for example with respect to sensitivity to rounding errors and limited coefficient precision. We will only show in a simplified example that the state equation describes a system of first-order subsystems which are interconnected and work simultaneously. We shall see that a system of m such subsystems is equivalent to a certain linear time-invariant system of mth order, with a transfer function as in eqn (5.26).

Let us have m memory registers, the outputs of which form the state-variable vector $\mathbf{q}_k$ of components , $^i q_k$, $i = 1, 2, \ldots, m$. The mutual interconnection of these registers is expressed by the matrix $\mathbf{A}$ of size $m \times m$. The input signal $\{x_n\}$ is supposed scalar, i.e. $\mathbf{x}_k = [x_n]$ and it enters, as previously, the sum forming the input of the first register. Therefore, matrix $\mathbf{B} = [1, 0, \ldots, 0]^T$; the sum $^1 q_{k+1}$ forming the output of the first subsystem will be denoted according to the previous convention y_n as the output of the system. There is naturally no reason why the complete memory input vector $\mathbf{y}_n = \mathbf{q}_{k+1}$ should not be understood more generally as the output of the system as it is obviously available in the kth sampling period. Then, $\mathbf{C} = \mathbf{A}$ and $\mathbf{D} = \mathbf{B}$. This notation enables us to rewrite the state equation into a form closer to the previous convention,

$$\mathbf{y}_n = \mathbf{A}\mathbf{y}_{n-1} + \mathbf{B}\mathbf{x}_n, \qquad (5.63)$$

i.e.

$$^1y_n = a_{11}\,^1y_{n-1} + a_{12}\,^2y_{n-1} + \ldots + a_{1m}\,^my_{n-1} + x_n$$

$$^2y_n = a_{21}\,^1y_{n-1} + a_{22}\,^2y_{n-1} + \ldots + a_{2m}\,^my_{n-1}$$

$$\vdots$$

$$^my_n = a_{m1}\,^1y_{n-1} + a_{m2}\,^2y_{n-1} + \ldots + a_{mm}\,^my_{n-1},$$

which represents the structure depicted in Figure 5.27. Term-by-term Z-transforming provides, under zero initial conditions, a linear-equation system

$$Y_1(z) = a_{11}\,Y_1(z)z^{-1} + a_{12}\,Y_2(z)z^{-1} + \ldots + a_{1m}\,Y_m(z)z^{-1} + X(z)$$

$$Y_2(z) = a_{21}\,Y_1(z)z^{-1} + a_{22}\,Y_2(z)z^{-1} + \ldots + a_{2m}\,Y_m(z)z^{-1}$$

$$\vdots$$

$$Y_m(z) = a_{m1}\,Y_1(z)z^{-1} + a_{m2}\,Y_2(z)z^{-1} + \ldots + a_{mm}\,Y_m(z)z^{-1}$$

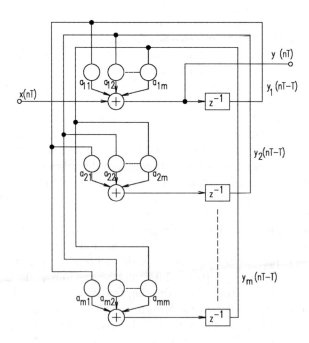

Figure 5.27 General system of simultaneous first order subsystems

and after a rearrangement

$$
\begin{bmatrix}
a_{11} - z & a_{12} & \cdots & a_{1m} \\
a_{21} & a_{22} - z & \cdots & a_{2m} \\
\vdots & & & \\
a_{m1} & a_{m2} & \cdots & a_{mm} - z
\end{bmatrix}
\begin{bmatrix}
Y_1(z) \\
Y_2(z) \\
\vdots \\
Y_m(z)
\end{bmatrix}
=
\begin{bmatrix}
-X(z) \\
0 \\
\vdots \\
0
\end{bmatrix}.
$$

Solving the system by Cramer's rule, we obtain for the transform $Y_1(z)$ of the output $y_n = {}^1 y_n$

$$
Y_1(z) = \frac{
\begin{vmatrix}
-X(z) & a_{12} & \cdots & a_{1m} \\
0 & a_{22} - z & \cdots & a_{2m} \\
\vdots & & & \\
0 & a_{m2} & \cdots & a_{mm} - z
\end{vmatrix}
}{
\begin{vmatrix}
a_{11} - z & a_{12} & \cdots & a_{1m} \\
a_{21} & a_{22} - z & \cdots & a_{2m} \\
\vdots & & & \\
a_{m1} & a_{m2} & \cdots & a_{mm} - z
\end{vmatrix}
} = \frac{P(z)}{Q(z)} X(z). \tag{5.64}
$$

It can be seen that by eqn (5.64) we have obtained a relationship between the transforms of the output and input in the usual form $Y(z) = H(z)X(z)$ and that the transfer function $H(z)$ is expressed as a ratio of polynomials in z. Indeed, the mth order characteristic polynomial of the system is the denominator and the numerator is a polynomial derived from a subdeterminant of the same matrix. The transfer function is therefore a rational fractional function with m poles which are obviously eigenvalues of the system. Therefore, such a system of simultaneous first-order subsystems is equivalent to a certain linear time invariant (LTI) system of mth order described by the difference equation (5.25).

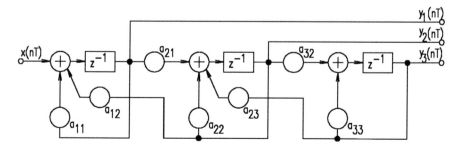

Figure 5.28 System of first-order subsystems with only a stripe matrix A

From a practical point of view, it is clear that the realisation of such a system is generally very complicated, as there are m^2 operations of multiplication and addition per sample. This is why only less general systems are usually used, in which most of the coefficients a_{ij} are *a priori* set to zero; an example of such a system with a stripe matrix **A** is shown in Figure 5.28. Even such simplified systems can still provide rather general possibilities for transfer functions and be advantageous with respect to particular practical properties.

Chapter 6
Signal enhancement by averaging

6.1 Principle of averaging

In practice, it is frequently the case that a signal of limited duration is repeated in time several or many times, always after a certain – not necessarily constant – period; such a signal is called a *repetitive signal*. Should such a received signal be corrupted by additive noise, it is possible, after receiving more repetitions, to improve the signal to noise ratio by averaging. We utilise the fact that, for every time instant t_l from the beginning of the finite useful signal, there exist more measurements of the corrupted signal values (i.e. of the mixture of the signal and noise for the time instants $t_k = t_{0i} + t_l$, which have a constant distance from the beginnings of repetitions, t_{0i}). While the signal component value is identical in all the measurements, the noise assumes different values and, if it is generated by a stationary stochastic process with a zero mean, it will tend to disappear in the calculated average of all the measurements. The signal value, on the contrary, naturally remains untouched by the averaging. Such measurements and calculations should be done independently in parallel for a set of time instants t_l, $l = 0, 1, \ldots N - 1$, separated by a suitably selected sampling period T, thus providing estimates of sampled signal values. Note that the term average should be understood in the more general sense of weighted average in which the individual measurements may have unequal effects. In this way – by cumulating more measurements – it is possible to improve the signal to noise ratio (SNR) for repetitive signals; therefore, the approach is also known as the group of *cumulating methods*, which perhaps describes the principle more precisely.

The basic requirement of all the averaging techniques is exact coherence of the cumulated signal runs; it is therefore necessary to determine exactly the beginning of each repetition and synchronise (register) all the repetitions before calculating the averages. This is easy if the repetitions are precisely periodic and the (constant) period is known, or if the averaged signals are artificially stimulated and the stimuli, although possibly irregular, are accessible. On the other hand, if the information on the start of every repetition is not *a priori* available, it must be determined from the measured signal. Such detection of the signal start then becomes a difficult problem as every repetition is usually deteriorated by noise which complicates determination of its beginning. Also, the complexity of the detection methods commonly requires an appreciable amount of time and, consequently, a delay (or even recording) has to be introduced into the signal path in order not to lose the front part of the signal.

The principle of cumulative methods can be seen in Figure 6.1. The real-time axis t of the repetitive signal is in the upper part; the sections containing the signal repetitions are to be extracted and unified on the auxiliary time axis τ in the lower part. They must be registered so that the starts of the repetitions agree, and the repetition runs are to be multiplied by proper weights and summed. We can assume that the signals are already discretised and that the beginnings of the repetitions coincide with certain instants of discrete time. Moreover, we suppose that the repetitions do not overlap, i.e. that the distances between beginnings of repetitions are of at least the same magnitude as the length NT of the repetitive signal sections. Below we shall use dual indexing for the time axes: index k as running from the origin of the real time axis t, with l used for indexing from the beginning of every repetition and therefore also of the auxiliary time axis, τ. It can be seen from the figure that, should the beginning of the ith repetition $(i = 0, 1, \ldots)$ be denoted $m_i T$, obviously $l = k - m_i$ in this repetition.

The input signal $x(kT)$ is formed by an additive mixture of the useful signal $s(kT)$ and noise $n(kT)$, $x(kT) = s(kT) + n(kT)$; it is assumed that both components are independent. The lth sample of ith repetition will be denoted $_i x_l = {}_i x(lT) = x((l + m_i)T)$.

If we implement the averaging in real time and follow the development of the cumulated signal at the output during the averaging process, we obtain, in the course of the jth repetition $(j = 0, 1, \ldots)$ from the beginning of the averaging, the output signal

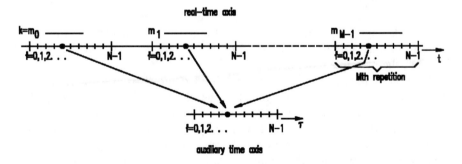

Figure 6.1 Principle of averaging of repetitive signals

$$y(kT) = y((l + m_j)T) = \sum_{i=0}^{j} [a_i \cdot {}_{(j-i)} x(lT)], \tag{6.1}$$

where a_i, $i = 0, 1, \ldots, j$ are the weight coefficients belonging to individual repetitions. For reasons that will be clarified later, the weight of the last – the newest – repetition is a_0, and a_j refers to the oldest repetition. A particular averaging technique and its properties are determined by the selection of a set of these weights.

We can express this sum by means of the running index k. Obviously $_{j-i} x_l = x_{l+m_{j-i}} = x_{k-m_j+m_{j-i}}$ so that

$$y(kT) = \sum_{i=0}^{j} a_i x((k - (m_j - m_{j-i}))T). \tag{6.2}$$

The concept of generating this sum corresponds to the structure of Figure 6.2, where the lth samples of all repetitions provided by a long chain of delay elements are summed with appropriate weights to form the lth averaged sample. If the useful signal does not repeat periodically, the tapping points on the line are generally different in each repetition. These would have to be determined at the beginning of every repetition in such a way that only the beginnings of each repetition would be taken into the sum; during a particular repetition the structure would remain unchanged. The variability of the structure is naturally a serious drawback, apart from the enormous number of memory registers needed to realise the very long delaying chain. The structure provides the cumulated output values only in synchronism with every incoming repetition; during the pauses between repetitions the output is only cumulated noise. The practical realisations are therefore based on a different structure; Figure 6.2 is only intended to help in understanding the properties of averaging techniques.

Practical realisations of cumulating (averaging) techniques are usually based on the generic structure given in Figure 6.3, which uses a bank of N parallel filters forming the accumulators for the individual time instants lT. The time

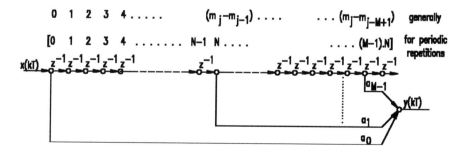

Figure 6.2 Nonrecursive structure clarifying the principle of averaging techniques

distances between successive repetitions are then irrelevant. At the time instant of the beginning of a repetition, the input channel is connected to the 0th cumulating channel. In the course of the repetition, the input is successively switched to further channels at the speed of sampling, so that at the lth sampling instant of the ith repetition, the sample $_i x_l$ of the input signal is brought to the input of the lth channel. Because a considerable amount of time may be needed for detection of the beginning of a repetition, so that the switching controller obtains the information on the start of a repetition with a delay, a corresponding delay must also be included between the signal input and the filter bank so that the beginning of the repetition is not lost. The output switch enables us to read the accumulated values at the same (or even a different) speed as the sampling rate. It can easily be verified that, should both switches be synchronised, the output during processing of a repetition will be the same as that which is provided by the structure of Figure 6.2. In this sense, the structures are equivalent. The structure of Figure 6.3 is, nevertheless, substantially more practical, primarily because it needs several orders less of registers for any chosen type of averaging. It also allows us to read the result, accumulated so far, at any time, independently of the state of input and at any speed (e.g. as needed for a display on an oscilloscope).

Every cumulating channel is paced just once during a repetition. Consequently, the structure of every one of them (Figure 6.4) is, with respect to Figure 6.2, simpler provided a delay element (denoted z'^{-1}) represents a delay between successive repetitions regardless of whether it is constant. The

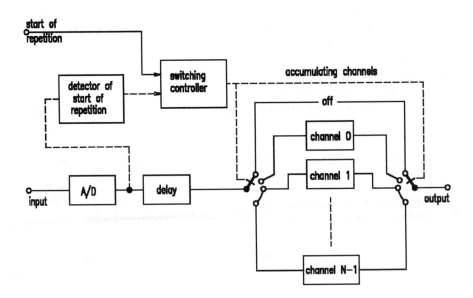

Figure 6.3 Basic realisation structure of an averaging system

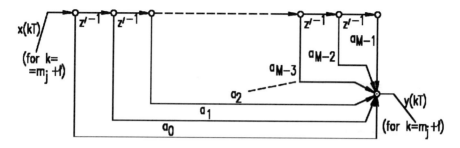

Figure 6.4 Nonrecursive structure explaining the function of a single cumulative channel

inner discrete time of a channel is therefore given by the occurrence of repetitions and not by the sampling frequency; consequently, the channel structure will have only j delay elements when processing the jth repetition. Now, it is also clear why we have introduced the indexing of weights as in eqn (6.1): the indices of weights increase with the delay of the samples weighted by them, as is usual with FIR structures. In spite of the simplification, this nonrecursive structure is still rather complicated and, if the number of averaged repetitions is not limited by the chosen method, even unrealisable, as the length of the delay chain would grow without limit. The cumulative channels usually are realised by means of equivalent but more economic recursive structures, as will be shown later.

Evaluating the frequency properties of averaging can be approached from two different standpoints. On the one hand, the averaging is under certain circumstances, as we shall see, a type of linear filtering and therefore we can investigate how the spectrum of the processed signal is influenced. On the other hand, the frequency properties of an individual cumulative channel are also interesting, as it is also a filter although paced by another frequency (or even irregularly).

In the special case of periodical repetitions, we can suppose without loss of generality that the useful section length NT is equal to the period of repetition so that eqn (6.2) simplifies to

$$y(kT) = \sum_{i=0}^{j} a_i x((j - iN)T). \qquad (6.3)$$

The structure according to Figure 6.2 is then (for a fixed j) fixed and is obviously an FIR filter. The impulse $\{h_k\}$ response of such a filter is then naturally finite, but gets longer with every repetition,

$$\{h_k\}: \quad h_k = \begin{cases} a_i, k = iN \\ 0, k \neq iN \end{cases}, \quad i = 0, 1, \cdots, j. \qquad (6.4)$$

The corresponding frequency response is given by the transfer $H(z) = \mathbb{Z}\{h_k\}$ as

$$G(\omega) = H(e^{j\omega T}) = \sum_{i=0}^{j} a_i e^{-j\omega i NT}, \qquad (6.5)$$

which is a periodic function with the period $2\pi/N$, called a *comb filter*. The averaging therefore transfers all the harmonic components of the input signal, that form the useful (periodic) component of such a repetitive signal, equally well, and all the other signal components that are noncoherent with the repetitions, are more or less attenuated.

The structure of an individual cumulative channel, according to Figure 6.4, is always a nonrecursive filter. Here, the requirement of repetition periodicity need not be postulated provided that the channel is paced once per repetition, regardless of the actual time difference between repetitions. As the impulse response of this filter is obviously

$$\{_{ch}h_k\}: \quad _{ch}h_k = a_k, \quad k = 0, 1, \cdots, j,$$

its frequency response is

$$G_{ch}(\omega) = H_{ch}(e^{j\Omega}) = \sum_{i=0}^{j} a_i e^{-ji\Omega}, \qquad (6.6)$$

where Ω is the normalised circular frequency (the real frequency relating to time cannot be used as the system under description is, in general, paced irregularly). We shall see later for the specific averaging methods that basically it is always a response of a lowpass type filter which transfers maximally only the DC (i.e. signal) component of the incoming sequence of samples.

It remains to determine the degree to which the signal-to-noise ratio can be generally improved by averaging. By substituting in eqn (6.1) the respective sum of components for the signal, taking into account the fact that the signal component is independent of the index of repetition, we obtain

$$y(kT) = \sum_{i=0}^{j} a_i ((j-i)s(lT) + (j-i)n(lT))$$

$$= s(lT) \sum_{i=0}^{j} a_i + \sum_{i=0}^{j} [a_i \cdot (j-i)n(lT)]. \qquad (6.7)$$

The first term expresses the signal component after cumulation, the second the noise component. While the signal component will change into a $\sum_{i=0}^{j} a_i$ — multiple of the original sample value s_l, the concrete value of the noise component, as a linear combination of j random values of noise, is naturally also a stochastic quantity and therefore only the mean noise power can be investigated.

Providing that the original continuous-time noise $n(t)$ before discretisation has been generated by a stationary and ergodic stochastic process described by the probability density $p(n)$, its mean power is

$$P_n = \lim_{T' \to \infty} \frac{1}{T'} \int_0^{T'} n^2(t)\,dt = \int_{-\infty}^{\infty} n^2 p(n)\,dt = \sigma_n^2;$$

the power of noise is therefore given by the variance of its distribution. With respect to the ergodicity, the instantaneous values $n(t)$ at the instants kT will have the same variance, so that the variance σ_n^2 is a measure of the average noise power even in the discrete input signal. Similarly, the noise level of the output is also characterised by the variance of the output noise component which is given by the sum of j realisations of identical stochastic variables weighted by coefficients a_i. From probability theory, the variance $\mathbb{D}$ of a linear combination of stochastic variables v_i is given by

$$\mathbb{D}\left(\sum_i a_i v_i\right) = \sum_i a_i^2 \sigma_i^2 + \sum_i \sum_l a_i a_l \sigma_{il},$$

where σ_i^2 are variances of individual variables and σ_{il} are covariances of pairs of the variables. With respect to the stationarity, the noise has the same variance σ_n^2 at every time instant; hence the output noise power σ_{nc}^2 is given by the variance of the second term in eqn (6.7),

$$\sigma_{nc}^2 = \sigma_n^2 \sum_{i=0}^{j} a_i^2 + \sum_{i=0}^{j} \sum_{l=0}^{j} a_i a_l \sigma_{il}. \tag{6.8}$$

It can be seen that eventual dependence between noise contributions from different repetitions increases the resulting variance and consequently reduces the efficiency of the averaging techniques. Thus, the possibilities are optimal in the case of independent contributions, which fortunately is the common case in practice. Then, the noise power is changed by averaging into a $\sum_{i=0}^{j} a_i^2$ – multiple of the original power.

The assumption of zero (or weak) correlation among the realisations of noise in the individual repetitions, and also that the noise is a centred (zero-mean) process, is decisive for the chance of success of averaging. On the other hand, further unnecessary conditions are often erroneously mentioned in the literature, such as a requirement for normal distribution or for whiteness – uniform spectral density etc. Possible correlations among successive samples of a repetition obviously have no influence; the form of the autocorrelation function in the range of one repetition is therefore irrelevant and, consequently, the noise spectrum can also be arbitrary. The cumulating process will, for example, be as effective if the noise is a harmonic signal with a random phase with respect to the beginnings of the repetitions.

The working hypotheses of zero (or low) noise correlation among individual repetitions can be verified in the case where the autocorrelation function of the pure noise (interference without signal) can be provided. If the function values converge for increasing delay to zero and are negligible for time differences corresponding to intervals between repetitions, the assumption is valid. Also *vice versa*: from knowledge of the autocorrelation function, the necessary minimum interval between successive repetitions may follow, which would influence the decision in the case where the repetition rate can be selected arbitrarily as, for example, with stimulated responses (in technical or biological systems). Should the noise have a narrow frequency band (e.g. power-line interference), the situation is more complicated as the autocorrelation function does not become negligible for any delays. Then, the low correlation of noise contributions can only be achieved by random interrepetition intervals, which again can be most easily realised for artificially stimulated responses or can follow from the nature of the source of the repetitive signal.

The average signal power is proportional to the average of the squares of the signal values; as all these values were changed by averaging (by the factor $\sum_{i=0}^{j} a_i$), the signal power was modified by the factor $(\sum_{i=0}^{j} a_i)^2$. Utilising the result mentioned after eqn (6.8), we could conclude that the achievable *improvement in power signal-to-noise* ratio is

$$K_p = \frac{\left(\sum_{i=0}^{j} a_i\right)^2}{\sum_{i=0}^{j} a_i^2}. \qquad (6.9)$$

Then, the improvement of average amplitude signal-to-noise ratio (e.g. in terms of signal voltage or current) is

$$K_U = \frac{\sum_{i=0}^{j} a_i}{\sqrt{\sum_{i=0}^{j} a_i^2}}. \qquad (6.10)$$

Thus, it can be seen that the averaging properties depend both on the number of repetitions taken into account and on the coefficients by which the individual repetitions are weighted.

It should be emphasised that, although we usually expect the interesting signal component to be deterministic, the noise component must always be stochastic and consequently even the result of cumulation is a random signal. The result derived in the previous paragraphs is the mean improvement that will be approached by the average improvement based on a large set of realisations. It must be taken into account that, especially if only a low number of repetitions can be cumulated, not only a rather low average improvement can be expected, as follows from eqns (6.9) and (6.10), but moreover some samples of the result will probably be encumbered by high errors. Such a gross error can, although rarely, appear even when cumulating a high number of repetitions. When interpreting the results of averaging, we must therefore take into consideration the possibility of such errors and treat the result with appropriate reserve. The fact that the derived improvement is only statistically valid is sometimes omitted, which can lead even to gross misinterpretations of the measurements.

6.2 Averaging with uniform weights

6.2.1 Uniform fixed-window averaging

The simplest type of averaging is the uniform-weight, fixed-window processing which takes into account an *a priori* chosen fixed number M of useful signal repetitions. Usually, those weight values selected preserve the original signal level,

$$a_i = \frac{1}{M}, \quad \forall i, \tag{6.11}$$

so that eqn (6.1) is modified into

$$y(kT) = \sum_{i=0}^{j} \left[\frac{1}{M} \cdot_{(j-i)} x(lT) \right], \quad j = 0, 1, \cdots, M-1. \tag{6.12}$$

This means that the set of the first M repetitions is accumulated and then the process is stopped. When using the system according to the basic scheme in Figure 6.3, it is possible to retrieve and analyse the result after stopping the averaging, as it is saved in the memories of the cumulative channels.

The improvement of the magnitude signal-to-noise ratio (SNR) according to eqn (6.10) during the cumulating process after the processing of j repetitions is

$$K_U = \frac{\displaystyle\sum_{i=0}^{j-1} 1/M}{\sqrt{\displaystyle\sum_{i=0}^{j-1} (1/M)^2}} = \frac{j/M}{\frac{1}{M}\sqrt{j}} = \sqrt{j}. \tag{6.13}$$

This increases with the square root of the number of processed repetitions and, after finishing the averaging process, is $\sqrt{M}$. It can be shown that this is the maximum possible improvement for the averaging of M repetitions, and, therefore, the weight set (6.11) is optimal in this sense. The level of useful signal in the cumulative channels obviously increases linearly with the number of repetitions.

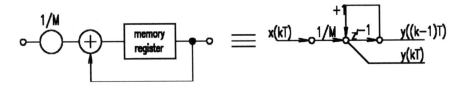

Figure 6.5 Structure of a cumulative channel for uniform, fixed-window averaging

The course of SNR improvement as dependent on the number of repetitions for a concrete number of repetitions, $M = 100$, is shown in Figure 6.6; the improvement always returns to one after reaching the maximum, i.e. when starting a new cycle of averaging.

The nonrecursive structure of a cumulative channel for this method (Figure 6.4) has only $M - 1$ delay elements, the contents of which are always deleted at the beginning of every averaging cycle. During the averaging, the structure of the registers is gradually filled from the left and the process is finished when the oldest sample reaches the end of the chain. The equivalent recursive structure is extremely simple in this case, as shown in Figure 6.5. Apart from the common multiplication of inputs by $1/M$ that may be realised easily in the common input branch, the channel is formed by the simplest first order recursive system realising the digital integrator. The system works at the border of stability but this does not endanger the function as, after a finite number of steps, the operation is always stopped and the registers initialised, so that the output always remains finite.

Uniform fixed-window averaging is fully satisfactory if we need the best possible improvement of averaged signal from a given number of repetitions, but only as a single-shot result. The possibility of following slow changes in the averaged signal is limited by the necessity to initialise the registers and

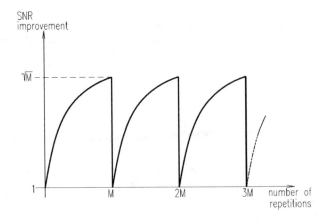

Figure 6.6 Dynamic properties of uniform fixed-window averaging

thus to delete the result repeatedly after processing every M repetitions. If we try to follow the repetitive signal continuously, a full quality signal (with the SNR improvement corresponding to the chosen M), with original amplitude, is available only once in M repetitions; between those instants the quality and amplitude are substantially lower, as shown in Figure 6.6.

As this type of system cannot, for fundamental reasons, work without external intervention (zeroing the registers) for unlimited time, it is not possible to characterise it in the frequency domain.

6.2.2 Uniform sliding-window averaging

The method of sliding (floating) window in uniform averaging removes the drawback of the fixed-window approach, which is the inability to follow continuously the slow development of a repetitive signal. Let us emphasise, however, that no averaging method can exactly follow any continuous development in the shape of repetitions, and that we made an assumption of fixed, invariable repetitions when deriving the properties of the averaging methods. We are now considering the case where changes are so slow that, in the frame of M repetitions, they will only be slightly apparent. Alternatively, we can consider the case of sudden changes, for which the instants of appearance are not known ahead and it is sufficient to detect them only after a number of repetitions. Nevertheless, the new values of the signal are again known exactly only after M repetitions if the signal did not change in the meantime.

The principle of the sliding window method is that, after receiving the first M repetitions, the contents of the cumulative registers are not deleted but rather refreshed before the processing of each new repetition by subtracting the oldest saved value. Thus, the register contents always carry information on the last M repetitions so that the coefficients weighting the repetitions can be expressed as follows,

$$a_i = \begin{cases} 1/M, & i = 0, 1, \cdots, M-1 \\ 0, & i \geq M \end{cases} . \tag{6.14}$$

The fixed number of terms in the sums is expressed by zero weights for terms older than M cycles of repetition. Thus, the cumulated result can be expressed, on the basis of eqn (6.1), for any j by the general formula

$$y(kT) = \sum_{i=0}^{\max(j, M-1)} \left[\frac{1}{M} \cdot {}_{(j-i)}x(lT) \right], \quad j = 0, 1, 2, \cdots. \tag{6.15}$$

The nonrecursive structure of the cumulative channel (Figure 6.4) remains the same as that for the fixed-window method. The only difference is that, after filling in the whole delay chain, this is not emptied before the next repetition but the values are shifted along, as in a common FIR filter, so that only the samples

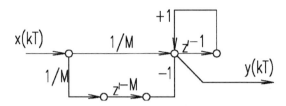

Figure 6.7 Recursive realisation of a cumulative channel with sliding-window averaging

from the last M repetitions form the output. Nevertheless, it is clear that the recursive structure of Figure 6.5 does not meet the requirements, because the information on the oldest sample, which should be removed from the sum in the following step, is missing. To provide this information, a long delay chain of M registers must complement the structure, as shown in Figure 6.7. The resulting structure is thus even more complicated than that for the nonrecursive model, only the number of additions in every step is lower.

A comparison of the complexity of uniform averaging with fixed window and averaging with sliding window clearly shows that the latter is orders of magnitude more complex. As N cumulative channels are always needed, N registers will suffice to implement the fixed-window system but $(M + 1)N$ registers are needed for the sliding-window method. For common values (N of the order of hundreds, M of the order of hundreds to hundreds of thousands), the sliding method is substantially more complicated and usually too expensive for a hardware realisation. That is why it is most commonly used in measuring systems using the services of computers.

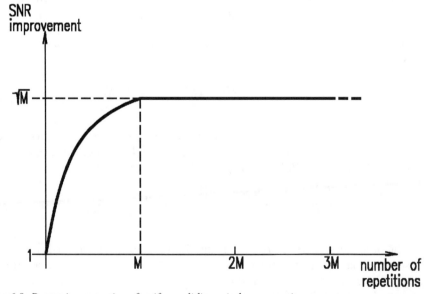

Figure 6.8 Dynamic properties of uniform sliding-window averaging

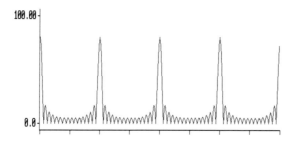

Figure 6.9 Frequency response of uniform sliding-window averaging for periodic repetitions
(M = 16)

The dynamic properties of sliding-window averaging are depicted in Figure
6.8 for the same conditions as in Figure 6.6. It can be seen that, when reaching
the steady state after the first M repetitions, both the signal level and the SNR
improvement are already constant. In the case of a sudden change in the signal
which leads to a new signal form, the output changes linearly during the following M repetitions and then stabilises in the new form. This is obviously the
optimum possible dynamic behaviour.

To conclude, let us show the properties of this type of averaging in the
frequency domain. We shall first analyse the overall frequency transfer of the
sliding-window averaging in the case where the repetitions are periodic. By substituting (6.14) into eqn (6.5), we obtain

$$G(\omega) = \sum_{i=0}^{M-1} \frac{1}{M} e^{-j\omega i NT}. \tag{6.16}$$

A concrete example of frequency response for $M = 16$ is in Figure 6.9. It can be
seen that this is a comb filter maximally emphasising the components of
frequencies $\omega = m(2\pi/NT)$, $m = 0, 1, 2, 3, \cdots$, which are the spectral lines of
the periodic signal with the period NT, which is, according to the assumption,
the repetitive signal to be processed. The noise components contained at other
frequencies are relatively suppressed, the higher the value of M.

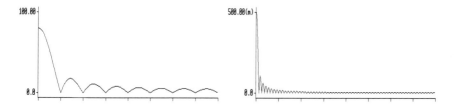

Figure 6.10 Frequency response of individual cumulative channel for uniform sliding-
window averaging (left M = 16, right M = 128)

We can also arrive at a similar conclusion on the basis of the frequency response of an individual cumulative channel according to eqn (6.6). After substitution we obtain

$$G_{ch}(\omega) = \sum_{i=0}^{M-1} \frac{1}{M} e^{-ji\Omega}, \qquad (6.17)$$

which, as seen in Figure 6.10, is the characteristic of a lowpass filter, as requested. Indeed, when calculating an individual sample y_l of the output, we want to enhance the invariant components of the input sequence and suppress the nonzero frequency components. The advantage of analysis using a single cumulative channel is obviously that the frequency-domain interpretation of properties is not limited to the case of periodic repetitions.

6.3 Exponential averaging

The weight coefficients of exponential averaging decrease as the index grows to the past,

$$a_i = q^i, \quad q \in (0, 1), \quad i = 0, 1, 2, \cdots, \qquad (6.18)$$

so that the most recent repetition has the greatest weight in the result and the influence of the previous repetitions is reduced as they become older. Compared with the previous method where the contribution of every repetition influenced the result with its full weight during the window duration (of M repetitions) and then was completely removed, the older values are now being gradually 'forgotten'. This is therefore also a sliding-window method but the window is not a finite-length rectangle as in the previous case; rather, it descends exponentially into the past and gets longer with every incoming repetition. Theoretically, the contributions of repetitions from the beginning of cumulating process are all included in the result (6.1); nevertheless, the contributions of very old values are very weak and they can be considered to be forgotten and neglected. This means that the result can also reflect slow changes in the signal shape in a similar way to uniform-weight sliding-window averaging.

By substituting (6.18) into eqn (6.1) we obtain

$$y(kT) = \sum_{i=0}^{j} [q^i \cdot_{(j-i)} x(lT)], \quad j = 0, 1, 2, \cdots. \qquad (6.19)$$

This formula means that the cumulative channel is a stable filter and can therefore work for an infinite time. Utilising the first term of the result (6.7), we obtain, by summing the geometrical series, the amplification factor for the useful signal $\sum_{i=0}^{j} a_i = \sum_{i=0}^{j} q^i = (1 - q^{j+1})/(1 - q)$, which gives, in the limit for a great number of repetitions, $1/(1 - q)$, so that the useful signal will be amplified against the original repetitions. Similarly, according to eqn (6.10), the running average improvement of amplitude signal-to-noise ratio will be

$$K_U = \frac{\displaystyle\sum_{i=0}^{j} a_i}{\sqrt{\displaystyle\sum_{i=0}^{j} a_i^2}} = \sqrt{\frac{1 - q^{j+1}}{1 + q^{j+1}}} \sqrt{\frac{1 + q}{1 - q}}$$

thus in the limit for $j \to \infty$

$$K_U = \sqrt{\frac{1 + q}{1 - q}}. \tag{6.20}$$

The resulting signal amplitude, as well as the average SNR improvement, thus depends on the feedback coefficient q – the closer it is to 1, the higher both parameters are, but also the longer it lasts before it approaches the steady-state limit.

Uniform fixed-window averaging may, as the optimum method, serve as a certain standard. The design of exponential averaging is then often based on a requirement that its properties should approach those of the uniform-weight method with a chosen M. Should we require that the average (limit) SNR improvements are identical, then q must be determined so that $\sqrt{M} = \sqrt{(1 + q)/(1 - q)}$, i.e.

$$q = \frac{M - 1}{M + 1}. \tag{6.21}$$

Figure 6.11 presents the courses of signal amplitude and SNR improvement of exponential averaging for $q = 0.980198$ in comparison with the uniform-sliding-window method with $M = 100$, which is the corresponding value according to eqn (6.21). In the upper part, the relative output signal level is depicted as being dependent on the number of received repetitions; the case shown describes a signal which remained constant until the 200th repetition and then its level dropped to one half. In the lower part of the figure, the average SNR improvement is also plotted against the number of received repetitions. It can be concluded that, from a practical point of view, exponential averaging is almost equivalent although slightly slower: after M repetitions it reaches 86 per cent of the final improvement and about the same percentage of the final ampli-tude; after 1.5 M repetitions the results differ from final ones by less than five per cent. On the other hand, exponential averaging reacts faster to sudden changes in the repetitive signal.

The nonrecursive structure of the exponential cumulative channel of Figure 6.4 will have a delay chain of the length corresponding to the number of so-far processed repetitions, i.e. the length will be increasing without a limit. The channel therefore cannot be realised nonrecursively. On the other

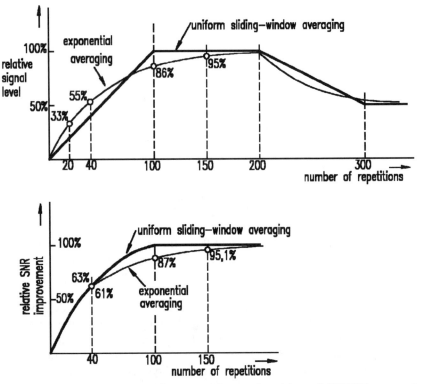

Figure 6.11 Dynamic properties of exponential averaging with q − 0.980198 in comparison
with uniform sliding-window averaging for M = 100

hand, the recursive realisation (Figure 6.12), which has the same impulse response, is very simple and differs from the channel for fixed-window uniform averaging only by the feedback coefficient equal to q. If q is selected so that $1 - q = 2^{-k}$, k natural, then the channel can be realised according to the equivalent scheme as in Figure 6.13, where the multiplication can be substituted for by bit-shift.

Note that the influence of rounding errors in exponential averaging may manifest itself adversely by causing so-called dead bands, which means that the exponentially changing curves do not exactly reach their limit values. Alternating or random rounding, or adding a certain amount of noise (*dithering*), can

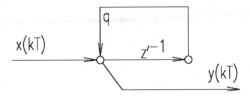

Figure 6.12 Recursive realisation of a cumulative channel for exponential averaging

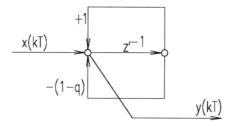

Figure 6.13 Alternative recursive realisation of exponential cumulative channel

solve this problem. Nevertheless, the accuracy of today's signal processors allows for neglecting the finite precision phenomena like this unless extremely high SNR improvement is needed, requiring hundreds of thousands or more repetitions to be averaged.

Using such 'forgetting' cumulative channels, we obtain a simple floating-window averaging system which is only slightly more complex (by N multiplications per repetition) than the fixed-window system but enables almost as good observation of slow development in analysed repetitive signals as does the substantially more complex uniform-weight sliding-window system.

As a closing consideration, let us compare the properties of exponential averaging in the frequency domain with those of the sliding-window method. The overall frequency transfer of exponential averaging will approach, according to eqns (6.5) and (6.18) in the limit for a large number of processed periodical repetitions, the expression

$$G(\omega) = \sum_{i=0}^{\infty} q^i e^{-j\omega i NT} = \frac{e^{j\omega NT}}{e^{j\omega NT} - q}. \tag{6.22}$$

The concrete amplitude frequency response for the value of q, corresponding to the value of M from Figure 6.9, is depicted in Figure 6.14. It can be seen that, again, the system behaves as a comb filter with similar properties as those for the sliding-window method but the response is smoother (the visible ripple is due to a finite number – 16 – of included repetitions).

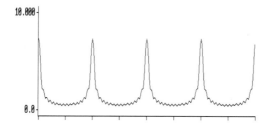

Figure 6.14 Overall frequency response of exponential averaging for periodic repetitions
($q = 0.88235$, number of cumulated repetitions: 16)

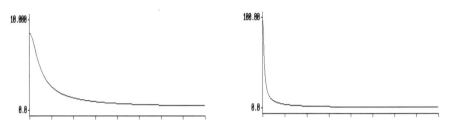

Figure 6.15 Frequency responses of individual exponential cumulative channel for unlimited number of repetitions (left: q = 0.88235, right: q = 0.984496)

The frequency response of an individual cumulative channel, according to eqn (6.6), is

$$G_{ch}(\omega) = \sum_{i=0}^{\infty} q^i e^{-ji\Omega}. \tag{6.23}$$

From Figure 6.15 it can be seen that this is again a lowpass-type characteristic; in comparison with Figure 6.10, we may conclude that the difference with respect to the sliding-window channel is similar to that for the overall characteristics. A simple example of averaging is in Figure 6.16.

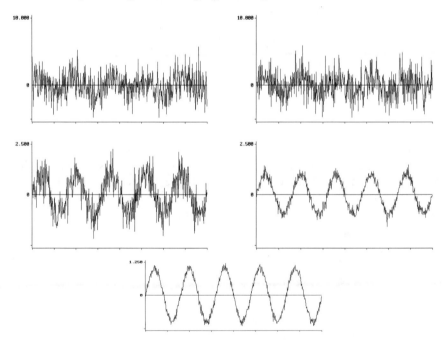

Figure 6.16 Simulation of uniform averaging; upper row, two different realisations of the noisy signal; middle row: results of averaging after processing of M = 10 and M = 100 repetitions; lower row: result of averaging M = 400 repetitions

Chapter 7
Complex signals and their applications

7.1 Representation of complex signals

Signals in their classical analogue form, represented by a suitable physical quantity, e.g. by electrical voltage at a certain point of a circuit, naturally acquire only real values in every time instant. Two such voltages would be needed to represent a signal, the values of which could be complex; nevertheless, to construct reliable circuits maintaining the proper relationship between the component signals would be extremely difficult. On the other hand, digital representation enables us to represent simply signals with samples of complex value – such signals will be called *complex signals*. Subsequently, advanced methods using complex signals can be conceived that would not be feasible with analogue signal representation.

A pair of numbers, which are interpreted as the real and imaginary components, respectively, of the complex sample value, represents every sample of a complex signal,

$$f(t_n) = f_n = \text{Re}(f_n) + j\,\text{Im}(f_n) = f_{Rn} + jf_{In}. \tag{7.1}$$

Alternatively, the sample may be represented in polar form by its magnitude and phase,

$$f_n = |f_n| \exp(j\arg(f_n)) = f_{An} e^{j\varphi_{fn}}. \tag{7.2}$$

In place of a single sequence of scalar values as in the case of a common scalar signal, the complex signal is therefore represented by a sequence of complex vectors or, in other words, by a pair of scalar sequences. Which of the above representations will be chosen depends on the prevailing type of operation to which the complex samples are to be submitted. Let us recall that the sum of two complex samples is

$$f_n + g_n = (f_{Rn} + g_{Rn}) + j(f_{In} + g_{In}),$$

and the product can be calculated as

$$f_n g_n = (f_{An} g_{An}) e^{j(\varphi_{fn} + \varphi_{gn})} = (f_{Rn} g_{Rn} - f_{In} g_{In}) + j(f_{Rn} g_{In} + f_{In} g_{Rn}).$$

Obviously, the product is easier to implement in polar representation but addition can reasonably be calculated using only Cartesian components so that,
usually, with only rare exceptions, the representation (7.1) is preferred in spite
of more complicated multiplication.

Notice that, evidently, the complex sequence of a finite length of N samples
can carry generally twice the amount of information as the real signal of the
same length and number representation precision.

7.2 The Hilbert transform and the analytical signal

The one-dimensional continuous *Hilbert transform* can be defined as the convolution of the transformed function and the inverse value of the relevant variable,

$$\mathcal{H}\{f(t)\} = \frac{1}{\pi} f(t) * \frac{1}{t} = \frac{1}{\pi} \int_{-\infty}^{\infty} f(\tau) \frac{1}{t - \tau} \, dt. \tag{7.3}$$

(The improper integral is to be evaluated in the sense of the principal value, i.e.
the limit has to be applied symmetrically with respect to the singular point.)

As signal theory shows, this transform expresses the relationship between real
parts $F_R(\omega)$ and imaginary parts $F_I(\omega)$ of the spectra of so-called causal signals
which fulfil the condition $f(t) = 0, t < 0$,

$$F_I(\omega) = -\frac{1}{\pi} \int_{-\infty}^{\infty} \frac{F_R(\omega')}{\omega - \omega'} \, d\omega', \quad F_R(\omega) = \frac{1}{\pi} \int_{-\infty}^{\infty} \frac{F_I(\omega')}{\omega - \omega'} \, d\omega'. \tag{7.4}$$

Realising that the inverse Fourier transform is almost symmetrical to the
forward transform and has, therefore, quite analogous properties, we might
expect that a symmetrical relationship to eqn (7.4) could also exist. It can be
shown that this is actually the case, i.e. if the signal is complex and has components which form a Hilbert-transform pair, the spectrum will be nonzero only
for positive frequency values. This is an advantageous property, especially
when frequency translation of signals is intended, as we shall see (recall that
the spectrum of every real signal is distributed on both sides of zero frequency
as $F(\omega) = F^*(-\omega)$). A complex signal $f(t)$ defined in this way, for which

$$f_I(t) = \mathcal{H}\{f_R(t)\}, \tag{7.5}$$

is called the *analytical signal*; as far as we are able to realise the Hilbert transform, the analytical signal can be generated for every real signal f_R. This
signal, besides being characterised by a one-sided spectrum, also has other inter-
esting properties: its absolute value $|f(t)|$ forms the so-called *envelope* of the
signal $f_R(t)$ and the derivative of its phase, $\partial/\partial t \arctan[f_r(t)/f_R(t)]$, forms the
instantaneous frequency of the signal. Both these quantities are particularly
useful when analysing narrowband signals, e.g. amplitude or frequency

modulated. Notice that the analytical signal – owing to the fixed relation (7.5) between its components – does not carry more information than any one of its components.

As the continuous-variable Hilbert transform cannot be directly converted into a discrete transform, we will derive the discrete version of the analytical signals, with analogous properties, independently. Let us try to generate a complex signal $v_n = v(nT)$ that will have a one-sided spectrum in the general sense appropriate to discrete signals,

$$Z\{v_n\}|_{z=\exp(j\omega T)} = V(e^{j\omega T}) = 0 \quad \text{for } -\pi \leq \omega T < 0. \tag{7.6}$$

Denote

$$v_n = x_n + jy_n. \tag{7.7}$$

As, of course, both the real component x_n and the imaginary component, y_n, are real signals, each of them has its own spectrum $X(e^{j\omega T})$ and $Y(e^{j\omega T})$, respectively. According to eqn (7.7), with respect to the linearity of the Z-transform,

$$V(e^{j\omega T}) = X(e^{j\omega T}) + jY(e^{j\omega T}). \tag{7.8}$$

Therefore, with respect to property (7.6), it must be valid on the lower semicircle, i.e. in the range $-\pi \leq \omega T < 0$,

$$Y(e^{j\omega T}) = jX(e^{j\omega T}). \tag{7.9}$$

The partial (naturally complex) spectra can be rewritten in greater detail as

$$X(e^{j\omega T}) = X_R(e^{j\omega T}) + jX_I(e^{j\omega T})$$
$$Y(e^{j\omega T}) = Y_R(e^{j\omega T}) + jY_I(e^{j\omega T}). \tag{7.10}$$

As x_n, y_n are real signals, their spectra must acquire complex conjugate values in the symmetrical position $z = e^{-j\omega T}$,

$$X(e^{-j\omega T}) = X_R(e^{j\omega T}) - jX_I(e^{j\omega T}),$$
$$Y(e^{-j\omega T}) = Y_R(e^{j\omega T}) - jY_I(e^{j\omega T}). \tag{7.11}$$

Let us now determine the value $Y(e^{j\omega T})$ in the upper semicircle, i.e. in the interval $0 \leq \omega T < \pi$. Obviously $Y(e^{j\omega T}) = Y^*(e^{-j\omega T})$, and as the variable $e^{-j\omega T}$ in Y^* is now in the range $-\pi \leq \omega T < 0$, Y^* can be substituted according to (7.9) and further X according to eqn. (7.11), thus obtaining

$$Y(e^{j\omega T}) = Y^*(e^{-j\omega T}) = [jX(e^{-j\omega T})]^* = [j(X_R(e^{j\omega T}) - jX_I(e^{j\omega T}))]^*$$
$$= -j(X_R(e^{j\omega T}) + jX_I(e^{j\omega T})) = -jX(e^{j\omega T}) \tag{7.12}$$

The signal y_n (the imaginary part of the analytical signal v_n) can therefore be obtained from the real part x_n according to eqns (7.9) and (7.12), which means processing by a discrete linear time-invariant system, the frequency response of which is

$$G_{\mathbb{H}}(\omega) = \begin{cases} -j, & 0 \leq \omega T < \pi \\ j, & -\pi \leq \omega T < 0, \end{cases} \tag{7.13}$$

and which we shall call the *discrete Hilbert transformer*. Its frequency response, which is naturally periodic, is depicted in Figure 7.1.

Finally, we shall derive the impulse response of the Hilbert transformer. As its frequency response is, according to eqn (2.26), given by the Fourier series $G(\omega) = H(e^{j\omega T}) = \sum_{n=-\infty}^{\infty} h_n e^{-j\omega nT}$ where the coefficients h_n are the values of the impulse response, we obtain

$$h_n^{\mathbb{H}} = \frac{1}{2\pi} \int_{-\pi}^{\pi} G_{\mathbb{H}}(\omega) e^{j\omega nT} d(\omega T) = \frac{1}{2\pi} \left(\int_0^{\pi} -je^{j\omega nT} d(\omega T) + \int_{-\pi}^{0} je^{j\omega nT} d(\omega T) \right)$$

$$= \begin{cases} \dfrac{1 - e^{jn\pi}}{n\pi}, & n \neq 0 \\ 0, & n = 0. \end{cases}$$

It is obvious that the Hilbert transformer is noncausal so that it is impossible to realise it exactly. One of the possibilities of acceptable approximation is an FIR linear-phase realisation obtained by symmetrically shortening the impulse response and delaying it by half of its length (Figure 7.2). The frequency response of the same approximation is in Figure 7.3.

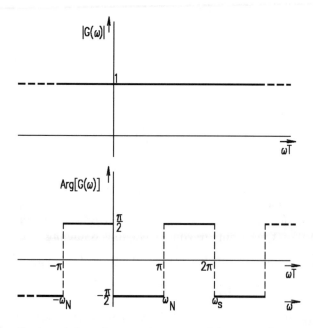

Figure 7.1 Amplitude and phase frequency responses of discrete Hilbert transformer

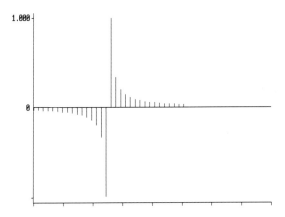

Figure 7.2 Impulse response of a causal FIR approximation (N = 64) of the discrete Hilbert transformer

Notice that even the theoretical discrete impulse response, all odd values of which are zero, is not given by samples of the impulse response $h(t) = 1/\pi t$ of the continuously working Hilbert transformer. Should we try to approximate the discrete Hilbert transformer by a filter derived from the continuous transformer using the impulse-invariance method, we would obtain a quite useless result as the frequency response of the analogue model is not band limited.

The inverse Hilbert transformer will obviously have the frequency transform

$$G_{\mathbb{H}^{-1}}(\omega) = G_{\mathbb{H}}^{-1}(\omega) = \begin{cases} j, & 0 \leq \omega T < \pi \\ -j, & -\pi \leq \omega T < 0 \end{cases} = G_{\mathbb{H}}^{*}(\omega),$$

and, consequently, its impulse response will be

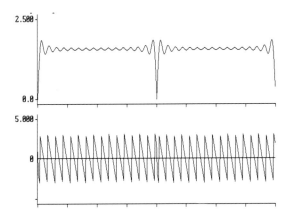

Figure 7.3 Frequency response of FIR approximation of the Hilbert transform as in Figure 7.2, in the range $\langle 0, \omega_s \rangle$

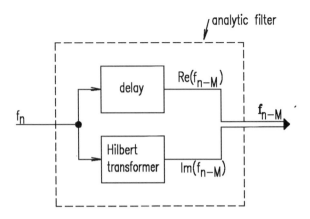

Figure 7.4 Principal block diagram of analytical filter

$$h_n^{\mathbb{H}^{-1}} = h_{-n}^{\mathbb{H}} = -h_n^{\mathbb{H}}.$$

Calculation of the analytical signal (more precisely, of its approximation) can be described by the block diagram in Figure 7.4. The system is called the *analytical filter*; the original real signal $f(nT)$ forms its input, and its output is the complex signal $f(nT)$, the imaginary part of which, $f_I(nT)$, is the output of the Hilbert transformer and the real part $f_R(nT) = f(nT - MT)$ is the delayed version of the input signal. The delay by M sampling periods in the real-component branch serves to compensate for the delay caused by the causal Hilbert transformer approximation; both delays must be identical in order to preserve coherence of the analytical signal components. The frequency response of the complete analytical filter using the approximation of the Hilbert transformer (Figure 7.2) is depicted in Figure 7.5.

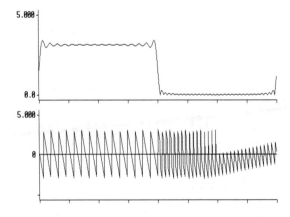

Figure 7.5 Frequency response of approximated analytical filter in the range $\langle 0, \omega_s \rangle$

It is worth noting that only the relation of components in a Hilbert transform pair is important to the analytical signal, regardless of what were the primary and secondary (derived) components. It is therefore equally possible to arrange the filter in the opposite way: inverse Hilbert transform in the real-component branch and the corresponding delay in the remaining branch.

Another approach to approximating the analytical filter based on translating the frequency response of a lowpass filter will be described in Section 7.3.3.

7.3 Translation of spectra and frequency responses

7.3.1 Plain multiplicative modulation and demodulation

A frequent task in telecommunications (and, though less frequently, in other areas) is the modification of the signal spectrum in such a way that the signal could be transferred by a channel with given, for the original signal unsuitable, frequency properties. A similar problem arises should the signal be archived onto a medium the properties of which only allow saving signals with a modified spectrum. This problem is generally solved by *modulation*, which is the subject of specialised literature. Here we shall only deal with the basic (and perhaps most frequent) requirement: to shift the spectrum $X(\omega)$ (Figure 7.6) of a band-limited (BL) signal $x(t)$, if possible without an increase in the bandwidth, to a different position on the frequency axis.

Discrete modulation methods use (in contrast to analogue methods) the ease of digital multiplication. The simplest method is plain multiplicative modulation which provides the modulated signal $u(t)$ by multiplication of the original signal $x(t)$ by a *carrier* signal $c(t) = \cos(\omega t)$. (For the sake of comprehensibility, we shall first treat the case of continuous signals; the influence of discretising will be mentioned later.) Recall that

$$c(t) = \cos(\omega t) = (e^{j\omega t} + e^{-j\omega t})/2,$$

so that the spectrum of the carrier is

$$C(\omega) = \pi(\delta(\omega - \omega_0) + \delta(\omega - \omega_0)),$$

Figure 7.6 Schematic spectrum of a BL signal (dotted – periodic extension due to discretisation)

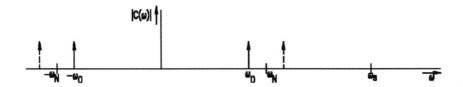

Figure 7.7 Spectrum of a real carrier signal (dashed – periodic extension)

(Figure 7.7). As the modulated signal is the product $f(t) = x(t)c(t)$, its spectrum is given by the convolution of partial spectra

$$F(\omega) = \frac{1}{2\pi} X(\omega) * C(\omega) = \frac{1}{2} \int_{-\omega}^{\omega} X(\omega - u)[\delta(u - \omega_0) + \delta(u + \omega_0)]\,du$$

$$= \frac{1}{2} X(\omega - \omega_0) + \frac{1}{2} X(\omega + \omega_0). \tag{7.14}$$

Instead of the original spectrum surrounding zero frequency in the range $\langle -B, B \rangle$, we obtain two shifted replicas of the spectrum around the frequencies ω_0 and $-\omega_0$ (Figure 7.8). These obviously correspond to a real-valued signal of the original information content but in the physical frequency range $\langle \omega_0 - B, \omega_0 + B \rangle$. The bandwidth of the modulated signal is doubled in comparison with the original one, and the carrier frequency is suppressed completely. Should interference between the two replicas be avoided, the carrier frequency must fulfil the condition $\omega_0 > B$.

If we work with discrete signals provided by sampling continuous signals, the complete spectral representation will become periodic, as shown in Figure 7.9. It can be seen that, should the aliasing be prevented, the sampling frequency ω_s must fulfil the inequality $\omega_s > 2(\omega_0 + B)$. Nevertheless, it should be mentioned that the relatively narrow band (bandwidth $2B$) enables *undersampling*. This means selection of a lower sampling frequency such that the unavoidable aliasing does not cause interference between spectra but only leads to filling up the unused parts of the frequency range. For communication purposes, if an analogue signal should be transferred, a bandpass filter can be used to select the proper frequency band of this spectrum.

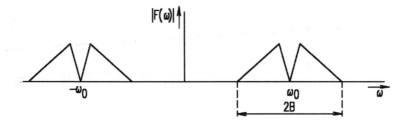

Figure 7.8 Spectrum of a continuous-time modulated signal

Figure 7.9 Spectrum of discrete modulated signal with too low sampling frequency

Demodulation – i.e. obtaining the original signal from its modulated version – is provided, after eventual sampling, again by multiplication by the auxiliary carrier signal followed by limiting of the frequency band to the original range $\langle -B, B \rangle$. Let us first show again the basic idea for the continuous signal; the product will be $v(t) = f(t) . c(t)$ and therefore the corresponding spectrum

$$V(\omega) = \frac{1}{2\pi} F(\omega) * C(\omega)$$

$$= \frac{1}{4} \int_{-\infty}^{\infty} [X(\omega - \omega_0 - u) + X(\omega + \omega_0 - u)][\delta(u - \omega_0) + \delta(u + \omega_0)] \, du$$

$$= \frac{1}{4} X(\omega - 2\omega_0) + \frac{1}{4} X(\omega) + \frac{1}{4} X(\omega) + \frac{1}{4} X(\omega + 2\omega_0), \tag{7.15}$$

as depicted in Figure 7.10. It can be seen that the spectrum contains components of the modulated signal with doubled carrier frequency, which can be suppressed by a lowpass filter with cut-off frequency B. The useful component in the lower-frequency part of the spectrum is a precise replica of the original-signal spectrum so that the filtered signal is identical to the original (if change of magnitude is disregarded).

When working with sampled signals, the spectrum will of course be periodic. Undersampling, i.e. use of a sampling frequency lower than $2(2\omega_0 + B)$, is again possible but the sampling frequency must be selected in such a way that no products caused by spectral periodicity would fall into the baseband $\langle -B, B \rangle$.

The requirement for complete coherence of the auxiliary carrier with the modulating carrier is fundamental – both the frequency and relative phase with respect to the translated signal (i.e. including possible transport-delay influence) must be identical. We will not go into details concerning the problems

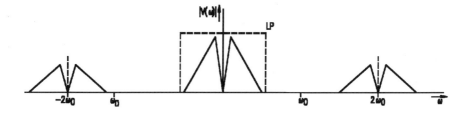

Figure 7.10 Spectrum of continuous signal after demodulation multiplication

of synchronisation of both carriers, possibly a great distance apart from each other, but we shall show the influence of improper frequency or phase. Should the auxiliary signal $c'(t)$ have the frequency $\omega_1 = \omega_0 - \Delta\omega$, we obtain by modifying eqn (7.15)

$$V(\omega) = \frac{1}{2\pi} F(\omega) * C'(\omega)$$

$$= \frac{1}{4} \int_{-\infty}^{\infty} [X(\omega - \omega_0 - u) + X(\omega + \omega_0 - u)][\delta(u - \omega_1) + \delta(u + \omega_1)]\,du$$

$$= \frac{1}{4} X(\omega - \omega_1 - \omega_0) + \frac{1}{4} X(\omega + \Delta\omega) + \frac{1}{4} X(\omega - \Delta\omega)$$

$$+ \frac{1}{4} X(\omega + \omega_1 + \omega_0). \tag{7.16}$$

All the replicas of the spectrum are thus shifted in frequency with respect to the previous case (Figure 7.11). Although the shift of high-frequency components that will be removed by subsequent filtering is irrelevant, the two baseband components are mutually shifted so that they cannot be properly added. A distortion of the resulting spectrum (and corresponding signal) follows which increases with growing $\Delta\omega$.

In the case where the frequency is precise but the phase is shifted just (exactly) by 90 degrees, the auxiliary carrier multiplying the modulated signal is in fact $c''(t) = \sin(\omega t)$ and by modification of eqn (7.15) we obtain

$$V(\omega) = \frac{1}{2\pi} F(\omega) * C''(\omega)$$

$$= \frac{1}{4j} \int_{-\infty}^{\infty} [X(\omega - \omega_0 - u) + X(\omega + \omega_0 - u)][\delta(u - \omega_0) + \delta(u + \omega_0)]\,du$$

$$= -j\left(\frac{1}{4} X(\omega - 2\omega_0) + \frac{1}{4} X(\omega) - \frac{1}{4} X(\omega) - \frac{1}{4} X(\omega + 2\omega_0)\right), \tag{7.17}$$

so that the useful component disappears completely. The same will apply for a phase error of 270 degrees. Similarly, it can be shown that, for a phase shift of

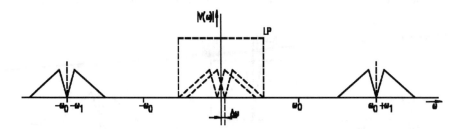

Figure 7.11 Spectrum after demodulation multiplication by auxiliary carrier with an imprecise frequency

180 degrees, the useful signal will again appear with the same amplitude as for 0 degrees but inverted (of opposite sign) with respect to the original signal. The demodulated signal varies between these extremes in the case of a slight frequency imprecision, which can be interpreted as a slow phase change.

7.3.2 Single-sideband modulation

The plain multiplicative modulation as described in the previous section has the disadvantage that the modulated signal has sidebands on both sides of the carrier frequency, each conveying complete information on the original signal. This obvious redundancy can be removed by a more sophisticated modulation method – SSB modulation – producing only single-sideband modulated signals.

Such a signal can be provided by a procedure the simple principle of which is illustrated by the block diagram in Figure 7.12 and by the spectrum development in the course of processing in Figure 7.13. For simplicity, we shall again restrict ourselves to the continuous signal case; the influence of discretisation has already been discussed and will be considered as understood. The first step of SSB modulation consists in removing the redundant left sideband of the original signal spectrum by analytical filtering, as explained in Section 7.2; the result is the complex analytical signal $x(t)$ with single-side spectrum $X_+(\omega)$. Next, the complex carrier $c(t) = e^{j\omega_0 t}$, the spectrum of which is a single line $C(\omega) = 2\pi\delta(\omega - \omega_0)$, multiplies the signal. Thus, the modulated signal is $f(t) = x(t)c(t)$ with the corresponding spectrum

$$F(\omega) = \frac{1}{2\pi} X_+(\omega) * C(\omega) = \int_{-\omega}^{\omega} X_+(\omega - u)\delta(u - \omega_0)\,du = X_+(\omega - \omega_0). \quad (7.18)$$

It is therefore, only a shift of the single sided spectrum by ω_0 to the desired new position on the frequency axis. However, the signal $f(t)$ is complex and as such rather inappropriate for the transfer either in analogue or digital form. If we use only the real part of this signal, $f_R(t) = \text{Re}\{f(t)\}$, we obtain a real signal with symmetrical spectrum as in Figure 7.13d, which obviously occupies only the same amount of bandwidth $2B$ as the original signal. Thus, we have finally

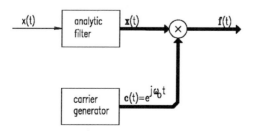

Figure 7.12 Block diagram of digital SSB modulation

obtained a real modulated signal in the proper frequency range without any increase in the frequency band requirements.

Such a signal can be summed with similarly modulated signals using different carrier frequencies, e.g. differing from ω_0 by integer multiples of B (Figure 7.13e). The spectra of individual signals obviously do not interfere, the mixture thus can be transferred as a single communication signal and, at the receiving end, the individual component signals can be separated from the mixture simply by bandpass filtering. This is the principle of *frequency multiplexing*.

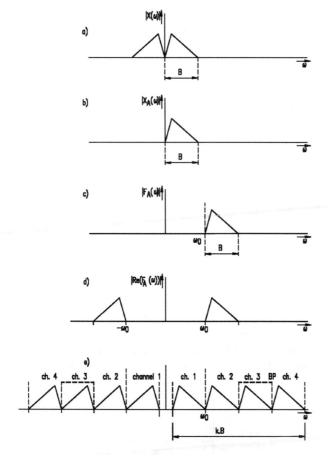

Figure 7.13 Spectrum development in steps of SSB modulation (only the basic period of the periodic spectrum is depicted)

    a Spectrum of original signal
    b Spectrum of analytical version of original signal
    c Spectrum of complex modulated signal
    d Spectrum of real component of signal c
    e Spectrum of sum of modulated real signals prepared for transfer in frequency multiplexing

Demodulation consists again in multiplication by the corresponding harmonic signal. If the modulated signal is analytical, as in Figure 7.13c, the auxiliary carrier must be $e^{-j\omega_0 t}$ as can be derived in a similar way to eqn (7.18); this will bring the analytical signal again to the original frequency position. Then, omitting the imaginary component of the signal will restore the original two-sided spectrum and therefore provide the original signal (disregarding the changed amplitude). Should the real SSB modulated signal corresponding to Figure 7.13d be demodulated, this can be done by multiplying the signal by the real auxiliary carrier $c(t)$. Similarly to eqn (7.15), we obtain in this way

$$V(\omega) = \frac{1}{2\pi} F_d(\omega) * C(\omega)$$

$$= \frac{1}{4} \int_{-\infty}^{\infty} [X_+(\omega - \omega_0 - u) + X_-(\omega + \omega_0 - u)] . [\delta(u - \omega_0) + \delta(u + \omega_0)] \, du$$

$$= \frac{1}{4} X_+(\omega - 2\omega_0) + \frac{1}{4} X_-(\omega) + \frac{1}{4} X_+(\omega) + \frac{1}{4} X_-(\omega + 2\omega_0). \tag{7.19}$$

After filtering out the high-frequency bands at the doubled carrier frequency, we again obtain the complete two-sided spectrum and therefore also the corresponding original signal, although with a lower amplitude than in the case of double-sideband modulation.

7.3.3 Approximation of filters with an asymmetrical frequency response

Let us recall that, after multiplying a signal by the sequence $e^{j\Delta\omega nT}$ term by term, the resulting product signal has a spectrum which is the exact replica of the original spectrum merely shifted on the frequency axis by $\Delta\omega$. This can be concluded on the basis of eqn (7.18) which is valid for any signals, not only analytical signals. When using this frequency-shift method, no interference between the symmetrical parts of the spectra can appear as can happen during plain multiplicative modulation. Therefore, the frequency shift can be arbitrary, even a fraction of the signal bandwidth, without leading to any irreversible information loss. This interesting fact can be utilised for designing filters with a frequency response which is asymmetrical with respect to the zero frequency, as is, for example, the case with the analytical filter.

The discrete analytical filter can also be interpreted as a bandpass filter having an asymmetrical frequency response as approximated in Figure 7.5, i.e. in an ideal case with the passband $\langle 0, \omega_s/2 \rangle$. This response can alternatively be considered as being derived by shifting the ideal lowpass response (with cut-off frequency $\omega_s/4$) by the half bandwidth (see the lower part of Figure 7.14).

The time-domain counterpart of such a frequency response is obviously the impulse response obtained from the lowpass filter impulse response by the frequency translation $\omega_s/4$. The resulting impulse response, as the product of multiplication by $e^{j(\omega_s/4)nT}$, is naturally a sequence of complex numbers.

This approach can be generalised: any bandpass filter with an asymmetrical frequency response can be designed by frequency translation $\Delta\omega$ of a suitably selected lowpass filter. The design procedure of such a filter has the following steps:

- design of an FIR lowpass filter with the required bandwidth and of the necessary quality given by the length of the filter and the design method used;
- term-by-term multiplication of the obtained impulse response by the sequence $e^{j\Delta\omega nT}$;
- realisation of the FIR filter with the obtained complex impulse response.

An example of a filter designed in this way and applied as an approximation of the analytical filter is depicted in Figure 7.14. The FIR analytical filter is represented here as a convolutor operating above the input signals by convoluting them with the impulse response provided by the above-mentioned method.

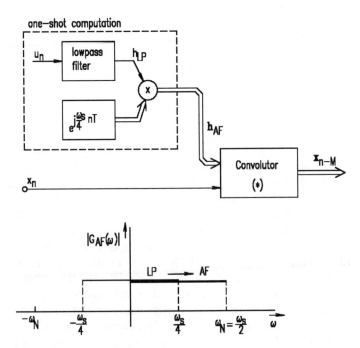

Figure 7.14 Principle of analytical filter design by frequency translation of a lowpass filter

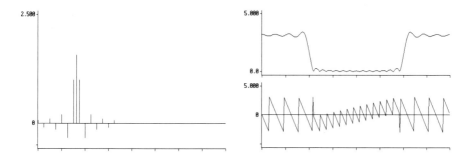

Figure 7.15 Responses of the parent lowpass filter (left: impulse response; right: frequency response in the range $\langle 0, \omega_s \rangle$)

Needless to say, the calculation of the time-invariant impulse response of the analytical filter will be done ahead, i.e. only once, in practical realisations. In the following Figures 7.15–7.17, properties of the initial lowpass filter, of the modified filter (the analytical filter approximation) and results of simulated processing of a narrowband signal are illustrated. Notice the impulse response of the analytical filter, realised in this way. It has a dual structure compared with the one in Figure 7.4: the inverse Hilbert transformer is now in the real branch and the pure delay is in the imaginary branch. It is interesting to realise that they have appeared without being explicitly designed.

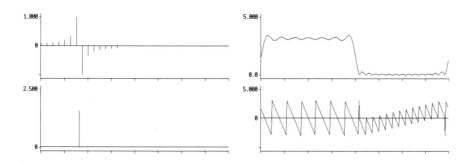

Figure 7.16 Responses of the approximated analytical filter obtained by frequency translation of the lowpass filter from Figure 7.15 (left: real and imaginary part of impulse response; right: amplitude and phase frequency responses in the range $\langle 0, \omega_s \rangle$)

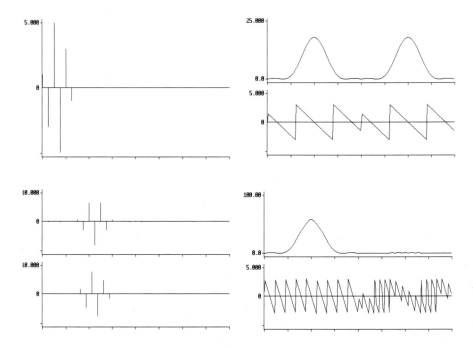

*Figure 7.17 Simulation of the effect of an approximated analytical filter from Figure 7.16
to a narrowband signal (upper part: input real signal and its spectrum; lower
part: real and imaginary components of complex output signal and its
spectrum)*

Chapter 8
Correlation analysis

8.1 Introduction

Correlation and covariance are quantities characterising relationships among stochastic variables; correlation and covariance functions then describe relationships inside or among stochastic processes, as we saw in Section 4.2. The present chapter will show properties of these functions and possibilities for their estimation based on received signals or measured data. Also, some important application areas for correlation analysis will be briefly described.

Correlation analysis always investigates a relationship between two stochastic variables, however many such couples may be analysed at one time, if passing from one couple to another can be expressed by suitable variable parameters, and if a functional rule can describe the corresponding change in the degree of correlation. This is the way to correlation and covariance functions.

This transition is vividly illustrated by the following elementary example documented in the first few figures.

Let us suppose that the stochastic process $a(t)$ is white noise, i.e. that there is no dependence between its values, however close, so that for any pair of time values, t_i, t_j, the correlation will be zero unless the times are identical. The estimate of correlation as the ensemble average of the products $a(t_i)a(t_j)$ will also have a value notably differing from zero only for $t_i = t_j$, if a sufficient number of terms are averaged. Such an estimate can be done for an arbitrary pair of time instants so that their correlation can be taken as a two-dimensional function (Figure 8.1) which is called the *autocorrelation function* because it describes intraprocess relations.

The example can be further generalised to a pair of white-noise processes: suppose that the process $b(t)$ is a replica of the process $a(t)$ delayed by Δt; we shall investigate the relationship between values of both processes $a(t_a), b(t_b)$ again for an arbitrarily chosen pair of time instants. According to the assumption, $a(t) = b(t + \Delta t)$; therefore, the correlation will be nonzero only for $t_b = t_a + \Delta t$ as both processes have maximally correlated (identical) values for such time instants, otherwise the values in a pair are independent. This

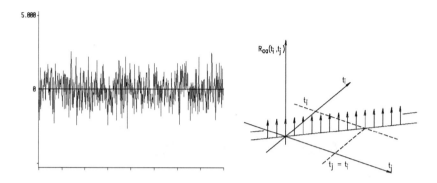

Figure 8.1 A realisation of white noise and the two-dimensional autocorrelation function for the corresponding process

conclusion can be understood as being a description of a function of two variables, which is called the *crosscorrelation function* (Figure 8.2). In this case, the interprocess relationships are obviously described by the function.

As far as the stochastic processes will be discrete in time, it will be possible to correlate only a finite number of pairs of their values. The correlation values are then usually arranged into *auto* or *crosscorrelation matrices* which describe the relevant two-dimensional discrete function.

If the process $a(t)$ – and consequently also $b(t)$ – is stationary, i.e. roughly speaking its statistical parameters will not vary in time, the mutual relationship of values in the time instants t_a, t_b will be given only by the time difference, and

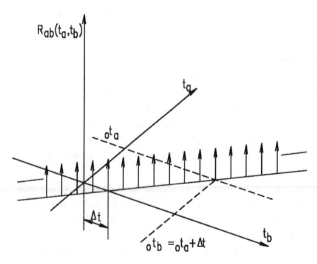

Figure 8.2 Two-dimensional crosscorrelation function of a pair formed by white noise and its delayed version

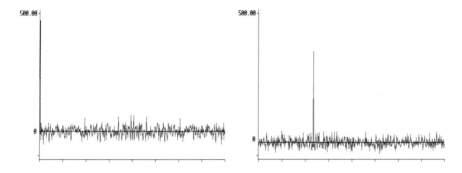

Figure 8.3 One-dimensional estimates of auto and crosscorrelation functions for previous examples

the absolute time values are irrelevant as was shown in Section 4.3. Both correlation functions will then be simplified to one-dimensional functions that are dependent only on the time difference, sometimes denoted as delay, which is $\tau = t_a - t_b$ for the continuous-time case. In the discrete case, the delay parameter is more commonly expressed by the difference of the indices, $\tau = i - j$, so that the absolute time delay is then τT.

So far we have spoken about correlations as defined by ensemble mean values (and estimated by ensemble averages, which is not usually easy in practice). Let us recall that, if the processes are not only stationary but also ergodic, estimates of the functions can be provided by means of time averages, on the basis of only a single realisation (for auto functions) or a single couple of corresponding realisations (for crossfunctions). Such estimates of one-dimensional auto and crosscorrelation functions for the previous example can be seen in Figure 8.3.

8.2 Properties of correlation and covariance functions

As providing estimates of two-dimensional correlation functions for non-stationary processes is extremely laborious and difficult to realise in practice, common correlation analysis is usually limited to the evaluation of stationary processes. Then, primarily, the correlation functions are only one-dimensional, thus substantially easier to describe and, moreover, the stationary processes met in practice are usually also ergodic so that their estimates can be provided from only a single realisation. We shall meet the general two-dimensional concept of correlation functions or matrices in this book again, in chapters on signal restoration and adaptive filtering, but even in this context, practically-estimated functions are often reduced to one-dimensional cases. The relevant matrices then have a special form. In the present chapter, we shall limit ourselves to properties, estimation and use of only one-dimensional correlation and covariance functions.

8.2.1 Properties of the autocorrelation and autocovariance function

We shall now summarise the basic properties of the autocorrelation function R_{ff} and autocovariance function C_{ff}. As has already been shown in Section 4.3, both these functions are even,

$$R_{ff}(\tau) = R_{ff}(-\tau) \quad \text{and} \quad C_{ff}(\tau) = C_{ff}(-\tau). \tag{8.1}$$

Here, τ means a time delay for continuous processes, or corresponding difference of indices for the discrete processes with which we shall mostly deal. The time delay is then τT, as already mentioned.

Further, especially for a stationary process, the following is valid according to eqn (4.11),

$$C_{ff}(\tau) = R_{ff}(\tau) - \mu_f^2; \tag{8.2}$$

a correlation function is therefore an upshifted version of the corresponding covariance function (or they are identical for centred processes).

The correlation-function value of a stationary process for zero delay is obviously

$$R_{ff}(0) = \mathbb{E}\{f_w(n)f_w(n)\} = \mathbb{E}\{f_w^2\}; \tag{8.3}$$

thus, it characterises the mean power of the signal. The initial value of the covariance function is given by the variance of the process,

$$C_{ff}(0) = \mathbb{E}\{(f_w(n) - \mu_f)^2\} = \sigma_f^2. \tag{8.4}$$

The values for zero argument are also the maximum values of both functions,

$$R_{ff}(0) \geq \pm R_{ff}(\tau), \tau \neq 0, \quad C_{ff}(0) \geq \pm C_{ff}(\tau), \tau \neq 0. \tag{8.5}$$

Indeed, taking into account the linearity of the mean-value operator and the nonnegativity of the mean of a square, we can write for stationary processes

$$\mathbb{E}\{(f_w(n) \pm f_w(n+\tau))^2\} = \mathbb{E}\{f_w^2(n)\} + \mathbb{E}\{f_w^2(n+\tau)\} \pm 2\mathbb{E}\{f_w(n)f_w(n+\tau)\}$$

$$= R_{ff}(0) + R_{ff}(0) \pm 2R_{ff}(\tau) \geq 0.$$

The mean values can be substituted, for stationary and ergodic processes, by limit time averages taken over a single realisation corresponding to the result w_i of the associated random experiment,

$$R_{ff}(\tau) = \lim_{N \to \infty} \frac{1}{N} \sum_{n=1}^{N} f_{w_i}(n)f_{w_i}(n+\tau). \tag{8.6}$$

Notice that $f_{w_i}(n)$ as a concrete realisation of the stochastic process is a deterministic function. The formula (8.6) can then be applied naturally, as a certain

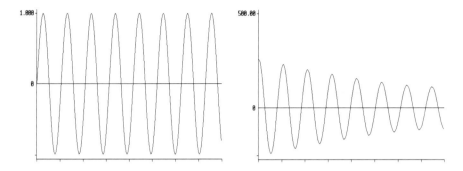

Figure 8.4 Periodic signal and (weighted) estimate of its autocorrelation function

functional, to any deterministic function; in this way, the autocorrelation function is defined for any time-domain signal. In particular, for the general harmonic signal in the discrete version, $x(n) = A \sin(\omega nT + \varphi)$, we obtain

$$R_{ff}(\tau) = \lim_{N \to \infty} \frac{A^2}{N} \sum_{n=1}^{N} \sin(\omega Tn + \varphi) \sin(\omega T(n + \tau) + \varphi) = \frac{A^2}{2} \cos(\omega T\tau). \quad (8.7)$$

The correlation function of a harmonic signal is therefore even, independently of the initial phase of the analysed signal, and periodic with the same period as the signal. Figure 8.4 shows the estimate from a finite number N of samples, weighted by the usual window $w(\tau) = (N - \tau)/N$, $N > \tau_{max}$. Put another way, the autocorrelation function preserves the information on amplitude and frequency of the signal but omits the information on initial phase.

If the analysed signal is generated by a bandlimited (BL) random process, we shall obtain the course of the autocorrelation function similar to that in Figure 8.5, which shows that the dependency of process samples decreases (perhaps nonmonotonically) when increasing their time separation. Let us denote $\Delta \tau$ the width of the delay interval around zero delay, in which the autocorrelation function values are above a certain relative level, e.g. above 50 per cent of the maximum. By a more detailed analysis, it can be shown that $\Delta \tau$ is inversely proportional to the frequency bandwidth $\Delta \omega$ of the analysed signal,

$$\Delta \tau \sim \frac{c}{\Delta \omega}; \quad (8.8)$$

where the constant c depends on the chosen level of dependency. Let us demonstrate this fact in two extreme cases: white noise has a uniform (maximally wide) amplitude spectrum and therefore zero width of interval for important dependencies (Figure 8.3); the other extreme is harmonic signals (including a constant, DC signal) which have zero frequency bandwidth and their autocorrelation functions therefore do not converge to zero even for infinitely increasing delay.

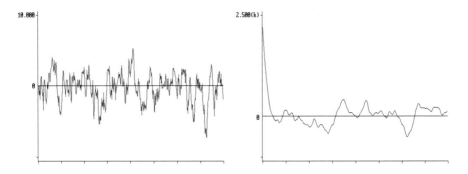

Figure 8.5 Random bandlimited signal and estimate of its autocorrelation function

The behaviour of the autocorrelation function of a mixture of several signals is noticeable. Let us analyse concretely the case of the sum of a useful signal $x(n)$ and noise $v_{w_i}(n)$ (for simplicity, we shall omit the index w_i denoting the realisation, and also a simplified notation of sequences will be used). We obtain for the autocorrelation function of such an additive mixture the following result,

$$R_{ff}(\tau) = \mathbb{E}\{(x_n + v_n)(x_{n+\tau} + v_{n+\tau})\}$$
$$= \mathbb{E}\{x_n x_{n+\tau}\} + \mathbb{E}\{x_n v_{n+\tau}\} + \mathbb{E}\{v_n x_{n+\tau}\} + \mathbb{E}\{v_n v_{n+\tau}\}$$
$$= R_{xx}(\tau) + R_{xv}(\tau) + R_{vx}(\tau) + R_{vv}(\tau). \tag{8.9}$$

The resulting autocorrelation function is thus composed of the sum of auto-correlation functions of each of the components and both crosscorrelation functions. If the signal components are independent, as in our case, the cross-correlation functions are identically equal to zero and may be omitted. An example of such a signal mixture is in Figure 8.6 together with its auto-correlation function.

A simple generalisation would lead to similar conclusions for a signal composed of more components.

Let us conclude the overview by recalling an important property of the one-dimensional autocorrelation function of a stationary random process, concerning its discrete Fourier transform. When weighted by the triangular window $w(\tau)$, the autocorrelation function forms a transform pair in $\mathbb{DTFT}$ with the discrete power spectrum $S_{ff}(\omega)$ of the same process, i.e. the Wiener–Khintchin theorem (4.24) for discrete processes applies,

$$S_{ff}(\omega) = \mathbb{DTFT}\{w(\tau)R_{ff}(\tau)\}. \tag{8.10}$$

In accordance with the findings concerning the loss of phase information in an autocorrelation function, we can state that the power spectrum, as the spectrum of an even function, is real-valued. Therefore, it does not carry any information on the phase relations of signal components.

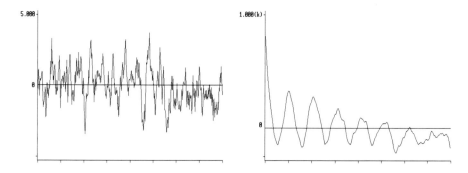

Figure 8.6 Additive mixture of the harmonic signal of Figure 8.4 and bandlimited noise of Figure 8.5, and estimate of its autocorrelation function

8.2.2 *Properties of crosscorrelation functions*

As we have already found in Section 4.3, the crosscorrelation function is not even,

$$R_{fg}(\tau) \neq R_{fg}(-\tau); \qquad (8.11)$$

but another property applies,

$$R_{fg}(\tau) = R_{gf}(-\tau), \qquad (8.12)$$

as follows from the meaning of the order of correlated processes and of the time delay, τ.

Similarly to the relation (8.5) for autocorrelation, the following inequality can be derived which expresses the magnitude limitation of a crosscorrelation function for arbitrary delay:

$$|R_{fg}(\tau)| \leq \frac{1}{2}(R_{ff}(0) + R_{gg}(0)). \qquad (8.13)$$

When starting from the relationship for the product of mean-square values of stochastic variables, as known from probability theory,

$$\mathbb{E}\{f_n^2\}.\mathbb{E}\{g_{n+\tau}^2\} \geq |\mathbb{E}\{f_n \cdot g_{n+\tau}\}|^2,$$

we obtain still another limitation

$$|R_{fg}(\tau)|^2 \leq R_{ff}(0)R_{gg}(0). \qquad (8.14)$$

Providing that the processes are (mutually) stationary and ergodic, the definition by ensemble means can, similarly as for autocorrelation functions, be substituted by limit time averages taken from a single pair of realisations belonging to the same result w_i of the associated stochastic experiment,

$$R_{fg}(\tau) = \lim_{N \to \infty} \frac{1}{N} \sum_{n=1}^{N} f_{w_i}(n) g_{w_i}(n + \tau). \tag{8.15}$$

The formula (8.15) can again be applied not only to realisations of stochastic processes but to any pair of deterministic functions, thus defining the cross-correlation function between them. Concretely, for a pair of real discrete harmonic signals of the same frequency,

$$x(n) = A \sin(\omega nT + \varphi) \quad \text{and} \quad y(n) = B \sin(\omega nT + \vartheta)$$

we obtain

$$R_{xy}(\tau) = \lim_{N \to \infty} \frac{AB}{N} \sum_{n=1}^{N} \sin(\omega Tn + \varphi) \sin(\omega T(n + \tau) + \vartheta)$$

$$= \frac{AB}{2} \cos(\omega T\tau + \varphi - \vartheta) \tag{8.16}$$

It is thus possible to extract, from the crosscorrelation function, information on the magnitude of one of the correlated signals if the other magnitude is known. In addition, information on the phase difference $\Delta\varphi = \varphi - \vartheta$ between both signals can also be retrieved; the frequency is also preserved. Therefore, if the parameters of one of the correlated signals are known, the other one can be completely reconstructed based on the parameters of the crosscorrelation function.

Let us investigate the behaviour of the crosscorrelation function of a mixture of more signals. We shall again concentrate, in a similar way as when deriving eqn (8.9), on the case of two signals both distorted by additive noise. The cross-correlation function of such additive mixtures is

$$R_{fg}(\tau) = \mathbb{E}\{(x_n + v_n)(y_{n+\tau} + \eta_{n+\tau})\}$$

$$= \mathbb{E}\{x_n y_{n+\tau}\} + \mathbb{E}\{x_n \eta_{n+\tau}\} + \mathbb{E}\{v_n y_{n+\tau}\} + \mathbb{E}\{v_n \eta_{n+\tau}\}$$

$$= R_{xy}(\tau) + R_{x\eta}(\tau) + R_{vy}(\tau) + R_{v\eta}(\tau). \tag{8.17}$$

The resulting correlation function is therefore given by the sum of all the cross-correlation functions for all signal-component pairs. Thus, should it be the common case, when each noise is independent of every signal and also both noises are mutually independent, then only the nonzero component $R_{xy}(\tau)$ remains, characterising the relationship between both signals. An analogous result could be obtained by generalisation for more complicated correlated signals consisting of more components.

An example of a crosscorrelation function between the noisy signal from Figure 8.6 and the reference signal $\sin(\omega nT)$ is presented in Figure 8.7. We can see that, compared with the autocorrelation function from the previous figure, the periodic component remains clean even for large delays. It not

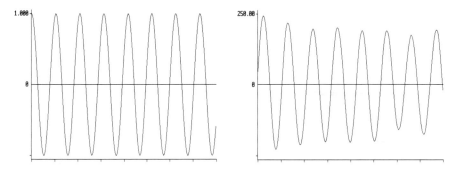

Figure 8.7 Reference cosine signal with zero phase and estimate of crosscorrelation function with the noisy signal from Figure 8.6

only provides information on the amplitude of the signal component, but also on its initial phase.

As the correlation function is not a linear operator, the completeness of the obtained information is not guaranteed. As an example, if the couple of correlated signals is

$$x_n = A \sin(\omega nT + \varphi) + B \quad \text{and} \quad y_n = C \sin(\omega nT + \vartheta) + D \sin(m\omega nT + \chi),$$

the crosscorrelation function is

$$R_{xy}(\tau) = \frac{1}{2} AC \cos(\omega T\tau + \varphi - \vartheta),$$

which can easily be shown. It is thus possible to extract information on one of the amplitudes A, C, and on the phase difference of the components with the frequency ω. Information on the DC component (B) as well as on the fourth component (i.e. D, m, χ) will be lost, although there may be important relationships. For instance, if m is an integer, the last component may be a higher harmonic of the other signal and therefore be closely connected with it; in spite of the close relationship, this component will not appear in the correlation. For a complete analysis of complicated signals, several different correlation analyses may be needed.

The one-dimensional weighted crosscorrelation function of a couple of stationary stochastic processes forms a DTFT transform pair with the cross-spectrum $S_{fg}(\omega)$ of the same process. According to eqn (4.27)

$$S_{fg}(\omega) = \mathbb{DTFT}\{w(\tau)R_{fg}(\tau)\}. \tag{8.18}$$

As the crosscorrelation function is not even, the crossspectrum is a complex-valued function and therefore also provides information on mutual phase relationships between corresponding harmonic components of the correlated signals, as we have mentioned already in Section 4.4.

8.3 Methods of estimating correlation functions

8.3.1 Direct estimation in the time domain

The direct method of estimating correlation functions from a single realisation (or a pair) in the time domain originates from the formulae (8.6) and (8.15), respectively, for auto and crosscorrelation functions. The expressions consider signals of unlimited length; but, in practice, measured signals are always limited to a finite length and thus only a finite number N of samples is available. The limit calculation must therefore be substituted by an approximating average of a finite number of terms. Taking into account that, for a certain delay of τ sampling periods, only $N - \tau$ pairs of samples with this time distance can be formed in the frame of a given signal sequence, we arrive at the classical expressions

$$R_{ff}(\tau) \approx \frac{1}{N - \tau} \sum_{n=1}^{N-\tau} f_{w_i}(n) f_{w_i}(n + \tau)$$

or

$$R_{fg}(\tau) \approx \frac{1}{N - \tau} \sum_{n=1}^{N-\tau} f_{w_i}(n) g_{w_i}(n + \tau). \tag{8.19}$$

As the precision of an estimate calculated by means of an average generally deteriorates with decreasing number of averaged terms, we have to accept the gradually lowering accuracy of the correlation function with increasing τ. Expressed more rigorously, we obtain an unbiased estimate for large τ but its variance is great and a possible large error must be envisaged. As can be shown by a more detailed analysis, the cause of the large error is division by the number $N - \tau$. This decreases for increasing τ and thus emphasises the relative magnitude of the error component which, on the difference to the right value term, is multiplied by $(N - \tau)^{-1}$. If the previous formulae are modified to

$$R_{ff}(\tau) \approx \frac{1}{N} \sum_{n=1}^{N-\tau} f_{w_i}(n) f_{w_i}(n + \tau)$$

or

$$R_{fg}(\tau) \approx \frac{1}{N} \sum_{n=1}^{N-\tau} f_{w_i}(n) g_{w_i}(n + \tau), \tag{8.20}$$

we obtain values with smaller variance for large τ at a price of the estimate not being fair any more: it will be systematically biased by the multiplicative factor $(N - \tau)/N$. Notice that, in fact, this means weighting of the resulting correlation function by a triangular window; it is the user who must decide on the acceptability of such a modification. It should nevertheless be stated that a usably reliable estimate can in general be obtained only for $|\tau| \ll N$, that is, we must analyse a signal sequence which is substantially longer than the extent of the argument of the correlation function. In this case, however, both types of formulae give almost identical results.

Both types of formulae as stated above are rather demanding because their computational complexity, evaluated by the number of multiplications and additions, is of the order of N^2. Because multiplication is much more complex than addition in classical computer systems, algorithms were sought which would replace it by simpler operations. One of these substitutes multiplication by algebraic expressions containing squares. When taking the equality

$$xy = ((x+y)^2 - x^2 - y^2)/2,$$

we can obtain the formula of so-called *half-squares method*

$$R_{fg}(\tau) \approx \frac{1}{2N} \left[\sum_{n=1}^{N-\tau} (x_n + y_{n+\tau})^2 - \sum_{n=1}^{N-\tau} (x_n)^2 - \sum_{n=1}^{N-\tau} (y_{n+\tau})^2 \right], \qquad (8.21)$$

in which multiplication is replaced by addition and searching a table of squares. Such an approach is practical only when a low precision (say eight bit) of number representation is used. A similar *quarter-squares method* will be obtained if the multiplication is substituted for by $xy = ((x+y)^2 - ((x-y)^2)/4$. With the advent of signal processors that perform multiplication as fast as addition, these methods lose on practical appeal.

Another approach to simplification of correlation-function estimation is coarse quantisation of sample values which utilises the fact that averaging, inherent to correlation calculation, can smooth out errors. Every element entering the average is *a priori* in certain error, the origin of which is naturally irrelevant; errors can be accepted as long as they have zero mean values, which is also the case for rounding errors. Then, a very low sample precision is used (two to five bits); in spite of this, relatively precise correlation results can be achieved (eight to 12 bits). This can only be done at the cost of increasing the length N of processed sequences so that the errors would converge more closely to zero. Surprisingly, even one-bit signal representation (only the sign bit of samples) may be sufficient if the signal is generated by a process close to Gaussian, and sufficiently long signal sections are available. About two to five times longer sequences are needed than in the case of full word length of samples to achieve the required precision. This approach, sometimes called *logical correlation* (although providing numerical results), may form the basis for constructing simple hardware correlators.

8.3.2 *Estimation* via *the frequency domain*

Estimation of correlation functions *via* the frequency domain utilises the similarity of formulae (8.20) with the definition relation of discrete convolution

(2.17). As can easily be verified, the correlation is equal to the convolution of the same sequences with the only difference being that the second of the sequences to be correlated must be reversed in time. It is worth asking whether it would not be possible to use, for correlation-function calculation, the discrete Fourier transform in a way similar to the frequency-domain method which was shown to be very effective for convolution calculations. We will show now that this is feasible.

Let us have the original sequences $\mathbf{x}$, $\mathbf{y}$ of the same length N, the discrete spectra of which are $\mathbf{X}$, $\mathbf{Y}$. A new spectrum $\mathbf{V}$ as the vector of products $V_k = X_k^* Y_k$ will be formed (the star denotes complex conjugate) and the original sequence $\mathbf{r} = \mathrm{DFT}^{-1}\{V_k\}$, corresponding to it, is found as follows:

$$r_\tau = \frac{1}{N} \sum_{k=0}^{N-1} (X_k^* Y_k) e^{j\tau k \frac{2\pi}{N}}$$

$$= \frac{1}{N} \sum_{k=0}^{N-1} \left(\sum_{n=0}^{N-1} x_n e^{jnk\frac{2\pi}{N}} \right) \left(\sum_{m=0}^{N-1} y_m e^{-jmk\frac{2\pi}{N}} \right) e^{j\tau k \frac{2\pi}{N}}.$$

By rearranging terms and setting common factors out of the inner sum we obtain

$$r_\tau = \frac{1}{N} \sum_{m=0}^{N-1} \sum_{n=0}^{N-1} x_n y_m \left(\sum_{k=0}^{N-1} e^{j(\tau - m + n)k \frac{2\pi}{N}} \right) = \sum_{n=0}^{N-1} x_n y_{[n+\tau]}. \tag{8.22}$$

Here, we have utilised the fact that the sum in brackets is equal to N, if $(\tau - m + n) = pN$ (integer p), but otherwise is zero; it follows that $m = (n + \tau) + pN$ (with p selected such that $m = [n + \tau] = (n + \tau) \bmod N$), so that $[n + \tau] \in \langle 0, N - 1 \rangle$ which is the principal value of the index. We can see that the sequence $\{(1/N)r_\tau\}$ has elements similar to those of eqn (8.20), except that the number of terms in the sum is always N and the index of the second sequence repeats from the beginning when it should exceed the upper limit. Expression (8.22) is therefore called a *circular correlation*. This would indeed bring a distortion to the correlation-function values for all $\tau \neq 0$, but it can be prevented by padding both correlated sequences with zeros to double their length. Thus, there will be formally $2N$ terms in every sum (8.22) but only $N - \tau$ of them will be nonzero. It can easily be verified that the elements of the vector $\mathbf{r}/N$ will be exactly equal to the values obtained by means of formulae (8.20), and the sequence $r_\tau/(N - \tau)$ is the same as (8.19).

The algorithm for calculating the correlation function *via* the frequency domain thus consists of the following steps (Figure 8.8):

1 Padding of both sequences to be correlated by zeros to length $2N$.
2 Discrete Fourier transform of both padded sequences.
3 Conjugation of the spectrum of the first sequence.
4 Term-by-term products of the spectra.

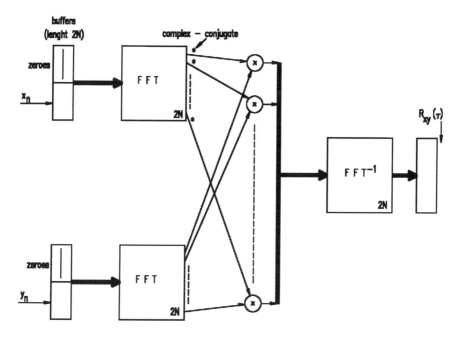

Figure 8.8 Algorithm for correlation-function calculation via *the frequency domain*

5 Inverse DFT of the resulting spectrum consisting of the products.
6 Multiplying all terms of the resulting original-domain sequence $\{r_\tau\}$, $\tau \in \langle -N, N \rangle$ by either or $1/N$ or $1/(N - \tau)$, depending on the chosen type of the correlation-function weighting.

Taking into account the availability of efficient and well elaborated algorithms of the FFT, this way of computation is today the most effective method of determining correlation functions for sequences with lengths which are above several tens of samples. For such longer sequences, the lower calculation complexity, which is of the order $3N \log_2 N$ in comparison with the complexity of the order N^2 for the direct time-domain computation, more than outweighs the overhead caused by more complicated organisation of the computation. When maximum speed is needed, it is of course helpful to work with sequences where the length is an integer power of 2; should this be impossible, a lower transform speed must be allowed for.

8.3.3 Estimates based on power or cross-spectra

In Section 4.4.1 we derived the Wiener–Khintchin theorem (4.24), which allows us to obtain the autocorrelation function of a stochastic process by the inverse discrete Fourier transform of the corresponding power spectrum. Similarly, according to eqn (4.27), the crosscorrelation function of a pair of processes can be provided by the inverse transform of their cross-spectrum. Although in principle such an approach is correct, it does not usually yield sufficiently accurate results in practice. This claim, at a first glance surprising, has two sources. First, the measured power spectra are only estimates which generally suffer from large random and sometimes even systematic errors. The other cause, which is closely connected with the first, is the fact that the estimates of power or cross-spectra, as used in frequency analysis (see Section 9.1), usually have to be modified in order to provide useful information on the frequency content of analysed processes. To obtain a reasonably smooth estimate in spite of the commonly large variance and, at the same time, to prevent too much leakage, it is necessary to pre and postprocess the data in several ways. These include weighting the input data by a suitable window and/or convolving the resulting spectrum with a smoothing function (apart from taking ensemble averages) etc. Weighting the input sequences by windows means convoluting the spectra of realisations with the window spectrum, which is followed by the non-linear operation of amplitude squaring so that the influence of the weighting is rather complicated. Also, smoothing the resulting spectra by averaging of a number of individual spectra, or by convolution with a smoothing function, wipes the spectral details. The mutual relationships among the values in the original domain, as reflected in the spectra, may thus be totally distorted. Moreover, relatively small errors in the frequency domain, namely in the power or cross-spectra, may lead to gross errors in the original domain of the correlation functions owing to DFT properties.

Should we want to obtain satisfactory estimates of correlation functions in this way, the power or cross-spectra used must not be modified in any way. It is necessary to use the square of the *unmodified* magnitude DFT spectrum of a signal to determine its autocorrelation function and corresponding-terms products of *unmodified* DFT spectra of both signals in the case of the cross-correlation function (the first factor in each product is to be complex conjugated). However, this is then exactly the algorithm described in the previous subchapter where it was interpreted as a computationally efficient numerical method equivalent to direct calculation in the original domain. Here, we have shown a different interpretation of this approach and also noticed that inversely DFT transforming of modified power or cross-spectra may lead to misleading results as far as correlations in the time-domain are concerned.

8.4 Correlation analysis of signals

8.4.1 Correlation detection of a signal in noise, linear matched filter

A frequently required task in practice is to detect the occurrence of a signal $x(n)$ of a known form and usually of finite duration in an additive mixture, e.g. in combination with noise, $y(n) = ax(n - \tau_0) + v(n)$. The purpose is to determine the signal appearance and its location on the time axis given by the time instant τ_0. A suitable mechanism for solving such a problem is provided by the cross-correlation function between the noisy signal and the signal $x(n)$ as a reference

$$R_{xy}(\tau) = \mathbb{E}\{x(n)y(n+\tau)\} = \mathbb{E}\{x(n)ax(n+\tau-\tau_0)\} + \mathbb{E}\{x(n)v(n+\tau)\}$$

$$= aR_{xx}(\tau - \tau_0) + R_{xv}(\tau). \tag{8.23}$$

As can be seen, this consists of a shifted autocorrelation function of the signal to be detected and of the crosscorrelation function between signal and noise. The maximum of the autocorrelation function appears for its zero argument, i.e. for the delay $\tau = \tau_0$, which provides an indication of the signal existence and also determines its position in time. The magnitude of the detection maximum is clearly

$$aR_{xx}(0) = \frac{a}{N} \sum_{n=1}^{N} |x(n)|^2$$

and is thus given by average signal power modified by the attenuation a of the received signal. If the noise is independent of the signal, the values of $R_{xv}(\tau)$ are zero and even its estimates will be small for any delay. An example of two different signals that are to be identified in noise, the differently shifted signals mixed with noise and estimates of the crosscorrelation functions between this mixture and each of the signals is given in Figure 8.9. The clear peaks visible on the correlation functions correspond to the ends of the signals being sought, i.e. to time instants when all the available information on the respective signals has been received.

Because the classical analysis of signal-to-noise ratio improvement as presented in Reference [2] is not correct, we shall estimate if there is any improvement, and its degree, in another way. The original power signal-to-noise ratio of the received signal is

$$SNR_1 = \frac{\mathbb{E}\{a^2 x^2(n)\}}{\mathbb{E}\{v^2(n)\}} = \frac{a^2 R_{xx}(0)}{R_{vv}(0)},$$

while the power ratio of the correlation functions at the time instant of detection is

$$SNR_2 = \frac{a^2 R_{xx}^2(0)}{\mathbb{E}\{R_{xv}^2(\tau_0)\}},$$

so that the relative improvement is given by the expression

$$\frac{SNR_2}{SNR_1} = \frac{R_{xx}(0)R_{vv}(0)}{\mathbb{E}\{R_{xv}^2(\tau_0)\}} \geq 1, \tag{8.24}$$

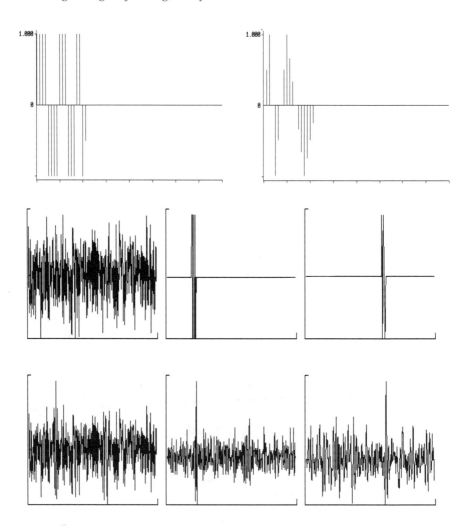

*Figure 8.9 Example of correlation detection of known signals in noise (upper row: two sig-
nals to be detected in detail; middle row: components of the mixture – noise,
shifted signal A, shifted signal B; lower row: mixture of signals with noise, crosscorrelation functions with reference signal A and with B)*

where the last inequality follows from (8.14). If the signal and noise are independent, the values of the crosscorrelation function estimates will be, on average, small and therefore the factor of improvement will be on average much greater than one. The magnitude of this improvement will obviously be greater the more pronounced the small values of crosscorrelation, i.e. for longer correlation intervals and also for greater frequency bandwidth of at least one of the correlated signals. It is obvious that the paradox conclusion of the cited work, that the improvement is inversely proportional to the input signal-to-noise ratio, is false.

Often there is a need to determine the precise time position of a signal in noise, such as when ascertaining the delay of the received signal with respect to the transmitted signal in radar or sonar technology. It is suitable then to choose a signal form that enables us to detect the time instant of the signal appearance uniquely, in spite of the signal's relatively long duration which is necessary for a sufficiently long correlation interval. Obviously, it must be a signal the auto-correlation of which has a narrow peak at zero and declines quickly with increasing delay without having important sidelobes. According to relation (8.8), it should be a wideband signal; thus it can be neither harmonic nor any other periodic signal, the autocorrelation function of which is also periodic. Suitable signal forms can be obtained by formalised optimisation, but we can estimate intuitively that only the shapes that match well in only one precisely defined position are suitable, i.e. for zero mutual shift of replicas. One such signal is the *chirp signal* – a 'sine' signal with increasing or decreasing frequency; similar forms have also been used in the above example.

As already mentioned, correlation can also be interpreted as convolution with the signal reversed in time. As the signal to be sought is time invariant, it is easily possible to construct a discrete linear time-invariant system that realises such a convolution. The supposed finite length of the sought signal is a linear filter of FIR type, the impulse response of which is given by

$$h(i) = x(N - i - 1), \quad i = 0, 1, \cdots, N - 1. \tag{8.25}$$

A filter designed in this way is called the *matched filter* (see example in Figure 8.10). Here, the received signal passes through a delaying chain. In every sampling period, an output sample is produced which is the value of

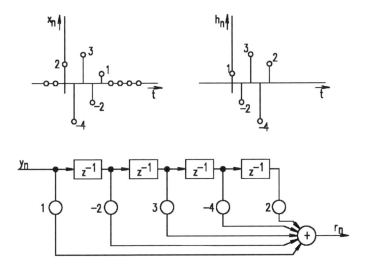

Figure 8.10 Example of the classical matched filter

correlation expressed by the dot product $r_n = \mathbf{h}^T . \mathbf{y}_n$ between the weight vector $\mathbf{h} = (x_{N-1}, x_{N-2}, \cdots, x_0)^T$ and the vector of instantaneous outputs of the delay elements $\mathbf{y}_n = (y_n, y_{n-1}, \cdots, y_{n-N+1})^T$. The output of the filter will be usually maximum (i.e. the occurrence of the signal detected) when the signal sought (mixed with noise) is just present completely in the delaying chain. A related problem is then how to select the threshold of detection – if it is too high, the signal can be overlooked but with too low a threshold there will be many false detections. This is a problem of decision theory; the threshold may even be adaptive, thus controlled by usually slowly varying noise properties.

The assumptions conditioning the proper function of the linear matched filter are rather demanding – stationarity of processes which generate the noise signals, zero mean, sufficiently wide frequency band with respect to the correlation interval. When these are not well fulfilled, the error rate may exceed an acceptable level. Under such circumstances, nonlinear matched filters based on other similarity criteria than the correlation function may be more effective; they will be described in greater detail in Chapter 12.

8.4.2 Correlation-based restoration of an unknown signal in noise

Restoration of an original signal distorted by noise is naturally a more complicated task than the mere detection of the presence of a known signal section. In the case where the signal is hidden in noise and only one appearance is available, so that averaging techniques cannot be used, correlation methods are useful. However, this restoration method (sometimes called correlation reception), based on a combination of auto and crosscorrelation analysis, is rather complicated.

Correlation reception uses the fact that every finite signal can be decomposed into harmonic components. It is then sufficient to determine the frequencies, amplitudes and initial phases of all such components and to synthesise the signal based on this knowledge. It should be pointed out that, in practice, not all signal components can be precisely identified as the weakest ones might have insufficient signal-to-noise ratio, even after correlation, and their parameters thus could not be reliably determined. Such components should then be neglected, resulting in an only approximate restoration; the degree of precision depends both on the *a priori* properties of the original signal and on the perfection of the utilised correlation estimates.

The correlation-restoration method can be described as the following iterative process:

1   Reset the order index i to zero. Assign the additive finite input sequence $\{x_n + v_n\}$ of the original signal mixed with noise for a variable sequence $\{y_n\}$.
2   Estimate the autocorrelation function $R_{yy}(\tau)$.
3   Test on end of the iteration: if there is an observable periodic component in $R_{yy}(\tau)$, continue at step 4, else go to step 8.

4   Find the strongest periodic component in $R_{yy}(\tau)$, concentrating attention on the function part with large τ, where the autocorrelation function of the noise is sufficiently weak. Determine the period (or frequency ω_i) of this component; this is also the frequency of the strongest component of the signal $\{x_n\}$ remaining[1] in the noisy mixture $\{y_n\}$.
5   Estimate the crosscorrelation function $R_{ys}(\tau)$ between the analysed part of the noisy mixture $\{y_n\}$ and the auxiliary signal $\{s_n\} = \{\cos(\omega_i T.n)\}$. From the almost harmonic form of $R_{ys}(\tau)$, estimate the amplitude A_i and phase φ_i of the signal component $\{_i a_n\} = \{A_i \cos(\omega_i Tn + \varphi_i)\}$.
6   Subtract the determined component from the analysed mixture; i.e. assign the sequence $\{y_n - {}_i a_n\}$ for $\{y_n\}$.
7   Increment i and continue again from step 2.
8   End of the analysis. Now the signal can be approximately synthesised as the sum of finite Fourier series,

$$x(n) \approx \sum_{i=0}^{i_{max}} A_i \cos(\omega_i Tn + \varphi_i).$$

Results of the simulation of such an analysis can be seen in Figure 8.11. The original signal was composed of two harmonic components, as is also its approximation, derived by means of the above-described procedure. Although the resulting signal is only approximate (all the parameters of the components are only estimated), it is clear that the restored signal is rather similar to the original when compared with the received noisy signal. The evident error in the mutual phase of both components, increasing with time, is caused by differing deviations in frequencies of components.

The method will be more efficient the easier the signal can be expressed by harmonic components, which are well identifiable in the autocorrelation function. This is particularly the case for periodic signals. The difficulties for non-periodic signals follow from the need for too high a number of harmonic components. Resolving their traces in rather rough estimates of the auto-correlation function based on only finite signal sections may be difficult or even infeasible.

8.5 Correlation-based system identification

Identification of unknown linear time-invariant systems (or systems which can be considered sufficiently close to being LTI in the working range of variables) aims at estimating their characteristics in the time or frequency domain. If the system to be identified is isolated and reasonably sized, such as an electronic

---

[1] During the first pass, naturally the strongest component of all.

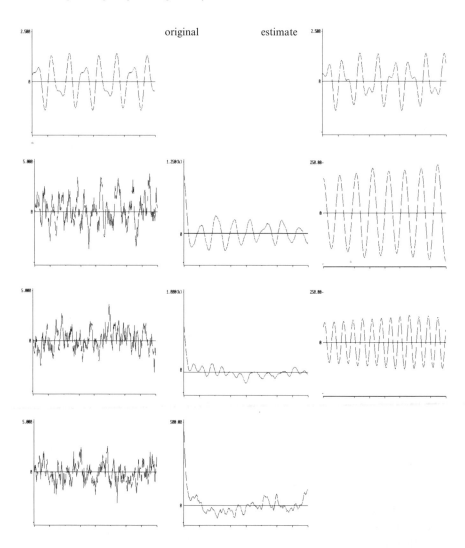

Figure 8.11 Example of correlation-based restoration of a signal in noise (upper row: the original signal (left) and its restoration; row 2: noisy signal y, estimate of R_{yy}, estimate of R_{ys1}; row 3: noisy signal y_1 after subtraction of the first estimated harmonic signal component, estimate of R_{y1y1}, estimate of R_{y1s2}; lower row: noisy signal y_2 after subtraction of the second estimated harmonic component, estimate of R_{y2y2}, already without observable periodicity)

amplifier, its characteristics can easily be measured according to their definitions: estimate of the impulse response as the reaction to a very narrow impulse
or by recalculation from the step response; the frequency response by, for
example, measuring it point-by-point by means of a harmonic signal generator.
The correctness of the identification can then be checked in each of the domains
by comparison of the directly measured response with that obtained by trans-

formation of the other domain characteristic. The measured characteristics should form (in the frame of the desired precision) a Fourier transform pair.

In industrial applications, measuring systems with nonelectrical elements (e.g. mechanical, chemical etc.), large systems, high-power systems or those that can usually be measured only under normal heavy-duty service conditions (e.g. complex control systems, production lines or their integral components) may be needed. Several important problems then arise which disqualify the above-mentioned basic methods from practical use:

1   The test signals can lead, owing to their rather unnatural character which does not occur under normal working conditions, to overload of the measured system; examples being congestion after the input step or intrinsic resonance under excitation by harmonic signals. Such phenomena may cause overcharging of some parts of the measured system, leading to a transition to a nonlinear working regime and thus deteriorating the measurements, if not causing a collapse of the system.
2   The presence of normal-operation (production) signals, nonavoidable in an industrial environment and possibly even several orders stronger than acceptable measuring signals, can substantially complicate or even preclude evaluation of the measurement.
3   Measured systems are often sources of strong interfering signals – internal noise which is generated on the way between the system's input and output – which can also influence or deteriorate the conclusions on input–output characteristics.

Correlation methods enable us to overcome these problems to a certain extent. Nevertheless, as they work on probabilistic principles, we must count on random errors deteriorating the measurements and the derived characteristics. The detailed quantification of bias and variance of the results is a subject of specialised literature; here we can only claim that these two characteristics are usually conflicting and estimation methods differ in their ways of making a balance between them. In this chapter, we shall concentrate on the principal concept and basic properties of the method. It can be roughly stated that, when sufficiently long signal sections are taken into account for correlation analysis and/or the measurements can be repeated with subsequent averaging of the results, we may achieve any reasonably required precision. The achieved precision can be roughly judged based on, for example, the smoothness of the obtained characteristics or by statistical stabilisation of the results of convergent averaging.

We shall suppose in this chapter, in accordance with many practical problems, that the systems to be identified work continuously in time. This does not exclude the fact that some parts of them – usually more or less autonomous – are discrete, as is the case in most contemporary controlling sub-systems, such as those for production lines. The identification signal analysis itself is, of course, performed exclusively in digital form today.

8.5.1 Autocorrelation-based identification

Autocorrelation-based identification deals with the first of the mentioned problems as it enables us to use wideband noise as the measuring signal $x(t)$. The principle of the measurement is documented in Figure 8.12.

The unknown system is excited by a white, or wideband, noise signal $x(t)$, which may be processed (after analogue-to-digital conversion) by the first correlator to estimate its autocorrelation function, $R_{xx}(\tau)$. Similarly, the output signal of the system, $y(t)$, is digitised and by means of the second correlator the estimated autocorrelation function $R_{yy}(\tau)$ is obtained. Both estimates are then transformed by the DTFT to obtain estimates of the power spectra of both the input and output process, $S_{xx}(\omega)$, $S_{yy}(\omega)$; in practice, only sampled versions of the spectra are provided by the DFT. According to eqn (4.32), which is also valid for continuous-time systems, we obtain the continuous power-frequency response

$$|G(\omega)|^2 = \frac{S_{yy}(\omega)}{S_{xx}(\omega)}, \tag{8.26}$$

or, in the more frequent case of using an N-sample DFT, its sampled version

$$|G(k\Omega)|^2 = \frac{S_{yy}(k\Omega)}{S_{xx}(k\Omega)}, \quad \Omega = \frac{2\pi}{NT}. \tag{8.27}$$

It is obvious that the method enables us to determine only the power-frequency characteristic, or equivalently, its square root, the amplitude frequency response $|G(\omega)|$. The simplicity of measurement is in allowing dislocated and independent measurement of each of the correlation functions so that it is even possible to measure both consecutively using the same equipment. On the other hand, it is paid for by the unavailability of phase characteristics and also by being highly sensitive to extraneous signals; thus the other two problems remain.

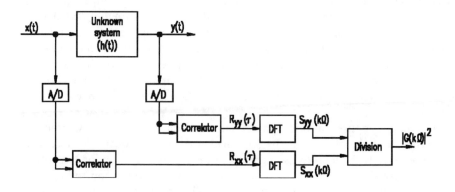

Figure 8.12 Principle of autocorrelation-based identification

A further simplification is possible if the character of the measured system allows generation of the signal $x(t)$ as a sufficiently precise approximation of white noise of known power, i.e. with a uniform amplitude spectrum in the working range of the identified system. In this case the measurement of $R_{xx}(\tau)$ can obviously be dropped.

8.5.2 Crosscorrelation-based identification

The concept of crosscorrelation-based identification is presented in Figure 8.13. The test-signal generator produces wideband noise, which is added to the normal-operation (production) signal $f(t)$ and the sum $u(t) = x(t) + f(t)$ forms the input to the identified system. The system is modelled by an ideal linear system which does not generate any internal noise, to the output $y(t)$ of which a noise signal $v(t)$ is added. This noise, generally independent of both $x(t)$ and $y(t)$, models the noise which is internally generated by any real system.

The signal $x(t)$ is digitised and its discrete version $\{x_n\}$ is connected to the first input of the correlator, the other input of which is supplied by the additive signal, $z(t) = y(t) + v(t)$ as measured at the output of the system and digitised. The correlator thus produces an estimate of the crosscorrelation function $R_{xz}(\tau)$. The discretisation of both signals must be synchronous in order to preserve their time relationships; this means that the equipment has to fulfil higher requirements in comparison with those for the previous method.

The internal linear block is described by the input–output convolution relationship $y(t) = \int_0^\infty h(s)u(t-s)\,ds$, where $h(t)$ is the impulse response of the block. Let us disregard, for a while, the fact that the correlation functions are calculated discretely for practical reasons. If the correlation had been realised in continuous time, we would obtain the crosscorrelation function dependent on the continuous delay ξ as $R_{xz}(\xi) = \mathbb{E}\{x(t)z(t+\xi)\}$ and, after substitution,

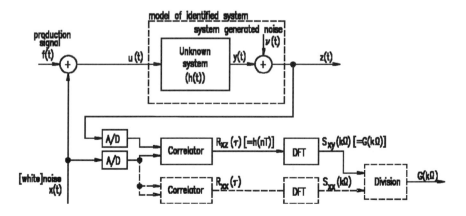

Figure 8.13 Principle of crosscorrelation-based identification

$$R_{xz}(\xi) = \mathbb{E}\{x(t)(y(t+\xi) + v(t+\xi))\}$$

$$= \mathbb{E}\left\{x(t)\left(\int_0^\infty h(s)u(t+\xi-s)\,ds + v(t+\xi)\right)\right\}.$$

Expanding the product and using the linearity of the mean-value operator which enables us to interchange it with the integration operator, we obtain

$$R_{xz}(\xi) = \mathbb{E}\{x(t)v(t+\xi)\} + \int_0^\infty h(s)\mathbb{E}\{x(t)(x(t+\xi-s) + f(t+\xi-s))\}\,ds$$

$$= R_{xv}(\xi) + \int_0^\infty h(s)(\mathbb{E}\{x(t)x(t+\xi-s)\} + \mathbb{E}\{x(t)f(t+\xi-s)\})\,ds$$

$$= R_{xv}(\xi) + \int_0^\infty h(s)(R_{xx}(\xi-s) + R_{xf}(\xi-s))\,ds. \qquad (8.28)$$

With respect to the assumption of independence of both the noise $v(t)$ and the production signal $f(t)$, on the auxiliary measurement signal $x(t)$, the cross-correlation functions $R_{xv}(\xi)$ and $R_{xf}(\xi)$ are identically equal to zero and we finally obtain

$$R_{xz}(\xi) = \int_0^\infty h(s)R_{xx}(\xi-s)\,ds. \qquad (8.29)$$

This is the relationship named after its discoverers as the *Wiener–Lee theorem*. It can be formulated in words as follows: the autocorrelation function of an input signal of an LTI system is transformed into the crosscorrelation function between this signal and the system output by a fixed operator, independent of the applied signals. It is the same operator as that transforming any input signal of the same system into its output signal. Notice that this relationship is not influenced by the presence of any other signals in the system, generated either inside or outside of the system, as far as they are independent of the auxiliary input signal.

If the auxiliary signal is a sufficiently precise approximation of white noise (in the sense mentioned in the previous section), its autocorrelation function would approximate the unit Dirac impulse sufficiently well. Then we obtain, based on eqn (8.29) and utilising the sifting property of the δ distribution,

$$h(t) \approx R_{xz}(t). \qquad (8.30)$$

Therefore the impulse response of the identified system is directly approximated by the measured crosscorrelation function. If the spectrum of the auxiliary signal $x(t)$ is nonuniform in the working frequency range of the system, it is also necessary to measure the autocorrelation function $R_{xx}(\xi)$ (as sketched by dotted lines in the figure). When eqn (8.29) is transformed into the frequency domain, the frequency response of the system can be determined as

$$G(\omega) = \frac{S_{xz}(\omega)}{S_{xx}(\omega)}, \tag{8.31}$$

and is thus given by the ratio of the cross and power spectrum which can be obtained by Fourier transforming the measured correlation functions.

Equation (8.29) is theoretically exact, but is valid only for precise correlation functions. When working with their estimates, we have to return to eqn (8.28) and observe that the estimates $R_{xv}(\xi)$ and $R_{xf}(\xi)$ will not be identically zero. We can only suppose that they will acquire, on average, relatively small values in comparison with the desired components so that their practical influence will be negligible if the estimates are reasonably made.

The precision of the estimates is, as with every correlation analysis, influenced by the length of the processed signal sequences, with regard to the frequency bandwidth of the analysed signals. Another crucial factor that can radically influence the correctness of the results is substitution of the continuous correlation function by its discrete version

$$_D R_{xz}(\tau) = R_{xz}(\tau T), \ \tau \in \langle -N + 2, N - 2 \rangle.$$

When disregarding the imprecision of estimates, the result of identification is therefore a discrete impulse response, identical to that obtained by sampling the theoretical continuous-time impulse response as determined according to eqn (8.30) or transformed from the result given by eqn (8.31). Thus it is actually a discrete model of the analysed continuous-time system obtained by the method of impulse invariance. As we analysed in detail in Section 5.3.2.2, this method is applicable to discrete modelling of continuous-time systems only when the upper limit of their working frequency band is sufficiently lower than the Nyquist frequency of the sampling used. The modelled systems must therefore have the character of lowpass or bandpass filters with only a negligible transfer above $\omega_s/2$. However, most systems which are likely to be considered for identification *via* correlation analysis contain parts with mechanical or other inertia, and so are of the desired character. Thus, it is only necessary to choose the sampling frequency properly with respect to the above requirement in order to achieve reasonable results.

The described method is illustrated, together with the previous method, by simulation documented in Figure 8.14. The 'identified system' is a discrete bandpass filter and precise impulse and frequency responses can be determined by direct measurement (as the response to the unit impulse and, subsequently, by the DFT of this response). These precise characteristics are depicted in Figure 8.14*a* (A – impulse response, B – amplitude and phase frequency responses). The results of correlation-based identification in the presence of strong production signals are presented in Figure 8.14b. The system was supplied by an additive mixture $u(t_n)$ of a strong harmonic ('production') signal and sufficiently precise white noise (part C). In part D, the estimate of the amplitude frequency response is depicted, provided by the autocorrelation method according to eqn (8.27). It can be seen that the estimate of the amplitude

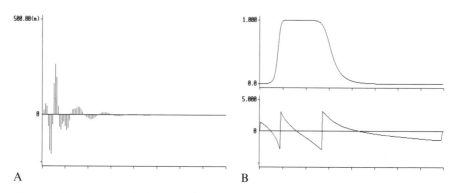

Figure 8.14a   Theoretical characteristics of an example system (explanation in text)

characteristic is strongly deteriorated by the presence of the narrowband production signal; the phase characteristic naturally cannot be determined in this
way at all and, consequently, neither can the impulse response.

A rough estimate of the crosscorrelation function R_{xz}, according to eqn (8.30)
of the impulse response h of the identified system, is given in part E. This estimate, based on a single realisation of only 512 samples, is obviously in gross
error as can be seen from a comparison of parts A and E. However, even this
rough measurement already provides (according to eqn (8.31)) a relatively
informative description namely of the phase characteristic (compare parts F
and B). Averaging of a greater number of realisations has provided a much
better estimate of R_{xz}, which is depicted in part G. Good agreement with the
theoretical function in part A is obvious; subsequently the frequency response
(H), calculated from estimated R_{xz} (as in G), is also a relatively good approximation of the theoretical response (B). It can be seen that the crosscorrelation
method provides not only more information (time relations) than does the autocorrelation approach but also, for the same number of realisations, substantially better results. However, it is achieved at the cost of more demanding
measurements. It is worth mentioning the very well identified phase characteristic in the passband; the incorrect values outside of the band are, of course,
irrelevant as no signal components are passed at these frequencies anyway.

Preference for the crosscorrelation approach is given primarily owing to the
fact that disturbance by the 'production' narrowband signal of markedly higher
amplitude than the mean amplitude of the measuring noise has been almost
entirely suppressed. The simulation could be complemented by disturbance of
the system output signal with strong (possibly rosy) noise, independent of the
measuring noise and representing the simulated internally-produced noise of
the measured system; even this disturbance would be eliminated (almost)
completely by the crosscorrelation method while the results of autocorrelation
identification would be totally hidden in errors of this kind.

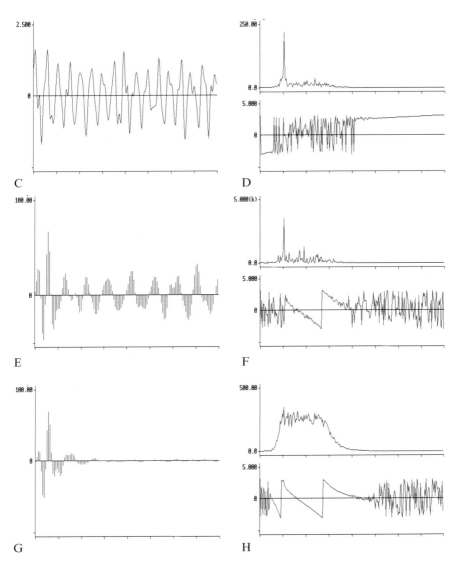

Figure 8.14b Auto and crosscorrelation-based identification of an example system (explanation in text)

Chapter 9
Spectral analysis

9.1 Introduction

Spectral (or frequency) analysis generally serves to describe a signal in terms of its components in the frequency domain. We shall deal in this chapter only with spectra in the sense of the Fourier transform; thus, we will have in mind harmonic components of different frequencies and unlimited duration. If we can find the description of a signal in the frequency domain, i.e. magnitudes and possibly even mutual phase (or time) shifts of its harmonic components, we can make certain conclusions about the character of the signal. This may enable us to classify or to recognise the signal, to use the information to design a suitable communication channel or archiving medium for such a signal or to consider restricting information about less important components in order to compress the data describing the signal. Applications of spectral analysis are very broad; we shall meet some illustrative examples in this and further chapters. More detailed information on concrete applications, such as in the area of speech recognition, nondestructive testing in different technical fields, biomedical diagnostic applications, multimedia signal processing, tele-communications etc. can be found in specialised literature.

We meet in principle two different approaches in the field of spectral analysis: either a concrete individual signal to be analysed or a whole class of partly differing signals to be described. In the former case, description in the frequency domain, called the *spectrum*, should usually be so detailed as to enable complete recovery of the signal, based on spectrum knowledge. On the other hand, in the latter case, common features of the signals belonging to the class under analysis are sought in order to characterise the whole class in the frequency domain. The concepts of both types of spectral analysis are of course significantly different.

Analysing a concrete signal described by a deterministic function of time is about finding, with given means, as precise as possible coefficients of the Fourier series or samples of the Fourier transform; both complex, thus including the phase information. Then, if the frequency-domain description is complete, i.e.

determines the given signal uniquely, it enables in principle its backward reconstruction, mostly based on discrete representation. We are usually also interested in the signal spectrum in the sense of the integral Fourier transform as the original analysed signal is often, if not mostly, an analogue signal. It is, of course, in principle impossible to obtain such a precise spectrum based on a finite and sampled section of the signal. We shall therefore analyse the distortions following from this signal representation and from the use of the discrete Fourier transform, in order to interpret the results properly and to be aware of what the discrete analysis is unable to show. The integral Fourier transform describes the signal by harmonic components of constant parameters on a two-sided infinite time interval. For signals of transient character, the nature of which is changing in time (e.g. speech signals), it is often more appropriate to apply so-called short-time spectrum analysis which enables the development of the signal's frequency content in time to be followed. This type of spectra and their sequences – *spectrograms* – are the subject of the concluding part of the section on analysing deterministic signals which forms the first part of the present chapter.

As we have already shown (see Section 4.4.4.1), the description of common spectral properties of a class of signals by means of the average of their (complex) spectra is not possible as such averages usually converge to identically zero functions. It is therefore common in such analysis to sacrifice the information on mutual time relationships of individual harmonic signal components contained in the phase part of the spectra and to work only with magnitude spectra, or their squared versions. These are *individual power spectra* of single signals, which can already be averaged. The processed signals may then be considered to be members of a family of functions constituting a stochastic process or, conversely, the individual signals can be regarded as realisations of the stochastic process. Consequently, the derived averaged spectrum can be given the name of *process power spectrum*. In Section 4.4.4.2 we became familiar with the concept of the *cross-spectrum* of a pair of stochastic processes, which is in a sense a generalisation of the power-spectrum concept. We shall deal with methods of providing power and cross-spectra of stochastic processes, as based on frequency analysis of random signals, in the second part of this chapter.

Let us mention that spectral analysis can also be based on other transforms, such as the cosine, Walsh, Haar transform etc., but their practical usefulness seems to be lower and the interpretation of the results is less straightforward. This may also be a consequence of the fact that the theory of the Fourier series and transforms is well known and accepted by most users, compared with the theory of other transforms. An important exception is the recently discovered class of *wavelet transforms*, a concept aiming at time–frequency analysis (or more generally time-scale analysis), the simplest forms of which are represented by spectrograms or by the Haar transform. Wavelet transforms (see Section 3.5) have proven to be a powerful tool in different areas of signal processing, among others in the particular tasks of short-time frequency (or scale) analysis.

9.2 Spectral analysis of deterministic signals

As deterministic signals are a special case of stochastic signals, we would expect that it is not necessary to treat methods for their spectral analysis separately. In fact, on the contrary, only a detailed study of these methods enables us to investigate their properties and application possibilities. In addition, it is necessary to ascertain sources of some unavoidable systematic errors caused by limitations following from the finite and discrete character of both the analysed signals and their corresponding spectra. Quite often, we have to deal with the analysis of a given signal, such as a measurement sequence, the features of which are to be discovered, and this is a typical case of deterministic-signal analysis. On the other hand, these systematic errors influence even the estimates of characteristics of stochastic processes, because the relevant methods are based on analysis of individual known realisations of the analysed processes, which are naturally deterministic signals. It is useful for a user, whose final aim is to interpret the results properly, to be able to distinguish between the error sources. This means, on one hand, understanding deterministic-signal methods and considering separately the distortion following from working with finite and discrete sequences instead of continuous signals; this is our present topic. On the other hand, the errors in estimates caused by the probabilistic character of the processes and by statistical processing are important as well; these will be discussed later.

9.2.1 Analysis of periodic signals

Periodic signals, the analysis of which is common in, for example, acoustical applications, can be analysed most easily and precisely by means of the *Fourier series method.* As is known from mathematics every piecewise continuous periodic function with a period Π can be expressed by the infinite series

$$f(t) = \sum_{k=-\infty}^{\infty} c_k \, e^{jk\Omega t}, \quad \Omega = \frac{2\pi}{\Pi,} \tag{9.1}$$

in which the complex coefficients c_k are determined by integrals over one period of the analysed function

$$c_k = \frac{1}{\Pi} \int_0^{\Pi} f(t) e^{-jk\Omega t} \, dt. \tag{9.2}$$

We shall show that the discrete Fourier transform has, under certain assumptions, a very close relationship to the Fourier series. Let us suppose, first, that the sampling has been chosen in such a way that the period of the analysed signal is an integer multiple of the sampling period T, i.e. $\Pi = NT$. Further, it is natural to assume that $f(t)$ is a bandlimited signal with the upper frequency limit ω_{max} and, also, that the sampling used fulfils the sampling theorem,

$$\omega_{max} < \frac{\pi}{T} = \frac{N\Omega}{2}. \tag{9.3}$$

With respect to this condition, all the coefficients c_k in eqn (9.1) will be zero for $|k| > N/2$ and the series will be finite,

$$f(t) = \sum_{k=-\text{int}(N/2)}^{\text{int}(N/2)} c_k e^{jk\Omega t}. \tag{9.4}$$

When expressing the discrete version of the same signal by means of the inverse DFT, we obtain

$$f(nT) = \frac{1}{N} \sum_{k=0}^{N-1} F_k e^{jnTk\Omega} = \frac{1}{N} \sum_{k=-\text{int}(N/2)}^{\text{int}(N/2)} F_k e^{jnTk\Omega}, \tag{9.5}$$

where the identity of the first and second sum follows from the periodicity of the DFT coefficients.[1] When switching in eqn (9.4) from continuous time t to discrete time nT, the expression will be equivalent to (9.5) and consequently we see that

$$c_k = \frac{1}{N} F_k. \tag{9.6}$$

It is therefore possible to calculate the coefficients of the Fourier series exactly by means of the discrete Fourier transform. At first sight it might be surprising that the coefficient values given by the integral (9.2) can also be calculated as the DFT definition sum $F_k = \sum_{n=0}^{N-1} f(nT) e^{-jk\Omega nT}$, that is by the simplest rectangular approximation of the integral. This is possible owing to the special properties of the integrand under the assumed conditions.

Because any practical signals are bandlimited and adherence to the sampling theorem is an implied condition, it remains to ensure that $NT = \Pi$, i.e. that the sampling frequency is the precise N-multiple of the basic repetition frequency of the periodic signal. (This might be arranged by, for example, a phase-lock loop of the digitiser used to the analysed signal, or by posterior resampling using suitable interpolation.) Should this condition be violated, the situation as depicted in Figure 9.1B will appear – the coefficients of the series are false. Consequently, although the function described by this series goes through all the sample points, in between its course is different from that of $f(t)$. The Fourier series is a very effective way of describing periodic signals because,

---

[1] The thoughtful reader might object that the right-hand sum has a greater number of terms (by one) for even N. Nevertheless, when considering the condition (9.3), the identity applies.

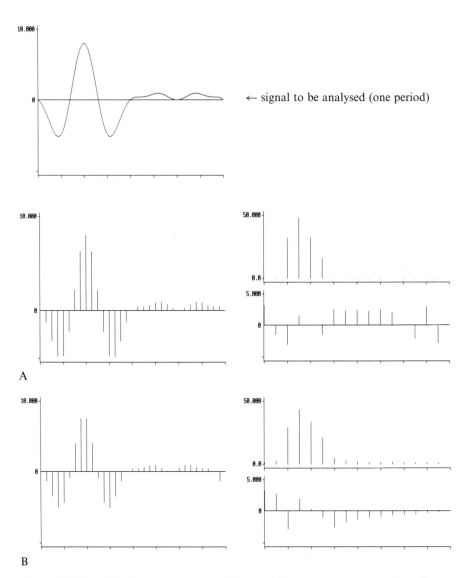

← signal to be analysed (one period)

Figure 9.1 Example of expressing a periodic signal by a Fourier series with coefficients calculated by the DFT (the original signal as depicted in the upper corner has four harmonic components: 2Hz/2V, 3Hz/3V, 4Hz/2V and 5Hz/1V, A: analysis with NT = Π, left – sampled signal; right – Fourier series, upper part: amplitudes, lower part: phases; B: analysis with NT ≠ Π)

among others, it has the advantageous property that when adding a next higher frequency term to improve the precision, the previously determined terms remain unchanged. Thus, given the usefulness of the Fourier series and the fact that the DFT is a generally available procedure, the possibility of calculating Fourier-series coefficients precisely using an FFT algorithm is undoubtedly beneficial.

9.2.2 Analysis of general signals

The spectrum of continuous signals[2] is generally given by the integral Fourier transform. However, when working with discrete signal representation and the spectrum is calculated by means of the discrete Fourier transform, differences appear that should be carefully analysed in order that the obtained results are properly interpreted. This section will therefore be devoted to the analysis of what is actually provided by the mentioned procedure.

First, observe that a finite section of N samples of a discrete signal $\{f_n = f(nT)\}$, $n = 0, 1, \cdots, N - 1$ can be expressed in quasicontinuous representation as a sum of the weighted and shifted Dirac distributions (Section 3.1),

$$f_s(t) = \sum_{n=0}^{N-1} f_n \delta(t - nT), \tag{9.7}$$

and its spectrum in the sense of the integral Fourier spectrum is therefore (Section 3.3)

$$F_s(\omega) = \mathbb{F}\left\{ \sum_{n=0}^{N-1} f_n \delta(t - nT) \right\} = \sum_{n=0}^{N-1} f_n \mathbb{F}\{\delta(t - nT)\}$$

$$= \sum_{n=0}^{N-1} f_n e^{-j\omega nT} = \mathbb{DTFT}\{f_n\}. \tag{9.8}$$

When sampling this continuous spectrum, which is of course periodic with period $2\pi/T$, by N samples in one period, we obtain

$$\{F_k\} = \{F_s(k\Omega)\} = \left\{ \sum_{n=0}^{N-1} f_n e^{-jk\Omega nT} \right\} = \mathbb{DFT}\{f_n\}. \tag{9.9}$$

Thus we can conclude that the discrete Fourier transform provides exact samples of the spectrum (in the sense of the integral Fourier transform) of a finite and sampled section of the analysed signal. Nevertheless, our aim is to approximate the spectrum of the original continuous and infinite signal. Let us determine what kind and extent of changes in the spectrum will appear as

---

[2] See the definition in Section 1.1.

a consequence of signal shortening and discretisation, and of the subsequent discretisation of the calculated spectrum.

Let us follow the development in the spectrum of a signal when the mentioned modifications are applied successively. This is illustrated in Figures 9.2 and 9.3 by an example of a simple harmonic signal $f_1(t) = \cos(\omega_1 t)$, the exact spectrum of which, in the sense of an integral Fourier transform, is well known. The mathematical description of individual steps is given in Table 9.1. As in the figures, there is representation in the time domain on the left-hand side of the table and the corresponding representation in the frequency domain – spectra in the sense of the integral Fourier transform – on the right-hand side of the table.

The original time-unlimited and continuous signal is shortened in the first step to a finite length by being multiplied by a window of length NT. This may – in the simplest case – be rectangular (this is used in the example), but may also have another shape. This operation is represented in the spectral domain by convolution of the original spectrum with the window spectrum $W(\omega)$. It can be said that every line in the original spectrum will be 'smeared' to a properly shifted version of $W(\omega)$ so that the phenomenon of *leakage* of power to improper frequencies in the spectrum appears. Subsequent sampling of the signal can also be interpreted as multiplication, this time by a sequence of Dirac impulses; the spectrum then becomes periodic with the period equal

Table 9.1 Mathematical description of effects of discretising signal and spectrum

Signal description	Representation in the time domain	Representation in the frequency domain
original signal	$f_1(t) = \cos(\omega_1 t)$	$F_1(\omega) = \pi(\delta(\omega - \omega_1) + \delta(\omega + \omega_1))$
time window	$w(t) = \begin{cases} 1, & t\langle -NT/2, NT/2\rangle \\ 0, & \text{otherwise} \end{cases}$	$W(\omega) = NT\, \dfrac{\sin(\pi(\omega/\Omega))}{\pi(\omega/\Omega)}, \ \Omega = \dfrac{2\pi}{NT}$
limited section of signal	$w(t).f_1(t)$	$\dfrac{1}{2\pi} W(\omega) * F_1(\omega)$
sampling signal	$s(t) = \displaystyle\sum_{n=-\infty}^{\infty} \delta(t - nT)$	$S(\omega) = \dfrac{2\pi}{T} \displaystyle\sum_{k=-\infty}^{\infty} \delta(\omega - kN\Omega)$
sampled and limited signal section	$s(t).w(t).f_1(t)$	$\dfrac{1}{4\pi^2} S(\omega) * W(\omega) * F_1(\omega)$
sampling function in spectral domain	$s_F(t) = NT \displaystyle\sum_{k=-\infty}^{\infty} \delta(t - kNT)$	$S_F(\omega) = 2\pi \displaystyle\sum_{k=-\infty}^{\infty} \delta(\omega - k\Omega)$
periodised original corresponding to sampled spectrum	$(s(t).w(t).f_1(t)) * s_F(t)$	$(S(\omega) * W(\omega) * F(\omega)).S_F(\omega)$

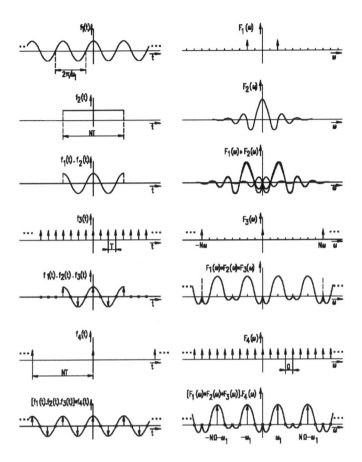

Figure 9.2 Development of a simple signal and its spectrum when gradually modified from a continuous-time, integral spectrum case to a discrete-time, DFT spectrum version (original harmonic signal frequency corresponds to one of the sampling points in the frequency domain)

to the sampling frequency. Summarising the consequences of discretisation of the analysed signal, we can state the following:

- *Frequency resolution* in the spectrum is lowered as a consequence of shortening the signal, which leads to leakage in the spectrum. This effect can be reduced primarily by using a longer window, thus providing the spectral function $W(\omega)$ with a narrower mainlobe and faster decline of sidelobes. A secondary precaution is the use of a differently shaped window $w(n)$ for weighting the signal, with a lower level of sidelobes in $W(\omega)$, which would reduce the leakage without increasing the required length of the measured signal. The influence of the window shape[3] on the spectra can be seen in Figure 9.4.

---

[3] Shapes of common windows are shown in Figure 5.5.

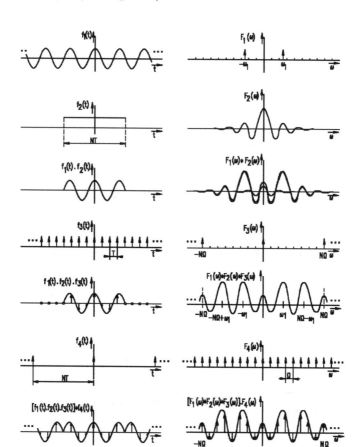

Figure 9.3 Development of a simple signal and its spectrum when gradually modified from a continuous-time, integral spectrum case to a discrete-time, DFT spectrum version (original harmonic signal frequency does not correspond to any of the sampling points in the frequency domain)

- The spectrum becomes periodic as a consequence of signal sampling. This periodicity may also lead to distortion of the spectrum by *aliasing* if the signal has significant components with frequencies above the Nyquist frequency $\omega_s/2$. (This may be caused not only by the properties of the original (infinite length) analysed signal but also as a result of leakage owing to signal shortening.) A remedy is possible primarily by increasing the sampling frequency or alternatively by preprocessing the signal using an antialiasing lowpass filter before sampling; also, application of a low-leakage window as mentioned in the previous paragraph may positively contribute to this end.

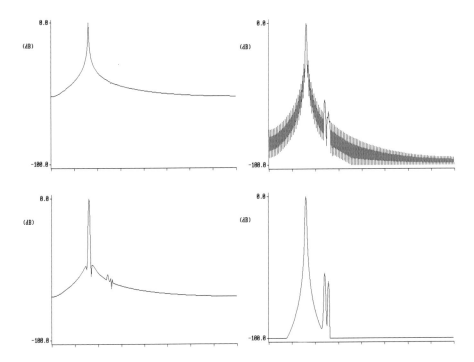

Figure 9.4 Influence of different signal-weighting windows on the resolution and leakage in the spectral domain (Analysed signal: three harmonic components – 1Hz/1V, 1.5Hz/0.02V a 1.58Hz/0.01V; depicted spectra on dB scale: upper row – rectangular and Bartlett window; lower row – Hamming and Hann window)

When determining the spectrum digitally, it is necessary (and the definition of DFT includes it) to sample also the originally continuous spectrum of the discrete-time signal. This operation is expressed on the side of the spectrum as a multiplication by a sampling impulse train; it leads in the time domain to repeating the signal periodically (which is natural, as the discrete spectrum must correspond to a periodic signal). When discretising the spectrum in accordance with the DFT definition, the corresponding signal periodicity is given by a period equal to the length of the input window, so that the analysed section of the signal remains unchanged. Nevertheless, discrete presentation of the spectrum may lead to a misleading display of spectral information for the following reasons:

- The difference between an originally line spectrum and an originally continuous spectrum may not be obvious. The original individual lines of the spectrum will only remain represented as isolated, when the samples are situated at maximums of the 'smeared' lines, and thus the other samples will represent the zero nodes of the shifted function $W(\omega)$. This is the situation arising when the window width is an integer multiple of the signal component

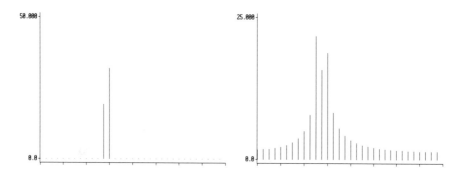

Figure 9.5a Dual possibility of spectrum appearance after sampling the originally two-line spectrum (left: component frequencies are equal to nodes of sampling in the frequency domain; right: the condition not fulfilled)

period for all the components (Figure 9.5a, left). When this condition is not fulfilled, the 'smearing' functions are sampled at nonzero values so that even for an originally line spectrum, all the spectral samples are nonzero although the samples closest to original lines are maximum (Figure 9.5a, right). Should it be known ahead that the signal is periodic, then the task is about calculating the Fourier coefficients and it is useful to utilise the approach described in the previous section which leads to precise results. More generally, it may help to interpret the spectrum better if the frequency-domain sampling is made denser, as described in the next paragraph.

• Spectrum sampling, according to the DFT definition, although perfect in preserving information completely, may be visually insufficient so that the spectrum shape, in particular the existence and position of peaks, are hardly recognisable. In such a case, it is useful to sample the spectrum in greater detail; m-times denser sampling will be achieved when an m-times longer original domain sequence is transformed, which begins with the analysed N-sample signal and is padded by $(m - 1)N$ zeros (Figure 9.5b).

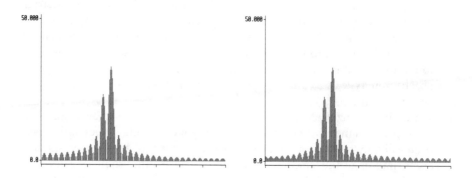

Figure 9.5b Improvement of previous spectra readibility by denser sampling

Only informal reasoning for this operation will be given, as follows. It is obvious that the continuous spectrum $S(\omega) * W(\omega) * F(\omega)$ will not be changed by setting zeros explicitly to signal samples which were already zero owing to shortening of the signal by the window. Formal extension of the transformed sequence length nevertheless leads to a corresponding increase in the length of the spectral coefficient sequence. However, this prolonged sequence describes the same range of frequencies because the sampling frequency in the time domain remains unchanged; consequently, the sampling of the spectrum is m-times denser.

The discussion shows what types of spectrum distortion must be taken into account when spectral analysis is based on the discrete Fourier transform, and how to suppress the distortions by changing the analysis parameters. When this is not possible for any reason, the practical influence of the distortions should be limited at least by a proper interpretation of the results obtained in applications. The estimates of power spectra of stochastic processes, which we shall deal with in Section 9.3, are in principle based on computations of spectra of individual process realisations, which are deterministic signals. It is therefore possible to apply the knowledge of this section adequately even for random signal analysis.

9.2.3 Time–frequency analysis

When analysing transient or nonstationary signals, the character of which is changing in time, for instance speech signals, it is often useful to consider the frequency content of relatively short sections of the analysed signals and to follow the development of such *short-time spectra* in time. This concept, enabling us to formulate the spectrum as a two-dimensional function dependent not only on frequency but also on time, is called *time–frequency analysis*. Although the integral Fourier transform theoretically works only with signals of infinite length, time-windowing leads in fact to analysing only finite pieces of signals. It can therefore be used for time–frequency analysis if the window has a suitable length and is sliding on the time axis. We have already used windowing in the previous section as a necessary step in DFT spectral analysis; in principle, the same approach can also be used here, although the philosophy of the analysis is different. While the purpose of classical spectral analysis is to determine magnitudes and phases of harmonic signal-components of different frequencies and unlimited duration, we now aim at as precise as possible a location of occurrences of every spectral component on both the frequency and time axes. A different design approach from the observation windows follows from the changed goal. In classical analysis, it was desirable to maximise the window length in order to minimise the distortions. For time–frequency analysis, the window length is a compromise between the requirements of frequency resolution directly proportional to the window length (the resolvable difference of frequencies is inversely proportional to the window length), and the as high as possible time resolution, which is given as being inversely proportional to the window length determining approximately the shortest resolvable time difference.

One of these requirements is usually decisive, and the signal window length (or the corresponding number of samples N with a given sampling frequency ω_s) must be adapted to it. Transforming such a signal section by the DFT yields a so-called discrete *short-time spectrum* characterising the frequency content and phase relations of the analysed signal in the respective time period. Notice that the values of the short-time spectrum describe the whole time period and it is not possible to resolve any development inside of the window duration – its length basically determines the time resolution. On the other hand, the window length also determines the frequency resolution, which is approximately the Nth part of the range $\langle -\omega_s/2, \omega_s/2 \rangle$ and is therefore constant in the whole range of the analysed frequencies.

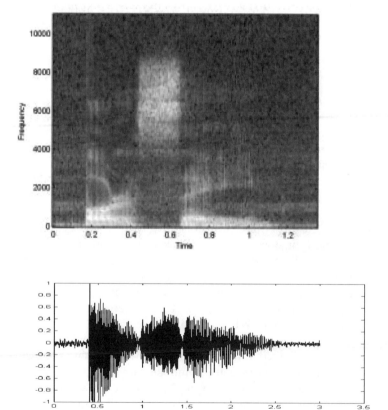

Figure 9.6 Example of a spectrogram: time-course of the acoustic signal corresponding to the word 'Orsay' (lower part) and its spectrogram (above)

The short time spectra are usually provided as a whole series, based on data describing a longer signal sequence, in the frame of which we want to follow the development of the frequency content. The simplest organisation of the analysis then consists in dividing the whole available sequence of M samples into sections of N samples, thus obtaining int(M/N) spectra. The frequency resolution is therefore determined by the window length NT; this period also determines the minimum resolvable difference in time. The time resolution can be slightly increased by using partial overlap of the windows, e.g. by half of their length. In this way, we obtain more spectra along the time axis and a possible time development can be better followed, particularly on the side of high frequencies. Such a set of spectra, called a *spectrogram*, can be vividly presented as a two-dimensional image in which one axis corresponds to frequency, the other one to time. The colour of a suitable pallette or a degree of grey expresses the amplitude (or exceptionally also the phase) of the spectral components of a particular frequency and a particular time location (see Figure 9.6).

Such plain spectrograms suffer from the drawback of DFT, consisting in the constant absolute frequency resolution. The length of the window must therefore be determined by the necessary frequency resolution on the side of low frequencies and in this way limits the time resolution which might be better for higher frequencies. It would usually be more useful in practical applications if the relative frequency resolution were constant, i.e. if the minimum resolvable frequency interval were a certain fraction of the absolute frequency. (This is also, for example, the case with human hearing – a trained musician can recognise a change of sound pitch by several per cent of a half tone, which is a relative frequency resolution of about 0.1 per cent.) Then, of course, a lower absolute resolution would be needed on the side of higher frequencies, consequently a shorter window would be needed and the time resolution could be better for higher frequencies. The physical interpretation is obvious: the high-frequency components can be recognised and identified with the relevant precision in a shorter time.

The above discussion suggests the idea of analysing the available signal by means of several spectrograms with different window lengths. If the number of samples in a window needed for the desired frequency resolution on the low-frequency side is N, series of spectrograms can be constructed conveniently e.g. for windows with N, $N/2$, $N/4$, $N/8$ etc. samples. A spectrogram from such a series always has a halved frequency resolution compared with the previous one, but it also has a doubled time resolution. In this way, the signal-spectrum development can be captured more completely although at the cost of an enormous increase in data amount in comparison with a single spectrogram. On the other hand, it is obvious that every spectrogram of the series describes only a certain frequency range optimally. With the chosen window sequence, the optimal range has approximately the extent of one octave (i.e. with the limit frequencies ratio $1:2$); it has insufficient frequency resolution for lower frequencies and too low time resolution for higher frequencies. It is thus possible and useful to reduce the data by only preserving the best described band of frequencies from each spectrogram (in our case, just one octave). Such bands of all spectrograms can then be concatenated on the frequency axis thus providing a new composite spectrogram. The scales on both axes can be arranged efficiently so that the time axis remains linear (the spectra at lower frequencies should be appropriately stretched to cover the whole time range as formed by the series of spectra for the highest octave). The frequency axis can be most easily formed in a piecewise linear manner preserving the original linear scale of the octave stripes which leads to an approximately logarithmic frequency scale – every octave has the same width.

It is obvious that the composite (multiresolution) spectrogram of the previous paragraph illustrates transients substantially better than the plain fixed-resolution spectrogram, although the amount of data describing it remains about the same; the useful new data was added at the cost of throwing away the unnecessary data. Nevertheless, high computational requirements are an important disadvantage of this approach. All the partial spectrograms have in practice to be calculated completely, although only a small part of them is used. This is because the fast DFT algorithms usually do not allow the calculation of only a part of the spectrum effectively.

For this reason, algorithms that are more effective are sought enabling the computation of differently modified spectrograms. One of the possibilities is the use of a logarithmic filter bank in which every next higher-frequency filter of a set of bandpass filters working in parallel has a q times wider band than the previous one (for instance, $q = \sqrt[3]{2}$ for the so-called third-octave filter banks, compare Section 9.3.2.1 where constant-width filters are used). Again, approximately constant relative frequency resolution is achieved in this way, which also means faster reaction of higher-frequency wider-band filters and thus higher time resolution on the side of higher frequencies.

An elegant and obviously effective instrument of a kind of the time–frequency analysis appeared recently as the wavelet transform, which has the principle of multiresolution already inherent in its definition (see Section 3.5). Its function can also be described in terms of certain logarithmic filter banks (mostly dyadic, $q = 2$). Moreover, this transform removes the basic disadvantage of all the frequency-analysis methods that are based on the Fourier transform and thus are using in principle time-unlimited harmonic functions as their basis: the need to use many harmonic components to express transients. As the name suggests, the base functions of the wavelet transforms are finite-duration smoothly starting and ending 'wavelets'. These are all generated from a single pattern by time dilation so that, simultaneously with increasing wavelet length, its frequency content is shifted towards lower frequencies. Expressing the short-time signal components is then easier and usually needs a much lower number of active components than in the case of harmonic-base functions. More details on the wavelet transform, besides those presented in Section 3.5, can be found in specialised literature; one of the basic sources is the monograph [33].

9.3 Spectral analysis of random signals

9.3.1 *Probabilistic estimates of spectra of stochastic processes*

When speaking about random signals, we have in mind the signals the time course of which cannot be exactly predicted; of course, only such signals are capable of bringing any information. On the other hand, should we need to analyse such a signal, its values (e.g. discrete samples) must already be known, and then the signal is not random any more but clearly deterministic. This observation may lead to the conclusion that the problem has been converted into that of the previous case and seemingly there is no more to discuss.

Nevertheless, there is the important aspect substantiating the need of random signal analysis, or more precisely, the necessity for the analysis and identification of the stochastic processes that are generating the random signals. It is about detecting and evaluating common features of all available realisations of a particular stochastic process which is used to model the operation of the equipment producing the signal, e.g. acoustic noise. We can then expect, with a certain probability, that further realisations, so far unknown, will have similar features or properties. Based on such knowledge, it is possible to design systems and procedures to process and evaluate the signals, to communicate or archive them etc. We can reasonably expect, then, that the designed systems or methods will be suitable at least for most of the newly appearing signals. On the other hand, the data obtained by identifying and describing such a stochastic process can be used to analyse the inner mechanism which is behind the origination of the random signals. This is the so-called *signature analysis* aiming at the non-destructive testing or noninvasive diagnostics of systems (e.g. mechanical machinery but also biological systems) on the basis of the signals produced by them. The description in the frequency domain belongs to most important characteristics of stochastic processes from the point of view of signal analysis.

It should be emphasised that the problem of estimating all the signal characteristics is a probabilistic matter. The realisations available for analysis have been randomly chosen from the family of functions constituting the stochastic process, according to results of the associated stochastic experiment and there is no way of proving that the selection is representative. All the derived characteristics, including the spectra, are therefore only statistical estimates burdened by systematic and random errors which are dependent on methods of data selection and on approaches to their processing. Formulated in another way, the calculated values of estimated characteristics (e.g. of spectra) are themselves stochastic variables with their own statistical parameters, namely mean and variance, although the theoretical quantities themselves are deterministic, being given by ensemble mean values.

We are naturally aiming, by selecting suitable data and processing methods, to the end where the mean values of the estimated variables are equal to the theoretical parameters of the analysed processes – i.e. that the estimates are unbiased, otherwise they are denoted as *biased* (systematically in error). In addition, we are trying to achieve as small variances of the estimated parameters as possible. Then we can expect the concrete error of an individual estimate not to be too high (and often we have to rely on a single available estimate in practical applications). In many situations, including the estimation of the spectral description of stochastic processes, it will be possible to determine in advance if the estimate, made by a particular method, will be unbiased. Theoretical analysis may show how much bias should be expected, and what will be the variance of the estimates. On this basis, the plausibility of the obtained characteristics can be ascertained. As a rule, minimising the bias and variance with a given amount of measuring data are mostly conflicting goals and a compromise must be sought. Theoretical analysis of the precision of statistical estimates is a subject of specialised literature, e.g. References [32, 35].

Detailed analysis of the precision and reliability of the estimates is beyond the scope of this section, the purpose of which is primarily explanation of the concepts and principles of spectral-analysis methods, and also clear physical interpretation of the obtained results. We shall, however, repeatedly call the reader's attention to the probabilistic character of all the analyses and consequently to the necessity to verify the results. This can be done by repeating the measurements and/or by trying to obtain consistent results by alternative methods of data processing, if an exact probabilistic analysis is unavailable. The statistical stability of estimates and a reasonable degree of agreement among the results obtained by different approaches to estimation are usually relatively reliable indication of their legitimacy.

9.3.2 Estimates of power spectra

9.3.2.1 Nonparametric methods

Nonparametric methods of estimating power (as well as cross) spectra of stochastic processes are distinguished by the property that the complete analysis is based only on measured or received signal data without making any models of signal generation. Classical, and still basic, methods of power-spectrum estimation are the nonparametric methods of periodogram and of correlogram existing in many modifications. We shall also briefly introduce in this section the method of floating-power spectrum estimation by means of filter banks and the method of minimum variance as an example of a modern approach.

The *periodogram method* is the most straightforward one; it utilises the definition relation of eqn (4.23) of the power spectrum based on digital data,

$$S_{ff}(\omega) = \mathbb{E}\left\{\frac{1}{N}|F_w(\omega)|^2\right\} \approx \frac{1}{M}\sum_{w_i=w_1}^{w_M}\frac{1}{N}|F_{w_i}(\omega)|^2. \qquad (9.10)$$

Recall that, in principle, this is an ensemble average of the individual power spectra of M realisations, each N samples long. The coefficient $1/N$ is a consequence of the requirement that the discrete version of the Wiener–Khintchin relation (eqn (4.24)) be valid. Computation according to the right-hand side of eqn (9.10) is digitally realised by means of FFT followed by squaring absolute values and therefore provides only samples of the spectrum, $S_{ff}(k\Omega)$, $\Omega = 2\pi/(NT)$. Several alternatives are applied for the average calculation.

Obviously, the simplest approach (Figure 9.7) is to choose $M = 1$, i.e. to suppose that the properties of an individual power spectrum are sufficiently close to the average properties of the process. This is reasonably possible if a sufficiently long section of a stationary-process realisation is available, and primarily in cases when narrowband or even harmonic components are to be evaluated. We then utilise fully the available frequency resolution given by the signal window length of NT. However, a large variance of estimates of individual spectrum samples must be expected, so that the spectrum course as yielded at the output A in Figure 9.7 will not be smooth. The input-signal samples may be weighted by a suitable window $w(n)$ in order to limit the leakage phenomenon, as was explained in Section 9.2.2.

The rough spectrum thus obtained may be smoothed if we can suppose that the background stochastic process is wideband in character and, consequently, that the neighbouring spectrum values are close in value, i.e.

$$S_{ff}(0) \approx S_{ff}(\Omega) \approx S_{ff}(2\Omega) \approx \cdots \approx S_{ff}((N-1)\Omega)$$

but, of course,

$$S_{ff}(k\Omega) \neq S_{ff}(l\Omega) \quad \text{for} \quad k \ll l.$$

Then it is possible to obtain new estimates of individual spectral samples by weighted averaging of neighbouring samples, i.e. by convoluting the estimated spectrum with a (usually) symmetrical weighting function, $W'(k)$. This provides a smoothed estimate (Figure 9.7, output B)

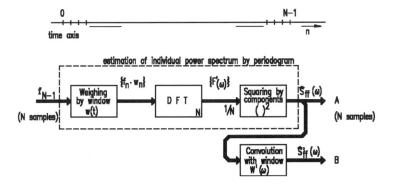

Figure 9.7 Basic procedure of periodogram computation

$$S'_{ff}(k\Omega) = \sum_{l=-\mathrm{int}(K/2)}^{\mathrm{int}(K/2)} W'(l)S_{ff}((k+l)\Omega), \qquad (9.11)$$

with the (odd) extent K in the usual range of 3 to 33 samples. The simplest such spectral window is the uniform function, providing a plain sliding average of K samples. The spectrum course becomes smoother in this way – the variance of individual samples is partially suppressed, but it is achieved at the cost of biasing the values owing to the influence of neighbouring samples. It will also lead to a deterioration of frequency resolution – close narrowband peaks may merge. As this modification is a convolution in the frequency domain, it is equivalent to a multiplication weighting of the input signal by a window the shape of which is given by the inverse Fourier transform of $W'(k)$. Thus, for example, for uniform $W'(k)$, the corresponding window in the time domain is of type sinc(*), which in consequence of its zeros omits some input data – in any case a part of the available input information will be lost. It is important to make sure that it is primarily the information specific to a particular realisation which would be suppressed, while the common features typical for all realisations should be preserved as much as possible. It is not easy to fulfil this requirement when we do not have *a priori* information on the signal-generating process.

If the process is stationary (and ergodic so that we could in principle infer the properties of the whole process on the basis of a single realisation) and the available signal sequence is sufficiently long, another approach is possible. We may then achieve the variance reduction at the price of frequency – resolution deterioration – i.e. again by introducing a bias – according to Figure 9.8. Here, the input signal sequence is divided into shorter segments of $N' = N/M$ samples (M is usually in the range 8 to 16). An individual power spectrum is then determined for each segment and the results averaged according to

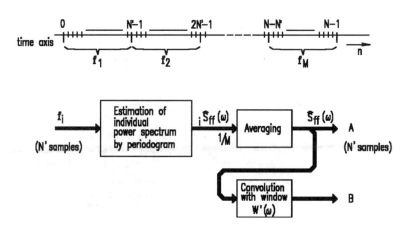

Figure 9.8 Principle of periodogram calculation based on segmented data

eqn (9.10), where naturally N will be substituted for by N'. The result will be smoother not only because of higher leakage due to shorter signal sections, but also owing to variance suppression by averaging of multiple spectra. With respect to the supposed ergodicity, the result is the same as if we had averaged more realisations; such an averaging thus limits the variance without leading to further biasing of the estimates. If the process of averaging segment spectra is combined with convolutional smoothing according to the previous paragraph, or by equivalent weighting of the input by the corresponding window $w'(n)$, then the described approach is probably the most commonly used *Welch method* of spectral estimation.

Finally, the most precise but also practically most difficult to realise approach is the method of averaging M different realisations, each with the original number of N samples. If M is sufficiently large, the variance is adequately low and the resulting average spectrum is thus rather smooth so that additional smoothing is unnecessary. The original frequency resolution corresponding to the signal length NT therefore remains preserved and, at the same time, the spectral sample estimates are unbiased. The difficulty with this method is mainly in providing a number of independent realisations of the process; the previously emphasised great computational burden of this approach is less important with the contemporary equipment available.

Often, an opinion can be met in the literature that weighting of the input signal or its segments by a window is improper when calculating power spectra. Let us observe that this opinion has no substantiation: primarily, because the signal is weighted anyway, even without this being explicit, by the rectangular window corresponding to a finite duration of the signal. If we replace this window, which has unsuitable spectral properties, by a more appropriate one which suppresses leakage to distant frequencies, it would influence every individual power spectrum of a concrete realisation as favourably as it did for a regular deterministic-signal spectrum. Consequently, the average power spectrum of the process would also be adequately improved. The chosen shape of the window used may of course also be influenced by other issues than those considered when analysing simple deterministic signals: the effort to minimise leakage and maximise frequency and level resolution may be subordinated to the aim of minimisation of variance in the spectra.

The periodogram method has already been introduced by statisticians in the nineteenth century (although with a different notation) as the first method of statistical spectral analysis to investigate the time series of different origin. After introducing the concept of the correlation function after 1920 and namely after the discovery of the Wiener–Khintchin theorem, the correlogram method which will be described in the next few paragraphs prevailed and interest in the periodogram method receded temporarily. Nevertheless, after the efficient algorithms of DFT calculations were (re)discovered and implemented in their many variants, the periodogram again became the basic and most frequently used method for calculating power-spectrum estimates.

An alternative to the above method is represented by the equally classical *correlogram method* based on a discrete version of the Wiener–Khintchin theorem eqn (4.24),

$$S_{ff}(\omega) = \mathbb{DTFT}\{w(\tau)R_{ff}(\tau)\} = \sum_{\tau=-N+1}^{N-1} w(\tau)R_{ff}(\tau)e^{-j\omega\tau T}, \quad w(\tau) = \frac{N-\tau}{N}. \quad (9.12)$$

In consideration of the many misunderstandings, the following commentary is probably appropriate here. As has been shown in Section 4.4.1, eqn (9.12) is a relation which is exactly valid for theoretical functions – the power spectrum and the autocorrelation function of the process. Therefore, it does not only represent a relationship between estimates, possibly even only approximate, as is sometimes claimed in the literature. The rating of the theorem as only approximate is nevertheless appropriate, once the weighing function $w(\tau)$ is not explicitly included (its omission is usually the case). Then the relationship is really not valid for the correlation function but rather for its commonly used biased estimate

$$R'_{w_i}(\tau) \approx \frac{1}{N} \sum_{n=0}^{N-1-\tau} f_{w_i}(n)f_{w_i}(n+\tau), \quad (9.13)$$

substituting the unbiased (but suffering with a greater variance for large τ) estimate

$$R_{w_i}(\tau) \approx \frac{1}{N-\tau} \sum_{n=0}^{N-1-\tau} f_{w_i}(n)f_{w_i}(n+\tau). \quad (9.14)$$

The estimate (9.13) can be obtained from the unbiased value given by (9.14) by multiplying it by the weighting function $w(\tau)$, i.e. $R'(\tau) = ((N-\tau)/N)R(\tau)$. Nevertheless, this biasing is so radical that the correlation function is substantially changed by it (even in the limit for $N \to \infty$) and thus it is more appropriate to speak about a weighted estimate. It is therefore obvious that the estimated correlation function according to eqn (9.13), which in fact is weighted, should be taken as the original to be transformed by the DTFT in order to obtain a fair power-spectrum estimate. Note that this is usually done in practice without explicitly mentioning that a weighted function is being used. If an unbiased estimate according to eqn (9.14) is available, it is of course necessary to modify it by the triangular window $w(\tau)$ before submitting it to the transform. This is probably an explanation of some published experimental findings where weighting the autocorrelation function by a window yields 'better' spectral estimates than those achieved by applying the window to the original time-domain signal. It may remain valid even with other than the triangular window; the used window serves in this case as an unintentional coarse approximation of the triangular one. Such a windowing, of course, serves quite a different purpose to that explained in the previous section.

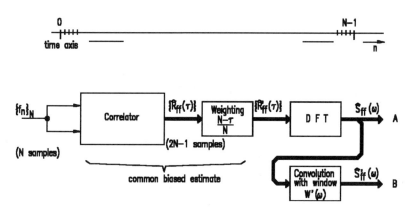

Figure 9.9 Basic procedure of correlogram computation

When using the correlogram method, the computation consists of two successive steps (Figure 9.9):

1 Computation of the weighted estimate of the autocorrelation function, usually directly according to eqn (9.13). Should the estimate be obtained by a method which does not impose automatic weighting or provides a different type of weighting, multiplication by a suitable weighting function must follow the correlation (as, for example, when using a substantially greater number of signal samples than corresponds to the extent of delay in correlation).

2 Discrete Fourier transform computation of the weighted autocorrelation function (usually using one of the FFT algorithms). It should be noted that the discrete estimate of the autocorrelation function is a vector of $2N - 1$ components and therefore the DFT must operate on sequences of this length according to eqn (4.24a), although the length of the original input sequence is only N.

The estimate according to eqn (9.12), based on the estimate (9.13), already includes the averaging inherent to the correlation procedure; the averaging effect is more pronounced the longer the signal section that was available. The resulting spectra (output A in Figure 9.9) therefore usually have an acceptable variance. It is of course possible to proceed with smoothing either by the optimum method of averaging the power spectra of more realisations, or by the substantially less demanding but certain distortion-introducing method of smoothing by convolution according to eqn (9.11) (output B in Figure 9.9) or equivalently by additional weighting of the correlation function before transformation, i.e. by multiplying by $w'(\tau).w(\tau)$. The use of signal segmentation similar to the Welch periodogram method is naturally also possible with the correlogram method, but less common (Figure 9.10). This averaging may

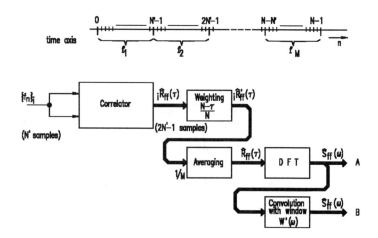

Figure 9.10 Principle of the correlogram calculation based on segmented data

concern either the resulting power spectra or, with advantage, the correlation functions which are real; in this way repeated use of the DFT can be minimised compared with what would be needed when many spectra are calculated prior to averaging.

Both classical methods of power-spectrum estimation often use the process of increasing the density of the spectral samples in order to improve visual evaluation of the spectra. This is arranged by means of prolonging the sequences entering the DFT (i.e. signal sections for periodograms or autocorrelation functions for correlograms) by padding them with zeros. This approach, naturally, does not add any further information.

To conclude this section on classical methods, we should try to point out their advantages and possible drawbacks. Concerning the computational requirements and quality of results, it can be said that their main advantages are, first, the simplicity and speed of calculation as they are both based on very efficient FFT algorithms and, secondly, the transparency and easy interpretation of the results on the basis of generally known elements of discrete signal theory. On the other hand, both methods are characterised by relatively low frequency-resolution for a given quality of estimates expressed by variance and perhaps also bias.

Another nonparametric approach to power-spectrum estimation is the use of *filter banks*, illustrated in its most general form by Figure 9.11. The analysed signal is connected in parallel to inputs of a set of M bandpass filters. The frequency responses of the filters are such (in the ideal case) that the passband of the ith filter, $\langle {}_d\omega_i, {}_h\omega_i \rangle$, is linked to the next band, ${}_h\omega_i = {}_d\omega_{i+1}$. These cover the required frequency range, i.e. maximally ${}_d\omega_0 = 0$, ${}_h\omega_{M-1} \cong \omega_s/2$, for discrete signal analysis; then, all the signal power is processed by the filter bank. The output of every filter is squared and integrated with a sliding window of rectangular or another shape, most often exponentially decreasing into the

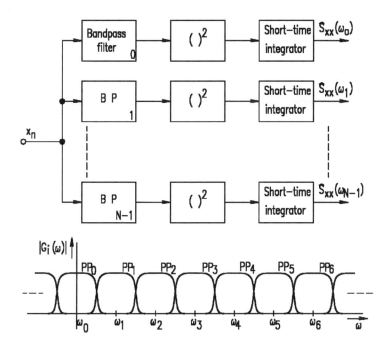

Figure 9.11 Principle of spectral analysis by filter banks

past. The output of each frequency-selective channel is thus proportional to the average signal power in the given frequency band. The result depends on both the bandwidth and the equivalent time of integration (defined as the rectangular window length providing the same stabilised output level for a stationary signal). Therefore, to obtain estimates of average power spectral densities in the relevant frequency bands, the channel outputs have to be divided by both the mentioned quantities which may be specific for each channel. The results then provide a staircase approximation of the power spectrum of the analysed signal; to obtain a reasonably detailed spectrum estimate, tens of filters are usually needed.

   This principle brings certain advantages: parallel work and consequently real-time availability of short-time spectra, user-selectable integrating times and possibly also filter bandwidths. The filter-bank approach is particularly suited to time–frequency analysis as every channel can have different properties, independent of other filters. Particularly, it is possible to build a filter bank with exponentially increasing bandwidth of individual filters thus approximating spectra with logarithmic scale of frequency, such as the so-called octave filters or third-octave filters. In addition, the integration times of individual channels can be arranged in a decreasing sequence so that the product of bandwidth and integration time remains constant for all channels. The time resolution then increases with frequency and the relative frequency resolution remains approximately constant, as suitable for time–frequency analysis (see Section 9.2.3).

This system can also be realised by analogue technology, although the digital realisation will be mostly preferred today. With respect to frequency-band chaining, the digital-filter elements can be shared and simplified in various ways. When building the spectrum analyser as a standalone apparatus, it is possible to manage even with only a single measuring channel: the idea is to measure the individual frequency bands successively providing that the analysed signal is stationary. The channel bandwidths and integration times may differ in the measurement sequence. The system can be even further simplified if both constant bandwidth $\Delta\omega$ and constant integration time are acceptable. Then it is possible to insert a modulator enabling frequency translation by $k\Delta\omega$ prior to such a channel and, by changing k, provide the results for the whole relevant range of frequencies (Figure 9.12). This concept is particularly advantageous with analogue realisations.

When evaluating the filter banks as a good and conceptually simple approach with the advantages as mentioned above, we should also take into account the fact that the filters do not have exactly rectangular frequency responses and the spectral estimates therefore suffer more or less from leakage, depending on the quality of filters. The reaction speed of channels, which determines the time to stabilise the outputs after a sudden change in the analysed signal properties, should be considered. The corresponding delay increases with an increase in the integration times, which in turn must be chosen appropriately to the reaction times of individual filters of possibly different bandwidths. On the other hand, the variance of results decreases with longer integration.

At the end of the section on nonparametric spectral estimates, we shall mention another concept which can be useful for narrowband signal analysis when maximum resolution of close frequency components is needed. Although a certain conceptual filter bank is considered when deriving the method, neither of the filters is in fact applied to signals nor do they represent models of signal generation. Therefore, this *minimum-variance method* is also a nonparametric method and provides the estimates solely based on the signal data.

The algorithm originates from the idea of a parallel structure of FIR filters of the degree P. Such a typical filter is described by its impulse response vector $\mathbf{h} = [h_0, h_1, \cdots, h_{P-1}]'$ (the symbol $'$ denotes transposition) and the nth sample

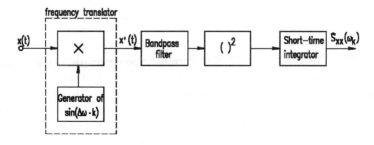

Figure 9.12 Power-spectrum analyser with frequency translation of the measured signal

of its output is $y_n = \mathbf{h}'.\mathbf{x}_n$ where $\mathbf{x}_n = [x_n, x_{n-1}, \cdots, x_{n-P+1}]'$ is the vector of the P last input samples. The following requirement is imposed on the filter: the variance of a general output sample y_n, characterising the filter's output power, should be minimised subject to the constraint that the frequency transfer of the filter at a chosen frequency ω_0 will be unity,

$$G(\omega_0) = H(z)|_{z=e^{j\omega_0 T}} = \sum_{n=0}^{P-1} h_n e^{-j\omega_0 nT} = \mathbf{h}'\mathbf{e}(\omega_0) = 1, \qquad (9.15)$$

where $\mathbf{e}(\omega_0) = [1, e^{-j\omega_0 T}, e^{-j\omega_0 2T}, \cdots, e^{-j\omega_0(P-1)T}]'$. The interpretation of this requirement is that, although the transfer at ω_0 remains constant, the components with other frequencies are being suppressed; the power (density) at the frequency ω_0 is then proportional to the minimum variance and approximates the value $S_{ff}(\omega_0)$. We are therefore seeking a vector $\mathbf{h}$, which minimises the mentioned variance under the given constraint.

The variance, as the ensemble mean value is (when the signals are supposed to have zero means)

$$\mathbb{E}\{y_n^2\} = \mathbb{E}\{(\mathbf{h}'\mathbf{x}_n)(\mathbf{h}'\mathbf{x}_n)'\} = \mathbf{h}'\mathbb{E}\{\mathbf{x}_n\mathbf{x}_n'\}\mathbf{h} = \mathbf{h}'\overline{\overline{\Phi}}_{xx}\mathbf{h}, \qquad (9.16)$$

where $\overline{\overline{\Phi}}_{xx}$ is obviously the autocorrelation matrix of the vector $\mathbf{x}_n$. By minimisation of (9.16) with respect to the components of $\mathbf{h}$ under the constraint (9.15), the following result for the optimum impulse response is obtained:

$$\mathbf{h}_{opt} = \frac{\overline{\overline{\Phi}}_{xx}^{-1}\mathbf{e}(\omega_0)}{\mathbf{e}'^*(\omega_0)\overline{\overline{\Phi}}_{xx}^{-1}\mathbf{e}(\omega_0)},$$

which, after substitution into eqn (9.16), gives the minimised variance at the filter output

$$S_{xx}(\omega_0) \approx \sigma_y^2 = \frac{1}{\mathbf{e}'^*(\omega_0)\overline{\overline{\Phi}}_{xx}^{-1}\mathbf{e}(\omega_0)}. \qquad (9.17)$$

This last expression thus provides an estimate of the power-spectrum value at an arbitrarily chosen frequency ω_0. It can be seen that calculation of the spectral values for an arbitrarily chosen sequence of frequencies is entirely based on the $P \times P$ autocorrelation matrix of the analysed signal. The matrix can be estimated by any of the previously mentioned methods utilising the available signal data. The formula (9.17) therefore presents an alternative expression for estimating the power spectrum. Experience shows that, for a given length of signal, the quality of harmonic-component estimation, as far as both the frequency resolution and the real power-spectral densities are concerned, is much better than with classical methods, even in the presence of additive wideband noise. Notice that the result is naturally influenced by the length P of the conceptual filters, which can be chosen rather arbitrarily; however, the quality of the estimates does not necessarily improve monotonically with P.

9.3.2.2 Parametric methods

The basis of all parametric methods of power-spectrum estimation is the formulation of a suitable model of signal generation (in short: the *signal model*). The structure of the model should correspond to a particular class of signal. A few parameters of such a model then describe a particular signal – therefore also its spectrum – in an economical way and represent thus, besides the analytical description, also a way to data reduction. Parametric spectral analysis uses the concept of approximating the power spectrum by frequency responses of the signal models; these are usually rational fractional functions and are therefore smooth functions of frequency. This corresponds to the expected shape of the estimated spectra of many common signal types which, in practice, are usually generated by systems of a rather low order.

Usually, we do not have enough information on the mechanisms of signal generation to allow us to formulate a precise model, or such a model is too complicated for practical use. The simple conception as depicted in Figure 9.13 is therefore often used. Here, the source generates wideband noise $v(n)$, forming the input of a linear time-invariant system with the transfer function $H(z)$ which in turn provides the signal $\xi(n)$ at its output. This signal is then considered to be a model of the real analysed signal in a certain defined sense. Usually, we require that the power spectrum $S_{\xi\xi}(\omega)$ of this signal (more precisely: of the process generating the signal) is as good as possible an approximation of the spectrum of the analysed signal $x(n)$,

$$S_{xx}(\omega) \approx S_{\xi\xi}(\omega). \tag{9.18}$$

According to eqn (4.32), the output spectrum is

$$S_{\xi\xi}(\omega) = |H(e^{j\omega T})|^2 S_{vv}(\omega).$$

Usually, the source signal $v(n)$ is chosen to be white noise in which case its power spectrum is uniform, $S_{vv}(\omega) = \sigma_v^2$, and the previous relation simplifies to

$$S_{\xi\xi}(\omega) = |H(e^{j\omega T})|^2 \sigma_v^2. \tag{9.19}$$

Then the spectrum of the model signal $\xi(n)$ is fully determined and described by the structure and parameters of the linear system in the model (when disregarding the noise-power factor).

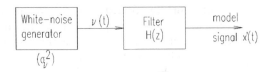

Figure 9.13 Basic stochastic model of signal generation

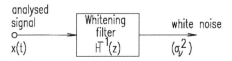

Figure 9.14 Concept of whitening filter

Parameter estimation of this internal system is based on the concept of the so-called *whitening filter* (Figure 9.14). This filter transforms the analysed signal $x(n)$ so that its output signal $e(n)$ will be white noise with a uniform spectrum $S_{ee}(\omega) = \sigma_e^2$. If the parameters and transfer function $H_B(z)$ of the whitening filter can somehow be determined for a given analysed signal, the following relationship among the transfers of both involved systems is obviously valid providing that $\sigma_v^2 = \sigma_e^2$ is chosen for the model,

$$|H(z)|^2 = \frac{1}{|H_B(z)|^2}. \qquad (9.20)$$

Thus, the estimated power spectrum of the analysed signal is

$$S_{xx}(\omega) \approx \frac{\sigma_e^2}{|H_B(e^{j\omega T})|^2}. \qquad (9.21)$$

Power-spectrum estimation by this method therefore consists of the following two stages:

- identification of whitening filter parameters and determination of the variance of its output signal (see later);
- spectrum computation according to expression (9.21).

The remaining difficult problem is how to ascertain the proper structure and parameters of the model filter corresponding to a particular signal. For the filter structure, the recursive system of Figure 2.9, which contains delays both in feedforward as well as in feedback branches, is naturally the most general structure and therefore covers all possible cases. As the nonrecursive part of the system provides a weighted *moving average* (MA) of a certain number of input values and concurrently the recursive part – or *autoregressive* (AR) part – provides a weighted average of some delayed output values, the signal model based on such a system is sometimes called the ARMA model. The identification of such a model is not easy and thus often simpler models, either purely nonrecursive MA models or purely recursive AR models, are used.

In the latter case (Figure 9.15), which we shall deal with in detail with respect to its advantages, the model yields the signal

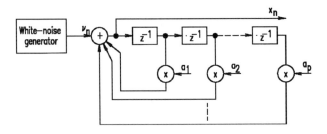

Figure 9.15 Recursive model of signal generation

$$\xi(n) = v(n) + \sum_{i=1}^{P} a_i \xi(n-i)$$

and the transfer function $H(z)$ therefore is

$$H(z) = \frac{1}{1 - \sum_{i=1}^{P} a_i z^{-i}}. \tag{9.22}$$

The inverse – whitening – filter will obviously be a nonrecursive system with the transfer function

$$H_B(z) = 1 - \sum_{i=1}^{P} a_i z^{-i}, \tag{9.23}$$

the output of which is

$$e(n) = x(n) - \sum_{i=1}^{P} a_i x(n-i). \tag{9.24}$$

The structure of the filter following from this equation is depicted in Figure 9.16. As indicated in the Figure, the filter can be understood as being divided into two branches entering the output sum. One branch is the direct connection of the signal $x(n)$; the other branch can be interpreted as an FIR filter fed by the delayed version $x(n-1)$ of the same signal. This filter produces the signal

$$\tilde{x}(n) = \sum_{i=1}^{P} a_i x(n-i), \tag{9.25}$$

which can be regarded as an estimate of the signal value $x(n)$. Interpreted in this way, the latter branch is a predictive filter providing a linear estimate of the current signal value based on P previous values of the input signal. The output signal of the whole system is then the sequence of differences between the real and predicted signal values; therefore, it may be denoted as the *error signal*.

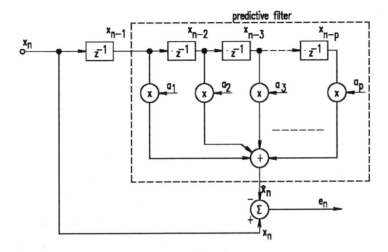

Figure 9.16 Nonrecursive whitening filter

Let us verify that the system of Figure 9.16 has, under certain assumptions which will be derived, the properties of a whitening filter, i.e. that the spectrum of the sequence $e(n)$ is uniform, or equivalently, the autocorrelation function $R_{ee}(\tau)$ has a nonzero value only for zero argument.

In the interpretation mentioned, the signal $e(n) = x(n) - \tilde{x}(n)$ is the difference between the random signal value and its linear estimate according to eqn (9.25). According to the principle of orthogonality (4.40), the estimation error will be uncorrelated with every previous signal value $x(n - \tau)$, $\tau > 0$,

$$\mathbb{E}\{e(n)x(n - \tau)\} = 0 \qquad (9.26)$$

if the linear estimate minimises the mean square error. In this case, we obtain for $\tau \neq 0$,

$$R_{ee}(\tau) = \mathbb{E}\{e(n)e(n - \tau)\} = \mathbb{E}\left\{e(n)\left(x(n - \tau) - \sum_{i=1}^{P} a_i x(n - \tau - i)\right)\right\}$$

$$= \mathbb{E}\{e(n)x(n - \tau)\} - \sum_{i=1}^{P} a_i \mathbb{E}\{e(n)x(n - \tau - i)\} = 0, \qquad (9.27)$$

as according to eqn (9.26) all the mean values present here are identically zero.

On the other side, for $\tau = 0$ we obtain a nonzero value

$$R_{ee}(0) = \sigma_e^2 = \mathbb{E}\{(e(n))^2\} = \mathbb{E}\left\{e(n)\left(x(n) - \sum_{i=1}^{P} a_i x(n-i)\right)\right\}$$

$$= \mathbb{E}\{e(n)x(n)\} - \sum_{i=1}^{P} a_i \mathbb{E}\{e(n)x(n-i)\} = R_{ex}(0). \qquad (9.28)$$

Here, only the mean values inside the sum are zero while the first term is non-zero, as it is not a correlation between the estimate error and a quantity on which the estimate would be based. We see that the autocorrelation function fulfils the above requirement. The filter is thus really a whitening filter, providing that the estimation is optimal in the least-square sense, i.e. the vector of prediction coefficients **a** is designed to be optimal in the sense of this criterion.

Still, the following comment may be interesting. The maximum value of the output autocorrelation function, meaning the output power given by the variance, is according to eqn (9.28) equal to the crosscorrelation between input and output of the whitening filter for zero delay. When substituting for $e(n)$ and expanding, we obtain

$$\sigma_e^2 = R_{ex}(0) = \mathbb{E}\{(x(n))^2\} - \mathbb{E}\{\tilde{x}(n)x(n)\} = \sigma_x^2 - R_{\tilde{x},x}(0); \qquad (9.29)$$

the power of the whitening-filter output signal is smaller than its input-signal power. The difference is the value of correlation between the estimates and the original values. The requirement that the filter output be white noise is thus equivalent to the optimality of prediction; in this case, the correlation is maximal and therefore the variance σ_e^2 of the output noise is minimised.

We have proved that the system as in Figure 9.16 is really a whitening filter as far as the internal prediction filter is designed to be optimum in the least-square sense. How to design the weight vector **a** solely on the basis of the properties of the signal $x(n)$ will be the subject of further chapters dealing with optimal and adaptive filtering. Let us only mention here preliminarily that the weights are in principle derived either from correlations among signal samples or from their frequency-domain counterparts. If estimates of these quantities can be provided *a priori*, based on either a theoretical analysis or some preliminary measurements, it will lead essentially to the design of a kind of optimal Wiener filter (Chapter 10). Another possible approach is that of using an adaptive predictive filter (Chapter 11), which generates the estimated vector **a** by successive approximations based on permanent comparison of predictions with the original values.

Note that choosing a suitable length P for the predictive filter is a substantial part of the task of parametric power spectral estimation. In this respect we are usually dependent on experimenting and experience as only rarely is a suitable order for the signal model (9.22) known ahead. Depending on the character of the concrete problem, either smoothness of the estimate or a more complex spectrum may be preferred. The former requirement leads to a low-order model, which naturally provides smooth spectral estimates but may be insufficient for more complex signal sources. The latter attitude, on the other hand, leads to higher-order models enabling a better resolution of close frequencies, but the spectral estimates may suffer from a higher variance and will also be computationally more demanding. A clue to suitable order selection is that expressing a pronounced spectral maximum in the frequency range $\omega \in \langle 0, \omega_s/2 \rangle$ requires a complex-conjugate pair of poles in the model (9.22), i.e. a pair of zeros in the prediction filter (9.23); every such pair naturally increases the order by two. Several more formalised criteria for determining P have appeared in the specialised literature, based on different assumptions concerning the analysed signal. As these properties are usually not known *a priori*, it is often again necessary to experiment. It is obvious that the order of the model must be substantially less than the length of the available analysed signal sequences, $P \ll N$. This follows intuitively from the requirement for greater smoothness than in the case of periodograms, and can be formally shown by precision analysis of the prediction-filter design. Let us emphasise that the precision of the estimated spectrum of noisy signals is generally not a monotonous function of the model order, or of the prediction degree.

When the optimum prediction filter and consequently also the whitening filter are found, the power-spectrum estimate (9.21) can be expressed using (9.23) in terms of components of the weight vector **a** and of the power of whitening filter output as

$$S_{xx}(\omega) \approx \frac{\sigma_e^2}{|H_B(e^{j\omega T})|^2} = \frac{\sigma_e^2}{\left| 1 - \sum_{i=1}^{P} a_i e^{-j\omega i T} \right|^2}. \tag{9.30}$$

Parametric power-spectrum estimation is thus realised in two principal steps:

1 Finding parameters of the whitening filter, i.e. the vector of predictor weights; this step can be realised in two consecutive steps:
   • finding estimates of correlation functions or matrices by theoretical analysis or by measurement;
   • design of an optimum prediction filter on the basis of this *a priori* information using the Wiener approach;

   or in a single step:
   • adaptive iterative estimate of the predictor using a form of adaptive filtering.

2 Calculation of the estimated spectrum according to expression (9.30).

We have dealt with the basic idea of parametric methods based on the concept of whitening filter. In detail, we have discussed perhaps the most practical variant of these methods which uses the autoregressive model of signal origin.

This method appears in the literature, with unimportant modifications, sometimes also as the *maximum entropy method* (with respect to maximisation of
difference-signal entropy which is nevertheless characteristic for the whole
class of parametric methods) or as *autoregressive spectral analysis.* The methods
based on MA or ARMA signal models are applied more rarely because of their
greater computational requirements – the filter identification leads to nonlinear
optimisation or, alternatively, the iterative determination of parameters by
adaptation also becomes more complex. Deeper analysis of these methods
can be found in specialised literature. Note that the estimates using AR
models can express individual narrowband (i.e. also harmonic) components
of the analysed signal, therefore the so-called *emission spectra,* as AR models
can describe such components by suitably located poles of the transfer function.
On the other hand, the MA models are more appropriate in cases of *absorption
spectra,* corresponding to wideband signals with narrow rejection bands which
can be characterised by the positions of transfer-function zeros. ARMA models
include both the mentioned and all other cases, but their identification is more
difficult.

An example of a spectral-estimation method specialising in a particular type
of signals is *Pisarenko decomposition.* Its purpose is to eliminate the degrading
influence of additive white noise, present in the analysed signal, to the frequency
resolution of parametric methods; it is particularly suited to the case where
mixtures of harmonic signals have been deteriorated by noise. The basic idea
of the method is as follows.

Every signal distorted by white noise can be expressed in principle as an additive mixture of white noise and harmonic signals of different amplitudes and
phases, at frequencies ω_i, $i = 1, 2, \cdots, M$. Naturally, the best fit of the model
appears for the periodic signals, while for nonperiodic signals the amount of
harmonic components may become unbearable. With respect to the supposed
independence of components, the discrete autocorrelation function is, according to eqns (8.9) and (8.7),

$$R_{ff}(\tau) = \sigma_v^2 u(\tau) + \sum_{i=1}^{M} \frac{A_i}{2} \cos(\omega_i \tau T), \qquad (9.31)$$

where $\tau, u(n), A_i$ are, respectively, delay in sampling periods, the discrete Dirac
function and amplitudes of the harmonic components. If we know the values of
the autocorrelation function from a previous estimate in the range
$\tau \in \langle -N + 1, N - 1 \rangle$, i.e. in $2N - 1$ points, eqn (9.31) represents a system of
$2N - 1$ equations where the unknown variables are σ_v^2 and components of
vectors $\mathbf{A}, \bar{\omega}$. When excluding the equation for $\tau = 0$, which is the only one influenced by noise, there remain $2N$ equations for $2M$ unknowns. As a rule,
$N \gg M$, so that the system is over-determined and the solution can be found
by optimisation. At the same time, optimisation appropriately suppresses the
influence of the imprecision of the correlation-function estimate and of possible
nonwhiteness of the noise. When substituting the solution into the remaining

equation, the noise power, σ_v^2, can be determined and subtracted from $R_{ff}(0)$. After this simplification, the following modified version of the estimated autocorrelation function is obtained,

$$R'_{ff}(\tau) = \sum_{i=1}^{M} \frac{A_i}{2} \cos(\omega_i \tau T), \tag{9.32}$$

in which the influence of noise is, in an ideal case, eliminated, and in practice substantially suppressed. Based on these function values, the parameters of the optimal prediction filter can be identified by the Wiener approach and consequently it is possible to find the parametric estimate of the power spectrum with a much higher resolution.

This approach can obviously be generalised even for the case of wideband, but not pure white, noise for which we know the shape of the (narrow) main lobe of the autocorrelation function. If this lobe encompasses only a few samples (for low values of τ), the corresponding equations of the system (9.31) can again be excluded and those few correction values can be evaluated in a similar way to the previous case.

9.3.2.3 Comparison of properties of parametric and nonparametric methods

The properties of spectral estimates obtained by nonparametric and by parametric methods differ considerably although they approximate the same functions. This is given by the fact that different methods utilise different and only partly overlapping parts of the available information given by the analysed signal section.

A fundamental property of classical nonparametric spectral estimates is the inverse proportionality of the resolvable frequency differences to the length of the processed signal section, which of course provides a low frequency-resolution when the available signal sections are short. On the other hand, this resolution is independent of the level of wideband noise as far as the narrowband components to be resolved do not get lost in the noise. The classical spectral estimates of stochastic processes also suffer from large variance; to limit it, averaging may be needed of estimates derived from several or many realisations which may be difficult to provide in practice. Alternative convoluting smoothing of resulting spectra brings systematic errors causing a bias which limits the already rather low-frequency resolution. Interpretation of classically provided results is mostly straightforward and easy for the user as it follows from the general background knowledge of signal and system theory and integral transforms. The computational demands of the classical methods are nowadays very reasonable owing to calculation of the DFT by means of effective FFT algorithms; the classical spectral analysis thus has become a standard part of all common signal-processing systems.

Modern methods of spectral analysis are designed so that they are better in a specified respect than the classical methods. This can be vaguely characterised by saying that the classical methods distribute their attention across the whole frequency range and the whole dynamic range. Modern methods, on the other hand, usually aspire to enhance a certain spectral feature at the cost of lower precision in other directions, unimportant in the given application. For instance, the nonparametric minimum-variance method yields a substantially better frequency resolution for harmonic components while preserving information on the signal dynamics only approximately both on harmonic components and on wideband noise background.

The use of parametric methods based on models of signal origin is complicated primarily by the necessity of choosing the type and order of the model. These methods are advantageous in yielding smooth estimates of spectra. However, by selecting the model order, for a reliable selection of which usually insufficient or no *a priori* information is available, we can change the character of the estimated spectrum even substantially – the ability of the model to reflect details in the analysed data spectrum is crucially dependent on the character and order of the model. Usually, it is necessary to find the order suited to a particular application by a repeated experiment. Another nice feature of parametric methods is that they provide frequency resolution which is usually substantially higher in comparison with classical methods, for a given length of available signal sequence. This high frequency-resolution is achieved owing to a certain inherent extrapolation of the corresponding autocorrelation function. It applies even for a low model order when the number of narrowband components to be resolved is small. This main advantage of parametric methods will be used especially when it is impossible to provide a sufficient amount of analysed data. A drawback of the parametric methods is that their frequency resolution deteriorates considerably with increasing levels of wideband noise. Also, the yielded information on power levels, namely of the narrowband components is rather unreliable.

9.3.3 Cross-spectra

The cross-spectrum was defined in Section 4.4.2 by eqn (4.25),

$$S_{fg}(\omega) = \frac{1}{N} \mathbb{E}\{F_w^*(\omega)G_w(\omega)\}. \tag{9.33}$$

The formula can be physically interpreted as expressing the frequency dependence of crosscorrelation between corresponding complex values of spectra of the two compared processes.

The basic method of estimating the cross-spectra follows from the right-hand side of eqn (4.25), where the mean value is approximated by an ensemble average of M realisations (each of N samples),

$$S_{fg}(\omega) \approx \frac{1}{MN} \sum_{w=w_1}^{w_M} F^*_{w_i}(\omega)G_{w_i}(\omega). \tag{9.34}$$

The process is therefore the averaging of individual cross-spectra $(1/N)F^*_{w_i}(\omega)G_{w_i}(\omega)$ which are products of complex spectra of individual concurrent realisations of both analysed processes. These coupled realisations are related in the sense that they are conditioned by the same result of the associated stochastic experiment; usually they appear at the same time, or in time sequence.

The individual cross-spectrum derived from only a single couple of related realisations is the simplest estimate of the cross-spectrum according to (9.34) for $M = 1$, which naturally suffers from a considerable variance.

The possibilities of variance reduction are quite analogous to those which we used for improving estimates of power spectra calculated *via* periodigrams. The optimum method is naturally averaging for $M \gg 1$, i.e. from a greater number of pairs of coupled realisations, with preserving the full length N of every realisation. Then there is no loss in frequency resolution and the estimate remains unbiased even after the averaging process; however, providing the data of many realisations is demanding. The method of data segmentation of a single realisation pair into M shorter sections with subsequent averaging of partial cross-spectra is well acceptable with similar limitations to those described earlier for power-spectrum estimation (Section 9.2.2). An analogue statement can be claimed for the method of smoothing by averaging of neighbouring spectral values (e.g. convoluting the resulting spectra with a window); the advantages and drawbacks are similar. It should nevertheless be emphasised that an estimate based on the product of averaged spectra is useless, even if special properties of the spectra would allow the averaging; because for dependent stochastic variables it is $\mathbb{E}\{xy\} \neq \mathbb{E}\{x\}\mathbb{E}\{y\}$.

An alternative way of estimating a cross-spectrum is represented by the discrete version of eqn (4.27),

$$S_{fg}(k\Omega) = \mathbb{DFT}\{w(\tau)R_{fg}(\tau)\} = \sum_{\tau=-N+1}^{N-1} w(\tau)R_{fg}(\tau)e^{-jk\Omega\tau T}, \tag{9.35}$$

where $w(\tau) = (N - \tau)/N$ is the triangular weighting function (window) that is a part of the relation, as was shown in Section 4.4. Notice that eqn (9.35) gives the discrete values of the spectrum precisely, the approximation is already in the crosscorrelation function which is usually available only as an estimate. The quality of this estimate, which can be obtained by the procedures described in Section 8.2, thus also determines the quality of the spectral estimation. Using an estimation of the crosscorrelation function has practical advantages in that the averaging may be done in the time domain, and thus with real numbers. This applies both to averaging, inherent in the correlation process providing an individual estimate of $R_{fg}(\tau)$, and to the possible consequential averaging of more crosscorrelation estimates. Notice that averaging of individual cross-spectra after separate DFTs is also possible, in contrast to normal spectra of individual realisations, although probably computationally more demanding. This can be done owing to the fixed useful part of the phase cross-spectra (while the individual normal spectra have random phase components).

The resulting cross-spectrum which, of course, is complex-valued is usually represented by its components in polar form, i.e. as amplitude and phase spectra. If the discrete *coherence spectrum* is needed according to the definition relation (4.26),

$$\kappa_{fg}(k\Omega) = \frac{|S_{fg}(k\Omega)|^2}{S_{ff}(k\Omega)S_{gg}(k\Omega)}, \tag{9.36}$$

besides the amplitude cross-spectrum estimate, we also need estimates of power spectra of both processes. All these estimates should be consistent in being provided from the same data set, by the same or analogous methods, including the methods of smoothing. A certain check of correctness of the result is that all the obtained coherence-spectrum values belong to the interval $\langle 0, 1 \rangle$.

Notice that none of the previously mentioned modern methods of power-spectrum estimation can be directly modified for providing estimates of cross-spectra as their concepts count on only one input signal; this is evident, for example, with the filter-bank method. A parametric estimate based on a couple of dependent signal models is conceivable but an elaborated method is not yet available.

Chapter 10
Inverse filtering and restoration of signals in noise

One of the fundamental problems of signal processing is the restoration of an unknown signal. Restoration is based on a distorted version of the original signal mixed with noise; deterioration may originate due to passing through a distorting and noisy system (e.g. a communication channel). We will try to recover the original signal form from its measured (observed, received) deteriorated version on the basis of some knowledge of the properties (or mechanism) of deterioration. In the previous chapters, we have dealt with the question of how the signal will be changed by passing through a system. Now we are going to solve the *inverse problem* of finding the input, based on knowledge of the output, in the more general case also influenced by noise interference.

10.1 Model of deterioration

A simplified but relatively general model of deterioration can be represented by a nonlinear operator with inertia, $\Psi(.)$ (Figure 10.1), which derives the output *(measured, observed) signal* from the *original signal* $\{x_n\}$ and *noise* $\{v_n\}$, both not available to the observer.

A problem formulated so generally is extremely difficult to solve; the routinely usable methods are therefore designed for only certain types of deterioration. A relatively simple and at the same time quite realistic model in many practically important cases is the combination of distortion by a linear

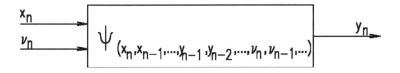

Figure 10.1 General model of deterioration

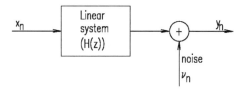

Figure 10.2 Simplified model with linear distortion and additive noise

time-invariant system and interference by *additive noise*, as depicted in Figure 10.2. In the continuous-time case, the model has the form

$$y(t) = \int_{-\infty}^{\infty} h(t - \tau)x(\tau)\,d\tau + v(t), \tag{10.1}$$

where $h(t)$ is the impulse response of the distorting system, $x(t)$ the original signal and $v(t)$ a realisation of the noise process. Similarly, for a discrete process, the model is

$$y_n = \sum_{i=0}^{\infty} h_i x_{n-i} + v_n. \tag{10.2}$$

The corresponding models in the Laplace transformed or in the frequency domains remain linear owing to the linearity of the transforms used. For the continuous-time model, we therefore obtain

$$Y_s(s) = H(s)X_s(s) + N_s(s), \quad \text{or} \quad Y(\omega) = G(\omega)X(\omega) + N(\omega) \tag{10.1a}$$

where, of course $Y(\omega) = Y_s(s)|_{s=j\omega}$, $G(\omega) = H(j\omega)$ etc., while the transform-domain version of the discrete model in the Z-transform is

$$Y_z(z) = H(z)X_z(z) + N_z(z), \quad \text{or} \quad Y(\omega) = G(\omega)X(\omega) + N(\omega) \tag{10.2a}$$

where $Y(\omega) = Y_z(z)|_{z=e^{-j\omega T}}$, $G(\omega) = H(e^{j\omega T})$ etc. We shall see later that some of the more advanced restoration methods allow for more complicated models, for example by including an inertialess nonlinearity and the like; the basic methods nevertheless come out of the mentioned models (10.1) and (10.2).

It is obvious today that even in the case of deterioration of continuous signals, restoration is realised digitally. The relationship between the degree of signal distortion owing to passing the linear system and to noise interference is very different in practical tasks. If the linear distortion prevails, the restoration problem is sometimes called *deconvolution*; if, on the contrary, noise is more important, the restoration aims at improving the signal-to-noise ratio (SNR). The requirements of removing linear distortion and of noise suppression are usually conflicting because of the character of common distorting systems (lowpass distortion, wideband or high-frequency noise). In problems where both requirements are combined, a compromise has to be sought according to a criterion of optimality formulated with respect to the particular task.

Different restoration methods require different levels of knowledge of the models mentioned above. Usually, rather detailed identification of characteristics of the inherent linear system is needed (and also possible), either in the time domain, i.e. $h(t)$ or $\{h_n\}$, or in the frequency domain – the frequency response $G(\omega)$. Based on these, or on theoretical considerations, it is possible to approximate the transfer function $H(s)$ or $H(z)$. If the linear system is accessible to measurement, it is possible to determine its characteristics by means of suitable test signals (unit impulse or step, or harmonic signals) according to the theory presented in Section 2.3; in more complex cases correlation methods as in Section 8.4 could be used. If the system cannot be identified, the problem leads to so-called *blind deconvolution*, to which we shall return in Chapter 12.

Knowledge of the noise may concern, with respect to its stochastic character, only the stochastic characteristics of the noise-generating process, which can either be theoretically derived or their statistical estimates measured when theoretical derivation is unavailable, as is often the case in practice. The requirements for the extent of the noise identification are different for different restoration methods; some can manage with only an estimate of noise power (i.e. variance), others need the power spectrum or autocorrelation function of the noise. If even nonstationary noise is admitted, the two-dimensional auto-correlation function or matrix (or perhaps only a time section of it) must be estimated, which is itself a complicated task. Estimation of noise characteristics as a stochastic-process identification problem is the subject of Sections 8.3 and 9.2.

Sometimes, we can meet a signal-deterioration model arranged according to Figure 10.3a. With respect to the linearity of the distorting system, the system is evidently equivalent to the model of part *b* and, consequently, also to the original model of Figure 10.1 where the noise is simply influenced by passing the linear system.

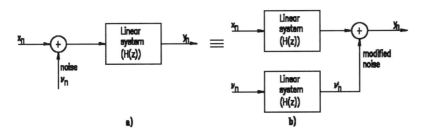

Figure 10.3 Modified model of deterioration

10.2 Plain deconvolution and pseudo-inversion

As far as the influence of the linear system (distortion) prevails in the deterioration according to models (10.1) or (10.2), the purpose of restoration is primarily
to compensate for the changes caused by the transfer of the signal through the
system. The task is most easily formulated in the frequency domain: if the
deterioration is given by the mentioned models and the noise level is low, the
plain inverse filter can be considered for restoration. The transfer function
$M_z(z)$ of such a (discrete) filter is given by the inverse of the transfer function
of the distorting system,

$$M_z(z) = \frac{1}{H(z)}. \tag{10.3}$$

The frequency response of the inverse filter is therefore

$$M(\omega) = \frac{1}{G(\omega)}, \tag{10.4}$$

so that the estimate $\hat{X}(\omega)$ of the spectrum $X(\omega)$ of the original signal will be, with
respect to eqns (10.1) and (10.2),

$$\hat{X}(\omega) = \frac{1}{G(\omega)}[G(\omega)X(\omega) + N(\omega)] = X(\omega) + \frac{N(\omega)}{G(\omega)}. \tag{10.5}$$

The middle expression allows for a vivid interpretation of the function of the
inverse filter (Figure 10.4): it compensates for the unevenness of the frequency
response of the distorting system so that the cascade connection of both systems
has a uniform (unit) frequency response. Notice that the configuration of poles
and zeros of the restoration filter is given by the configuration of the distorting
system; only poles and zeros are interchanged.

Let us now analyse the cascade connection of both linear systems in greater
detail. If the distorting system is purely recursive, of the order m, its transfer
function is

$$H(z) = \frac{1}{\sum_{i=0}^{m} a_i z^{-i}}, \quad a_0 = 1$$

and its poles must lie inside the unit circle if the distorting system is stable.
In such a case the restoration filter is of an FIR type with all zeros inside the
unit circle, thus a minimum phase system with

$$M_z(z) = \sum_{i=0}^{m} a_i z^{-i}.$$

Let us show that, when disregarding noise influence, a perfect restoration is
really possible in this case. If the Z-transform image of the observed signal is
given by a noiseless model of distortion, $Y(z) = H(z)X(z)$, so that the image

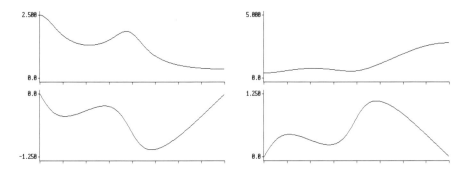

Figure 10.4 Amplitude and phase frequency response of a distortion (left) and corresponding frequency responses of the inverse filter

of the estimated restored signal is $\hat{X}(z) = M(z)Y(z)$, we have according to eqn (2.18) in the time domain

$$y_n = x_n - \sum_{i=1}^{m} a_i y_{n-i} \quad \text{and} \quad \hat{x}_n = y_n + \sum_{i=1}^{m} a_i y_{n-i}.$$

Thus, after substituting for y_n in the second relation, we obtain precisely $\hat{x}_n = x_n$. The restoration filter simply compensates for the weighted sum which damaged the signal; see the example in Figure 10.5.

By interchanging the distorting and restoration systems, we can obtain a similar result – the theoretical possibility of perfect restoration also for the case of nonrecursive distortion. By cascading the cases of recursive and nonrecursive distortions we obtain a generalisation of restoration possibilities for any linear distortion with a general transfer. Nevertheless, if the distorting system is of nonminimum phase type, i.e. with zeros outside the unit circle, the corresponding inverse filter with the transfer (10.3) will be unstable and thus practically useless (not counting the unrealistic case of zero noise and absolute precision of calculations). In the case of such a distortion, the exact causal and stable restoration filter does not exist and it only remains to design one of the different approximate filters. One of the possibilities for a stable filter design is to stabilise the recursive inverse filter by transforming all the poles, p_i, which lie outside the unit circle, into positions $1/p_i$. The amplitude frequency response thus remains unchanged and the resulting all-over amplitude frequency response of the cascade [distortion – restoration] will be uniform as requested; however, the phase characteristic will be changed and consequently the restored signal $\hat{x}_n$ will remain phase distorted. Alternatively, an approximate FIR restoration filter can be designed based on known characteristics of the distortion: the distortion frequency response will be inverted and the corresponding filter with this inverted characteristic can be designed by one of the methods described in Section 5.2.2. A stable exact inverse filter cannot naturally be

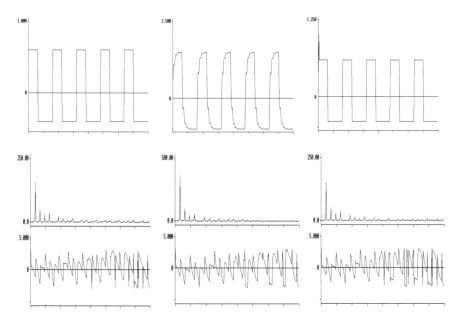

Figure 10.5 Example of the inverse filtering of a signal distorted by a purely recursive sysem of second order as in Figure 10.4. Although the distortion is of a rather disturbing type (edge smearing with ringing) it can be compensated for perfectly. Upper row from left: original, distorted and restored signals; lower row: corresponding amplitude and phase spectra

realised when the distortion has zeros on the unit circle. This is also physically obvious, as in this case some signal components are totally suppressed and thus not restorable. Even in this case, only an approximate restoration is in principle possible.

These considerations are specific to plain inverse filtering (deconvolution) without noise influence. However, as it is clear from eqn (10.5), once the distorting system generates any noise which is practically unavoidable, the output of the exact inverse filter suffers from the error expressed by the second term in the mentioned result. The magnitude of the error is dependent on the noise level at the given frequency but also on the relevant value of the frequency response of the distorting system. With respect to the usually wideband character of the noise, this term becomes large for frequencies at which the channel transfer is small so that the restoration must compensate for the loss by a high amplification. In the extreme case of zeros of the transfer $G(\omega)$, the error term increases without limits. The restoration of signals distorted by channels or systems with zero or very small values in the frequency response is therefore extraordinarily difficult, because even an imperceptible noise is selectively strongly amplified in frequency bands where the distorting system suppresses the signal components. The original-signal estimate may be (and usually is) heavily deteriorated or even totally obscured by the amplified noise. An example

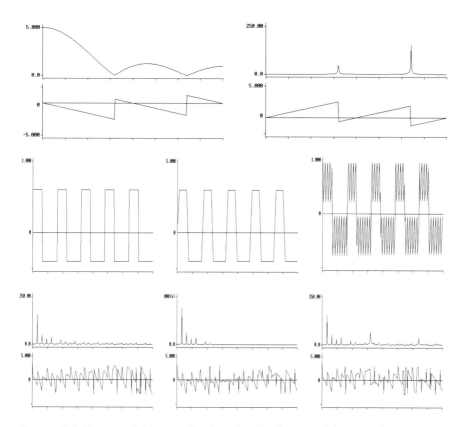

Figure 10.6 Unsuccessful inverse filtering of a signal distorted by a simple nonrecursive system (FIR filter with $\mathbf{h} = [1, 1, 1, 1, 1]$). Upper row from left: frequency response of distorting system, frequency response of the inverse filter; middle row: original, distorted and restored signals; lower row: corresponding amplitude and phase spectra

of an unsuccessful inverse restoration of signal distorted by simple FIR filtering (floating average of five samples) is presented in Figure 10.6.

In such cases, plain inverse restoration (deconvolution) is useless and the restoration filter must be modified in a way which takes into account the noise influence. Such modified filters are denoted as *pseudo-inverse filters*. The pseudoinverse primarily corrects the main causes of the difficulties, which are the extreme values of the frequency response of the restoration filter.

One of the possibilities of (approximate) pseudo-inverse filtering is the modification of the amplitude frequency response as follows

$$M(\omega) = \begin{cases} 1/G(\omega) & |G(\omega)| > \varepsilon \\ 0 & |G(\omega)| \le \varepsilon \end{cases}, \tag{10.6}$$

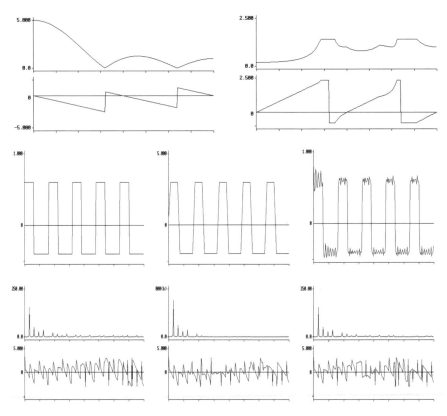

Figure 10.7 Pseudo-inverse restoration of the signal from Figure 10.6 (limited magnitude frequency response, the visible distortion of the phase characteristic is given by limited possibilities of the simulation program)

where ε is a suitably chosen threshold (in the theoretical definition of pseudo-inverse $\varepsilon = 0$). This modification leads to complete suppression of components of the restored signal in a (narrow) frequency band surrounding the points of small $G(\omega)$. This omission may cause a smaller error than that from admitting the devastating influence of the error term in eqn (10.5).

A similar consideration leads to another modification – limiting of the large magnitude response values,

$$M(\omega) = \begin{cases} 1/G(\omega) & |1/G(\omega)| < \xi \\ \xi \exp(j \arg(1/G(\omega))) & |1/G(\omega)| \geq \xi \end{cases}, \qquad (10.7)$$

where ξ is again a suitably chosen real constant, in this case meaning an acceptable maximum of frequency transfer. The advantage of this filter is that it only limits but does not totally refuse signal components in the neighbourhood of minima of $G(\omega)$. It can be seen from Figure 10.7 that the modification has improved the restoration – the noise part is substantially smaller than in

Figure 10.6 and the impulse-edge steepness has been significantly improved by the restoration. Such filters have proved useful namely for image restoration where preserving the phase information is crucial, even in frequency areas with low signal-to-noise ratio.

We shall see in Section 10.3.2 that, under certain conditions, Wiener filters may also be considered to be modified inverse filters.

10.3 Wiener filtering

10.3.1 Concept of minimum mean-square-error estimation

Wiener filtering is a classical method of optimal estimation of the *original signal* $x(t)$ or $\{x_n\}$ based on the *measured (observed) signal* $y(t)$, $\{y_n\}$ in the presence of stochastic *noise* $v(t)$, $\{v_x\}$. The noise component precludes the precise restoration of the original and therefore we have to be satisfied with only an approximate estimation $\hat{x}(t)$ or $\{\hat{x}_n\}$ which would be optimal in a suitably defined sense.

The task is, in its most general form, formulated using the concept that both the original signal and noise, and consequently even the observed signal as derived *via* the distortion model, are realisations of stochastic processes. Then we can interpret these signals as members of function families $\tilde{x}(t)$ or $\{\tilde{x}_n\}$, $\tilde{y}(t)$ or $\{\tilde{y}_n\}$, $\tilde{v}(t)$ or $\{\tilde{v}_n\}$ and the equations, which we shall deal with in the following paragraphs, therefore as members of families of equations where every member applies to a particular combination of realisations.

The criterion of optimality is based on the notion of the error signal $e(t) = x(t) - \hat{x}(t)$ or $\{e_n = x_n - \hat{x}_n\}$; even this signal is, of course, stochastic and all its possible realisations form the family $\tilde{e}(t)$ or $\{\tilde{e}_n\}$. The Wiener restoration considers as the optimum restoration such an approach that, when applied to all possible combinations of the mentioned process realisations, leads to such estimates that their ensemble mean value of the quadratic error is minimal for all time instants. A concrete set of processed signals is formed by such realisations of the processes involved, which correspond to a particular result of the associated stochastic experiment w; thus the means are to be taken over all possible results w. For continuous-time signals, the *criterion of optimality* is thus given by the ensemble mean

$$\varepsilon^2(t) = \mathbb{E}_w\{(x(t) - \hat{x}(t))^2\} \to \min, \quad t \in (-\infty, \infty),$$

while for discrete signals by

$$\varepsilon_n^2 = \mathbb{E}_w\{(x_n - \hat{x}_n)^2\} \to \min, \quad \forall n. \tag{10.8}$$

The task is to find a *universal approach* which minimises the mean quadratic error in every time instant and on average for all possible realisations. Therefore, an estimate obtained in this way does not necessarily need to be good in every individual case. However, it can be expected that common types of signal that have a high probability of occurrence in the frame of their family (and thus significantly influence the error mean) will usually be restored well. On the other hand, we have to put up with the fact that the derived procedure may not be optimal for rarely appearing signals, for the same reason. Should such signals represent an important case, it would be sensible to consider detaching them from the signal class and establishing a constricted class for which a special Wiener procedure could be derived.

The family of the original signal x is defined by a (eventually infinite) listing of the set of its members and by the distribution of their probabilities. An *a priori probability distribution* describes the statistical frequencies with which the individual original signals are generated, disregarding any further deterioration or processing. If, for example, the original signals are alphabetical characters, the *a priori* distribution of their appearance will obviously depend on the language used for the communication. This distribution describes how probable the occurrence of a particular signal x is, before any measurement or reception at all is performed. After the measurement, observation or reception of the distorted signal y, certain information is available (e.g. the distorted code of a character but more or less close to the right one and almost excluding some other characters). This information changes the probabilities with which we may suppose that the already realised transmission of individual original signals has happened. Thus, a new distribution is adjoined to the family of the original realisations after the execution of the measurement or reception; this is called the *posterior distribution*. We can intuitively expect a high probability for the original which was in fact transmitted and for similar originals; however, owing to the presence of noise, this assumption need not always be fulfilled, which may lead to errors that cannot be completely prevented.

Note that the simplified notion of probabilities corresponding to complete individual realisations should be regarded as being only introductory. In fact, the individual values of realisations (belonging to particular time instants) are stochastic variables, more or less mutually dependent; therefore, we have to consider the corresponding local (instantaneous) distributions. It is then possible to formulate, for example, a concept of *signal mean value* as the average signal formed by the local mean values. In general, to account for the mutual dependencies, multidimensional probability distributions must be considered.

It can be proved that the optimal estimate $\hat{x}$, in the sense of the Wiener criterion (10.8), is the signal given by the conditional mean values corresponding to the posterior distribution conditioned by reception of a corresponding particular signal y,

$$\hat{x}(t)_{opt} = \mathbb{E}_w\{x(t)\}|_{\{y(t)\}} \quad \text{or} \quad \hat{x}_n|_{opt} = \mathbb{E}_w\{x_n\}|_{\{y_n\}}, \tag{10.9}$$

where $\{y(t)\}$, $\{y_n\}$ denotes the complete run of the received signal. Notice that, naturally, the best *a priori* estimate (i.e. without any measurement or reception) is the unconditional (*a priori*) mean value of the original, $\hat{x}(t) = \mathbb{E}_w\{x(t)\}$ or $\hat{x}_n = \mathbb{E}_w\{x_n\}$.

It can be observed that formulations of the Wiener restoration which have been postulated so far did not need any specification of the deterioration model and in this sense they are very general. Computation of the estimate according to eqn (10.9), which is generally a nonlinear operator in y, is, however, extremely demanding. It requires knowledge of the multidimensional probability distribution which represents a concrete problem; both the *a priori* distribution and properties of the concrete deterioration model are projected into the posterior distribution. Finding such a complete probabilistic model of a concrete problem is usually not feasible and, even if it was possible, the related amounts of data and the calculation burden are mostly unbearable. For this reason, only *suboptimal approaches* are used in practice, among which the classical and the most important are the estimates, *linear* in the processed values of the received signal. Such restoration processing is realised by means of linear (superposition) systems; the restoration problem is thus reduced to finding the optimal system among all possible systems of this kind.

If we limit ourselves to the case of signals, generated by stochastic stationary processes, the superposition system will simplify to a convolutional system, i.e. a plain linear time-invariant filter which is usually called the *Wiener filter*. The design of such a filter in its classical frequency-domain formulation will be treated in Section 10.3.2 and its modern discrete formulation in Section 10.3.3. Further sections will then widen the generalisation to the restoration of signals generated by nonstationary processes.

10.3.2 Formulation of the Wiener filter in the frequency domain

In this section, which is devoted to the classical Wiener filter, we shall work with the concept of continuous-time signals to conform with the original, perhaps more straightforward, description. As already said, practical applications will today most probably be realised digitally. Then either the formulae will have to be used in its discrete version – for example, the discrete Fourier transform will substitute for the integral transform – or a digital counterpart to the final derived continuous-time filter can be designed using the methods of Section 5.3.2.2. Nevertheless, the principle of the filtering and its physical interpretation remain the same.

The estimation will be done in the sense of the closing note of the previous paragraph, i.e. in a suboptimal way, by a linear superposition operator

$$\hat{x}_w(t) = \int_{-\infty}^{\infty} m(t, \tau) y_w(\tau) \, d\tau, \tag{10.10}$$

where the indices indicate which of the functions are realisations of stochastic processes controlled by an associated stochastic experiment w, thus being members of the relevant families. The function $m(t, \tau)$ is generally a time-variable weighting function which is to be determined based on the optimisation criterion (10.8). Our aim is to derive a time-invariant system; therefore, we shall introduce the first limiting condition that the concerned stochastic processes are *stationary*. This means, on the one hand, a rather serious limitation of the class of treated problems but, on the other hand, it leads to a substantial simplification of the resulting filter. It is obvious that if the characteristics of the processes used for the filter design do not change in time, even the filter need not be time variant so that the integral of eqn (10.10) will simplify to the convolution

$$\hat{x}_w(t) = \int_{-\infty}^{\infty} m(t - \tau)y_w(\tau)\,d\tau. \tag{10.11}$$

The restoration system is thus a linear time-invariant filter with the impulse response $m(t)$, which is to be determined.

According to eqn (10.11), the values of $\hat{x}(t)$ are estimated linearly based on values of $y(s)$, $s, t \in \langle -\infty, \infty \rangle$ and, considering the principle of orthogonality of eqn (4.40), we see that it must be valid for all t and s

$$\mathbb{E}_w\{(x_w(t) - \hat{x}_w(t))y_w(s)\} = 0, \tag{10.12}$$

i.e. the estimation error for any t must be uncorrelated with (statistically orthogonal to) the signal value y at any time instant s. Substituting eqn (10.11) into eqn (10.12), we obtain

$$\mathbb{E}_w\left\{\left(x_w(t) - \int_{-\infty}^{\infty} m(t - \tau)y_w(\tau)\,d\tau\right)y_w(s)\right\} = 0.$$

With respect to the linearity of both mean value and integration operators, these can be interchanged and the deterministic factor taken out of the mean so that

$$-\int_{-\infty}^{\infty} m(t - \tau)\mathbb{E}_w\{y_w(\tau)y_w(s)\}\,d\tau + \mathbb{E}_w\{x_w(t)y(s)\} = 0.$$

The first mean value can be recognised as the autocorrelation function $R_{yy}(\tau, s)$, in the second one, the crosscorrelation function $R_{xy}(t, s)$, both being one-dimensional functions of the difference of parameters with respect to the assumption of stationarity. Therefore, we have

$$\int_{-\infty}^{\infty} m(t - \tau)R_{yy}(\tau - s)\,d\tau = R_{xy}(t - s)$$

and, introducing the substitution $t' = \tau - s$ and $t'' = t - s$, we obtain

$$\int_{-\infty}^{\infty} m(t'' - t')R_{yy}(t')\,dt' = R_{xy}(t''). \tag{10.13}$$

As both the correlation functions dependent on the time difference Δt are actually deterministic characteristics of stochastic processes, eqn (10.13), the left-hand side of which is clearly a convolution integral, can be transformed into the frequency domain as

$$M(\omega)S_{yy}(\omega) = S_{xy}(\omega), \quad \text{i.e.} \quad M(\omega) = \frac{S_{xy}(\omega)}{S_{yy}(\omega)}. \qquad (10.14)$$

Here, $M(\omega) = \mathbb{F}\{m(t)\}$ is the frequency response of the restoration filter, $S_{yy}(\omega) = \mathbb{F}\{R_{yy}(\Delta t)\}$ is the power spectrum of the deteriorated signals (more precisely, the spectrum of the stochastic process generating the observed signals) and $S_{xy}(\omega) = \mathbb{F}\{R_{xy}(\Delta t)\}$ is the cross-spectrum between original and observed signals. The formula (10.14) enables designing of the restoration Wiener filter in its most general form. Notice that when deriving it, we have so far introduced, besides the basic decision on limiting ourselves to linear restoration, the only (although important) limitation in assuming the associated processes to be stationary. Namely, we have not yet utilised the supposed model of deterioration. It can therefore be claimed that eqn (10.14) represents the optimal system in the class of linear filters usable for restoration of any deterioration, *even a nonlinear* one. It probably will not be very effective in this case but such a use is quite legitimate. Let us note that, in this respect, many misunderstandings can be found in the literature.

An application example of a Wiener filter designed in this way is depicted in Figure 10.8. It can be seen that the Wiener filter 'behaves' well in comparison with the restoration in Figure 10.6. When the input signal-to-noise ratio is high, a relatively good restoration with rather steep edges and a reasonable noise level is obtained. For a low input SNR, about the same acceptable noise level is preserved at the cost of deteriorated deconvolution properties of the filter; nevertheless, the steepness of the edges is still significantly improved in the restored signal compared to the observed one.

Filter design according to eqn (10.14) leads to the problem of estimating the spectra, or alternatively both corresponding correlation functions, on the basis of suitable measurements. While the autocorrelation function $R_{yy}(\Delta t)$ or the power spectrum $S_{yy}(\omega)$ can usually be measured without difficulty, as the observed signal $y(t)$ is naturally available, measurement of the crosscorrelation function $R_{xy}(\Delta t)$ or the cross-spectrum $S_{xy}(\omega)$ is only exceptionally possible. It requires, at least for a certain period, availability not only of the deteriorated but also of the original signal $x(t)$, which can only rarely be provided.

We shall therefore try to find a more practically suitable filter formulation which would allow us to determine the filter characteristics on the basis of more easily available measurements, although at the cost of additional limiting assumptions. We shall thus limit ourselves to the case of signal deterioration by linear distortion and additive noise as in the deterioration model (10.1),

$$y_w(t) = \int_{-\infty}^{\infty} h(t - \tau)x_w(\tau)\, d\tau + v_w(t), \qquad (10.15)$$

in which the impulse response $h(t)$ of the distorting system is supposed to be known. A further assumption is that the signal $x_w(t)$ and noise $v_w(t)$ are generated by independent processes, of which at least one (usually noise) has zero mean value so that

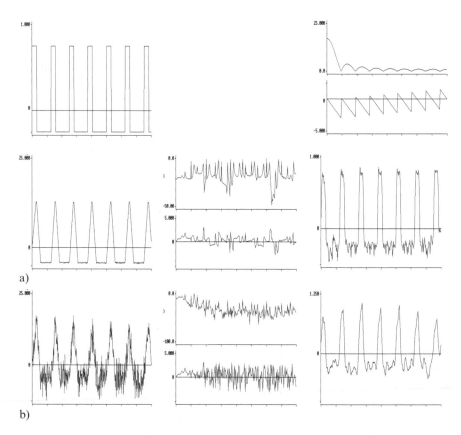

*Figure 10.8 Restoration of a deteriorated signal by a Wiener filter; two cases of different
noise levels: group a – noise variance 0.01; group b – noise variance 10.
Upper row – left: original signal, right: frequency response of the distorting
system (FIR filter with h = [1, 1, 1, 1, 1, 1, 1, 1]); middle row (a): deteriorated signal (high SNR), derived frequency response of the optimal restoration filter, restored signal; lower row (b): similarly, low SNR case*

$$\mathbb{E}\{x_w(t)v_w(t')\} = \mathbb{E}\{x_w(t)\} \cdot \mathbb{E}\{v_w(t')\} = 0. \tag{10.16}$$

Introducing the assumptions of a particular form of deterioration and of mutual
independence of the original signal and noise of course, further limits the class
of restoration problems to which the filter can be applied. However, the model
of deterioration (10.15) is still relatively general and the assumption of independence of both signal components is automatically fulfilled in many
practical tasks; thus, the class of problems covered still remains rather wide.
The model is therefore considered to be a base for formulating most of the
restoration approaches, not only for the Wiener filtering.

Under the mentioned assumptions, the crosscorrelation function can be
expressed using eqn (10.15) as

$$R_{xy}(t-s) = \mathbb{E}\{x_w(t)y_w(s)\}$$

$$= \mathbb{E}\left\{x_w(t)\int_{-\infty}^{\infty} h(s-\tau)x_w(\tau)\,d\tau\right\} + \mathbb{E}\{x_w(t)v_w(s)\}$$

$$= \int_{-\infty}^{\infty} h(s-\tau)\mathbb{E}\{x_w(t)x_w(\tau)\}\,d\tau$$

as the second term in the middle form is zero, according to the assumption. In the mean value inside the integral, the autocorrelation function $R_{xx}(t-\tau)$ can be recognised. Introducing the substitution $t' = t - s$, we obtain

$$R_{xy}(t') = \int_{-\infty}^{\infty} h(\tau' - t')R_{xx}(\tau')\,d\tau', \tag{10.17}$$

which is the correlation integral C_{hR} of two deterministic functions. As the Fourier transform of such an integral is known to be $\mathbb{F}\{C_{hR}\} = \mathbb{F}^*\{h\}\mathbb{F}\{R\}$, we obtain finally by transforming eqn (10.17) the relation

$$S_{xy}(\omega) = H^*(\omega)S_{xx}(\omega). \tag{10.18}$$

The power spectrum of the input signal $y(t)$, which is an additive mixture of two independent signals, is given by the sum of the original-signal power spectrum, modified by the linear distorting system according to eqn (4.32), and power spectrum of noise, thus

$$S_{yy}(\omega) = |H(\omega)|^2 S_{xx}(\omega) + S_{vv}(\omega). \tag{10.19}$$

By substitution of (10.18) and (10.19) into eqn (10.14) we obtain

$$M(\omega) = \frac{H^*(\omega)S_{xx}(\omega)}{|H(\omega)|^2 S_{xx}(\omega) + S_{vv}(\omega)} = \frac{1}{H(\omega)}\frac{|H(\omega)|^2}{|H(\omega)|^2 + \dfrac{S_{vv}(\omega)}{S_{xx}(\omega)}}. \tag{10.20}$$

Such a formulation of the Wiener-filter frequency response as a product of two factors has an interesting physical interpretation. The product can be interpreted as characterising a cascade connection of two subsystems: the first one is obviously the plain inverse filter according to eqn (10.4), the other subsystem is the so-called *Wiener correction factor*, the effect of which we shall analyse in detail. Primarily, we can easily see that it is always real so that it does not influence the phase characteristic of the complete filter, which is given solely by the phase properties of the inverse part. Further, taking into consideration the fact that all functions appearing in the correction factor are nonnegative, it may take on values only in the range $\langle 0, 1 \rangle$ so that it only lowers the amplitude transfer in certain frequency ranges.

Let us consider first the case of the noise produced by the deteriorating system being negligible in the whole range of frequencies. In such a case, the second term in the denominator of the Wiener factor may be neglected with respect to the first term, and the value of the whole fraction will be close to one.

In the noiseless case, the Wiener filter thus reduces to the plain inverse filter. If the noise is not negligible, transfer of the filter will obviously be reduced in some bands, which can have two causes. On one hand, the value of the correction factor will obviously decrease markedly at frequencies where the transfer of the distorting system is approaching zero and, in the same range of frequencies, the power level of the noise spectrum is nonzero. Then, the second term of the denominator guarantees its nonzero values and the whole fraction value becomes close to zero. On the other hand, the correction factor will also drop when the power noise-to-signal ratio as expressed by the second term of the denominator is high. Both influences are, of course, combined in practical cases and, in this way, they generate the 'purposeful behaviour'[1] of the Wiener filter. In frequency areas where there is a good ratio of original signal to noise and the transfer of the distorting system is sufficient to let pass relevant signal components, the Wiener correction falls away. On the other hand, frequency areas may also exist where the useful signal components are weak relative to noise, either because they were missing already in the original signal or due to suppression by the distorting linear system. Then, the transfer is limited or totally suppressed at such frequencies. Notice that, from this point of view, the intuitively modified inverse filters (10.6) and (10.7) can be considered to be rough approximations of the Wiener filter, although designed in a different way.

The expression (10.20) suggests the mentioned vivid interpretation and therefore it is the most frequently presented form of Wiener filter. However, for a practical design it is still not very satisfactory as it contains the power spectrum of the usually inaccessible original; this spectrum is thus not easy to identify. If we express $S_{xx}(\omega)$ from eqn (10.19), substitute for it into eqn (10.18) and then for $S_{xy}(\omega)$ into (10.14), we obtain an equivalent but rarely mentioned formulation, which is more practical,

$$M(\omega) = \frac{1}{H(\omega)} \frac{S_{yy}(\omega) - S_{vv}(\omega)}{S_{yy}(\omega)}. \tag{10.21}$$

As has already been mentioned, estimation of the power spectrum of the measured (observed) deteriorated signal is of course always possible. It is usually also feasible to organise the experiment in such a way that the deteriorating system is temporarily supplied by zero input. Then, its output is pure internally generated noise and thus estimation of the noise power spectrum is practicable as well.

We have already said that the proper restoration will, of course, be commonly done nowadays by a digital filter. The digital version of the classical Wiener filter may be designed as an IIR filter using the methods of Section 5.3.2; the filter frequency response would then approximate the characteristics given by eqns (10.14), (10.20) or (10.21). If the identification of the distorting system

---

[1] It is naturally not about a real purposeful behaviour of learning systems, the vague term only expresses good properties of the filter.

and the spectral estimates were also provided digitally, then there is no necessity to consider the connecting link to the continuous characteristics. The design can be directly based on the discrete data characterising the model of deterioration by using adequately modified formulae. An approach leading to FIR approximation of the classical Wiener filter will be presented in the next section.

10.3.3 Discrete, time-domain formulation of the Wiener filter

We shall now deal with designing Wiener filters constrained ahead to be discrete and of FIR type with a chosen fixed degree (filter length). As is obvious, such a limitation means in most cases that the derived filter, although designed to be optimal in the given class, will only approach the optimum properties of the more general filter designed according to eqns (10.14) or (10.21). On the other hand, the structure of the transversal FIR filter is suitable, owing to its simplicity, in many applications, and the following analysis will also be the first stage of introducing methods of nonstationary signal processing and adaptive approaches.

We are designing an FIR filter of degree N with the impulse response $\{h_n\}$, $n = 0, 1, \cdots, N-1$, the output of which – the estimate of the original – is given by a discrete convolution which can be expressed as the scalar product of corresponding vectors,

$$\hat{x}_n = \sum_{i=0}^{N-1} h_i y_{n-i} = [h_0 \quad h_1 \quad \cdots \quad h_{N-1}] \begin{bmatrix} y_n \\ y_{n-1} \\ \vdots \\ y_{n-N+1} \end{bmatrix} = \mathbf{h}^T \mathbf{y}_n = \mathbf{y}_n^T \mathbf{h}, \qquad (10.22)$$

where $\mathbf{y}_n$ is the vector of N last values of the input (observed) signal. The design of vector $\mathbf{h}$ is based again on minimising the criterion (10.8) for every discrete time instant indexed n,

$$\varepsilon_n^2 = \mathbb{E}\{(x_n - \hat{x}_n)^2\} = \mathbb{E}\{(x_n - \mathbf{h}^T \mathbf{y}_n)^2\} \to \min, \quad \forall n. \qquad (10.23)$$

The minimum will be reached if, for all $j = 0, 1, \cdots, N-1$

$$\frac{\partial}{\partial h_j} \varepsilon_n^2 = \mathbb{E}\left\{\frac{\partial}{\partial h_j}(e_n^2)\right\} = \mathbb{E}\left\{2e_n \frac{\partial e_n}{\partial h_j}\right\} = 0, \qquad (10.24)$$

where we have used the denomination $e_n = x_n - \hat{x}_n$. By substitution and simplification, we obtain

$$\frac{\partial}{\partial h_j} \varepsilon_n^2 = \mathbb{E}\left\{2e_n \frac{\partial}{\partial h_j}(x_n - \mathbf{h}^T \mathbf{y}_n)\right\} = \mathbb{E}\left\{2e_n \frac{\partial}{\partial h_j}(-h_j y_{n-j})\right\}$$

$$= \mathbb{E}\{-2e_n y_{n-j}\} = 0, \quad j = 0, 1, \cdots, N-1.$$

This conclusion of course could have been reached directly from the ortho-gonality principle (4.40). The last expression represents a system of N equations expressing the gradient of the mean quadratic error,

$$\nabla \varepsilon_n^2 = \begin{bmatrix} \partial \varepsilon_n^2/\partial h_0 \\ \partial \varepsilon_n^2/\partial h_1 \\ \vdots \\ \partial \varepsilon_n^2/\partial h_{N-1} \end{bmatrix} = -2\mathbb{E}\left\{ \begin{array}{c} y_n e_n \\ y_{n-1} e_n \\ \vdots \\ y_{n-N+1} e_n \end{array} \right\} = -2\mathbb{E}\{\mathbf{y}_n e_n\} = \mathbf{0}. \qquad (10.25)$$

Substituting for e_n and by further obvious manipulation, we obtain

$$\mathbb{E}\{\mathbf{y}_n(x_n - \mathbf{y}_n^T \mathbf{h})\} = \mathbb{E}\{\mathbf{y}_n x_n\} - \mathbb{E}\{\mathbf{y}_n \mathbf{y}_n^T\}\mathbf{h} = {}_n\overline{\overline{\Phi}}_{yx} - {}_n\overline{\overline{\Phi}}_{yy}\mathbf{h} = \mathbf{0}.$$

Thereby we have arrived at the following linear-equation system for compo-nents of the impulse-response vector of the filter being designed,

$$ {}_n\overline{\overline{\Phi}}_{yy}\,\mathbf{h}_{opt} = {}_n\overline{\Phi}_{yx}, \qquad (10.26)$$

where the matrix ${}_n\overline{\overline{\Phi}}_{yy}$ of mean values is the autocorrelation matrix of the observed signal and ${}_n\overline{\Phi}_{yx}$ is the vector of crosscorrelations among the last original-signal value and components of the input vector $\mathbf{y}_n$. If the matrix $\overline{\overline{\Phi}}_{yy}$ is nonsingular, a solution of this system exists,

$$\mathbf{h}_{opt} = \overline{\overline{\Phi}}_{yy}^{-1}\overline{\Phi}_{yx}. \qquad (10.27)$$

Here, we have omitted indices n with respect to the assumed stationarity of the problem. It can be proved that the system matrix is nonsingular and the solution therefore can be found if the power spectrum of the observed signal $\{y_n\}$ has no zero points. Nevertheless, as with most inverse problems, the solution (10.27) is badly conditioned, i.e. it is very sensitive to errors in correlation estimates and thus also to concrete noise values. The restoration system, the impulse response of which is obtained according to (10.27), is called the *Wiener–Levinson filter*. Notice that this is a very general formulation; as with the result (10.14), the only assumption that we have made is the stationarity of the problem. The validity of the solution is not constricted to any particular model of deteriora-tion (thus also not to its linearity as often incorrectly presented in the literature) nor does it require independence of the original signal and noise. In comparison with the formulation (10.14), which yields the optimal linear estimate of the ori-ginal signal, the derived FIR filter, as a less general linear system, naturally pro-vides a suboptimal and generally worse estimate.

Both the autocorrelation matrix and the crosscorrelation vector are generally connected with a particular discrete time instant n; it follows that the impulse response and consequently the filter as a whole will be time invariant only for stationary signals for which the mentioned probability characteristics are constant in time. Only then is it possible to omit the indices n in eqn (10.26), as we did in solution (10.27). The conclusion can also be reversed: the time-invariant Wiener filter, as derived, is only suitable for restoration of signals generated by stationary processes. In addition, the noise must also be stationary, as it influences the characteristics involved. If it is possible to measure the correlations forming the mentioned matrix and vector (i.e. to provide satisfactory statistical estimates of them), the filter can be designed. As for the cross-correlation vector, however, the same practical problem appears that we mentioned in connection with estimating the cross-spectrum in eqn (10.14). Because the designed filter is an approximation of the filter analysed in Section 10.3.3, the limitations and application properties mentioned there apply here as well.

So far, we have been speaking about correlations estimated by means of ensemble averages. If the processes are not only stationary but also ergodic, the difficult to obtain ensemble averages may be replaced by time averages, the calculation of which needs only one couple of corresponding realisations of original and measured (observed) signals. Moreover, as the correlation functions of stationary processes depend only on the difference of compared time instants, the autocorrelation matrix will be formed by only $2N - 1$ different but repeating elements of the one-dimensional autocorrelation function. The matrix will thus acquire Toeplitz form (i.e. with constant elements along the principal diagonal as well as along side diagonals).

Before concluding, let us realise that restricting ourselves to the stationary case, although practically advantageous in many instances, was not necessary. The fact that the correlation matrix and vector in eqn (10.26) contain ensemble mean values connected to particular time instants enables us to calculate them, at least in principle, exactly even if the involved stochastic processes are non-stationary. The matrix and the vector then naturally become time dependent and consequently the solution of the equation system is so too. It must be then rewritten more precisely as

$$_n\mathbf{h}_{opt} = {_n\overline{\overline{\Phi}}_{yy}^{-1}} \cdot {_n\overline{\Phi}_{yx}}, \tag{10.28}$$

i.e., with the index n also at the vector of filter coefficients. The filter thus becomes a time-variant system. The design of the filter is rather heavy going, as the elements of a new correlation matrix and of a new crosscorrelation vector must be estimated again for every sampling instant by means of ensemble averages. (Theoretically, we would therefore need many realisations to be available in parallel.) On the other hand, it is possible to determine the optimal estimate (in the above sense) of the original sample x_n in every sampling period. Its computation would be independent of both the previous estimated samples and of the filter properties in previous periods. We shall return to this idea in the next sections.

10.4 Kalman filtering

10.4.1 Introduction

A *Kalman filter* may be considered as a generalisation of the Wiener filter in two directions. Primarily, it does not require stationarity of the involved processes and therefore it can also be used to estimate nonstationary signals. Besides that does not *a priori* limit the information used for designing the filter to the last N samples as was the case with the Wiener–Levinson filter, but it is capable of utilising all the available empirical information which the observed signal offers from the beginning of measurement or reception. The amount of information increases with every further sampling period so that, particularly in the special case of stationary signals (or signals with properties which change slowly in time), the estimate improves in the course of time. The structure of a Kalman filter is recursive and its coefficients are modified, based on the available information, in every sampling period in order to provide an optimal estimate of the original signal. This recursivity also means that the filter can have (and usually does have) an infinite impulse response so that it is more general than the Wiener–Levinson filter.

On the other hand, the Kalman filter is restricted with respect to the Wiener filter in that it introduces an *a priori* model of the observed signal (based on Markov chains); the class of signal which can be restored is thus reduced. We shall see that, on the other hand, the order of the introduced model can be arbitrarily increased, thus widening the class of admissible signals sufficiently for the most part of practical cases. However, the identification of such a complex signal model, the parameters of which are necessary for designing the Kalman filter, becomes difficult too and also leads to increased filter complexity. The introduction of the mentioned type of signal model has enabled us to calculate the filter parameters recursively. A new filter therefore originates in every sampling period by correcting the filter parameters from the previous step utilising the newly arrived information without the need to remember explicitly all the previous values of the input signal.

10.4.2 First-order Kalman filter

Let us suppose that we have a Wiener–Levinson filter of order N and would like to design a more sophisticated one of order $N+1$, which would utilise the information contained in a longer observation sequence. This can be done by increasing the size of both the correlation matrix and vector in eqn (10.26) by adding the missing elements based on additional measurement and estimation; then, a new solution of the enlarged equation system must be found. Not only is such a procedure heavy going but also the complexity of the filter structure is correspondingly increased. Obviously, it is in principle impossible to improve the FIR-filter properties by increasing its length without limits.

Another possibility, which takes into account all previous input-signal samples and thus has the potential of an optimum estimate, taking into account all the available information, is to use a recursive filter. Such a filter provides the estimate $\hat{x}_{n+1}$ based on the previous estimate $\hat{x}_n$, which reflects the information included in the observation samples $y_0, y_1, \cdots, y_n$. This estimate is corrected by a quantity derived from the newly arriving sample of the observed signal y_{n+1}. The simplest possibility is obviously the linear estimate

$$\hat{x}_{n+1} = B_{n+1}\hat{x}_n + K_{n+1}y_{n+1}, \tag{10.29}$$

in which the coefficients B_{n+1}, K_{n+1} are generally time dependent as shown by the indices. The variable coefficients must be suitably determined in every discrete-time instant so that the condition (10.8) would be fulfilled. For reasons that will appear in the next section, we shall call the system which realises the estimate according to expression (10.29) a *scalar Kalman filter*.

We shall show that the mentioned linear estimate may be optimal, when proper values of coefficients are used, providing that the original signal $\{x_n\}$ is generated by a Markov process of the first order. The *model of signal generation* (Figure 10.9, left-hand side) is therefore described by the difference equation

$$x_{n+1} = a_{n+1}x_n + g_{n+1}. \tag{10.30}$$

Here, $\{g_n\}$ is white, generally nonstationary, *driving noise* described by a sequence of local variances $\{_g\sigma_n^2\}$, and $\{a_n\}$ is a sequence of feedback coefficients of the linear time-variant first-order system which is a part of the model. The *original signal* $\{x_{n+1}\}$ is further changed according to the *model of deterioration* depicted on the right-hand side of Figure 10.9, which provides the *observed signal*

$$y_{n+1} = c_{n+1}x_{n+1} + v_{n+1}, \tag{10.31}$$

where $\{c_n\}$ is a sequence of time-variant coefficients in the product that represents the *observation distortion* and can be considered to be the simplest form of convolution distortion by a time-variant FIR filter of degree 0. The sequence $\{v_n\}$ is additive generally nonstationary *observation noise* independent of the driving noise and characterised by a sequence of variances $\{_v\sigma_n^2\}$. If the model coefficients as well as the variances of both noise processes were constant in time, $a_n = a$, $c_n = c$, $_g\sigma_n^2 = _g\sigma^2$, $_v\sigma_n^2 = _v\sigma^2$, it would be a special case of the model describing stationary observed signals.

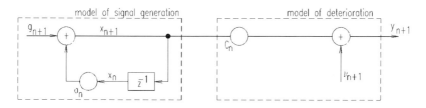

Figure 10.9 Markov model of observed signal

Whether or not the designed simple model represents the properties of the signal (or the mechanism of its origin) well, must be considered in every individual case with respect to the character of the task. In many cases, it is possible to determine the structure of the model and its parameters directly, based on knowledge of the internal structure and functioning of the real signal source. It can then be decided whether the time-invariant (or rather a variant) model is adequate and if the mentioned first-order model is sufficient or a rather more complex model is needed. (We shall deal with more complicated models in the following section.) When no such information about the signal source is available, we have no other choice than to identify the signal properties by means of observing and analysing the signal.

Let us show the principle of such identification on the simplest case of a stationary model for which the four mentioned constant parameters have to be determined. First, let us state that the deteriorated signal cx_{n+1} is non-correlated with the additive noise v_{n+1} (with respect to independence of both noise processes), so that the autocorrelation function of the observed signal is, according to eqn (8.9),

$$R_{yy}(\tau) = c^2 R_{xx}(\tau) + R_{vv}(\tau). \tag{10.32}$$

The autocorrelation function of the additive white noise has obviously only a single nonzero value, $R_{vv}(0) = {}_v\sigma^2$. As clearly (for zero initial conditions) $x_n = \sum_{i=0}^{n} g_i a^{n-i}$, i.e. a linear combination of stochastic variables g_i, the variance of this centred stochastic process can easily be determined, for large n, as the sum of a geometric series,

$$_x\sigma^2 = \frac{_g\sigma^2}{1 - a^2}. \tag{10.33}$$

The recursive part of the model obviously has the frequency response $G(\omega) = e^{j\omega T}/(e^{j\omega T} - a)$ and it shapes the uniform power spectrum of the driving noise into

$$S_{xx}(\omega) = |G(\omega)|^2 {}_g\sigma^2 = \frac{_g\sigma^2}{1 + a^2 - 2a \cos \omega}.$$

From here, after substituting from eqn (10.33), the following expression for the autocorrelation function can be obtained,

$$R_{xx}(\tau) = a^{|\tau|} {}_x\sigma^2. \tag{10.34}$$

Therefore according to eqn (10.32) it is

$$R_{yy}(0) = c^2 {}_x\sigma^2 + {}_v\sigma^2, \quad R_{yy}(\tau) = c^2 a^{|\tau|} {}_x\sigma^2, \quad \tau \neq 0, \tag{10.35}$$

so that we obtain the estimate of the constant parameter a as

$$\hat{a} \approx \frac{R_{yy}(\tau + 1)}{R_{yy}(\tau)}, \quad \tau \neq 0,$$

which can be improved by averaging this-way-determined values for different τ. The estimate of the disturbing noise power is then (using eqns (10.34) and (10.35))

$$_v\sigma^2 = R_{yy}(0) - c^2{}_x\sigma^2 \approx R_{yy}(0) - \frac{R_{yy}(1)}{\hat{a}}. \tag{10.36}$$

If the power $_g\sigma^2$ of driving noise is known, the parameter c can be estimated according to (10.36) after substitution from eqn (10.33),

$$c^2 \approx (1 - \hat{a}) \frac{R_{yy}(0) - {}_v\hat{\sigma}^2}{_g\sigma^2}.$$

It is therefore obvious that, as far as the driving noise power is known, the parameters of the model of signal generation and deterioration can be estimated based on the autocorrelation function of the observed signal.

A check of the model appropriateness and accuracy may be based on use of the Kalman filter, as will be described further, which provides an estimate of the original signal x_n from the observed signal y_n. Then the driving noise g_n can be estimated from $\hat{x}_n$ by means of an FIR filter, which is the inversion of the recursive part of the model,

$$\hat{g}_n = \hat{x}_n - \hat{a}\hat{x}_{n-1}.$$

The estimated power spectrum derived from this signal should be uniform, or the corresponding autocorrelation function should have the only important nonzero value in the origin. If the model does not pass this test, the model order is insufficient and a higher order must be used (see Section 10.4.3).

Let us now return to deriving values of filter coefficients in the time-variant filter (10.29). We will start from the conditions of orthogonality,

$$\mathbb{E}\{e_{n+1}y_i\} = 0, \quad i = 0, 1, \cdots, n, n+1. \tag{10.37}$$

Particularly, for $i = n$ we obtain using eqns (10.30), (10.29) and (10.31),

$$\mathbb{E}\{(x_{n+1} - \hat{x}_{n+1})y_n\} = \mathbb{E}\{(a_{n+1}x_n + g_{n+1} - B_{n+1}\hat{x}_n - K_{n+1}y_{n+1})y_n\}$$

$$= \mathbb{E}\{(a_{n+1}x_n + g_{n+1} - B_{n+1}\hat{x}_n$$

$$- K_{n+1}(c_{n+1}a_{n+1}x_n + c_{n+1}g_{n+1} + v_n))y_n\} = 0.$$

Three products in this expression have zero mean, as the relevant factors are evidently independent quantities for reasons of causality: twice this is the product $g_{n+1}y_n$ and once $v_{n+1}y_n$. (Although y_n is derived from the previous elements of the second sequence in both cases, it is not influenced by the new, later, noise element.) After simplification we obtain

$$\mathbb{E}\{[a_{n+1}(1 - c_{n+1}K_{n+1})x_n - B_{n+1}\hat{x}_n]y_n\} = 0. \tag{10.38}$$

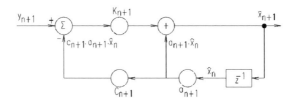

Figure 10.10 Structure of the Kalman scalar filter

Because it is also $\mathbb{E}\{e_n y_n\} = \mathbb{E}\{(x_n - \hat{x}_n)y_n\} = 0$ as follows from the principle of orthogonality, the previous equation will be fulfilled if the coefficient B takes on the values

$$B_{n+1} = a_{n+1}(1 - c_{n+1}K_{n+1}). \tag{10.39}$$

Under this assumption, the error value e_{n+1} will be orthogonal to $y_0, y_1, \cdots, y_n$, if the previous difference e_n, was orthogonal to them. Substituting from eqn (10.39) into (10.29), we obtain

$$\hat{x}_{n+1} = a_{n+1}\hat{x}_n + K_{n+1}(y_{n+1} - c_{n+1}a_{n+1}\hat{x}_n). \tag{10.40}$$

This equation has a straightforward physical interpretation and also determines the structure of the Kalman scalar filter, as is shown in Figure 10.10. The expression for the resulting value of $\hat{x}_{n+1}$ can be interpreted as the sum of the predicted value $a_{n+1}\hat{x}_n$ based on the previous sample of the estimated signal, and of a certain correction term. The magnitude of the correction is actually given by the difference of the incoming observed signal sample y_{n+1} and the value predicted, again on the basis of the previous estimate, by the term $c_{n+1}a_{n+1}\hat{x}_n$. The difference – the estimation error – is amplified by the coefficient K_{n+1} which is usually called the *Kalman gain*.[2] Notice that, if the predicted value is equal to the observed sample, the correction is zero and the filter output is given only by the above prediction.

Comparison of the diagrams of the signal generation-deterioration model in Figure 10.9 and of the Kalman restoration filter in Figure 10.10 shows that the Kalman filter contains the complete signal model (without additive noise). This model is only complemented by the part calculating the difference signal between the predicted and observed signals and by the branch with Kalman gain.

It remains to derive a formula for the time-variant Kalman gain. We will start again with eqn (10.37), now for $i = n + 1$, i.e. $\mathbb{E}\{(x_{n+1} - \hat{x}_{n+1})y_{n+1}\}$. After substituting here from eqns (10.29), (10.30) and (10.31), simplifying and removing deterministic quantities out of the mean value argument we obtain

$$c_{n+1}(1 - c_{n+1}K_{n+1})(a_{n+1}^2\mathbb{E}\{e_n x_n\} + g\sigma_{n+1}^2) - K_{n+1}v\sigma_n^2 = 0.$$

---

[2] It should rather be called amplification, but this is a traditional term.

When denoting $p_n = \mathbb{E}\{e_n x_n\}$, the following recursive relations for the Kalman gain are obtained,

$$K_{n+1} = \frac{c_{n+1}(a_{n+1}^2 p_n + g\sigma_{n+1}^2)}{c_{n+1}^2(a_{n+1}^2 p_n + g\sigma_{n+1}^2) + v\sigma_n^2},$$

$$p_n = (1 - K_n c_n)(a_n^2 p_{n-1} + g\sigma_n^2). \tag{10.41}$$

When the repeated factor in brackets is denoted as p', the previous relations can be rewritten into a form which will be generalised in the next section,

$$K_{n+1} = c_{n+1} p'_{n+1}(c_{n+1}^2 p'_{n+1} + v\sigma_n^2)^{-1},$$

$$p'_{n+1} = a_{n+1}^2 p_n + g\sigma_{n+1}^2,$$

$$p_n = (1 - K_n c_n)p'_n. \tag{10.42}$$

It can be seen that both computation of the Kalman gain and operation of the filter according to eqn (10.40) need to know the instantaneous values of the signal-model parameters. These must be identified experimentally, which is generally rather a complicated problem (as far as they do not follow directly from the nature of the task). When the problem is stationary, however, the parameters are constant, which simplifies the problem substantially, as we have already seen.

The recursive relations must be still complemented by an instruction on how to initialise the recursion. When supposing, rather naturally, that for $n < 0$, $x_n = 0$, it should of course be also $\hat{x}_n = 0$. With the lack of any other information, the best initial estimate is $\hat{x}_0 = y_0$. Consequently, with respect to the mentioned zero initial condition, from eqn (10.40) we obtain

$$K_0 = 1$$

and, by substituting into eqn (10.41),

$$p_0 = (1 - c_0)_g \sigma_0^2.$$

Here, p_n was used as the mean-square error (see next paragraph) of the optimal estimate which is of course perfect (zero) for negative n; the expected values of the original signal are also zero. The values of K_n and p_n for $n > 0$ can then be obtained by eqn (10.41).

Let us comment on the physical meaning of the quantity

$$p_n = \mathbb{E}\{e_n x_n\}. \tag{10.43}$$

The mean quadratic error $\mathbb{E}\{e_n^2\}$ of the nth sample of the optimal estimate can obviously be rewritten into

$$\mathbb{E}\{e_n(x_n - \hat{x}_n)\} = \mathbb{E}\left\{ e_n\left(x_n - \sum_{i=0}^{n} {}_n h_i y_i \right) \right\},$$

where $_n h_i$ is the weight of the signal sample y_i in the estimate of $\hat{x}_n$. (Notice that the length of the impulse response of the Kalman filter is finite in every step, but increases without limit with increasing n.) As the quantity e_n is the error of a linear estimate based on samples y_i, all the mean values $\mathbb{E}\{e_n y_i\}$ are zero according to the principle of orthogonality if the filter $\{h_i\}$ is designed as optimal; the result is thus (10.43). It can therefore be concluded that the quantity p_n, enumerated in every step of the filter operation, provides information on the time-dependent quality of the estimate as is characterised by its (instantaneous) mean quadratic error.

10.4.3 Higher-order Kalman filters

A scalar Kalman filter works with signal model of only the first order, which is not sufficient for most practical tasks. Generalisation to higher orders, when carried out by classical expansion of the model by adding further delay elements with the relevant coefficients, would lead to a complicated derivation and rather confusing complex formulae. Instead, we shall use the state representation approach which, as we have seen in Sections 2.3 and 5.3.3.3, enables us to formulate a system of higher order as a super system of simultaneously working and interconnected systems of the first order. The appropriate state equations for the model are then of the first order and the results obtained in the previous section can be generalised in a straightforward way by merely substituting the scalar quantities by vector ones. Another advantage of a Kalman filter formulated in this way is that the state vector need not contain only delayed values of one state variable but it may be composed of different quantities which appear in the system in parallel. The state variables may even have different physical meanings. In many cases it enables straightforward setting up of models of physical systems, the internal variables of which (understood as original signals) should be estimated by a Kalman filter on the basis of external observations. A simple example of this kind will be mentioned at the end of the section.

Let us introduce the following labelling for the values of the original and observed signals,

$$_1 x_n = x_n \qquad\quad _1 y_n = y_n$$
$$_2 x_n = x_{n-1}, \qquad _2 y_n = y_{n-1}.$$
$$\vdots \qquad\qquad \vdots$$

Further, these quantities will be arranged into vectors

$$\mathbf{x}_n = \begin{bmatrix} {}_1 x_n \\ {}_2 x_n \\ \vdots \\ {}_R x_n \end{bmatrix}, \quad \mathbf{y}_n = \begin{bmatrix} {}_1 y_n \\ {}_2 y_n \\ \vdots \\ {}_R x_n \end{bmatrix},$$

where R is the requested model order. Similarly, we shall also obtain the vectors of values of driving and disturbing noise, $\mathbf{g}_n$ and $\bar{v}_n$. The state equation of the model describing the signal generation is then

$$\mathbf{x}_{n+1} = \mathbf{A}_{n+1}\mathbf{x}_n + \mathbf{g}_{n+1}, \tag{10.44}$$

and the output equation is

$$\mathbf{y}_{n+1} = \mathbf{C}_{n+1}\mathbf{x}_{n+1} + \bar{v}_{n+1}. \tag{10.45}$$

In comparison with the standard form of state description (2.34) there is a difference in the output equation which does not include the system-input vector but the vector of disturbing noise. Further, obviously $\mathbf{B} = \mathbf{D} = \mathbf{I}$; the corresponding signal-flow block diagram is in Figure 10.11. When compared with Figure 10.9, the structural similarity of both models is obvious. The only changes are that the simple scalar-signal connections were substituted by parallel channels, the delay block described by the matrix $z^{-1}\mathbf{I}$ represents a parallel system of delaying registers, and the relevant coefficient matrices are included instead of scalar coefficients a, c. Replacing the multiplication of scalars by an operator of linear combination, expressed as a multiplication of the vector signal by a coefficient matrix, means a substantial generalisation. It allows for mutual sequential affecting of the state vector components *via* matrix $\mathbf{A}$ and for generating individual components of the output vector as linear combinations of state vector components *via* matrix $\mathbf{C}$. Multiplication by such a matrix can mostly be interpreted as FIR filtering of a degree up

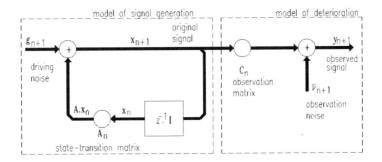

Figure 10.11 Vector version of Markov model of observed signal

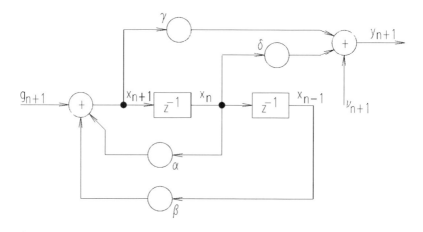

Figure 10.12 Scalar formulation of a second-order model

to R, as the state vector components are often delayed samples of signals to be incorporated in the output-vector components. The *vector model* as outlined is a rather powerful tool for generating signals of very complicated properties or for modelling of rather complex systems, should a sufficiently high-order R be chosen.

To clarify the idea, we shall present a simple example of a scalar second-order model according to the scheme in Figure 10.12. It is clear that the scalar model, as described by the system of classical difference equations

$$x_{n+1} = \alpha x_n + \beta x_{n-1} + g_{n+1}$$

$$y_{n+1} = \gamma x_{n+1} + \delta x_n + v_{n+1},$$

can be described as well by the corresponding vector eqns (10.44) and (10.45) with the following vector and matrix quantities:

$$\mathbf{A} = \begin{bmatrix} \alpha & \beta \\ 1 & 0 \end{bmatrix}, \quad \mathbf{C} = \begin{bmatrix} \gamma & \delta \\ 0 & 0 \end{bmatrix}, \quad \mathbf{x}_n = \begin{bmatrix} x_n \\ x_{n-1} \end{bmatrix},$$

$$\mathbf{g}_n = \begin{bmatrix} g_n \\ 0 \end{bmatrix}, \quad \bar{v}_n = \begin{bmatrix} v_n \\ 0 \end{bmatrix}, \quad \mathbf{y}_n = \begin{bmatrix} y_n \\ 0 \end{bmatrix}.$$

A *vector Kalman filter* can be derived in a way analogous to its scalar counterpart derivation. All that is needed is to replace all the scalar quantities by vector ones and the scalar operations by appropriate operations on vectors and matrices in such a way that the equations remain consistent. In this way, we obtain the recursive equations describing the process of higher-order filtering as a direct counterpart of eqns (10.41) and (10.42),

$$\hat{\mathbf{x}}_{n+1} = \mathbf{A}_{n+1}\hat{\mathbf{x}}_n + \mathbf{K}_{n+1}(\mathbf{y}_{n+1} - \mathbf{C}_{n+1}\mathbf{A}_{n+1}\hat{\mathbf{x}}_n)$$

$$\mathbf{K}_{n+1} = \mathbf{P}'_{n+1}\mathbf{C}_{n+1}[\mathbf{C}_{n+1}\mathbf{P}'_{n+1}\mathbf{C}^T_{n+1} + \mathbf{N}_n]^{-1}$$

$$\mathbf{P}'_{n+1} = \mathbf{A}_{n+1}\mathbf{P}_n\mathbf{A}_{n+1} + \mathbf{G}_{n+1}$$

$$\mathbf{P}_n = (\mathbf{I} - \mathbf{K}_n\mathbf{C}_n)\mathbf{P}'_n, \tag{10.46}$$

where $\mathbf{G}_n$, $\mathbf{N}_n$ are autocorrelation matrices of the driving and disturbing noise, respectively,

$$\mathbf{G}_n = \mathbb{E}\{\mathbf{g}_n\mathbf{g}^T_n\}, \quad \mathbf{N}_n = \mathbb{E}\{\bar{v}_n\bar{v}^T_n\}.$$

The signal-flow diagram representing the vector Kalman filter is schematically depicted in Figure 10.13. The changes with respect to the scalar case in Figure 10.10 are quite analogous to those between Figures 10.9 and 10.1 which have been commented upon earlier. The universality of the filter can be appropriately evaluated in similar terms, as has been done for the vector signal model. Our explanation started from the restoration point of view; however, the filter operation can be also interpreted in another way. If the filter describes the behaviour and perhaps even the structure of a certain physical system, the components of its state vector may represent values of internal system variables which are not directly observable (measurable). The information on the state of the system is only indirectly mediated by the vector of output (observed) signals on the basis of which it is possible to estimate the state-variable values by means of the filter. If used in this way, it is sometimes called the *estimation filter*. In this case, the importance of identification leading to a proper model of the system, the state of which is to be estimated, is particularly obvious. The system identification preceding the filter design crucially influences the precision and correctness of the estimates.

A Kalman filter can be interpreted as not only a restoration or estimation device but also as a *whitening filter* which was mentioned in Section 9.2.2.2 where we showed that the optimal estimator produces a white-noise error signal as its byproduct. This also applies to Kalman filters: from the signal-flow diagram in Figure 10.13 we see that the channel entering the Kalman gain carries the *innovation signal* $\mathbf{a}_{n+1} = \mathbf{y}_{n+1} - \hat{\mathbf{y}}_{n+1}$, where $\hat{\mathbf{y}}_{n+1} = \mathbf{C}_{n+1}\mathbf{A}_{n+1}\hat{\mathbf{x}}_n$ is obviously the optimum estimate of the new value of the observed signal based on its previous values. If we take the innovation signal as being the output of the filter (instead of state-vector estimates), such a system is a whitening filter. This property can be utilised for verification of the correctness of identification or of the chosen order of the model: if the innovation process has a uniform spectrum or corresponding correlation function with a narrow maximum at the origin, the model is satisfactory.

Let us demonstrate the formulation of a Kalman filter on a simplified problem of target tracking by radar. The radar provides a time sequence of noisy estimates of the target's distance r and azimuth φ, at the rate of the sampling period T,

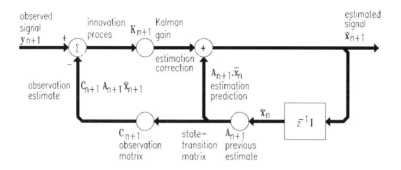

Figure 10.13 Structure of vector Kalman filter

$$_r y_n = r_n + {}_r g_n$$

$$_\varphi y_n = \varphi_n + {}_\varphi g_n,$$

where $_r g_n$, $_\varphi g_n$ are stochastic measurement errors caused by imprecision in determining the distance and azimuth, for example due to receiver noise and imperfections in the mechanical state of the antenna.

A simple linear model was chosen that is valid in the range of small changes of both polar coordinates; it is described by the system of equations

$$r_{n+1} = r_n + T r'_n$$

$$r'_{n+1} = r'_n + {}_r v_n$$

$$\varphi_{n+1} = \varphi_n + T \varphi'_n$$

$$\varphi'_{n+1} = \varphi'_n + {}_\varphi v_n,$$

where r' and φ' as derivatives of the coordinates are the radial and lateral velocities, and $_r v_n$, $_\varphi v_n$ are random differences in both velocities caused, for example, by wind gusts. Without these influences, with both velocities constant, the position would vary linearly (in polar coordinates) according to the chosen model. The vectors and matrices characterising the problem are in accordance with the notation of eqns (10.46)

$$\mathbf{x}_n = \begin{bmatrix} r_n \\ r'_n \\ \varphi_n \\ \varphi'_n \end{bmatrix}, \quad \mathbf{g}_n = \begin{bmatrix} 0 \\ {}_r g_n \\ 0 \\ {}_\varphi g_n \end{bmatrix}, \quad \mathbf{y}_n = \begin{bmatrix} {}_r y_n \\ {}_\varphi y_n \end{bmatrix}, \quad \bar{v}_n = \begin{bmatrix} {}_r v_n \\ {}_\varphi v_n \end{bmatrix},$$

$$\mathbf{A} = \begin{bmatrix} 1 & T & 0 & 0 \\ 0 & 1 & 0 & 0 \\ 0 & 0 & 1 & T \\ 0 & 0 & 0 & 1 \end{bmatrix}, \quad \mathbf{C} = \begin{bmatrix} 1 & 0 & 0 & 0 \\ 0 & 0 & 1 & 0 \end{bmatrix},$$

$$\mathbf{G}_n = \mathbb{E}\{\mathbf{g}_n\mathbf{g}_n^T\} = \begin{bmatrix} 0 & 0 & 0 & 0 \\ 0 & \,_r^g\sigma^2 & 0 & 0 \\ 0 & 0 & 0 & 0 \\ 0 & 0 & 0 & \,_\varphi^g\sigma^2 \end{bmatrix}, \quad \mathbf{N}_n = \mathbb{E}\{\bar{v}_n\bar{v}_n^T\} = \begin{bmatrix} \,_r\sigma^2 & 0 \\ 0 & \,_\varphi\sigma^2 \end{bmatrix}.$$

To finalise the formulation of the task, it is necessary to estimate the elements of the correlation matrices. For the signal model, we can suppose that the linear acceleration in each of the observable dimensions (radial and lateral) can be described by a stochastic variable with uniform distribution in the interval $\langle -a, a\rangle$, so that its mean value is zero and variance is $\sigma_a^2 = a^2/3$. As the velocity increments in radial or lateral directions are Ta_r or $(Ta_l)/(R + r_n) \approx (Ta_l)/R$, respectively, the relevant variances are

$$\,_r^g\sigma_n^2 = T^2\sigma_a^2 = a^2 T^2/3, \quad \,_\varphi^g\sigma_n^2 \approx a^2 T^2/(3R^2).$$

The elements of the disturbing-noise autocorrelation matrix are given by standard deviations of Gaussian measurement errors (e.g. in the radial dimension it is typically $\,_r\sigma = 1000\,m$, in the lateral dimension $\,_\varphi\sigma = 0.017\,rad$, so that $\,_r\sigma^2 = 10^6$ and $\,_\varphi\sigma^2 = 2.89 \times 10^{-4}$). The problem is formulated as essentially stationary, the only slowly varying model parameter being $\,_\varphi^g\sigma_n^2$; it is therefore possible, for short time sections, to project the filter with only a single variable matrix $\mathbf{K}_n$. Simulations, according to Reference [32], show very fast convergence of the matrix elements – the final state is reached during a few sampling periods, regardless of the choice of initial values.

10.5 Constrained deconvolution

Another concept of restoration is represented by *constrained deconvolution*. This method does not impose the requirement of minimising estimation errors but only requests that the original noise power in the restored signal be preserved. It comes from the general tendency of deconvolution methods to lead to a substantial degradation in signal-to-noise ratio and therefore it seeks an approximate approach which would correct the convolution distortion without increasing the noise level.

The method uses the notion of a discrete model of deterioration consisting in distortion caused by a discrete linear system with a finite impulse response $\{h_n\}$, $n = 0, 1, \cdots, J - 1$, and additive noise $\{v_n\}$,

$$y_n = \sum_{i=0}^{n} h_{n-i}x_i + v_n. \tag{10.47}$$

For a finite section $\{x_n\}$ of the input signal, M samples long, obviously $n \in \langle 0, M + J - 2\rangle$, $i \in \langle 0, M - 1\rangle$. The model equation can then be rewritten into vector form

$$\mathbf{y} = \mathbf{H}\mathbf{x} + \boldsymbol{v}, \tag{10.48}$$

where the nonzero elements of the matrix are $H_{n,i} = h_{n-i}$, $(n - i) \in \langle 0, J - 1 \rangle$ so that it is a circulant matrix. The noise energy of the observed signal, that is before restoration, is

$$\varepsilon = \sum_{n=0}^{M+J-2} v_n^2 = \boldsymbol{v}^T \boldsymbol{v}. \tag{10.49}$$

If the noise is centred, its energy is given by the variance,

$$\mathbb{E}\{v_n\} = 0, \forall n \implies \sum_{n=0}^{M+J-2} v_n \cong 0 \implies \varepsilon \cong (M + J - 1)\sigma_v^2.$$

We shall define the *residuum* $\mathbf{r}$ as being the difference vector dependent on the estimate $\hat{\mathbf{x}}$ of the original signal,

$$\mathbf{r}(\hat{\mathbf{x}}) = \mathbf{y} - \mathbf{H}\hat{\mathbf{x}}. \tag{10.50}$$

The restoration is constrained by the condition that the energy of residuum of the restored signal remains the same as the energy of noise in the observed signal,

$$G(\hat{\mathbf{x}}) = \mathbf{r}^T(\hat{\mathbf{x}}).\mathbf{r}(\hat{\mathbf{x}}) = \varepsilon. \tag{10.51}$$

Notice that, according to eqn (10.47), the noise in the observed signal is the residuum of the original signal so that the original $\mathbf{x}$ is one of the solutions satisfying the condition (10.51).

It can be shown that infinitely many solutions exist which fulfil this condition; one of these must be chosen based on an additional criterion reasonably following from the substance of the problem. Such a possible condition is that the estimate $\hat{\mathbf{x}}$ should be a 'reasonably' smooth function and the corresponding criterion to be minimised is then the measure of the second difference in the signal,

$$F(\hat{\mathbf{x}}) = \sum_i (\hat{x}_{i-1} - 2x_i + x_{x+1})^2 = (\mathbf{x}^T\mathbf{C}^T).(\mathbf{C}\mathbf{x}) \to \min, \tag{10.52}$$

where the matrix $\mathbf{C}$ of size $(M + 2) \times M$ is (zero components omitted)

$$\mathbf{C} = \begin{bmatrix} 1 & & & & \\ -2 & 1 & & & \\ 1 & -2 & 1 & & \\ & 1 & -2 & 1 & \\ & & 1 & -2 & 1 \\ & & & & \ddots \\ & & & & & 1 \end{bmatrix}. \tag{10.53}$$

The problem is therefore to find the estimate $\hat{x}$ minimising the criterion (10.52) while preserving the condition (10.51), so that a constrained minimum of the function $F(\hat{x})$ under the condition (constraint) $G(\hat{x}) - \varepsilon = 0$ is sought. This task can be solved using the method of Lagrange multipliers providing that both $F(.)$ and $G(.)$ have total differentials in a neighbourhood of the curve $G(\hat{x}) - \varepsilon = 0$ and at least one of the partial derivatives of $G(.)$ is nonzero. If this is fulfilled, the Lagrange functional can be introduced,

$$L(\hat{x}) = F(\hat{x}) + \lambda(G(\hat{x}) - \varepsilon) \to \min,$$

which is to be minimised (as proved by Lagrange) in order to find the constrained minimum of $F(\hat{x})$. The point $\hat{x}$ of the minimum must therefore fulfil the conditions

$$\frac{\partial L(\hat{x})}{\partial x_i} = \frac{\partial F(\hat{x})}{\partial x_i} + \lambda \frac{\partial G(\hat{x})}{\partial x_i} = 0, \quad \forall i. \tag{10.54}$$

This system of M linear equations together with nonlinear (10.51) enables us to determine uniquely the sought M components of $\hat{x}$ together with the proper value of the multiplier λ. After carrying out the differentiation, the obtained linear equations can be arranged into the following expression

$$\hat{x} = \left[H^T H + \frac{1}{\lambda} C^T C \right]^{-1} H^T y. \tag{10.55}$$

This vector formula expresses explicitly the sought estimate as a function of the observed signal samples, of the known samples of the impulse response of the distorting system and of the yet unknown coefficient λ.

The coefficient λ must be determined such that even the condition (10.51) is satisfied. As only a little is known ahead about the nonlinear equation, the coefficient must be searched for by a reliable simple method not imposing any additional requirements. A simple iteration has proved to work well, beginning with a choice of the initial estimate of λ and continuing further in the following iterative steps:
- compute the estimate $\hat{x}$ according to formula (10.55);
- calculate the residuum (10.50) and the value of $G(\hat{x})$ as in eqn (10.51);
- test whether the equation $G(\hat{x}) - \varepsilon = 0$ is satisfied with sufficient precision; if so, the iteration is stopped, else to be continued;
- modify the λ value (if $G(\hat{x}) > \varepsilon$ increase λ and *vice versa*) and start a new iteration step.

Considering the above analysis, the main properties of the method can be evaluated. The basic advantage is that it requires only minimal identification of the problem. As standard, the impulse response of the distorting system must be identified or estimated, but the noise identification is limited only to estimation of its variance which enters the condition (10.51). As this must be a constant, stationarity of the noise process is required while no particular limitations are imposed on the original signal. This is a substantial advantage in comparison with the Wiener filter which expects the stationarity of both signal and noise components which is often violated in practice. On the other hand, the constrained deconvolution makes the linear estimation formula (eqn (10.55)) specific for each restored signal vector (owing to the specificity of λ). It is therefore a case-specific method, unlike the Wiener filter which is always fixed for a class of signals. This *signal specificity* complicates processing of long signals which must be segmented. Furthermore, difficulties with joining the neighbouring sections may then appear as the method was originally designed for finite signals only. Although the linear operator does not seem to be generally a convolutional filter but rather a more general superposition operator, it will be shown in one of the subsequent paragraphs that simplification to convolution is always possible.

As a new λ must be determined by iteration for every processed signal section, the technique is rather demanding. Nevertheless, it is possible, when processing subsequent signal sections, to use the previous λ value as a good initial estimate for the next signal section, thus lowering the number of iterative steps. Another problem is the large size of the matrices involved, which are roughly $M \times M$ in size. Even for a reasonable length of signal sequence, of the order of thousands of samples, this means an enormous memory requirement and large computational burden as, according to eqn (10.55), it is necessary to invert a matrix of this size in every iteration step. This is the reason for usually realising the method in the frequency domain where the requirements are substantially lower, as we shall show in the next paragraphs.

Formulation in the frequency domain uses (as with frequency-domain realisation of ordinary FIR filters) signal and spectrum vectors of a higher dimension than M in order to prevent interperiod interference caused by circular convolution as provided by the DFT. As can be seen from eqn (10.55), the signal $\mathbf{y}$ is convoluted with the impulse response in fact twice; thus, the length P of all the involved sequences must fulfil the condition $P \geq M + 2J - 2$. The sequences of vector components will therefore be prolonged to this length by zero padding, thus providing the corresponding vectors of the dimension P. It can easily be shown that all the previously mentioned relations for the unmodified vectors remain valid also for the prolonged ones; consequently, the vector formulae remain the same and we shall not distinguish the former from the latter.

By a discrete Fourier transform we obtain from eqns (10.47), (10.48) and (10.52) successively (indexed capital letters denote discrete spectra of prolonged sequences as, for example, $\{x'_n\}$ in $\{X_w\} = DFT\{x'_n\}$, w is the index corresponding to frequency)

$$Y_w = PH_w X_w + N_w, \qquad (10.56)$$

$$P \sum_{w=0}^{P-1} |N_w|^2 = \varepsilon, \tag{10.57}$$

$$P \sum_{w}^{P-1} |L_w \hat{X}_w|^2 \to \min. \tag{10.58}$$

Here we have used the discrete versions of convolutional property and of Parseval's theorem; in the first equation we have also used the assumption of mutual independence of original signal and noise. The last equation has been derived by rewriting criterion (10.52) as a sum with the inner convolution

$$\sum_{n=0}^{M+J-1} \left[\sum_{m=0}^{M+J-1} l_m \hat{x}_{n-m} \right]^2 \to \min,$$

where $\mathbf{l} = [1, -2, 1]^T$ is a discrete approximation of the one-dimensional Laplacian.

Further, substituting (10.50) into eqn (10.51) and transforming, we obtain the condition

$$P \sum_{w=0}^{P-1} |Y_w - P\hat{X}_w H_w|^2 = \varepsilon. \tag{10.59}$$

The Lagrange functional will then be

$$U(\hat{\bar{X}}) = P \sum_{w=0}^{P-1} (|L_w \hat{X}_w|^2 + \lambda |Y_w - P\hat{X}_w H_w|^2) \to \min,$$

and for its minimum it must be valid

$$\frac{\partial U(\hat{X}_w)}{\partial \mathrm{Re}(\hat{X}_w)} = 0, \quad \frac{\partial U(\hat{X}_w)}{\partial \mathrm{Im}(\hat{X}_w)} = 0, \quad \forall w.$$

This is a system of $2P$ linear equations (as every element of the spectrum has its real and imaginary part). This system has a remarkable property that the equations are independent in the sense that they can be solved simply individually and the solutions arranged into the vector expression in the explicit form

$$\hat{X}_w = \frac{1}{P} \frac{H_w^*}{|H_w|^2 + \frac{1}{\lambda}|L_w|^2} Y_w = \frac{1}{P} \frac{1}{H_2} \frac{|H_w|^2}{|H_w|^2 + \frac{1}{\lambda}|L_w|^2} Y_w. \tag{10.60}$$

Substituting this result into eqn (10.59), we obtain the nonlinear equation expressing the requested constraint

$$\frac{P}{\lambda^2} \sum_{w=0}^{P-1} \frac{|Y_w|^2 |L_w|^4}{\left[\frac{1}{\lambda}|L_w|^2 + |H_w|^2\right]^2} - \varepsilon = 0. \tag{10.61}$$

The sought spectral components of the estimated signal are not present in this equation, so that all its quantities except λ are known. The frequency-domain approach therefore does not need repeated solution of the complete linear-equation system inside the iteration loop, as was the case with the time-domain approach. Instead, we only need to solve iteratively the single nonlinear equation (10.61), which is substantially simpler. Note that the condition of zero gradient is only a necessary but not sufficient condition of a minimum and thus the possibility that a maximum or a saddle would be found is not excluded. From a more detailed analysis of the second derivatives, the condition for a minimum follows,

$$\lambda > -\min_w \left(\left|\frac{L_w}{H_w}\right|^2\right).$$

We can summarise the properties of the constrained deconvolution as follows: the frequency-domain approach has proved that the solution of the problem has led again to linear filtering (thus the expression (10.55) must be a convolution). The formula for the frequency response of the resulting filter as follows from eqn (10.60),

$$G_w = \frac{1}{P}\frac{1}{H_w} \frac{|H_w|^2}{|H_w|^2 + \frac{1}{\lambda}|L_w|^2}$$

is somewhat similar to the Wiener filter (10.20). Again, it has the form of the plain inverse filter modified by a correction factor, with the only difference that instead of noise-to-signal ratio in the denominator of the correction factor, a term based on the smoothness criterion appears. The influence of this term is determined by the parameter λ, which has to be determined indi-vidually for every signal by solving the nonlinear equation (10.61); the filter is therefore case-specific. Let us emphasise once more the exceptional modesty of the method as far as the identification phase of the filter design is concerned.

Constrained deconvolution has become the basis of a class of modern non-linear adaptive methods aimed at correcting quasiconvolutional distortion together with generalised noise suppression. In two and three-dimensional versions they are related to the methods of semiflexible membranes, the purpose of which is the sharpening of image contours while suppressing continuously distributed noise as well as impulse noise in smooth regions.

10.6 Deconvolution *via* impulse-response optimisation

Another approach to deconvolution is represented by the method of optimising the shape of a specially defined impulse response. It is based on the notion of a cascade connection of the given deteriorating system and the linear restoration filter to be designed. Such a cascade should ideally have a unit transfer, i.e. its overall impulse response should be (in continuous version) $c(t) = \delta(t)$. This cannot be practically achieved, as was shown in Section 10.2. However, it is possible to introduce a suitable criterion evaluating the shape of the impulse response and to then use this criterion in the optimisation process constrained by a condition limiting excessive increase in noise in consequence of restoration.

The method is formulated assuming continuous-signal degradation by the convolutional effect of a continuously working linear system and by additive noise; the discretisation (and usually A/D conversion) is included only at the input of the discrete restoration system. We suppose a known impulse response $h(t)$ of the distorting system; the optimal impulse response $\{m_n\}$ of the FIR restoration filter of length M is to be found. The output signal of the complete chain can be represented quasicontinuously; for the overall impulse response expressed as convolution, we thus obtain

$$c(t) = h(t) * m(t) = h(t) * \sum_{i=0}^{M} m_i \delta(t - iT)$$

$$= \int_{-\infty}^{\infty} h(\tau) \sum_i m_i \delta(t - iT - \tau) dt$$

$$= \sum_{i=0}^{M} m_i h(t - iT). \tag{10.62}$$

A suitable measure of restoration quality is the slenderness of the resulting impulse response $c(t)$, characterised by the criterion

$$r^2 = \frac{\int_{-\infty}^{\infty} w(t) c^2(t) dt}{\int_{-\infty}^{\infty} c^2(t) dt} \to \min, \tag{10.63}$$

where $w(t)$ is the weighting function penalising the unwanted contributions of the function $c(t)$ off the time origin. One common type of weighting function is the quadratic rule $w(t) = t^2$, which penalises and consequently, *via* designing the filter, suppresses namely large deviations. An alternative is represented by the tolerance rule – the function equal to 1 everywhere outside of a certain chosen neighbourhood of the origin – $w(t) = 0$, $t < D$, which tolerates any course of the response inside the interval $t \in \langle 0, D \rangle$, while anything else is penalised evenly.

Noise limitation is achieved by requesting that the noise level after restoration, characterised by its variance σ_R^2, should not exceed a certain chosen threshold S,

$$\sigma_R^2 \le S. \tag{10.64}$$

Threshold selection can be based on the noise variance σ_0^2 in the observed signal; a common choice is $S = \sigma_0^2$.

Substituting expression (10.62) into criterion (10.63), we obtain

$$r^2 = \frac{\displaystyle\int_{-\infty}^{\infty} w(t) \sum_{i=0}^{M-1} \sum_{j=0}^{M-1} m_i m_j h(t - iT) h(t - jT)\, dx}{\displaystyle\int_{-\infty}^{\infty} \sum_{i=0}^{M-1} \sum_{j=0}^{M-1} m_i m_j h(t - iT) h(t - jT)\, dx}$$

$$= \frac{\mathbf{m}^T \mathbf{A} \mathbf{m}}{\mathbf{m}^T \mathbf{B} \mathbf{m}} \to \min, \tag{10.65}$$

where the elements of the matrices are

$$A_{ij} = \int_{-\infty}^{\infty} w(t) h(t - iT) h(t - jT)\, dx, \quad B_{ij} = \int_{-\infty}^{\infty} h(t - iT) h(t - jT)\, dx.$$

The denominator of the fraction (10.65) expresses the total energy of the impulse response and it is desirable that its value should be 1, i.e. the same as for the ideal impulse response,

$$\mathbf{m}^T \mathbf{b} \mathbf{m} = 1. \tag{10.66}$$

When assuming (usually well substantiated) independence of noise in the original signal, the statistical characteristics of the noise can be analysed separately. The noise variance after restoration therefore is

$$\sigma_R^2 = \mathbb{E}\{(m_n * v(nT))^2\} = \mathbb{E}\left\{ \left(\sum_i^{M-1} m_i v(nT - iT) \right)^2 \right\}$$

$$= \sum_{i=0}^{M-1} \sum_{k=0}^{M-1} m_i m_k \mathbb{E}\{v(nT - iT)v(nT - kT)\} = \mathbf{m}^T \mathbf{R}_{vv} \mathbf{m}.$$

Here we have recognised the mean value inside the sum as the autocorrelation matrix $\mathbf{R}_{vv}$ of the noise-generating process. Thus, the constraining condition (10.64) is (at the edge of the tolerance range)

$$\mathbf{m}^T \mathbf{R}_{vv} \mathbf{m} = S. \tag{10.67}$$

Determining the vector of the restoration-filter coefficients is thus based on minimising the expression:

$$\mathbf{m}^T \mathbf{A}\mathbf{m} \to \min$$

under the conditions (10.66) and (10.67). Again, this constrained optimisation problem can be solved by the method of Langrange's coefficients. The corresponding functional is

$$U(\mathbf{m}) = \mathbf{m}^T \mathbf{A}\mathbf{m} + \lambda_1(\mathbf{m}^T \mathbf{B}\mathbf{m} - 1) + \lambda_2(\mathbf{m}^T \mathbf{R}_{\nu\nu}\mathbf{m} - S),$$

and its minimum will be determined from the condition

$$\nabla U(\mathbf{m}) = \mathbf{0}, \quad \text{i.e.} \quad \partial U(\mathbf{m})/\partial m_i = 0, \quad \forall i.$$

Rewriting the equation system into vector form and rearranging it provides

$$\mathbf{B}^{-1}(\mathbf{A} + \lambda_2 \mathbf{R}_{\nu\nu})\mathbf{m} = \lambda_1 \mathbf{m}. \tag{10.68}$$

It can be seen that the solution – the vector of restoration-filter coefficients – is the eigenvector of the matrix $\mathbf{M} = \mathbf{B}^{-1}(\mathbf{A} + \lambda_2 \mathbf{R}_{\nu\nu})$ for the eigenvalue λ_1. It remains now to decide which of the eigenvalues to use.

Multiplying the equation (10.68) from the left by matrix $\mathbf{B}$ and vector $\mathbf{m}^T$, we obtain, when using the equality of (10.65) and the conditions (10.66, 10.67), the equation

$$r^2 = \lambda_1 + \lambda_2 S,$$

from which follows that the minimum value of the criterion corresponds to the minimal eigenvalue of the matrix $\mathbf{M}$, used as λ_1. The parameter λ_2 is not an eigenvalue and must be determined by iterative computation starting from any initial estimate and heading to estimates which would provide gradually smaller r^2. It is, of course, a demanding procedure.

When disregarding the tediousness of the design, the method has advantageous properties. It does not impose any limitations on the class of original signals or noise, namely it does not require stationarity of the original signals (noise is supposed stationary, however, at least as far as its power is concerned). To implement the method, we only need to identify the impulse response of the distorting system and to estimate roughly the noise power (variance) at the input of the restoration system. With respect to such a simple identification and considering that the processed signal does not enter the design process, the derived filter obviously applies to a very broad class of problem. When designed, the resulting filter is an ordinary FIR system. As such, it can process signals of any length and it may be realised by means of any method mentioned in Section 5.2.3.

10.7 Generalised discrete mean-square-error minimisation

The method that we shall introduce in this section is, in a sense a generalisation of Wiener filtering. The concept assumes that both the original signal and noise are realisations of stochastic, not necessarily stationary, processes and it also uses the optimisation criterion of mean-square error (10.8). The model of deterioration is again eqn (10.47). The restoration is a generalisation of filtering *via* frequency domain; we suppose that the vectors have already been prolonged to the length P and the matrices to size $P \times P$ by zero padding, as in the second part of Section 10.5.

A simplifying facet of this method is that the transform need not necessarily be of a DFT type, because the convolution property is not used. On the other hand, the restoration-filter frequency transfer is not expressed by a vector but rather by a matrix and the output in the transform domain is thus given by a regular matrix product of the frequency-response matrix and the input-signal spectrum. This leads to removing the rule, valid for linear convolution systems, that any output harmonic component can only originate based on an input component of the same frequency. The described filter therefore is generally *not convolutional*.

The estimate of the original is obviously

$$\hat{\mathbf{x}} = \mathbf{A}^{-1}[\mathbf{M}(\mathbf{A}\mathbf{y})], \tag{10.69}$$

where $\mathbf{A}$ is the core of the transform used and $\mathbf{M}$ is the matrix transfer of the filter in the transform domain. According to the principle of orthogonality, the differences between the original signal and its optimal estimate must be orthogonal to any component of the observed signal that is used in the estimation,

$$\mathbb{E}\{(\mathbf{x} - \hat{\mathbf{x}})\mathbf{y}^T\} = \mathbb{E}\{(\mathbf{x} - \mathbf{A}^{-1}\mathbf{M}\mathbf{A}\mathbf{y})\mathbf{y}^T\} = \mathbf{0}.$$

This equation can be rewritten utilising, e.g., $\mathbf{R}_{fg} = \mathbb{E}\{\mathbf{f}\mathbf{g}^T\}$, etc., into

$$\mathbf{R}_{xy} = \mathbf{A}^{-1}\mathbf{M}\mathbf{A}\mathbf{R}_{yy}.$$

If, as supposed, $\mathbf{x}$, $\bar{v}$ are uncorrelated, then $\mathbf{R}_{yy} = \mathbf{H}\mathbf{R}_{xx}\mathbf{H}^T + \mathbf{R}_{vv}$ and $\mathbf{R}_{yx} = \mathbf{R}_{xx}\mathbf{H}^T$, and by substituting into the previous equation, we obtain the resulting expression for the filter transfer matrix:

$$\mathbf{M} = \mathbf{A}\mathbf{R}_{xx}\mathbf{H}^T[\mathbf{H}\mathbf{R}_{xx}\mathbf{H}^T + \mathbf{R}_{vv}]^{-1}\mathbf{A}^{-1}. \tag{10.70}$$

To design the filter we therefore need to know the autocorrelation matrices of the original signal and of noise, the impulse response of the distorting system and also the core of the chosen transform.[3] With respect to the expected non-stationarity, the estimates of the autocorrelation matrices cannot be based on time averages and it is necessary to build them using ensemble averages, which is of course demanding.

It is interesting, from an interpretation point of view, to convert the relations formally into the transform domain. Let us introduce *generalised power spectra* as transforms of the autocorrelation matrices,

---

[3] Considering that $\hat{\mathbf{x}} = \mathbf{A}^{-1}[\mathbf{M}(\mathbf{A}\mathbf{y})]$, after substituting from eqn (10.70) we obtain a time-domain transformation matrix $\mathbf{m} = \mathbf{R}_{xx}\mathbf{H}^T[\mathbf{H}\mathbf{R}_{xx}\mathbf{H}^T + \mathbf{R}_{vv}]^{-1}$ so that the filtering can be realised in the original domain in a simpler way according to $\hat{\mathbf{x}} = \mathbf{m}\mathbf{y}$.

$$S_{xx} = AR_{xx}A^{-1}, \quad S_{vv} = AR_{vv}A^{-1},$$

and *generalised frequency responses* as

$$G = AHA^{-1}, \quad G' = AH^{T}A^{-1}.$$

Notice that, of course, these are not spectra in the common sense, not even when using the DFT as the transform, because the generalised spectra are two dimensional. This is due to the nonstationarity of the processes involved which leads primarily to two-dimensional autocorrelation matrices. If the transform is unitary, $A^{-1} = A^{*T}$ and consequently

$$S_{xx} \triangleq AR_{xx}A^{-1} = A[\mathbb{E}\{xx^{T}\}]A^{-1} = \mathbb{E}\{Ax\}\mathbb{E}\{[Ax]^{T}\} = \mathbb{E}\{XX^{T}\}.$$

Now it can be shown that, for stationary processes, the generalised power-spectrum definition is really a formal generalisation of the common one-dimensional power-spectrum definition of a stationary process (4.23). Note that the main diagonal of the generalised power spectrum carries the values of the commonsense one-dimensional power spectrum for stationary processes, while the other elements express the inner correlations among spectral components.

The expression for the filter transfer can be rewritten using these generalised spectra,

$$M = AR_{xx}A^{-1}AH^{T}A^{-1}A[HR_{xx}H^{T} + R_{vv}]^{-1}A^{-1}$$

$$= AR_{xx}A^{-1}.AH^{T}A^{-1}[AHA^{-1}.AR_{xx}A^{-1}.AH^{T}A^{-1} + AR_{vv}A^{-1}]^{-1}$$

$$= S_{xx}G'(GS_{xx}G' + S_{vv})^{-1}. \tag{10.71}$$

This is a noteworthy result showing that the filter transfer expressed in terms of generalised spectra can be understood as being formally identical to the Wiener-filter frequency transfer (10.20) derived for stationary processes under the assumption of independence of signal and noise. In this sense, the filter (10.70) or (10.71) really can be considered as a generalisation of a Wiener filter. In terms of applications, however, the 'spectral domain' formulation (10.71) does not provide any computational savings in comparison with the formulation in the original domain, because the dimension of the nonstationary problem is not reduced by being transformed into the 'spectral' domain.

10.8 Other approaches to signal restoration

We shall briefly mention two other approaches to restoration.

The first of these is the *method of maximum a posteriori probability* (MAP). The concept of this method is connected with the explanation of Section 10.3.1, where the conditioned mean value (10.9) was presented as the optimal estimate of the original. The method discussed now is based on the same posterior probability distribution, conditioned by reception (observation) of a particular signal $\{y_n\}$. It starts with the assumption that the conditional mean value of the signal vector would not differ substantially from the vector corresponding to the maximum of the conditional probability distribution, called the conditional modus. As determining this signal vector with maximum posterior probability is, in spite of all its complexity, still substantially easier than assessing the conditional mean value, the method discussed aims to find the mentioned maximum.

The method enables us to generalise, to a certain extent, the deterioration model which may contain an inertialess nonlinearity superposed on the convolutional distortion,

$$y_n = \Psi(\{h_n * x_n\}) + v_n,$$

thus in vector notation,

$$\mathbf{y} = \overline{\Psi}(\mathbf{Hx}) + \overline{v}. \tag{10.72}$$

The probability distribution for a discrete finite signal $\mathbf{x}$ of length N is obviously a scalar function $p(\mathbf{x})$ in N-dimensional space of the signal sample values. The *a priori* distribution $p(\mathbf{x})$ describes, roughly, the occurrence probabilities of individual admissible original signals; it is therefore a characteristic of the source process. If a signal $\mathbf{y}$ has been observed as the input to restoration, the distribution is modified into the conditioned probability distribution $p(\mathbf{x}|\mathbf{y})$ and the vector of its mean value

$$\hat{\mathbf{x}}_{opt} = \int_{-\infty}^{\infty} \cdots \int_{-\infty}^{\infty} \mathbf{x}\, p(\mathbf{x}|\mathbf{y})\, dV_{\mathbf{x}} \tag{10.73}$$

is the optimal estimate. Instead of determining this estimate, which is not practically feasible, we will try to find the position of the maximum of the conditioned distribution, its modus,

$$\hat{\mathbf{x}} \colon \; p(\hat{\mathbf{x}}|\mathbf{y}) = \max_{\mathbf{x}}(p(\mathbf{x}|\mathbf{y})). \tag{10.74}$$

According to Bayes theorem, for the occurrence distribution of a particular pair of signals $\mathbf{x}$, $\mathbf{y}$, it is $p(\mathbf{x}, \mathbf{y}) = p(\mathbf{x}|\mathbf{y})p(\mathbf{y}) = p(\mathbf{y}|\mathbf{x})p(\mathbf{x})$ thus

$$p(\mathbf{x}|\mathbf{y}) = \frac{1}{p(\mathbf{y})}\, p(\mathbf{y}|\mathbf{x})p(\mathbf{x}). \tag{10.75}$$

As the first factor on the right-hand side is independent of $\mathbf{x}$, it is possible to ignore it when seeking the maximum with respect to $\mathbf{x}$.

The *a priori* distribution $p(\mathbf{x})$ can be estimated in practical tasks on the basis of long-term observation (measurement) of signal sources, or sometimes it can be calculated directly based on the theoretical properties of the signal-generating mechanism. The conditioned distribution $p(\mathbf{y}|\mathbf{x})$ can be determined according to the following consideration: when, knowing the original signal $\mathbf{x}$, it is possible to determine the noiseless distorted vector $\mathbf{x}' = \overline{\Psi}(\mathbf{Hx})$ from

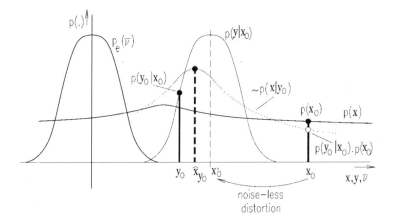

Figure 10.14 Probability distributions of vectors for one-dimensional parameterisation

eqn (10.72); with respect to nonstochastic functional dependence, it is of course $p(\mathbf{x}') = p(\mathbf{x})$. Because, according to the same model, $\bar{v} = \mathbf{y} - \mathbf{x}'$, the distribution $p(\mathbf{y}|\mathbf{x})$ is only a shifted version of the *a priori* distribution of noise $p_e(\bar{v})$,

$$p(\mathbf{y}|\mathbf{x}) = p_e(\mathbf{y} - \mathbf{x}') = p_e(\mathbf{y} - \overline{\Psi}(\mathbf{H}\mathbf{x})),$$

and therefore

$$p(\mathbf{x}|\mathbf{y}) \sim p_e(\mathbf{y} - \overline{\Psi}(\mathbf{H}\mathbf{x}))p(\mathbf{x}) = U_\mathbf{y}(\mathbf{x}). \tag{10.76}$$

It is schematically illustrated in Figure 10.14 how to determine this function point-by-point under the condition that we have observed the vector $\mathbf{y}_0$. The figure is simplified by the assumption that the vectors are all functions of a single scalar parameter and the distributions are therefore one dimensional. For an arbitrarily chosen original $\mathbf{x}_0$, the value $p(\mathbf{x}_0)$ can be read from the curve $p(\mathbf{x})$. Further, the vector of the noiseless distorted signal $\mathbf{x}'_0 = \overline{\Psi}(\mathbf{H}\mathbf{x}_0)$ must be found using the distortion model. The *a priori* noise distribution $p_e(\bar{v})$ will then be shifted so that its central value for $\bar{v} = \mathbf{0}$ is placed at $\mathbf{x}'_0$, as shown by the thin curve depicting the conditioned distribution $p(\mathbf{y}|\mathbf{x}_0)$. On this curve, the value $p(\mathbf{y}_0|\mathbf{x}_0)$ can be read for the particular observed vector $\mathbf{y}_0$. The resulting value $p(\mathbf{y}_0|\mathbf{x}_0)\,p(\mathbf{x}_0)$ provides one point on the dotted curve, the values of which are proportional to the sought conditioned probability $p(\mathbf{x}|\mathbf{y}_0)$. After having obtained the curve completely in this point-by-point manner, we could finally determine the modus estimate $\hat{\mathbf{x}}_{\mathbf{y}_0}$ of the original signal corresponding to the observed signal $\mathbf{y}_0$ as required by the MAP method. Complete evaluation of the course of the function is naturally not needed, as the maximum position, i.e. $\hat{\mathbf{x}}_{\mathbf{y}_0}$, can be determined analytically; it has only been described as a way of understanding the approach better.

The maximum of the function (10.76) is a point of zero gradient,

$$\nabla U_y(\mathbf{x}) = \nabla[p_e(\mathbf{y} - \overline{\Psi}(\mathbf{Hx}))p(\mathbf{x})] = \mathbf{0}$$

$$\text{i.e.} \quad \partial U_y(\mathbf{x})/\partial x_i = 0, \quad \forall i. \tag{10.77}$$

By solving this equation system, the sought estimate $\hat{\mathbf{x}}_y$ can be found for concrete $\mathbf{y}$ (only probably, as a zero gradient does not necessarily mean a maximum). It can be seen that identification, needed to implement the method, includes determination of the following functions: the linear-distortion impulse response and the nonlinear distortion function, the *a priori* probability distribution of the original signal source and the *a priori* probability distribution of the noise source. All these functions (or the parameters describing them) can in principle be obtained. However, the practical procedure is complicated by the high dimension of the problem, and therefore simplified versions of the approach have been derived, under more or less realistic assumptions. As these details do not belong to the basic concept of the method, they are beyond the scope of this book.

The *method of maximum entropy* is conceptually close to the constrained-deconvolution approach in that it maximises the 'smoothness' of the restored signal. In this case, the smoothness property of the signal estimate, or of the noise which is also estimated, is quantified by the functions

$$K_x = -\sum_{i=0}^{N-1} \hat{x}_i \ln(\hat{x}_i) \quad \text{or} \quad K_v = -\sum_{i=0}^{N-1} \hat{v}_i \ln(\hat{v}_i), \tag{10.78}$$

respectively. Although the expressions are formally similar to the expression for the entropy of stochastic systems, which gave the method its name, the entropy concept as such is not utilised in the method under discussion. The expression is only a suitable functional which has proved useful as a measure of the smoothness of the estimates. Indeed, the smoothest signal is a constant for which the expression becomes maximum and decreases with increasing sample diversity. The link to the entropy concept lies in the fact that when the signal values are normalised to $\langle 0, 1 \rangle$ and to unit sum, they could be considered to be probabilities of a certain stochastic experiment and, in the case of equal probabilities, the entropy expression is known to be maximum. The method estimates concurrently both the original signal values and the values of noise; this is why both 'entropies' have been introduced.

The method constrains the solution to have the identical sum of the signal elements as has the observed signal,

$$\sum_{i=0}^{N-1} \hat{x}_i = \sum_{i=0}^{N-1} y_i = S.$$

This is another heuristic precaution against divergence.

Apart from this, the values of signal and noise estimates are bound with the observed-signal values and values of the distorting impulse response by the model of deterioration

$$y_n = \sum_{i=0}^{n} h_{n-i}\hat{x}_i + v_n.$$

This is again a constrained optimisation problem, with multiple constraints. The Lagrange functional has in this case the form

$$U_y(\hat{x}, \hat{v}) = K_x + \rho K_v + \sum_{p=0}^{N-1} \lambda_p \left[\sum_{i=0}^{N-1} h_{p-i}(\hat{x}_i - B_x) + \hat{v}_p - B_v - y_p \right]$$

$$+ \beta \left(\sum_{i=0}^{N-1} \hat{x}_i - S \right),$$

where B_x, B_v are the maximally possible negative values of the original signal and noise (needed to shift both observed-signal components so that they are positive and, consequently, the functions K_x, K_v defined). The chosen parameter $\rho(\approx 20)$ expresses the relative importance of noise suppression in comparison with suppression of signal diversity. As well as the *2N* estimated values of signal and noise, values of $N+1$ coefficients λ_p, β must also be found. It can be shown that estimated signal and noise values can be expressed explicitly as nonlinear functions of these coefficients. Thus, the system of equations, derived in the standard way from the requirement of zero gradient of the above functional, is sufficient to determine all the sought quantities.

The primary advantage of this method is that it makes no limiting assumptions concerning the signal and noise properties. As the Lagrange functional depends on the observed signal, it is again a case-specific method. The preliminary identification is not demanding; it only includes the impulse-response measurement and determining of the extreme signal values B_x, B_v. Further, the parameters ρ, S must be chosen based on experience. The computational implementation of the estimation procedure is nevertheless rather complex, especially when restoring long signals, as every signal section is in principle restored in an individual way. The problem of joining consequent signal sections therefore reappears in this method.

10.9 A note on signal data compression

Signal data compression is not among the main themes of this book; nevertheless, it is worth investigating briefly to see if there are any links with the analysis and restoration of signals. So far, we have dealt with signals having in mind either obtaining a 'better' signal (in a sense) or a signal description for analytical or diagnostic purposes. When any kind of processing or design was to be evaluated, the criteria of quality have been based on some mathematical concept. Primarily, some kind of absolute or mean-square error was used, based on the differences between the desired and obtainable results (restored signals, responses of designed systems, estimation of stochastic parameters etc.). These criteria are transparent and easy to implement; also, consistent theories can be built on them to enable formalised analysis or restoration. They are designed from this point of view and therefore they may look somewhat arbitrary to a user of the signal.

The subjective quality of signals, as perceived by human beings *via* their sensory organs or as evaluated with respect to the practical use of the signal, need not necessarily correspond to the mathematically introduced criteria. The most prominent examples of this are multimedia signals – acoustic signals and image sequences to be observed by human beings. As another example, the quality of digitally restored or decompressed medical signals, such as ECG or X-ray images as evaluated by medical staff, cannot be simply related to anything like the LMS criteria. Thus, it is quite common for a signal to be evaluated as being excellent by its user although the mathematical criterion indicates a poor result, and *vice versa*. This complicates the situation as new criteria for quality are to be sought, but it also enables us to remove unnecessary signal components which do not influence the application quality.

In this way, that is by removing the components of signals which are redundant as far as the application is concerned, it is possible to lower the extent of the signal data without losing anything (or any important part) from its real information content. It is obvious that the signal shape may be substantially changed due to such an operation and therefore any difference criterion which compares it with the original would be useless. It is an important development in the last two decades that the need for *new quality criteria*, based on the user view, has been recognised; in many application areas these have already been found and applied. The result is a remarkable development in the field of signal and image data compression which has enabled the implementation of *digital* sound and video recording, multimedia communication, image archiving, teleconferencing etc. Until recently, the relevant digital methods were considered too demanding for practical application. This was primarily because the capacity of communication channels or frequency properties of archiving media have physical limits and simply cannot comply with the necessarily high bit rates or quantities of data in the uncompressed sampled versions of the signals. Only after achieving today's levels of compression, digital versions of the above services became not only feasible but also more economic and, in spite of high compression, provide the same or even better subjective quality.

The compression ratios which are available nowadays may be between units and several hundreds, depending on the needed quality, method of compression and character of the signal. The compression methods can be basically divided into two groups: methods of lossless compression and lossy compression methods.

Methods of *lossless compression* are independent of the applications or user acceptance and utilise the statistical redundancy in digital signals, which can be successfully evaluated and utilised by formalised methods. As the name suggests, no information is lost and the signals can be completely recovered from the compressed version by the inverse procedure – decompression. Statistical redundancy is due to nonzero correlations in the signal. These are primarily temporal and space correlations – near or even distant samples of signals or images may be mutually correlated. In video sequences, intraframe correlations, inside an image, and interframe correlations, among subsequent images, often differing by only a small amount, can be found. Another type is represented by intercomponent correlations, such as between spectral components of a signal, colour components in video or between audio channels in stereo. Lossless compression methods all aim to find (construct) a coding method which, primarily, uses a low-entropy signal description. This means that the probability distribution among transmitted 'symbols' (e.g. sample values) should be non-uniform, contrary to the distribution of original samples, which have all admissible values about equally probable. This is provided for mostly by a method of *predictive coding*; the differences between the predicted and real values usually have a much more compact distribution than do the original signal samples. Consequently, frequently-occurring high-probability symbols can be coded by short binary words while low-probability symbols would not contribute substantially to the length of the resulting bit-chain even when their codes are long – this is the principle of *entropy coding*. As for applying methods discussed elsewhere in the book, correlation analysis is often used in building stochastic models of signals, which can lead to more effective coding. Obviously, the different methods of predictive coding and filtering represent another link to subjects which we have dealt with already, while more detailed description of the entropy coding is out of the range of this book.

Lossy compression uses the above-mentioned fact that a part (perhaps most, in some cases) of the information carried by a signal is redundant for the user and would not be used anyway. The main problem, when designing such a method, is to determine the redundant components. This is usually a result of psychophysiological research (in the case of image, video and audio signals), of long-term comparison of the results of using the original and purposely deteriorated (depleted) images or signals, for example for diagnostic purposes, and so on. Generally, better discrimination between useful and redundant components is possible in the frequency domain or in other transformed domains; the type of suitable transform depends on the signal type. Most of the transforms decorrelate the signal components, i.e. spectral coefficients, which contributes to the efficiency of the compression. In this respect, the cosine transform is perhaps currently the most prominent one, being the best available fast approximation of the optimum Karhunen–Loeve transform. The cosine transform is massively used in image and video compression where it is applied to small blocks of image elements. Wavelet transforms are also becoming frequently used, with excellent results, in image compression. Wavelet-based methods do not suffer from 'blocking effects' as they are successfully applied to complete, undivided images. Subband coding *via* either DWT or other transforms has proved very useful.

In the field of audio signals, the classical discrete Fourier transform is primarily used owing to its similarity to the auditory analyser of humans. It is common to all transform-based methods that the redundant components are removed or suppressed in the frequency domain on the basis of some criteria, and possibly only a few spectral coefficients are preserved. In the simplest case, the weaker components are omitted but, in many cases, more complex criteria must be applied, corresponding to the use of the signal. As an example, we mention the audio signals where so-called frequency and temporal masking is in effect: a strong narrowband signal (a tone) masks the weaker components with close frequencies, and these may be discarded as not audible. The sounds following shortly after a strong sound are also hidden so that they too can be omitted without the listener noticing it. This means that the sound signal must be frequency analysed, the masking threshold, which is dependent on frequency and time, must be determined and, based on this information, some spectral components will be suppressed. The remaining spectral components are then coded and the bit stream communicated or archived. At the receiving end, the signal is reconstructed based on this incomplete information; thus the signal shape will be rather different from that of the original signal, but the listener's perception will not be impaired if the compression method is fair.

Apart from transform-based methods, there are many other lossy approaches, interpreted in the original domain, for example based on probabilistic models of signal generation, on lossy predictive coding or even on heuristic rules. Neural networks are also promising, primarily for discovering hidden features which might be utilised in compression. Usually several methods are combined in order to achieve a good compression ratio with a reasonable computing effort. An example of a special, very effective lossy compression method is inter-frame predictive coding of video sequences based on motion estimation and prediction. It is obvious that consequential images usually remain almost the same and, if the moving object can be identified and kept track of, only a very small part of the information is needed for the (approximate) update of the next images.

The data limited by lossy procedures is mostly lossless entropy coded to provide a highly compressed bit stream to be transmitted or archived.

When designing a compression method, a balance between the conflicting aspects of coding efficiency (expressed by achievable compression ratio), coding and decoding complexity and also coding delay must be found. For lossy methods, the allowable deterioration must also be prescribed and observed. The other aspects to be observed are, for example, robustness of the method with respect to transmission errors and to repeated compression–decompression, compatibility with other compression and transmission systems, accessibility of individual parts of the signal in compressed form (for editing) etc. An important requirement is scalability of the compression, i.e.

the ability to recover the decompressed signal or namely image gradually on the basis of so-far-available data, with a progressively increasing resolution, as is typical, for example, for wavelet-based compression.

Let us conclude this marginal note with the observation that multiple links exist between the area of signal compression and the material of this book. For more information, sources which are devoted to the topic include References [8], [26], [5].

Chapter 11
Adaptive filtering and identification

11.1 Concept of adaptive filtering

In the previous chapter, when designing restoration filters which should provide optimal estimates of original signals based on their observed noisy and distorted versions, we used explicit information obtained by *a priori* identification of signal-source properties. Apart from identifying the deterministic distortion (e.g. by the relevant impulse response), it was about measuring or estimating probability or statistical characteristics of related stochastic processes, such as correlation functions or matrices. These can reasonably be provided in advance in many practically important cases, namely when modelled by stationary processes. Alternatively, the stationary signal-source parameters could also be estimated from the signal itself providing that a suitable signal-generation model has been introduced. Consequently, it is possible to design an optimal or suboptimal restoration system; in the case of stationary processes, the system is, or aims at, a time-invariant filter, such as the classical Wiener filter.

Nevertheless, if the filter is to work in an unknown environment (either because the identification is impossible or the environment is time varying in an unpredictable way), it must be capable of adapting to such a situation. We shall therefore deal in this chapter with *adaptive filters* that are able to learn from a given environment, i.e. they are capable of providing the necessary information – estimates of the needed quantities – in the course of their work, without any *a priori* information. It is then possible to expect that such filters will be able to react (with a certain delay) even to changes in environmental properties and thus to also process signals generated by nonstationary processes. Compared with Kalman filters, the models of the processes need not be known ahead of time. The cost, to be paid for not providing the *a priori* information, is the need to supply the filter continuously with additional information in the form of a so-called *training signal*. The training signal is supplied to the filter besides the regular input signal to be processed. It is closely correlated with the requested output signal of the filter, usually being an approximation of it; in the simplest case it may be directly identical to the required output.

It might seem at first sight that, if a training signal closely approximating the required output is available, no filtering is actually needed or, at least, that it is unreasonable to proceed from the worse observed signal when a better training one is available. Nevertheless, as we will show in the last part of this chapter, there are many situations in practice when the concept of an adaptive filter is useful and the required training signal can somehow be provided. If it is available only temporarily, perhaps repeatedly, the filter can be adapted during periods of training-signal availability. In between these periods, it may operate as a time-invariant system under the assumption that the changes in the environment will be sufficiently small until the next adaptation period. In some cases, we may be able to generate the desired training signal approximately based on the observed signal according to some *a priori* assumptions, for example by means of a nonlinear transform. The time-variant adaptive filter then serves to provide continuously linear estimates which may be more precise or more generally valid over a greater time or dynamic range than those which have been preliminarily estimated. A typical application for adaptive filters is identification of input–output characteristics of a system. In this situation, both the input and output signals are available at the same time and the purpose of identification is to adapt the filter so that it mimics the identified system by having a similar transfer function. The output of the identification procedure is naturally not the filter's output signal but rather the filter parameters characterising the identified system; the parameters will be variable in time if the identified system is time variant.

Adaptive filters can be designed as filters with infinite or finite impulse response. General recursive filters (ARMA-type filters) promise naturally, in principle, better estimates. Their basic disadvantage is that they may become unstable in the course of adaptation; thus, complicated precautions in the adaptation mechanisms are needed to prevent parameter-adjustment leading to instability. We shall therefore limit ourselves in this book to common nonrecursive FIR adaptive filters (e.g. MA type) which are always stable. These also have favourable properties concerning the algorithmic complexity of their adaptation procedures, which aim at minimal quadratic differences. Let us note that it is sometimes possible to encounter discussions on the instability of such a filter in the literature. This is a misunderstanding owing to vague formulations – the analyses do not concern the stability of the filter itself but rather the convergence properties of the adaptation algorithms.

A general block diagram of such an adaptive filter is in Figure 11.1; the upper part presents the outside view with all the important external signals, while the lower part shows the basic internal structure. The external view shows that there are two inputs to the filter, the *observed signal* $\{y_n\}$ to be processed and the *training signal* $\{x_n\}$, which describes the desired output signal of the filter. The external outputs are, primarily, the filtered output, that is the *estimation signal* $\{\hat{x}_n\}$ which should be an approximation of $\{x_n\}$, further the *difference (error) signal* $\{e_n\} = \{x_n - \hat{x}_n\}$ and the *identification signal* $\{\mathbf{h}_n\}$, a sequence of instantaneous parameter vectors of the filter. Depending on the application, either of the output signals may be of interest. We see that the observed (input) signal is processed by an ordinary FIR filter, which is described in the time instant t_n by the vector of its weighting coefficients, that is by the impulse-response vector $\mathbf{h}_n$. The filter provides, at its output in every time-instant n, a more or less precise estimate $\hat{x}_n$ of the desired training-signal sample x_n. The precision of the approximation depends on the degree of adaptation (which usually increases with time) and of course also on the abilities of the filter given by its length. The filter is time variant and its instantaneous impulse response is determined by the output of the block of adaptation algorithm which calculates the vector $\mathbf{h}_n$ for every discrete time instant. The repeated calculation is based on two incoming signals, the input (observed) signal $\{y_n\}$ and the error signal $\{e_n\} = \{x_n - \hat{x}_n\}$; the training signal is needed to provide the error signal.

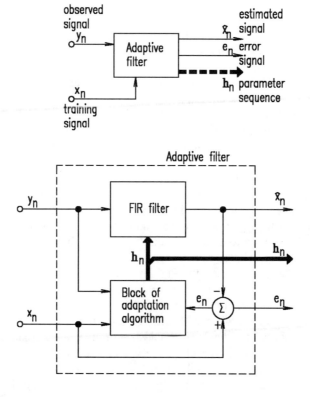

Figure 11.1 General structure of an adaptive filter

11.2 Algorithms of adaptive filters

11.2.1 Adaptive version of the discrete Wiener filter

We saw in Section 10.3.3 that the classical Wiener filter definition (in its discrete version) can easily be generalised so that the filter would provide optimal estimates even when the relevant signal and noise-generating processes are nonstationary. It is only necessary to calculate a new vector of the optimal filter parameters $_n\mathbf{h}_{opt}$ for each time-instant using eqn (10.28),

$$_n\mathbf{h}_{opt} = {_n\overline{\overline{\Phi}}_{yy}^{-1}} \, {_n\overline{\Phi}_{yx}} \tag{11.1}$$

where $_n\overline{\overline{\Phi}}_{yy}$ is the instantaneous (local) autocorrelation matrix (of size $N \times N$), of the process generating the observed signal, valid for the time instant n, and $_n\overline{\Phi}_{yx}$ is the vector of crosscorrelations between the actual original-signal sample x_n and elements of the input signal vector

$$\mathbf{y}_n = [y_n, y_{n-1}, \cdots, y_{n-N+1}]^T.$$

Let us emphasise that the auto and crosscorrelations must be estimated by means of ensemble averages; with respect to the nonstationarity of the processes, the time averages cannot be used and, also, the matrix will not be Toeplitz.

The relationship enables us in principle, for every discrete time instant, to calculate the corresponding filter-coefficient vector that would lead to an optimal estimate of the original x_n, as far as the matrix is nonsingular. Although the result would be optimum for the class of FIR filters of length N, this approach is not practically feasible, as providing the ensemble averages based on many realisations is usually very difficult if not entirely impossible to achieve. In addition, the computational demands connected with compiling and solving the equation system (11.1) are rather high. However, it is a theoretical advantage that the filter is reformed in every sampling period, independently of its properties in previous periods. Naturally, the individual vectors $_n\mathbf{h}_{opt}$ for different n are mutually dependent owing to dependencies among correlation characteristics in the individual time instants. The transfer of this time-dependent filter is equivalent to the ideal adaptive FIR filter of the chosen length: it provides optimal estimates with an instant reaction to changes in signal properties and may therefore be used as a golden standard for other approaches. Nevertheless, it is not an adaptive filter because its design depends on *a priori* information which cannot be derived from the incoming signals in real time.

If only sequences of both original and observed signals are available, it is possible to work with mere approximations of the correlation matrices derived entirely from the course of both signals as received (observed, measured) so far. The best estimate of the matrix $_n\overline{\overline{\Phi}}_{yy} = \mathbb{E}\{\mathbf{y}_n\mathbf{y}_n^T\}$ is then the sole available term of the ensemble average, i.e. $\mathbf{y}_n\mathbf{y}_n^T$. Similarly, the best available estimate of the vector of crosscorrelations is $_n\overline{\overline{\Phi}}_{yx} = \mathbb{E}(\mathbf{y}_n x_n) \approx \mathbf{y}_n x_n$. Nevertheless, these estimates suffer from a large variance and, as it is impossible to improve them by including more terms into the ensemble averages, they can only be improved by time averaging which assumes stationarity of the signals. However, should the statistical parameters of the relevant processes vary sufficiently slowly in time, satisfactory estimates can be obtained when taking into account only an adequately long finite history. We shall show later how to limit the influence of old values of the signals. For the time being, let us design an adaptive filter that would approach the properties of the Wiener filter in case of stationary processes.

For stationary signals, the matrix $_n\overline{\overline{\Phi}}_{yy} = \mathbb{E}\{\mathbf{y}_n \mathbf{y}_n^T\}$ can obviously be approximated by the time average $_n\mathbf{r}_{yy}/(n+1)$ and, similarly, the vector $_n\overline{\overline{\Phi}}_{yx}$ by the average $_n\mathbf{r}_{yx}/(n+1)$, where

$$_n\mathbf{r}_{yy} = \sum_{m=0}^{n} \mathbf{y}_m \mathbf{y}_m^T \quad \text{and} \quad _n\mathbf{r}_{yx} = \sum_{m=0}^{n} \mathbf{y}_m x_m. \tag{11.2}$$

If the signals are zero before the time origin, $y_n = 0$ for $n < 0$, the elements of the vector $\mathbf{y}_m$ for $m < N - 1$ are partly zero which means that some elements of the correlation matrices would also be zero as long as $n < N - 1$. For n above this limit, the matrices are already full although the number of summed products is complete only in elements with zero indices and it lowers when the indices increase. Division by $(n+1)$ thus yields, for most of the elements, an average influenced by a systematic error; this bias nevertheless decreases with increasing n and, for large n, it can be neglected. When substituting for the correlation matrices in eqn (11.1) by these estimates, we obtain the estimated members of the impulse response sequence as

$$_n\hat{\mathbf{h}}_{opt} = {_n\mathbf{r}_{yy}^{-1}} \, {_n\mathbf{r}_{yx}}, \tag{11.3}$$

which is already a practically applicable formula. Notice that besides values of the observed signal the algorithm also needs the original (training) signal values, as it corresponds to the concept of adaptive filtering. The time development of the vector $_n\hat{\mathbf{h}}_{opt}$ in a stationary environment naturally reflects only the improvement in the estimate of the constant optimal vector. The estimate at every time instant is thus optimum in the sense that it is not possible to design the filter any better with the given information. It is nevertheless always worse on average than the theoretical filter given by eqn (11.1) for any finite n.

If the environment is nonstationary, it is required that the filter would be able to adapt to its changing properties. This means that we may take into account only such a long history of the signals which occurred during the time in which the environment was approximately stationary. It would therefore be necessary to apply a floating window, say of the length W, to both input signals when calculating either of the estimates (11.2) (averaging of slowly varying repetition signals in Section 6.2 was organised similarly). When a rectangular window is applied, the estimates obviously become

$$_n\mathbf{r}_{yy} = \sum_{m=n-W+1}^{n} \mathbf{y}_m \mathbf{y}_m^T \quad \text{and} \quad _n\mathbf{r}_{yx} = \sum_{m=n-W+1}^{n} \mathbf{y}_m x_m. \tag{11.4}$$

Applying such a rectangular sliding window requires, of course, that we keep the last $W + N - 1$ of both signals in memory registers, which complicates the realisation.

This is why exponential averaging is more often used instead, as it provides for the successive forgetting of old values in a similar way to the method in Section 6.3. To this end, it is only necessary to modify the expressions for matrix estimation by introducing a damping parameter α,

$$_n\mathbf{r}_{yy} = \sum_{m=0}^{n} \mathbf{y}_m \mathbf{y}_m^T \alpha^{n-m} \quad \text{and} \quad _n\mathbf{r}_{yx} = \sum_{m=0}^{n} \mathbf{y}_m x_m \alpha^{n-m}, \tag{11.5}$$

where $\alpha \in (0, 1)$ is such a chosen constant that the equivalent length $W' = \alpha/(1 - \alpha)$ of this exponentially into-history-decreasing window would correspond to the required length W of the rectangular window.

The filter according to eqn (11.3), based on the correlation estimates (11.4) or (11.5), is capable of working in a slowly varying nonstationary environment. Fast or step changes in the characteristics of the relevant processes will lead to a worsening of the estimates during the adaptation time, similarly as at the beginning of the filter operation. The quality of estimates will of course be worse than those provided by the optimum filter (11.1). In addition, when comparing the 'forgetting' filter (with either a rectangular or exponential window) working in a stationary environment with the filter (11.3) which uses the original matrices according to eqn (11.2), the latter should be on average better. This is because the 'nonforgetting' matrices utilise, in contrast to 'forgetting' ones, all the available information. This partial loss of precision is the price to be paid for the ability of adaptation in a nonstationary environment. Naturally, estimate precision and adaptation speed are conflicting properties; they depend, in a given environment, on the parameters of the estimation method, i.e. on N and α or W.

11.2.2 Filter with recursive optimal adaptation

The filter derived in the previous section is an adaptive filter in the fullest sense as it utilises only information in both the available signal sequences. Nevertheless, repeated computation of the estimation of $_n\hat{\mathbf{h}}_{opt}$ according to eqn (11.3), which requires matrix inversion, and providing approximations of correlation quantities according to eqn (11.2) or eqn (11.5) in every step is very laborious. We shall therefore derive in this section a recursive version of the method that is functionally equivalent, but which substantially reduces the computational burden. Note that the method is traditionally described as the *RLS method* (recursive least squares) which is not very apt as many other methods are also based on recursive use of the least-squares approach.

The recursive computation of approximations of the correlation matrix and vector according to eqn (11.2) or (11.5) can obviously be introduced easily as

$$_n\mathbf{r}_{yy} = \alpha_{n-1}\mathbf{r}_{yy} + \mathbf{y}_n\mathbf{y}_n^T \quad \text{and} \quad _n\mathbf{r}_{yx} = \alpha_{n-1}\mathbf{r}_{yx} + \mathbf{y}_n x_n. \tag{11.6}$$

(Notice that, when $\alpha = 1$, the formulae are equivalent to eqn (11.2) for non-forgetting estimates, otherwise they represent an equivalent of eqn (11.5).) When returning to the equation system that has led to eqn (11.3) and denoting $_n\hat{\mathbf{h}}_{opt} = \mathbf{h}_n$, we obtain

$$_n\mathbf{r}_{yy}\,\mathbf{h}_n = {}_n\mathbf{r}_{yx}. \tag{11.7}$$

When substituting in the right-hand equation of (11.6) with recursive use of eqns (11.6) and (11.7), we obtain

$$_n\mathbf{r}_{yx} = \alpha(_{n-1}\mathbf{r}_{yy}\,\mathbf{h}_{n-1}) + \mathbf{y}_n x_n = \alpha\alpha^{-1}(_n\mathbf{r}_{yy} - \mathbf{y}_n\mathbf{y}_n^T)\mathbf{h}_{n-1} + \mathbf{y}_n x_n$$

$$= {}_n\mathbf{r}_{yy}\,\mathbf{h}_{n-1} - \mathbf{y}_n\mathbf{y}_n^T\mathbf{h}_{n-1} + \mathbf{y}_n x_n,$$

so that

$$_n\mathbf{r}_{yy}\,\mathbf{h}_n = {}_n\mathbf{r}_{yy}\,\mathbf{h}_{n-1} - \mathbf{y}_n(x_n - \mathbf{y}_n^T\mathbf{h}_{n-1}) = {}_n\mathbf{r}_{yy}\,\mathbf{h}_{n-1} + \mathbf{y}_n e_n.$$

Here, we notice that the expression in brackets gives the instantaneous error of the estimate if we take for the filter output

$$\hat{x}_n = \mathbf{y}_n^T\mathbf{h}_{n-1}. \tag{11.8}$$

Finally, by multiplying the above equation from the left by the inverted correlation matrix, we obtain the recursive relation for calculation of the new filter-coefficient vector $\mathbf{h}_n$ by modifying the vector from the previous time instant (i.e. the *approximation step*),

$$\mathbf{h}_n = \mathbf{h}_{n-1} + {}_n\mathbf{r}_{yy}^{-1}\,\mathbf{y}_n e_n. \tag{11.9}$$

It is evident that the adaptation algorithm does not require determination of the crosscorrelation vector $_n\mathbf{r}_{yx}$, the influence of which is included in the product term containing the observation vector $\mathbf{y}_n$. On the other hand, the price paid for the possibility of recursive calculation is the necessity to use the delayed coefficient vector $\mathbf{h}_{n-1}$, corresponding in fact to the previous time instant, when calculating an estimate of the original signal according to eqn (11.8). Although it would in principle be possible to recalculate the estimate more precisely as $\hat{x}_n = \mathbf{y}_n^T\mathbf{h}_n$ after having determined $\mathbf{h}_n$, this is not commonly done. The correction of $\mathbf{h}_n$ in a single approximation step is usually small and the gain in precision would not be adequate to cope with the increased computational requirements.

The recursive relation (11.9) requires inversion of the estimated correlation matrix in every iteration step. This would be a tedious action but, instead, as has been shown (Householder, 1964), it is also possible to provide new values of the inverted matrix by recursion. The new value of the inverted matrix can be calculated, without any loss in precision, based on the previous value by means of the recursive relation

$$
_n\mathbf{r}_{yy}^{-1} = \frac{1}{\alpha} \left(_{n-1}\mathbf{r}_{yy}^{-1} - \frac{_{n-1}\mathbf{r}_{yy}^{-1}\,\mathbf{y}_n\mathbf{y}_n^T\,_{n-1}\mathbf{r}_{yy}^{-1}}{\alpha + \mathbf{y}_n^T\,_{n-1}\mathbf{r}_{yy}^{-1}\,\mathbf{y}_n} \right), \tag{11.10}
$$

which we present here without derivation. To update the matrix, only the new observation vector is needed; evaluation of this formula is substantially less demanding than the inversion.

The recursive adaptive filtering thus runs in the following cycles: at the beginning of every step, we suppose knowledge of the previous coefficient vector $\mathbf{h}_{n-1}$, the previous inverted correlation matrix $_{n-1}\mathbf{r}_{yy}^{-1}$ and the vector $\mathbf{y}_{n-1}$ of N previous samples of the observed signal. After the arrival of the new sample y_n of observation, the following operations are to be realised:

1 updating of the observation vector $\mathbf{y}_n$ from $\mathbf{y}_{n-1}$ by appending the new sample y_n and omitting the oldest sample y_{n-N};
2 calculation of the output sample $\hat{x}_n$ according to eqn (11.8);
3 calculation of the instantaneous error $e_n = x_n - \hat{x}_n$;
4 updating of the inverted correlation matrix $_n\mathbf{r}_{yy}^{-1}$ according to eqn (11.10);
5 updating of coefficient vector $\mathbf{h}_n$ according to eqn (11.9);
6 (possibly recalculation of the corrected new output sample $\hat{x}_n = \mathbf{y}_n^T\mathbf{h}_n$).

The algorithm can be properly initialised by the initial values $\mathbf{h}_{-1} = \mathbf{0}$ and $_{-1}\mathbf{r}_{yy}^{-1} = (\delta\mathbf{I})^{-1}$, where δ is a small positive number. The block signal-flow diagram corresponding to the described algorithm is depicted in Figure 11.2. Notice that the vector $\mathbf{y}_n$ is automatically generated and saved in the delay chain of the FIR filter. A further N registers are needed to retain the coefficient vector $\mathbf{h}_{n-1}$ and an extensive memory-register block is used to save the inverted correlation-matrix estimate $_{n-1}\mathbf{r}_{yy}^{-1}$. The inertialess blocks to compute the correction $\Delta\mathbf{h}_n$ of the filter-coefficient vector and the correction of the inverted matrix are presented schematically. It should be mentioned that fast variants of this algorithm exist with a computational complexity which is of the order N, while the complexity of the algorithm as presented in its basic form is quadratic.

11.2.3 Filter with stochastic-gradient adaptation

In the previous section, we approached adaptive filtering, conditioned by least-mean-square error, as the approximation problem. Starting from the optimal theoretical filter (11.1) we approximated the unknown correlation quantities in this solution as well as possible, with respect to the properties of the processed signals. The (quasi)optimal coefficient vector can then be computed in every sampling interval directly by using the proper approximate formula. Nevertheless, it is possible to approach the same task alternately as an optimisation

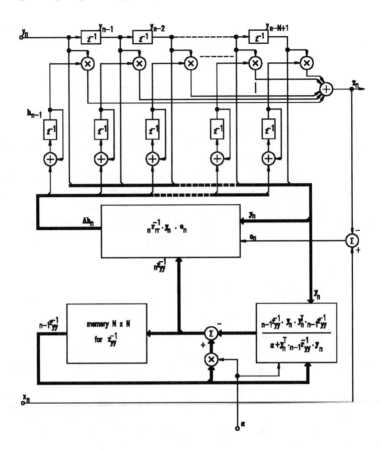

Figure 11.2 Block signal-flow diagram of RLS adaptive filter

problem to be solved by iteration, as we will do in the following paragraphs. Let us note at the beginning that we shall use and extend the results from Section 10.3.3. However, it does not change anything on the situation characterising the adaptive filtering, that the relevant autocorrelation matrix, crosscorrelation vector and any other parameters of the processed signals are not known. The derived relationships serve only as a general model on the basis of which the optimisation is designed.

The mean quadratic error that is to be minimised according to requirement (10.23) is

$$\varepsilon_n^2 = \mathbb{E}\{(x_n - \hat{x}_n)^2\} = \mathbb{E}\{(x_n - \mathbf{h}_n^T \mathbf{y}_n)^2\}$$

$$= \mathbb{E}\{x_n^2 - 2\mathbf{h}_n^T \mathbf{y}_n x_n + \mathbf{h}_n^T \mathbf{y}_n \mathbf{y}_n^T \mathbf{h}_n\}$$

$$= \mathbb{E}\{x_n^2\} - 2\mathbf{h}_n^T {}_n\overline{\Phi}_{yx} + \mathbf{h}_n^T {}_n\overline{\overline{\Phi}}_{yy} \mathbf{h}_n; \qquad (11.11)$$

its minimum value for the optimal filter coefficient vector $_{opt}\mathbf{h}_n$ according to eqn (11.1) is, after substitution,

$$_{opt}\varepsilon_n^2 = \mathbb{E}\{x_n^2\} - 2(_n\overline{\overline{\Phi}}_{yy}^{-1}\,_n\overline{\Phi}_{yx})^T\,_n\overline{\Phi}_{yx} + (_n\overline{\overline{\Phi}}_{yy}^{-1}\,_n\overline{\Phi}_{yx})^T\,_n\overline{\overline{\Phi}}_{yy}(_n\overline{\overline{\Phi}}_{yy}^{-1}\,_n\overline{\Phi}_{yx})$$

$$= {}_x\sigma_n^2 - {}_n\overline{\Phi}_{yx\,n}^T\overline{\overline{\Phi}}_{yy\,n}^{-1}\overline{\Phi}_{yx}. \tag{11.12}$$

It can be seen from expression (11.11) that the square error ε_n^2 is a quadratic function in components of the vector $\mathbf{h}_n$. The problem can therefore also be postulated in such a way that we are seeking, in the N-dimensional space of filter coefficients, the minimum-value point of the function (11.11), which is thus interpreted as the criterion function of the optimisation. At the optimum point, the criterion function obviously takes on the minimum value (11.12), but this fact can only be used in check-problems where the probability characteristics of the signal model are known *a priori*.

The *optimisation process* in the frame of every *approximation step* (i.e. for a given n) then runs in the standard way: some vector $_0\mathbf{h}_n$ is arbitrarily, or based on a preliminary estimate, selected as the initial point in the coefficient space and, by successive iteration steps, the gradually modified estimate approaches the optimum point $_{opt}\mathbf{h}_n$. If the process is convergent, the optimum point would be reached after a certain number of steps, or at least the solution should be close to it (see Figure 11.3). The direction and magnitude of the individual iteration steps is determined by the choice of optimisation method. Should the steepest-descent method be chosen, it will be

$$_{i+1}\mathbf{h}_n = {}_i\mathbf{h}_n - \mu_i \nabla(\varepsilon_n^2), \tag{11.13}$$

where i is the step number in the iteration sequence, μ is an arbitrarily chosen constant influencing the magnitude of the step and $\nabla(.)$ denotes the gradient operator. (To simplify notation, we shall suppose that μ remains constant during the optimisation, although it can easily be varied). Recall that the complete optimising sequence runs (for the present) in the frame of a particular (nth) approximation step (sampling period), i.e. many iteration steps are needed to obtain an estimate of the filter-coefficient vector and, consequently, a single output-signal sample.

According to eqn (10.25) the gradient is

$$_i\nabla(\varepsilon_n^2) = -2\mathbb{E}\{\mathbf{y}_{n\,i}e_n\} = -2\mathbb{E}\{\mathbf{y}_n(x_n - \mathbf{y}_n^T{}_i\mathbf{h}_n)\}.$$

When only current realisations of the processed signals are available, the indicated ensemble mean can only be roughly estimated as the 'average' of a single term,

$$_i\nabla(\varepsilon_n^2) \approx {}_i\hat{\nabla}(\varepsilon_n^2) = -2\mathbf{y}_{n\,i}e_n, \tag{11.14}$$

which naturally suffers with random error; this substantiates the name *stochastic gradient*. Of course, it is a very coarse but unbiased estimate. The result of the optimisation (iteration) step based on this estimation thus is

$$_{i+1}\mathbf{h}_n = {}_i\mathbf{h}_n + 2\mu\,\mathbf{y}_{n\,i}\,e_n, \tag{11.15}$$

which is the approximation of (11.13), and will usually be very imprecise. Nevertheless, as the estimate eqn (11.14) is unbiased and the errors in the successive iteration steps are independent, mutual compensation of errors may be expected in many successive steps. It can be shown by a detailed analysis that indeed, the mean value of the final point of iteration is $_{opt}\mathbf{h}_n$. The speed of the descent will naturally depend on the properties of the criterion function, that is on the statistical properties of the processed signals, length N of the filter and on the choice of the parameter μ. In Figure 11.3, a thin line shows schematically how slowly, with many deviations from the proper direction of negative gradient but with a correct trend, the estimate of the coefficient vector may approach the optimum value. For comparison, the optimum steepest-descent trajectory, leading from the starting to final position, is plotted by a heavy curve.

The presented method is correct and would lead in principle to the desired result. However, the problem is that the computational requirements for complete iteration inside each approximation step (i.e. in the frame of one signal-sample determination) are very high. If the problem is (almost) stationary so that the properties of the criterion function are (almost) fixed during the course of many sample periods, the iteration inside an approximation step can be substituted for by recursion in time,

$$\mathbf{h}_{n+1} = \mathbf{h}_n + 2\mu\,\mathbf{y}_n\,e_n. \tag{11.16}$$

Indeed, for the optimisation process it is unimportant whether (for a fixed n) the iteration uses the differences between the fixed sample x_n and its different

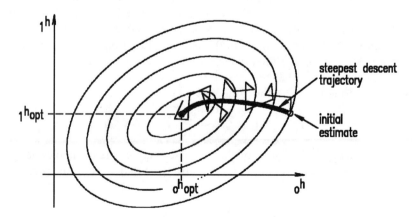

Figure 11.3 Optimisation in coefficient space for $N = 2$

estimates $_i\hat{x}_n$ derived from a fixed $\mathbf{y}_n$ by the filter of different successive approximations $_i\mathbf{h}_n$, or if we are similarly moving in the coefficient space of the same function in time, i.e. when the iteration is using differences between successive samples x_n and the corresponding estimates $\hat{x}_n$ calculated from the variable vectors $\mathbf{y}_n$ by means of a time sequence of gradually improving vectors $\mathbf{h}_n$. In a stationary environment, both ways lead on average to the same value of $\mathbf{h}$. Nevertheless, it takes longer by the second method (perhaps many sampling periods would be needed while the first method provides the proper estimate during a single sampling period). This is the price for the substantial computational and structural simplification of the corresponding adaptive filter.

An important question is how to select a suitable magnitude for the parameter μ. It is obvious, intuitively, that the choice will be a compromise between two viewpoints. On the one hand, a larger value of μ could lead more quickly to the neighbourhood of the optimum solution. However, it may also lead to the deterioration of an already rather good estimate, when the stochastic gradient is in great error or if the step overshoots the optimum position. This may then consequently increase the error in subsequent steps. On the other hand, small values of μ stabilise the iteration but make the convergence slower and consequently decrease the correctness of the filtering namely in a nonstationary environment. The adaptation may then lag too far behind the changes in environmental properties. A detailed theoretical analysis, which is already beyond the chosen scope, shows that the process converges if $\mu < 1/\lambda_{\max}$, with $\lambda_{\max}$ being the maximum eigenvalue of the autocorrelation matrix. The ratio $\lambda_{\max}/\lambda_{\min}$ can be shown to determine the speed of convergence

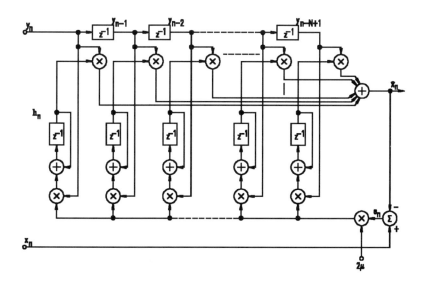

Figure 11.4 Structure of an adaptive LMS filter (with stochastic-gradient adaptation)

(λ_{min} being the minimum eigenvalue). In situations where adaptive filtering is applied, such information is usually unavailable and often we are only left with the possibility of finding a proper μ value experimentally. However, experience proves that the method is rather robust and its sensitivity to parameter values is low.

The recursive relation (11.16) for gradual improvement of the filter-coefficient vector is the basis of the simplest adaptive filter (Widrow, Stearns). This filter is often called the *LMS filter* (least-mean squares), although all other discussed versions of adaptive filters aim at minimisation of the same criterion. A more precise denomination emanates from the most prominent feature of this filter, the stochastic gradient. The corresponding detailed signal-flow diagram for this filter type is in Figure 11.4.

11.2.4 Filter with adaptation based on orthogonalised input data

Filtering by the stochastic gradient method is very attractive for practical applications owing to its simplicity, but the speed of convergence is often rather slow. Reaching the steady state of the vector $\mathbf{h}_n$ (i.e. approximately its optimum) may take hundreds to thousands of sampling periods which, especially in cases where the environment is nonstationary, may not be acceptable. The speed of convergence depends inversely on the condition factor of the observed signal autocorrelation matrix, $\lambda_{max}/\lambda_{min}$, as already mentioned. The optimum convergence speed is thus achieved when all the eigenvalues are (approximately) identical, which occurs when the autocorrelation matrix is diagonal; in the stationary case, all its elements are then equal to the variance. Then, obviously, the observed signal is white noise for which the algorithm speed is the maximum.

Thus, it is worth considering decorrelating the observed signal elements by a suitable transform characterised by its core matrix $\mathbf{P}$. The LMS algorithm would be applied to decorrelated data and the found optimal coefficient vector would be used so that the resulting filter would yield the required estimate of the training signal in the original domain. This is the main idea of adaptive filtering with orthogonalising data or the *self-orthogonalising algorithm* (SO).

The vector $\mathbf{z}_n$ of the modified (transformed) signal is thus

$$\mathbf{z}_n = \mathbf{P}\,\mathbf{y}_n, \tag{11.17}$$

where $\mathbf{P}$ is, in an ideal case, chosen such that the autocorrelation matrix of the transformed process is an identity matrix, so that, utilising the theorem for correlation matrices of transformed processes,

$$\overline{\overline{\Phi}}_{zz} = \mathbf{P}\,\overline{\overline{\Phi}}_{yy}\,\mathbf{P}^T = \mathbf{I}. \tag{11.18}$$

In this case, all the eigenvalues are equal to one and the convergence speed is optimum. The linear transform does not remove the dependence (should there be any) between the observed and training signals; it is therefore possible to approximate the values of the training signal x_n by filtering the transformed signal z_n as well as by filtering y_n. The estimate will be

$$\hat{x}_n = \mathbf{g}_n^T \mathbf{z}_n, \tag{11.19}$$

where $\mathbf{g}$ is the coefficient vector of the filter, the input of which is z_n. Thus, proper estimates may in principle also be obtained by filtering the decorrelated (transformed) observed signal by the modified adaptive filter. The signal x_n remains the training signal for the new filter. This is the *explicit form of the SO algorithm*.

By substituting and modifying, we have

$$\hat{x}_n = \mathbf{g}_n^T \mathbf{z}_n = \mathbf{z}_n^T \mathbf{g}_n = (\mathbf{P}\mathbf{y}_n)^T \mathbf{g}_n = \mathbf{y}_n^T \mathbf{P}^T \mathbf{g}_n = \mathbf{y}_n^T \mathbf{h}_n.$$

In this way we have obtained the relationship between the coefficient vector of the original filter and that of the modified filter, processing the transformed signal,

$$\mathbf{g}_n = (\mathbf{P}^T)^{-1} \mathbf{h}_n.$$

By comparison of the recursive relations for updating of coefficient vectors in both filters,

$$\mathbf{g}_{n+1} = \mathbf{g}_n + 2\mu \mathbf{z}_n e_n \quad \text{and} \quad \mathbf{h}_{n+1} = \mathbf{h}_n + 2\mu \mathbf{y}_n e_n,$$

we obtain, with respect to eqn (11.18), the update formula for the so-called *implicit form* of the SO adaptive filter

$$\mathbf{h}_{n+1} = \mathbf{h}_n + 2\mu \overline{\overline{\Phi}}_{yy}^{-1} \mathbf{y}_n e_n. \tag{11.20}$$

This operates on nontransformed observed data, but the speed of convergence corresponds to decorrelated data. Nevertheless, when disregarding the arbitrary factor 2μ, the derived algorithm is seen to be equivalent to the RMS algorithm and thus it does not provide the simplification expected from an LMS algorithm. The result (11.20) can therefore be interpreted rather as expressing a certain relationship between both these approaches.

Even the explicit form of SO filtering needs knowledge of the autocorrelation matrix $_n\overline{\overline{\Phi}}_{yy}$ (for a nonstationary environment, it is a time-variant matrix) in order to derive the orthogonalising matrix $\mathbf{P}_n$ based on eqn (11.18). As the approach has any advantage in comparison with the RMS algorithm only when it is substantially simpler, we should avoid estimating and inverting the matrix $_n\overline{\overline{\Phi}}_{yy}$ which excludes determining the transform matrix $\mathbf{P}_n$. Thus, we are left with the possibility of trying the decorrelating fixed transforms which can modify the observed data approximately so that their autocorrelation matrix more or less approaches the diagonal matrix. This may be the cosine transform, known to approximate quite well the decorrelating Karhunen–Loeve transform, under rather general conditions. Perhaps even DFT may be used as it can be expected that, in some cases, the harmonic components are less correlated than signal samples. The simulations in Reference [5] show that, although this approximation of the SO method is considerably slower than the RMS method, it compares favourably with the plain LMS algorithm in the case of observed signal samples being strongly mutually dependent.

11.3 Typical applications of adaptive filtering

We shall present a few applications of adaptive filtering that should show the practical usefulness of this approach. At the same time, we will try to demonstrate that, in essence, there are just a few typical connections of adaptive filters into the external world. Individual applications that differ only in details, or perhaps by interpretation of results, will be classified as belonging to one of the classes. Recall that, besides typical signal processing tasks such as noise reduction and spectral analysis, the applications also include system identification and tracking of internal signals of systems on the basis of externally observable signals.

11.3.1 Direct identification and modelling

One of the basic applications of adaptive filters is the direct identification or modelling of systems, in the connection as in Figure 11.5. The adaptive filter, driven by the same signal as the unknown system to be identified or modelled, produces an optimal estimate of the system's output signal in the presence of additive noise ν which increases the estimation error.

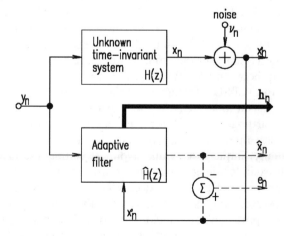

Figure 11.5 Direct adaptive system-identification and modelling

When the system is time invariant, the approach is usually spoken of as about (static) *identification*. If the noise influence can be neglected, and the filter degree (length) is sufficient, the input–output behaviour of the adaptive filter will become – after a certain time, needed for adaptation – (approximately) identical to the behaviour of the investigated system. Vector **h** of found filter weights will then characterise the properties of the identified system with the available precision.

Should the properties of the unknown system be time variant, as is often the case in automatic-control problems, the task of the adaptive filter is to keep track, as precisely as possible, of the varying parameters of the investigated (modelled) system. We then usually speak of (dynamic) *modelling*, its result is a sequence $\{\mathbf{h}_n\}$ of filter-coefficient vectors; every such vector should characterise (approximately) the instantaneous properties of the modelled system. Of course, a delay is necessarily involved in such modelling owing to finite adaptation time. The ability of the filter to follow faithfully the changes in system characteristics depends thus on the speed of adaptation, which should be sufficient with respect to the maximum speed with which the system properties could change. In this application, the output $\{\hat{x}_n\}$ of the filter is usually uninteresting and is only used to calculate the error signal that internally controls the adaptation algorithm of the filter. The state of adaptation reached is characterised by the degree of decorrelation of the samples in the error-signal sequence, as follows from the properties of the optimal estimation (Section 9.2.2.2.). Such modelling could provide the information needed for *meta-identification* of the system, i.e. a description of the dynamic processes controlling the time development of the *properties* of the system (not just the signals), should the deterministic or stochastic laws describing the development of system parameters be discovered.

11.3.2 Inverse identification and modelling

The second typical application of adaptive filters is *inverse identification* or modelling, which corresponds to a cascade connection of the unknown system and the adaptive filter as in Figure 11.6. Here, the adaptive filter is driven by the

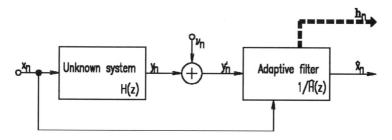

Figure 11.6 Inverse adaptive system-identification and modelling

output $\{y_n\}$ of the unknown system (perhaps with additive interference) and the original input $\{x_n\}$ is used as a training signal. In this way, the output of the adaptive filter, and thus of the whole cascade chain, is the estimate $\{\hat{x}_n\}$ of the original signal. It is obvious that when the transfer function of the unknown system is $H(z)$, the transfer of the adaptive filter will be, after adaptation, close to $1/H(z)$. This can be used for system identification, and then the coefficient vector $\mathbf{h}$ is the desired output; however, more often the result used is the filter output signal $\{\hat{x}_n\}$ which is, after adaptation, the optimal estimate of the original. This is obviously *deconvolution* processing applied to the received (observed) signal $\{y_n\}$; in other words, it can be interpreted as *frequency-response equalisation* of the chain.

Such *channel equalisation* is a frequent application in telecommunications where the unknown system is a communication channel with an unknown frequency response of inconvenient properties which need to be compensated for. It may be arranged in such a way that, for a certain period, both the original and observed (received *via* the channel) signals are available at the receiving end. During this time filter adaptation is performed with the original signal used as the training signal; after finishing training, the filter equalises the channel properties reasonably for a certain time before they change significantly. Then the adaptation must be repeated.

Providing the original signal at the receiving end is a separate problem. The simplest solution is to choose a suitable fixed signal form that can be known to the receiver in advance (as with mobile telephones, which need to equalise the rapidly varying channel properties quite often). Alternatively, the original can be temporarily communicated in parallel by a channel of higher quality (e.g. by a satellite link to equalise a surface cable channel); then a higher level of delay in one of the channels must be compensated for in the other channel before attempting equalisation. An interesting alternative is to use the special properties of the transmitted signal for providing an acceptable approximation of the original signal continuously, in order that it can be used for permanent training. If it is known that a signal may take on only a few discrete values (meaning, perhaps, different symbols of an alphabet), it is possible to recover the original precisely by means of quantisation, providing that the interference is sufficiently small. If the error rate in such a restoration is small, the training of the adaptive filter is satisfactory. Owing to continuous adaptation, the filter can keep the distortion so small that the nonlinear estimate is sufficiently reliable even when the channel properties vary to a great extent, exceeding by far the abilities of quantising restoration alone. The condition is that the changes would have a relatively long-term character; they must be sufficiently slow to enable the filter to keep track of them (as, for example, is the case with radio-wave fading). To initialise the filter and/or to readjust it after losing track of the channel changes, the method of short-time training by a known good approximation of the original may be used.

11.3.3 Linear adaptive prediction

Many modern applications are based on *linear prediction* by adaptive filtering, according to Figure 11.7. The adaptive filter here is driven by the original signal delayed by k sampling periods (most often $k = 1$, exceptionally more). The training signal is the original $\{x_n\}$ so that the output of the adaptive filter – after adaptation – is the estimate $\{\hat{x}_n\}$. The current sample of the original signal is thus obviously linearly predicted by the filter on the basis of previous samples of the same signal.

In Section 9.2.2.2, we derived that *difference predictive filter* according to Figure 9.16, which produces the difference between the input signal and its predicted value for $k = 1$, is a precise whitening filter, as long as the prediction is optimal in the sense of least-mean-square error. In Figure 11.8, a variant of such a filter is presented in which the predictive part is realised as an adaptive filter. If the adaptive filter is capable of modifying its coefficients so that the mentioned requirement is fulfilled, it can be used in the frame of a whitening filter as an estimator of the signal properties, particularly of its power spectrum. We have discussed the properties of such a spectral estimate in comparison with alternative approaches in Section 9.2.2.3. Let us recall that when deriving these properties, we supposed the signal-generation model to be in the form of white noise shaped by a purely recursive (AR) system. Thus, the estimate will be more precise the more closely the model approximates the reality.

Probably the most important practical use of the discussed approach is *linear predictive coding* (LPC) of speech which provides substantial data reduction when transmitting or recording speech signals. The method is based on

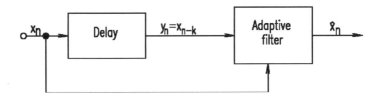

Figure 11.7 Adaptive linear predictor

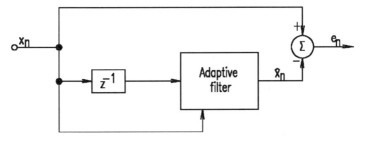

Figure 11.8 Adaptive whitening filter

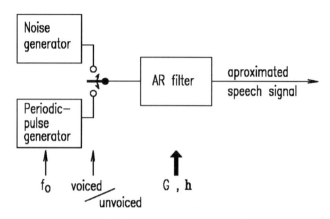

Figure 11.9 Model of speech-signal synthesis

the concept of speech-signal synthesis according to the model depicted in Figure 11.9, which roughly approximates the generation of sound signals of real speech. Two sources of driving signal correspond to two different types of phonemes, voiced (periodic driving) and unvoiced (driving by noise), which are switched between, corresponding in reality to involvement or exclusion of resonating vocal chords. The following filter models the function of the vocal tract, the frequency response of which is influenced by the shape of relevant cavities and by the position of tongue and lips. The approximating synthesiser is thus controlled by only a few time-varying quantities – controlling signals. The generating part of the system is controlled by a binary entry indicating whether the respective phoneme is voiced or unvoiced and, in the case of a voiced phoneme, by an added numerical entry on the required pitch of the periodic impulse train. Controlling the filter requires supplying its coefficient vector and perhaps even an explicit entry on the required gain if the transmission, as given by **h** is normalised. As this data set (a frame) characterises a relatively long signal section (some 10 to 30 ms), which may be considered approximately stationary, it is sufficient to transmit the data with a frame rate of tens per second only. A substantial data reduction is thus achieved in comparison with transmitting a full train of speech samples.

The basic block diagram of a speech coder based on linear predictive coding is illustrated in Figure 11.10. The speech signal is divided into sections determined by a time window; these are consequently processed by a detector which decides whether the phoneme is voiced and, if so, also determines the pitch. In parallel, the signal frame is processed by the difference predictive filter which, after adaptation that must occur in the frame of the same time section, yields the identified filter parameters, G and **h**. The four parameters are consequently coded into a form suitable for transmission or recording. An improvement in the joining of successive signal sections can be achieved by initialising the adaptive filter in every section by the resulting parameters of the previous section.

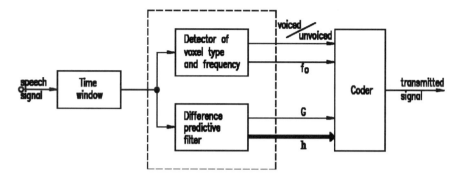

Figure 11.10 Block diagram of an LPC vocoder

11.3.4 Adaptive interference suppression

A further typical application of adaptive filtering is the suppression of interference in a situation when additional information either on the useful signal
or on the interfering signal (e.g. noise) is continuously available. Typically, it
may be in the form of another signal containing a component which is derived
from (or dependent on) either of the two mentioned signals.

The *subtractive decomposition* of a mixture of two signals into components is,
in its basic concept, illustrated in Figure 11.11. Here, the input to the system is
formed by two composite signals, $\{x_n\} = \{s_n + q_n\}$ and $\{y_n\} = \{r_n + p_n\}$ that are
partly interrelated as follows. The components p_n and q_n are supposed somehow
mutually dependent and therefore (probably) also correlated; on the contrary,
there are no mutual dependencies in all the other couples s_n, q_n, r_n, p_n and
r_n, s_n so that members of each of these couples are mutually uncorrelated.
The purpose of the scheme is to decompose one of the system-input signals,
say x_n, into estimates of its components $\hat{x}_n, \hat{q}_n$ by subtracting the component
estimate $\hat{q}_n$ from the mixture $x_n = s_n + q_n$. The other signal $y_n = r_n + p_n$
forms the input to the adaptive filter, the training signal of which is $x_n = s_n + q_n$.

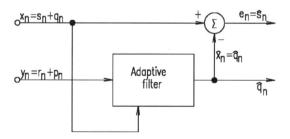

Figure 11.11 Subtractive interference suppression by adaptive filtering

We shall show that the output of the adaptive filter is, in our case, not only the optimal estimate of the training signal x_n but concurrently also the best possible estimate of q_n. The desired difference output $\hat{s}_n$ of the system is then identical with the filter error signal e_n, the mean quadratic value of which is minimised (after adaptation) by the filter,

$$\mathbb{E}\{e_n^2\} = \mathbb{E}\{(x_n - \hat{x}_n)^2\} \to \min.$$

When expressing the mean quadratic error in terms of signal components, we obtain

$$\mathbb{E}\{(x_n - \hat{x}_n)^2\} = \mathbb{E}\{x_n^2 - 2x_n\hat{x}_n + \hat{x}_n^2\}$$
$$= \mathbb{E}\{(s_n + q_n)^2 - 2(s_n + q_n)\hat{x}_n + \hat{x}_n^2\}$$
$$= \mathbb{E}\{(q_n - \hat{x}_n)^2 + s_n^2 + 2s_n q_n - 2s_n\hat{x}_n\}$$
$$= \mathbb{E}\{(q_n - \hat{x}_n)^2\} + \mathbb{E}\{s_n^2\} + 2\mathbb{E}\{s_n q_n\} - 2\mathbb{E}\{s_n\hat{x}_n\}.$$

As the last two terms are zero, being correlations of independent quantities, we obtain

$$\mathbb{E}\{e_n^2\} = \mathbb{E}\{(q_n - \hat{x}_n)^2\} + \mathbb{E}\{s_n^2\}. \tag{11.21}$$

The signal s_n is not influenced by the filter, so that the second term expressing the mean power of the signal s_n for a given n is invariant with respect to the filter coefficients. Therefore, the signal $\hat{x}_n$ is obviously also the optimum estimate of the component q_n,

$$\hat{q}_n = \hat{x}_n, \tag{11.22}$$

which is correlated with a component of the adaptive-filter input signal. The estimate $\hat{x}_n$ is, at the same time, the best available estimate of the signal x_n from the signal y_n. We can therefore conclude that the optimal training-signal estimate provided by an adaptive filter is always the best available estimate of only this component that is correlated with the input signal of the filter. Should the signals x_n and y_n contain no mutually correlated components, also the filter output would be evidently uncorrelated with x_n and thus the estimate would be useless.

The result (11.22) may be interpreted in alternative ways, depending on whether the correlated components are understood as being the useful signal or the interference. This is the same as considering whether the additional information (the input signal of the adaptive filter) is related to the useful signal or to the interfering component. In the first case, the optimum estimate of the desired signal is the output of the adaptive filter, $\hat{x}_n = \hat{q}_n$ (and evaluation of the difference outside of the filter is unnecessary). On the contrary, in the second case the optimal estimate of the useful signal is obviously the difference signal $e_n = \hat{s}_n$. Notice that, in this case, the resulting signal is the error signal which is computed also internally in the adaptive filter. Double calculation is, of course,

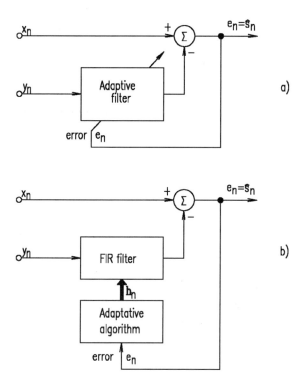

Figure 11.12 Alternative diagrams for Figure 11.11

unnecessary; therefore, the system of Figure 11.11 can be redrawn in the block diagrams depicted in Figure 11.12, which can often be found in descriptions of concrete applications. In variant *b*, which is reproduced in the form commonly found in the literature, there is an inaccuracy in the missing input of the signal y_n into the adaptation algorithm.

One of the common applications using the described principle is the method of *suppressing narrowband interference* m_n (e.g. whistle) in a wideband signal, when the input to the adaptive filter is formed by a delayed version of the signal x_n (Figure 11.13). The delay must be chosen such that the wideband

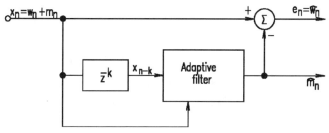

Figure 11.13 Adaptive suppression of a narrowband interference, or enhancement of a narrowband signal

components of both signals would be practically uncorrelated while the correlation of the narrowband components would remain important. Therefore, we obtain the estimate $\hat{m}_n$ of the narrowband component at the output of the adaptive filter. This can be subtracted from the input composite signal, thus providing a difference signal which is the estimate $\hat{w}_n$ of the wideband signal. We see that the difference signal is the estimate of the wideband component of the input mixture, while the output of the adaptive filter is the estimate of the narrowband component. Therefore, the same circuit can be used alternatively for adaptive *suppression of wideband noise* mixed with narrowband useful signal (then it is so-called *line enhancer*), in which case the useful signal is found at the adaptive filter output. The mean frequency of the narrowband component as well as its bandwidth may change with time in both mentioned cases; owing to its adaptivity, the system can cope with such changes. Of course, the acceptable speed of the changes is limited by the ability of the system to keep track of them.

A more general case of suppressing noise in an additive mixture x_n is schematically illustrated in Figure 11.14. This time, only a linearly distorted and noisy version y_n of the interfering signal r_n is available. The properties of the distorting system as well as of the added noise are unknown. In spite of this, the adaptive filter would properly derive the best available estimate of the interference, $\hat{r}_n$. It is possible because of the correlation between the interfering component r_n of the processed signal and the auxiliary signal y_n; the correlation has not been removed by the unknown linear processing or by adding the uncorrelated noise v_n.

A basically complementary case to the previous one is the system of Figure 11.15, which serves to remove interference caused by reflections in a communication channel due to imprecise impedance matching at different locations. At duplex communication, the useful received signal u_n is disturbed at a terminal due to the reflecting phenomena by an added mixture of up to several versions of the differently weakened and distorted own transmitted signal s_n. The adaptive filter converts the original transmitted signal s_n to a version of it which is deteriorated by reflections, and which can then be subtracted from the mixture of the useful received signal, interference and noise, thus ensuring

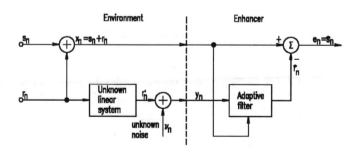

Figure 11.14 Adaptive suppression of interference, the distorted version of which is known

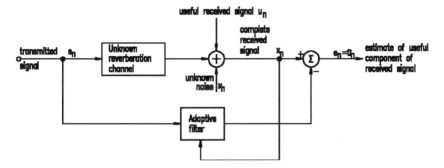

Figure 11.15 Adaptive corrector of channel echoes

undisturbed reception even during transmission of the own message. Here, the training signal is deteriorated but again the filter would provide the estimate corresponding only to correlated components, that is it would model the unknown distorting system. Naturally we suppose that the transmitted, received and noise signals are mutually independent. Such adaptive filters are common parts of telecommunication systems.

Before concluding this chapter, let us mention an interesting application for adaptive filtering – the adjustment of the directional patterns of receiving antennas. The antennas under discussion are phased arrays consisting of a number of usually identical antenna elements distributed in a regularly spaced network. Every element receives independently of others (when neglecting the mutual impedance influence); their signals are individually weighted, perhaps phase shifted and summed together to provide the input to the receiver. The resulting directional pattern depends not only on the fixed directional character-istic of a single element, but (and namely) also on how their contributions are combined in the resulting sum. This can be controlled by adjusting the gain (or attenuation) and phase shift (delay) for individual antenna elements using FIR filters in the individual signal paths. In this way, radical changes in the resulting directional pattern of the antenna system can be achieved; for example a rejecting dip may be oriented towards the direction of an unwanted signal. The coefficients of the filters can be adaptively modified with the aim of minimising the interference. Notice that, compared with previous applications, this is a case of the parallel processing of more signals (array signal processing), which needs a generalisation of the analysis methods, as treated, for example, in Reference [28].

Chapter 12
Nonlinear filtering

12.1 Introduction

The linear methods that we have mainly dealt with so far are still the primary means of signal processing. Their dominant role is given, on the one hand, by historical development as they are genealogically older and thus more broadly implemented, and the general degree of understanding, based on formalised analysis using common mathematical means, is higher. On the other hand, they are also theoretically and structurally simpler, which enables further development of the standard analysis and synthesis methods of the relevant algorithms and realisation structures in an easy to understand way. Their simple description makes the operation of signal-processing systems and possible system changes in time – as with adaptive systems – transparent for the user and easily applicable. The class of linear methods is defined by validity of the superposition principle; owing to this definition, the class is clearly delimited, the knowledge and approaches can be generalised well and the methods lucidly classified.

Nonlinear methods and systems, on the contrary, are delineated only negatively – by invalidity of the superposition principle; therefore, they are all the methods and systems which remain after separating out the linear methods. This is of course a very vague demarcation, the consequence of which is that it is very difficult to formulate any generally applicable theorems and rules which would be valid in all nonlinear systems. Consequently, it is also impossible to provide general approaches of description, classification, analysis and synthesis of nonlinear methods. However, there are many different practical tasks for which linear methods are not appropriate, due to principal reasons. Therefore, the use of nonlinear approaches is indispensable; in many cases, it has already proved very successful. As examples, some frequently met and seemingly simple cases can be mentioned: suppression of nonadditive (e.g. multiplicative) noise, processing of signals generated or influenced by systems with nonlinear characteristics (e.g. quantization or saturation) or seeking relationships between signals with spectra which are nonoverlapping.

In such a situation, the basic problem for an expert is to choose a suitable type of processing from the inexhaustible spectrum of nonlinear methods and to analyse the method mathematically in order to optimise its effect. The only reasonable way of managing the problem of choice from such an extensive but not easy-to-survey offer is to detach certain narrower, less general classes of nonlinear methods or systems. With a better defined class, it is easier to formulate some general principles and to investigate characteristic properties of the methods and their applications. Numerous such excursions into the world of nonlinear methods are currently topical; in some directions, such a degree of understanding and development of the methods has been already reached that relatively easy implementation in practice is possible. In the context of such well understood nonlinear methods, more advanced and well tried concepts known in linear methods, such as adaptivity, can be implemented.

A detailed study of the nonlinear methods of signal processing known today is beyond the scope of this book, partly because of the advanced mathematical concepts involved. Nevertheless, basic information on some already classical concepts belongs to fundamental knowledge and therefore we shall devote a brief discussion to them in the present chapter. If we start from the classical model of the difference equation and generalise the formulation of the corresponding discrete system response so that it includes, besides linear combinations of delayed input and output samples, also the products of these values, we obtain the important class of polynomial (especially Volterra) filters. Polynomial filters can be considered as a special case of a more general class of all dynamic generally recursive systems with an arbitrary nonlinear function forming the output. Another class that we shall mention is so-called order statistics filters, based on sorting of signal values, the best known example of which is the median filter. Historically, one of the oldest clearly defined groups is the class of homomorphic systems based on the formulation and use of the generalised superposition principle; we shall also briefly mention these and their applications to homomorphic filtering. As a concrete example of improving the processing properties by transition from linear to nonlinear filtering, we shall show several variants of nonlinear matched filters.

An important and fast expanding area of nonlinear signal processing is the application of neural networks to the different tasks of signal filtering and analysis. Although some common features with the approaches covered so far can be found, it is a markedly different approach. Therefore, we shall devote Chapter 13 to the fundamental ideas and main features of neural networks, and also to several typical applications in the field of signal processing.

12.2 Nonlinear discrete dynamic systems

12.2.1 Generic and polynomial nonlinear discrete dynamic systems

In a generic linear discrete dynamic system according to eqn (2.18), the output signal is formed as a linear combination of differently delayed values of the input and output signal; the special case of nonrecursive systems according to eqn (2.30) is a linear combination of only a certain number of the last values of the input signal. The schematic diagrams of these systems (Figures 2.9 and 2.11) can be generalised by replacing the linear combination with an arbitrary nonlinear function of the corresponding number of variables. For a generic system of mth order we thus obtain

$$y_n = \Psi(x_n, x_{n-1}, \cdots, x_{n-r}, y_{n-1}, y_{n-2}, \cdots, y_{n-m}), \tag{12.1}$$

where $\Psi(.)$ is an inertialess scalar operator of a vector argument of $(r + m + 1)$ components. Such a generally recursive system of mth order is schematically depicted in Figure 12.1. A less general nonrecursive nonlinear system of degree r is described by the formula

$$y_n = \Psi(x_n, x_{n-1}, \cdots, x_{n-r}), \tag{12.2}$$

where of course the operator $\Psi(.)$ has only $(r + 1)$ scalar variables. The block diagram of such a system is given in Figure 12.2. This system can naturally be regarded as a special case of the previous one in which the group of variables representing the delayed output values does not influence the function value.

Unfortunately, most concepts and established characteristics that we have used to describe linear systems fail with nonlinear systems. This is obvious

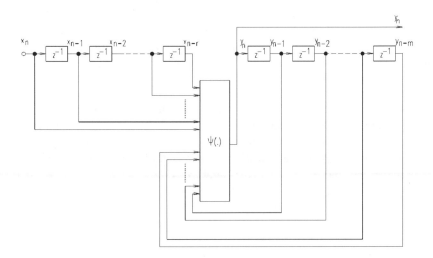

Figure 12.1 General nonlinear dynamic discrete system

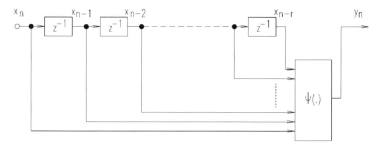

Figure 12.2 Nonrecursive nonlinear dynamic discrete system

already in the impulse-response concept the character of which (shape, length) depends fundamentally on the magnitude of the driving impulse. This is an important difference compared with linear systems, for which an input-magnitude change only leads to the corresponding magnitude alteration in the output. (As an elementary example, when the nonlinearity consists in neglecting sample values under a certain threshold, the length of the nonzero part of a monotonically decreasing impulse response depends on the amplitude of the driving impulse.) We may obviously claim that a nonrecursive nonlinear system can have only finite impulse-response length, at maximum correspond-ing to the length of the delay chain. It is therefore correct if we denote systems described by the equation (12.2) as nonlinear FIR systems. Recursive systems described by eqn (12.1) can have an infinite impulse response owing to the existence of feedback. However, whether or not the response really is infinite depends on the character of internal nonlinearities, the amplitude of the driving impulse and on the initial state of the system (the content of the delaying registers at the beginning instant). It is also obvious then, that the responses to successive impulses are not superimposed so that the convolution relation (2.24) does not apply to nonlinear systems.

With respect to the invalidity of the superposition principle, the fundamental analytical methods, based on decomposition of signals into components and on subsequent combining of partial responses, cannot be used for nonlinear systems. It primarily applies to Fourier analysis using decomposition into harmonic components, but also to the application of the Z-transform which also uses the superposition principle. Therefore, concepts such as the transfer function or frequency response are meaningless for nonlinear systems. Notice that when the frequency response of nonlinear systems is sometimes referred to, it is correct only when discussing the quasilinear mode of operation, i.e. for small signals and under concrete operating conditions ensuring sufficiently precise local linearity of the function $\Psi(.)$ in the operating range. Otherwise, either it is meant in a figurative sense or it is simply an unwise use of the term. For the same reason, it is also impossible to use the stability criteria derived for linear systems. The invalidity of the superposition theorem further disables decomposing complex nonlinear systems into cascade or parallel connections of simpler subsystems, in the general case.

Nonlinear systems can also be characterised (often with advantage) by the state model which is a generalisation of the equation system (2.34). The originally matrix relations would be naturally replaced by general nonlinear vector operators,

$$\mathbf{q}_{n+1} = \overline{\Psi}_q(\mathbf{q}_n, \mathbf{x}_n) \quad \text{and} \quad \mathbf{y}_n = \overline{\Psi}_y(\mathbf{q}_n, \mathbf{x}_n). \tag{12.3}$$

The simplest but not least important group of nonlinear systems is formed by inertialess systems which of course are a special case of systems, according to eqn (12.1) or (12.2), described only by a single-variable nonlinear operator

$$y_n = \Psi(x_n). \tag{12.4}$$

They usually find their use as functional converters, realising a prescribed mathematical function (like logarithm, limitation and the like) and then become parts of more complex systems. In some cases, they represent the complete nonlinearity of the whole system concentrated into one or several such isolated blocks; this view substantially simplifies the analysis of such a system as we shall see when discussing homomorphic systems. The use of functional converters that compensate for known nonlinearities of cooperating systems, such as sensors, is common. In image processing, functional converters represent point-wise operations providing very effective contrast transforms. By generalisation of inertialess scalar systems we obtain vector systems, with a greater number of simultaneously acting input quantities and perhaps also with a number of parallel scalar outputs, arranged into an output vector

$$\mathbf{y}_n = \overline{\Psi}(\mathbf{x}_n). \tag{12.5}$$

Examples of such systems are the operators $\Psi(.)$ in eqns (12.1)–(12.3) where they represent nonlinear inertialess parts of the dynamic systems. They may also be autonomous systems providing output signals derived from a number of simultaneously acting input signals; examples are a multiplier, or systems equivalent to combinatory logical circuits etc.

A subclass of generic systems according to eqns (12.1) and (12.2) are the systems with nonlinear functions $\Psi(.)$ which are polynomials; such systems are usually denoted as *polynomial filters*. The conceptually simpler nonrecursive case is described by the relation

$$y_n = h_0 + \sum_{m_1=0}^{r} h_1(m_1)x_{n-m_1} + \sum_{m_2=0}^{r}\sum_{m_1=0}^{r} h_2(m_1, m_2)x_{n-m_1}x_{n-m_2}$$

$$+ \cdots + \sum_{m_p=0}^{r}\cdots\sum_{m_2=0}^{r}\sum_{m_1=0}^{r} h_p(m_1, m_2, \cdots, m_p)x_{n-m_1}x_{n-m_2}\cdots x_{n-m_p}, \tag{12.6}$$

if we choose the length of the filter (i.e. the number of delay elements) to be r and the degree of the polynomial, p. The constant term h_0 is usually set to zero. An example of such a filter structure for $r = 2, p = 2$ can be found in Figure 12.3.

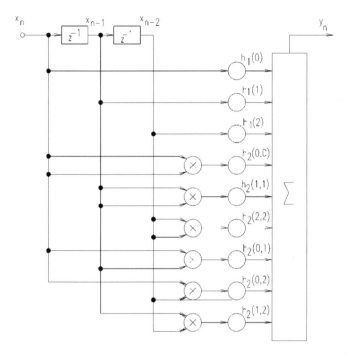

Figure 12.3 Structure of a polynomial (Volterra) filter with r = 2 and p = 2

Note that the structure is related to the finite Volterra series and therefore such systems are sometimes called *Volterra filters*. From eqn (12.6) and from Figure 12.3 we can see that the output is a linear combination of products of different orders, in which the weights are given by the components of the vectors $\mathbf{h}_1, \mathbf{h}_2, \cdots \mathbf{h}_p$. This property is convenient for designing adaptive filters, as the approach to optimisation of the coefficient vectors may remain in principle similar to that which we have seen in Chapter 11.

The more general recursive case is described by the equation

$$y_n = P_p(y_{n-1}, y_{n-2}, \cdots, y_{n-m}, x_n, x_{n-1}, \cdots, x_{n-r}), \qquad (12.7)$$

where $P_i(.)$ is a general polynomial of k variables and ith degree,

$$P_i(u_1, u_2, \cdots, u_k) = a_0 + \sum_{j=1}^{k} {}^1 a_j u_j + \sum_{j_2=1}^{k}\sum_{j_1=1}^{k} {}^2 a_{j_1,j_2} u_{j_1} u_{j_2}$$

$$+ \cdots + \sum_{j_i=1}^{k} \cdots \sum_{j_2=1}^{k}\sum_{j_1=1}^{k} {}^i a_{j_1,j_2,\cdots,j_i} u_{j_1} u_{j_2} \cdots u_{j_i}.$$

It can be seen that in both cases – recursive and nonrecursive systems – the number of coefficients is very high for a higher degree of polynomial and larger lengths of delaying chains, as the coefficient number is proportional to k^i.

This is why some coefficients are often, with respect to the character of the task, set *a priori* to zero, as is also the case in the following example of a *bilinear system* described by the equation

$$y_n = \sum_{i=0}^{r} a_i x_{n-i} + \sum_{i=0}^{m} b_i y_{n-i} + \sum_{i=0}^{r} \sum_{j=0}^{m} c_{i,j} x_{n-i} y_{n-j}.$$

Here, compared with more general second-order systems, the squares of the individual variables are omitted. Notice that this system, the signal-flow graph of which is in Figure 12.4, differs from the linear system described by eqn (2.18) only by adding linearly weighted products of state variables.

The problem of an explosive increase in the coefficient number is particularly limiting, from a practical point of view, in the case of nonrecursive filters as they need, in order to model a more complicated nonlinear behaviour, rather high values of p and r. For this reason, recursive filters are often preferred, because they can manage with a substantially lower number of coefficients for the same requirements concerning their properties. However, their analysis and design are more difficult.

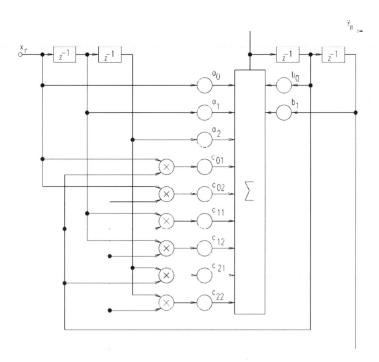

Figure 12.4 Example of recursive polynomial system – bilinear filter with $r = m = 2$

A more detailed analysis of the properties of polynomial filters can be found in specialised literature, an overview of which can be found, e.g., in Reference [21].

12.2.2 Filters based on sorting

Another type of nonlinear system is the group of filters based on sorting, also called *order-statistics filters*. Their operation consists in selecting, as the output sample, one of the sorted neighbouring samples of the input signal vector in every sampling period. The basic structure is nonrecursive and corresponds to Figure 12.2; it therefore processes the vector of observed values $\mathbf{x}_n = [x_n, x_{n-1}, \cdots, x_{n-r}]$. The operator $\Psi(.)$ realises, in the simplest case of the *plain median filter*, the following operations:

- sorting of values x_i according to their magnitudes;
- selection of the middle element of the sorted sequence, i.e. the median of the set,

$$y_n = \text{med}\{x_i\}, \tag{12.8}$$

($r + 1$ is usually an odd number so that the middle term is unique);
- presenting of this value y_n as the output.

Attempts to provide a formal analysis of the filter operation are hindered by the complexity of the realised operator, the behaviour of which is very variable dependent on the input values. The basic properties can reasonably be shown in examples like that in Figure 12.5.

Here, the effects of the plain median filter of length $r + 1 = 3$ on different input sequences are compared with those of a linear FIR filter of the same length and coefficients $h_0 = h_1 = h_2 = 1/3$. The behaviour of the median filter can easily be determined: the three signal values included in the range of the window sliding along the signal are sorted and the middle value becomes the output. In contrast, the linear filter provides the average of the three samples as its output. The first three rows deal with the reactions to rectangular impulses which, when short, are usually interference; while the longer ones are, as a rule, elements of the useful signal. It can be seen that this median filter ignores and therefore completely suppresses impulses of length 1 or 2, while longer ones are transferred without any distortion. On the contrary, the linear filter suppresses the amplitude of the impulses more the shorter they are, but at a cost of deteriorating their edges which can be interpreted as the widening and distortion of impulses. It is similar for the edge of the step function in the following row. A linear increase or decline is transferred by both filters more or less identically. The transition from the increase to decline is deteriorated in both filters; while the median filter only trims away the peak of the signal but

Input signal   Median−filtered signal   Linearly filtered signal

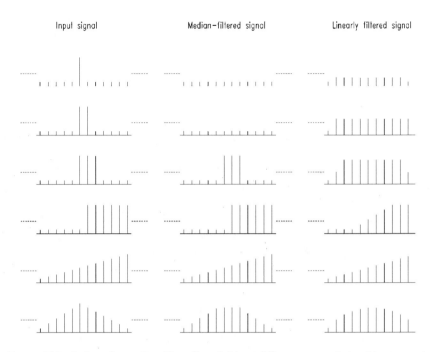

Figure 12.5 Action of a median filter (length 3) on different types of signal in comparison with a smoothing (time–average) filter of the same length

preserves the rest of the linear parts, the averaging filter distorts (rounds) the whole course.

It can be claimed based on the example – and more detailed analyses justify such a generalisation – that the basic feature of a median filter is to suppress impulse interference without distorting the sharp transitions of the signal. The smallest element preserved by the filter is approximately of the size corresponding to the filter length. On the other hand, the median filter is ineffective in cases of continuous (e.g. thermal) noise, affecting more or less all signal samples.

Note that simple median filters are particularly effective in the suppression of impulse noise of both polarities (so-called pepper and salt noise) in image data, where the historically older smoothing filtering has a very unpleasant side effect of blurring the image although it also partly suppresses the noise.

The described filter can easily be somewhat generalised. First, it is possible to derive the output not just as the middle term of the sorted sequence but rather as any chosen (but then fixed) kth term, $k \in \langle 1, r \rangle$ which leads to partially different results. The extreme cases are *maximum* and *minimum filters* (i.e. for $k = 1$ and $k = r$). Although such modified systems are sometimes still called median filters, this is clearly not correct and a better designation would be (r, k) – *sorting filter* (or order statistics filter). It is clearly possible to provide concurrently the results for more (or all) filters for different values of k with a minimum of extra effort, as the main computational burden is in the repeated sorting. If there is enough time to decide which output is the best in a given context (e.g. when off-line processing image data), the optimum output can be selected based on a formalised criterion.

Another generalisation that may have a similar but more finely graduated effect than the previous modification is in affiliating different integer weights $w_i \geq 0$ to individual components of the vector $\mathbf{x}_n$. This can be considered as being analogous to the weighting windows of linear filters. The multipliers are interpreted as follows: the sequence to be sorted contains every element $x_{n-i}\, w_i$ – times so that it has altogether $\sum_{i=0}^{r} w_i$ elements. The multiple appearance of the element x_{n-i} increases the probability of this element becoming the median, approximately proportionally to w_i, which naturally influences the properties of the filter. A filter formulated this way thus has $r + 1$ parameters by means of which its effect can be modified. These parameters can even be varied automatically, derived from the properties of the signal (possibly even local or instantaneous ones). This leads to the idea of a certain type of *adaptive median filter* that has found its use in suppressing specific types of noise in image data.

Another direction in generalisation is represented by the *recursive median filter* marked by including the output value of the median from the previous step into the sequence to be sorted. Such a filter is successfully used in speech processing.

12.3 Homomorphic filtering

12.3.1 Canonical form of homomorphic systems

Homomorphic systems form a subclass of generally nonlinear systems which fulfil the *generalised superposition principle*. Let us denote $\mathbb{M}(.)$ an operator realising a (generally nonlinear) transform of input sequences into output sequences, $\{y_n\} = \mathbb{M}(\{x_n\})$. A system fulfils the generalised superposition principle if, for any couple $\{u_n\}, \{v_n\}$ from the set of input sequences admissible to the operator $\mathbb{M}(.)$, it is valid

$$\mathbb{M}(\{u_n\} @ \{v_n\}) = \mathbb{M}(\{u_n\}) \, \$ \, \mathbb{M}(\{v_n\}),$$

$$\mathbb{M}(c \,\&\, u_n) = c \,\#\, \mathbb{M}(\{u_n\}). \tag{12.9}$$

Here, @ and $ mean some, but for a given system fixed, *characteristic operations* among signal sequences. @ is called the input operation, $ the output operation of the system, c is an arbitrary scalar constant and &, # are some, for a given system fixed, operations between a scalar and a sequence. A symbolic representation of such a system with indications of the input and output operations is given in Figure 12.6.

Figure 12.6 Homomorphic system with indicated characteristic operations

An example of a homomorphic system is, for example, every linear system; then both the characteristic operations @ and $ are additions, and the operations & and # are both multiplications. Another example is an inertialess system realising the transform $y_n = e^{x_n}$ which is also homomorphic; here the input operation @ is addition and the output operation $ is multiplication, as obviously it is in this case

$$\mathbb{M}(u_n + v_n) = \mathbb{M}(u_n)\mathbb{M}(v_n) \quad \text{and further} \quad \mathbb{M}(cu_n) = [\mathbb{M}(u_n)]^c,$$

so that the operation & is multiplication and the operation # is raising to a power.

Homomorphic systems form rather a general class of nonlinear systems. Owing to the validity of the generalised superposition theorem, it is possible to apply some useful artifices; particularly useful is the conversion of a general homomorphic system into a special cascade form described as a *canonical realisation*. Its structure is derived based on the following considerations.

It can be proved that, for a very broad class of operations @, it is possible, for every operation of the class, to find a system which would realise the corresponding inversible operator $\varphi(.)$ with the properties

$$\varphi(\{u_n\} @ \{v_n\}) = \varphi(\{u_n\}) + \varphi(\{v_n\}) \quad \text{and} \quad \varphi(c \& \{u_n\}) = c\varphi(\{u_n\}). \qquad (12.10)$$

Note that the system fulfilling the equations (12.10) is obviously also a homomorphic system. Then, of course, an inverse system exists realising the operator φ^{-1} such that (when denoting $\varphi(\{u_n\}) = \{u'_n\}$) it fulfils the equations

$$\varphi^{-1}(\{u'_n\} + \{v'_n\}) = \varphi^{-1}(\{u'_n\}) + \varphi^{-1}(\{v'_n\}) \quad \text{and}$$

$$\varphi^{-1}(c\{u'_n\}) = c\varphi^{-1}(\{u'_n\}). \qquad (12.11)$$

The cascade connection of the blocks realising the operators φ and φ^{-1} provides unit transfer so that when connected before the system of Figure 12.6, the system transfer remains unchanged. Similarly, for every output operation $ a system can be found realising the invertible transformation $\psi(.)$ with properties analogous to eqn (12.10). If the cascade connection of blocks with transfers ψ and ψ^{-1} is connected at the output of the system of Figure 12.6, the original transfer of the system would also be preserved. The resulting chain of five blocks, as depicted in Figure 12.7, therefore has the same transfer as the original homomorphic system of Figure 12.6. When regarding the chain of the three inner blocks as a certain newly defined system, as delimited by the dotted

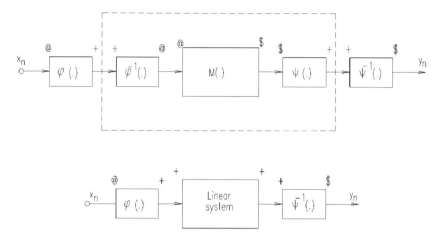

Figure 12.7 Canonic realisation of homomorphic system

frame, both its input and output operations are addition. Such a system is naturally a linear system; we shall call it the *linear core* of a homomorphic system.

Every homomorphic system can thus be represented in the *canonical form* as shown in the lower part of Figure 12.7, i.e. as a cascade connection of three subsystems. These are the linear core and the two marginal generally non-linear systems the properties of which are determined only by input and output operations of the original system (together with the sets of admissible signals for these operations). This is naturally an advantageous representation, as the non-linearities are thus concentrated in the two marginal systems, while the substantial remaining part of the system is represented by the linear core. This is a subsystem, which can be analysed and synthesised by well known methods of a wide palette for linear systems. When we choose the input and output operations as being fixed, the properties of input and output blocks are also firm. In this way, a *class of homomorphic systems* is defined where the individual systems differ only in the linear part.

It can be proved that if (and only if) the characteristic operations are memory-less (inertialess), the systems with transfers φ and ψ^{-1} are also memoryless, which is frequently the case in practice. Then, the whole memory of the homo-morphic system is concentrated in the linear part, that is only the linear part shows inertial properties. This of course remarkably simplifies the design of such a system and its analysis.

12.3.2 Homomorphic filtering and deconvolution

The purpose of filtering a signal is generally the separation of the signal components based on a certain chosen criterion. Usually, the problem is formulated so that one component is emphasised to the detriment of others or, on the contrary, one particular component is suppressed. Additive combinations of signal components can be filtered successfully by linear filters if the spectral properties of the components are sufficiently different. Thus, the criterion used to discriminate among the components is their spectral properties. Separation of components from a nonadditive mixture, generated, for example, by multiplication, is not usually possible by linear methods. In such cases, however, it may be possible to apply filtering successfully, using homomorphic systems.

Should the processed signal be composed of its components by an operation @,

$$\{x_n\} = \{u_n\} @ \{v_n\},$$

the corresponding *homomorphic filter* in canonical representation will be formed according to the block diagram of Figure 12.8. The input block is a homomorphic subsystem realising the transform φ, for which

$$\varphi(\{u_n\} @ \{v_n\}) = \varphi(\{u_n\}) + \varphi(\{v_n\}); \tag{12.12}$$

the output block is a subsystem with the inverse transfer so that its function is described by the relation

$$\varphi^{-1}(\{r_n\} + \{s_n\}) = \varphi^{-1}(\{r_n\}) @ \varphi^{-1}(\{s_n\}), \tag{12.13}$$

where $r_n + s_n$ is the output signal of the linear part of the filter. The input block thus transforms the nonadditive mixture of signals into an additive one that can be separated into components by a linear system optimally designed by known methods. The output signal of the linear part will be an additive mixture in which, of course, some components will be suppressed to a negligible amplitude while others will be conversely emphasised. This mixture is then transformed by the output system in such a way that the resulting output signal $\{y_n\}$ is again made up of a component mixture formed by the operator @. The transformation removes the distortion of the useful component. Should this transform be omitted, the output signal would be distorted or, more generally, transformed into another space by the operator φ.

If we know the operation characterising a particular given signal combination, the first step in designing a homomorphic filter is to determine the operators φ and φ^{-1}. This is not a simple task, as a general procedure to

Figure 12.8 General homomorphic filter

determine such transforms for a given operation is not known. It is usually necessary to utilise heuristic, intuitive approaches to the transform design and to prove afterwards that they have the properties requested by equations (12.12) and (12.13). Should such a pair of transforms be found, it would then define a whole class of homomorphic filters differing mutually only in their linear parts. In this class, we are then seeking the optimal filter by methods known for linear filtering, or perhaps the choice can be based on experiment. It should be stressed, however, that the spectral content of the components might be changed by the input transform, which must be taken into account when designing the linear filter section.

A rather frequent case is the requirement of filtering a signal component from a multiplicative mixture. This can originate from transferring a signal *via* a time-variant channel when the signal may be regarded as the product of the useful component and (slowly) changing channel transfer. Examples of such variability may be fading in a radio electromagnetic-wave channel or the nonlinear imperfect contact of a sensor of biomedical signals. A similar situation is with amplitude modulation as the modulated signal may be interpreted as a multiplicative mixture of the modulating signal (perhaps shifted by adding a constant) and the higher-frequency harmonic carrier signal. Another type of practical problem is the case of optical images originating under nonuniform illumination. In this case the useful signal is the two-dimensional reflectivity of the scene and the disturbing component is the nonuniform illumination; the resulting image data is obviously given by the product of both quantities. In this case it can be supposed that the illumination is a slowly changing function of space coordinates, thus being represented by low space–frequency components while the reflectivity representing the details of the scene is primarily expressed by high frequencies.

In the cases mentioned, the frequency ranges of the components are rather different but the nonadditivity of the mixtures doesn't allow for separating them by linear filtering. Taken exactly, it would be necessary to analyse how the spectra of components are changed by the nonlinear transform used. Published attempts nevertheless show that even heuristic use of the mentioned assumptions on the spectra gives reasonable results, regardless of the transform influence, probably owing to the character of the nonlinearity. This is monotonous and smooth, thus not changing the spectra properties substantially.

If the processed signal is a product

$$x_n = u_n v_n,$$

the suitable input transform φ is the logarithmic function $x'_n = \ln(x_n)$. The corresponding inverse transform φ^{-1} is therefore the exponential $y_n = \exp(y'_n)$. A homomorphic filter to separate components of a multiplicative mixture is thus formed by the cascade of a logarithmic converter, a linear filter and an exponentiator. The entire memory of the system is thus concentrated in its linear core. Realisation of such a system is not difficult for real signals providing that all the input signals are positive. This can easily be arranged even when they were originally changing polarity, by adding, to all the samples, a suitable constant, which does not change the information content of the signal.

If the signal is complex and its original version before sampling is represented by a continuous curve $x(t)$ in the complex plane, only the limitation that the curve does not contain the origin must be observed. Nevertheless, the curve may even repeatedly to circumvent it; this may be utilised for an approximation of a real signal of both polarities. The situation is however complicated by the fact that the complex logarithm is an ambiguous function

$$\log(z) = \log|z| + j[\arg(z) + 2m\pi], \quad m = 0, 1, 2, \cdots$$

while the input operator must be unique. Use of the main branch of the logarithm is not acceptable as it is not analytic – its imaginary part has a discontinuity for points on the real axis. It is therefore useful to suppose that the curve lies on the Riemann surface in such a way that the origin of the curve, $x(0)$, and the whole first loop up to the point $x(t_1)$: $\arg(x(t_1)) = \pm 2\pi$ (the sign corresponding to the sense of circulation) lies on the initial surface leaf. The other loop up to the point $x(t_2)$: $\arg(x(t_2)) = \pm 4\pi$ then lies on the next leaf (or on the previous one for the opposite sense of circulation) etc. If the function $x(t)$ is continuous, even the function $\log(x(t))$ defined in this way is continuous and unique. When such a signal is represented by discrete samples, there will not be any difficulties as far as the sampling frequency will be high enough to ensure that the phase difference between neighbouring samples will be less than 2π. In this case, obviously it is possible to keep track of phase development. The inverse transform is then a complex exponential function, which does not cause any difficulties as it is a unique operator. We shall meet a complex multiplicative signal mixture, among others, when discussing homomorphic deconvolution in the following paragraph.

When dealing with an input signal formed by convoluted components,

$$\{x_n\} = \{u_n\} * \{v_n\}, \tag{12.14}$$

and none of the components is known, as, for example, after passing a signal *via* an unknown channel, it is possible to try removing the convolutional distortion also by means of homomorphic filtering – this is so-called *blind deconvolution*. It will be possible, providing that we are able to find a system transforming the input operation of convolution into the operation of summing and, further, that we can also find a system inverse to the former. Let us show that such systems exist.

Indeed, if we transform the equation (12.14) by the Z-transform, we obtain a product of (complex) functions

$$X(z) = U(z)V(z),$$

which can further be submitted to the logarithmic transform (using logarithm base e.g. *e*), thus

$$\log(X(z)) = \log(U(z)) + \log(V(z)).$$

Although this mixture is additive, it is not suitable for linear filtering as it is not a time sequence. Therefore, the inverse Z-transform follows and returns the signal back into the original domain,

$$\{x'_n\} = \mathbb{Z}^{-1}\{\log(X(z))\} = \mathbb{Z}^{-1}\{\log(U(z))\} + \mathbb{Z}^{-1}\{\log(V(z))\}.$$

The sequence $\{x'_n\}$, generated from the original signal $\{x_n\}$ by successively applying the Z-transform, complex logarithm (as defined in the previous paragraph) and inverse Z-transform, is called the *complex cepstrum* of the signal $\{x_n\}$. It is obvious that this is an additive mixture of two time-sequences.

However, from the point of view of realisation, it is hardly acceptable that the first transform increases the dimension of the signal – it converts the one-dimensional signal into a two-dimensional function in the *z*-domain. This 2D function would have to be discretised to be represented digitally, thus replacing vectors by much greater matrices. However, when realising that, according to eqn (2.14), the inverse Z-transform utilises only values of the transformed function on a closed curve, which in practical cases is usually the unit circle, it is sufficient to use only this one-dimensional Z-transform representation. As even this single-parameter function must be discretised, we arrive at the common discrete Fourier transform which can thus replace the Z-transform in the described signal transform chain providing that the effects of discretisation are compensated for.

The inverse system on the output side of the filter is again formed by a cascade of three transforms – the Z-transform, exponential function and inverse Z-transform. Again, the Z-transform will be replaced by the DFT for numerical computations.

The linear part of the filter will naturally be designed based on some knowledge of the spectral components of the complex cepstrum of the signal to be processed. It is usually supposed that the frequency bands of the interference and of the useful signal do not overlap significantly; often the interference spectrum is concentrated in the area of low frequencies while the useful signal spectrum occupies higher frequencies. The precise specifications of the limit frequencies are usually not known, and the spectra of components partly overlap. Therefore, filters with frequency responses which are smoothly and slowly changing with frequency, not sharp cut-off filters, are usually used.

Notice that the linear part of a homomorphic filter can be a linear filter of any type, i.e. also a Wiener, Kalman filter, adaptive filter or even a cumulative (averaging) system. The idea of such an *adaptive homomorphic filter* is attractive, because it enables us to circumvent the uneasy task of identifying the spectral properties of the signal-mixture components generated by the input block of the homomorphic filter.

12.4 The power cepstrum and its applications

In the previous section, we introduced the notion of the complex cepstrum as an intraproduct in homomorphic blind deconvolution. Historically older is the concept of the *power cepstrum* of a signal, which is defined as the product of chaining of the Fourier transform of the signal, logarithm of the absolute value of the spectrum and another Fourier transform. It is obvious that such processing, often denoted simply as cepstrum, is nonlinear; we shall show some of its practical applications.

The cepstrum can be utilised for blind deconvolution in a similar way to the complex cepstrum. If the analysed signal is given by convolution as in eqn (12.14), its spectrum is $X(\omega) = U(\omega)V(\omega)$ and therefore its power spectrum is

$$S_{xx}(\omega) = |U(\omega)V(\omega)|^2 = S_{uu}(\omega)S_{vv}(\omega).$$

Application of the natural-logarithm operator gives

$$\ln(S_{xx}(\omega)) = \ln(S_{uu}(\omega)) + \ln(S_{vv}(\omega)),$$

which is an additive mixture of logarithms of individual power spectra (these quantities are sometimes abbreviated as log spectra). This mixture can be split in principle by linear techniques applied this time in the frequency domain. Again, *a priori* assumptions on the different character of both components are utilised; usually the assumption is that one of the log spectra is changing slowly and the other quickly with frequency. It is the purpose of the second Fourier transform in the chain to determine the content of the different harmonic components in the log-spectra. (Notice that we are speaking about 'frequencies' of these components of log spectra as behaving on the axis of frequency, not about frequencies describing the speed of signal variations in the time domain.)

A frequent problem is to remove convolutional distortion caused by a linear system through which the signal has passed, thus becoming convolved with its impulse response v_n. If the log spectrum of the useful signal u_n could be substantially suppressed, the remaining term can approximate, after exponential transform, the amplitude square of the frequency response $G_v(\omega)$ of the linear system,

$$|G_v(\omega)|^2 \approx \exp[\ln(S_{vv}(\omega))] = S_{vv}(\omega).$$

Based on the amplitude frequency response estimated in this way, it is possible to try designing a corresponding approximate deconvolution system. The phase characteristic should be complemented based on a certain assumption, such as of the minimum phase property of the distorting system.

Another possibility is to submit the mentioned mixture of log spectra to a further (possibly inverse) Fourier transform and to obtain in this way again a time sequence, cepstrum, which could be processed by standard linear filtering. By means of the second transform, it is well possible to detect periodic components in log spectra that will appear in the cepstrum as pronounced peaks. This is used in particular to identify distortion caused by reverberation, i.e. by adding, to the original signal, some repeated, delayed and possibly amplitude modified versions of the original. This kind of distortion appears, for example, owing to poorly matched communication lines or because of a long reverberation in a hall etc. Let us illustrate the case for a signal with a single reverberation; we will use continuous-time presentation for simplicity. Should the analysed signal consist of the original with a single echo of identical amplitude,

$$x_1(t) + x_1(t + \Delta t),$$

its spectrum is $X(\omega) + X(\omega)e^{-j\omega \Delta t}$ (utilising the linearity property of the Fourier transform and the time-shift theorem) and consequently the power spectrum is

$$|X(\omega)|^2(1 + e^{j\omega \cdot \Delta t})(1 + e^{-j\omega \Delta t}) = S_{xx}(\omega)(2 + 2\cos(\omega \Delta t)).$$

After applying the logarithmic transform, we obtain

$$\ln(S_{xx}(\omega)(2 + 2\cos(\omega \Delta t))) = \ln(S_{xx}(\omega)) + \ln(2 + 2\cos(\omega \Delta t)).$$

It can be seen that there is a periodically varying component in the log spectrum, which is oscillating with the basic 'frequency' Δt along the axis ω; this 'frequency' corresponds to the delay of the echo. The following Fourier transform detects this component as a remarkable maximum at the corresponding point Δt on the time axis.

12.5 Nonlinear matched filters

The classical (linear) matched filters that we have discussed in Section 8.3.1 serve to detect known signal sections in an observed (received) signal perhaps distorted by additive noise. The purpose of such a filter is to respond with a maximum peak in its output in the time instant of recognition of such a signal section specific to a particular filter. We have shown that under certain conditions – sufficient signal-section length with respect to the frequency properties of the signal to be detected, interference with white noise or at least sufficiently wideband, zero-mean noise – the detection can be performed efficiently by an FIR filter. If the sought signal section of length $L(\mathbf{s})$ is described by a vector $\mathbf{s}$, this optimal linear detection is provided by correlation of the section with the observed signal $\mathbf{x}$. The section $\mathbf{s}$ is successively shifted along the signal so that the sample y_k of the output vector $\mathbf{y}$ is

$$y_k = \mathbf{x}_k^T \mathbf{s},$$

where $\mathbf{x}_k = [x_{k-L(s)+1}, \cdots, x_{k-1}, x_k]^T$. The above scalar product can be recognised as an element of the convolution sequence

$$\{y_n\} = \{x_n\} * \{h_n\},$$

which can be realised by an FIR filter with the impulse response formed by the sequence of the sought signal section reversed in time,

$$\mathbf{h} = [s_{L(s)-1}, \cdots, s_1, s_0]^T.$$

We shall show that, if the mentioned conditions are not properly fulfilled, which is frequently the case in practice, the linear matched (correlation) filter is not a good detector of the sought signal occurrence. Obviously

$$y_k = \sum_{i=0}^{L(s)-1} s_i x_{k'+1} = \sum_{i=0}^{L(s)-1} (s_i - S)(x_{k'+1} - X_k) + \sum_{i=0}^{L(s)-1} SX_k,$$

where $k' = k - L(s) + 1$, $X_k = 1/L(s) \sum_{i=k'}^{k} x_i$ and $S = (1/L(s)) \sum_{i=0}^{L(s)-1} s_i$. Of course, the local average X_k does not carry any information about the similarity of both the signal sections, but it can substantially influence the value of y_k. Thus, the peak of this signal is not a reliable indicator of the presence of $\mathbf{s}$ in $\mathbf{x}_k$, if the local average is time variable as is often the case. This drawback of the matched filter can be removed by substituting for the vector $\mathbf{s}$ by its centred version $\mathbf{s}'$: $s_i' = s_i - S$, that is by a corresponding modification of the impulse response of the filter; in this way we obtain the *covariance filter*.

If the frequency band of the noise is not sufficiently wide (in order to approach the white-noise ideal), there still remains a rather high probability of a false detection. Alternatives are then open in the form of other similarity criteria than the mentioned correlation or covariance. Nonlinear versions of the similarity detector may be based on comparison of the vectors $\mathbf{x}_k$ and $\mathbf{s}$ in signal space. One of the detection possibilities is the minimisation of the norm of the difference vector,

$$\|\mathbf{x}_k - \mathbf{s}\|^2 = \sum_{i=0}^{L(s)-1} (x_{k'+1} - s_i)^2,$$

which, after omitting the constant term $\sum s_i^2$, leads to the output signal formed of samples

$$y_k = \sum_{i=0}^{L(s)-1} x_{k'+i} s_i - \frac{1}{2} \sum_{i=0}^{L(s)-1} x_{k'+i}^2.$$

Notice that this is actually a modification of the classical matched filter, from the output of which the sum of squares of input samples, delimited by a sliding window, is subtracted. We shall call this filter a (Euclidean) *distance filter* (Figure 12.9). A substantial disadvantage of this filter (as of the classical matched filters) is its sensitivity to the magnitude of the vector $\mathbf{x}_k$, which often varies to a great extent in practical tasks, thus adversely influencing the precision of determining the maximum positions.

Another and rather excellent criterion of similarity, as experience shows, is the angle between vectors $\mathbf{x}_k$ and $\mathbf{s}$, which is fundamentally invariant to the variable

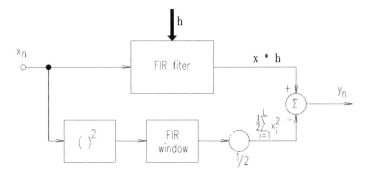

Figure 12.9 Distance-controlled matched filter

magnitude of the observed signal and also rather insensitive to its nonlinear distortions. When replacing the angle by its cosine,

$$\frac{\mathbf{x}_k \cdot \mathbf{s}}{\|\mathbf{x}_k\| \, \|\mathbf{s}\|} \, ,$$

which in the extent used is a monotonous function of the angle, and when omitting the constant factor $\|\mathbf{s}\|$, we obtain another nonlinear matched detector, the output of which is

$$y_k = \frac{\displaystyle\sum_{i=0}^{L(s)-1} x_{k'+i} \, s_i}{\sqrt{\displaystyle\sum_{i=0}^{L(s)-1} x_{k'+i}^2}} .$$

Such a modification of the matched filter, the signal-flow diagram of which is in Figure 12.10, we shall call an *angle* or *cosine filter*.

Both the distance and cosine filters provide the detection peak appearing with a high probability in the proper time instant, which is the end of sought-signal occurrence. Nevertheless, they have a common drawback in that the detection peaks, although maximal, are usually of amplitudes differing only slightly from other samples. A detector based on any of these filters thus must contain a maximum-searching algorithm, which will detect the absolute maximum in the complete observed signal or in its reasonable part where the occurrence of the sought signal can be expected. This is a complication in comparison with classical filters, which allow, without a substantial increase in the (generally higher) error rate, use of only a simpler thresholding algorithm with a chosen or even automatically determined threshold. In this respect, an improvement in the angle filter could be expected if both the compared vectors were centred,

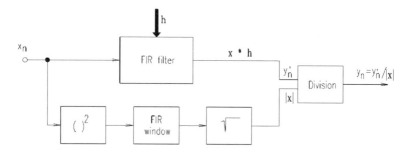

Figure 12.10 Angle-controlled (cosine) matched filter

$$
y_k = \frac{\displaystyle\sum_{i=0}^{L(s)-1} (x_{k'+i} - X_k)(s_i - S)}{\sqrt{\displaystyle\sum_{i=0}^{L(s)-1} (x_{k'+i} - X_k)^2}},
$$

at a cost of a considerable increase in the filter complexity owing to repeated calculation of the sliding mean value X_k.

The results of statistical verification [13] for both one-dimensional and two-dimensional (image) signals show that an extremely minimal error rate is achieved by the angle detector. Somewhat worse are the results of the distance detector, unless the observed signal amplitude varies; then the effectiveness deteriorates close to that of the classical covariance filter. Surprisingly enough, the last mentioned version, the centred-vector angle filter, has shown properties inferior to those of the plain angle detector. The positive properties of the nonlinear filtering-based detectors remain preserved even under rather unfavourable conditions (varying mean value and amplitudes of the signal, comparable frequency bandwidth of the signal and noise), when the classical linear detectors fail completely. Naturally, the price to be paid for the remarkably higher reliability is a computationally more intensive algorithm. The angle detector has proved to be clearly the best among all the similarity criteria, in the problem of two-dimensional disparity analysis of pairs of images where all the other approaches lead to an unacceptably high error rate.

Chapter 13
Signal processing by neural networks

13.1 Concept of neural networks

Neural networks are a relatively new means of data processing. Interpreted in this way, it can be said that a neural network realises a mapping from an input vector space into the output vector space,

$$\{x\} \rightarrow \{y\},$$

(Figure 13.1); the dimensions of both spaces are generally different. The physical separation of inputs and outputs, as indicated in the Figure, need not be kept with some types of neural networks; the same nodes may carry input or output values in different time instants according to a convention and mode of experimenting. Understood so generally, neural networks can be applied in very different ways. We shall concentrate our attention primarily on neural-network applications as signal processors, when the input and output vectors represent the relevant signals. Another, perhaps more frequent use is their application as classifiers – then the input vector represents a section of a signal or image and the output indicates to which class the section belongs. Further, it is possible to utilise the ability of some networks to solve optimisation problems; they can be used for signal restoration with respect to chosen criteria. An important application of certain networks is their use as associative memory able to retrieve information on the basis of incomplete assignment. It is also possible to design neural nets in such a way that the transferred information is passed through a 'bottleneck' – a part of the network

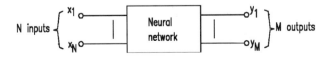

Figure 13.1 Neural network as a data processor

capable of transferring only a limited rate of information. Some networks are capable of arranging their structure and properties so that only a small fraction of original data is transferred through the bottleneck with practically untouched information content – data reduction is achieved automatically in this way.

All the mentioned functions can of course also be realised by the classical means that have already been discussed in the previous chapters of this book; the substantial difference is in their design methods. While the classical approaches were precisely defined by their purpose and it was possible to analyse their efficiency exactly, a neural network is always only a frame represented by a chosen network architecture. The mode of operation and the operators realised by the networks are, to a great extent, dependent on the methods of experimenting with them. These determine which methods are used to modify their parameters in the process of learning and how the output quantities (or, more generally, the behaviour of network) are interpreted. In comparison with classical algorithms, we can state initially several characteristic distinctions of neural networks:

- Processing elements are typically *very simple processors* but a large number of them are usually operating at one time.
- It is therefore a *parallel processing* method, which can provide for a radical increase in processing speed (notice, however, that this claim applies primarily to hardware realisations while common simulations on sequential computers tend to be rather slow).
- Individual processing elements (so-called neurons) typically work (almost) autonomously, there is usually no central synchronisation in the networks and thus the networks operate in *asynchronous mode* with *distributed control*.
- Neurons are more or less densely interconnected with the connections being characterised by different *connection weights* expressing the degree of one-way or mutual influence.
- The weights, which together with the chosen structure determine the network properties, are not usually determined *a priori* (as is the case for the parameters of classical algorithms). They are generated and modified in the process of *learning* based on the processed information and perhaps (in the case of *supervised learning*) also on some additional *a priori* information.
- The variable set of weights, reflecting in a way the properties of the processed information, means the ability for *internal knowledge representation*.
- From the above properties, the *adaptability* property of the networks follows, which also manifests itself in remarkable *robustness*, i.e. immunity with respect to failures of parts of the network and to inaccuracies in the input information. A properly designed and run network is in principle capable of maintaining its operability even with some faulty elements by modifying the remaining functional parts so that the overall function remains (basically) preserved. In addition, it can process appropriately even incomplete and deteriorated input information.

Let us note that these properties were not usable until recently owing to the complexity of the necessary equipment. With today's large-scale integration technology, neural networks of an interesting size are not only realisable but they can even inversely influence the philosophy of hardware design. The ability of regeneration after a failure allows us to utilise extremely large-scale integration which inherently suffers from a nonnegligible probability of some-elements failure. (Circuit producers claim that it is easier and cheaper to produce a VLSI circuit with 10^9 elements of which 95 per cent are functional than a circuit of 10^6 elements which all must be perfect, as in the case of today's microcomputers and signal processors.)

These generally positive properties, together with the fact that nowadays good simulation programs are commercially available, enabling use of neural networks even to entire dilettantes, have led during the last two decades to an enormous boom in this area of information processing. A potential user should nevertheless be aware of the main pitfall of this approach: the already classical neural architectures almost ensure yielding a certain result in a concrete application. However, it is not guaranteed by far that the result is reasonable not to mention optimal. This is primarily related to the fact that, in spite of many advances in neural network theory, it is still impossible to interpret the weight ensembles obtained during the learning process in relation to the required or even to the obtained result. We are simply unable to explain why the network yields, under certain circumstances (input sequence, learning method etc.), some result or another, certain decision and suchlike. Therefore, formalised analysis or even synthesis of the networks is limited mainly to certain probabilistic characteristics, the relationship of which to the problem to be solved is usually rather detached. This is probably also the source of a certain scepticism, namely of theoreticians with respect to neural approaches.

Although technical neural networks originated initially as simplified models of biological neuron nets, it should be emphasised that, today, the similarity is already rather vague. Technical networks have already been developing independently of the real properties of their former biological models for quite a long time. Today's models of biological neurons, taking into account the transport phenomena in cell membranes, different mechanisms of excitement propagation on neural fibres etc., are incomparably more complex than the processing elements in technical networks which still carry the same name for historical reasons. No less different is the situation at the level of complete networks and their parts. It should not be understood, however, that both areas cannot positively influence each other in the future. In the next paragraphs we shall use the notions of neuron and neural network in a purely technical sense, without claiming to keep closely to the analogy with biological neural networks.

Although technical neural networks represent a distinctly different paradigm from everything that we have dealt with so far, certain common features of the concepts that have been described so far, can be found. Also, they obviously form such a practically promising approach that including them at least in a brief and review form seems to be necessary. We shall describe the notion of an individual neuron as the processing element as well as the concepts and properties of basic types of neural networks. Our explanation will concentrate mainly on the most commonly applied multilayer feedforward networks (illogically usually called 'backpropagation networks'), to self-learning structures of the Kohonen net type and finally we shall briefly also mention feedback networks with mutual interconnections. The concluding section will be devoted to several typical applications of neural networks in the area of signal processing.

13.2 A single neuron

A *neuron* will be defined as a processing element (Figure 13.2), which has N inputs and one output and is characterised by the equation

$$y = f\left(\sum_{i=1}^{N} w_i x_i - \vartheta\right),$$ (13.1)

describing the output of the neuron as the response to an input vector $\mathbf{x} = [x_1, x_2, \cdots, x_N]^T$, where $\mathbf{w} = [w_1, w_2, \cdots, w_N]^T$ is the current vector of weights, ϑ is the current threshold of the neuron and $f(\alpha)$ is a chosen (but fixed) usually nonlinear function that is called the *neuron characteristic*. The argument of the function in eqn (13.1) is called *activation* of the neuron. Some typical characteristics of neurons are depicted in Figure 13.2. Besides the linear and clipped linear characteristics, these are the functions sign(α) or its modification sign(α)/2 + 1/2 which generate the output with binary ('logical') values 0, 1, and the *sigmoidal function*

$$f(\alpha) = \frac{1}{1 + e^{-\alpha/T}},$$ (13.2)

the advantageous properties of which are used primarily by feedforward multilayer networks. Notice that the function is continuous and has continuous derivatives and, further, that the parameter T allows us to adjust the steepness of the function transition in the neighbourhood of zero.

Subtraction of the threshold ϑ in eqn (13.1) has the same effect as if the characteristic of the neuron with respect to the active inputs were shifted by the corresponding amount in the opposite horizontal direction. To simplify the formalism, we shall introduce the designation $w_0 = -\vartheta$. When defining the corresponding fictive input as $x_0 \equiv 1$, the activation can be rewritten as

$$\alpha = \sum_{i=0}^{N} w_i x_i,$$ (13.3)

and eqn (13.1) can then be modified to

$$y = f(\mathbf{w}^T \mathbf{x}).$$ (13.4)

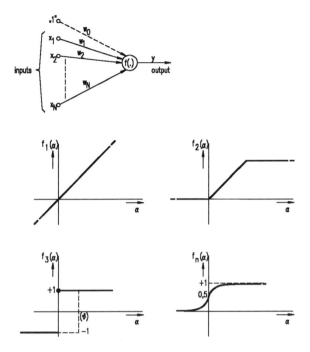

Figure 13.2 Neuron as a processing element

The definition region of a neuron is usually the N-dimensional space of real numbers $\mathfrak{R}^N$. The region of output values is commonly a certain interval of real numbers (e.g. for the function (13.2) it is $(0, 1)$), or, in the case of so-called logical neurons, the binary set $\{0, 1\}$ or the like. Vectors of weights are, in the sense of the simplified form of activation notation, from the space $\mathfrak{R}^{N+1}$.

Let us first briefly analyse the properties of the historically older *binary* ('logical') *neuron*, which provides classification of the input vectors into two classes. The space of input vectors is (for a given $\mathbf{w}$) divided into two subspaces, one of which contains all the vectors $\mathbf{x}$ that lead to the unitary output of the neuron, the other subspace contains the remaining vectors. The border surface is obviously a hyperplane determined by the equation

$$\sum_{i=0}^{N} w_i x_i = 0.$$

The neuron is thus only capable of classifying problems which can be characterised by *linearly separable* sets of input vectors.[1] The equation of the border

[1] It was this discovery that led, at the end of the 1960s, to the formulation of the so-called 'hard-learning' elementary problems that are not linearly separable. The resulting scepticism caused almost twenty years of stagnation in the field of neural nets, which ended only after the ideas of feedback networks and multilayer networks emerged. The classical example of a hard-learning (i.e. linearly nonseparable) problem is a realisation of the logical function *exclusive-OR*.

hyperplane shows that its position is uniquely given by the weight vector – **w** is obviously the normal vector of the hyperplane, which contains the origin of the coordinates. By changing the weights in the process of learning, the border-plane position is correspondingly modified.

Supervised learning of a neuron assumes that there exists a *training set* of pairs $(\mathbf{x}, y_d)$ representing the desirable correspondence; y_d is the required neuron response to the input vector **x**. The learning process consists in 'showing' the vectors of the pairs to the neuron (i.e. bringing the vector components to the neuron inputs in the corresponding order) and comparing the real response of the neuron with the required response. Based on the output difference (error) the weight vector **w** is modified.

A number of learning algorithms have been designed; many of them are of a heuristic character. Of these, let us present what is historically probably the oldest *Hebbian rule* for a logical neuron with binary inputs and output that illustrates the philosophy of such approaches (*y* is the real response of the neuron). If $y = 1$, then:

- if the result is proper, strengthen the weights of all 'live' inputs
  $_{n+1}w_i = {}_nw_i + \Delta,\ \forall i: x_i = 1,\ \Delta > 0;$
- if the result is improper, weaken the weights of all 'live' inputs
  $_{n+1}w_i = {}_nw_i - \Delta,\ \forall i: x_i = 1,\ \Delta > 0;$
- the weights belonging to 'dead' (zero-valued) inputs remain unchanged as they have not influenced the result.

If $y = 0$, the weights remain unchanged.

We shall concentrate on certain more formalised algorithms which also have a relationship to the theory discussed in the previous parts of the book. A commonly used rule of weight modification is the (originally also heuristic) *δ-rule*, which encompasses even the case of generally real (noninteger-valued) components of the input vector and of the real output,

$$_{n+1}w_i = {}_nw_i + \mu(y_d - y)x_i.$$

The rule is applied in every learning step to all components of the weight vector, thus, in vector notation:

$$_{n+1}\mathbf{w} = {}_n\mathbf{w} + \mu(y_d - y)\mathbf{x}. \tag{13.5}$$

Here μ is a suitably chosen constant, influencing the iteration speed. It can be shown that the algorithm converges to the proper position of the border (if it exists), although the convergence is usually slow. Notice the close similarity with the recursive rule (11.15) for FIR linear adaptive filters. This is basically the same problem – minimisation of (mean-square) error by successive modifications of the set of weights. The exact derivation of eqn (11.15) was certainly based on the linearity of the estimate, while for neurons this assumption is fulfilled precisely only by neurons with linear characteristics; with other continuous and monotonous characteristics it is satisfied only roughly. We shall see later, in Section 13.3.2, that the rule with a certain modification is precisely valid even for nonlinear neurons. For the linear neuron, it is possible to derive quite analogous relationships for the calculation of the weight vector as were the expressions for the Wiener filter in eqns (11.1) and (11.13). It is – when using the same criterion for the optimum – an analogous problem. However, the practical meaning of these relationships is limited, as the necessary correlation matrices are not available in problems that are reasonably considered for solving by neural networks.

Rather interesting is the precise optimisation approach for a neuron with real inputs and a Boolean output designed by Widrow. The rule originates from the idea that if the (binary) classification is proper, no modifications are needed. If, on the contrary, the classification of the input vector x_0 is false, it means that the point x_0 lies on the improper side of the border hyperplane in the input vector space. In this case, its distance $w^T x_0 / \|w_0\|$ from the border may form a part of the error quantifier. This criterion, quantifying the error corresponding to a given fixed-weight vector w, is the sum E of distances of all falsely classified vectors from the training set,

$$E(w) = \sum_{x \in X_F} |w^T x|,$$

where X_F is the set of all falsely classified vectors and the constant $1/\|w_0\|$ could have been omitted. This criterion can further be expressed as

$$E(w) = \sum_{x \in X_F} w^T(\pm x) = \sum_{x} \sum_{i=0}^{N} \pm w_i x_i,$$

where the positive sign is valid for falsely negative classification (improper zero result) and the negative sign for the classification which is falsely positive. The gradient of the criterion function is

$$\nabla E(w) = \sum_{i=0}^{N} \frac{\partial E}{\partial w_i} j_i = \sum_{x} \left(\pm \left[\sum_{i=0}^{N} x_i j_i \right] \right) = \sum_{x} \pm x,$$

where j_i is the unit vector in the direction of the ith variable. The gradient is therefore given by the sum of all falsely classified vectors summed with respect to the above-mentioned sign convention. We are thus approaching the optimal weight vector by successive iterations

$$_{n+1}w = {}_n w - \mu \nabla E(_n w).$$

The vector is always modified after finalising one epoch of learning, i.e. after 'showing' all the learning vectors, when the sum meaning the gradient is available. Starting from a random initial estimate, we can obtain gradually improving estimates of weights. If all the vectors are properly classified in the last epoch, or alternatively, if the error rate (ratio of falsely-classified vectors) is sufficiently low, the iteration is stopped. This approach is noteworthy as it shows that a precisely formalised optimisation has been found although the characteristic of the neuron is strongly nonlinear and even discontinuous function.

13.3 Feedforward networks

13.3.1 Concept and architecture of feedforward networks

The conceptually simplest neural network is a *single-layer perceptron* (Figure 13.3). As can be seen, it is just a set of M neurons working in parallel without any mutual interaction. Every one of the neurons realises its transform of the input vector, say $y_j = f(_j\mathbf{w}^T\mathbf{x})$ according to its own weight vector $_j\mathbf{w}$. The characteristics of all the neurons in a network are usually identical. It is obvious that such a network realises a mapping from the space $\Re^N$ into the space $\Re^M$ if the neurons have continuous characteristics, or a mapping between binary spaces of the same dimensions if the neurons are Boolean. With networks of continuously working neurons, frequent configuration is a cascade of a single-layer perceptron and another joint network the purpose of which is to find and indicate the output y_k, which became the maximum, as needed, for example, in competitive learning. This can be interpreted, under certain assumptions, so that the vector $_k\mathbf{w}$ is the optimum approximation of the 'shown' input vector $\mathbf{x}$. Let us mention that the historical Rosenblatt perceptron was basically organised in this way. The inputs of the neurons were randomly connected to so-called receptors which formed the layer of primary inputs of the perceptron. In the case of a network with binary neurons, this is a realisation of a Boolean M, N-pole the function of which naturally varies during the course of learning.

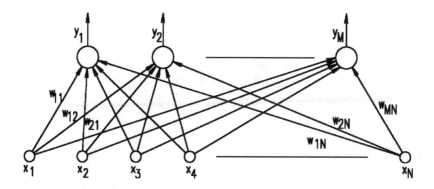

Figure 13.3 Single-layer perceptron

Before becoming acquainted with the general structure of feedforward networks and their possibilities, let us first present an example of a practically used network with fixed *a priori* designed weights, which serves as a specialised parallel processor. This is the *Hamming network,* the purpose of which is to evaluate the similarity of a shown input N-dimensional binary vector to all of the M binary patterns retained in the network, to choose the most similar one and to evaluate quantitatively its similarity. The network, depicted in Figure 13.4, consists of two parts: the first one is a single-layer perceptron formed by M linear neurons whose weight vectors $_j\mathbf{w}$ are binary, of the dimension N and representing the mentioned pattern. If the auxiliary weight substituting the threshold of each neuron is $_jw_0 = N$, $\forall j$ and if all the neurons have the same characteristics $y = \alpha/2$, the output of the jth neuron is obviously (when the network is supplied with the input vector $\mathbf{x}_p$)

$$_jy_p = \frac{1}{2}\left(\sum_{i=1}^{N} {}_jw_{i\,i}x_p + N\right).$$

If the binary elements of the weight vectors and of the input vector are represented by the numbers ± 1, it can easily be shown that the output of a neuron will be equal to the number of complying bits in both compared vectors. The expression $N - {}_jy_p$ is thus the so-called Hamming distance between both vectors.

The second stage of the Hamming network is the maximum selecting network, the output of which is, on one hand, the integer value $z = \max[_1y_p, {}_2y_p, \cdots, {}_My_p]$ and, on the other hand, M binary outputs that indicate which of the patterns was the closest (in code 1 of M, i.e. the order index of

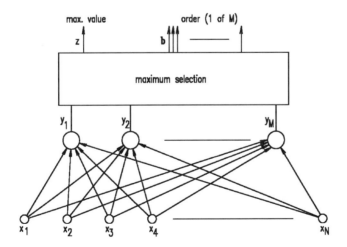

Figure 13.4 Hamming network

the relevant neuron). A building stone of this partial network is the circuit depicted in the upper part of Figure 13.5 in which there are three types of neurons. The type denoted A is linear, $z = \alpha$, type B has a characteristic with the negative part clipped off, i.e. $z = \alpha$ for $\alpha \geq 0$ and $z = 0$, $\alpha < 0$, and type C are logical neurons with Boolean output which have a threshold characteristic with zero threshold. It can easily be found that the network will choose the higher of both its input values to the output v. Also, the logical value 1 will be assigned to this one of two logical outputs b_1, b_2 which corresponds to the higher input, while the other will be zero. When denoting this circuit as $M2$, it is shown in b of Figure 13.5 that a block $M4$ determining the maximum of four inputs can be formed of $M2$-blocks and of D-type neurons realising a Boolean product. The construction for a higher number of input variables would proceed recursively in an obvious manner.

Let us mention that networks, similar to, but more general than, the Hamming network, form a base structure also for other important neural nets. The generalisation is then in real input vector components, not fixed but variable patterns developing in the process of learning and possibly also in maximum determination based on a competitive procedure.

The limitations of a single-layer perceptron can be demonstrated in the simplest case of a general network with $N = 2$ and one binary output. In contrast, extending the possibilities by increasing the number of layers is shown in Figure 13.6. The input vectors can be interpreted as point positions in the

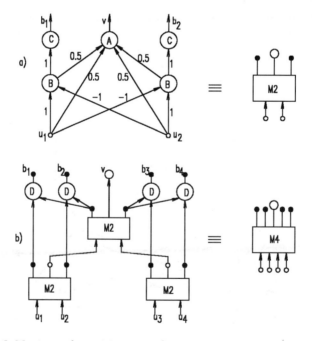

Figure 13.5 Maximum determining network

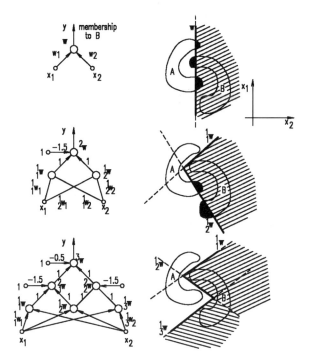

Figure 13.6 Classification possibilities for single and multilayer feedforward networks

plane (x_1, x_2); two point sets A, B are given in this plane and the input vector should be classified as belonging to one of them. In the upper part of the figure, which is devoted to the possibilities of a single-layer perceptron, it is shown that exact classification is impossible by such a network. The perceptron, in this case represented by a single neuron with the characteristic of type 3 in Figure 13.2, provides only a single border hyperplane, which degenerates to a line in the case of two inputs. Even when this line is optimally positioned, some areas of points remain which would be classified improperly.

Adding further neurons to the layer does not bring the desired effect of shaping the border, as the possibility of combining a number of different classifications with distinct borderlines is absent. The middle part of the figure shows that a two-layer network, the second layer of which is formed by neurons realising a logical product,[2] partly eliminates this drawback. The logical products generate areas which are intersections of half planes formed by the classification possibilities of individual neurons. By intersection of a sufficient number of half planes, it is evidently possible to form any convex area; however, this is still not sufficient to formulate a proper border for the given shapes of

---

[2] A neuron with weights $w_0 = -(m - 0.5)$, $w_i = 1$, $i = 1, 2, \cdots, m$

point classes. An idea then emerges to approximate any nonconvex area by the union of a finite number of convex areas, which is always possible. The Boolean operation corresponding to the set union is a logical sum which can be realised in the third layer.[3] In the lower part of the figure, it can be seen that classification formulated in this way is already perfect, if classification of points not belonging to any of the areas A, B is not requested. Anyway, should it be required, an increase in the number of classification classes would only need to add further neurons to the layers but the layer number – three – is sufficient for an arbitrarily complicated problem of this kind. It can easily be shown that, using this approach, it is possible to form the areas of any shape, including discontinuous ones and areas with holes. It is then also possible to realise any Boolean function of N variables if a neuron is available providing logical inversion.[4]

It is noteworthy that, if we realise a standard three-layer network according to the concept described in the following paragraphs and let it learn the problem discussed above, the weights generated in the process of learning will very probably be quite different from those that have been mentioned in the example. Also, the functions realised by individual neurons will be quite different; moreover, every new learning process will lead to a different set of weights. The purpose of the above example was only to demonstrate the existence of a network realising the required classification and, at the same time, to show the necessity of using multilayer networks.

The example mentioned was a special case of a *multilayer perceptron*, the general form of which is sketched in Figure 13.7. We can recognise here the highest *output layer* of M neurons, below which we see the so-called *hidden layers* of neurons and, at the bottom of the figure, the lowest layer of N input nodes. The network is generally completely interconnected, that is, the output of every neuron (except naturally those in the output layer) is connected to the inputs of all the neurons of the following layer. This assumption does not cause any loss in generality as the possible nonexistence of a connection can be expressed by zero weight. The architecture, which we shall call a *feedforward network*, is the most commonly used type of neural network in practice. The name follows from the way in which the signals proceed in the network: their flow is unidirectional from the input to the output layer. Notice that there is an alternative, frequently used and rather misleading name for the same architecture – *back propagation network* – which is derived from the method of learning, not from the operation of the system. In the frame of this architecture, the individual network types are distinguished by their structure, that is by the number of layers and numbers of neurons contained in the layers. Further, in the frame of a certain structure, a concrete network is determined by the used characteristics of the neurons and, in particular, by the set of weights; these

---

[3] By a neuron with weights $w_0 = 0.5$, $w_i = 1$, $1, 2, \cdots, m$
[4] A neuron with $w_0 = 0.5$, $w_1 = -1$

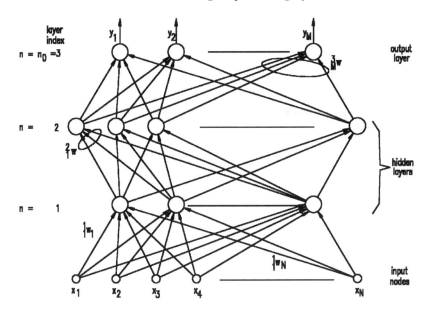

Figure 13.7 Generic feedforward network

parameters uniquely determine the mapping of the input space onto the output space.

For further analysis, we shall introduce the following designation (Figure 13.7): the serial layer number (starting from the bottom) $n = 1, 2, \cdots, n_o$, where n_o is thus the number of layers; number of neurons in the nth layer $N_n (N_{n_o} = M)$; further, $^n_j \mathbf{w}$ is the weight vector of the jth neuron in the nth layer and $^n_j w_i$ is its ith component, i.e. the weight of the connection from the ith neuron in the previous layer. For the indices in the layer, obviously $j = 1, 2, \cdots, N_n$ and with respect to completeness of connections with the previous layer also $i = 1, 2, \cdots, N_{n-1}$.

The set of weights is of course usually variable, particularly in the course of learning but possibly even during data processing, and in this way the input–output correspondence is modified. The feedforward networks normally use neurons with the same characteristics in the whole network; with respect to the requirements of the learning method of error backpropagation, these are most often sigmoidal functions. However, the above example shows that other neuronal characteristics may also be useful, when using alternative learning methods or working with fixed *a priori*-determined weights.

Feedforward networks seem to be very widely usable. The idea of universality can also be supported on the basis of the Kolmogoroff theorem, which says that *any* function of N variables can be expressed by mere linear combinations and a single but repeatedly available nonlinear monotonous function of one variable. These are exactly the means provided by networks such as the ones discussed. We can thus deduce that, should the network be extensive enough, it can induce at its outputs arbitrary functions (transformations) of the input variables. Certain published (not quite convincing) considerations lead to the conclusion that even a two-layer network with $N(2N+1)$ sigmoidal neurons is in principal capable of generating any functions of N variables. This conclusion justifies the rather optimistic approach, as far as the range of application is concerned. Nevertheless, it does not say anything about how to design the weight vectors and the parameter of the sigmoid for a particular selected network structure and a required transform function.

13.3.2 Network learning by error backpropagation

Apart from the convenience of the architecture with its universality of realisable transforms, wide use of feedforward networks is also supported by the existence of a formally derived method of learning (although originally this was also a rather heuristic algorithm). Similarly, as was the case with a single neuron, the learning of whole networks is also based on the use of a *training* set, now consisting of a certain finite (rather high) number of couples $(\mathbf{x}_p, \mathbf{d}_p)$, where $\mathbf{x}_p$ is an input vector of dimension N and $\mathbf{d}_p$ the corresponding (desired) output vector of the dimension M. An individual learning step consists in supplying the vector $\mathbf{x}_p$ to the input layer of the network – again, it is often said that the vector is 'shown' to the network – and in finding the difference between the induced output vector of the network

$$\mathbf{y}_p = \overline{\Psi}(\mathbf{x}_p),$$

and the desired vector $\mathbf{d}_p$. Based on the determined difference, the interconnection weights are modified either immediately in the individual steps, or after several steps or even after the whole epoch, on the basis of integrated difference information. By a *learning epoch,* we shall understand execution of learning steps successively using all the couples of the training set. As the convergence of the weight set to the state, when the network would induce the required transform function, is rather slow, many learning epochs are usually needed to achieve a reasonable error rate for the performed transform or classification.

Let us present first the approximate considerations which have led to the formulation of the most frequently used learning algorithm, called the error backpropagation, and which will simplify for the reader an understanding of the formal derivation that will follow. We shall start with the assumption that the (quasi-) optimal way of learning of an individual neuron is the δ-rule (13.5) and that it would therefore be useful to use it locally for all neurons of the network. If the network has n_o layers, the error of a single, say jth, output of the network when showing the learning vector $\mathbf{x}_p$, is obviously

$$^{n_o}_j e_p = {}_j d_p - {}_j y_p.$$

Although the errors of the output-layer neurons are thus easily determined, it is doubtful how to define the errors of the inner neurons (i.e. in the first layer and in the hidden layers). The reason is that we are only able to determine the actual neuronal output values induced by local activations $\binom{(\cdot)}{(\cdot)}\alpha_p$ caused by showing the vector $\mathbf{x}_p$ to the network with its instantaneous weights, but the desired values are unknown. We shall therefore use a heuristic conception that the error ${}^n_j e_p$ of any (jth) neuron in the layer n will be distributed among all the neurons of the previous layer ($n-1$) proportionally to the weights of the relevant connections. For the error of the ith neuron of the lower layer we thus obtain

$$
{}^{n-1}_{\ i} e_p \sim \sum_{j=1}^{N_n} {}^n_j e_p \, {}^n_j w_i,
\tag{13.6}
$$

where the meanings of N_n and ${}^n_j w_i$ have been introduced in Section 13.3.1. Therefore, if we can, using this concept, generally transfer the errors from the nth layer to the previous one, then the known errors of the output layer can be transferred to the last-but-one layer, and from this to the previous one etc., until we reach the first layer. This procedure is called backpropagation of error which gave the method its name.

In every step of learning, the modification of weights is performed as follows:
- showing a vector $\mathbf{x}_p$ to the network and finding its response $\mathbf{y}_p$;
- calculating the error vector $\mathbf{e}_p = \mathbf{d}_p - \mathbf{y}_p$;
- calculating distributed errors of individual neurons by error back-propagation according to expression (13.6);
- modifying the weight vector of each single neuron according to the δ-rule (13.5) using the known activation of the neuron when showing $\mathbf{x}_p$ to the network.

With respect to the practical importance of the algorithm of learning feed-forward networks, we shall derive a precise expression for iterative corrections of the neuronal weights more formally. To simplify the formalism, we shall suppose only a two-layer network (with one hidden layer) i.e. $n_o = 2$; a general-isation to multilayer networks will be easy. All the neurons in the network are of identical sigmoidal type. Let us recall that the activation of the jth neuron in the nth layer when the vector $\mathbf{x}_p$ is shown to the network will be denoted ${}^n_j \alpha_p$, the ith component of the weight vector ${}^n_j \mathbf{w}$ of this neuron will be marked ${}^n_j w_i$. The learning will be interpreted as an adaptation problem of mean-length minimisation of the difference (error) vector $\mathbf{e}_p$.

A feedforward network (multilayer perceptron) realises the mapping $\mathbf{y} = \Psi(\mathbf{x})$, i.e. when showing a vector $\mathbf{x}_p$ in any learning step, the network response is

$$
\mathbf{y}_p = \overline{\Psi}(\mathbf{x}_p);
\tag{13.7}
$$

therefore, the corresponding error vector is

$$\mathbf{e}_p = \mathbf{d}_p - \mathbf{y}_p = \mathbf{d}_p - \overline{\Psi}(\mathbf{x}_p) \tag{13.8}$$

and thus the (instantaneous) quadratic error is

$$\varepsilon_p = \mathbf{e}_p^T \mathbf{e}_p = \sum_{j=1}^{M} (_jd_p - _jy_p)^2. \tag{13.9}$$

The criterion of quality of the mapping $\overline{\Psi}(.)$ is the ensemble mean-square-error for the ensemble of all admissible input vectors (i.e. theoretically also encompassing vectors not contained in the training set),

$$\varepsilon = \mathbb{E}\{\varepsilon_p\}, \quad \forall p.$$

This criterion is to be minimised by modifying the set $\{_j^n w_i\}$ of the network weights that can be arranged into the vector $\mathbf{w}$. The minimisation can then be done by iterative corrections as given by the steepest-descent method,

$$\mathbf{w}(t+1) = \mathbf{w}(t) - \mu_i \nabla \varepsilon,$$

which in components is

$$_j^n w_i(t+1) = _j^n w_i(t) - \mu_i \frac{\partial \varepsilon}{\partial _j^n w_i}(t). \tag{13.10}$$

Here, t denotes the iteration step, usually identical with the learning step.

The needed mean-error value is not available during the process of learning; rather, only the series of instantaneous square errors ε_p is provided. If we approximate the mean-square-error by an unbiased (though imprecise) estimate $\varepsilon \approx \varepsilon_p$ and take into account that $\varepsilon_p = \varepsilon_p(f(_j^n \alpha_p(_j^n w_1, \cdots, _j^n w_i, \cdots)), \cdots)$, we obtain the correcting term as

$$-\mu_t \frac{\partial \varepsilon}{\partial _j^n w_i} \approx -\mu_t \frac{\partial \varepsilon_p}{\partial _j^n w_i} = \frac{\partial \varepsilon_p}{\partial f(_j^n \alpha_p)} \frac{\partial f(_j^n \alpha_p)}{\partial _j^n \alpha_p} \frac{\partial _j^n \alpha_p}{\partial _j^n w_i}. \tag{13.11}$$

Notice that the influence of the neuronal output $_j^n y_p = f(_j^n \alpha_p)$ on ε_p may of course be mediated by other neurons, as we shall see later.

We shall evaluate the expression (13.11) first for the weights of neurons of the last layer, i.e. for $n = 2$. When calculating the first factor, the derivative of the quadratic expression (13.9), we realise that only one term of the sum depends on the neuronal output $f(_j^2 \alpha_p)$. The second factor – the derivative of a known function – can be expressed symbolically. Finally, when evaluating the last factor, we should consider that only one term of the sum (13.3) is dependent on $_j^2 w_i$; it is the product of this weight and the input value transferred *via* this weight. Also, realise that this input is at the same time the output $_i^1 y_p = f(_i^1 \alpha_p)$ of the ith neuron in the first layer. In this way we obtain

$$-\mu_t \frac{\partial \varepsilon}{\partial \, _j^2 w_i} \approx 2\mu_t (\, _jd_p - f(\, _j^2\alpha_p)) f'(\, _j^2\alpha_p) f(\, _i^1\alpha_p)$$

$$= 2\mu_t f'(\, _j^2\alpha_p) \, _j^2 e_p \, _i^1 y_p. \qquad (13.12)$$

Substituting this result into eqn (13.10) and arranging the components into a vector, we obtain the correction formula for the weight vector of the jth output-layer neurone

$$_j^2\mathbf{w}(t+1) = \, _j^2\mathbf{w}(t) + 2\mu \, f'(\, _j^2\alpha_p) \, _j^2 e_p \, ^1\mathbf{y}_p. \qquad (13.13)$$

The derived iterative correction that gradually minimises the local error of the jth network output (and in this way also that of the total square error ε), is obviously an application of the δ-rule (13.5), the validity of which is thus proved even in the case of nonlinear neurons. The nonlinearity manifests itself only in influencing the iteration (speed) constant given by the product $2\mu_t f'(\, _j^2\alpha_p)$.

To evaluate the expression (13.11) for neurons of the first layer, we have to take into account the fact that, because of the complete interconnection, the output of a single first-layer neuron influences all neurons of the output layer, therefore also their outputs. When ε_p is given by eqn (13.9), the influence of every first-layer output will be characterised by the function chain

$$\varepsilon_p = \varepsilon_p(f(\, _1^2\alpha_p(\, _i^1 y_p)), \, f(\, _2^2\alpha_p(\, _i^1 y_p)), \cdots, \, f(\, _M^2\alpha_p(\, _i^1 y_p)))$$

and

$$_i^1 y_p = f(\, _i^1\alpha_p). \qquad (13.14)$$

Considering the general rule

$$\frac{dg}{dt} = \sum_{i=1}^{m} \left(\frac{\partial g}{\partial x_i} \frac{dx_i}{dt} \right),$$

if $g = g(x_1, x_2, \cdots, x_m)$ and $x_i = x_i(t)$, $\forall i$, we obtain for the first factor in formula (13.11), when taking into account eqns (13.9) and (13.3),

$$\frac{\partial \varepsilon_p}{\partial f(\, _i^1\alpha_p)} = \sum_{j=1}^{M} \left(\frac{\partial \varepsilon_p}{\partial \, _j^2\alpha_p} \frac{\partial \, _j^2\alpha_p}{\partial \, _i^1 y_p} \right) = \sum_{j=1}^{M} \left(\frac{\partial (\, _jd_p - \, _jy_p)^2}{\partial \, _j^2\alpha_p} \, _j^2 w_i \right),$$

as, in the sum on the right hand side of eqn (13.9), only the difference at the jth output of the network is influenced by the activation $_j^2\alpha_p$. Further, we have

$$\frac{\partial \varepsilon_p}{\partial f(_i^1\alpha_p)} = \sum_{j=1}^{M} \left(\frac{\partial (_jd_p - f(_j^2\alpha_p))^2}{\partial _j^2\alpha_p} \, _j^2 w_i \right)$$

$$= \sum_{j=1}^{M} \left(\frac{\partial (_jd_p - f(_j^2\alpha_p))^2}{f(\partial _j^2\alpha_p)} \, \frac{\partial f(_j^2\alpha_p)}{\partial _j^2\alpha_p} \, _j^2 w_i \right)$$

$$= -2 \sum_{j=1}^{M} ((_jd_p - f(_j^2\alpha_p)) f'(_j^2\alpha_p) _j^2 w_i)$$

$$= -2 \sum_{j=1}^{M} (_j^2 e_p f'(_j^2\alpha_p) _j^2 w_i),$$

and finally, after substituting into (13.11) we obtain

$$-\mu_t \frac{\partial \varepsilon}{\partial _i^1 w_k} \approx -\mu_t \frac{\partial \varepsilon_p}{\partial _i^1 w_k} = 2\mu_t \sum_{j=1}^{M} (_j^2 e_p \, f'(_j^2\alpha_p) _j^2 w_i) f'(_i^1\alpha_p) _k x_p.$$

To preserve a formal similarity with the modified δ-rule (13.12), we shall denote the sum as the error transformed from the network outputs to the output of the jth first-layer neuron,

$$_i^1 e_p = \sum_{j=1}^{M} (_j^2 e_p \, f'(_j^2\alpha_p) _j^2 w_i). \tag{13.15}$$

We can easily see that this result approximately corresponds to the heuristically-designed expression (13.6). The only difference is in multiplying every term in the sum by the derivative of the higher-level neuron characteristic. Therefore, after distributing the errors according to 'back propagation', eqn (13.15), the corrections of weights of every first-layer neuron are calculated locally according to the δ-rule, analogously to eqn (13.13),

$$_i^1 w(t+1) = _i^1 w(t) + 2\mu_t f'(_i^1\alpha_p) _i^1 e_p \, \mathbf{x}_p. \tag{13.16}$$

In the case of multilayer networks, it is possible to use a generalised procedure: using the derived formula (13.15) we can determine the distributed errors in the last-but-one layer when simply substituting the layer indices $2 \to n$, $1 \to n-1$. Then, based on these errors, the errors in the layer $n-2$ will be similarly determined etc. until the first layer.

As the derived weight-correcting expressions contain derivatives of neuronal characteristics, the characteristics must be smooth (continuously differentiable) and, with respect to the desired elimination of local minima of optimisation criterion, also monotonous. Both the requirements are fulfilled by the sigmoidal characteristics; therefore, these are the ones most frequently used. Obviously the methods described cannot be used for learning of networks with thresholding neurons.

Learning by means of a training set leads to modifications of the network weights so that the network gradually approximates the required input–output transform more closely; nevertheless, the improvement in this sense is not necessarily a monotonous function of the number of pattern vectors shown. To quantify the degree to which the network has come near to the required behaviour (formulated by a concrete problem), we shall introduce the term *network effectiveness*. In classification tasks, the effectiveness is defined simply by the relative frequency of proper classifications on the whole class of admissible patterns. In simple (scalar output) approximation tasks it is given, for example, by mean-square error with respect to desired values; in multi-dimensional approximations it may be by the mean length of the error vector or the mean of the angle difference between the required and resulting vector, and the like. The practically unavailable mean error values can usually be approximated by averages of a certain (rather high) number of last experimental results so that the influence of the inherent variance is reasonably limited. Often, the averages are taken over the last learning epoch, that is over the actual results for all the couples of the training set.

A typical course of the effectiveness, as determined during learning by the training-set couples, is depicted by the upper curve in Figure 13.8. The effectiveness improves rather quickly at the beginning, then the increase slows down remarkably and possibly stops completely; the so-called plateau of effectiveness is reached. When learning with the same training set continues, its effectiveness (with respect to this training set) will start growing again after a certain number of experiments and it may approach the optimum.

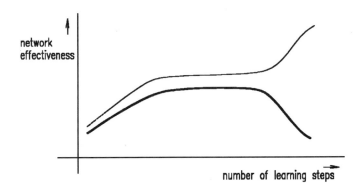

Figure 13.8 Typical development of network effectiveness during learning with respect to training and testing sets

For practical reasons, the training set is always finite. Therefore, it represents the required transform, which is to be realised by the network, only by selected samples shown to the network usually repeatedly in the course of the learning process. The common organisation of learning assumes that all the available learning patterns will be shown to the network in the frame of one epoch, perhaps in a different order in every epoch. With respect to the generally low learning efficiency, many epochs are usually needed. The network naturally has to process other than only the learning vectors, so that a certain ability for learned *knowledge generalisation* is required. This is to be understood so that the input vectors which differ only slightly from learning vectors should also lead to only slightly different answers for the network. Thus, for instance in a classification problem, vectors differing from the learning vector only by some defects (e.g. noise), should be classified identically. Only the network's effectiveness with respect to the testing set, i.e. to vectors that were not a part of the training set, is a realistic measure of its usefulness. If the network is independently tested during learning by vectors of couples with known answers that form the *testing set* (e.g. always after a certain number of learning steps), the course of the effectiveness evaluated in this way is markedly different from the previous one. The typical curve is depicted in Figure 13.8: at the beginning, the curve basically follows the course of effectiveness with respect to the training set although the effectiveness with respect to the testing set is naturally always somewhat lower. However, after reaching the plateau, this effectiveness does not increase any more and, after the number of experiments when the first curve started to grow again, it usually declines.

This phenomenon is explained by *over-training* of the network. While the first ascending section of the curve probably corresponds to the representation of the essential features of the mapping which enable good generalisation, reaching the plateau means exhaustion of detectable general properties. The new increase in effectiveness with respect to the training set is then explained by finding detailed specific features of individual training vectors to which the network then closely adapts. However, this occurs at the cost of the possibility of generalisation because these particular features do not already carry substantial, characteristic information but rather unimportant details. Thus the over-trained network, in which possibly the individual neurons or their groups are directly adapted to concrete pattern vectors, loses the ability for generalisation in the sense that even a negligible difference in the pattern leads to improper classification. The network then becomes a mere memory without intelligence.

Elementary prevention of over-training naturally consists in well timed termination of learning, which should end at the instant of reaching the plateau when the effectiveness stops growing to an important extent. Another effective possibility is to alter moderately the training vectors by random noise, which disables the adaptation to unimportant details; however, the deterioration must not be systematic, or so large, that a wrong classification would emerge. Finally, probably the smartest method of preventing over-training is formation of a 'bottleneck', a narrow path in the network, which would not allow internal representation of the erratic detailed transformation to form. In feedforward networks this can be achieved easily if a hidden layer consists of only a low number of neurons so that the amount of information transferred to higher layers is limited. It turns out that networks of this kind are capable of forming such weight structures that only the most important characteristic information is passed through the bottleneck. This approach has interesting implications also in signal-data compression.

13.4 Feedback networks

In this section we shall deal briefly with networks in which mutual inter-connections and/or feedback connections exist, thus not only the unidirectional information transfer, as was the case with feedforward nets. There exist many different paradigms of such networks with different types of connections among neurons and consequently with different types of behaviour. The use of such networks is still rather exceptional in signal processing; we shall there-fore limit ourselves to only basic information on the types where successful application in signal processing or classification has been reported on in the literature.

A milestone in neural-network development that led to a revival of interest after stagnation in the 1970s was the introduction of the *Hopfield network* paradigm, the basic structure of which is presented in the example of Figure 13.9. The network formed by N neurons is generally fully interconnected (possibly with some couplings being zero). The couplings w_{ik} are mutual, i.e. the transfer is identical in both directions; the right-hand part of the figure depicts how such a coupling can be interpreted in terms of classical neurons. The characteristics of neurons are typically of the threshold type with Boolean output values $(0, 1)$; the threshold ϑ_i is the individual parameter of each

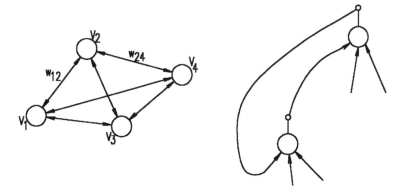

Figure 13.9 Hopfield network

neuron. Neurons operate in principle independently with the limitation that, in a certain instant of the discrete time used, the state (output) of only one neuron may be changed in the frame of the whole network. Which neuron obtains the chance to change its state is random, and commonly the probability of this chance is equal for all neurons in the network. The result, that is whether the state of the chosen neuron will really be changed, depends on its instantaneous activation. This is given, in relation to the threshold of the neuron, by the states of all connected neurons mediated by the weights of the interconnections.

The state of the network in a certain time instant is defined as the vector of all individual neuronal states. The state diagram is then a graph of 2^N nodes which correspond to individual states of the network. The edges (links) of it correspond to admissible transitions among the states – of course only transitions leading from a state to the states which differ in the state of only one neuron are admissible. It can be shown for a concrete network that certain transitions (possible in principle) cannot occur, as the previous state does not provide the activation needed to change the state of the concrete neuron. For instance, the state diagram of the network from Figure 13.9 will have 16 nodes; without knowing the concrete weights and thresholds defining the network it is nevertheless impossible to determine which transitions are excluded.

The notion of *energy of the ith neuron* is introduced which is defined as

$$E_i = -V_i\alpha_i = -V_i\left(\sum_j w_{ij} V_j - \vartheta_i\right), \tag{13.17}$$

where V_i is the state (output) of the neuron and α_i is its activation. (Of course, the energy concept is just a mathematical abstraction and has nothing to do with physical energy unless specifically defined so for some application problem modelled by the network.) The total *energy of the network* is given by the sum of individual neuronal energies,

$$E = -\sum_i V_i\alpha_i. \tag{13.18}$$

The energy of a single neuron (13.17) can only drop or remain unchanged when the neuron changes its state. Indeed, the change is $\Delta E_i = -\Delta V_i\alpha_i$ as the activation given by the states of other neurons is fixed in the transition of the single neuron. Then, if the state change is $0 \rightarrow 1$, so that $\Delta V_i > 0$, this is only possible if $\alpha_i > 0$ and therefore $\Delta E_i < 0$. In the case of the opposite change, $1 \rightarrow 0$, $\Delta V_i < 0$ and $\alpha_i \leq 0$ so that $\Delta E_i \leq 0$. The global result is that even the total network energy can only decrease or at maximum remain on the previous level,

$$\Delta E \leq 0. \tag{13.19}$$

This result has a fundamental importance for behaviour and, consequently, for applications of Hopfield networks and networks derived from them. It means that only basically unidirectional progression is possible in the state diagram, from states with a higher energy to those of a lower (or maximally equal) one. Although the state diagram has stochastic transitions, it is obvious that, after a sufficiently high number of steps, the network will reach (with probability approaching one) a state from which there is no escape. Such network states where there is no transition to a state of a lower or equal energy are denoted as *attractors*. A network can have, depending on its configuration and set of parameters (weights and thresholds), a single attractor, or it may have more attractors; in this case, the total energies belonging to the individual attractors are generally different. It depends then on the character of the application whether the purpose is to reach the absolute minimum of energy or if, on the contrary, we want to utilise the fact that a number of attractors is available.

An example of a simple Hopfield network and the corresponding state flow diagram is in Figure 13.10. The states (nodes in the diagram) are represented by rectangles with the state as a binary vector $[V_1, V_2, V_3]$ mentioned at the top; the decimal number expresses the state energy. The links of the graph are denoted by the probabilities of the respective transitions. There are two attractors in the network, labelled A and B, of which B represents the absolute minimum of energy. In brackets, the Hamming distances from the relevant state to the attractors are mentioned in the order (to A, to B).

In applications concerning data processing (including signals) the network is usually used in the mode where the binary input vector of length N is assigned as the network state at the beginning of work. This means that the states of the individual neurons must be set correspondingly before the first cycle of operation. The output vector is normally defined as the vector of the same length

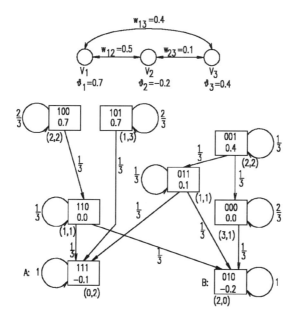

Figure 13.10 Concrete Hopfield network and its state-flow diagram

represented by the final state of the network at the end of its work, which is usually terminated when the network is trapped into an attractor. Let us add that the possibilities of the network will be markedly widened if we introduce intrinsic (hidden) nodes. These do not become parts of input and output vectors, but increase the number of network states; then, naturally, the number of neurons in the network is higher than the length N of data vectors.

The network can be utilised in several different modes. An interesting application is the use of the Hopfield network as *associative memory*. This application assumes that the network has a greater number of attractors; the corresponding states represent the memorised (saved) information vectors. The network must be suitably adjusted (usually by means of learning), so that transitions from other states representing the partially modified vectors are (always or at least with a high probability) heading to the attractor which is most similar to the shown vector. In the example in Figure 13.10, it can be seen that the degree of similarity of individual state vectors to the vectors of attractors, as represented by Hamming distances, is different. Different also are the probabilities that the network will recover one or other of the attractors as the response to an initial state – 'distorted' input vector, as can be seen from Table 13.1.

It is therefore possible to submit incomplete information to the network in the form of differently distorted vectors – initial states of the network; after a number of steps, the network will recover (by transition to an attractor) the related memorised vector. From a practical point of view, it should be observed that the memory capacity, given by the number of realisable attractors, is only a negligible fraction of the memory capacity needed for realisation of the network. This is the price for the robustness of the memory addressed by imprecise (or incomplete) data.

The required attractors (more precisely, the corresponding weight set) can theoretically be provided by solving extensive systems of nonequalities, but this is so clumsy and laborious a procedure that, in practice, almost only adjustment of weights by learning is used. However, the learning usually leads to the

Table 13.1

Initial state	Final state:	A		B	
	Hamming distance	transition probability	Hamming distance	transition probability
001	2	0.75	2	0.25
000	3	0	1	1
011	1	0.5	1	0.5
100	2	0.5	2	0.5
110	1	0.5	1	0.5
101	1	1	3	0
A: 111	0	1	2	0
B: 010	2	0	0	1

result that, apart from the required attractors, even undesirable attractors (false patterns) emerge, to which the memory can converge improperly. In this way, the associative memory performance may be deteriorated. We will not deal with the mentioned algorithms of learning, with respect to so-far lesser importance of this application in the field of signal processing.

Another application of this type of network is solving optimisation problems. The basic idea consists in formulating the optimisation task in such a way that the network states describe, possibly indirectly, the parameters of the task (e.g. signal values). The criterion of optimality, as defined for the given problem, is somehow transformed so that it corresponds to the energy of the network. The optimisation is performed in such a mode that the initial state of the problem is represented by the initial state of the network. The network is then working autonomously, and hopefully, after a number of steps, it will arrive at the state with the minimum energy corresponding to the optimum solution of the task. Of course, it is desirable to achieve the absolute minimum in this case, so that trapping in a local minimum should be avoided. Sometimes it is possible to formulate the problem in such a way that the side attractors will not emerge at all, or the probability of transition to them is sufficiently small.

More often, such prevention is unavailable and then a significant modification in the concept of the network may be used which enables transitions even to states with a higher energy, thus allowing escaping from local minima. The modification consists in replacing the *deterministic neurons* by *stochastic* ones that are distinguished by the characteristics in which the activation does not determine uniquely the new state of the neuron but only the probabilities of both possible new states. In the course of the network operation, the stochastic characteristics are gradually modified so that the uncertainty decreases until the network ends as deterministic, but with increased probability of reaching the absolute minimum. This approach is called 'simulated annealing' in analogy with a metallurgical process, aiming for a similar goal of minimising inner energy. Networks utilising this concept are usually denoted as *Boltzmann machines*.

Before concluding this section, let us briefly mention some other types of neural network with mutual couplings or feedback connections. One such type is represented by *competitive networks* which realise, usually in a sequential manner, selection of one competing hypothesis. The simplest example is the MAXNET, a fully interconnected synchronous net of M neurons with characteristics limited from left and with weights $w_{ij} = 1$ for $i = j$, and $w_{ij} = -\varepsilon$ for $i \neq j$, $0 < \varepsilon < 1/M$. These latter inhibition couplings give that, after a sufficient number of cycles, only a single important nonzero component of the output vector remains of all the initially nonzero components. The 'winning' component is the one the value of which was maximum at the start of operation. At this place, it is possible to state that the operation of a recursive network can usually be described by a finite or infinite feedforward network which originates by recursive expansion of the feedback net, as shown in Figure 13.11. It points to the fundamental possibility of teaching these networks by the

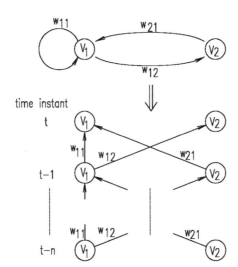

Figure 13.11 Principle of recursive expansion of networks

error backpropagation method, if the limitations following from the expansion can be reflected.

It is also possible to generalise feedforward networks by introducing feedback connections from the output to the input of the whole network. At the same time, local feedbacks are provided in certain neurons which then serve as memory elements. In this way, so-called *Jordan networks* are introduced that were devised to simulate the operation of dynamic systems and to produce not only static vectors but rather time sequences of output vectors as the response to a fixed controlling vector.

13.5 Self-organising maps

Self-organising maps form another group of algorithms that are able to learn from the processed information. The purpose of these algorithms is mostly classification of input vectors into groups – classes which usually are generated autonomously in the course of data processing, i.e. not given *a priori* by a chosen classification. The process of generating such classification is sometimes called *self learning (unsupervised learning)* in contrast to learning under the guidance of a teacher (supervised learning), which is typical for feedforward networks.

We shall concentrate on *Kohonen maps* which represent a contemporary effective means of automatic creation of classification; they are also widely used in the area of signal processing. Let us mention that, although the maps are generally considered to be one of the fundamental classes of neural network, the algorithm is not commonly realised by means of neurons although some partial steps could be performed by them. The idea of using the network is rather an instrument to introduce certain metrics based on the notion of distance in an auxiliary space. This space plays a crucial role in the concept of these networks.

A *Kohonen map* realises a mapping from a continuous space of n-dimensional signal vectors onto a discrete set of vectors from the same space, which will be denoted as original space (left part of Figure 13.12),

$$\{\mathbf{x}\} \rightarrow \{\mathbf{m}_i\}, \quad \mathbf{x}, \mathbf{m}_i \in \Re^n. \tag{13.20}$$

As the process of data evaluation and self learning is performed in discrete steps, we shall denote $\mathbf{x} = \mathbf{x}(t)$, $\mathbf{m}_i = \mathbf{m}_i(t)$, $t = 1, 2, \cdots$. The mapping is defined as follows: the vector $\mathbf{x}(t)$ is compared with all the patterns $\mathbf{m}_i(t)$, $i = 1, 2, \cdots, K$ in their instantaneous state, and the pattern $\mathbf{m}_c(t)$, for which the criterion of similarity with the input vector is optimum, is considered the result of the mapping. Thus, if the criterion is the minimum distance (magnitude of the difference vector), the pattern found is the vector

$$\mathbf{m}_c(t) : \|\mathbf{x}(t) - \mathbf{m}_c(t)\| = \min_i \|\mathbf{x}(t) - \mathbf{m}_i(t)\|.$$

The set of patterns is then modified in every step, as will be shown further, and in this way a suitable set of patterns in the mentioned space is generated. Let us specify more precisely what is meant by a suitable set.

It can be observed that the mapping (13.20) can be understood as being *vector quantisation*, by which the vector $\mathbf{x}$ is approximated by the nearest of the patterns. Optimal distribution of patterns in the original space can be defined as such that leads to minimisation of the mean-square error of this approximation. Should the probability distribution of $\mathbf{x}$ occurrence in the original space be $p(\mathbf{x})$, the mean-square error will be equal to the sum

$$\varepsilon = \sum_c \left(\int \cdots_{\Omega_c} \int \|\mathbf{x} - \mathbf{m}_c\|^2 p(\mathbf{x}) dV_{\mathbf{x}} \right),$$

$$\Omega_c = \{\mathbf{x} : \|\mathbf{x} - \mathbf{m}_c\| = \min_i \|\mathbf{x} - \mathbf{m}_i\|\}, \tag{13.21}$$

in which the individual terms express the contributions to the error caused by vectors belonging to individual areas Ω_c. Every such area is represented by the corresponding pattern $\mathbf{m}_c$. It can be derived that ε will be minimum if the density of patterns as a function of position vector (characterised approximately by averages in small volumes) will approximate the function $(p(\mathbf{x}))^{n/(n+2)} \approx p(\mathbf{x})$ (for common values $n \gg 1$). This could be expected, even intuitively. In the high-probability areas of vector $\mathbf{x}$ occurrence, a high density of patterns is needed in order to keep the errors due to quantisation small enough, as they will appear frequently thus substantially influencing the mean value of error. The desired set of generated patterns should therefore have approximately this property.

It is possible to arrive at such a distribution iteratively by means of *competitive learning (self learning)* in which the individual steps consist in two phases. In the first phase, the optimum pattern $\mathbf{m}_c(t)$ is found for a given input vector $\mathbf{x}(t)$; in the second phase, this pattern is modified according to the relation

$$\mathbf{m}_c(t+1) = \mathbf{m}_c(t) + \mu_t[\mathbf{x}(t) - \mathbf{m}_c(t)], \qquad (13.22)$$

(where μ_t is a chosen iteration constant, $\mu_t \in (0, 1)$), while the other patterns remain untouched. It is seen that the correction moves the nearest pattern closer to the input vector (for $\mu_t = 1$, the pattern would be substituted for by the input vector). During many steps, the patterns thus gradually become cumulated in areas of the original space with a high probability of input-vector occurrence. It can be proved that the correction according to eqn (13.22) is also the modification step in the sense of the steepest descent of the error criterion (13.21), so that, after a sufficient number of steps, the pattern distribution reaches the optimum. It is sensible to decrease the value of the iteration constant gradually in the course of learning. In this way, a faster convergence in the initial stage of learning and a stable descent during the final stage, even in the neighbourhood of a minimum, could be achieved. So far, only a well known approach to finding the optimum pattern lexicon for vector coding by means of competitive learning has been discussed; learning of Kohonen networks is partly modified as will be presented next.

The central idea of Kohonen maps consists in their second property: n-dimensional patterns are mapped into space of a generally lower dimension k (Figure 13.12, right-hand part), in which every pattern $\mathbf{m}_i$ is represented by a so-called detector $\mathbf{u}_i$,

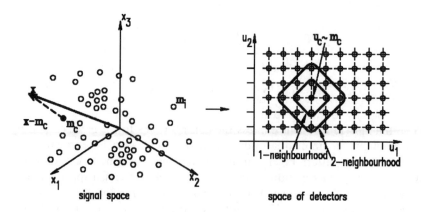

Figure 13.12 Double space of Kohonen maps

$${\mathbf{m}_i} \to {\mathbf{u}_i}, \quad \mathbf{m}_i \in \mathfrak{R}^n, \mathbf{u}_i \in \mathfrak{R}^k, \forall i, k \leq n,$$

(usually, $k = 1$ or $k = 2$). This mapping is fixed and given by the organisation of the experiment. The *space of detectors* is created in this way: commonly, a line or a plane on which the detectors are distributed – on the line usually equidistantly; on the plane in nodes of a rectangular or hexagonal grid. We shall introduce a suitable *metrics in the space of detectors* which would enable us to determine the mutual distance $d(\mathbf{u}_i, \mathbf{u}_j)$ for any couple of detectors; it may be, for example, the absolute value of difference of indices for the linear arrangement. On the plane, the distance can be defined as e.g. the sum of absolute differences of both indices, or as another distance, e.g. Euclidean. Then it is possible to introduce the notion of the *L-neighbourhood* of the detector $\mathbf{u}_i$, which is the set of detectors

$${\mathbf{u}_j : d(\mathbf{u}_j, \mathbf{u}_i) \leq L}. \tag{13.23}$$

In the course of learning, the components of pattern vectors are changing so that the corresponding points which represent the patterns are moving in the original space. At the beginning of learning process, the points are distributed randomly in the space; they should only be mutually different in order that it is always possible to find the closest (although perhaps distant) pattern to each input vector. The pattern-modification rule in the learning mode is modified in Kohonen networks: the correction analogous to (13.22) is applied not only to the determined optimal pattern but also to all other patterns which have their corresponding detectors in a chosen *L-neighbourhood* of the detector $\mathbf{u}_c$,

$$\mathbf{m}_j(t+1) = \mathbf{m}_j(t) + \mu_t[\mathbf{x}(t) - \mathbf{m}_j(t)], \quad \mathbf{m}_j : d(\mathbf{u}_c, \mathbf{u}_j) \leq L,$$

where $\mathbf{u}_c, \mathbf{u}_j$ are detectors belonging to the patterns $\mathbf{m}_c, \mathbf{m}_j$. According to experience, L is to be chosen such that, at the beginning of learning, the neighbourhood encompasses almost the whole space of detectors. During the learning, this is gradually reduced and, in the final stage, it could be limited even to $L = 0$. This allows fine tuning of individual patterns to the optimum distribution according to eqn (13.22) without other patterns being influenced concurrently. Experiments show that, after a sufficient number of steps, the optimal distribution of the set of patterns in the sense of minimal mean error is created. Furthermore, the created patterns are then represented in the space of detectors in such a way that detectors of patterns with similar features are positioned closely in this space and usually form clusters. It should be stressed that the detector positions are fixed during the whole learning process; only points representing the corresponding patterns in the original space move. The features appearing to be significant, according to which the clustering of detectors occurs, emerge automatically in the course of learning, without using any *a priori* classification and without any intervention of the operator. Thus, the process may lead to a new classification, independent of established rankings.

The neighbourhood definition according to (13.23) together with the modified correction mechanism (13.24) mean that all the patterns, corresponding to the detectors of the neighbourhood, are corrected by the same amount. It turns out that a modification may be useful which modifies the correcting term by multiplying it with a suitable weight function $\eta(d)$ dependent on the distance between the optimum detector and the detector of the pattern to be modified. Such a suitable function is, for example, a Gaussian bell of selectable variance which determines the size of the equivalent (uniformly weighted) neighbourhood. It can then be understood as a definition of a certain 'fuzzy' neighbourhood and the weight can be interpreted as the measure of the membership degree of individual detectors. The mentioned modification probably corresponds better to similar organisational processes in biological neural nets but a precisely formalised analysis is still not available (as generally for Kohonen networks, with the exception of extremely simplified cases).

13.6 Applications of neural networks in signal processing

The most frequently used neural networks in the signal processing field are feed-forward networks. The simplest straightforward application of a neural network functioning as a signal processor is presented in Figure 13.13. Here, the input vector of the neural network is directly a section of the input signal $\{x_n\}$. The system can thus be regarded as an FIR nonlinear filter, in which the network realises the nonlinear operator providing the current output sample y_n as dependent on the vector $\mathbf{x}_n = [x_n, x_{n-1}, \cdots, x_{n-N+1}]^T$. Whether the network is fixed with the weights set *a priori* based on some rules or learns in the course of signal processing depends on the application. Notice that the principle of the neural network enables its output to be a vector; this case will be discussed in one of the following paragraphs.

It is obvious that a nonlinear *neural adaptive filter* can be designed, the principle of which corresponds to the concept in Figure 11.1; the signal flow diagram of such a filter is shown in Figure 13.14. Filters of this type have been successfully verified in applications for the correction of nonlinearities of sensors and for local image filtering.

The concept of a neuronal filter can naturally be generalised to the recursive case of the IIR neuronal filter as in Figure 13.15; nevertheless, the probable problems of instability of such a filter should also be pointed out. The fact that the neural network in principle realises a vector function of a vector argument can find its natural utilisation in the state representation of a nonlinear dynamic system according to eqns (12.3). The nonlinear functions of this representation – $\overline{\Psi}_q(.)$, $\overline{\Psi}_y(.)$ – are of the type mentioned and can be realised by means of feedforward neural networks. In the general case, both the input and output signals may then be sequences of vectors.

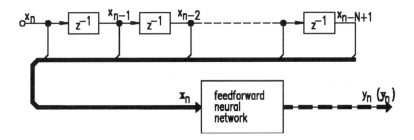

Figure 13.13 Nonrecursive processing of signals by a feedforward network

More often than direct processing of input signals into the corresponding output signals, we can meet applications of neural networks for the *classification of signals*. Then, the output of the network in every working cycle is a decision consisting of determining which class a set of classes the signal belongs to. In principle, it is of course possible to utilise the concept according to Figure 13.13 with a vector output meaning symbols of classes; interpreted in this way the system classifies sliding segments of the input signal, N-samples long. The coded symbols of successively recognised classes form the output sequence $\{\mathbf{y}_n\}$. This approach is only rarely possible as practical classification aspects are seldom given by distinctive features in the original (time) domain. If it is barely possible to define such original domain features, reliable results of the network, trained on patterns with such hard-to-define features, cannot be expected. In spite of this, some successful applications were published concerning *recognition* of characteristic waves in signals (namely in biological signals, particularly EEG) or characteristic shapes in two-dimensional image signals. The latter case commonly concerns local filtering in relatively small windows encompassing a neighbourhood of several pixels in diameter. Interesting and rather successful experiments concerned classification of phonems (speech-signal sections) by their recognition from the lips of a speaker, as visible on a sequence of video images. The images were directly recognised in the original domain by a two-layer feedforward network with the necessary number of alternative parallel outputs corresponding to the individual phonems.

The effectiveness of learning and consequently even exploitation of the network can often be substantially increased when the network is supplied not by the original signal sections but rather by a certain signal description (Figure 13.16). Such a description by features, in other than the original domain, can be obtained by means of a suitable analytical method, such as by spectral or correlation analysis. This approach is particularly successful in cases where the original domain description requires a large amount of data and signals evidently belonging to different classes are not easily distinguishable, although their properties in the transformed feature space can be described by a few parameters and the differences are obvious. A suitable transform is

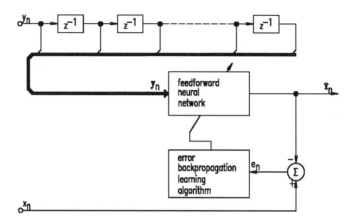

Figure 13.14 Adaptive FIR nonlinear filter with learning neural network

therefore one which possibly leads to data reduction without markedly influencing the information content. Then, the network can not only be much simpler, having by orders of magnitude a lower number of inputs, but primarily, owing to easier recognition, the complexity and length of the learning process may decrease substantially. Consequently, much more reliable classification can be expected.

The most commonly used kinds of transform are different types of spectral analysis, as many practically important tasks are optimally described in the frequency domain, in consequence of their physical substance or with respect to the character of their final evaluation. In most published applications, short-time amplitude or power spectra are utilised which are derived by means of the FFT from finite signal sections that are either partly overlapping or just joined together. Very extensive literature deals with the analysis of speech signals oriented in this direction; the authors differ in their choice of signal-

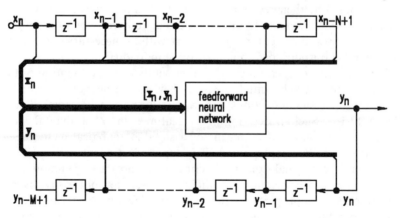

Figure 13.15 Recursive neural filter

section length, their overlap, number of frequency coefficients used and range of frequency bands described by these coefficients. The neural network evaluating the spectral information is mostly a multilayer feedforward structure of different architectures. It seems that neither the choice of layer number nor the number of neurons in the layers is critical. After sufficiently long supervised learning, an acceptable classification can usually be achieved, if the properties expressed by the feature vectors obtained by the transform were chosen properly.

An alternative solution for the recognition part of the system may be a self-organising classifier based on a Kohonen network or a similar algorithm using competitive learning. Such a system would generate the classification itself, often with a higher degree of respect for the real character of the signal, such as speech (transition of phonems etc.), than an *a priori* man-designed classification which often suffers from unjustifiable assumptions. Recognition of words with an acceptable error rate, which requires learning sequences of at least thousands of words, is still mostly bound to a particular speaker. However, it is already possible to re-learn the algorithm to another speaker quickly using learning sequences of only several hundred words.

Based also on the power or amplitude spectrum, although in other frequency ranges, it is possible to analyse acoustic (also sub or ultrasonic) signals or mechanical vibrations caused by operation of rotating or vibrating mechanisms. In this way, the quality or wear of the machines can be evaluated. Another application of a similar kind is recognition of character of sounds developed

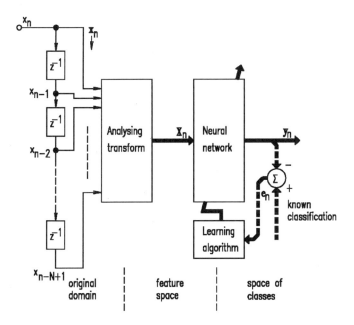

Figure 13.16 Classification of signals by a neural network in feature space

in the respiratory tract of humans. Surprisingly good results have been achieved by analysing electromyographic signals sensed on an operator's wrist in only one or two channels (in the latter case, by slightly displaced electrodes). Frequency analysis in roughly the acoustic range has yielded ten-component vectors of spectral coefficients which the following two-layer feedforward network was able to classify after a relatively long period of learning. The classification led either to one of five classes meaning movements of different fingers or to ten-component vectors expressing required mutual angles of finger elements in ten different joints. The robot hand controlled by these data copied surprisingly well the movement of the operator's hand. This example shows how learning-based classification may enable us to gain the needed information from a very modest measurement. When realising that tens of muscles had to be controlled, it could be expected that the relevant amount of information could only be provided from measurements directly on these muscles. It is surprising that the necessary information could have been obtained from rather noisy and seemingly, with the finger-movements, uncorrelated signals, moreover sensed in the location where all the controlling signals are necessarily passing and thus mutually interfering. It is of course possible that, in consequence of the 'bottleneck', mentioned earlier, of the biological communication channel, a single suitably compressed signal is passing in the mentioned place. The compression code of the biosignal might have been partially deciphered by the neural network. Unfortunately, this does not mean that it is possible to formulate explicitly the mentioned coding on the basis of the weight set of the network, which carries the information in a hidden form.

A very interesting result, mentioned in Reference [30], is the successful restoration of images, degraded by convolution and additive noise, by means of a Hopfield-type network. The network is formulated so that it describes the image directly by its states – the individual pixel values are characterised by states of groups of neurons. The restoration criterion is defined basically as in the restoration method of constrained deconvolution (see Section 10.5). Owing to a suitable network structure, the criterion is, in each step of network operation, numerically equal to the energy of the network, as defined in Section 13.4. The image is gradually restored by progressive descent of the network state in the state diagram of the network, towards lower energy levels. When reaching a minimum, the image turns out restored with a quality comparable to the results of classical approaches, although it cannot be guaranteed that the absolute minimum has been reached. However, a network, designed for this purpose, had huge dimensions.

Chapter 14
Multidimensional signals

14.1 Continuous multidimensional signals and systems

14.1.1 Concept of multidimensional signals

The purpose of this section is to outline a generalised version of the theory that we have used so far in this book for the field of signals dependent on more than just a single variable. We shall define a *multidimensional continuous signal* as a scalar function of a continuous vector argument

$$f(\mathbf{x}),$$

where the physical meaning of the function value and of the components of $\mathbf{x}$ is arbitrary. Probably the most common example of a multidimensional signal is a static greyscale plane image, which is described by the brightness (or reflectivity) function of two space coordinates, $f(x, y)$. Examples of three-dimensional signals are a time-variable image $f(x, y, t)$ or tomographic space–image data $f(x, y, z)$. In advanced tomography, four-dimensional time-dependent space–image data $f(x, y, z, t)$ is already dealt with. Contemporary computing technology enables the practical solution of many problems relating to multidimensional signals in spite of the enormous computational and memory requirements which follow from such tasks. We shall illustrate the discussion by some simple examples of this kind. It may be expected that future developments will make it possible to process and analyse multidimensional signals by highly sophisticated methods that would be capable of utilising complex inner relationships among elements and components of such signals, although their practical applications are currently rather hypothetical.

Notice that the concept of multidimensional signals can be further generalised to vector signals,

$$\mathbf{f}(\mathbf{x}).$$

This is, for example, the case of colour images: a static colour image is a two-dimensional signal having three-dimensional vector values; the vector elements are the individual colour components, e.g.

$$\mathbf{f}(\mathbf{x}) = [f_R(x, y), f_G(x, y), f_B(x, y)]^T.$$

Another example is given by complex-valued two-dimensional signals as they can be obtained when measuring time-dependent profiles of physical fields,

$$\mathbf{f}(\mathbf{x}) = f_R(x, t) + jf_I(x, t).$$

On the contrary, we do not usually understand as multidimensional the vector-valued signals that are dependent only on one parameter, such as the time-dependent vector signals in the state representation of continuous-time systems.

In further discussion, we shall limit ourselves to the simplest case of multi-dimensional signals, that is *two-dimensional signals* (often denoted as '2D'); as a possible example we shall usually have in mind static greyscale images. Here, an important comment concerning a possible misunderstanding in terminology is needed. In the world of one-dimensional, namely time-dependent signals, the term 'image' usually refers to the transformed counterpart of an original signal (e.g. Fourier spectrum or image in the Z-transform). In this section, we shall reserve the term 'image' for original two-dimensional (2D) signals, and their transformed versions will be called spectra, frequency-domain data and suchlike.

14.1.2 Two-dimensional Fourier transform and linear two-dimensional systems

Many concepts that we used for the processing and analysis of one-dimensional signals can be generalised to the multidimensional case in a straightforward way. They are namely: the Fourier transform, spectra, notion of linear systems and their characteristics, stochastic processes etc., all in continuous and discrete versions. We shall deal first with continuous concepts, then with multidimensional sampling and finally with discrete versions of the individual concepts.

The *two-dimensional Fourier transform* is the straightforward generalisation of the one-dimensional transform,

$$F(u, v) = \mathbb{E}\{f(x, y)\} = \int_{-\infty}^{\infty} \int_{-\infty}^{\infty} f(x, y)e^{-j(ux+vy)}\, dx\, dy. \qquad (14.1)$$

It is therefore a mapping from the original plane (x, y) onto the spectral plane of the so-called *space angular frequencies* (u, v). In this short note, it is not possible to discuss more deeply the interpretation of the result of the transform, which is called the *2D spectrum*. Let us only mention that the absolute space frequency (e.g. $u/2\pi$, more generally $\sqrt{u^2 + v^2}/2\pi$) indicates the number of cycles of an individual harmonic image component on a unit length (i.e. per metre). The transform $F(u, v)$ expresses, similarly as for one-dimensional spectra, the parameters of the harmonic components of which the image consists.

These components are strip-structures with a harmonic course of brightness in profiles perpendicular to the stripes. The space density of stripes corresponds to the absolute space frequency, the image contrast – the difference between the maximum and minimum value of the structure – to the amplitude of the component. The distance of the nearest maximum ridge of this function from the origin of the plane (x, y) is given by the phase of the component. Finally, the last parameter not having any counterpart in the one-dimensional case, the ratio of space frequency components, u/v, determines the direction of 'propagation', that is the orientation of stripes with respect to the coordinate axes. As the transform base consists of complex exponential functions, the spectral representation of a real harmonic component is formed (as in the one-dimensional case) of a couple of impulses, which are now located in the spectral plane symmetrically to the origin. The radial distance from the origin corresponds to the frequency of the component, the magnitude (absolute value of generally complex impulse weight) to the amplitude of the component. The phase of the weight determines the shift of the structure in the original plane with respect to the origin of coordinates. Finally, the angle between the join of both points and the axis u in the frequency domain characterises the direction of 'propagation' of the 'wave' (harmonic component) in the original domain, that is the direction of the perpendicular to ridges of stripes with respect to the x-axis. It is obvious that image rotation by a certain angle around the origin in the original domain corresponds to the rotation of its spectrum by the same angle around the origin in the spectral domain.

The Fourier transform exists for all physically realisable images; also, the inverse transform of the obtained spectra exists which can be derived as

$$f(x, y) = \int_{-\infty}^{\infty} \int_{-\infty}^{\infty} F(u, v) e^{j(ux + vy)} \, du \, dv, \qquad (14.2)$$

so that the 2D Fourier transform is invertible. The definition range and properties of the 2D transform are analogous to those for the one-dimensional case. The most important property of the 2D Fourier transform is the convolutional property: the product of two original functions is transformed into the convolution of the individual spectra of both original components. *Vice versa*, convolution in the original domain corresponds to the product of individual spectra.

A *two-dimensional linear operator* realised by a two-dimensionally and continuously working linear system (e.g. a projection system) transforms an image from the plane of originals (input images) into the plane of output images.[1] The

---

[1] Usually, it is unnecessary to distinguish between coordinates in both planes, as in one-dimensional systems where also only a single variable t is used.

basic property influencing the imaging (mapping) is naturally the validity of the superposition principle. The operator realised by such a linear 2D system is described by the following relationship between the input image $f(x, y)$ and the output image $g(x, y)$,

$$g(x, y) = \int_{-\infty}^{\infty} \int_{-\infty}^{\infty} h(x, y, \xi, \eta) f(\xi, \eta) \, d\xi \, d\eta, \tag{14.3}$$

which is the so-called *superposition integral*. It can be interpreted so that, roughly speaking, every point of the input plane influences every point of the output plane with the intensity given by the weight function $h(.)$. The physical meaning of this function will be clearly understood when a special type of input image is processed, namely the shifted 2D Dirac impulse

$$f(x, y) = \delta(x - x_0, y - y_0),$$

which can be interpreted in the input plane as a single bright point of co-ordinates x_0, y_0 on the black background. Using the sifting property of the Dirac impulse, we obtain from eqn (14.3)

$$g(x, y) = h(x, y, x_0, y_0), \tag{14.4}$$

which means that the function is the response to a point excitation of the system, generally dependent on the position of the source point x_0, y_0. This is why the function is often denoted as the PSF – *point spread function*.

If the response is invariant to the position, that is the shape of the function $h(.)$ is fixed and is only shifted in the output plane correspondingly to the source point position in the input plane, the function will acquire a special form

$$g(x, y) = h(x - x_0, y - y_0). \tag{14.5}$$

The operator of such a linear system is described by the *convolution integral*

$$g(x, y) = \int_{-\infty}^{\infty} \int_{-\infty}^{\infty} h(x - \xi, y - \eta) f(\xi, \eta) \, d\xi \, d\eta = h(x, y) * f(x, y). \tag{14.6}$$

Systems realising this type of operator are called *isoplanar*. They represent an analogy to one-dimensional time-invariant systems and therefore similar characteristics are used to describe them: *two-dimensional impulse response* $h(x, y)$ and its Fourier transform, *two-dimensional frequency response*, also denoted as the *frequency-* or *spectral transfer*,

$$H(u, v) = \mathbb{F}\{h(x, y)\}. \tag{14.7}$$

With respect to the validity of superposition, the output of the system can also be determined *via* the frequency domain, as an alternative way to direct calculation in the original domain according to eqn (14.3). If we determine the spectrum of the input image as

$$F(u, v) = \mathbb{F}\{f(x, y)\},$$

we obtain, using the convolution theorem, the spectrum of the output image as

$$G(u, v) = H(u, v) F(u, v). \tag{14.8}$$

The output image in the original domain can then be obtained by the inverse Fourier transform,

$$g(x, y) = \mathbb{F}^{-1}\{G(u, v)\}.$$

Let us remark that, compared with the widespread use of Laplace and Z-transforms for the analysis of one-dimensional systems and signals, the application of multidimensional versions of these transforms for multidimensional problems appears rather rarely. This is primarily caused by an increase in dimensionality when using any of the transforms; in the case of 2D originals, the Laplace transform and Z-transform are both four-dimensional functions. These are cumbersome to visualise and, should their discretisation be needed, they represent too large an amount of data. Besides that, the theory of these multidimensional transforms still suffers from deficiencies in certain respects.

14.1.3 Stochastic fields

The theory of one-dimensional stochastic processes (Chapter 4) can also be generalised to the multidimensional case in a straightforward manner. Instead of speaking of stochastic processes, we shall prefer the name two-dimensional *stochastic fields* (the term 'process' implies more or less a time dependence). The stochastic fields are characterised by local characteristics analogous as in the case of one-dimensional processes: local *probability distribution* and its moments, namely local mean and variance. To characterise relations inside a stochastic field, which can generate individual images as its realisations, it is necessary (similarly as in the one-dimensional case) to introduce multidimensional joint probability distributions, perhaps even of high orders. As such a description is usually unbearably clumsy, this concept is most often used merely in theoretical considerations and, in practice, only mixed second-order moments are used, namely *correlation* and *covariance functions*, which are generally four dimensional for two-dimensional original space. For instance, the crosscorrelation function of two stochastic 2D fields formed by the function families $f_w(\mathbf{r})$, $g_w(\mathbf{r})$ is defined as the ensemble mean (over all possible results of the associated experiment w),

$$R_{fg}(\mathbf{r}_1, \mathbf{r}_2) = \mathbb{E}\{f_w(\mathbf{r}_1) g_w(\mathbf{r}_2)\} \tag{14.9}$$

where $\mathbf{r}_i = (x_i, y_i)$ is a position vector.

The concept of the two-dimensional *homogeneous field* corresponds to the notion of one-dimensional stationary process; the homogeneous field is commonly defined only in the wider sense, that is fulfilling the conditions of mean-value and correlation-function position invariance, thus

$$\mu_f(\mathbf{r}) = \mu_f(\mathbf{r} + \mathbf{d}) = \mu_f;$$

$$R_{ff}(\mathbf{r}_1, \mathbf{r}_2) = R_{ff}(\mathbf{r}_1 + \mathbf{d}, \mathbf{r}_2 + \mathbf{d}) = R_{ff}(\mathbf{r} - \mathbf{r}_2) = R_{ff}(\Delta\mathbf{r}) \qquad (14.10)$$

where $\mathbf{d}$ is an arbitrary vector. Should a relationship similar to the last one be valid for a crosscorrelation function $R_{fg}(\mathbf{r}_1, \mathbf{r}_2) = R_{fg}(\Delta\mathbf{r})$ of two stochastic fields, the fields will be called *mutually homogeneous*. It is obvious that the homogeneity reduces the dimension of the correlation and covariance functions to a half so that they become much easier-to-handle 2D functions.

As the autocorrelation and crosscorrelation functions are deterministic functions, they can be transformed by a two-dimensional Fourier transform. In this way we obtain the 2D *power spectrum* of a homogeneous field, or 2D *cross-spectrum* of a mutually homogeneous couple of fields,

$$S_{ff}(u, v) = \mathbb{F}\{R_{ff}(\mathbf{r})\} \quad \text{or} \quad S_{fg}(u, v) = \mathbb{F}\{R_{gf}(\mathbf{r})\}. \qquad (14.11)$$

It can be shown that, as in the one-dimensional case, these spectra are mean values of individual power spectra of single realisations or, in the case of cross-spectra, mean values of individual cross-spectra of realisation couples,

$$S_{ff}(u, v) = \mathbb{E}\{F_w(u, v)F_w^*(u, v)\} \quad \text{or} \quad S_{fg}(u, v) = \mathbb{E}\{F_w(u, v)G_w^*(u, v)\}. \qquad (14.12)$$

A special case of homogeneous fields is *ergodic fields* characterised by the possibility of substituting the estimates of stochastic-field characteristics based on ensemble averages (which approximate ensemble mean values) by estimates derived from a single image as space averages, performed over the plane (x, y). A more precise formulation can be obtained by a straightforward generalisation of a one-dimensional ergodicity explanation as given in context with eqns (4.19)–(4.22).

At the end of this section, we shall investigate the effect of linear operators on stochastic fields. In analogy with one-dimensional stochastic processes, it should be understood that, of course, a linear system does not literally process a field, but only its concrete realisations which are deterministic functions and in this sense common two-dimensional signals. The linear-system impact on an individual input-field realisation, $f_{w_i}(\mathbf{r})$ corresponding to the result w_i of the associated experiment, leads according to eqn (14.6) to the output,

$$g_{w_i}(\mathbf{r}) = \iint\limits_{S \in \Xi} h(\mathbf{r} - \mathbf{s}) f_{w_i}(\mathbf{s}) \, dS_{\mathbf{s}},$$

where Ξ denotes the unlimited plane (x, y). All the output functions $g_{w_i}(\mathbf{r})$ $\forall i$, form the family of realisations $g_w(\mathbf{r})$ which constitutes, together with the associated random experiment, w, the output stochastic field. In this sense, it is possible to speak about the processing of stochastic fields by the system.

It can be shown that the output field of an isoplanar system is homogeneous if the input field was homogeneous. Both fields are then characterised by their power spectra which are related as

$$S_{gg}(u, v) = |H(u, v)|^2 S_{ff}(u, v). \qquad (14.13)$$

14.2 Discrete multidimensional signals and systems

14.2.1 Two-dimensional sampling and reconstruction

A discrete representation of an image can be obtained by *rectangular sampling* its continuous version; therefore, in analogy to the one-dimensional case, theoretically by multiplying the image with the sampling function (Figure 14.1),

$$s(x, y) = \sum_{i=-\infty}^{\infty} \sum_{k=-\infty}^{\infty} \delta(x - i\,\Delta x, y - k\,\Delta y),$$

so that the image, sampled in nodes of an equidistant rectangular grid with the space increments Δx, Δy, may be described in the quasicontinuous representation as

$$f_s(x, y) = f(x, y)s(x, y) = \sum_i \sum_k f(i\,\Delta x, k\,\Delta y)\delta(x - i\,\Delta x, y - k\,\Delta y). \qquad (14.14)$$

Providing that the sampling theorem has been observed, the *image matrix* of samples,

$$\bar{\bar{f}} = [_s f_{i,k}], \quad _s f_{i,k} = f(i\,\Delta x, j\,\Delta y), \qquad (14.15)$$

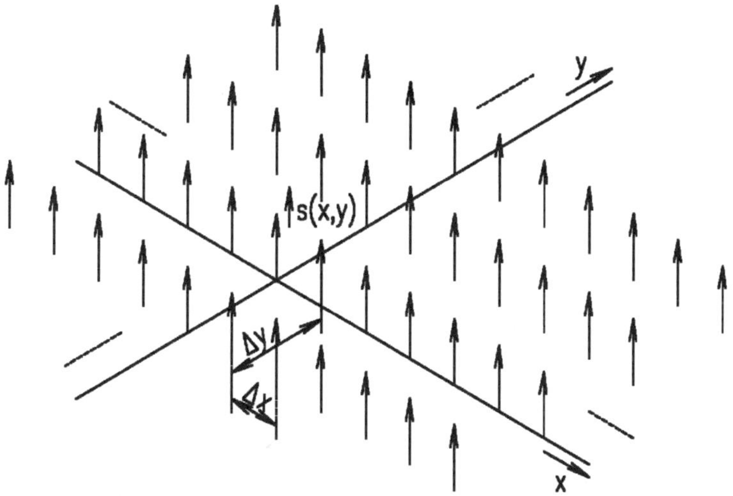

Figure 14.1 Two-dimensional sampling function

carries the complete information on the image. (The vectors and matrices in the original domain will be represented by symbols like $\overline{\overline{\mathbf{f}}}$ or $\overline{\overline{\mathbf{f}}}$, while capital letters $\overline{\overline{\mathbf{F}}}$, $\overline{\overline{\mathbf{F}}}$ will be reserved for representation of data in the frequency domain, or for denoting the transform matrices describing linear operators, e.g. $\mathbf{H}$.)

It should be said that rectangular sampling is not the only possibility; it is possible to sample even in differently formulated grids such as a hexagonal one; however, we shall not deal with these less frequent modes.

The product (14.14) is transformed into the frequency domain as the convolution

$$\mathbb{F}\{f(x, y)s(x, y)\} = \frac{1}{4\pi^2} F(u, v) * S(u, v)$$

$$= \frac{1}{\Delta x \, \Delta y} \sum_{m=-\infty}^{\infty} \sum_{m=-\infty}^{\infty} F(u - mU, v - nV),$$

$$U = \frac{2\pi}{\Delta x}, V = \frac{2\pi}{\Delta y}. \tag{14.16}$$

The *spectrum of a sampled image* is therefore periodic; it is formed by replicas of the primary spectrum shifted by integer multiples of the sampling frequencies U, V (Figure 14.2). If a distortionless reconstruction of the original image from its sampled version should be possible, the individual spectral replicas must not overlap in the frequency domain. This will be guaranteed only if the

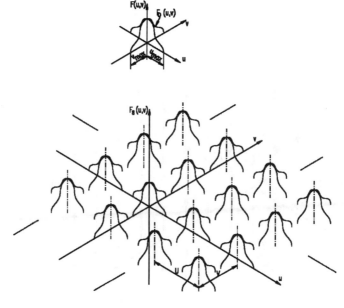

Figure 14.2 Bandlimited 2D spectrum (above) and its periodisation due to image sampling

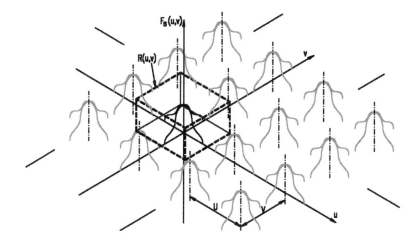

Figure 14.3 Reconstruction of a two-dimensional signal from samples by means of a low-pass filter (spectral representation)

primary spectrum is bandlimited by the limit frequencies u_{max}, v_{max} and if the *2D sampling theorem*

$$\Delta x < \frac{\pi}{u_{max}}, \quad \Delta y < \frac{\pi}{v_{max}} \tag{14.17}$$

is fulfilled by choosing sufficiently dense sampling.

The *reconstruction* of the original image from its sampled version can then be interpreted, in the frequency domain, as suppressing all of the spectral replicas except the basic one in the original position, i.e. in the neighbourhood of the frequency-plane origin. This can be done by a suitable two-dimensional low-pass filter (theoretically the ideal one) with the frequency response $R(u, v)$ (Figure 14.3) so that

$$F_r(u, v) = F_s(u, v)R(u, v) \cong F(u, v).$$

If the function of the reconstruction filter is interpreted in the original domain, it can be found that it represents a continuous interpolation among the samples,

$$f_r(x, y) = f_s(x, y) * r(x, y) = \sum_i \sum_k {}_s f_{i,k} r(x - i\,\Delta x, y - k\,\Delta y),$$

where the interpolation function $r(.)$ is obviously the impulse response (PSF) of the reconstruction filter, similarly as in the one-dimensional case.

14.2.2 Matrix and vector representation of images, two-dimensional systems and unitary transforms

The most natural representation of the sampled image is to arrange the samples in a matrix such as (14.15). However, to represent the effects of linear operators by simple equations we would need a mathematically more suitable representation of images. This is representation by vectors which can be provided from matrices (14.15) by linear arrangement of their elements, for example by scanning them along individual columns,

$$\bar{\mathbf{f}} = [f_{00}, f_{10}, \cdots, f_{N-1,0}, f_{01}, \cdots, f_{N-1,1}, \cdots, f_{0,M-1}, \cdots, f_{N-1,M-1}]^T,$$

(when the initial size of the matrix was $M \times N$). Let us remark that, besides the obvious algorithmic description of the conversions in both directions, $\bar{\mathbf{f}} \rightarrow \bar{\bar{\mathbf{f}}}$, $\bar{\bar{\mathbf{f}}} \rightarrow \bar{\mathbf{f}}$, the conversions can also be described by matrix-algebra formulae using some specially defined auxiliary vectors and matrices. This description, although computationally ineffective, is useful in theoretical analyses.

A generic *discrete linear operator,* analogous to the continuous operator described by the integral (14.3), transforms the initial matrix $\bar{\bar{\mathbf{f}}}$ into the output matrix $\bar{\bar{\mathbf{g}}}$ usually of the same size according to the superposition relation

$$g_{mn} = \sum_{i=1}^{N} \sum_{k=1}^{N} h(i, k, m, n) f_{ik}, \tag{14.18}$$

(for simplicity, we consider square matrices). Thus again, every sample of the input image generally influences every sample of the output image. It is possible to describe such an operator much more concisely by the vector relationship between vector representations of both images,

$$\bar{\mathbf{g}} = \mathbf{T}\bar{\mathbf{f}}. \tag{14.19}$$

The form of the transform matrix $\mathbf{T}$ follows from eqn (14.18) – it is, in the simplest case, obviously a matrix of the size $N^2 \times N^2$, hence very large. The expression (14.19) would be therefore rather ineffective for practical computations but, for theoretical considerations, the mentioned representation is very useful. Moreover, let us remark that this relation comprises, besides linear image processing in the original domain as just presented, also discrete two-dimensional transforms, that is calculating of spectral representations of original discretised images.

If the matrix $\mathbf{T}$ is nonsingular, eqn (14.19) may be multiplied from the left by the inverse matrix $\mathbf{T}^{-1}$, which shows (at least theoretically) the possibility of restoration of the original image $\bar{\mathbf{f}}$ from its linearly distorted version $\bar{\mathbf{g}}$,

$$\mathbf{f} = \mathbf{T}^{-1}\mathbf{g}. \tag{14.20}$$

Unfortunately, the inverse problem of the two-dimensional deconvolution formulated in this way is usually rather stiff (badly conditioned). As in the one-dimensional version, even here very small errors caused by noise (e.g. even mere quantising noise) give rise to an unacceptable distortion of the result. This is why more advanced restoration methods must usually be applied, which are two-dimensional analogies of the methods described in Sections 3 to 8 of Chapter 10.

The general form of the operator encompasses some special cases. Let us name first the *separable operators*, i.e. those the operation of which can be separated into column processing and row processing. In column processing individual columns of the input matrix influence only corresponding columns of the output, an analogous statement defines row processing. It can be shown that the transform matrix of a separable operator can be factorised into the product of two equally sized but sparse matrices of column and row transforms

$$\mathbf{T} = \mathbf{T}_C \mathbf{T}_R,$$

which leads to a substantial reduction in the number of operations. Further simplification can be achieved if the column-transform of every column to the corresponding one is expressed by a fixed matrix (of size $N \times N$) for all columns, and the row transform is similarly fixed. A cardinal computational simplification will be obtained, as the column and row transforms can be expressed by the relationships (respectively)

$$\bar{\bar{\mathbf{g}}}_C = \mathbf{T}'_C \bar{\bar{\mathbf{f}}} \quad \text{and} \quad \bar{\bar{\mathbf{g}}}_R = \bar{\bar{\mathbf{f}}} \mathbf{T}'^{T}_{R}.$$

Here, the matrices $\mathbf{T}'_C, \mathbf{T}'_R$ are only of size $N \times N$. By cascade application of both operators, we obtain the output matrix expression

$$\bar{\bar{\mathbf{g}}} = \mathbf{T}'_C \bar{\bar{\mathbf{f}}} \mathbf{T}'^{T}_{R},$$

which naturally represents in order a lower number of operations than the general expression given by eqn (14.19). The order of both transforms is irrelevant in the calculation. The property of separability in this strict sense is also typical for unitary transforms, including the two-dimensional discrete Fourier transform.

Another special case of an operator in eqn (14.19) is *isoplanar operators* for which the individual output samples are given by eqn (14.18) with a special type of weight function,

$$h(i, k, m, n) = h(m - i, n - k).$$

In this case, the sum is obviously convolutional and it can be shown that the matrix $\mathbf{T}$ will have then a certain special (block circulant) form.

Still another type of linear operators is represented by the group of *local operators*. These are characterised by the property that the result $g_{m,n}$ is not contributed to by all elements of the input matrix but rather only by elements of a certain (usually small) submatrix, surrounding the element $f_{m,n}$. This corresponds to a common case of imaging by, for example, an imperfect optical system in which the contributions of each point of the input image are spread into a certain finite neighbourhood of the corresponding point of the output image. In such a case, only those weight values $h(i, k, m, n)$ are nonzero for which the differences $m - i$, $n - k$ are in certain limits given by the size of the influencing neighbourhood. Taken rigorously, the output matrix then becomes greater in consequence of the spread as certain marginal elements emerge in the output because of it; in spite of this, the size of the resulting matrix is often left unchanged in the course of processing for practical reasons. Local operators can be expressed, without a loss in generality, by the following expression which clearly represents their substance. Providing that the influencing neighbourhood is of size $(2M + 1) \times (2M + 1)$ and that $M < N/2$ (usually $M \ll N/2$), we have

$$g_{mn} = \sum_{i=-M}^{M} \sum_{k=-M}^{M} h(i, k, m, n) f_{m+i, n+k}, \qquad (14.21)$$

where the weight function is, for a particular position of the calculated (output) point, dependent only on the indices i, k. The expression therefore means the so-called *mask operation*: the mask $h(.)$ is laid on the input matrix so that its centre would merge with the point m, n of the input image. The value of the output element of the same coordinates is then calculated as the linear combination of covered input elements weighted by the mask values. If the form of the mask and its values do not depend on its position m, n, it represents an *isoplanar operator* and thus a convolutional operation. It can easily be shown that the result is the convolution between the input image and the mask matrix spatially inverted by 180 degrees. Therefore, this is FIR filtering with the impulse response given by the elements of the mask. The mask operations form the basic and most common outfit of image processors and enable effective processing in many practically important cases, in spite of their simplicity.

Moreover, let us mention that the mask operations need not only be linear as given by eqn (14.21), but the elements selected by the mask may be used as input values of any operators, including nonlinear. The practically very useful two-dimensional *median filter*, which works with the set of inputs defined by the mask quite analogously to the one-dimensional case, may serve as a good example. The original 2D arrangement of elements sorted by the median operator is naturally irrelevant, rather the size and geometrical shape of the mask influence the behaviour of the operator.

Two-dimensional discrete linear transforms are generally also described by eqns (14.18) or (14.19); their output is nevertheless interpreted differently. It is not taken as an image in the original domain but rather as a spectrum $\overline{\mathbf{F}}$, that is, as an invertible description of the input image $\bar{\mathbf{f}}$ in the frequency domain,

$$\overline{\mathbf{F}} = \mathbf{A}\bar{\mathbf{f}}, \quad \bar{\mathbf{f}} = \mathbf{A}^{-1}\overline{\mathbf{F}}. \tag{14.22}$$

For the sake of simpler notation, we have used the vector representation of both the image and its spectrum. However, both can also be represented by matrices $\bar{\bar{\mathbf{f}}}$, $\overline{\overline{\mathbf{F}}}$ composed of the vector elements and consequently they can both be interpreted as images expressing their values by brightness level. Notice that a spectrum, which generally has complex values, needs two grey-level images to be expressed completely, commonly one for amplitude spectrum and another one for the phase spectrum (Figure 14.4).

To comply with the relations (14.22), the basic required property of all transforms is the nonsingularity of their core matrix. If it is further valid that

$$\mathbf{A}^{-1} = \mathbf{A}^{*T},$$

the transform is denoted as *unitary*, in the special case of the real matrices as *orthogonal*.

Unitary transforms are not isoplanar and cannot therefore be expressed by convolution, on the other hand they are separable so that

$$\overline{\overline{\mathbf{F}}} = \mathbf{A}_C \bar{\bar{\mathbf{f}}} \mathbf{A}_R^T,$$

which means that it is possible to initially perform one-dimensional transforms of individual rows and then the same for columns, or *vice versa* with the same result. Moreover, usually $\mathbf{A}_C = \mathbf{A}_R$. The form and values of the transform matrix depend naturally on the kind of transformation; for example for the discrete Fourier transform a general element of the matrix is

$$A_{iN+k,\,uN+v} = e^{-j\frac{2\pi}{N}(ui+vk)},$$

where j, k are indices in the input image matrix and u, v are indices of the resulting discrete spectrum.

The application possibilities of two-dimensional discrete transforms are analogous to their use in one-dimensional cases: fast convolution calculations based on the convolution property, spectra estimation as a means of feature extraction in recognition problems, image-data compression *via* frequency domain etc. Besides the mentioned 2D DFT which is of course realised by means of fast algorithms (FFT), many other transforms are also used in the two-dimensional version, usually exploiting the property of separability. Perhaps the most important currently is the 2D *cosine transform*, widely used in contemporary block-oriented image-compression algorithms (e.g. in JPEG and MPEG2 standards). Now very topical 2D *wavelet transforms* prove to be excellent tools, particularly in non-block-oriented image-data compression, interpolation and restoration, the oldest but still frequently used among them being the 2D Haar transform. Also, other classical transforms are enjoying a

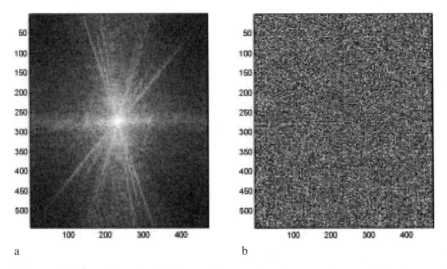

a   b

Figure 14.4 Two-dimensional discrete Fourier transform spectrum of the image in
Figure 14.5a
a   Amplitude
b   Phase

revival, Hadamard and Walsh transforms being recognised as the simplest
wavelet-packet transforms.

14.2.3 Discrete stochastic fields

In comparison with continuous stochastic fields as described in Section 14.1.3,
the main differences of *discrete stochastic fields* are naturally given by the
discrete-space character of them. As the dimensions of images are always
finite, discrete stochastic fields are formulated in terms of a finite number of
stochastic variables – random values of image elements in the node points of
the discretisation grid. In digital representation, even the values of the variables
are discrete owing to quantising which is often rather rough for common image
data. Then, the probability distributions are described by tables of probabilities
(rather than by continuous probability densities).

Similarly as in the one-dimensional case, every individual variable is locally
described by its table of probability distribution and, in a simplified way, by
moments of the distribution. Further, joint probabilities can be formulated
for combinations of image values at more or many points, starting with pairs
of points which leads to the important concept of correlation functions. This
idea may be generalised to a greater number of stochastic point variables
involved until finally (in contrast to the continuous case) it is theoretically possible to determine the probabilities of particular value combinations of all image
points. These, of course, are probabilities of particular images which can be
realised with the chosen size of image matrix and selected type of quantising.

Obviously, the number of such images is finite although very large and, in principle, the corresponding probability table may be meditated on.

The definitions of discrete-field characteristics are direct counterparts of the definitions of continuous fields and, from another aspect, they are also two-dimensional variants of the characteristics of one-dimensional discrete processes. The definition formulations are thus direct generalisations of formulations from Chapter 4, considering the generalisation to multidimensionality made in Section 14.1.3, so we will not discuss them here in a greater detail.

As a demonstration of the efficiency of vector notation, we shall only mention some relationships which characterise the processing of stochastic fields by linear systems in the sense considered for one-dimensional processes in Section 4.5, and for continuous two-dimensional processes in Section 14.1.3. If every realisation of a stochastic field is processed by a linear system according to eqn (14.19), the mean value it is naturally

$$\mathbb{E}\{\bar{\mathbf{g}}\} = \mathbb{E}\{\mathbf{T}\,\bar{\mathbf{f}}\} = \mathbf{T}\mathbb{E}\{\bar{\mathbf{f}}\}.$$

Hence, the ensemble mean value of the output field is equal to the image obtained by the particular linear processing of the image representing the mean value of the input field. Similarly, for the autocorrelation function of the output stochastic field (four-dimensional and thus expressed by an $N^2 \times N^2$ matrix, as the requirement of stationarity has not been imposed), we obtain

$$\mathbf{R}_{gg} = \mathbb{E}\{\mathbf{g}\mathbf{g}^{*T}\} = \mathbb{E}\{\mathbf{T}\,\mathbf{f}\mathbf{f}^{*T}\,\mathbf{T}^{*T}\} = \mathbf{T}\mathbb{E}\{\mathbf{f}\mathbf{f}^{*T}\}\mathbf{T}^{*T} = \mathbf{T}\mathbf{R}_{ff}\,\mathbf{T}^{*T}.$$

As we can see, even in a quite general case it is possible to derive the output autocorrelation-function matrix from the autocorrelation matrix of the input field by a mere double transform based on the linear operator matrix. The advantages of vector formulation become obvious, should we try to derive the adequate individual-component relationships on the basis of eqn (14.18). Simplification *via* the frequency-domain derivation is not possible here, as the inhomogeneous stochastic fields do not have spectra in the usual sense.

14.3 Processing and analysis of images as two-dimensional signals

A typical and very developed application field, dealing with two-dimensional signals, is the processing and analysis of images. We shall present a very brief overview of the possibilities of some methods based on a generalisation of digital signal-processing approaches. The listing showing the principles of basic methods is naturally not complete by far; other approaches of rather different theoretical starting points also exist, particularly in the area of computer vision. These methods rely heavily on *a priori* knowledge in concrete practical tasks and their background is often rather heuristic, combining intuitively designed procedures based on experience with formalised methods; many of them are closely connected with computer graphics techniques. Computer vision is devoted primarily to the interpretation of image data (analysis of motion, of the third dimension as radial distances or surface estimation, of shapes of objects including estimation of occluded parts) rather than providing improved or transformed images. Computer vision, the final aim of which is scene recognition, is already beyond the scope of this book and we shall refer to other sources as far as related topics are concerned, e.g. in Reference [10]. Nevertheless, there is no strict border between the area of processing images as signals and that of computer vision. *A priori* knowledge (as expected shapes, size and space arrangement of objects, admissible degree of surface curvature, knowledge of illumination mode etc.) is often used even in formalised solutions as constraints in optimisation procedures. Such methods thus approach those of Chapter 10. However, the reader should be warned that too heavy a use of *a priori* information might impose an improper interpretation on the analysed image data.

14.3.1 Application of point operators

Point operators of the type

$$g_{i,k} = \lambda(f_{i,k}), \qquad (14.23)$$

where $\lambda(.)$ is a chosen continuous or discrete function, are the simplest means of processing images; they generally serve to contrast or colour scale transformations. It is evident that they are a degenerated case of local operator with a mask size of 1×1. In spite of their obvious simplicity, they are very effective instruments for image enhancement.

The basic type of point operator is represented by *global contrast transforms*, the function $\lambda(.)$ of which does not depend on the position in the image. A number of typical functions exist that are commonly used, mostly to increase the contrast in a certain part of the greyscale. As the dynamic range of image-element brightness is always limited, it necessarily leads to a decrease of contrast in another part of the scale. Therefore, contemporary image processors mostly allow for interactive control of the steepness and range of modified scale sections, so that different parts of the processed image can successively be inspected with differently adjusted contrast. It is usually required that the functions used be increasing and monotonous in order that the greyscale is not inverted in certain brightness ranges. An important exception is the dependence denoted as the 'zebra' or saw-tooth function consisting of several adjoining usually linear sections which all individually use fully the admissible range of output brightness values. An enormous increase in contrast can be achieved in this way at the cost of creating false edges in the image locations where the areas of brightness belonging to two such neighbouring sections are in touch. However, emerging edges can also be utilised as a good approximation of isolines of brightness. Another exception from the rules is a monotonously decreasing function used for providing the negative of the input image, which naturally inverts the brightness values on purpose. (See examples on Figure 14.5, a–d.)

A more general mode of image point processing is so-called *pseudo-colouring* in which the function $\lambda(.)$ acquires vector values – its elements express values of colour components. The purpose of this operation is to express levels of grey in the colour scale which, owing to a much higher resolution of human sight in colours than in greyscale, enables us to resolve many more shades in the output colour image than in the original greyscale image. When the input image is in colour, the application of a point operator leads to a colour transformation; the function $\lambda(.)$ is then obviously a vector function of a vector argument.

A suitable contrast-transform function can be formally derived based on the requirement that all levels of grey should have equal relative statistical frequencies in the output image. Although this does not lead to an increase in the information content of the image, as sometimes claimed, the transformed data represents a well contrasted image which is better suited to evaluation by an observer. The derivation can be based on the criterion requesting *histogram equalisation* of greyscale shades. While the histogram of the original image, expressing the relative frequencies of individual grey shades, is usually rather uneven (see Figure 14.5e), the histogram of the transformed image should be as uniform as possible (certain residual nonuniformity is caused by the discrete character of the problem). The result of the histogram equalisation procedure is a certain derived function $\lambda(.)$ which can be applied further in the same way as any other contrast transform. Another formalised contrast modification is the transform which is inverse to a known characteristic of the light sensor used to provide the image data, so that its nonlinearity will be compensated for in this way.

Point operations can also be used for *segmentation* of images on the basis of brightness. The simplest operator of this kind is plain *thresholding* which displays everything under a chosen brightness threshold as black and the rest of the image as white (or *vice versa*); in this way, it is possible, for example, to separate bright or dark objects from a grey background. Another possibility is multithreshold segmentation representing, for example, a certain medium range of input brightness as white, and the other grades as black. Determining the proper thresholds is crucial for accuracy of segmentation and this is rather a difficult problem, which can also be solved based on using the greyscale histogram, apart from by other methods.

The realisation of a global contrast transform for a known operator function $\lambda(.)$ is very simple: every input pixel value is submitted to the same transform and the image is thus transformed point-by-point. When represented digitally, the transform is expressed by a simple look-up table containing the required discrete function. The contrast transform may even be performed in real time, when displaying the picture, without the need to modify the original image; the look-up table then modifies the transferred pixel values on their way from

Figure 14.5 *Applications of contrast transforms by isoplanar point operators*
   a   Original image
   b   Enhanced by a monotonous nonlinear transform
   c   Negative
   d   Modified by nonmonotonous transform
   e,f Histograms of images a) and b)

the image matrix to the display. Any change in the table thus immediately influences the displayed image.

In many cases, a global point operator is not satisfactory, for example in the case of a nonuniformly illuminated scene where different contrast transforms are needed in bright and shadow parts of the image. Similarly, the segmentation transforms should also be chosen as adapted to local image properties in such cases. The automatic change of the look-up table, dependent on the local image characteristics (e.g. on local mean and variance as determined from a small neighbourhood of the transformed point) then means a realisation of an *adaptive contrast transfor*m or *adaptive segmentation*. In such cases, the adaptation algorithm may be considerably more complicated then the point operator itself. The operation of *field homogenisation* also belongs to the same category of space-variant contrast transforms; it is needed when the image is provided by a two-dimensional plane sensor (perhaps a CCD element) with spatially non-uniform sensitivity. The correction of contrast then needs individual modification functions for different image areas, perhaps up to the level of individual pixels. Parameters of these correction functions can be determined based on identification of the nonuniform sensitivity by means of sensing a uniformly grey image, if linear correction is sufficient. Depending on the complexity of the functions, which may reflect not only different sensitivities but also variant dead bands and saturation levels, several such phantom images of different density or reflectivity may be needed.

14.3.2 Application of local operators

Local operators, according to eqn (14.21) also denoted as mask operations, are, apart from contrast transforms, the most frequently used means of routine image processing. The used size of the mask – i.e. also of the input image area contributing to an individual output value – is from 3×3 pixels (the most frequently applied size) to matrices sized several tens of pixels on one side. Such great masks are nevertheless used rather rarely because of difficult design and high computational requirements; common sizes are up to about 9×9. From the point of view of the previous discussions, the local operators are two-dimensional linear or nonlinear FIR filters, mostly shift invariant but in some cases dependent on their position in the image. The applications of local operators are very wide – for example:

- noise suppression;
- sharpening of images;
- preparation to segmentation – edge and line detection etc.;
- morphological operations.

Noise suppression in images by local operators assumes the additive white-noise model, i.e. as generated by a stochastic field with zero mean and mutually independent values in neighbouring pixels, which is summed with the useful image content. Providing that the useful signal – image brightness values – in the elements covered by the mask is (almost) constant, it is possible to obtain a better signal-to-noise ratio by weighted averaging of pixel values covered by the mask. The results correspond to the number of averaged values and therefore to the size of the mask. If the weights (elements of the mask) are h_{ik}, the amplitude of SNR improvement is given as in eqn (6.10) as

$$K_U = \frac{\sum_i \sum_k h_{ik}}{\sqrt{\sum_i \sum_k h_{ik}^2}},$$

where it is summed over all the elements of the mask operator. The improvement in SNR will be maximum for uniform weighting; it is then equal to $\sqrt{(2M+1)^2}$, thus proportional to the square root of the number of mask elements. Unfortunately, the assumption that signal values under the mask are constant is not always properly fulfilled, such as in the neighbourhood of edges in the image. This leads to distortion of the output image, which is visible as blurring – a loss of spatial resolution. It is then necessary to find a compromise between noise suppression and preserving the image quality, which can be influenced primarily by the mask size and by different weighting elements. If the central element and elements close to it have relatively greater values, the blur is limited to the cost of deteriorating the noise-suppression effect. The following 3×3 masks show the development from a uniform mask to a mask limiting the influence of more distant elements:

$$\frac{1}{9} \begin{bmatrix} 1 & 1 & 1 \\ 1 & 1 & 1 \\ 1 & 1 & 1 \end{bmatrix}, \quad \frac{1}{10} \begin{bmatrix} 1 & 1 & 1 \\ 1 & 2 & 1 \\ 1 & 1 & 1 \end{bmatrix}, \quad \frac{1}{16} \begin{bmatrix} 1 & 2 & 1 \\ 2 & 4 & 2 \\ 1 & 2 & 1 \end{bmatrix}.$$

The blurring effect of such operators can be partially eliminated by *adaptive size control* of the mask: in image areas with a small brightness variance in the frame of the chosen neighbourhood, the mask size can be greater as (probably) no edge is present here. On the other hand, in the vicinity of edges indicated by a great variance of the pixel values, a small mask size must be chosen or the smoothing even dropped completely, in the interest of preserving the resolution. The greater areas of continuously varying brightness in the resulting image are then smoothed, while in the vicinity of the edges, where the noise is less perceived by human sight, the sharpness is preserved. The criteria for adaptation and mask-size variations can naturally be chosen differently, depending on the concrete image type to be processed. Generally, it can be said that the adaptation algorithms are usually much more demanding than the local operator is itself.

Linear local operators come in useful when random noise, affecting on average all the image elements to the same extent, is to be suppressed. In practice, another type of interference is also common, which touches only individual isolated elements of the image but has a large magnitude, so-called 'salt and pepper' noise; this is often caused by impulse interference during image communication. The generic approach to this type of noise removal consists in two phases: first, the false pixels should be detected (usually by comparison with the average of surroundings, obtained, for example, by a suitable local operator). Secondly, new values of these points are determined by interpolating from the surrounding points, perhaps by means of the same or another local operator. Notice that there is a nonlinear step in the procedure, consisting in the decision on whether the point under consideration is false or untouched. Simpler and in practice often an equipotential approach is the use of a *median filter* which does not need to detect explicitly the damaged pixels. The median filter sorts the image elements that are covered by the mask of the chosen size and it assigns the median of the sorted sequence to the output. It is an example of a conceptually simple (although computationally intensive) and very effective filter, see Figure 14.7.

Image *sharpening* is an operation that is, to a certain extent, in conflict with the previously discussed intention of noise suppression. This property follows from the spectral interpretation of both procedures. Local averaging (smoothing) has the character of a lowpass filter so that it suppresses the high-frequency components which are assumed to suffer most from noise. The sharpening operators, on the contrary, increase the share of high-frequency components as they carry most of the information on edges and details of the image. As both deteriorating components are usually present at any one time, a compromise must be sought: sharpening is only possible to the extent that would not lead to an unbearable deterioration of signal-to-noise ratio.

The design of local sharpening operators is based on the idea that the loss of resolution which is to be compensated for has been caused by integrating (in the discrete version, averaging) operation of the imaging or communication system. Therefore, the desired sharpening would occur when applying suitable differentiating (difference) operators. Usually, isotropic operators are required but in some special cases only the edges of a certain direction should be emphasised. The common sharpening operators are derived on the basis of either first or second-order differences.

Gradient operators are based on differences of the first order and they approximate usually only the absolute value, sometimes also the direction, of the gradient of a two-dimensional image-brightness field,

$$\nabla f(x, y) = \frac{\partial f}{\partial x}\,\mathbf{i} + \frac{\partial f}{\partial y}\,\mathbf{j}, \tag{14.24}$$

where $\mathbf{i}$, $\mathbf{j}$ are unit directional vectors along coordinate axes. Although the absolute value of the gradient

$$|\nabla f(x, y)| = \sqrt{\left(\frac{\partial f}{\partial x}\right)^2 + \left(\frac{\partial f}{\partial y}\right)^2} \tag{14.25}$$

is an isotropic operator and therefore it responds equally well to edges of all directions, the gradient direction, expressed as angle in the (x, y) plane is, of course, anisotropic. The partial derivatives in eqn (14.24) or eqn (14.25) may be approximated by the first differences oriented to different directions, which can be expressed by the following linear operator masks; in the simplest case therefore

$$
\begin{bmatrix} 0 & -1 & 0 \\ 0 & 1 & 0 \\ 0 & 0 & 0 \end{bmatrix}, \quad
\begin{bmatrix} 0 & 0 & 0 \\ 0 & 1 & -1 \\ 0 & 0 & 0 \end{bmatrix}, \quad
\begin{bmatrix} -1 & 0 & 0 \\ 0 & 1 & 0 \\ 0 & 0 & 0 \end{bmatrix}, \quad
\begin{bmatrix} 0 & 0 & -1 \\ 0 & 1 & 0 \\ 0 & 0 & 0 \end{bmatrix}.
$$

If all the four masks are used successively, we shall obtain the approximations of four directional derivatives with maximum sensitivities (from the left) to edges that are horizontal, vertical and parallel to the axis of the first and of the third quadrant. The absolute value can then be determined from two perpendicular components according to eqn (14.25), or approximately (and much less laboriously) as the average of two or even of all four components. The direction is usually only roughly evaluated as that of the four mentioned directions for which the absolute difference was maximal; the demanding angle computation may thus be dropped. The notion of so-called *compass masks*, which are usually somewhat more complicated variants of the above four masks, is based on this principle.

As the first differences determined in this way are rather sensitive to image noise, averages of neighbouring values of differences are often used instead. In addition, differences over two image elements, in which case the operators become symmetrical with respect to the mask centre, may be used. The gradient value belonging to the centre row or column may be accented. All the possibilities mentioned are demonstrated by examples of operators sensitive to horizontal edges, as follows:

$$
\frac{1}{3}\begin{bmatrix} -1 & -1 & -1 \\ 1 & 1 & 1 \\ 0 & 0 & 0 \end{bmatrix}, \quad
\frac{1}{6}\begin{bmatrix} -1 & -1 & -1 \\ 0 & 0 & 0 \\ 1 & 1 & 1 \end{bmatrix}, \quad
\frac{1}{8}\begin{bmatrix} -1 & -2 & -1 \\ 0 & 0 & 0 \\ 1 & 2 & 1 \end{bmatrix}.
$$

The masks for the other directions would be obtained by rotation in an obvious way.

The discrete *operators of Laplacian type* approximate the Laplace differential operator of the second order

$$
\nabla^2 f(x, y) = \frac{\partial^2 f}{\partial x^2} + \frac{\partial^2 f}{\partial y^2} \tag{14.26}
$$

by means of the second differences, for the calculation of which in different directions the following masks can be used,

$$\begin{bmatrix} 0 & 1 & 0 \\ 0 & -2 & 0 \\ 0 & 1 & 0 \end{bmatrix}, \begin{bmatrix} 0 & 0 & 0 \\ 1 & -2 & 1 \\ 0 & 0 & 0 \end{bmatrix}, \begin{bmatrix} 1 & 0 & 0 \\ 0 & -2 & 0 \\ 0 & 0 & 1 \end{bmatrix}, \begin{bmatrix} 0 & 0 & 1 \\ 0 & -2 & 0 \\ 1 & 0 & 0 \end{bmatrix}.$$

The Laplacian based on differences in the directions of coordinate axes is then approximated by the mask which is the sum of the first two matrices from the previous line. Similarly, the approximate Laplacian coming out from the directions rotated by 45 degrees is given by the sum of the second couple of matrices. Finally, the average of both approximations mentioned is proportional to the sum of all the four matrices, as shown (from the left) in the following line

$$\begin{bmatrix} 0 & 1 & 0 \\ 1 & -4 & 1 \\ 0 & 1 & 0 \end{bmatrix}, \begin{bmatrix} 1 & 0 & 1 \\ 0 & -4 & 0 \\ 1 & 0 & 1 \end{bmatrix}, \begin{bmatrix} 1 & 1 & 1 \\ 1 & -8 & 1 \\ 1 & 1 & 1 \end{bmatrix}. \tag{14.27}$$

As the last mask gives an estimate based on a weighted average of two simpler estimates based on mostly different measurements, it can be expected that the corresponding operator will be somewhat less sensitive to noise. However, these operators generally amplify the noise extraordinarily; they can thus be applied only to low-noise images.

It can be shown that a sharpened image, corresponding to an original blurred linearly by an approximately Gaussian point-spread function, can be obtained by subtracting the Laplacian image from the original. Taking into account that the mask plainly reproducing the original has the only nonzero (unit) element in its centre, the mentioned sharpening operator may be expressed by a single mask. For instance, with the use of the first form of the Laplacian, we obtain the mask of often-used *sharpening operator* as

$$\begin{bmatrix} 0 & -1 & 0 \\ -1 & 5 & -1 \\ 0 & -1 & 0 \end{bmatrix}. \tag{14.28}$$

Its effect can be seen by comparison of Figures 14.6c (sharpened) and 14.5a (original).

Detectors of edges and lines in an image serve to find so-called *edge representation*, i.e. a derived image in which the edges and lines are first emphasised by difference operators. Consequently, only the edge features that are found to be sufficiently 'important' are preserved. Their importance may mean that they are strong enough as determined, for example, by thresholding, also sufficiently long and perhaps also well connected etc.; these properties are to be evaluated by rather complex algorithms. Such an edge representation (as in Figure 14.6d) can serve, in subsequent processing, for a more advanced edge or *region-based segmentation* of the image.

Local operators of the gradient type as well as Laplacians are used to emphasise the edges. These operators nevertheless are not well suited to emphasise or

Figure 14.6 Examples of applications of linear local (mask) operators – two-dimensional
*   FIR filters*
*   a   Lowpass filtered version of image in Figure 14.5a*
*   b   Highpass filtered image*
*   c   Result of sharpening by the mask (14.28)*
*   d   Result of applying an edge detector*

detect the details of thin-line type. For this purpose, special *line detectors* are
formulated, which are mostly heuristic linear local operators commonly 5×5
pixels in size.

Morphological operations are also based on the use of some masks but their
interpretation is different and the processing is nonlinear as it involves decision
making. The masks contain so-called *structural elements*, the shape of which
can influence the results of otherwise identical operators. The purpose of these

a   *b*

Figure 14.7 Example of effect of nonlinear filtering
    a   Image deteriorated by salt-and-pepper noise
    b   The same image after filtering by a median filter

transforms, which are mostly used for post processing of binary images provided by previous image segmentation, is usually noise suppression, smoothing of object boundaries, separation of falsely aggregated objects or, on the contrary, merging of falsely separated objects. Morphological operations such as finding the boundaries, determining skeletons of the objects etc. are oriented more towards preparation of image analysis; they allow us to evaluate subsequently the number of objects, to characterise their shapes and orientations and such like. We shall limit ourselves to this brief information, as the principle of morphological transformations is rather different from the concepts that we are dealing with in this book.

14.3.3 Advanced methods of image processing and analysis

The advanced methods that are all connected with the theoretical frame of this book encompass a number of different approaches and procedures of which some are generally known and routinely used; others are perhaps considered rather theoretically interesting. We shall mention here only some of them.

Advanced methods can mostly be interpreted as *global operators* that are characterised by the property that every output element is influenced by all the elements of the input image. The most frequently used operator of this kind, although perhaps not belonging itself to advanced procedures, is undoubtedly the *two-dimensional discrete Fourier transform* (2D DFT) which serves as the base of many if not most advanced methods. It primarily enables us to obtain discrete spectra of images, or estimations of power spectra of stochastic fields based on computing averages of a number of individual power spectra of a number of related images. Further, it is possible to perform fast convolution *via* the frequency domain (with large operator matrices having several tens or hundreds of elements on a side) either as globally fixed, or even piecewise adaptive operators. As in the one-dimensional case (Section 5.2.3.2), the matrices must be adequately padded by zeros in order to prevent interperiodic interference owing to circular convolution. The spectra of images are also used as feature sets in recognition problems, e.g. in some methods of texture analysis, or for identifying objects in the image etc. The DFT also plays a key role in the field of reconstruction of images from their tomographic projections as will be discussed later. Using the DFT, it is also possible to identify *a posteriori* the properties of a linear imaging system, by analysing its response to line or edge objects in an image provided by the system.

The point and local operators served primarily to *enhance* the image, i.e. for operations used heuristically to improve its appearance. The criterion of success was therefore good subjective judgement of either the image appearance or the possibility of obtaining the necessary information when inspecting the image. On the contrary, advanced operators and the procedures combined with them enable *restoration* of the observed (measured, received) image by means of a formalised approach based on some knowledge of the mechanism of image deterioration. The purpose of the restoration is thus not to 'improve' the image but to restore it as closely as possible to its original state (or to a defined state as, for example, in tomographic reconstruction) according to a suitably chosen criterion.

The first step of the restoration procedure is thus *identification of deterioration* (geometrical and convolutional distortion, eventual anisoplanar transforms, possible nonlinearities, noise and its statistical properties, the way in which the noise is combined with the image – additively, multiplicatively, convolutionally etc.). The methods of identification are in many cases analogous to those used in one-dimensional cases.

We shall briefly discuss the following methods of formalised image restoration and their application fields:
• geometrical restitution;
• modified inverse filtering, Wiener filtering and other deconvolution procedures;
• suppression of noise and interference with identified properties;
• reconstruction from tomographic projections;
• reconstruction of depth information from stereo pairs.

Geometrical restitution corrects the distortion caused, for example, by imperfection of the imaging system, or owing to the geometry of image recording (e.g. perspective distortion), or distortions which are part of the imaging principle (e.g. the necessary transform from polar to Cartesian coordinates in ultrasonic scanning, radar, sonar etc.). The identification of a global geometric distortion consists in finding the analytical expression representing the mapping from the original image space (x, y) in the observed (distorted) image space (x', y'), which follows from the character of image sensing. If we know the transform equations

$$x' = q_1(x, y), \quad y' = q_2(x, y),$$

it is in principle possible to find, for every point in the restituted image $g(x, y)$, the corresponding point (x', y') in the distorted image and to transfer its value $f(x', y')$ to the proper place. The complications, evoked by the discrete character of data which disables the direct realisation of the procedure, can easily be solved by interpolating in the distorted-image data matrix. Such an approach denoted as *inverse restitution* prevents the generation of unpleasant artefacts in the resulting image which appear when applying the direct restitution method. If the distortion is too complicated, as is the case for topographic satellite-picture distortion owing to uneven film shrinkage, global transform equations in the closed form may not be available. In such a case, the distortion must be identified by providing a sufficiently dense although possibly irregular grid of reference points on the picture with known coordinates. Then we know the exact coordinate transform for each point of the grid; the transform inside the triangles delimited by the points may usually be expressed, with sufficient precision, by the linear transform

$$x' = ax + by + c, \quad y' = dx + ey + f.$$

The coefficients can be calculated from a linear equation system compiled based on known coordinates of the relevant triangle apexes in the original and the distorted image. Naturally, even higher-order interpolating functions, such as spline functions, can be used which would provide not only a continuous but also a smooth transition between neighbouring triangles.

Formalised *inverse filtering* usually assumes a two-dimensional version of the deterioration model (10.1) or (10.2), consisting of distortion by a linear iso-planar convolutional system and by additive noise, independent of the original image content. Restoration methods are often summarised under the common name of *deconvolution*. The first step common to all the methods is *identification of the linear distortion*, that is determination of the point-spread function (PSF) $\bar{\mathbf{h}}$ of the linear system or, alternatively, of its frequency transfer. This can be done in the simplest way by preliminary imaging of a scene or a phantom containing point sources; in this way, the required PSFs including the degree of isoplanarity would be directly (*a priori*) determined. If this is not feasible, a less straightforward approach is possible, where a scene can be imaged that contains line or edge objects, the responses to which would supply estimates of line-spread or step-spread functions. Thus, by measuring the perpendicular brightness profiles of such objects, we can derive an estimate of PSF (even a posterior one if the objects are a part of the image to be restored). It can be shown that the profiles are projections of PSF (or integrals of such projections in the case of edge profiles) so that the PSF can in principle be computed by utilising any of the methods of reconstruction from projections that will be mentioned later.

The *identification of a stochastic field,* namely noise, requires – dependent on the restoration method to be used – more or less detailed determination of its statistical properties. It is usually necessary to determine the mean value and variance which is generally variable, and perhaps, in a homogeneous case, to also estimate the 2D autocorrelation function or 2D power spectrum. Similar statistical characteristics may also be needed for the stochastic field generating the images, should such a model be used in the chosen restoration method, namely with Wiener-approach-based methods. A rather demanding measurement on a set of images may be needed for this purpose. With respect to the complexity of such measurements, should they be performed based on ensemble averages, it is common to assume that both the fields generating the image and noise are homogeneous and ergodic. The estimates may then be based on space averages from single realisations that are much easier to provide. It is usual that verification of the ergodicity hypothesis is only possible *a posteriori,* on the basis of the success of performed restoration or by comparison with results obtained in different ways which should be consistent.

As already said, the plain inverse filtering according to eqn (14.20) is usually useless owing to reasons that were discussed in detail for the one-dimensional case in Section 10.2. Inverse filters must usually be modified to suppress their singularities. This leads to so-called *pseudo-inversion,* or alternatively, more advanced methods can be used; namely, methods based on the two-dimensional *Wiener filtering.* These methods often yield acceptable results even when the assumptions used in deriving the filter formula, such as homogeneity of involved fields, linearity and isoplanarity of distortion, are not exactly fulfilled. The explanation may be that the formula derivation was based on these assumptions as sufficient, but not necessary conditions (see example in Figure 14.8 [40]). Almost all other advanced methods of restoration, mentioned in one-dimensional versions in Chapter 10, have also been utilised for image restoration, with a noticeable degree of success. Because generalisation of them from the one-dimensional description to the two-dimensional case is straightforward when using vector and matrix notation (Section 14.2.2), we will not discuss them here in a detail. Modern restoration methods are used routinely in demanding applications, such as in orbital remote sensing or in the processing of images provided by spaceships; however, they have so far penetrated to general applications only to a limited extent. Note that successful experiments have been published [39] on using neural networks in advanced image processing, particularly on utilising Hopfield-type networks for optimisation-based restoration by a method similar to constrained deconvolution (Section 13.4).

A special case of the restoration is mere noise suppression without a request for sharpening by deconvolution. It is obvious that all the advanced deconvolution methods can manage to solve this problem easily by introducing the simplifying condition $\bar{\bar{\mathbf{h}}} = [u_{i,k}]$, i.e. if PSF of the (non)distorting system is a discrete two-dimensional unit impulse. In this context a special note should

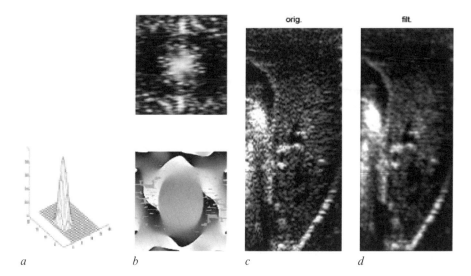

Figure 14.8 Example of a Wiener filter application. It can be seen that the textural noise, specific to the ultrasonic imaging modality (so-called speckles) is substantially suppressed without losing edge sharpness of anatomical structures; moreover, the organ borders are smoother thus enabling better segmentation

a   Measured PSF of the imaging system used (ultrasonic scanner)
b   Frequency response of Wiener filter derived on the basis of the PSF, power spectra of the observed image and of noise (upper part: amplitude transfer, lower part: phase transfer)
c   An observed image
d   Corresponding restored image

be devoted to the method of constrained deconvolution from which some modern nonlinear noise-suppression methods are inferred. These methods model the brightness function as smooth semi-stiff surfaces in areas outside the neighbourhood of edges and the continuous region borders by means of curves with controlled flexibility.

A special type of image data processing is *reconstruction from projections*, which may also be included in the group of restoration methods. It is about restoring two-dimensional (or three-dimensional) image data on the basis of measured one-dimensional vectors, the set of which can be interpreted as a distorted representation of the original image. The essential notions of the projection theory can be seen from Figure 14.9.

A transversal plane of usually a three-dimensional object, carrying a certain characteristic parameter (e.g. X-ray absorption, distribution density of a radioactive isotope etc.) as a three-dimensional distribution described by $f(x, y, z)$, is defined by $z = z_0$. Then the object parameter forms a two-dimensional image $f(x, y, z_0)$ on this plane, the so-called *tomographic plane* or *layer*. The core of tomographic imaging is to reconstruct this image from projections which are measurable from outside without interfering with the inside of the object,

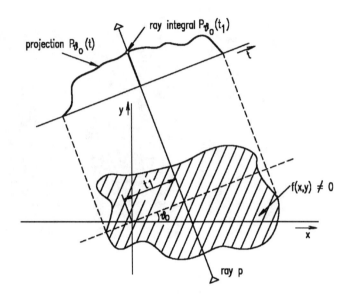

Figure 14.9 Projection generation in tomographic imaging

which may be a patient body or a technical object to be noninvasively tested. By changing the shift parameter z_0 successively, the complete object function $f(x, y, z)$ can be reconstructed in discrete parallel planes thus providing a three-dimensional data set from which any section or profile may be extracted.

We shall concentrate on the fundamental problem of obtaining the two-dimensional image from projections. Let us assume, for simplicity and without a loss of generality, $z = 0$. Then the image $f(x, y)$ formed by the object parameter in the plane x, y is to be reconstructed. The image is perpendicularly projected onto the axis t by means of *rays*, which are straight lines along which the object parameter is integrated. A value obtained by integration along a particular ray p is the *ray integral*

$$P_{\vartheta_0}(t_1) = \int_p f(x, y) \, ds,$$

corresponding to the geometrical parameters of the ray – the angle of projection ϑ_0 and the ray position t_1.

The continuous function of the parameter t, given by the values of ray integrals on parallel lines with different distances t from the origin of coordinates, is called the *projection*, relevant to the angle ϑ_0. When this angle is varied continuously, a continuous set of projections is generated which can be understood as being a continuous function of two variables,

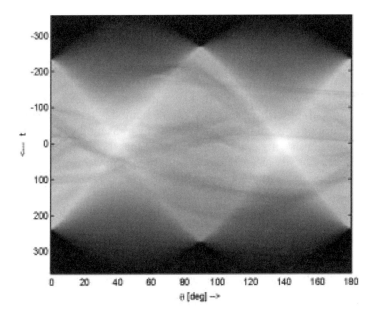

Figure 14.10 Radon transform of the image of Figure 14.5a (vertical profiles are formed by individual parallel projections). Reconstruction from projections means to restore the mentioned image from this data

$$P_\vartheta(t) = P(t, \vartheta) = \int_{p_{t,\vartheta}} f(x, y) \, ds$$

$$= \int_{-\infty}^{\infty} \int_{-\infty}^{\infty} f(x, y) \delta(x \cos \vartheta + y \sin \vartheta - t) \, dx \, dy.$$

This two-dimensional function is called the *Radon transform* of the function $f(x, y)$ (see Figure 14.10) and, in continuous formulation, the task of reconstruction from projections is the problem of finding the inverse Radon transform. Practically, it is only possible to scan a finite number of projections and each of these is in turn represented by a vector of discrete samples so that the real task can be formulated as an approximate discrete inverse Radon transform. At present, three differently based approaches are available to solve this problem numerically.

The *algebraic approach* is based on consistent discretisation, which comes from the notion of dividing the object into rectangular small cells so that the imaged parameter is constant in each of them (equal to f_i in the ith cell). Further, the rays are supposed to be actually stripes of finite width so that the influence of the jth cell to the ith ray, denoted as w_{ij} is given by the area of their intersection. The ray sum approximating the ray integral is then

$$p_i = \sum_{j=1}^{N} w_{ij} f_j,$$

where N is the total number of cells (the great majority of weight coefficients are naturally zero for a particular ray). The system of equations for all i, corresponding to different rays in different projections, is linear and can, in principle, be solved for the vector $\mathbf{f}$ of cell parameter values. The difficulty of the problem is in its extraordinarily high dimensionality – the number of simultaneous equations is of the order of 10^4 to 10^5 so that only iterative procedures can be used. An established such procedure is the Kaczmarz method, which can also manage with the presence of noise in the measurements by utilising the over determination of the equations owing to a great number of measurements. In the context of current developments in available computational power and memory size, this conceptually simple although computationally intensive method again gains on interest.

The classical method of reconstruction from projections is based on application of the *projection-slice theorem*. This says that the spectrum of (one-dimensional) projection acquired from a certain direction is equal to the central slice (at the corresponding angle) of the two-dimensional spectrum of the image to be reconstructed,

$$S_\vartheta(w) = \mathbb{F}_{1D}\{P_\vartheta(t)\} = F(w \cos \vartheta, w \sin \vartheta),$$

where

$$F(u, v) = \mathbb{F}_{2D}\{f(x, y)\}.$$

Based on this, it is in principle sufficient to reconstruct, by interpolation, the 2D spectrum of the sought image from the individual slices that are each given by the corresponding one-dimensional projection spectrum. The original image may then be obtained by the inverse two-dimensional Fourier transform. The disadvantage of the realisable discrete form of the method is in deficiencies in the interpolation. Samples of the projection spectra are positioned in the frequency plane (u, v) in an equidistant manner with respect to polar coordinates, and the samples needed for the inverse 2D DFT must be arranged in a rectangular grid. The necessary interpolation in the frequency domain brings some systematic errors which manifest themselves in the reconstructed image as artefacts that are the more pronounced the less the number of projections.

Nowadays, the most frequently used reconstruction approach, found in commercial systems, is the method of *filtered back-projection* which combines, to a certain extent, the advantages of both previous approaches. It works basically in the original domain but the result is achieved by a straightforward procedure without iteration. The method is functionally similar to the historic heuristic reconstruction approach by so-called backprojection. This consisted in 'back-projecting' every projection $P_\vartheta(t)$ into all elements of the reconstructed image, in the same direction in which the projection was provided, so that a certain 'smeared' stripe structure originated in the image from a single projection. It was expected that summing all these structures for all projections would provide an approximation of the original image but it turned out that such a reconstruction suffers from significant defects (artefacts). It can be proved by detailed theoretical analysis that a similar procedure can be used correctly providing that, instead of the original projections, their modified versions are used. The required modification consists in one-dimensional filtering of each projection with a transfer which linearly increasing with frequency; it therefore basically corresponds to differentiation in the original domain, which also means that the DC components of projections are suppressed. Such a reconstruction procedure is already theoretically correct. Owing to its relative simplicity, it is also advantageous for routine use, which contributed to its widespread application.

Let us note that contemporary tomographic systems commonly provide the data in *fan projections*, instead of the parallel projections as explained. This allows us to provide a whole fan projection during a single exposure which is more time saving and, namely, limits the dose of irradiation of the object, e.g. a patient. The individual ray integrals, i.e. the samples of the fan projections, can be resorted under certain conditions concerning the geometry of the measurement, so that data sets are obtained, each corresponding to a constant angle of projection; in this way the problem is in principle transformed to the previous case. Another possibility is to modify the filtered backprojection especially for fan-projection tomography; this is described, with respect to some additional weighting of the backprojected filtered projections, as *weighted (and filtered) backprojection*.

The last comment on a method which directly uses the results of signal-processing theory belongs to reconstruction of the third dimension, that is of a surface, on the basis of couples of stereo images. Such a stereo pair consists of two pictures taken from different sites with respect to the imaged object so that the pictures differ in details. The geometry of the imaging arrangement may have a very different character (it need not necessarily simulate the position of the eyes of a human observer); the reconstruction algorithm must then consider the geometry appropriately. The input of the reconstruction algorithm is formed, apart from the description of measurement geometry primarily by the data on differences between both images. In the ideal case, these are provided as a two-dimensional difference image of the same size as the original stereo-pair pictures. This *disparity map* supplies, for each pixel, the magnitude and direction of the difference vector between position vectors of the points mutually corresponding in both images. Providing such disparity maps, needed in the stereo-analysis case but also in other practically important tasks (motion analysis, scene-, time-development or perspective-change analysis etc.), is the subject of *disparity analysis*. Although seemingly simple, and in spite of the availability of different sophisticated approaches, the problem is not yet completely solved for arbitrary images. Often, some unavailable *a priori* knowledge is requested by a display analysis method or a rather limiting constraint is imposed, which may exclude the sophisticated methods from routine application. Commercial systems usually require interactive intervention of a human operator to ensure sufficient reliability.

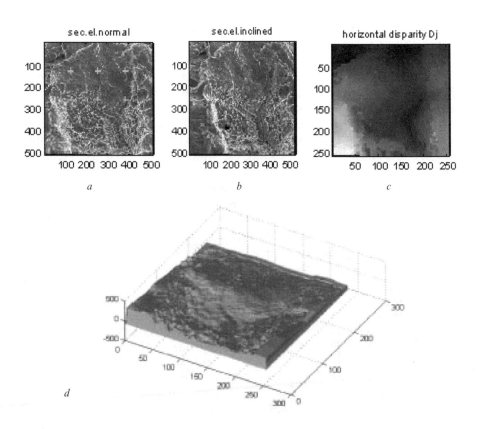

Figure 14.11   Example of stereo analysis
*   a, b   Couple of images of an electron-microscopic sample*
*   c   Corresponding disparity map*
*   d   Calculated reconstructed surface of the sample*

In principle, the core of disparity analysis is very simple: it is about finding details of one member of the stereo pair in the other picture. It is generally believed that this task of finding corresponding pixels can be solved by classical correlation methods, which can also be interpreted as repeated application of two-dimensional matched filters. However, to ensure sufficient robustness and low error rate, criteria of similarity other than the classical correlation or covariance functions should be used, as was already mentioned for the one-dimensional case in Section 12.5. The most effective of the direct methods, not requiring any assumptions, has proved to be the application of two-dimensional versions of nonlinear matched filters. Among these, the distinctly lowest error rate with different types of image has been shown by the so-called 2D cosine filter, analogous to the one-dimensional filter (12.15). A concrete result of such an analysis [41] can be found in Figure 14.11.

When concluding this chapter on multidimensional signals, its limited purpose should once more be emphasised. It should have served primarily to draw the reader's attention to the close relationships between the processing of one-dimensional time-domain signals and the methods of multidimensional signal processing which are only seemingly conceptually different. The main ideas have been demonstrated on methods of processing and analysis of two-dimensional space-domain images, which is a fast developing field. A more detailed description of the methods that were only briefly mentioned here and of many other approaches may be found in specialised literature on image processing and computer vision, e.g. References [10], [28], [31].

References

1 *Aleksander, I., and Morton, H.:* 'An introduction to neural computing' (Chapman & Hall, 1991)
2 *Banks, S.:* 'Signal processing, image processing and pattern recognition' (Prentice Hall Int. (UK) Ltd., 1990)
3 *Beauchamp, K.G., and Yuen, C.K.:* 'Digital methods for signal analysis' (G. Allen & Unwin Ltd., London, 1979)
4 *Bellanger M.:* 'Digital processing of signals, theory and practice' (J. Wiley & Sons Ltd., 1990)
5 *Bhaskaran, V., and Konstantinides, K.:* 'Image and video compression standards, algorithms and architectures' (Kluwer Academic Publ., 1997, 2nd edn.)
6 *Gold, B., and Rader, C.M.:* 'Digital processing of signals' (McGraw-Hill, 1969)
7 *Grant, P.M., Cowan, C.F.N., Mulgrew, B., and Dripps, J.H.:* 'Analogue and digital signal processing and coding' (Chartwell-Bratt Ltd., 1989)
8 *Haykin, S.:* 'Adaptive filter theory' (Prentice Hall Int., 1991, 2nd edn.)
9 *Haykin, S.:* 'Modern filters' (Maxwell Macmillan, 1990, int. edn.)
10 *Jain, A.K.:* 'Fundamentals of digital image processing' (Prentice Hall Int., 1989)
11 *Jan, J.:* 'Averaging methods of signal processing', *Slaboproudý Obzor*, 1981, **42**(12), pp. 565–572 (in Czech)
12 *Jan, J.:* 'Discrete methods of biosignal processing', (SNTL Praha – VUT Brno, 1976) (in Czech)
13 *Jan, J.:* 'Nonlinear matched filters'. Proceedings of COFAX '95, Bratislava (SK), 1995, pp. 565–572
14 *Kamas, A., and Lee, E.A.:* 'Digital signal processing experiments' (Prentice Hall, Englewood Cliffs, NJ, 1988)
15 *Kamen, E.W.:* 'Introduction to signals and systems' (Macmillan Publ. Comp., 1990, 2nd edn.)
16 *Kosko, B. (Ed.):* 'Neural networks for signal processing' (Prentice Hall Int., 1992)

17 *Kosko, B.:* 'Neural networks and fuzzy systems' (Prentice Hall Int., 1992)

18 *Kreyszig, E.:* 'Advanced engineering mathematics' (J.Wiley & Sons, 1979, 4th edn.)

19 *Kuc, R.:* 'Introduction to digital signal processing' (McGraw-Hill Int., 1988)

20 *Lau, C. (Ed.):* 'Neural networks, theoretical foundations and analysis' (IEEE Press, NY, 1992)

21 *Mathews, V.J.:* 'Adaptive polynomial filters', *IEEE-SP Mag.*, 1991, (7), pp. 10–26

22 MATLAB Image Processing Toolbox v.2, The Math-Works Inc., 1997

23 MATLAB Signal Processing Toolbox v.2, The Math-Works Inc., 1997

24 MATLAB v. 5.1 manual, The Math-Works Inc., 1997

25 *Misiti, M.Y., Oppenheim, G., and Poggi, J-M.:* 'MATLAB wavelet toolbox user's guide' (The Math-Works Inc., 1996)

26 *Mulgrew, B., Grant, P., and Thompson, J.:* 'Digital signal processing, concepts and applications' (MacMillan Press Ltd., 1999)

27 *Oppenheim, A.V., and Schafer, R.W.:* 'Digital signal processing' (Prentice-Hall, Englewood Cliffs, NJ, 1975)

28 *Pratt, W.K.:* 'Digital image processing (J. Wiley & Sons, 1991, 2nd edn.)

29 *Proakis, J.G., Rader, C.M., Ling, F., and Nikias, C.L.:* 'Advanced digital signal processing' (Maxwell Macmillan Int., 1992)

30 *Rabiner, L.R., and Gold, B.:* 'Theory and application of digital signal processing' (Prentice Hall Inc., NJ, 1975)

31 *Rosenfeld, A., and Kak, A.C.:* 'Digital picture processing' (Academic Press, 1982, 2nd edn.)

32 *Schwartz, M., and Shaw, L.:* 'Signal processing: discrete spectral analysis, detection and estimation' (McGraw-Hill Kogakusha Ltd., 1975)

33 *Strang, G., and Nguyen, T.:* 'Wavelets and filter banks' (Wellesley-Cambridge Press, 1996)

34 *Šonka, M., Hlaváč, V., and Boyle, R.D.:* 'Image processing, analysis and machine vision' (PWS Boston, 1998, 2nd edn.)

35 *Uhlíř, J., and Sovka, P.:* 'Digital signal processing' (Vydavatelství ČVUT Praha, 1995) (in Czech)

36 *Vaidyanathan, P.P.:* 'Multirate systems and filter banks' (Prentice Hall PTR, Englewood Cliffs, NJ, 1993)

37 *Vích, R.:* 'Z-transform theory and applications' (D. Reidel Publ. Comp., 1987)

38 *Wickerhauser, M.V.:* 'Adapted wavelet analysis from theory to software' (IEEE Press, A.K. Peter, Ltd., 1994)

39 *Zhou, Y.T., and Chellappa, R.:* 'Image restoration with neural networks' *in KOSKO B. (ed.):* 'Neural networks for signal processing' (Prentice-Hall Int., 1992)

40 *Jan, J., and Kilian, P.:* 'Modified Wiener approach to restoration of ultrasonic scans via frequency domain', *in* Proc. of 9th IAPR Scandinavian Conference on Image Analysis, Uppsala (Sweden) 1995, pp. 1173–1180

41 *Janová, D., and Jan, J.:* 'Robust surface reconstruction from stereo SEM images' *in V. Hlavac, R. Sara (Eds.):* 'Computer analysis of images and patterns', series 'Lecture Notes in Computer Science no. 970', pp. 900–905, Springer Int., 1995

Index

All you need is . . .

love.

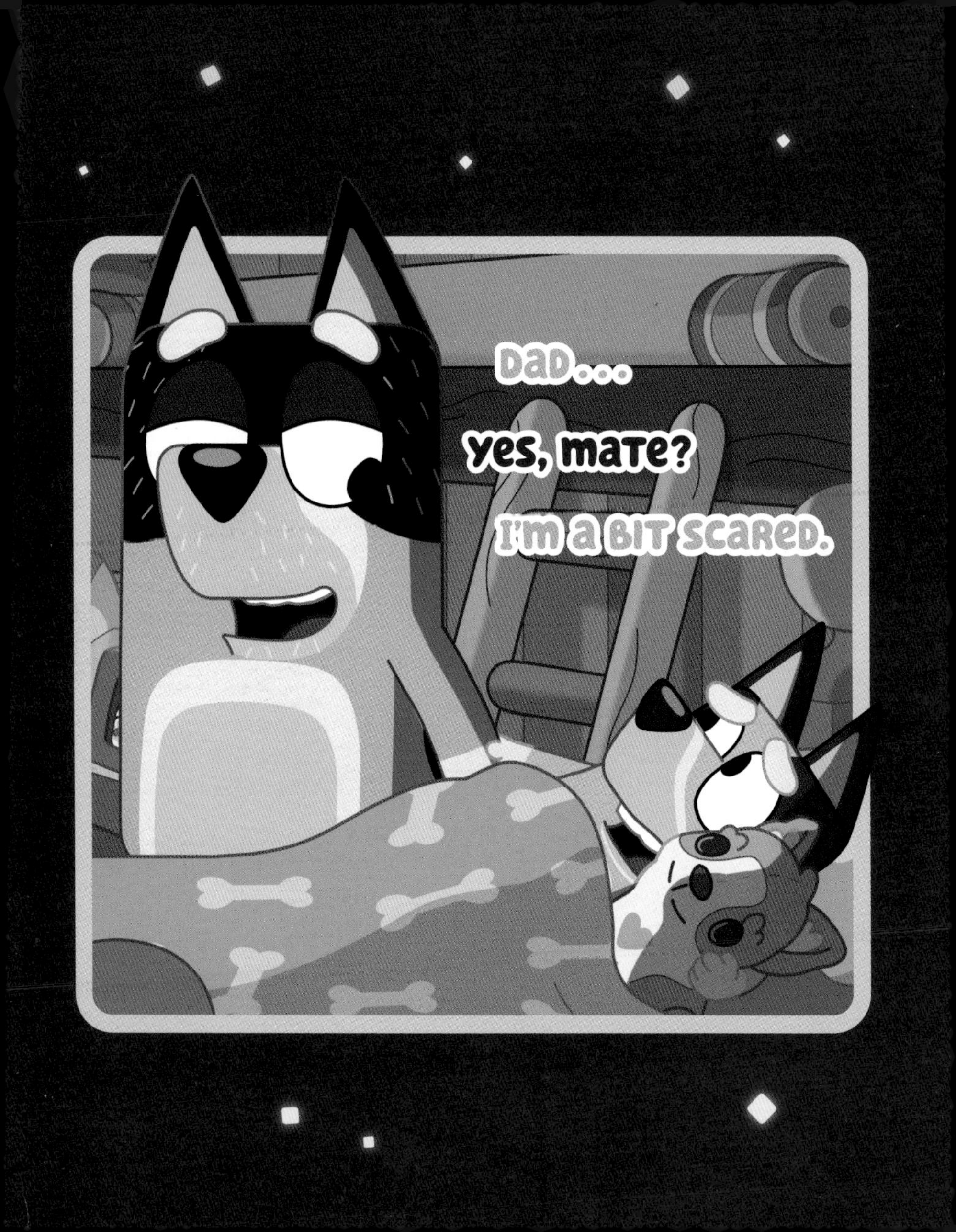
Dad...
Yes, mate?
I'm a bit scared.

LOVE CONQUERS ALL OUR FEARS.

Love...

...goes the extra mile.

Love is...

...little acts of kindness.

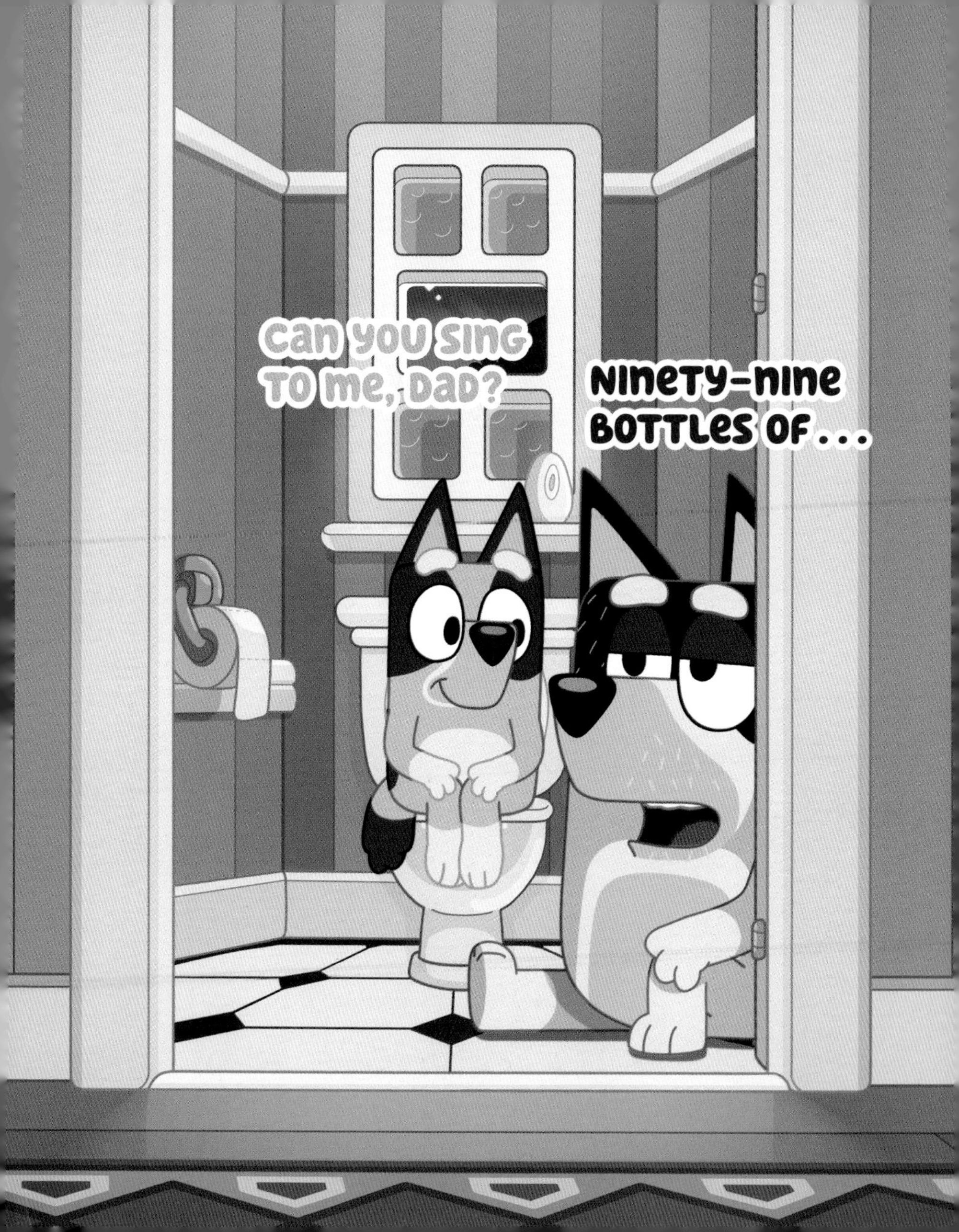
Can you sing to me, Dad?
Ninety-nine bottles of . . .

Love...

...solves every problem.

Love...

...always lifts you up.

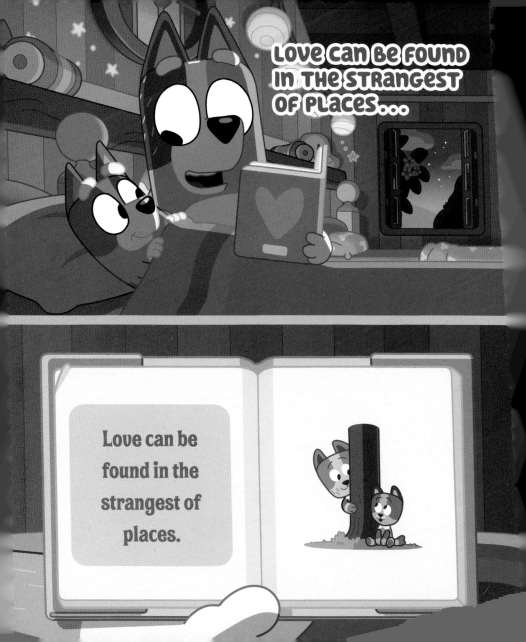

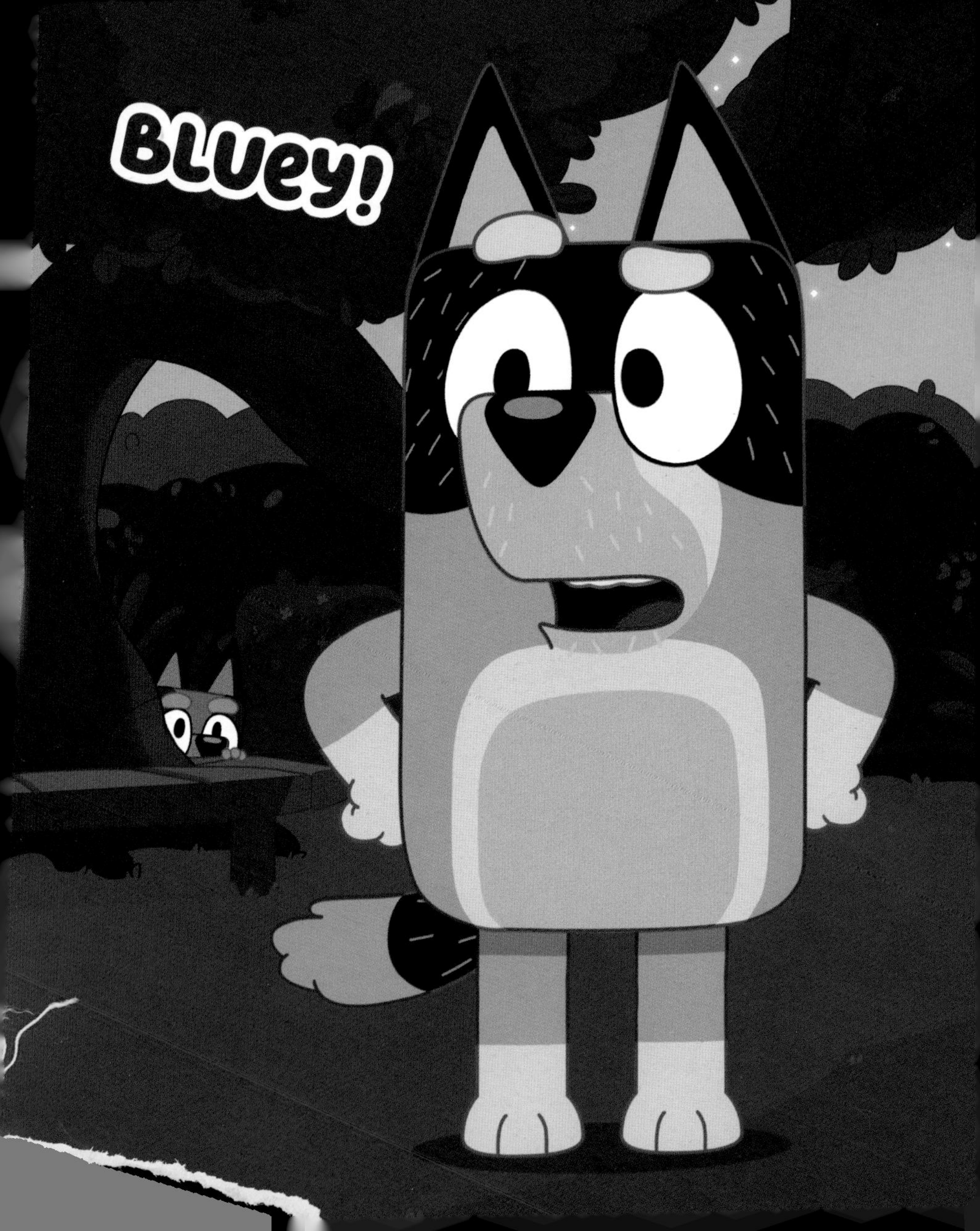
Bluey!

TEETH!

HAIR!

FLOPPY!

ALL DONE.

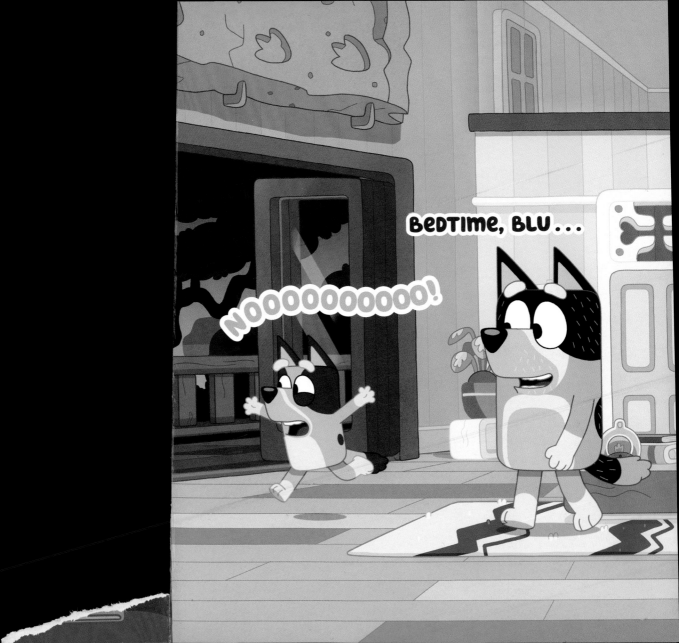

It is almost time for bed in the Heeler house.

PENGUIN YOUNG READERS LICENSES
An imprint of Penguin Random House LLC, New York

First published in the United States of America by Penguin Young Readers Licenses,
an imprint of Penguin Random House LLC, New York, 2023

This book is based on the TV series *Bluey*.

BLUEY ™ and BLUEY character logos ™ & © Ludo Studio Pty Ltd 2018.
Licensed by BBC Studios. BBC logo ™ & © 1996.

Text by Suzy Brumm

Penguin supports copyright. Copyright fuels creativity, encourages diverse voices,
promotes free speech, and creates a vibrant culture. Thank you for buying an authorized
edition of this book and for complying with copyright laws by not reproducing, scanning,
or distributing any part of it in any form without permission. You are supporting writers
and allowing Penguin to continue to publish books for every reader.

Visit us online at penguinrandomhouse.com.

Manufactured in China

ISBN 9780593658444   10 9 8 7 6 5 4 3 HH